Louise Palmer Heaven

Chata and Chinita

A Novel

Louise Palmer Heaven

Chata and Chinita
A Novel

ISBN/EAN: 9783743348868

Manufactured in Europe, USA, Canada, Australia, Japa

Cover: Foto ©Andreas Hilbeck / pixelio.de

Manufactured and distributed by brebook publishing software (www.brebook.com)

Louise Palmer Heaven

Chata and Chinita

CHATA AND CHINITA

A Novel

BY

LOUISE PALMER HEAVEN

BOSTON
ROBERTS BROTHERS
1889

CHATA AND CHINITA.

I.

On an evening in May, some forty years ago, Tio Pedro, the *portero*, or gate-keeper, of Tres Hermanos, had loosened the iron bolts that held back the great doors against the massive stone walls, and was about to close the hacienda buildings for the night, when a traveller, humbly dressed in a shabby suit of buff leather, urged his weary mule up the road from the village, and pulling off his wide sombrero of woven grass, asked in the name of God for food and shelter.

Pedro glanced at him sourly enough from beneath his broad felt-hat, gay with a silver cord and heavy tassels. The last rays of the setting sun flashed in his eyes, allowing him but an uncertain glimpse of the dark face of the stranger, though the shabby and forlorn aspect of both man and beast were sufficiently apparent to warn him from forcing an appearance of courtesy, and he muttered, grumblingly, —

"Pass in! Pass in! See you not I am in a hurry? God save us! Am I to stand all night waiting on your lordship? Another moment, friend, and the gate would have been shut. By my patron saint," he added in a lower tone, "it would have been small grief to me to have turned the key upon thee and thy beast. By thy looks, Tia Selsa's mud hut for thee, and the shade of a mesquite for thy mule, would have suited all needs well enough. But since it is the will of the saints that thou comest here, why get thee in."

"Eheu!" ejaculated a woman who stood by, "what makes thee so spiteful to-night, Tio Pedro, as if the bit and sup were to be of thy providing? Thou knowest well enough that Doña Isabel herself has given orders that no wayfarer shall be turned from her door!"

"Get thee to thy hand-mill, gossip!" cried the gate-keeper, angrily. "This new-comer will add a handful of corn to thy stint for grinding; he has a mouth for a *gordo*, believe me."

The woman, thus reminded of her duty, hurried away amid the laughter of the idlers, who, lounging against the outer walls or upon the stone benches in the wide arch-way, exchanged quips and jests with Pedro, one by one presently sauntering away to the different courtyards within the hacienda walls or to their own homes in the grass-thatched village, above which the great building rose at once overshadowingly and protectingly.

The stranger, thus doubtfully welcomed, urged his mule across the threshold, throwing, as he entered, keen glances around the wide space between the two arches, and beyond into the dim court; and especially upon the rows of stuffed animals ranged on the walls, and upon the enormous snakes pendent on either side the inner doorway, twining in hide-ous folds above it, and even encircling the tawdry image of the Virgin and child by which the arch was surmounted. These trophies, brought in by the husbandmen and shep-herds and prepared with no unskilful hands, gave a grim aspect to the entrance of a house where unstinted hospi-tality was dispensed, the sight of whose welcoming walls cheered the wayfarer across many a weary league, — it being the only habitation of importance to be seen on the extensive plain that lay within the wide circle of hills which on either hand lay blue and sombre in the distance. For a few moments, indeed, the western peaks had been lighted up by the effulgence of the declining sun; the last rays streamed into the vestibule as the traveller entered, then were suddenly withdrawn, and the gray chill which fell upon the valley deepened to actual duskiness in the court to which he penetrated.

Careless glances followed him, as he rode across the broad flagging, picking his way among the lounging herds-men, who, leaning across their horses, were recounting the adventures of the day or leisurely unsaddling. He looked around him for a few moments, as if uncertain where to go; but each one was too busy with his own affairs to pay any attention to so humble a wayfarer. Nor, indeed, did he seem to care that they should; on the contrary, he pulled his hat still further over his brows, and with his dingy striped blanket thrown crosswise over his shoulder and almost muffling his face, followed presently a confused noise of horses and men, which indicated where the stables stood, and disappeared within a narrow doorway leading to an inner court.

Meanwhile, Tio Pedro, his hands on the gate, still stood exchanging the last words of banter and gossip, idly delaying the moment of final closure. Of all those human beings gathered there, perhaps no one of them appreciated the magnificent and solemn grandeur by which they were surrounded any more than did the cattle that lowed in the distance, or the horses that ran whinnying to the stone walls of the enclosures, snuffing eagerly the cool night air that came down from the hills, over the clear stream which rippled under the shadow of the cottonwood trees, across the broad fields of springing corn and ripening wheat, and through the deep green of the plantations of chile and beans and the scented orchards of mingled fruits of the temperate and torrid zones. For miles it thus traversed the unparalleled fertility of the Bajio, that Egypt of Mexico, which feeds the thousands who toil in her barren hills for silver or who watch the herds that gather a precarious subsistence upon her waterless plains, and which gives the revenues of princes to its lordly proprietors, who scatter them with lavish hands in distant cities and countries, and with smiling mockery dole the scant necessities of life to the toiling thousands who live and die upon the soil.

Many are these fertile expanses, which, entered upon through some deep and rugged defile, lie like amphitheatres inclosed by jagged and massive walls of brescia and porphyry, that rise in a thousand grotesque shapes above their bases of green, — at a near view showing all the varying shades of gray, yellow, and brown, and in the distance deep purples and blues, which blend into the clear azure of the sky. One of the most beautiful of such spots is that in which lay the hacienda or estates of the family of Garcia, and one of the most marvellously rich; for there even the very rocks yield a tribute, the mine of the Three Brothers — the " Tres Hermanos " — being one of those which at the Conquest had been given as a reward to the daring adventurer Don Geronimo Garcia. It was surrounded by rich lands, which unheeded by the earliest proprietors, later yielded the most important returns to their descendants. But at the time our story opens, the mines and mills of Tres Hermanos, though they added a picturesque element to the landscape, had become a source of perplexity and loss, — still remaining, however, in the opinion of their owners, a proud adjunct to the vast stretches of field and orchard which encircled them.

The mines themselves lay in the scarred mountain against which the reduction-works stood, a dingy mass of low-built houses and high adobe walls, from the midst of which ascended the great chimney, whence clouds of sulphurous smoke often rose in a black column against the sky. These buildings made a striking contrast to the great house, which formed the nucleus of the agricultural interests and was the chief residence of the proprietors, and whose lofty walls rose proudly, forming one side of the massive adobe square, which was broken at one corner by a box-towered church and on another by a flour-mill. The wheels of this mill were turned in the rainy season by the rapid waters of a mountain stream, which lower down passed through the beautiful garden, the trees of which waved above the fourth corner of the walls, — flowing on, to be almost lost amid the slums and refuse of the reduction-works a half-mile away, and during the nine dry months of the year leaving a chasm of loose stones and yellow sand to mark its course. Along the banks were scattered the huts of workmen, though, with strange perversity, the greater number had clustered together on a sandy declivity almost in front of the great house, discarding the convenience of nearness to wood and water, — the men, perhaps, as well as the women, preferring to be where all the varied life of the great house might pass before their eyes, while custom made pleasant to its inmates the nearness of the squalid village, with its throngs of bare-footed, half nude, and wholly unkempt inhabitants.

These few words of description have perhaps delayed us no longer than Tio Pedro lingered at his task of closing the great doors for the night, leaving however a little postern ajar, by which the tardy work-people passed in and out, and at which the children boisterously played hide-and-seek (that game of childhood in all ages and climes); and meanwhile, as has been said, the traveller found and took his way to the stables. Before entering, he paused a moment to pull the red handkerchief that bound his head still further over his bushy black brows, and to readjust his hat, and then went into the court upon which the stalls opened. Finding none vacant in which to place his mule, he tethered it in a corner of the crowded yard; and then, with many reverences and excuses, such as rancheros or villagers are apt to use, asked a feed of barley and an armful of straw from the "major-domo," who was giving out the rations for the night.

"All in good time! All in good time, friend," answered this functionary, pompously but not unkindly. "He who would gather manna must wait patiently till it falls."

"But I have a *real* which I will gladly give," interrupted the ranchero. "Your grace must not think I presume to beg of your bounty. I—"

"Tut! tut!" interrupted the major-domo; "dost think we are shop-keepers or Jews here at Tres Hermanos? Keep thy *real* for the first beggar who asks an alms;" and he drew himself up as proudly as if all the grain and fodder he dispensed were his own personal property. "But," he added, with a curiosity that came perhaps from the plebeian suspicion inseparable from his stewardship, "hast thou come far to-day? Thy beast seems weary, — though as far as that goes it would not need a long stretch to tire such a knock-kneed brute."

"I come from Las Vigas," answered the traveller, doffing his hat at these dubious remarks, as though they were highly complimentary. "Saving your grace's presence, the mule is a trusty brute, and served my father before me; but like your servant, he is unused to long journeys, — this being the first time we have been so far from our birthplace. Santo Niño, but the world is great! Since noon have my eyes been fixed upon the magnificence of your grace's dwelling-place, and, by my faith, I began to think it one of the enchanted palaces my neighbor Pablo Arteaga, who travels to Guadalajara, and I know not where, to buy and sell earthenware, tells of!"

The major-domo laughed, not displeased with the homage paid to his person and supposed importance, and suffering himself to be amused by the villager's unusual garrulity. Las Vigas he knew of as a tiny village perched among the cliffs of the defile leading from Guanapila, whence fat turkeys were taken to market on feast-days, when its few inhabitants went down to hear Mass, and to turn an honest penny. They were a harmless people, these poor villagers, and he felt a glow of charity as if warmed by some personal gift, as he said. "Take a fair share of barley and straw for thy beast, and when thou hast given it to him, follow me into the kitchen, and thou shalt not lack a tortilla, nor frijoles and chile wherewith to season it."

"May your grace live a thousand years!" began the villager, when the major-domo interrupted him.

"What is thy name? So bold a traveller must needs have a name."

"Surely," answered the villager, gravely, "and Holy Church gave it to me. Juan — Juan Planillos, at your service."

The major-domo started, laid his hand on the knife in his belt, then withdrew it and laughed. "Truly a redoubtable name," he exclaimed; then, as they passed into another court over which the red light of charcoal fires cast a lurid glare, illuminating fantastically the groups of men who were crouching in various attitudes in the wide corridors, awaiting or discussing their suppers, "I hope thou wilt prove more peaceful than thy namesake: a very devil they say is he."

The villager looked at him stupidly, and then with interest at the women who were doling from steaming shallow brown basins the rations of beans and pork with red pepper, — a generous portion of which, at a sign from the major-domo, was handed to the stranger, who looked around for a convenient spot to crouch and eat it.

The major-domo turned away abruptly, muttering, "Juan Planillos! Juan Planillos! a good name to hang by. What animals these rancheros are! Evidently he has never heard of the man that they say even Santa Anna himself is afraid of. Well, well, Doña Isabel, I have obeyed your commands! What can be the reason of this caprice for knowing the name and business of every one who enters her gates? In the old time every one might come and go unquestioned; but now I must describe the height and breadth, the sound of the voice, the length of the nose even, of every outcast that passes by."

He disappeared within another of the seemingly endless range of courts, perhaps to discharge his duty of reporter, and certainly a little later, in company with other employees of the estate, to partake of an ample supper, and recount to Señor Sanchez the administrador, with many variations reflecting greatly on his own wit and the countryman's stupidity, the interview he had held with the traveller from Las Vigas. Any variation in the daily record of a country life is hailed with pleasure, however trifling in itself it may be; and even Doña Feliz, the administrador's grave mother, listened with a smile, and did not disdain to repeat the tale in her visit to her lady, Doña Isabel, which according to her usual custom she made before retiring for the night.

The apartments occupied by the administrador and his family were a part of those which had been appropriated to the use of the proprietors and rulers of this circle of homes within a home, which we have attempted to describe. The staircase by which they were reached rose, indeed, from an inferior court, but they were connected on the second floor by a gallery; and thus the inhabitants of either had immediate access to the other, although the privacy of the ruling family was most rigidly respected; while at the same time its members were saved from the oppression of utter isolation which their separation from the more occupied portions of the building might have entailed. This was now the more necessary, as one by one the gentlemen of the family had, for various reasons or pretexts, gone to the cities of the republic, where they spent the revenues produced by the hacienda in expensive living, and Doña Isabel Garcia de Garcia, — still young, still eminently attractive, though a widow of ten years standing, — was left with her young daughters, not only to represent the family and dispense the hospitality of Tres Hermanos, but to bear the burden of its management.

She was a woman who, perhaps, would scarcely be commiserated in this position. She was not, like most of her countrywomen, soft, indolent, and amiable, a creature who loves rather than commands. A searching gaze into the

depths of her dark eyes would discover fires which seldom
leapt within the glance of a casual observer. Seemingly
cold, impassive, grave beyond her years, Doña Isabel
wielded a power as absolute over her domains as ever did
veritable queen over the most devoted subjects. Yet this
woman, who was so rich, so powerful, upon the eve on
which her bounty had welcomed an unknown pauper to her
roof, was less at ease, more harassed, more burdened, as
she stood upon her balcony looking out upon the vast extent and variety of her possessions, than the poorest peon
who daily toiled in her fields.

Her daughters were asleep, or reading with their governess; her servants were scattered, completing the tasks of
the day; behind her stretched the long range of apartments throughout which, with little attention to order,
were scattered rich articles of furniture, — a grand piano,
glittering mirrors, valuable paintings, bedsteads of bronze
hung with rich curtains, services of silver for toilette and
table, — indiscriminately mixed with rush-bottomed chairs
of home manufacture, tawdry wooden images of saints,
waxen and clay figures more grotesque than beautiful, the
whole being faintly illumined by the flicker of a few candles in rich silver holders, black from neglect. Doña
Isabel stood with her back to them all, caring for nothing,
heeding nothing, not even the sense of utter weariness and
desolation which presently like a chill swept through the
vast apartments, and issuing thence, enwrapped her as
with a garment.

She leaned against the stone coping of the window.
Her tall, slender figure, draped in black, was sharply outlined against the wall, which began to grow white in the
moonlight; her profile, perfect as that of a Greek statue
unsharpened by Time yet firm as Destiny, was reflected
in unwavering lines as she stood motionless, her eyes
turned upon the walls of the reduction-works, her thoughts
penetrating beyond them and concentrating themselves
on one whom she had herself placed within, — who, successful beyond her hopes in the task for which she had
selected him, yet baffled and harassed her, and had planted
a thorn in her side, which at any cost must be plucked
thence, must be utterly destroyed.

The hour was still an early one, though where such primitive customs prevailed it might well seem late to her when she left the balcony and retired to her room, which was somewhat separated from those of the other members of the family, though within immediate call.　Soothed by the cool air of the night, the peace that brooded over village and plain, the solemn presence of the everlasting hills, — those voiceless influences of Nature which she had inbreathed, rather than observed, — her health and vigor triumphed over care, and she slept.

II.

MEANWHILE, the moon had risen and was flooding the broad roofs and various courts of the great buildings with a silvery brilliancy, which contrasted sharply with the inky shadows cast by moving creatures or solid wall or massive column. While it was early in the evening, the sound of voices was heard, mingling later with the monotonous minor tones of those half-playful, half-pathetic airs so dear to the ear and heart of the Mexican peasantry; but as night approached, silence gradually fell upon the scene, broken only by the mutter or snore of some heavy sleeper, or the stamping of the horses and mules in their stalls.

The new-comer Juan Planillos, who had joined readily in jest and song, — though his wit was scarce bright enough, it seemed, to attract attention to the speaker (while absolute silence certainly would have done so),— at length, following the example of those around him, sought the shaded side of the corridor, and wrapping himself in his striped blanket lay down a little apart from the others, and was soon fast asleep.

Men who are accustomed to rise before or with the dawn sleep heavily, seldom stirring in that deep lethargy which at midnight falls like a spell on weary man and beast; yet it was precisely at that hour that Juan Planillos, like a man who had composed himself to sleep with a definite purpose to arise at a specified time, uncovered his face, raised himself on his elbow, and glancing first at the sky (reading the position of the moon and stars), threw then a keen glance at the prostrate figures around him. The very dogs — of which, lean and mongrel curs, there were many — like the men, fearing the malefic influences of the rays of the moon, had retired under benches, and into the farthest corners, and upon every living creature profound oblivion had fallen.

It was some minutes before Planillos could thoroughly satisfy himself on this point, but that accomplished, he rose to his feet, leaving the sandals that he had worn upon the brick floor, and with extreme care pushing open the door near which he had taken the precaution to station himself, passed into the first and larger court, which he had entered upon reaching the hacienda. As he had evidently expected, he found this court entirely deserted, although in the vaulted archway at the farther side he divined that the gate-keeper lay upon his sheepskin in the little alcove beside the great door, of which he was the guardian.

As he stepped into this courtyard, Juan Planillos paused to draw upon his feet a pair of thin boots of yellow leather, so soft and pliable that they woke no echo from the solid paving, and still keeping in the shadow, he crossed noiselessly to a door set deep in a carved arch of stone, and like one accustomed to its rude and heavy fastenings, deftly undid the latch and looked into the court upon which opened the private apartments of the family of Garcia. He stood there in the shadow of the doorway, still dressed, it is true, in the ranchero's suit, — a soiled linen shirt open at the throat, over which was a short jacket of stained yellow leather, while trousers of the same, opening upon the outside of the leg to the middle of the thigh, over loose drawers of white cotton, were bound at the waist by a scarf of silk which had once been bright red ; his blanket covered one shoulder ; his brows were still circled by the handkerchief, but he had pushed back the slouching hat, and the face which he thrust forward as he looked eagerly around had undergone some strange transformation, which made it totally unlike that of the stolid mixed-breed villager who had talked with the major-domo a few hours before. Even the features of the face seemed changed, the heavy fleshiness of the ranchero had given place to the refinement and keenness of the cavalier. The bushy brows were unbent, there was intelligence and vivacity in his dark eyes, a half-mocking, half-anxious smile upon his lips, which utterly changed the dull and ignorant expression, and of the same flesh and blood made an absolutely new creation.

It was not curiosity that lighted the eyes as they glanced lingeringly around, scanning the low chairs and tables scattered through the corridor, resting upon the rose-entwined columns that supported it, and then upon the fountain in

the centre of the court, which threw a slender column
in the moonlight, and fell like a thousand gems into the
basin which overflowed and refreshed a vast variety of
flowering shrubs that encircled it. It was rather a look
of pleased recognition, followed by a sarcastic smile, as
if he scorned a paradise so peaceful. There was indeed
in every movement of his well-knit figure, in the clutch of
his small but sinewy hand upon the door, something that
indicated that the saddle and sword were more fitting to
his robust physique and fiery nature than the delights of
a lady's bower.

Nevertheless, he was about to enter, and had indeed
made a hasty movement toward the staircase that led to
the upper rooms, when an unexpected sound arrested him.
Planillos drew back into the shadow and listened eagerly,
scarce crediting the evidence of his senses; gradually he
fell upon his knees, covering himself with his dingy blanket,
transforming himself into a dull clod of humanity, which
under cover of the black shadows would escape observation except of the most jealous and critical eye. Yet this
apparent clod was for the time all eyes and ears. Presently
the sound he had heard, a light tap on the outer door,
was repeated; a shrill call like that of a wild bird —
doubtless a pre-arranged signal — sounded, and in intense astonishment he waited breathlessly for what should
further happen.

Evidently the gate-keeper was not unprepared, for the
first wild note caused him to raise his head sleepily, and
at the second he staggered from his alcove, muttering an
imprecation, and fumbling in his girdle for the key of the
postern. He glanced around warily, even going softly to
places where the shadows fell most darkly; but finding no
one, returned, and with deft fingers proceeded to push
back noiselessly the bolts of the small door set in a panel
of the massive one which closed the wide entrance. It
creaked slowly upon its hinges, so lightly that even a bird
would not have stirred in its slumbers, and a man cautiously entered. He had spurs upon his heels, and after
effecting his entrance stooped to remove them, and Planillos had time and opportunity to see that he was not
one of Pedro Gomez's associates, — not one of the common people.

The midnight visitor was tall and slender, the latter though, it would seem, from the incomplete development of youth, rather than from delicacy of race. The long white hand that unbuckled his spurs was supple and large ; his whole frame was modelled in more generous proportions than are usually seen in the descendants of the Aztecs or their conquerors.

"Ingles," thought Planillos, using a term which is indiscriminately applied to English or Americans. "A man I dare vow it would be hard to deal with in fair fight!"

But evidently the Englishman, or American, was not there with any idea of contest; a pistol gleamed in his belt, but its absence would have been more noticeable than its presence, — it was worn as a matter of course. For so young a man, in that country where every cavalier native or foreign affected an abundance of ornament, his dress was singularly plain, — black throughout, even to the wide hat that shaded his face, the youthful bloom of which was heightened rather than injured by the superficial bronze imparted by a tropical sun.

Planillos had time to observe all this. Evidently the late-comer knew his ground, and had but little fear of discovery. "A bold fellow," thought the watcher, "and fair indeed should be the Dulcinea for whom he ventures so much. It must be the niece of Don Rafael, or perhaps the governess — did I hear she was young?"

But further speculation was arrested by the movements of the stranger, who, after a moment's parley with Pedro, came noiselessly but directly toward the door near which Planillos was lying.

Once within it, he paused to listen. Planillos expected him to make some signal, and to see him joined by a veiled figure in the corridor, but to his unbounded amazement and rage the intruder passed swiftly by the fountain, under the great trees of bitter-scented oleanders and cloying jasmine, and sprang lightly up the steps leading to the private apartments. His foot was on the corridor, when Planillos, light as a cat, leaped up the steep stair. His head had just reached the level of the floor above, when with an absolute fury of rage he caught the glimpse of a fair young face in the moonlight, and beheld the American in the embrace of a beautiful girl. Instinct, rather than recognition, revealed to his initiated mind the young heiress, Herlinda Garcia. Absolutely paralyzed by astonishment and rage, for one moment dumb, almost blinded, in the next he saw the closing of a heavy door divide from his sight the lovers whom he was too late to separate.

Too late? No! one blow from his dagger upon that closed door, one cry throughout the sleeping house and the life of the man who had stolen within would not be worth a moment's purchase! It required all his strength of will, a full realization of his own position, to prevent Planillos from shouting aloud, from rushing to the door of Doña Isabel, to beat upon it and cry, "Up! up! look to your daughter! See if there be any shame like hers! see how your own child tramples upon the honor of which you have so proudly boasted!"

But he restrained himself, panting like a wild animal mad with excitement. The thought of a more perfect, a more personal revenge leaped into his mind, and silenced the cry that rose to his lips, — held him from rushing down to plunge his dagger into the heart of the false door-keeper, completely obliterated even the remembrance of the purpose for which he had ventured into a place deemed so sacred, so secure! and sustained him through the long hour of waiting, the horrible intentness of his purpose each moment growing more fixed, more definitely pitiless.

For some time he stood rooted to the spot upon which he had made the discovery which had so maddened him, but at last he crouched in the shadow at the foot of the staircase; and scarcely had he done so, when the man for whom he waited appeared at the top. He saw him wave his hand, he even caught his whispered words, so acute were his senses: "Never fear, my Herlinda, all will be well. I will protect you, my love! In another week at most all this will be at an end. I shall be free to come and go as I will!"

"Free as air!" thought the man lying in the shadow, with grim humor, even as he grasped his dagger. Crouching beneath his blanket he had drawn from his brows the red kerchief. The veins stood black and swollen upon his temples as the foreigner, waving a last farewell, descended the stairs. He passed with drooping head, breathing at the moment a deep sigh, within a hand's breadth of an incarnate fiend.

Ah, devoted youth! had thy guardian angel veiled her face that night? Oh, if but at the last moment thy light foot would wake the echoes and rouse the sleepers, already muttering in their dreams, as if conscious that the dawn was near. But nothing happened; the whole world seemed wrapped in oblivion as he bent over the gate-. keeper, and with some familiar touch aroused him. He stooped to put on his spurs, as Pedro opened the postern, and instantly stepped forth, while the gate-keeper proceeded to replace the fastenings. But as the man turned nervously, with the sensation of an unexpected presence near him, he was absolutely paralyzed with dismay. A livid face, in which were set eyes of lurid blackness, looked down upon him with satanic rage. The bulk that towered over him seemed colossal. "Mercy! mercy!" he ejaculated. "By all the saints I swear—"

"Let me pass!" hissed Planillos in a voice scarce above a whisper, but which in its intensity sounded in the ears of Pedro like thunder. "Villain, let me pass!" and he cast from him the terrified gate-keeper as though he were a child, and rushed out upon the sandy slope which lay between the great house and the village. He was not a moment too soon. In the dim light he caught sight of the lithe figure of the foreigner, as he passed rapidly over the rough ground skirting the village, the better to escape the notice of the dogs, which, tired with baying the moon, had at last sunk to uneasy slumbers.

Planillos looked toward the moon, and cursed its rapid waning. The light grew so faint he could scarce keep the young man in sight, as he approached a tree where a dark horse was tied, which neighed as he drew near. Planillos clutched his dagger closer; would the pursued spring into his saddle, and thus escape, at least for that night? On the contrary, he lingered, leaning against his horse, his eyes fixed on the white walls of the house he had left. All unconscious of danger, he stood in the full strength of manhood, with the serene influences of Nature around him, his mind so rapt and tranced that even had his pursuer taken no precaution in making his approach from shrub to shrub, concealing his person as much as possible, he would probably have reached his victim unnoticed. Within call slept scores of fellow-men; behind him, scarce half a mile away, rose the walls and chimneys of his whilom home; not ten minutes before he had said, "I shall be as safe on the road as in your arms, my love!" He was absolutely unconscious of his surroundings, lost in a blissful reverie, when with irresistible force he was hurled to the ground; a frightful blow fell upon his side, — the heavens grew dark above him. Conscious, yet dumb, he staggered to his feet, only to be again precipitated to the earth; the dagger that at the moment of attack had been thrust into his bosom, was buried to the hilt; the blood gushed forth, and with a deep groan he expired.

All was over in a few moments of time. John Ashley's soul, with all its sins, had been hurled into the presence of its Judge. The self-appointed avenger staggered, gasping, against the tree; an almost superhuman effort had brought a terrible exhaustion. Every muscle and nerve quivered; he could scarcely stand. Yet thrusting from him with his foot the dead body, he thirsted still for blood. "If I could but return and kill that villain Pedro," he hissed; "if his accursed soul could but follow to purgatory this one I have already sent! But, bah! a later day will answer for the dog! Ah, I am so spent a child might hold me; but," looking toward the mountains, "this horse is fresh and fleet. I shall be safe enough when the first beam of the morning sun touches your lover's lips, Herlinda."

The assassin glanced from his victim toward the house he had left, with a muttered imprecation; then, trembling still from his tremendous exertions, he approached the steed, which, unable to break the lariat by which it had been fastened, was straining and plunging, half-maddened, after the confusion of the struggle, by the smell of blood already rising on the air.

Planillos possessed that wonderfully magnetic power over the brute creation which is as potent as it is rare, and which on this occasion within a few moments completely dominated and calmed the fright and fury of the powerful animal, which he presently mounted, and which — though man and horse shook with the violence of excitement and conflict — he managed with the ease that denoted constant practice and superb horsemanship. With a last glance at the murdered man, whom the darkness that precedes the dawn scarce allowed him to distinguish from the shrubs around, he put spurs to the restive steed, and galloped rapidly away.

2

III.

It is not to be supposed that this bloody deed occurred entirely unsuspected. Pedro, the gate-keeper, lay half-stunned upon the stones where he had been cast by the man who called himself Planillos, and listened with strained ears to every sound. No indication of a struggle reached him, but his horrified imagination formed innumerable pictures of treacherous violence, in which one or the other of the men who had left him figured as the victim. He dared give no alarm; indeed, at first he was so unnerved by terror that he could neither stir nor speak. At length, after what appeared to him hours but was in reality only a few minutes, he heard the shrill neigh of the horse and the sound of rearing and plunging, followed by the dull thud of retreating footsteps and shrill whistles in challenge and answer from the watchmen upon the hacienda roof, who, however, took no further steps toward investigating what they supposed to be a drunken brawl which had taken place, almost out of hearing and quite out of sight, and which therefore, as they conceived, could in no wise endanger the safety or peace of the hacienda.

Their signals, however, served to arouse Pedro, who shaking in every limb, his brain reeling, his heart bursting with apprehension, crawled to the postern, and after many abortive efforts managed to secure the bolts. He then staggered to the alcove in which he slept, and searching beneath the sheepskin mat which served for his bed, found a small flask of *aguardiente*, and taking a deep draught of the fiery liquor, little by little recovered his outward composure.

For that night, however, sleep no more visited his eyes; and he spent the hour before dawn in making to himself wild excuses for his treason, in wilder projects for flight, and in mentally recapitulating his sins and preparing himself for death; so it can readily be imagined that it was a haggard and distraught countenance that he thrust forth from the postern at dawn, when with the first streak of light came a crowd of excited villagers to the gate, to beat upon it wildly, and with hoarse groans and cries to announce that Don Juan had been found murdered under a mesquite tree.

"Impossible! Ye are mad! Anselmo, thou art drunk, raving!" stammered forth the gate-keeper. "Don Juan is is at the reduction-works!"

"Thou liest!" cried an excited villager; "he is in purgatory. God help him! Holy angels and all saints pray for him!"

"Ave Maria! Mother of Sorrows, by the five wounds of thy Son, intercede for him!" cried a chorus of women, wringing their hands and gesticulating distractedly.

"Open the gate, Pedro!" demanded the throng without, by this time almost equalled by that within, through which the administrador, Don Rafael Sanchez, was seen forcing his way, holding high the great keys of the main door. He was a small man, with a pale but determined face, before whom the crowd fell back, ceasing for a moment their incoherent lamentations, while he assisted Pedro to unlock and throw open the doors.

"Good heavens, man, are you mad?" he exclaimed, as Pedro darted from his side and rushed toward the group of rancheros, who, bearing between them a recumbent form, were slowly approaching the hacienda. "Ah! ah, that is right," as he saw that Pedro, with imperative gestures and a few expressive words, had induced the bearers to turn and proceed with the body toward the reduction-works; "better there than here. What could have induced him to roam about at night? I have told him a score of times his foolhardiness would be the death of him;" and with these and similar ejaculations Don Rafael hastened to join the throng which were soon pouring into the gates of the reduction-works.

Meanwhile from within the great house came the cries of women, above which rose one piercing shriek; but few were there to hear it, for in wild excitement men, women, and children followed the corpse across the valley and thronged the gates of the works which were closed in their faces, or surrounded with gaping looks, wild gesticulations, and meaningless inquiries, the tree beneath which the murdered man had been found, thus completely obliterating the signs of the struggle and flight of the murderer even while most eagerly seeking them.

John Ashley had been an alien and a heretic. No longer ago than yesterday there had been many a lip to murmur at his foreign ways. In all the history of the mining works never had there been known a master so exacting with the laborer, so rigorous with the dishonest, so harsh with the careless ; yet he had been withal as generous and just as he was severe. The people had been ready to murmur, yet in their secret hearts they had respected and even loved the young *Americano*, who knew how to govern them, and to gain from them a fair amount of work for a fair and promptly paid wage ; and who, from a half ruinous, ill-managed source of vexation and loss, was surely but slowly evolving order and the promise of prosperity.

The bearers and the crowd of laborers belonging to the reduction-works were admitted with their burden, and as they passed into the large and scantily-furnished room which John Ashley had called his own, they reverently pulled off their wide, ragged straw hats, and many a lip moved in prayer as the people, for a moment awed into silence, crowded around to view the corpse, which had been laid upon a low narrow bed with the striped blanket of a laborer thrown over it. As the coarse covering was thrown back, a woful sight was seen. The form of a man scarce past boyhood, drenched from breast to feet in blood, yet still beautiful in its perfect symmetry. The tall lithe figure, the straight features, the downy beard shading cheeks and lips of adolescent softness, the long lashes of the eyelids now closed forever, and the fair curls resting upon the marble brow, all showed how comely he had been. The women burst into fresh lamentations, the men muttered threats of vengeance. But who was the murderer? Ay, there was the mystery.

"He has a mother far off across the sea," said a woman, brokenly.

" Ay, and sisters," added another ; " he bade us remember them when we drank to his health on his saint's day. 'In my country we keep birthdays,' he said (I suppose, poor gentleman, he meant the saints had never learned his barbarous tongue) ; and then he laughed. 'But saint's day or birthday, it is all the same ; I'm twenty-three to-day.'"

" Yes, 't was twenty-three he said," confirmed another ; " and do you remember how he reddened and laughed when I told him he was old enough to think of wedding?"

" But vexed enough," added another, " when I repeated our old proverb, ' Who goes far to marry, goes to deceive or be deceived.' I meant no ill, but he turned on me like a hornet. But, poor young fellow, all his quick tempers are over now ; he'll be quiet enough till the Judgment day — cursed be the hand that struck him ! "

" Come, come ! " suddenly broke in Don Rafael, " no more of this chatter ; clear the room for the Señor Alcalde," and with much important bustle and portentous gravity the official in question entered. He had in fact been one of the first to hasten to the scene of the murder, for the time forgetting the dignity of his position, of which in his ragged *frazada*, his battered straw hat, and un-kempt locks, there was little to remind either himself or his fellow villagers. However, on the alcalde being called for, he immediately dropped his *rôle* of idle gazer, and proceeded with the most stately formality to the reduction-works. After viewing the dead body, he made most copious notes of the supposed manner of assassination, which were chiefly remarkable in differing entirely from the reality ; and he gave profuse orders for the following of the murderer or murderers, delivering at the same time to Don Rafael Sanchez the effects of the deceased, for safe keeping and ultimate transmission to the relatives, mean-while delivering himself of many sapient remarks, to the great edification of his hearers.

It appeared upon examination of various persons con-nected with the reduction-works that the young American had been in the habit of riding forth at night, sometimes attended by a servant, but often alone, spending hours of the beautiful moonlight in exploring the deep cañons of the mountains, having, seemingly, a peculiar love for their wild solitudes and an utter disregard of danger. More than once when he had ventured forth alone, the gate-keeper or clerk had remonstrated, but he had laughed at their fears ; and in fact it was the mere habit of caution that had suggested them, the whole country being at that time remarkably free from marauders, and the idea that John Ashley — almost a stranger, so courteous, so well liked by inferiors, as well as by those who called themselves his equals or superiors — should have a personal enemy had never entered the mind of even the most suspicious. But for once the cowards were justified; the brave man had fallen, the days of his young and daring life were ended.

The alcalde and Don Rafael were eloquent in grave encomiums of his worth and regret for his folly, as they at last left the reduction-works together. They had agreed that a letter must be written to the American consul in the city of Mexico, with full particulars, and that he should be asked to communicate the sad event to the family of the deceased; but as several days, or even weeks, must necessarily elapse before he could be heard from, it was decided that the murdered man should be buried upon the following day. To wait longer was both useless and unusual. And so, these matters being satisfactorily arranged, the alcalde and administrador, both perhaps ready for breakfast, parted.

The latter at the gate of the hacienda met the major-domo, who whispered to him mysteriously, and finally led him to the courtyard, where the forsaken mule was munching his fodder. A pair of sandals lay there. Pedro, had he wished, could have shown a striped blanket and hat that he had picked up near the gateway and concealed; but the mule and sandals were patent to all.

"Well, what then?" cried Don Rafael, impatiently, when he had minutely inspected them, turning the sandals with his foot as he stared at the animal.

"Oh, nothing," answered the major-domo; "I am perhaps a fool, but the ranchero is gone."

Don Rafael started — fell into a deep study — turned away — came back, and laid his hand upon the major-domo's arm. This was the first suggestion that had been advanced of the possibility of the murderer having sought his victim from within the walls of the great house. "Silencio!" he said; "what matters it to us how the man died? There is more in this than behooves you or me to meddle with."

The two men looked at each other. "Why disturb the Señora Doña Isabel with such matters? The American is dead. The ranchero can be nothing to her," said Don Rafael, sententiously. "He who gives testimony unasked brings suspicion upon himself. No, no! leave the matter to his countrymen; they have a consul here who has nothing to do but inquire into such matters."

"True, true! and one might as well hope to find again the wildbird escaped from its cage, as to see that Juan Planillos! God save us! if he was indeed the true Juan Planillos!" and the mystified major-domo actually turned pale at the thought. "They say he is more devil than man; that would explain how he got out of the hacienda, for Pedro Gomez swears he let no man pass, either out or in."

Don Rafael had his own private opinion about that, and of whom the disguised visitor might be. Yet why should he have attacked the American? Had Ashley too been within the walls, — and for what purpose? These questions were full of deep and startling import, and again impressing upon his subordinate that endless trouble might be avoided by a discreet silence, he walked thoughtfully away, those vague suspicions and conjectures taking definite shape in his mind. He went to the gate with some design of warily questioning Pedro, but the man was not there; for once, friend or foe might go in or out unnoticed. But it was a day of disorder, and Don Rafael could readily divine the excuse for the gate-keeper's neglect of duty. Remembering that he had not broken his fast that day, he went to his own rooms for the morning chocolate; and from thence he presently saw Pedro emerge from the opposite court, and with bowed head and reluctant steps repair to his wonted post. Don Rafael Sanchez knew his countrymen, especially those of the lower class, too well to hasten to him and ply him with inquiries as he longed to do. He knew too well the value of patience, and more than once had found it golden. Rita, his young wife, had come to him, and through her tears and ejaculations was relating the account of the murder the servants had brought to her, which was as wild and improbable as the reality had been, though not more ghastly, when a servant entered with a hasty message from Doña Isabel.

IV.

WHILE the discovery of the murder had caused this wild excitement outside the walls of the hacienda, a far different scene was being enacted within. Mademoiselle La Croix, the governess of the two sisters Herlinda and Carmen Garcia, had arisen early, leaving her youngest charge asleep, and, hurriedly donning her dressing-gown, hastened to the adjoining apartment, where Herlinda was enjoying that deep sleep which comes to young and healthy natures with the dawn, rounding and completing the hours of perfect rest, which youthful activity both of body and mind so imperatively demands.

A beautiful girl, between fifteen and sixteen, in her perfect development of figure, as well as in the pure olive tints of her complexion, revealing her Castilian descent, — Herlinda Garcia lay upon the white pillows shaded by a canopy of lace, one arm thrown above her head, the other, bare to the elbow, thrown across a bosom that rose and fell with each breath she drew, with the regularity of perfect content. Yet she opened her eyes with a start, and uttered an exclamation of alarm, as Mademoiselle La Croix lightly touched her, saying half petulantly, as she turned away, "Oh, Mademoiselle, why have you wakened me? I was so happy just then! I was dreaming of John!"

She spoke the English name with an indescribable accent of tenderness, but Mademoiselle La Croix repeated it after her almost sharply.

"John! yes," she said, "it is no wonder he is always in your thoughts; as for me, Heaven knows what will happen to me! I am sure, had I known—" and the Frenchwoman paused, to wipe a tear from her eye.

"Ah, yes, it was thoughtless, cruel of us!" interrupted Herlinda, penitently, yet scarcely able to repress a smile as her glance fell upon the gayly flowered dressing-gown which formed an incongruous wrapping for the thin, bony figure of the governess; " but, dear Mademoiselle, nothing worse than a dismissal can happen to you, and you know John has promised — "

The governess drew herself up with portentous dignity. " Mademoiselle wanders from the point," she interrupted; " it is of herself only I was thinking. This state of affairs must be brought to a close," she added solemnly, after a pause. " At all risks, Herlinda, John must claim you."

" So he knows, so I tell him," answered Herlinda, suddenly wide awake, and ceasing the pretty yawns and stretchings with which she had endeavored to banish her drowsiness. " Oh, Mademoiselle," a shade of apprehension passing over her face, " I have done wrong, very wrong. My mother will never forgive me ! "

" Absurd ! " ejaculated the governess. " Doña Isabel, like every one else in the world, must submit to the inevitable."

" So John said; but, Mademoiselle, neither you nor John know my mother, nor my people. She will never forgive : in her place, I would never forgive ! "

" And yet you dared ! " cried Mademoiselle La Croix, looking at the young girl with new admiration at the courage which stimulated her own. " Truly, you Mexicans are a strange people, so generous in many things, so blind and obstinate in others. Well, well ! you shall find, Herlinda, I too can be brave. If I were a coward, I should say, wait until I am safely away; but I am no coward," added the little woman, drawing her figure to its full height and expanding her nostrils, — " I am ready to face the storm with you."

" Yes, yes ! " said the young girl, hurriedly and abstractedly. " What," she added, rising in her bed, and grasping the bronze pillar at the head, " what is that I hear? What a confusion of voices ! " She turned deadly pale, and her white-robed figure shook beneath the long loose tresses of her coal-black hair. " My God ! Mademoiselle, I hear his name ! "

The governess too grew pale, though she began incoherently to reassure the young lady, who remained kneeling in the bed as if petrified, her hands clasped to her breast, her eyes strained, listening intently, as through the thick walls came the dull murmur of many voices. Like waves they seemed to surge and beat against the solid stones, and the vague roar formed itself into the words, " Don Juan! Ashley!"

Although a moment's reflection would have reminded her that a hundred other events, rather than that of his death, might have brought the people there to call upon the name of their master, one of those flashes of intuition which appear magnetic revealed to Herlinda the awful truth, even before it was borne to her outward ear by the shrill voice of a woman, crying through the corridor, " God of my life! Don Juan is killed! murdered! murdered!" She even stopped to knock upon the door and reiterate the words, in the half-horrified, half-pleasurable excitement the vulgar often feel in communicating dreadful and unexpected news; but a wild shriek from within suddenly checked her outcry, and chilled her blood.

" Fool that I am! I should have remembered," she muttered. " Paqua told me there was certainly love between those two; she saw the glance he threw on the young Señorita in church one day. But that was months ago, and she certainly is to marry Don Vicente."

At that moment a middle-aged, plainly-dressed woman, with the blue and white reboso so commonly worn thrown over her head, entered the corridor. Her figure was so commanding, the glance of her eyes so impressive, that even in her haste she lost none of her habitual dignity. The woman turned away, glad to escape with the reproof, " Cease your clamor, Refugio! What! is your news so pressing that you must needs frighten your young mistress with it? Go, go! Doña Isabel will be little likely to be pleased with your zeal."

The woman hastened away, and Doña Feliz, waiting until she had disappeared, laid her hand upon the door of Herlinda's chamber, which like those of many sleeping apartments in the house opened directly upon the upper corridor, its massive thickness and strength being looked upon as more than sufficient to repel any danger which could in the wildest probability reach it from the well guarded interior of the fort-like building.

As Doña Feliz touched the latch, the door was opened by the affrighted governess, who had anticipated the entrance of Doña Isabel. The respite unnerved her, and she threw herself half fainting in a chair, as Herlinda seized the new-comer by the shoulders, gasping forth, "Feliz, Feliz, tell me! tell me it is not true! He is not dead! dead! dead!" her voice rising to a shriek.

"Hush! hush, Herlinda! O God, my child, what can this be to thee?" Doña Feliz shuddered as she spoke. She glanced at the closed window; the walls she knew to be a yard in thickness, yet she wished them double, lest a sound of these wild ravings should escape.

"Feliz, you dare not tell me! — then it is true! he is murdered! lost, lost to me forever!" The young girl slipped like water through the arms that would have clasped her, crouching upon the floor, wringing her hands, tearless, voiceless, after her last despairing words. Feliz attempted to raise her, but in vain.

Carmen, aroused by the sounds of distress, appeared in the doorway which connected the two rooms. "Back! go back!" cried Doña Feliz, and the child frightened and whimpering, withdrew. Feliz turned to the governess, — the deep dejection of her attitude struck her; and at that moment Doña Isabel appeared.

"Herlinda," she began, "this is sad news; but remember—" she paused, looked with stern disapprobation, then her superb self-possession giving way, she rushed to her daughter and clasped her arm. "Rise! rise!" she cried; "this excess of emotion shames you and me. This is folly. Rise, I say! He could never have been anything, child, to thee!"

Herlinda did not move, she did not even look up. She had always feared her mother; had trembled at her slightest word of blame; had been like wax under her hand. Yet now she was as marble; her hands had dropped on her lap; she was rigid to the touch; only the deep moans that burst from her white lips proved that she lived.

The attitude was expressive of such utter despair that it was of itself a revelation; and presently the moans formed themselves into words: "My God! my God! I am undone! he is dead! he is dead!"

The words bore a terrible significance to the listeners. Doña Isabel turned her eyes upon Feliz, and read upon her face the thought that had forced its way to her own mind. Her face paled; she dropped her daughter's arm and drew back. The act itself was an accusation. Perhaps the girl felt it so. She suddenly wrung her hands distractedly, and sprang to her feet, exclaiming, "My husband! my husband! Let me go to him! he cannot be dead! he is not dead!"

The words "My husband" fell like a thunderbolt among them. Herlinda had rushed to the door, but Doña Feliz caught her in her strong arms, and forced her back. "Tell us what you mean!" she ejaculated; while the frightened governess plucked her by the sleeve, reiterating again and again, "Pardon! pardon! entreat your mother's pardon!"

But the terrible turn affairs had taken had driven the thought of pardon, or the need of it, from her mind. "I tell you I am his wife! Ah, you think that cannot be, but it is true; the Irish priest married us four months ago in Las Parras. Let me go, Feliz, let me go! I am his wife!"

"This is madness!" interrupted Doña Isabel, in a voice of such preternatural calmness that her daughter turned as if awestricken to look at her. "Unhappy girl, you cannot have been that man's wife. You have been betrayed! Child! child! the house of Garcia is disgraced!"

A chill fell upon the governess, yet she spoke sharply, almost pertly: "Not disgraced by Herlinda, Madame. She was indeed married to John Ashley, in the parish church of Las Parras, by the missionary priest, Father Magauley."

The long, slow glance of incredulity changing into deepest scorn which Doña Isabel turned upon the governess seemed to scorch, to wither her. She actually cowered beneath it, faltering forth entreaties for pardon, rather, be it said to her honor, for the unhappy Herlinda than for herself. Meanwhile, with lightning rapidity, the events of the last few months passed through the mind of Doña Isabel. Yes, yes, it had been possible; there had been opportunity for this base work. Her eyes clouded, her breast heaved; had she held a weapon in her hand, the intense passion that possessed her might have sought a method more powerful than words in finding for itself expression. As it was, she turned away, sick at heart, her brain afire. Doña Feliz had placed a strong, firm hand over Herlinda's lips. "It is useless," she said in a voice like Fate. "You will never see him again."

Herlinda comprehended that those words but expressed the unspoken fiat of her mother. She shuddered and groaned. "Mother! mother!" she said faintly, "he loved me. I loved him so, mother! Mother, I have spoken the truth; Mademoiselle will tell you all; I was indeed his wife."

Doña Isabel would not trust herself to look at her daughter. She dared not, so strong at that moment was her resentment of her daring, so deep the shame of its consequences. "Vile woman!" she said to the governess, in low, penetrating tones of concentrated passion; "you who have avowed yourself the accomplice of yon dead villain, tell me all. Let me know whether you were simply treacherously ignorant, or treacherously base. Silence, Herlinda! nor dare in my presence shed one tear for the wretch who betrayed you."

But her commands were unheeded. The present anguish overcame the habits and fears of a whole life, — as, alas! a passionate love had once before done. But then she had been under the domination of her lover, and had been separated from the mother, whose very shadow would have deterred and prevented her. Now, even the deep severity of that mother's voice fell on unheeding ears. Though tears came not, piteous groans, mingled with the name of her love, burst from the heart of the wretched girl, who leaned like a broken lily upon the breast of Doña Feliz, who from the moment that Herlinda had declared herself a wife gazed upon her with looks of deep compassion, alternating with those of anxious curiosity toward Doña Isabel, whose every glance she had learned to interpret. She was a woman of great intelligence, yet it appeared to her as though Doña Isabel, who was queen and absolute mistress on her own domain, had but to speak the word and set her daughter in any position she might claim. The supremacy of the Garcias was her creed, — that by which she had lived; was it to be contradicted now?

"Tell me all," reiterated Doña Isabel, in the concentrated voice of deep and terrible passion, as the cowering governess vainly strove to frame words that might least offend. "How did this treachery occur? Where and how did you give that fellow opportunity to compass his base designs?"

Herlinda started; she would have spoken, but Doña Feliz restrained her by the strong pressure of her arm; and the faltering voice of the governess attempted some explanation and justification of an event, which, almost unparalleled in Mexico, could not have been foreseen perhaps even by the jealous care of the most anxious mother.

"This is all I have to tell," she stammered. "You remember you sent us to Las Parras six months ago, just after you had refused your daughter's hand to John Ashley, and promised it to Vicente Gonzales. We remained there in exile nearly two months. Herlinda was wretched. What was there to console or enliven her in that miserable village? Separated from her sister, from you, Madame, whom she deeply loved even while she feared, what had she to do but nurse her grief and despair, which grew daily stronger on the food of tears and solitude? At first she was too proud to speak to me of that which caused her sleepless nights and unhappy days. But my looks must have expressed the pity I felt. She threw herself into my arms one day, and sobbed out her sad tale upon my bosom. She had spoken to this Ashley but a few times, and then in your presence, Madame; but in your country the eye seems the messenger of love. She declared that she could not live, she would not, were she separated from John Ashley; that the day of her marriage with Vicente Gonzales should be the day of her death."

"To the point," interrupted Doña Isabel in an icy tone. "I had heard all this. Even in John Ashley's very presence Herlinda had forgotten her dignity and mine. This is not what I would know."

"But it leads to it, Madame," cried the governess, deprecatingly, "for while I was in the state of mingled pity and perplexity caused by Herlinda's words, a message was brought to me that John Ashley was at the door. I went to speak to him. Yielding to his entreaties, I even allowed him to see Herlinda. How could I guess it was to urge a course which only the most remarkable combination of events could have made possible?"

"Intrigante," muttered Doña Isabel, bitterly.

"You," continued the governess, piqued and emboldened by the adjective, "angered by the sight of him as you passed the reduction-works, had yourself invented a pretext for sending him to San Marcos. You could not well dismiss him altogether from a position he filled so well. He might, you thought, reveal the reason."

"Deal not with my motives," interrupted the lady haughtily. "It is true I sent him to San Marcos. And what then?"

"Then, by chance, he learned what here no servant had dared to tell him, — the name of the village to which Herlinda had been sent, so near your own hacienda, too, that he had never once suspected it. And there he met a countryman. These English, Irish, Americans, — they are all bound together by a common language ; and he, this poor priest, entirely ignorant of Spanish, coldly received even by his clerical brethren, was glad to spend a few days in a trip with Ashley ; and as they rode together over the thirty leagues of mountain and valley between San Marcos and Las Parras, he formed a great liking for the pleasant youth, and beyond gently rallying him, made no opposition to staying over a night in the village, and joining him in holy matrimony to the woman of his choice, whom he imagined to be a poor but pretty peasant, so modest were our surroundings."

Doña Isabel's face darkened. "Hasten ! hasten !" she muttered. "I see it all ; deluded, unhappy girl."

"Unhappy, yes !" cried the governess. "Prophetic were the tears that coursed over her cheeks, as she went with me to the chapel in the early morning, and there in the presence of a few peasants who had never seen her before, or failed to recognize her under the dingy reboso she wore, was married to the young American."

"Ignorant imbeciles !" ejaculated Doña Isabel, but so low that no one distinctly caught her words. "And this *marriage* as you call it, in what language was it performed?"

"Oh, in English," answered Mademoiselle La Croix, readily. "The priest knew no other. Immediately after the ceremony the bell sounded, the groom and bride separated, the people streamed in, and Holy Mass was celebrated, thus consecrating the marriage. Reassure yourself,

Doña Isabel, all was right; the good priest gave a certificate in due form, which doubtless will be found among
John Ashley's papers."

In spite of the stony yet furious gaze with which Doña
Isabel had listened to these particulars, the governess had
gathered confidence as she proceeded, and ended with a
feeling that the most jealous doubter must be convinced,
the most inveterate opponent silenced.

But far otherwise was the effect of her narrative upon
Doña Isabel; she had been deceived by her own daughter,
befooled by her hirelings. Her keen intelligence declared
to her at once the fatal irregularity of the ceremony. It
indeed vindicated the purity of Herlinda, but could it save
her from dishonor? Thoughts of vague yet terrible meaning tormented her. The horrors of a past day returned
with fresh complications to menace and torture her; and
even had it been possible at that moment for her by one
word to prove her daughter the honorable widow of John
Ashley, it would have caused her a thousand pangs to have
uttered it; and could one single word have brought him to
life, she would have condemned herself to perpetual dumb-
ness. A frenzy of shame and baffled intents possessed her.
But her thoughts were not of these. She knew that this marriage as it stood was void; it met the requirements of neither
Church nor State. Yet — yet — yet — there were possibilities: her family were powerful, her wealth was great.

Doña Feliz watched her with deep, inquiring eyes. Her
child stood there, a voiceless pleader, her utter abandonment of grief appealing to the heart of the mother; but
between them was an impregnable wall of pride and a
cloud of possibilities which confused and distracted her.
She came to no determination, made no resolve, but clasping her hands over her eyes, stood as if a gulf had opened
in her path, — from which she could not turn, and over
which she dared not pass. Slowly, at last, she dropped
her arms, resumed her usual aspect of composure, and
passed from the room. For some moments the little
group she had left remained motionless. A profound stillness reigned throughout the house. Time itself seemed
arrested, and the one word breathed through the silence
seemed to describe the whole world to those within the
walls, — "dead! dead! dead!"

V.

As Doña Isabel Garcia turned from her daughter's apartment, she stepped into a corridor flooded with the dazzling sunshine of a perfect morning, and as she passed on in her long black dress, the heavily beamed roof interposing between her uncovered head and the clear and shining blue of the sky, there was something almost terrible in the stony gaze with which she met the glance of the woman-servant who hurried after her to know if she would as usual break her fast in the little arbor near the fountain. It terrified the woman, who drew back with a muttered "Pardon, Señora!" as the lady swept by her, and entered her own chamber.

The volcano of feeling which surged within her burst forth, not in sobs and cries, not in passionate interjections, but in the tones of absolute horror in which she uttered the two names that had severally been to her the dearest upon earth, — "Leon!" and "Herlinda!" and which at that moment were equally synonymous of all most terrible, most dreaded, and were the most powerful factors amid the love, the honor, the pride, the passions and prejudices which controlled her being.

For a time she stood in the centre of her apartment, striking unconsciously with her clenched hand upon her breast blows that at another time would have been keenly felt, but the swelling emotions within rendered her insensible to mere bodily pain. Indeed, as the moments passed it brought a certain relief; and as her walking to and fro brought her at last in front of the window which opened upon the broad prospect to the west, she paused, and looked long and fixedly toward the reduction-works, as if her vision could penetrate the stone walls, and read the mind which had perished with the man who lay murdered within them.

As she stood thus, she presently became aware that a sound which she had heard without heeding, — as one

ignores passing vibrations upon the air, that bring no
special echo of the life of which we are active, conscious
parts, — was persistently striving to make itself heard;
and with an effort she turned to the door, upon which fell
another timid knock, and bade the suppliant enter; for
the very echo of his knocking proclaimed a suppliant.
She started as her eyes fell upon the haggard face of
Pedro the gate-keeper.

He entered almost stealthily, closing the door softly
behind him. "Señora," he whispered, coming up to her
quite closely, extending his hands in a deprecating way,
"Señora, by the golden keys of my patron, I swear to
you I was powerless. Don Juan told me he had your
Grace's own authority; he told me they were married!"

Doña Isabel started. In the same sentence the man
had so skilfully mingled truth and falsehood that even
she was deceived. By representing to his mistress that
Ashley had used her name to gain entrance to the hacienda, he had hoped to divert her anger from himself, —
and what matter though it fell unjustly upon the dead
man? But in fact the second phrase of the sentence,
"He told me they were married," was what struck most
keenly upon the ear of Doña Isabel, and chilled her very
blood. How much, then, did this servant know? How far
was she in his power? Until that moment she had not
known — had not suspected — that the murdered man
and the murderer had been within the walls of the hacienda buildings. This knowledge but confirmed her intuitions! Partly to learn facts which might guide her, and
partly to gain time, she looked with her coldest, most petrifying gaze upon the man, and asked him what he meant,
and bade him tell her all, even as he would confess to the
priest, for so only he might hope to escape her most
severe displeasure.

As she spoke, she had glided behind him and slipped
the bolt of the door, and stood before the solid slab of
unpolished but time-darkened cedar, a very monument of
wrath. Pedro trembled more than ever, but was not for
that the less consistent in his tale of mingled truth and
falsehood. He had begun it with the name "The Señorita Herlinda," but Doña Isabel stopped him with a
portentous frown.

" Her name," she said, " my daughter's name need not
be mentioned. She knows nothing of the woman John
Ashley came here to see, if there is one ; the Señorita
Herlinda has nothing to do with her, nor with your tale.
Proceed."

Pedro, not so deeply versed in the dissimulation of the
higher class as was Doña Isabel in that of the lower,
looked at her a moment in utter incredulity. He learned
nothing from her impassive face, but with the quickwitted-
ness of his race divined that one of the many dark-eyed
damsels who served in the house was to be considered
the cause of Ashley's midnight visits. In that light, his
own breach of trust seemed more venial. Unconsciously,
he shaped his story to that end, and even took to himself
a sort of comfort in feigning to believe, what in his heart
he knew to be an assumption — whether merely verbal
or actual he knew not — of Doña Isabel.

The arguments by which he had been induced by Ashley to open the doors of the hacienda for his midnight
admittance he would have dwelt on at some length, but
Doña Isabel stopped him. " Tell me only of what happened last night," she said ; and in a low whisper he
obeyed, shuddering as he spoke of the man whom he
had admitted under the guise of a peasant, and who had
rushed out to encounter the devoted American, as a madman or wild beast might rush upon its prey.

At his description, eloquent in its brevity, Doña Isabel
for a moment lost her calmness ; her face dropped upon
her hands ; her figure shrank together.

" Pedro !" she murmured, " Pedro ! you knew him?
You are certain ? " she continued in a low, eager voice.

" Certain, Señora ! Should I be likely to be mistaken?
I, who have held him upon my knees a thousand times ;
who first taught him to ride ; who saw him when — "

Doña Isabel stopped the enumeration with a gesture.
She paused a moment in deep thought ; then she extended
her hand, and the man bent over it, not daring to touch it,
but reverently, as if it were that of a queen or a saint.

" Silence, Pedro !" she said. " Silence ! One word,
and the law would be upon him, — though God knows
there should be no law to avenge these false Americans,
who respect neither authority nor hospitality, and would

take our very country from us. Pedro, this deed must
not bring fresh disaster; 't was a mistake; but as you
live, as I pardon you the share you bore in it, keep
silence!"

The words were not an entreaty; they were a command. Doña Isabel understood too well the ascendency
which as lords of the soil the Garcias held over all who
had been born and bred on their estates, to take the false
step of lessening it by any act of weakness. She comprehended that that very ascendency had led him to open
the gates to the declared husband of Herlinda — ay! as to
her lover he would have opened them. It was the *house*
of Garcia he served, as represented by the individual possessing the dominant influence of the hour. As occasion
offered, he and his associates would have favored the interests of any member in affairs of love, believing the intrigue
the natural pleasure of youth, and conceiving it presumption to impugn the actions of one of the seigneurial family.

Doña Isabel became, at this time, when the terrible
consequences of his levity overpowered him, the controlling power, and with absolute genius in a few words, admitting nothing, explaining nothing, offering no reward,
she made the conscience-stricken man the keeper of the
honor of the powerful house of which he was but the veriest minion.

Within the hour, while the people still thronged the
walls of the reduction-works, Doña Feliz left the great
house. The few who witnessed her departure were accustomed to the peremptory commands of the Señora
Doña Isabel and the instant obedience of her confidential
servant, and had as little speculation in their minds as in
the gaze with which they followed the carriage and its
outriders, — yet murmured a few words of pity for those
who, after the horror of the tragedy, would lose the
sombre splendor of the rites which must necessarily
follow.

Upon the next day, John Ashley, carried in procession
by the entire population of men, women, and children of
Tres Hermanos, excepting only the immediate family of
Doña Isabel and Pédro the gate-keeper, was borne across
the wide valley, up the bleak hillside, and laid in a corner

of the low-walled, unkempt graveyard, among the lowly dead of the *plebe.*

Not a sound escaped Herlinda, as from the windows of her mother's room she watched the funeral procession. She had intuitively guessed the time it would issue from the gates of the reduction-works, and her mother placed no restraint upon her movements. Through the clear atmosphere of the May day she could perfectly distinguish the form, ay the very features of her beloved, as he lay stretched upon a wide board surrounded by flowering boughs, his fair curls resting upon the greenery, his hands clasped upon his breast.

To steady their steps perhaps, rather than from any religious custom, the people sang one of those minor airs peculiar to the country, and which are at once so sad and shrill that the piercing wail reached even so far as the great house, — a weird accompaniment to the swaying of the ghostly white lengths of candles borne in scores of hands, and the pale flames of which burned colorless in the brilliant sunshine.

Strangely impressive, even to an indifferent eye, might well have been that scene; the slow march of Death and Woe across the smiling fields, blotting the clear radiance of the cloudless sky, and awesome then even to a careless ear that wail of agony. Mademoiselle La Croix burst into tears and threw herself upon the floor. Doña Isabel, deadly pale, covered her eyes with a hand as cold and white as snow. Herlinda sank upon her knees with parted lips and straining eyes to watch the form upborne before that dark and sinuous procession; but when it became lost to view amid the throng which encircled the open grave, she fell prone to the floor with such a moan as only woe itself can utter, — a moan that seemed the outburst of a maddened brain and a bursting heart.

That night instead of lamentation the sounds of festivity began to be heard, and days of revelry among the peasants followed the hours of horror and gloom which had for a brief period prevailed. In the midst of them Doña Feliz returned to the hacienda. Wherever her journey had led her it had outwardly been unimportant, and drew but little comment from the men who had attended her, and was speedily forgotten. She herself gave no

description of it, nor volunteered any information as to
its object or result.   Even to Doña Isabel, who raised inquiring eyes to the face of her emissary as she entered her
private room, she said, briefly, "No, there is no record;
absolutely none."

Doña Isabel sank back in her chair with a deep-drawn
breath as if some mighty tension, both of mind and body,
had suddenly relaxed.   She had herself sought in vain
through the papers of Ashley for proofs of the alleged
marriage with Herlinda, and Feliz had scanned the public
records with vigilant eyes.   Part of these records had in
some *pronunciamiento* been destroyed by fire, but the
book containing those of the date she sought was intact.
The names of John Ashley and Herlinda Garcia did not
appear therein; the marriage, if marriage there had been,
was unrecorded, and as secret as it was illegal.   Conscience was satisfied, and Doña Isabel was content to
be passive.   Why bring danger upon one still infinitely
dear to her?   The heart of Doña Isabel turned cold at
the thought.   Why rouse a scandal which could so easily
be avoided?   Why strive to legalize a marriage which
could but bring ridicule upon herself, and shame and contempt upon Herlinda?

That day, for the first time in many, Doña Isabel could
force a smile to her lip; for even for policy it had not been
possible for her to smile before.   She was by nature
neither cold nor cruel, but she had been brought up in
the midst of petty intrigues, of violent passions and narrow prejudices; and while she had scorned them, they
had moulded her mind, — as the constant wearing of rock
upon rock forms the hollow in the one, and rounds the
jagged surface of the other.   What would have been
monstrous to her youth became natural to her middle age.
She had suffered and striven.   Was it not the common
lot of woman?   What more natural than that her daughter
should do the same?   And what more natural than that the
mother should raise her who had fallen? — for fallen indeed, in spite of the ceremony of marriage, would the world
think Herlinda.   But why should the world know?   She
pitied her daughter, even as a woman pities another in
travail; yet she looked to the future, she shrank from
the complexities of the present; and so silently, relent-

lessly, shaping her course, ignoring circumstance, she, like a goddess making a law unto herself, thus unflinchingly ordered the destiny of her child. Could she herself have divined the various motives that influenced her? Nay, no more perhaps than the circumstances which will be developed in this tale may make clear the love, the woman's purity, the high-born lady's pride, that all combined to bid her ignore the marriage, which, though irregular, had evidently been made in good faith; and for which, in spite of open malice or secret innuendo, the power and influence of her family could have won the Pope's sanction, and so silenced the cavillings if not the gossip of the world.

AND thus in that remote hacienda — a little world in itself, with all the mingled elements of wealth and poverty, and all those subtile differences of caste and character which form society, in circles small as well as great — began a drama, which to the initiated was of deep and absorbing interest. To the common mind despair and agony can have no existence if they do not declare themselves in groans and tears, and to such Herlinda's deep pallor and her silence revealed nothing; but there were a few who watched in solemn apprehension, feeling hers to be like the intense and sulphurous calm with which Nature awaits the coming of the tempest.

But there were indeed few who saw in her any change other than the events and anxieties of the time rendered natural. At first indeed there had been whispers in corners, and half-pitying, half-fearful shrugs and glances; but almost from the day of Ashley's burial a new and fearful cause of public interest drew attention from Herlinda, from her pallor and her wide-eyed gaze of horror, to the consideration of a more personal anxiety.

The common people declared that from the night of the murder, death, unsatisfied with one victim, had hovered over the hacienda. The rains which should have fallen after the long dry winter, with cleansing and copious force, flooding the ravines and carrying away the accumulated impurities of months, had but moistened and stirred the infected mud of the stagnant water-courses and set loose the fevers which lingered in their depths. Years afterward the peasants dated many a widowhood and orphanage from those plague-stricken weeks. There was one death or more in every hut, and even the great house did not escape its quota of victims. One after another, members of the families of the clerks and officers succumbed, — the major-domo of the courts among the first, and then Mademoiselle La Croix, who indeed, it was afterward observed, had from the first sickened and fallen into a dejection, from which it was almost impossible she should rally. The governess was the object of the most devoted care even from the usually cold and stately Doña Isabel, while the panic-stricken Herlinda, careless of her own danger, bent over her with agonized and fruitless efforts to recall the waning life, or soothe the parting and remorseful soul.

But in all that terrible time this was the only event that seemed to touch or rouse her; for the rest, one might have thought those dreadful days but the ordinary calendar of Herlinda's life. Indeed, it is to be supposed that they suited so well the desolation of her spirit, and that they presented so congruous a setting to her melancholy, that it became merged and absorbed as it were in her surroundings, and so was unperceived, save as the fitting humor of a time when ease and mirth would have been an insult to the general woe.

Doña Isabel had announced her intention of replacing the director of the reduction-works; but time went on, and in the general consternation produced by the epidemic nothing was done. There was much sickness at the works; many of the most experienced hands died; and one day when the clerk in charge was at the crisis of the fever, the men who were not incapacitated from illness went by common consent to the *tienda* to stupefy themselves with fiery native brandy; and Doña Isabel, who was fearlessly passing from one poor hovel to another, aiding the village doctress and the priest in their offices, ordered the mules to be taken from the *tortas*, and the stamps to be stopped. Thus, as the masses half mixed lay upon the floors, they gradually dried and hardened; and as the great stone wheels ceased to turn in the beds of broken ores, so for years upon years they remained, and the works at Tres Hermanos gradually fell into ruin, — a fit haunt for the ghost which, as years went by, was said to haunt their shades. But this was long afterward, when the memory of the handsome and hapless youth had become almost as a myth, mingled with the thousand tales of blood which the fluctuating fortunes of years of international and civil war made as common as they were terrible.

This fertile spot until now had been singularly free from the terror and disorder that had affected the greater part of the country; and though sharing the excitement of party feeling, the actual demands of strife had never invaded it. But quick upon the typhoid, when the peasants who had been spared began to think of repairing their half-ruined hovels, many of them were summoned away with scant ceremony. Don Julian Garcia appeared at the hacienda, his uniform glittering with gold braid, buttons, and lace, the trappings of his horse more gorgeous even than his own dress. He was raising a troop to join his old commander, Santa Anna, who had returned in triumph to the land from which he had been banished, to lead the arms of his countrymen against the foreign foe, which already had begun its victorious march within the sacred borders of their country. In a word, the American War had begun, and involved all factions in one common cause, giving a rallying cry to leaders of every party, to which even the most ignorant among the people responded with intuitive and unquestioning ardor.

Don Julian was uncertain in his politics, but not in his hatreds. He heard the tale of the murder of the American with complacency; the taking off of one of the heretics seemed to him natural enough, — it was scarcely worth a second thought, certainly not a pause in his work of collecting troops. If Isabel, he commented, had writhed under wounded patriotism as he had done, the American would never have had an opportunity of finding so honorable a service in which to die. Evidently the grudge of some bold patriot, this. What would you? Mexicans were neither sticks nor stones!

Herlinda heard and trembled; a faint hope, a half-formed resolve, had wakened in her breast when she had heard of the arrival of Don Julian. He was a distant cousin, a man of some influence in the family. She remembered him as more frank and genial than others of her kindred. An impulse to break the seal of silence came over her, as she heard his voice ringing through the courts and the clank of his spurs upon the stairs; but it was checked by the first distinct utterance of his lips, which, like all that followed, was a denunciation of the perfidious, the insatiable, the licentious and heretical Americans. For the first time, to the indifference with which she had regarded the desirability of establishing her position as the acknowledged wife of Ashley was added a sensation of fear. What had been in her mind an undefined and incomplete idea of the anger and scorn which the knowledge of her daring would cause among her family connections, became now a terrifying dread as the impetuous but unrepented act assumed the proportions of treason. The words which at the first opportunity she would have spoken died upon her lips, and she became once more hopeless, impassive, unresisting, cold, waiting what time and fate should bring.

And time passed on unflinchingly, and fate was unrelenting. Carmen, after a slight attack of fever, had been sent to some relative in Guanapila, and there she still remained. Doña Isabel's household consisted only of herself, Herlinda, and the aged priest her cousin Don Francisco de Sales, who though in his dotage still at long intervals read Mass in the chapel, baptized infants, and muttered prayers over the dying or dead, not the less sincere because he who breathed them himself stood so far within the shadow of the tomb. The old man was kindly in his senility, and spent long hours dozing in the chair of the confessional, while penitents whispered in his ear their faults and sins, for which they never failed to obtain absolution, little imagining that the placid mind of the old man, even when by chance he was awake, dwelt far more upon the scenes of his youth than the follies and wickednesses of the present. Sometimes he babbled harmlessly of days long past, even of sights and doings far from clerical; but the priestly habit was second nature, and even if he heeded the confidences reposed in him, in his weakest moments they never escaped his lips. To him Herlinda was free to go and disburden her mind, complying with the regulations of her Church, and seeking relief to her troubled soul. To him, too, Doña Isabel resorted; and these two women with their tales of woe, which as often as repeated escaped his memory, roused faintly within his heart an echo of the pain which he uneasily and confusedly remembered dwelt in the world, from which he was gliding into the peace beyond.

Sometimes at the table, or as he sat with them in the corridor, — the priest in the sunshine, they in the shade, — he looked at them with puzzled inquiry in his gaze, which changed to mild satisfaction at some caress or fond word; for this gentle old man was tenderly beloved, with a sort of superstitious reverence. Even Doña Isabel attributed a special sanctity to his blessing, looking upon him as an automaton of the Church, which without consciousness of its own would — certain springs of emotion being touched — respond with admonition or blessing, fraught with all the authority of the Supreme Power. Doña Isabel, as a devout Romanist, had ever been scrupulous in the observances of her Church, submitting to the spiritual functions of the clergy absolutely, while she detested and openly protested against their licentiousness and greed, as also their pernicious interference in worldly affairs. Therefore throughout her life, and especially during her widowhood, she had studiously avoided the more popular clergy, and had sought the oracle of duty through some clod of humanity, who, though dull, should be at least free from vices, — choosing by preference one of her own family to be the repository of her secrets and the judge of her motives and actions. Unconsciously to herself, while outwardly and even to her own conscience fulfilling the requirements of her Church, she had interpreted them by her own will, which, in justice let it be said, had often proved a wise and loyal one; in a word, Doña Isabel Garcia, with exceptional powers within her grasp, had skilfully and astutely freed herself from those trammels which might at the present crisis have forced her into a diametrically opposite course from that which she had determined to pursue, or would at least have forced her to acknowledge to her own mind the doubtful nature of deeds that she now suffered herself to look upon as meritorious. For years, unconsciously, her will had imbued the judgments of her spiritual adviser, as the Padre Francisco was called, and it was not to be supposed that she should cavil now, when with complacent alacrity he echoed yea to her yea, and nay to her nay, — and as she left him, sank back into his chair with a faint wonder at her tale, to forget it in his next slumber, or until recalled to him by the anguished outpourings of Herlinda, for whom he found no words of guidance other than those which throughout his life he had given to young maidens in distress, the commendable ones, " Do as your mother

directs;" though, as he listened to her words, the tears
would pour down his cheeks, and pitying phrases fall from
his trembling lips. Poor Herlinda would be comforted
for a moment by his simple human sympathy, — even
weeping perhaps, for at such times the blessed relief of
tears was given her, — yet found in her darkness no
light, either human or divine.

Had Mademoiselle La Croix lived, Herlinda would doubtless have received from her the impetus to throw herself
upon the pity and protection of her cousin Don Julian,
which in spite of his prejudices he could scarcely have refused ; for the governess, though she was at first stunned
and terrified by the knowledge of the invalidity of the
marriage, was no coward, and would have braved much
to reinstate the girl she had through compassion — and,
she had with a pang been obliged to own, through cupidity — aided to bring into a false position. But she had
scarcely recovered her bewildered senses, the more bewildered by the incomprehensible calm of Doña Isabel, when
she was attacked by the fever, — to which she succumbed
a month before the appearance of the doughty warrior,
whose blustering fierceness would not have appalled her or
deterred her from urging Herlinda to lay before him the
matter, whose vital importance the stunned young creature failed to comprehend.

Later it burst upon her, but it was then too late, —
Don Julian had marched away with his troops. She was
alone, — no help, no counsellor near. Alone? Ah, no!
there were human creatures near, who could behold and
suspect and shake the head. Herlinda awoke to the
shame of her position, as a bird in a net, striving to fly,
first learns its danger. O God! where should she fly?
Were these careless, laughing women as unconscious as
they seemed? Where might she hide herself from these
languid, soft eyes, which suddenly might become hard and
cruel with intelligence? Herlinda drew her reboso around
her, and with flushing cheek traversed the shadiest corridors in her necessary passages from room to room, her
eyes, large with apprehension, burning beneath her down-
cast lids. Every day she grew more restless, more beautiful. She walked for hours in the walled garden, which
the servants never entered. They began to whisper, for-

getting the gossip of months before, that the chances of war were secretly stealing the gayety and buoyancy of Herlinda's youth, by keeping from her side the playmate of her childhood, her lover Vicente Gonzales. Feliz smiled when a garrulous servant spoke thus one day, but ten minutes later entered the room of Doña Isabel.

The next morning it was known that the Señorita Herlinda was to have change, was to go to the capital, that Mecca of all Mexicans. Doña Isabel and Feliz were to accompany her. The clerks and overseers wondered, and shook their heads wisely. They had heard wild tales of the political factions which rendered the city unsafe to woman as to man; Santa Anna's brief dictatorship had ended in trouble. Still, in that remote district nothing was known with certainty, and these bucolic minds were not given to many conjectures upon the motives or movements of their superiors. If anything could arouse surprise, it was the fact that the ladies were not to travel by private carriage, as had been the custom of the Garcias from time immemorial, attended by a numerous escort of armed rancheros; but being driven to the nearest post where the public diligence was to be met, were to proceed by it most unostentatiously upon their way. This aroused far more discussion than the fact of the journey itself; though it was unanimously agreed that if Doña Isabel could force herself to depart from the accustomed dignity of the family, and indeed preserve a slight incognito upon the road, her chances of making the journey in safety would be greatly increased.

Her resolve once made it was acted upon instantly, no time being allowed for news of her departure to spread abroad and to give the bandits who infested the road opportunity to plan the *plajio*, or carrying off, of so rich a prize as Doña Isabel Garcia and her daughter would have proved. And thus, early one November morning, — when the whole earth was covered with the fresh greenness called into growth by the rainy season which had just passed, and the azure of a cloudless sky hung its perfect arch above the valley, seeming to rest upon the crown-like circlet of the surrounding hills, — Herlinda passed through the crowd of dependents who, as usual on such occasions, gathered at the gates to see the travellers off. Doña

Isabel, who was with her, was affable, smiling and nodding to the men, and murmuring farewell words to the nearest women; but Herlinda was silent, and it was not until she was seated in the carriage that she threw back the reboso which she had drawn to her very eyes, revealing her face, which was deadly pale. As she gazed lingeringly around, half sadly, half haughtily, with the proud curve of the lip (though it quivered) which made all the more striking her general resemblance to her beautiful mother, a thrill, they knew not of what or why, ran through the throng. For a moment there was a profound silence, in the midst of which the aged priest raised his hand in blessing. Suddenly a flash of memory, a gleam of inspiration, came over him; he turned aside the hand of Doña Isabel, which had been extended in farewell, and laid his own upon the bowed head of her daughter. "Fear not, my daughter," he said, "thou art blessed. Though I shall see thee no more, my blessing, and the blessing of God, shall be with thee."

The old man turned away, leaning heavily upon Doña Rita, the wife of the administrador, who led him tenderly away, and a few minutes later he was sitting smiling at her side, while without were heard the farewell cries of the women. "May God go with you, Niña! May you soon return! Adios, Niña! more beautiful than our patron saint! Adios, and joy be with thee!" And in the midst of such good wishes, as Herlinda still leaned from the window, a smile upon her lip, her hand waving a farewell, the carriage drove away and the people dispersed; leaving Pedro, the gate-keeper, standing motionless in the shadow of the great door-post, his eyes riveted on the sands at his feet, but seeing still the glance of agony, of warning, of entreaty, which had darted from Herlinda's eyes, and seemed to scorch his own.

VII.

Upon the death of Mademoiselle La Croix, or rather perhaps from the time of her return to the hacienda after her ineffectual quest, Doña Feliz had virtually become the duenna of Herlinda. Not that such an office was formally recognized or required in the seclusion of Tres Hermanos, but it was nevertheless true that Herlinda had seldom found herself alone, even in the walled garden. Though she paced its narrow paths without companionship, she had been aware that her mother or Doña Feliz lingered near; and it was this consciousness that had steeled her outwardly, and forced her to restrain the passionate despair that under other circumstances would have burst forth to relieve the tension of mind and brain. When she at last roused from the apathy of despair, her days became periods of speechless agony, but sometimes at night, when she had believed that Feliz — who, since Carmen's departure, had occupied the adjacent room — was asleep, for a few brief moments she had yielded to the demands of her grief, and given way to sobs and tears, to throw herself finally prostrate before the little altar, where she kept the lamp constantly burning before the Mother of Sorrows. Thence Feliz at times had raised her, and led her to her bed, — chill, unresisting, more dead than alive, yet putting aside the arm that would have supported her, and by mute gestures entreating to be left to her misery.

Fortunately for her reason, there were times when in utter exhaustion Herlinda had slept heavily and awoke refreshed, — and this had occurred a night or two after she had learned, by a few decisive words from her mother, of her imminent removal from Tres Hermanos. She had retired early, and awoke to find the soft and brilliant moonlight flooding her chamber. Every article in the room was visible; their shadows fell black upon the tiled floor, and the lamp before the altar burned pale. A profound stillness reigned. Herlinda raised herself on her pillow, and looked around her. The scene was weird and ghostly, and she presently became aware that she was utterly alone. She listened intently, — not the echo of a breath from the next room. Her heart leaped; for a moment its pulsations perplexed her; another, and she had moved noiselessly from her bed and crossed the room. She glanced into that adjoining. That too was flooded in moonlight, which shone full upon the bed. Yes, it was empty. Doña Feliz had doubtless been called to some sick person; she had left Herlinda sleeping, thinking that at that hour of the night there could be no danger in leaving her for a brief half hour alone.

In an instant these thoughts darted through Herlinda's mind, followed by a project that of late she had much dwelt upon, but had believed impossible of realization. With trembling hands she took from her wardrobe a dress of some soft dark stuff, and a black and gray reboso, and put them on. Without pausing a moment for thought that might deter her, she glided from the room, crossed the corridor, and descended the stairs, taking the same direction in which Ashley had gone to his death. She paused too at the gate, to do as he had done; for she touched the sleeping Pedro lightly upon the shoulder, at the same instant uttering his name.

The man started from his sleep affrighted, — too much affrighted to cry out; for like most haciendas, Tres Hermanos had its ghost. From time to time the apparition of a weeping woman was seen by those about to die. Had she come to him now? His tongue clove to the roof of his mouth; he shook in every limb. The moonlight shone full in the court, but the archway was in shade : who or what was this that stood beside him, extending a white arm from its dark robes, and touching him with one slight finger? A repetition of his name restored him to his senses, and he staggered to his feet, muttering, " Señorita ! My Señorita, for God's sake why are you here? You will be seen ! You will be recognized ! "

" ' In the night all cats are gray,' " she answered, with one of those proverbs as natural to the lips of a Mexican as the breath they draw. " No one would distinguish me in this light from any of the servants; but still my words

must be brief, for my absence from my room may be discovered. Pedro, I have a work to do; it has been in my
mind all this time. You, you can help me! "

She clasped her hands; he thought she looked at the
door, and the idea darted into his mind that she contemplated escape, or that she had a mad desire to throw
herself upon her lover's grave and die there.

" Niña ! Niña, of my life ! " he said imploringly, using
the form of address one might employ to a child, or some
dearly loved elder, still dependent. " Go back to your
chamber, I beg and implore ! How can I do anything for
you? How can Pedro, so worthless, so vile, do anything?"

The adjectives he applied to himself were sincere enough,
for Pedro had never ceased to reproach himself for his share
in the tragedy which, in spite of Doña Isabel's words, he
had never really ceased to believe concerned Herlinda,
though he had striven for his own peace of mind, as well
as in loyalty to the Garcias, to affect a contrary opinion,
until this moment, when his young mistress's appearance
and appeal rendered self-deception no longer possible.
Again and again he reiterated, " What can the miserable
Pedro do for you?"

Apparently with an instinct of concealment, Herlinda
had crouched upon the stones, and as the man stood before
her she raised her face and gazed at him with her dark
eyes. How large they looked in the uncertain light! how
the young face quivered and was convulsed, as her lips
parted ! Pedro, with an inward shrinking, expected her to
demand of him the name of Ashley's murderer; but the
thought of vengeance, if it ever crossed her mind, was far
from it at that moment. " Yes, yes, there is perhaps
something you can do for me," she said. " Men are able
to do so much, while we poor women can only fold our
hands, and wait and suffer. I thought differently once,
though. John used to laugh at what he called our idle
ways; he said women were made to act as well as men.
But what can I do? What could any woman do in my
place? Nothing! nothing! nothing!"

Pedro was silent. He knew well how powerless, what
a mere chattel or toy, was a young woman of his people.
It seemed, too, quite natural and right to him. In this
particular case the mother was acting with incompar-

able severity, but she was within her right. Even while he pitied the child, it did not enter his mind to counsel her to combat her mother's will. He only repeated mechanically, " What can I do? What would you have your servant do? "

" Not so hard a thing," she said with a sob in her voice ; " even a woman, had I one for my friend, could do this thing for me; and yet it is all I have to ask in the world. Just a little pity for my child, Pedro!" She rose to her feet suddenly, and spoke rapidly. " Pedro, they say that I was not truly married ; they say my beautiful, golden-haired husband, my angel of light, deceived me. It is false, Pedro! all false! But they say the world will not believe me, and so I must go away ; and my child, like an offspring of shame, must be born in secret, and I must submit. It will be taken from me, and I must submit. There is no help! no help!"

She spoke in a kind of frenzy, and her excitement communicated itself to Pedro. He understood, far better than she could, the motives of Doña Isabel; he did not condemn her, neither did he attempt to justify her to her daughter. He only muttered again in his stoical way, " What can I do? "

Herlinda accepted the words as they were meant, as an offer of devotion, of service. " Pedro, you can do much," she said rapidly. " You can watch over my child. Years hence, when I come to ask it, you can give me news of it. Ah, they think when they take my child from me, it will be as dead to me ; but Pedro," she added in an eager whisper, " I have found what they will do. Never mind how I learned it. They will bring my child here, — here, where only the peasants will ask a few useless questions, where there will be no person of influence to interfere. Yes, it will be brought here, and — forgotten! But Pedro, promise me you will watch for it, you will protect it. Promise! promise! promise!"

Pedro was startled, but not incredulous. This would not be the first child that had been found at the hacienda doors, left to the charity of the señoras ; more than one half-grown boy, of whose parents no one knew anything, loitered in the courts, and even the maid who served Doña Isabel was a foundling of this class.

" But how shall I know," he stammered, after he had satisfied her with the promise she desired. " True enough, it may be brought here, but how shall I know?"

Herlinda scarcely heeded his words. She was busy in taking a small reliquary from her neck. It was square, made of pale blue silk, and in no way remarkable. " See, I will put this around its neck," she said. " No one will dare remove a reliquary. There is a bit of the true cross in it. It will keep evil away; it will bring good fortune. The first day I wore it I met John; and " she added, nervously fingering the jewel at her ear, " take this, Pedro. The other I will put in the reliquary, with a prayer to San Federigo. When you see the strange child that will come here, look for these signs, and as you hope for mercy hereafter, guard the child that bears them."

She had placed in his hand a flat earring of quaint filagree work, one of the marvels of rude and almost barbaric workmanship that the untaught goldsmiths of the haciendas produce. Pedro would have returned it to her, swearing by all he held sacred to do her will; but some sound had startled her. She slipped the reliquary into her bosom, drew her scarf around her, and glided away. He saw her pass the small doorway like a spectre. He could scarcely believe that she had been there at all, that she had actually spoken to him. He crossed himself as he lost sight of her, and looked in a dazed way at the earring in his palm.

" Would to God," he muttered, " I had told Doña Isabel all the truth, as I meant to, when I went to her from the dead man's side. Why did I not tell her plainly I knew her daughter Herlinda to be the woman Ashley had come here to meet, — would she have dared then to say she was not his wife? Fool that I was! I myself doubted. What, doubt that sweet angel! Beast! imbecile!" and Pedro flung his striped blanket from him with a gesture of disgust. "And now, what would be the use, though I should trumpet abroad the whole matter? No, my hour has passed. Doña Isabel must work her will; I will not fail her, for only by being true can I serve her daughter. But who knows? — Herlinda may be deceived; her fears may have turned her brain. Yet all the same I will keep this token; " and he looked

at the earring reverently, then placed it in his wallet.
Two days later, when she left Tres Hermanos and he saw
its fellow in Herlinda's ear, he caught the momentary
glance in her dark eye, and stood transfixed.

Pedro Gomez hitherto had been a careless, idle, rollick-
ing fellow ; thenceforward he became grave, watchful, and
crafty, — the change which, had there been keen observers
near, all might have noticed in the outward man being as
nothing to that from the specious fellow whom Ashley had
found it an easy matter to bribe, to the conscience-stricken
man who stood at the gates of the great hacienda of the
Garcias, cognizant of its conflicting interests, and sworn
to guard them ; his crafty mind inclining to Doña Isabel
and the cause she represented, his heart yearning over the
erring daughter.

VIII.

Though Herlinda Garcia had forced a smile to her lips as she left, perhaps forever, the house where she was born, as the carriage was driven rapidly across the fertile valley her eyes remained fixed with melancholy, even despairing, intensity upon the walls wherein she had learned in her brief experience of life much that combines to make up the sum of woman's wretchedness.

Herlinda had ever been an imaginative child, even before she had attained the age of seven years, at which she had been taught to consider herself a reasoning, responsible being; she had been conscious of vague feelings and desires, which had in a measure separated her from her family and the people who surrounded her, and had set her in sullen opposition to the aimless and inane occupations which served to while away days that her eager nature longed to fill with action. Though she had not been conscious of any especial direction into which she would have thrown her energies, she had been most keenly conscious that she possessed them, and early rebelled against the petty tasks that curbed and strove to stifle them, — such tasks as the embroidering of capes and stoles, or drawing of threads from fine linen, to be replaced with intricate stitches of needle-work, to form the decoration of altar cloths, or the garments of the waxen Lady of Sorrows above the altar in the chapel, or of the Virgin of Guadalupe in the great *sala*, — as she did also against the endless repetition of prayers, for which she needlessly turned the leaves of her well-thumbed breviary. How she had longed for freedom to run with the peasant children over the fields! How many hours she had hung over the iron railing of her mother's balcony, and gazed upon the far hills, and wondered what sort of world lay in the blue beyond them.

Sometimes Herlinda had attempted to talk to Vicente Gonzales of these things when he came from the city,

privileged as the son of an old friend, and the scion of a
wealthy and influential family, to form an early intimacy
with the pretty child, whom later he would meet but in
her mother's presence with all the restrictions of Spanish
etiquette. She had always liked the proud, handsome
boy, but he was far slower in mental development than
she, and could only laugh at her fancies. And so as they
grew older, and he in secret grew more fond, she had
become indifferent, restlessly longing for an expansion
of her contracted and aimless existence, yet finding no
promise in the prospects of war and political strife which
began to allure Gonzales, and in which she could not
hope to take part, — and to sit a spectator was not in the
nature of Herlinda. Her mother delighted to watch the
fray, to counsel and direct. It was perhaps this trait in
Doña Isabel's character that, while it had awakened her
daughter's admiration, had chafed and fretted her, checking the natural expression of her lively and energetic
spirit, even as the cold and stately dignity of her manner repressed the affections which lay ardent within her,
waiting but the magnetic touch of a responsive nature.

Such an one had not been found within her home ; all
were cold, preoccupied, absorbed in the every-day affairs
of life. Sometimes, when by chance Herlinda had caught
a glimpse of the repressed inner nature of Doña Feliz, the
mother of the administrador, she had felt for a moment
drawn toward her ; but although all her life she had lived
beneath the same roof with her, there had occurred no
special circumstance to draw them into intimacy, or in
any way lessen the barrier that difference in age and
position raised between them, — for perhaps in no part of
the world are the subtle differences of caste so clearly
recognized and so closely observed as in those little
worlds, the Mexican *haciendas de campo*.

Sometimes, in her unhappiest moods, when her unrest
had become actual pain and resolved itself into a vague
but real feeling of grief, Herlinda had thought of her
father, in her heart striving to idealize what was but an
uncertain memory of an elderly, formal-mannered man,
handsome according to the type of his race, — sharp-featured, eagle-eyed, but small of stature, with small effeminate hands which Herlinda could remember she used to kiss,

in the respectful salutation with which she had been taught to greet him. He had died when Herlinda was eight years old, just after the second daughter, Carmen, was born; and though Doña Isabel seldom mentioned him, it was understood that she had loved him deeply, and for his sake lived the life of semi-isolation which her age, her beauty, her talents, and wealth seemed to combine to render an unnatural choice. As she grew older, Herlinda began to wonder, and sometimes repine, at this utter separation from the world of which in a hurried visit to the city of Guanapila she had once caught a glimpse. Especially was this the case after the arrival of Mademoiselle La Croix, who was lost in wonder that any one should voluntarily resign herself to exile even in so lovely a spot; and although she opened for Herlinda a new world in the studies to which she directed her, they had been rather of an imaginative than a logical kind, and stimulated those faculties which should rather have been repressed, while personally the governess had answered no need in the frank yet repressed and struggling nature of her pupil.

These had been the conditions under which Herlinda had met John Ashley, and we know with what result. As the tiny stream rushes into the river and is carried away by its force, their waters mingling indistinguishably, so the mind, the very soul of Herlinda had felt the power of that perfect sympathy which, in the few short words uttered in the pauses of a dance (for they had first met at Guanapila) and the expressive glances of his eyes, she believed herself to have found in the mind and heart of the alien,—a man in her mother's employ, one whom ordinarily she would have treated with perfect politeness, but would have thought of as set as far apart from her own life as though they were beings of a separate order of creation. The fact that he was a handsome young man would primarily have had no effect upon Herlinda, though undoubtedly it served to render to her mind more natural and delightful the ascendency which, in spite of all obstacles, he rapidly gained over her entire nature.

Needless is it for us to analyze the mind and character of Ashley. It is certain he loved Herlinda passionately, and in the opposition of Doña Isabel to his suit saw but irrational prejudice and mediæval tyranny. His entire freedom from sordid motives, and his fears of the consequences of delay, — knowing as he did of the desired engagement between Herlinda and the young Vicente Gonzales, — justified to his mind a course which the canons of honor would have forbidden, but of the legality of which he certainly had had no question, the intricacies and delicacies of marriage laws having engaged no share in the attention of a somewhat adventurous youth.

This very heedlessness and activity of John Ashley's nature had formed an especial charm to Herlinda; she would have shrunk from and pondered over a more cautious nature, — perhaps would have ended in loving, but she never would have cast aside all the traditions of her youth. All her life she had been like a bird in the cage. For a brief space she had seen the wide expanse of the sky opening above her, she had fluttered upward; but death had struck her down to darkness, — death, which had pierced the strong and loving one who would have guided and protected her! She moaned, and turned her face to the corner of the carriage. An arm stole around her; it was that of Doña Feliz.

THE pale dawn, creeping over the hills behind which the sun was still hidden, revealing to the accustomed sight of Doña Feliz a narrow, irregular street of adobe hovels; a tiny church with a square tower, where the swallows were sleepily chirping; around and behind, stray trees and patches of gardens; upon the waste of sand, where cacti and dusty sagebrush grew, up to the hills where the pines began, a road of yellow sand, winding like a sinuous serpent over all; two or three early loiterers, with eyes turned toward the diligence, which thus early was making its way from the night's resting place toward the distant city, — such was the scene upon which the trusted servant and friend of the Garcias looked on a morning early in November. She was standing in the low gateway that gave entrance to a garden overgrown with weeds and vines. These vines spread from the fig and orange trees, and half covered the ruinous walls of a house which had once, where the surroundings were so humble, ranked as an elegant mansion, and which indeed had served in years gone by as a temporary retreat, small but attractive, for such of the family of Garcia as desired a few days' retirement from their accustomed pursuits. Here the ladies had wandered amid the flowers, and sat under the arbors where the purple grapes clustered, and honeysuckle and jessamine mingled their rich odors; and the gentlemen had smoked their cigarettes in luxurious ease, or sallied forth to shoot the golden plover in its season, or hunt the deer amid the surrounding hills. This had in fact been a *quinta*, or pleasure resort, but since the days of revolutions and bandits it had been utterly abandoned to the rats and owls, or to the nominal care of the ragged brood who huddled together in the half-ruinous kitchen; and here the romance of Herlinda's life had been enacted.

When Doña Isabel Garcia had desired to send her daughter from the hacienda of Tres Hermanos, in order to remove her from the neighborhood of Ashley and give her the benefit of change, she had at first been sadly perplexed where to send her. Should she go to her relatives in the city, it was possible that her dejected mien and unguarded words might give them a suspicion of the truth, — and Doña Isabel detested gossip, particularly family gossip; besides, she looked upon Herlinda's marriage with Vicente Gonzales as certain, and dreaded lest the faintest rumor of the young girl's attachment should reach his ears, and awaken in him the slumbering demon of jealousy, — which, though it might rouse the young soldier as a lover to fresh ardor only, might incite him later as her husband to a tyranny which the mind of Herlinda was ill disposed to bear. In this dilemma the house at Las Parras had occurred to her. Once in her own girlhood she had visited the place, and she remembered it as a most charming sylvan retreat; and although she knew it to be situated in the outskirts of a small hamlet scarce worthy of the name of village, and that it had been abandoned for years, its isolation and abandonment at that juncture precisely constituted its attractions; and thither, under the care of Don Rafael the administrador and of Mademoiselle La Croix, Herlinda had been sent. Precautions had been taken to baffle the inquiries of Ashley as to their route and destination, which, as has been said, an accident revealed to him just when his mind was most strongly excited by the mystery which his disposition and training, as well as his love, led him passionately to resent. Hither, too, when a new and still more important need had risen, Herlinda had been brought.

Doña Isabel had been unaffectedly shocked, when, after a tortuous journey by diligence in order to evade conjecture as to their destination, they had at nightfall arrived at this deserted mansion, and had passed through the narrow door-way set in the high stone-wall that surrounded the garden, and had looked upon its tangled masses of half tropic vegetation, and entered the ruin, to find that only three or four small rooms opening upon the vineyard were habitable. But in these few rooms they and their secret were safe, — safe as if buried in the caves of the earth. Herlinda looked around her for familiar faces, but all she saw were strange to her. Doña Isabel

had guarded against recognition of Herlinda, and even her
own identity was disguised. To the women and the old
man who performed the work of the kitchen and went the
necessary errands, but who were rigidly excluded from the
private rooms, she was known only as a friend of Doña
Isabel Garcia, — one Doña Carlota, whose family name
awoke no interest or inquiry.

After satisfying her hungry anxiety to catch a glimpse
of the servants, and finding them strangers, Herlinda
made no further effort to encounter them. She was very
ill after arrival, and it is doubtful whether the attendants —
dull, apathetic creatures — ever saw her face plainly from
the day she entered the house until that of which we
speak, when Doña Feliz stood in the low doorway in the
garden wall, and looked toward the diligence which
appeared indistinctly, a moving monster in the distance.
She glanced back occasionally, half impatiently, half sorrowfully, to the house. Through the open door of it
presently glided Doña Isabel. Her head was bent, her
olive cheeks were deadly pale, and she shivered as with
cold as she stepped out into the dusk of early morning,
— or rather late night, for it was an hour when not a
creature around the place was stirring, not even the birds;
a wide-eyed cat stared at her as she passed down the narrow walk, and she shrank even from its gaze. She held
something under her black reboso, which upon reaching
Feliz she passed to her with averted eyes.

"Take it," she said; "Herlinda is asleep. We trust
you, Feliz. I in my shame, she in her despair, we give
this child to you, never to ask it of you again, never to
know whether it lives or dies."

The passionless composure with which she said these
words, the absolute freedom from any tone of vindictiveness, gave to them the accent of perfect trust. There was
nothing of cruelty, nothing of hesitancy in the tone or
words or manner with which Doña Isabel Garcia laid in the
arms of Feliz a new-born sleeping infant, and thus separated herself and her family from the fate which with absolute confidence she placed in the hands of the statuesque,
cold-faced woman who stood there to receive it.

But with the child in her arms a great change swept
over the face of Feliz. One could not have told at a

glance whether it was loathing and resentment, or an agony of pity, that convulsed her features, or all combined. "My words are all said," she murmured. "Herlinda is, you say, resigned. Oh, Doña Isabel, Doña Isabel, you will rue this hour! I do your will; do not you blame or accuse me in the future!"

The diligence had driven through the village. To the astonishment of the idlers it stopped before the wall that circled the half-ruined *quinta;* a woman stepped through the doorway, and was helped to her seat. She had evidently been expected by the driver. They would have been still more surprised had they also seen the lady who waved a white hand at parting, and who turned back into the garden with a deep-drawn sigh of relief, followed by a groan that seemed to rend and distort the lips through which it came, and which she vainly strove to keep from trembling as she entered the house, and answered the call of her awakened daughter.

What can I say of the scene that followed? What that will awaken pity, unstained with blame, for that poor creature, so powerless in that land that her sisters, in others more blessed, perhaps, find it impossible to put themselves in imagination in her place even for a single moment? But the captive slave can writhe; woman, the pampered toy, may weep: and where woman was both (for even in Mexico a new era is dawning on her), she could struggle and despair and die,—but, as Herlinda knew too well, in youth at least she could not assert her womanhood, and make or mar her own destiny. In such a land, in such a cause, what champion would arise to beat down the iron laws of custom which manacled and crushed her? Not one!

X.

One day Pedro Gomez, half-sleeping half-meditating as he sat on the stone bench beneath the hanging serpents that garnished the vestibule of Tres Hermanos, thought he saw a ghost upon the stairs which led from one corner of the wide court into which he had glanced, to the corridor of the upper floor. An apparition of Doña Feliz, he thought, had passed up them; and with ready superstition he decided in his own mind that some evil had befallen her in her journeyings. He was so disturbed by this idea that a few moments later, as her son Don Rafael passed through the vestibule, he ventured to stop him and tell him what he had seen; whereat Don Rafael burst into a loud laugh.

"What, do you not know," he said, "that my mother has returned? Ah, I remember you were at Mass this morning. She came over from the post-house on donkey-back. A wonderful woman is my mother; but she knew we had need of her, and she came none too soon. I opened the door to her myself;" and Don Rafael hastened to his own apartments, where it was understood Doña Rita his wife hourly awaited the pangs of mother-hood, and left Pedro gazing after him in open-mouthed astonishment.

In the first place nothing had been heard of the proba-bility of the return of Doña Feliz; in the second, the manner of her return was unprecedented. She was a woman of some consequence at the hacienda. It was an almost incredible thing that under any circumstances she should arrive unexpectedly at the diligence post, and ride a league upon a donkey's back like the wife of a laborer. And thirdly it was a miracle that he Pedro had himself gone to Mass that morning, — he could not remember how it had come about, — and that discovering his absence from the gate Don Rafael had himself performed his functions, and had not soundly rated him for his unseasonable devotion; for Don Rafael was not a man to confound the claims of spiritual and secular duties.

Pedro Gomez did not put the matter to himself in precisely these words; nevertheless it haunted and puzzled him, and kept him in an unusual state of abstraction, — which perhaps accounted for the fact that later in the day, just at high-noon, when the men were afield and the women busy in their huts, and Pedro had ample leisure for his siesta, he was suddenly aroused by a voice that seemed to fall from the skies. Springing to his feet, he almost struck against a powerful black horse, which was reined in the doorway; and dazzled by the sun, and confused by the unexpected encounter, he gazed stupidly into the face of a man who was bending toward him, his broad hat pushed back from a mass of coal-black hair, his white teeth exposed by the laugh that lighted up his whole face as he exclaimed, —

"Here, brother! here is a good handful for thee! I found it on the road yonder. *Caramba!* my horse nearly stepped on it! Do people in these parts scatter such seeds about? I fancy the crop would be but a poor one if they did, and I saw a good growth of little ones in the village yonder. Well, well! I have no use for such treasure; I freely bestow it on thee," — and with a dexterous movement the stranger placed a bundle, wrapped in a tattered scarf, in the hands of the astounded Pedro, and without waiting question or thanks, whichever he might have expected, put spurs to his horse and galloped across the dusty plain.

Twice that day had Pedro Gomez been left, as he would have said, open-mouthed. Almost unconscious of what he did, he stood there watching the cloud of dust in which the horse and rider disappeared, until he felt himself pulled by the sleeve, and a sharp voice asked, "In the name of the Blessed, Tio, what have you there? Ay, Holy Babe! it is a child!"

A faint cry from the bundle confirmed these words; a tiny pink fist thrust out gave assurance to the eyes.

Pedro Gomez, strong man as he was, trembled in every limb, and sank on a seat breathless; but even in his agitation he resisted the efforts of his niece to unwrap the child.

"Let it be," he said; "I will myself look at this gift which the Saints have sent me."

With trembling hands he undid its wrappings. The babe was crying lustily; red, grimacing, struggling, it was still a pretty child, — a girl only a few days old. Around its neck, under the little dress of white linen, was a silken cord. Pedro drew it forth, certain of what he should find. Florencia pounced upon the blue reliquary eagerly. "Let us open it," she said; "perhaps we shall find something to tell us where the babe comes from, and whose it is."

"Nonsense!" said Pedro, decidedly; "what should we find in it but scraps of paper scribbled with prayers? And who would open a reliquary?"

Florencia looked down abashed, for she was a good daughter of the Church, and had been taught to reverence such things.

"No, no, girl! run to the village and bring a woman who can nourish this starving creature;" and as the girl flew to execute her commission, Pedro completed his examination of the child.

It was clothed in linen, finer than rancheros use even in their gala attire, and the red flannel with white spots, called *bayeta*, was of the softest to be procured; but beyond this there was nothing to indicate the class to which the child belonged. Upon a slip of paper pinned to its bosom was written the name *Maria Dolores* (what more natural than that such a child should bear the name, and be placed under the protection of the Mother of Sorrows?), and upon the reverse was "Señora Doña Isabel Garcia." Was this to commend the waif to the care or attention of that powerful lady? Pedro rather chose to think it a warning against her. "What! place the bird before the hawk?" With a grim smile he thrust the paper into his bosom. Doña Isabel was he knew not where, — later would be time enough to think of her; meanwhile, here were all the women and children, all the old men, and halt and lame of the village, trooping up to see this waif, which in such an unusual manner had been dropped into the gate-keeper's horny palms.

Some of the women laughed; all the men joked Pedro when they saw the child, though a yellow nimbus of hair around its head and the fineness of its clothing puzzled them.

Pedro had hastily thrust the slip of paper into his breast, scarce knowing why he did so; for though some instinct as powerful as if it were a living voice that spoke, urged him to secrete the child, to rush away with it into the fastnesses of the mountains, rather than to render it to Doña Isabel, he did not doubt for a moment that she herself had provided for its mysterious appearance at the hacienda, that it might be received as a waif, and cared for by Doña Feliz as her representative.

These thoughts flashed through his mind, and he heard again Herlinda's despairing cry: "Watch for my child! Protect it! protect it!" Was it possible that she had actually known that this disposition would be made of her child? Involuntarily his arms closed around it, and he clasped it to his broad breast, looking defiantly around.

"Tush, Pedro, give it to me!" cried one stout matron, longing to take the little creature to her motherly breast. "What know you of nursing infants? A drop of mother's milk would be more welcome to it than all thy dry hugs. Ah, here comes the Señor Administrador," and the crowd opened to admit the passage of Don Rafael, who attracted by the commotion had hastened to the spot in no small anger, ordering the crowd to disperse; but he was greeted with an incomprehensible chorus of which he only heard the one word "baby," and exclaimed in indignation, —

"And is this the way to show your delight, when the poor woman is at the point of death perhaps? Get you gone, and it will be time enough to make this hubbub when it comes."

The women burst out laughing, the men grinned from ear to ear, and the children fell into ecstasies of delight. Don Rafael was naturally thinking of the expected addition to his own family, and was enraged at what he supposed to be a premature manifestation of sympathy. Pedro alone was grave, and stepping back pointed to the infant, which was now quiet upon the bosom of Refugio, her volunteer nurse. "This is the child they speak of, Señor," he said, and in a few words related the manner in which it had been delivered to him.

5

If he had expected to see any consciousness or confusion upon the face of Don Rafael, he must certainly have been disappointed, for there was simply the frankest and most perfect amazement, as he turned to the woman who had stepped out a little from the crowd and held the infant toward him. He saw at a glance that it was no Indian child,—the whiteness of its skin, the fineness of its garments, above all the yellow nimbus of hair, already curling in tiny rings around the little head, struck him with wonder. He crossed himself, and ejaculated a pious "Heaven help us!" and touched the child's cheek with the tip of his finger, and turned its face from its nurse's dusky breast in a very genuine amaze, which Pedro watched jealously. The child cried sleepily, and nestled under the reboso which the woman drew over it, hushing it in her arms, murmuring caressingly, as her own child tugged at her skirts,—"There, there, sleep little one, sleep! nothing shall harm thee; sleep, *Chinita*, sleep!"

But the little waif—whose soft curls had suggested the pet name—was not yet to slumber; for at that moment Doña Feliz appeared. Pedro noticed as she crossed the courtyard that she was extremely pale. Some of the women rushed toward her with voluble accounts of the beauty of the child and the fineness of its garments. She smiled wearily, and turned from them to look at the foundling. A flush spread over her face as she examined it, not reddening but deepening its clear olive tint. She looked at Rafael searchingly, at Pedro questioningly. He muttered over his thrice-told tale. "Was there no word, no paper?" she said, but waited for no answer. "This is no plebeian child, Rafael. What shall we do with it? Doña Isabel is not here, perhaps will not be here for years!"

There was a buzz of astonishment, for this was the first intimation of Doña Isabel's intended length of absence. In the midst of it Pedro had taken the sleeping child from Refugio's somewhat reluctant arm, and wrapping it in a scarf taken from his niece's shoulders, had laid it on the sheepskin in the alcove in which he usually slept. This tacit appropriation perhaps settled the fate of the infant; still Doña Feliz looked at her son uneasily, and he rubbed his hands in perplexity. "Of all the days in the year for a babe like this to be left here," he said, " when, the Saints willing, I am to have one of my own! No, no, mother, Rita would never consent."

" Consent to what?" she answered almost testily. " What! Because this foundling chances to be white, would you have your wife adopt it as her own, when after so many years of prayer Heaven has sent her a child? No, no, Rafael, it would be madness!"

" There is no need," interpolated Pedro, with a half-savage eagerness, and with a look which, strangely combined of indignation and relief, should have struck dumb the woman who thus to the mind of the gate-keeper was revealed as the incarnation of deceit,—" there is no need. I will keep the child; ' without father or mother or a dog to bark for me,' who can care for it better? Here are Refugio and Teresa and Florencia will nurse it for me. It will want for nothing." A chorus of voices answered him : " We will all be its mother."—" Give it to me when it cries, and I will nurse it." — " The Saints will reward thee, Pedro!"—in the midst of which, in answer to a call from above, Doña Feliz hastened away, saying, " Nothing could be better for the present. Come, Rafael, you are wanted. I will write to Doña Isabel, Pedro; she will doubtless do something when you are tired of it. There is, for example, the asylum at Guanapila."

Pedro gazed after her blankly. In spite of that momentary flush on the face, Doña Feliz had seemed as open as the day. He never ceased thereafter to look upon her in indignant admiration and fear. Her slightest word was like a spell upon him. Pedro was of a mind to propitiate demons, rather than worship angels. There was something to his mind demoniacal in this Doña Feliz.

Half an hour after she had ascended the stairs, and the idlers had dispersed to chatter over this event, leaving the new-found babe to its needed slumber, the woman who acted the part of midwife to Doña Rita ran down to the gate where Pedro and his niece were standing, to tell them that there was a babe, a girl, born to the wife of the administrador. A boy, who was lounging near, rushed off to ring the church bell, for this was a long-wished-for event; but before the first stroke fell on the air, the voice of Doña Feliz was heard from the window: "Silence! Silence! there are two. No bells, no bells!"

Two! Doña Rita still in peril! The midwife rushed back to her post. The door was locked, and there was a momentary delay in opening it. "Where have you been," said Doña Feliz severely, "almost a half an hour away?"

The woman stared at her in amaze,—the time had flown! Yes, there was the evidence,—a second infant in the lap of Doña Feliz, puny, wizened. She dressed it quickly, asking no assistance, ordering the woman sharply to the side of Doña Rita.

"A thousand pities," said Don Rafael as he looked at it, "that it is not a boy!" Then as the thought struck him, he laughed softly: "Ay, perhaps it is for luck, — instead of the three kings, who always bring death, we have the three *Murias*."

Doña Rita had heard something of the foundling, and smiled faintly. "Thank God they were not all born of one mother," she said. "Ay! give me my first-born here;" and with the tiny creature resting upon her arm, and the second presently lying near, Doña Rita sank to sleep.

THOUGH the three Marias, as Don Rafael had called them, thus entered upon life, or at least into that of the hacienda of Tres Hermanos, almost simultaneously, except at their baptism they found nothing in common. On that occasion, a few days later than that of which we have written, the aged priest, in the name of the Trinity, severally blessed Florentina, Rosario, and Dolores, — each name as was customary being joined to that of the virgin Queen of Heaven ; but as they left the church their paths separated as widely as their stations differed. Dolores, for whom in vain—were it designed to subdue or chasten her—was chosen so sad a name, was taken to the dusky little hut, a few rods from the gate, that was, when he chose to claim it, Pedro's home, and there cared for by his niece Florencia with an uncertain and somewhat fractious tenderness, and nourished at the breast of whomsoever happened to be at hand. She passed through babyhood, losing her prettiness with the golden tinge of her hair, and as she grew older looking with wide-opened eyes out from a tangle of dark elf-locks, which explained the survival of her baby pet-name Chinita, or "little curly one."

Meanwhile the two children at the great house were seldom seen below stairs, so cherished and guarded was their infancy. Rosario grew a sturdy, robust little creature, with straight shining brown hair, drawn back, as soon as its length would permit, from her clear olive temples, in two tight braids, leaving prominent the straight dark eye-brows that defined her low forehead. Long curling lashes shaded her large black eyes,—true Mexican eyes, in which the vivacity of the Spaniard and the dreamy indolence of the Aztec mingled, producing in youth a bewitching expression perhaps unequalled in any other admixture of races. She had, too, the full cheeks, of which later in life the bones would be proved too high, and the slightly prominent formation of jaw, where the lips, too full for beauty, closed over perfect teeth of dazzling whiteness. Rosario was indeed a beauty, according to the standard of her country; and Florentina so closely followed the same type, that she should have been the same, but there was a certain lack of vividness in her coloring which beside her sister gave her prettiness the appearance of a dimly reflected light. Rosario was strong, vivid, dominant; Florentina, sweet, unobtrusive, spirituelle,—though they had no such fine word at Tres Hermanos for a quality they recognized, but could not classify; and so it came about, as time went on, and Rosario romped and played and was scolded and kissed, reproved and admired, that Florentina grew like a fragrant plant in the corner of a garden, which receives, it is true, its due meed of dew and sunshine, but is unnoticed, either for praise or blame, except when some chance passer-by breathes its sweet perfume, and glances down in wonder, as sometimes strangers did at Florentina. In the family, ignoring the fine name they had chosen for her, they called her little " snub-nose,"—Chata,—not reproachfully, but with the caressing accent which renders the nicknames of the Spanish untranslatable in any other tongue.

So time passed on until the children were four years old. The little Chinita made her home at the gateway rather than at the hut with Florencia, who by this time had married and had children of her own, and indeed felt no slight jealousy at the open preference her uncle showed for his foundling. For Pedro was a man of no vices, and his food and clothing cost him little; so in some by-corner a goodly hoard of sixpences and dollars was accumulating, doubtless, for the ultimate benefit of the tiny witch who clambered on his knees, pulled his hair, and ate the choicest bits from his basin unreproved; who thrust out her foot or her tongue at any of the rancheros who spoke to her, or with equally little reason fondled and kissed them; and who at the sight of the administrador or clerk or Doña Feliz, shrank beneath Pedro's striped blanket, peeping out from its folds with half-terrified, half-defiant eyes, which softened into admiration as Doña Rita and her children passed by.

They also in their turn used to look at her with wonder, she was so different from the score or more of half-naked, brown little figures that lolled on the sand or in the door-ways of the huts, or crept in to Mass to stare at them with wide-opened black eyes. They used to pass these very conscious of their stiffly-starched pink skirts, their shining rebosos, and thin little slippers of colored satin. But though this wild little elf crouching by Pedro's side was as dirty and as unkempt as the other ranchero children, they vaguely felt that she was a creature to talk to, to play with, not to dazzle with Sunday finery, — for even so young do minds begin to reason.

As for Chinita, after the rare occasions when she saw the children of the administrador, she tormented Pedro with questions. "What sort of a hut did they live in? What did they eat? Where did their pretty pink dresses come from?"

This last question Pedro answered by sending by the first woman who went to the next village for a wonderful flowered muslin, in which to her immense delight Chinita for a day glittered like a rainbow, but which the dust and grime soon reduced to a level with the more sombre tatters in which she usually appeared. When these were at their worst, Doña Feliz sometimes stopped a moment to look at her and throw a reproving glance at Pedro; but she never spoke to him of the child either for good or ill.

One day, however, — it was the day, they remembered afterward, on which the Padre Francisco celebrated Mass for the last time, — the two little girls accompanied by their mother and followed by their nurse went to the church in new frocks of deep purple, most wonderful to see. Chinita could not keep her eyes off them, though Rosario frowned majestically, drawing her black eyebrows together and even slyly shaking a finger half covered with little rings of tinsel and bright-colored stones. But the other child, the little Chata, covertly smiled at her as she half guiltily turned her gaze from the saint before whose shrine she was kneeling; and that smile had so much of kindliness, curiosity, invitation in it that Chinita on the instant formed a desperate resolution, and determined at once to carry it through.

Now, it had happened that from her earliest infancy

Pedro had forbidden her to be taken, or later to go, into the court upon which the apartments of the administrador opened. Everywhere else, — even into the stables where the horses and mules, for all Pedro's confidence, might have kicked or trodden her; to the courtyard where the duck-pond was; to the kitchen, where more than once she had stumbled over a pot of boiling black beans — anywhere, everywhere, might she go except to the small court which lay just back of the principal and most extensive one. How often had Chinita crossed the first, and in the very act of peeping through the doorway of the second had been snatched back by Pedro and carried kicking and screaming, tugging at his black hair and beard, back to the snake-hung vestibule to be terrified by some grim tale into submission; or on occasion had even been shut up in the hut to nurse Florencia's baby, — if nursing it could be called, where the heavy, fat lump of infant mortality was set upon the ragged skirt of the other rebellious infant, to pin her to her mother earth. Florencia perhaps resented this mode of punishment more than either of the victims, for they began with screams and generally ended by amicably falling asleep, — the straight coarse locks of the little Indian mingling with the brown curls, still tinged with gold and reddened at the tips by the sun, of the fairer-skinned girl.

Upon this day, Chinita in her small mind resolved there should be no loitering at the doorway; and scarcely had the two demure little maidens passed into the inner court and followed their mother up the stairway, when she darted in and looked eagerly around. There was nothing terrible there at all, — an open door upon the lower floor showing the brick floor of a dining-room, where a long table set for a meal stood, and a boy was moving about in sandalled feet making ready for the mid-day dinner. There was a great earthen jar of water sunk a little in the floor of a far corner, and some chairs scattered about. A picture of the Virgin of Guadalupe, under which was a small vessel of holy water, met her eyes as she glanced in. She turned away disappointed and went to another door, that of a sitting-room, as bare and uninviting as the dining-room, but with an altar at one end, above which stood a figure of Mary with the infant Jesus in her arms. Even the saints in the church were not so gorgeous as this. Chinita gazed in admiration and delight; if she could have taken the waxen babe from the mother's arms she would have sat down then and there in utter absorption and forgetfulness. As it was, she crossed herself and ran out among the flower-pots in the courtyard and anxiously looked up. Yes, there leaning over the railings of the corridor were those she sought. At sight of her Rosario screamed with delight, her budding aristocratic scruples yielding at once to the charms of novelty. Chata waved her hand and smiled, both running eagerly to descend the stairs and grasp their new play-fellow.

"What is your name?" asked both in a breath. "Why are you always with Pedro, at the gate? Who is your mother, and why have you got such funny hair? Who combs it for you? Does n't it hurt?"

Chinita answered this last question with a rueful grimace, at the same time putting one dirty little finger on Rosario's coral necklace, — a liberty which that damsel resented with a sharp slap, which was instantly returned with interest, much to Rosario's surprise and Chata's dismay.

At the cry which Rosario uttered, following it up with sobs and lamentations, both Doña Feliz and Doña Rita appeared. Rosario flew to her mother. "Oh, the naughty cat! the bad, wicked girl! she scratched me! she slapped me!" she cried, between her sobs.

Chata followed her sister, still keeping Chinita's hand, which she had caught in the fray. "Poor Rosario! poor little sister," she said pityingly; "but, *Mamacita*, just look where Rosa slapped the poor pretty Chinita," and she softly smoothed the cheek which Chinita sullenly strove to turn away.

"Why, it is that wretched little foundling of Pedro's!" cried Doña Rita, indignantly, as she wiped Rosario's streaming cheeks. "Get you gone, you fierce little tigress! Chata, let go her hand; she will scratch you, she may bite you next."

"Oh, no," cooed Chata, quite in the ear of the ragged little fury beside her; while Doña Feliz, who had been silent, placed her fingers under the chin of the little waif, and lifted her face to her gaze. "Be not angry at a children's quarrel," she said; "they will be all the better friends for it later."

"But I don't wish them to be friends," cried Doña Rita, — though the absolute separation of classes rendered intimate association possible and common between them which neither detracted from the dignity of the one caste, nor was likely to arouse emulation in the other. "What a wild, savage little fox! No, no, my lamb, she shall not come near thee again!"

But the mother's lamb was of another mind, for suddenly she stopped crying, pulled the new-comer's ragged skirt, and said, "Come along, I'll show you my little fishes;" and in another moment, to Doña Rita's amazement and Doña Feliz's quiet amusement, the three children were leaning together, chatting and laughing, over the edge of the stone basin in the centre of the court.

In the midst of their play, a sudden fancy seized Doña Feliz. Catching up a towel that lay at hand, she half-playfully, half-commandingly caught the elf-like child and washed her face. What a smooth soft skin, what delicately pencilled brows appeared! how red was the bow of that perfect little mouth! Doña Rita sighed for very envy; Doña Feliz held the little face in her hands, and looked at it intently. But Chinita, already rebellious at the water and towel, absolutely resented this; and in spite of the cries of the children she broke away and ran from the courtyard, arriving breathless at the knees of Pedro, to cover herself with the grimy folds of his blanket.

Little by little he drew from her what had passed, comforting her though he made no audible comment; and an hour later Doña Feliz, catching sight of the child, wondered how it had been possible for her to get her face so dirty in so short a time, though a suspicion of the truth soon caused her to smile gravely. While Chinita had been telling her adventures, Pedro had drawn his grimy fingers tenderly over her cheeks, in this way at once resenting Doña Feliz's interference, curiosity, interest, whatever it was, and manifesting his sympathy with the aggrieved one. Nor did he scold the child for her intrusion to the court, or forbid her to go again; and when after some days of hesitation, anger, and irresistible attraction she found her way thither, she wore on her neck a string of coral beads which made Rosario cry out with envy, and which Chata regarded with wide-eyed and solemn admiration.

XII.

THE acquaintance thus unpromisingly begun among the three children grew apace. At first, Chinita's visits were as infrequent as Pedro's watchfulness and Doña Rita's antipathy to the foundling could render them, although neither openly interfered, — Pedro, for reasons best known to himself, and Doña Rita out of respect to her mother-in-law, who she saw, in her undemonstrative and quiet way, seemed inclined to regard the child with an interest differing from that with which she favored the children of the herdsmen and laborers. Doña Feliz seldom gave Chinita anything, even in the way of sweets, with which on special festival days she sometimes regaled the others; but in the chill days of the rainy season, or when the norther blew, she it was who chid her if she ran barefooted across the courts, or left her shoulders and head uncovered, and who set all the children to string wonderful beads of amber and red and yellow, placing the painted gourd which contained them close to the brasier of glowing coals, so that the shivering little creature might benefit by its warmth.

Not that the waif was neglected, according to the customs of Pedro's people, — indeed he was lavish to her of all sorts of rural finery. But where all children ran barefoot, where none wore more clothing than a chemise, a skirt, and the inevitable reboso (a long striped scarf of flexible cotton), and in a clime where this was usually more than sufficient for protection, it did not occur either to Florencia or Pedro to provide more against those few bitter days, when it seemed quite natural to shiver, perhaps grow ill, and to mutter against the bad weather; and so, very often the child he would have given his life to shelter had run a thousand risks of wind and weather, which custom had inured her to, and a robust constitution defied.

Still Chinita was glad of shelter and warmth, though like others, she bore the lack of them stoically, and at first in the bad weather went to the administrador's for such comforts, as much as from the attraction which Rosario's spiteful fondness and Chata's soft friendliness offered; while so it chanced that she was suffered to go and come as the dogs did, sometimes caressed, sometimes greeted with a sharp word, often enough unnoticed except by Chata, who looked for the visit each day, never forgetting to save in anticipation a tiny bit of the preserved fruit she had been given at dinner, or a handful of nuts. These offerings of affection often proved efficacious in soothing the irritation caused by Rosario's uncertain moods. Yet it was to Rosario that this perverse little creature attached herself; with her she romped, and chased butterflies in the garden; with her she laughed and quarrelled; and Chata looked on the two with a precocious benignity pretty to see, leaning often upon Doña Feliz's lap, and, with a quaint little way she had, smoothing down with one little finger the tip of her tiny nose which obstinately turned skyward, giving just the suggestion of sauciness to features which otherwise would have been inanely uncharacteristic.

Doña Rita was of opinion that all that was necessary in the education of girls was to teach them to hem so neatly that the stitches should not show in the finest cambric, and to make conserves of various sorts, — adding, by way of accomplishment, instruction in the drawing of threads and the working of insertions in many and quaint designs, or the modelling of fruits and figures in wax, to be used in the wonderful mimic representation of the scene of the birth of the Saviour made at Christmas. But Doña Feliz held more liberal views, and much as she esteemed accomplishments, considered them of inferior value to the arts of reading and writing, which she had herself acquired with infinite difficulty, at the pain of disobedience to well-beloved parents.

Reading and writing, according to Feliz's father, were inventions of the arch-enemy, dangerous to men, and fatal to the weaker sex. What could a woman use writing for, asked he, but to correspond with lovers, — when she should only know of the existence of such beings when one was presented as her future husband, by a wise and discreet father. What could a woman desire to read but her prayers? — and those she should know by heart. In vain,

therefore, had been Feliz's appeal to be taught to read
and write. At last she and the Señorita Isabel had puzzled
out the forbidden lore together, both copying portions of
stolen letters, or the crabbed manuscripts in which special
prayers to patron saints were written, thus acquiring an
exquisite caligraphy, and learning the meanings of words
as they noticed them appear and reappear in the copies of
prayers they knew by heart. By a similar process the
art of reading printing was acquired, — all in secret, all
with trembling and fear. Isabel, much assisted by Feliz,
who was older and had sooner begun her task, had successfully concealed her knowledge until it could be revealed with safety; and great was the indignation and
surprise of Feliz's father, when on her wedding day the
bride took up the pen and signed her marriage contract,
instead of affixing the decorous cross which had been expected of her, — while the groom, too, was perhaps not
over pleased to find himself the husband of a wife of such
high acquirements.

But these acquirements, added to her natural penetration, had been powerful factors in the life of Doña Feliz.
Her husband had been weak and inefficient, yet had through
her tact retained throughout his life the management of the
Garcia estates; in which he had been succeeded by his son,
a man of more character, which perhaps the preponderating
influence of his mother as much overshadowed as it had
sustained and lent a deceptive brilliancy to that of his
father, who, like many a man who goes to his grave respected and admired, had shone from a reflected light as
unsuspected and unappreciated as it was unobtrusive
and unfaltering.

Doña Feliz had all her life, in her quiet, self-assured
way, ruled in her household, — in her husband's time because he had accepted her opinions and acted upon them,
unconscious that they were not his own; while now by her
son she was deferred to from the habitual respect a Mexican yields to his mother, and from the steadfast admiration
with which from infancy he had recognized her talents.
Thus, it is not an exaggeration to say that Don Rafael,
whatever might have been his temptations to do otherwise,
invariably identified himself in thought as well as act with
the mother to whom he felt he owed all that was strong

or fortunate or to be desired, not only in his station, but in mind or person. Therefore it was not to be expected that he would interfere when Doña Rita complained to him that his mother made Rosario cry by keeping her poring over the mysteries of the alphabet, and that Chata inked her fingers and frocks over vain endeavors to form the bow-letters at a required angle, and that both would be better employed with the needle. And indeed Don Rafael thought it a pretty sight, when he came upon his mother seated in her low chair, with the two sisters before her, Rosario's mouth forming a fluted circle as she ejaculated " Oh ! " in a desperate attempt at " O," and Chata follow-ing the lines painfully with one fat forefinger, her eyes almost touching the book, — no dainty primer with pret-tily colored pictures, but a certain red-bound volume of " Letters of a Mother," containing advice and admoni-tion as alarming as the long and abstruse words in which they were conveyed.

With all her inattention and impatience, Rosario learned her tasks with a rapidity which roused the pride of her mother's heart; but Chata, in those early years, stumbled wofully on the road to learning. At lesson-time Chinita, not a whit less grimy than of old, used to hasten to crouch down behind her victimized little patroness, and sometimes whisper impatiently in her ear, sometimes give her a sly tweak of the hair, when her impatience grew beyond bounds, and at others vociferate the word with startling force and suddenness ; until one day it occurred to Doña Feliz, who had made no effort to teach her anything, and had often been oblivious of her very presence, that this little elf-locked rancherita was her aptest pupil. That day, when the others unwillingly seated themselves to their copy-books, she watched the gate-keeper's child, and saw her write the words she had set for her little pupils upon the brick floor with a piece of charcoal taken from the kitchen, then covertly wipe them off with the hem of her skirt.

Doña Feliz was touched. Here was a child of five doing what she herself at fifteen had painfully acquired. She did not pause to think that what with her had been the result of deep thought, was here but parrot-like though effective imitation. She took away the charcoal from the child's blackened fingers, bade her stand at the table, and gave her pen and ink.

After the lesson Chinita flew rather than ran across the court, leaving Rosario and Chata astounded and offended that she would not play, and thrust into Pedro's hand a piece of dirty paper covered with cabalistic characters. She had already confided to him that she could read, and had even once spelled out to him a scrap of printed paper which had come in his way, amazing him by her knowledge; but now that she could write, a veritable superstitious awe of this elfish child befell him.

That evening Pedro stole into the church, and lighted two long candles before the image of the Virgin. Were they an offering of thanks for a miracle performed, or a bribe against evil? The man went back to his post thoughtful, his breast swelling with pride, his head bowed in apprehension. He never had heard that those the gods love die young, yet something of such a fear oppressed him, — though as he found Chinita in flagrant disgrace with Florencia because she had drunk the last drop of thin corn-gruel which the woman had saved for her uncle's supper, he had reasonable ground for believing that the healthful perversity of her animal spirits and moral nature might counteract the malefic effect of mental precocity; and as he was thirsty that night, so might have been interpreted the muttered "A dry joke this!" with which he looked into the empty jar, and swallowed his tough tortillas and goat-milk cheese.

"Ay! but Florencia is cross to poor Chinita," whispered this astute little damsel, seizing the opportunity to creep up behind him when he was not looking, of stealing a brown arm around his neck, and interposing her shock of curls between his mouth and the morsel he destined for it. "Who has poor Chinita to love her but Pedro, good Pedro?" And so Pedro's anger was charmed away, even as he thought evil might be turned from his wilful charge by the faint glow of the two feeble candles he had lighted. Were her coaxing ways as evanescent, as little to be relied on, as their flicker? Ay, Chinita!

XIII.

THESE few years of which the flight has been thus briefly
noted, had wrought a subtle change in the appearance of
Tres Hermanos as well as in the life of its inhabitants.
Gradually there came over it that almost indescribable
suggestion of absenteeism which falls upon a dwelling
when there is death within, and which is wholly different
from the careless untidiness of a house temporarily closed.
True, there was movement still at Tres Hermanos, —
people came and went, the fields were tilled, the herds of
horses roamed upon the hillside, the cattle lowed in the
pastures, the village wore its accustomed appearance of
squalid plenty, the children played at every doorway, the
same numbers of heavily-laden mules passed in at the
house-gates, the granaries were as richly stored, — and yet,
even to the casual observer, there was a lack. At first,
one would attribute it wholly to the pile of deserted buildings to the west. No smoke ever issued from the tall
stack of the reduction-works; the lizards ran unmolested
upon the walls, which already had crumbled in a place or
two, affording entrance to a few adventurous goats, which
browsed upon the herbage that sprang up in the court, and
even around the great stones in the reduction-sheds. But
turning the eyes from these, there was something desolate
in the appearance of the great house itself. The upper
windows opening upon the country were always closed, dust
gathered in the balcony where Doña Isabel had been wont
to stand, and a rose, which had long striven against neglect, waved its slender tendrils disconsolately in the evening breeze. Some one pathetically calls a closed window
the dropped eyelid of a house; and so seemed those barred
shutters of cedar, upon which beat the last rays of the
setting sun.

The great event of the American War had despoiled
Tres Hermanos of many of its young men. Others had

from time to time been drawn into the broils that followed, and which had been augmented by the dictatorship of Santa Anna ; yet the estate itself had escaped invasion. Its great storehouses of grain remained intact, its fields were untrodden by the horses of soldiery either hostile or friendly ; but a change menaced it, — a hoarse murmur as of the sea seemed to gather and break against the bulwark of mountains that environed it. News of the great events of the day penetrated the remote valley, and with them vague apprehensions and disquiet. Even the laborers in the fields felt the oppression of the storm which was raging without, and which threatened to break upon them. Their hearts quaked ; they knew not what an hour might bring forth. For the first time they realized that the great events which had been transpiring, and were still in progress beyond their cordon of hills, meant more to them than food for gossip, or an attraction to some idle boy to whom army life meant a frolic and freedom from work.

These events had followed one another in such rapid succession, and were seemingly so contradictory, that to the onlooker they appeared irrational, childish, even traitorous. But in truth they were the vague, blind outstretchings of a people groping for self-government, for a liberty and peace which they were both by nature and training as yet unprepared to enjoy. The thraldom of Spain had left them madly impatient of fetters, yet they clung to the stake to which they had been chained. Were the prop called King or President, an individual rather than abstruse principles was demanded to uphold them. This it was which in the chaos that followed the war with the United States led them to recall the man whom they had exiled, — the man who had failed them in their greatest need, yet whose unaccountable ascendency over the minds of the masses led them to turn to him again as a deliverer, and whose triumphant march through the land intensified a thousand times the prevailing misery. As one of the historians of Mexico says of Santa Anna, —

" On his lips had been heard the words of brotherhood and reconciliation. The majority had believed in them, because they thought that in the solitude of exile the experience of years and the spectacle of his afflicted country must have purified and instructed the man. It is impossible to say whether his was hypocrisy or a flash of good faith; but certain it is he deceived those who believed, and silenced those who had no faith in his words, and none can imagine the days of distress and mourning which followed.

"His term of office was to last a year; his promises were to redeem his nation from the yoke of slavery, to announce a code of wise and just measures which should insure its happiness and prosperity. A hopeless task, perhaps, in the midst of a nation distracted by years of foreign and civil wars; but at least an attempt was possible. But when once the sweets of power were tasted, all sense of honor and patriotism was lost in the intoxication of personal ambition. Beguiled by promises of protection of their interests, so often and so violently assailed by the Liberal and Conservative parties, the clergy and their adherents in all parts of the Republic secured the passage of an Act which declared him perpetual ruler, with the title of Serene Highness, with his will as his only law, and his caprices his only standard."

Those not lost in the inconceivable stupor which the deadly upas in their midst cast far and near, opened wide eyes of amaze. A trumpet cry rang through the land! Liberals and Conservatives, even the less bigoted of the clerical party, sprang to arms. The entire nation, grieving and reduced to misery by the loss of ninety thousand men who had been dragged from their homes to support the pomp and power of the tyrant, to become a prey upon the land, and upon the helpless families of whom they should naturally have been the support, had refused long to be dazzled by the spectacle of military pomp, or to be beguiled by the *fiestas* and processions which in every town and village made the administration one that appeared a prolonged carnival and madness. These continued insults to the public misery; the daily proscriptions of men who dared to raise the voice or write a line against the Dictator or his senseless policy; the oppressions of the army; the cold, cruel, implacable espionage which made life unendurable, — these wrought quickly their inevitable consequences among a people accustomed to disorder and revolutions, and who in their blind, irrational way longed for liberty. Disgust and detestation of the dictatorship became general. As suddenly as it had sprung into being it was met and crushed. Rebellions sprang up on every hand; the populace rose in mass; the statues of Santa Anna were thrown down in the streets, his portraits stoned;

the houses of his adherents were sacked, their carriages destroyed. The popular fury culminated in the practical measure of the promulgation of the plan of Ayutla, which condemned to perpetual exile the ambitious demagogue who had disappointed and betrayed all parties, mocking with cruel levity his country's woes, and which declared for the establishment of a Republic based upon the broadest platform of civil rights. Gomez Farias gave form to this act; but Ignacio Comonfort became its soul when he proclaimed it in Acapulco, and in the almost inaccessible recesses of the South raised the standard of a rebellion, which rapidly extending throughout the land hurled from its pedestal the idol of clay, that for a brief moment had been taken for gold, to place in its stead a new favorite.

Then another exile returned to his country, heralded by neither trumpets nor acclamations. Calm, astute, watchful, he took his place amid the revolutionary forces; but without seeming effort, from a follower he became a leader. His was the brain that was to develop from the imperfect plan of Ayutla liberties more daring and precious than men had learned to dream of to that hour. Comonfort the last President was the figure toward which all eyes turned; but behind him stood the quiet, insignificant Indian, successful general now, Benito Juarez, shaping the destinies of those who ignored or despised him.

Comonfort was daring, impulsive, utterly devoid of physical fear; a man of action, prone to plunge into difficulties, yet ready to compromise where he could not fight, antagonistic to the temporal power of the Church, yet superstitiously bound by its traditions, he was at once the initiator and the enemy of reform. Finding himself in triumphant opposition to the clergy, he recklessly attacked their most cherished institutions; to open a passage for his troops he threw down their finest convent; to pay his soldiery he levied upon their treasures. Yet he trembled before their denunciations, — upon one day sending the bishop into exile; on the next, he cowered before the meanest priest who threatened him with the Virgin's ire. The terrors of excommunication unnerved him. Scared by his own audacity; unable to quell the storm he had roused; viewing with dismay the reaction that his ill-considered boldness had created in the minds of a people dominated by ghostly fears, even while they groaned under the material oppressions of priestcraft; led beyond his depth by unscrupulous counsellors, or by those who like Juarez had ideas beyond the epoch in which he lived, — Comonfort, while he maintained a kingly state, looked forth upon the new aspect of distraction which his country wore, and vainly sought a method of compromise to evoke order from chaos. He who had dared all physical dangers shrank before a revolution of sentiment. His vacillating demeanor — above all his conciliations of the clergy whom he had so short a time before defied — awoke distrust on every hand.

Such was the political aspect, so far as known at Tres Hermanos, upon the eve when the first straggling band of soldiery crossed the peaceful valley, and its doors opened to receive the first of those armed guests, which in the near future were to become so numerous and so dreaded.

In one far corner of the great house there was a little balcony with its high iron railing; and behind it, scarce reaching to its top, stood two children on tip-toe, looking with wide eyes upon the glory of the purpling mountains, and then with mundane curiosity dropping them upon the more homely attractions within hearing as well as sight. And upon that special afternoon in October these chanced to be of a somewhat unusual character; for across the plain rode one of those predatory bands, which in those wild days sprang up like magic even in the most isolated regions, — the arid mountains and the fertile plains alike furnishing their quota of material, which blindly, ignorantly, but for that none the less furiously, became sacrifices to the ambition of a score or more contesting chiefs. Yet amid the cupidity, unscrupulousness, and barbarity of these chiefs still lingered the spirit of liberty, which though drenched in blood, and bound down by ecclesiastical as well as military despotism, was yet to rise triumphant, perhaps after its years of long struggle stronger, purer, holier than the world before had known it.

But license rather than liberty seemed to animate those wild spirits who, invigorated after a long day's march by the sight of a halting place, urged their steeds with wild shouts and blows with the flat side of their sabres, as well as with applications from their clanking spurs, across the plain, where scattered at intervals might be seen the laggards of the party, chiefly women, on mule or donkey back, with their cooking implements hanging from the panniers upon which they squatted in security and comfort, nursing their babies or quieting the more fractious older children, as the animals they rode paced quietly on or broke into a jog-trot at their own wills.

It was a cause of great excitement and delight to the children in the balcony to see the soldiers — most of them still arrayed in their ranchero dress of buff leather, but some of them resplendent in blue-and-red cloth, with stripes of gilt upon their arms and caps — stop at the huts along the principal street or lane of the village, and laughingly take possession, bidding Trinita and Francisca and Florencia, and the rest of them, to go or stay as it pleased them. Some of the women were frightened and began to cry and bewail, but others found acquaintances among the new arrivals; and there was much laughing and talking, in the midst of which two personages who appeared to be the leaders of the party, and who were followed by a dozen or more companions and servants, rode up to the hacienda gates, and one, scarcely pausing for an answer from the astonished Pedro whom he saluted by name, rode into the courtyard, whither he was followed by the gate-keeper, who with stoical calm yet evident amazement saluted him as Don Vicente; and holding his stirrup as he dismounted added in a low voice, —

"The Saints defend us, Don Vicente! The sight of you is like rain in May, — it will bless the whole year! Heaven grant your followers leave untouched the harvest of new maize! Don Rafael would go out of his senses if it were broached and trampled on by this rabble, — begging your Grace's pardon a thousand times!"

Don Vicente, as the young man was called, laughed as he stamped his feet on the brick pavement until his spurs and the chains and buttons on his riding suit clanked again, — though he looked half sadly, half furtively around.

"Have no fear, Pedro good friend, the men have their orders. The General, José Ramirez, is not to be trifled with;" and he glanced at his companion, a man older than himself, but still in the prime of life, who had also dismounted

and was shaking hands with Don Rafael, with many polite
expressions of pleasure at meeting the courageous and
prudent administrador of Tres Hermanos.

These compliments were returned with rather pallid
lips by Don Rafael, who however upon being recognized
by Don Vicente, who advanced to embrace him with the
cordiality of a friend, though with something of the condescension of a superior, regained his composure with the
rapidity natural to a man who having fancied himself in
some peril finds himself under the protection of a powerful
and generous patron. He hastened in the name of Doña
Isabel to place everything the hacienda contained at the
disposal of the visitors, making a mental reservation of
the new maize and sundry fine horses that happened to be
in the courtyards.

Chinita, who had pushed her way through the crowd of
children and half-grown idlers that had been attracted to
the court, and were gazing in silent and opened-mouthed
wonderment and admiration at the imposing personage
called the General José Ramirez, was so absorbed in the
contemplation of his half-military, half-equestrian bravery
of riding trousers of stamped leather trimmed with silver
buttons, and wide felt hat gorgeous with gold and silver
cords and lace, his epauletted jacket, and scarlet sash
bristling with silver-handled pistols and stilletto, that she
took no heed when a servant came to lead away the
charger upon which the object of her admiration had been
mounted, and so narrowly escaped being knocked down
and trampled upon.

" Have a care thou !" cried Don Vicente, as he sprang
forward and clutched the child by the arm, drawing her out
of danger, while a score of voices — the General's perhaps the most indifferent among them — reiterated epithets
of abuse to the servant and admonition to the child. In
the midst of the commotion, Don Rafael conducted the
two officers to rooms which were hastily assigned them.

As they disappeared, Chinita's eyes followed them. She
was not especially grateful for her escape : it was not the
first time she had been snatched from beneath the feet of
a restive horse ; the incident was natural enough to her,
and perhaps for this reason her rescuer was not specially
interesting to her mind. Somewhat to her disgust, an

hour later, when she had managed to steal unobserved into the supper-room, where she crouched in a corner, she saw Rosario and Chata from their seats at their mother's side regarding the young officer with amiable smiles,— Rosario with infantile coquetry, drooping her long lashes demurely over her soft dreamy black eyes ; and Chata, with her orbs of a nondescript gray, frankly though coyly taking in every detail of his face and dress, while they averted themselves as if startled or repelled from the dark countenance of his companion. It might have been thought that Doña Feliz shared her dread, for more than once she looked at the General with an expression of perplexity and aversion, as he lightly entertained Doña Rita with an account of his family and his own exploits, — topics strangely chosen for a Mexican, but which seemed natural rather than egotistical when lightly and wittily expatiated upon by this gay soldier of fortune.

Meanwhile, Don Vicente Gonzales was talking in a low voice to Doña Feliz. He ate little and drank only some water mixed with red wine, while Don Rafael and the General Ramirez partook freely of more generous stimulants, growing more talkative as the evening advanced ; and at last, as the ladies rose from the table, and Doña Rita went with the children to the upper rooms, the two walked away together to inspect the horses and talk of the grand reforms initiated by Comonfort, which in reality had but filled the country with discontent and bloodshed. The poison of personal ambition was working in the new President slowly — as it had done more rapidly in his renowned predecessor Santa Anna — the change from the patriot to the demagogue. He who had talked and worked and fought for the liberties of Mexico, dallied with the chains he should have broken.

XIV.

As Don Rafael in an unwonted state of complacency, which drew the anxious eyes of his mother upon him, disappeared with his jovial guest the General, the younger officer, Don Vicente Gonzales, drew a long breath of relief, and at a sign from Doña Feliz followed her to the window, with the half-sombre, half-expectant air of one who is about to speak of past events with an old and tried friend; and throwing himself into a chair, he turned his face toward her with the air and gesture which says more plainly than words, "What have you to tell, or ask? We are alone; let us exchange confidences."

In truth they were not quite alone. Chinita had half-sulkily, half-defiantly, crept after Doña Feliz, and had sunk down in her usual crouching attitude within the shadow of the wall. She would have preferred to follow Don Rafael and the General in their rounds, but she knew that was impracticable; Pedro would have stopped her at the gate, and sent her to Florencia, or kept her close beside him, — and so even the inferior pleasure of seeing and listening to the less attractive stranger would have been denied her. Chinita was an imaginative child; she used sometimes to stand upon the balcony with Chata, and gaze and gaze far away into the blue which seemed to lie beyond the farthest hills, and wonder vaguely what strange creatures lived there. Sometimes her wild imagination pictured such uncouth monsters, such terrifying shapes, that she herself was seized with nervous tremblings, and Chata and Rosario would clasp each other and cry out in fright; but oftener she peopled that world with cavaliers such as she had occasionally seen, and stately dames such as she imagined Doña Isabel and the *niña* Herlinda must be, — for the accidental mention of those names was as potent as would have been the smoke of opium to fill her brain with dreams. By the sight of

Don José Ramirez in his picturesque apparel, part of these vague dreams seemed realized; and even the quiet figure of Don Vicente and the sound of his stranger voice had the charm of novelty. She placed herself where she could best see his face, with infantile philosophy contenting herself with the next best where the actual pleasure desired was unattainable. She was very quiet, for she had naturally the Indian stealthiness of movement, and she had besides a vague instinct that her presence upon the corridor might be forbidden. Still she did not feel herself in any sense an intruder; she felt as a petted animal may be supposed to do, that she had a perfect right in any spot from which she was not driven.

But as Doña Feliz and the new-comer were long silent, she became impatient, and half-resolved to settle herself to sleep there and then. She had drawn her, feet under her, covering them with the ragged edges of her skirt, and drawing her scarf over her head and shoulders, tightly over the arms which clasped her knee, looked out as from a little tent, and instead of sleeping became gradually absorbed in the contemplation of the face and figure which, when seen beside those of the dashing Ramirez, had appeared gloomy and insignificant. The young man was dressed in black; the close-fitting riding trousers, the short round jacket, the wide hat, which now lay on the ground beside him, being relieved only by a scanty supply of silver buttons, — a contrast to the usual lavishness of a young cavalier; and in its severe outlines and its expression of gloom, his face, as he sat in the moonlight, was in entire harmony with his dress. How rigid looked the clear-cut profile against the dead whiteness of the column against which it rested, his close-cropped head framed in black, his youthful brow corrugated in painful thought. Suddenly he lifted the dark eyes which had rested upon Doña Feliz, and turned them on the fountain which was splashing within the circle of flowering plants and murmured : —

"I feel as though in a dream. Is it possible I am here, and she is gone, gone forever? How often I have seen her by the side of the fountain, raising herself upon the jutting stone-work to pluck the red geraniums and place them in her hair! Even when I was a boy her pretty unstudied ways delighted me, — and Herlinda as naturally as she breathed acted her dainty coquetries. And to fancy now that all that grace and beauty is lost to me, to the world, forever! that she is sacrificed — buried!"

He spoke bitterly and sighed, yet with that tone of renunciation which more completely than to death itself, marks the voices of the children of the Church of Rome as they yield their loved ones to her cloisters. It was in the voice of Doña Feliz, as she presently replied, —

"It seems indeed a strange destiny for so bright a life; but against the call of religion we cannot murmur, Vicente. Many and great have been the sins of the Garcias. May Herlinda's prayers, her vigils, her tears condone them!" She crossed herself and sighed heavily.

"I cannot accept even the inevitable so calmly," cried the young man in sudden passion. "I loved her from a child; I never had a thought but for her! She was promised me when we were boy and girl! She used to tease me, saying she hated me, and then with a soft glance of her dark eyes disarmed my anger. She would thrust me from her with her tiny foot, and then draw me to her with one slender finger hooked in the dangling chain of a jacket button, and laughingly promise to be good, breaking her word the next moment. She would taunt me when I sprang toward her in alarm as she leaped from the fountain parapet, and in turn would cry out in agonies of fright as I hung from the highest boughs of the garden trees, or when I dashed by her on the back of a half-broken horse, stopping him or throwing him perhaps on his haunches, with one turn of the cruel bit. Through all her vagaries I loved her, and perhaps the more because of them; and I fancied she loved me. Even later, when she had grown more formal and I more ardent, I believed that her coy repulses were but maiden arts to win me on."

"I always told Doña Isabel," interrupted Feliz, "that such freedom of intercourse between youth and maiden would but lead to weariness on one side or the other. But she was a hater of old customs. She said there was more danger in two glances exchanged from the pavement and the balcony than in hours of such youthful chat and frolic."

"Yet this freedom was designed to bind our hearts together," said Vicente. "The wish of Doña Isabel's heart for years was to see us one day man and wife. Yet she changed as suddenly — more suddenly and completely than Herlinda did. What is the secret? Is not Tres Hermanos productive enough to provide dowers for two daughters? Is all this to be centred on Carmen? Rich men have immured their daughters in convents to leave their wealth undivided. Can it be that Doña Isabel —"

"Be silent!" interrupted Doña Feliz, as she might have done to a foolish child. "Let us talk no more of Herlinda, Vicente; it makes my heart sore, and can but torture thine."

"No, it relieves me; it soothes me," cried Vicente. "I have longed to come here to talk to you. Doña Isabel is unapproachable. She has relapsed once more into the icy impenetrability that characterized her in that terrible time so many years ago. I can just remember —"

"Let the dead rest," cried Doña Feliz, sharply. "That is a forbidden subject in Doña Isabel's house. You are her guest."

Vicente accepted the reproof with a shrug of his shoulders, and Doña Feliz added, as if at once to turn his thoughts and afford the sympathy he craved, "Talk to me then, if you will, of Herlinda. Do you know where she is now?"

"Yes, in Lagos, in that dreariest of prisons the convent of Our Lady of Tribulation. Think you Maria Santisima can desire such scourgings, such long fastings, such interminable vigils as they say are practised there? God grant the scoffers are right, and that the reputed self-immolations are but imaginings, — tales of the priests to attract richer offerings to the Church shrine. When I saw it, it was groaning beneath vessels of gold and silver and wreaths of jewels. Oh, Feliz! Feliz! higher and heavier than the treasures they pile on their altars are the woes these monks and nuns accumulate upon our devoted country!"

Doña Feliz glanced around warily, but an expression of genuine acquiescence gleamed from her eyes.

"You are where I have always hoped to see you," she said in a low tone; "but beware of a too indiscriminate zeal. They say Comonfort himself has been too hasty, must draw back — retract — "

"Retract!" cried Vicente. "Never! Down, I say, with these tyrants in priestly garments, — these robbers in the guise of saints! The land is overrun with them; their dwellings rise in hundreds in the sunlight of prosperity, and the hovels of the poor are covered in the darkness of their oppressions. The finest lands, the richest mines, the wealth of whole families have passed into their cunning and grasping hands. There is no right, either temporal or spiritual, but is controlled by them. Better let us be lost eternally than be saved by such a clergy. What, saved by bull-baiters, cock-fighters, the deluders of the widow and orphan, the oppressors of the poor!"

"You are bitter and unjust," interrupted Doña Feliz; "remember, too, the base ministers of the Church take nothing from the sanctity of her ordinances."

"So be it," answered Vicente. "Perhaps," he added, with a short laugh, "you think I have lost my senses. No, no; but my personal loss has quickened my sense of public wrongs. In losing Herlinda, I lost all that held me to the past, — old superstitions, old deceptions. The idle boyish life died then, and up sprang the discontented, far-seeing, turbulent new spirit which spurns old dogmas, breaks old chains, and cries for freedom."

Vicente had risen to his feet; his face lighted with enthusiasm; his pain was for a moment forgotten. The listening child felt a glow at her heart, though his words were as Greek to her. Doña Feliz thrilled with a purer, more reasonable longing for that liberty which as a child she had heard proclaimed, but which had flitted mockingly above her country, refusing to touch its ground. Her enthusiasm kindled at that of the young man, though his sprung from bitterness. How many enthusiasms own the same origin! Sweetness and content produce no frantic dissatisfactions, no daring aims, no conquering endeavors.

"You belie yourself," she said, after a pause. "It is not merely the bitterness of your heart which has made you a patriot. The needs, the wrongs, the aspirations of the time have aroused you. Had Herlinda been yours, you still must have listened to those voices. With such men

as you at his call, Comonfort should not falter. The cause
he espoused must triumph."

"Humph!" muttered Vicente, doubtfully, while Feliz,
with a sudden qualm at her outspoken approbation of
measures subversive of an authority that her training had
made her believe sanctioned by heaven cried : —

"Ave Maria Santisima! what have I said? In blam-
ing, in casting reproach upon the clergy, am I not casting mud upon our Holy Mother the Church?"

"Feliz!" cried Vicente, impatiently, "that question too
asks Comonfort. Such irrational fears as these are the real
foes of progress ; and so deeply are old prejudices and superstitions rooted, that they find a place in every heart ;
no matter how powerful the intellect, how clear the comprehension of the political situation, how scrupulous or
unscrupulous the conscience, the same ghostly fears hang
over all. What spells have those monks with their oppressions and their shameless lives thrown over us that we
have been wax in their hands? Think of your own father,
— a man of parts, generous, lofty-minded, but a fanatic.
He shunned the monté table, the bull-fight, and all such
costly sports as the *hacenderos* love ; he almost lived in
the Church. But that could not keep misfortune from his
door : his cattle died ; his horses were driven away in the
revolution ; his fields were devastated ; and he was forced
to borrow money on his lands. And to whom should he ·
look but the clergy, — who so eager to lend, who so suave
and kind as they? And when he was in the snare, who so
pitiless in winding it around and about him, strangling,
withering his life?"

"But, Vicente," said Feliz, in a hard, embittered voice,
"in our lot there was a show of justice. If you would
have a more unmitigated use of pitiless craft, think of the
fate of your own cousin Inez."

The child within the shadow of the wall was listening
breathlessly. Her innate rebellion against all authority
made her quick to grasp the situation ; a secret detestation of the coarse-handed, loud-voiced village priest who
had succeeded Padre Francisco at Tres Hermanos quickened her apprehension. She looked at Vicente with glistening eyes. "Ah, well I remember poor Inez," he said ;
"forced by her father to become a nun, that at his death

he might win pardon for his soul by satisfying the greed of his councillors, she implored, wept, raved, fell into imbecility, and died; and her sad story, penetrating even the thickness of convent walls, was blackened by the assertion that she was possessed of devils foul and unclean, — she, the whitest, purest soul that ever stood before the gates of heaven."

His voice choked; he was silent and sank again into his chair. "And Comonfort," he muttered presently, "strives to conciliate wretches such as these. He is a man, Feliz, who with all his courage believes a poor compromise better than a long fight. Ah, the world believes Mexicans savage, unappeasable, blood-thirsty. How can they be otherwise with these blind leaders who precipitate them into those ditches which they fondly hope will prove roads to liberty and peace!"

Feliz looked at him with disquietude. "What, Vicente," she said, "are you a man to be blown about by every wind, — a mere ordinary revolutionist seeking a new chief for each fresh battle?"

Vicente flushed at the insinuation. "One cause and a *thousand* chiefs if need be," he said. "But there is now a man in Mexico, Feliz, who must inevitably become the head of this movement, — who, like the cause, will remain the same through all mischances. To-day he is the friend of Comonfort, but who knows? To-morrow —"

"He may be his enemy," ejaculated Feliz. "I wonder if in all this land there can be found one man who can be faithful!"

"To-morrow," said Vicente, completing his sentence, "he may be the friend and leader of all the lovers of freedom in Mexico; and if so, *my* leader. I have talked with that man, and he sees to the farthest ramifications of this great canker that is eating out the very vitals of our land. You will hear of him soon, Feliz, if you have not done so already. His name is Benito Juarez."

Feliz smiled. "What, that Indian?" she said. "It is a new thing for a gentleman of pure Spanish blood to choose such a leader. Ah, Vicente, you disappoint me! It must be this Ramirez, who has in his every movement the air of a guerilla, a free-fighter, who has infected you."

" No," answered Vicente, sullenly, " Ramirez has no influence over me ; only the fortune of war has thrown us together, — a blustering fellow on the surface, but so deep, so astute, that none can fathom him. He is not the man I could make my friend."

" Where does he come from ? " asked Doña Feliz with interest. " There is something familiar to me in his voice or expression."

" A mere fancy on your part," answered Vicente ; " just such a fancy as makes me glance at him sometimes as he rides silent at my side, and with a sudden start clap my hand upon my sword. I have an instinctive dread of him, — not a fear, but such a dread as I have of a deadly reptile. I wonder," he added gloomily, " if it is to be my fate to take his life."

Feliz shuddered. Chinita's eyes flashed.

" And yet once I saved him, when we were fighting against the guerillas of Ortiz. He was caught in a defile of the mountains ; four assailants dashed upon him at once with exultant cries ; and though he fought gallantly, had I not rushed to the rescue he must have been killed there. Together we beat the villains off, and he fancies he owes me some thanks ; and perhaps too I have some kindness for the man I saved, — and yet there are times when I cannot trust myself to look upon him."

" Strange ! strange indeed ! " said Doña Feliz, musingly. " I have heard his name before. Is he not the man who stopped the train of wagons by which the merchants of Guanapila were despatching funds to make their foreign payments, and who took fifty thousand dollars or more to pay his troops ? "

" The same," answered Vicente ; " and those troops were reinforced by a chain-gang he had released the day before, — vile miscreants every one. We quarrelled over each of these acts ; but he laughed us all — the merchants, the government, myself — into good-humor again. He is one of those anomalies one detests, and admires, — crafty, daring, licentious, superstitious, yielding, cruel, all in turn and when least expected. He will rob a city with one hand, and feed the poor or enrich a church with the other. But here he comes ! "

The man thus spoken of was, indeed, crossing the court

with Don Rafael, who seemed to reel slightly in his walk, and was laughing and talking volubly. "Yes, yes," he was saying, as he came within hearing, "you are right, Señor Don José; the herd of brood mares of Tres Hermanos is the finest in the country. There are more than a hundred well-broken horses in the pasture, besides scores upon scores that no man has crossed. I sent a hundred and fifty to Don Julian a month ago. Doña Isabel begrudges nothing to the cause of liberty."

"Then I will take the other hundred to-morrow," said Ramirez, lightly. Don Rafael stared at him blankly. There was something in the General's face that almost sobered him. The countenance of Gonzales darkened.

"Believe me, Señor Comonfort shall know of your good-will, and that of the excellent lady Doña Isabel," continued Ramirez, suavely. "She will lose nothing by the complacency of her administrador," and as he spoke, he smiled half indulgently, half contemptuously, upon Don Rafael.

"You promised me that here at least no seizures should be made," exclaimed Don Vicente, in a low indignant voice, hot with the thought that even the men he had himself mustered and commanded were so utterly under the spell of Ramirez that upon any disagreement they were likely to shift their allegiance, — for those free companies were even less to be depended upon than the easily rebellious regulars.

"There have been no seizures, nor will there be," answered the General, laughing. "Don Rafael and I have been talking together as friends and brothers; he has told me of his amiable family, and I him of my foot-sore troops."

Vicente, silenced but enraged, glared upon Ramirez as he bade farewell to Doña Feliz. As he took her hand, he bent and lightly kissed it. The action was a common one, — Doña Feliz scarcely noticed it; her eyes rested upon her son, who shifted uneasily from one foot to the other, his garrulity checked, his gaze confused and alarmed.

"We shall be gone at daybreak. You will be glad to be rid of us," the General said laughingly; "yet we are innocent folk, and would do you no harm. Hark! how sweetly our followers are singing," — and, indeed, the plaintive notes of a love ditty faintly floated on the air. "My adieus to the Señora de Sanchez and her lovely children."

While the General spoke thus, with many low bows and formal words of parting, he was quite in the shadow of the wall. Doña Feliz could scarce see his face, but Chinita's eyes never left it. As he turned away, a sob rose in her throat; but for a sudden fear, she would have darted after him. Her blood seemed afire. There was something in the very atmosphere stirred by this man that roused her wild nature, even as the advent of its fellow casts an admonishing scent upon the air breathed by some savage beast.

Don Rafael stole away to bed, but Don Vicente and Doña Feliz continued their interrupted conversation far into the night. Chinita sat in the same place, and slumbered fitfully, and dreamed. All through her dreams sounded the voice of the General Ramirez; all through her dreams Gonzales followed him, with hand upon his sword.

It was near morning, when at last the child awoke, chilled and stiff, and found herself alone in the corridor. The moon had sunk, and only the faint light of the stars shone on the vast and silent building; but she was not afraid. She was used to dropping asleep, as did others of the peasant class, where best it suited her, and at best her softest bed was a sheep-skin. She sleepily crept to the most sheltered part of the corridor and slept again. But the stony pillow invited to no lengthy repose; and when the dawn broke, the sound of movement in the outer court quickly roused her, and she ran out just in time to see the officers hastily swallowing their chocolate, while Don Rafael, Pedro, and a crowd of laborers, shivering in their *jorongos*, were looking on, while the sumpter mules were being laden. At the village, the camp women were already making their shrill adieus, taking their departure upon sorry beasts, laden with screeching chickens, grunting young pigs, and handfuls of rice, coffee, chile, or whatever edibles they had been able to filch or beg, tied in scraps of cloth and hung from their wide panniers, where the children were perched at imminent risk of losing their balance and breaking their brown necks. It was not known, however, that such accidents had ever happened, and the women jogged merrily away, to fall into the rear when outstripped by their better mounted lords.

Don Rafael wore a gloomy face. A squad of soldiers had already been despatched for the horses; his own herders were lassooing them in the pastures, and they were presently driven past the hacienda gates, plunging and snorting. He felt that had he not in Doña Isabel's name yielded them, they would have been forcibly seized; yet his conscience troubled him. The night before he had drunk too much; the wine had strangely affected him, — he had been maudlin and garrulous. These were times when no prudent man should talk unnecessarily, and especially to such a listener as the adventurer General José Ramirez.

The neighing and whinnying of the horses, the hollow ringing of their unshod hoofs upon the road-way, the shouts of the men, the shrill voices of the women, all combined to fill the air with unwonted sounds, and brought the family of the administrador early from their beds. As Vicente Gonzales, after shaking hands coldly with Don Rafael, rode away at the head of his band, he half turned in his saddle to glance at Doña Isabel's balcony. At the rear of the house, a faint glow was beginning to steal up the sky and touch the tops of the trees which rose above the garden wall, and tinge with opal the square towers of the church; he remembered the good Padre Francisco, and piously breathed a prayer for his soul. The drooping rose on the balcony of what he knew to be Doña Isabel's chamber seemed the very emblem of death and desolation. With a sigh he pulled his hat over his eyes and rode on; but the General, José Ramirez, who had been longer in his adieus, caught sight of Doña Rita in the corner balcony, leaning over her two half-dressed children. Their two heads were close together, their laughing faces side by side, their four eyes making points of dancing light behind the black bars of the balcony railing.

Don José Ramirez was in a gentle mood; a sudden impulse seized him to turn his horse and ride close to the building, turning his eyes searchingly upon the children. Both coquettishly turned their faces away. Rosario covered her eyes with her fingers, glancing coyly through them ; then kissing the tips of the other hand, opened them lightly above him in an imaginary shower of kisses. No goddess could have sprinkled them more deftly than did this infantine coquette.

Ramirez answered the salute laughingly, then turned away with a frown on his brow. The slight delay had left him behind the troop, amid the dust of the restive horses. Yet he made no haste to escape the inconvenience, but yielding for the moment to some absorbing thought rode slowly. The voice of a child suddenly caused him to arrest his horse with an ungentle hand. He looked around him with a start, — an object indistinctly seen under a mesquite tree caused his heart to bound. The blood left his cheek, he shook in his saddle. His horse, as startled as he, bounded in the air, and trembled in every limb. A moment later and José Ramirez laughed aloud. His name was repeated. "What do you there, child?" he cried ; "thou art a witch, and hast frightened my horse. And by my patron saint," he added in a lower tone, "I was startled myself!"

Chinita the foundling came forward calmly, though her skirt was in tatters, and her draggled scarf scarce covered her shoulders ; but there was an air about her as if she had been dressed in imperial robes. "Ah!" she said quite calmly, "it is the smell of the blood that has startled your horse ; they say no animal passes here without shying and plunging, since the American was killed!"

Ramirez glanced around him with wild eyes. "Oh, you cannot see him now," cried the child ; "that happened long ago. No, no, there is nothing here that will hurt you. Why do you look at me like that? It is not I — a poor little girl — who could injure you, but men like those," and she pointed to the columns of soldiers whose bayonets were glistening in the rising sun. Her eye seemed to single out Gonzales, though he was beyond her vision. The thought of Ramirez perchance followed hers, yet he only sat and stared at her, his eyes fixed, his body shrunken and bowed.

"See here," she said slowly, raising herself on tiptoe, and with eager hand drawing something from beneath her clothing, "I have a charm of jet : Pedro put it on my neck when I was a baby. It will ward off the evil eye.

Take it; wear it. An old man gave it to Pedro on his death-bed; he had been a soldier, a highwayman; he had fought many battles, killed many men, yet had never had a wound! Take it!" She took from her neck a tiny bit of jet, hanging from a hempen string, and thrust it into his hand.

Ramirez was astounded. He looked upon her as a vision from another world, — he who was accustomed to outbursts of strange eloquence, even from the lips of un-clothed children amid those untutored peasantry. She seemed to him a thing of witchcraft. His eyes fixed themselves on the child's face as if fascinated; he saw it grimy, vivacious, beautiful but weird, tempting, mysterious. No angel, he felt, had stopped him on his way. He took the charm mechanically, and the child, with a joyous yet mocking laugh, fled away. He roused as from a spell, called after her, tossed the charm into the air, and caught it again, and called once more, but she neither answered nor stopped. He gazed around him once again. A superstitious awe, akin to terror, crept over him; he shuddered, thrust the tailsman into his belt, and put spurs to his horse.

That day, for the most part, he rode alone, and when for a time he joined Gonzales, he was silent; silent, too, was his companion, and neither one nor the other divined the thoughts of the man who rode at his side.

XV.

YEARS passed. The nine days' feast of the Blessed Virgin, one of the most charming of all the year, was being celebrated with unusual pomp in the church at Tres Hermanos. Since the death of Padre Francisco, no priest had been regularly stationed there; but at the expense of Doña Isabel, one had been sent there to remain through the nine days sacred to Mary, and the people gave their whole time to devotional exercises, much to the neglect of the usual hacienda work. The crops in the fields were untended, while the men crowded to Mass in the morning, and spent their afternoons at the tavern-shop playing monté and drinking pulque; while the women and children streamed in and out of the church, — the women to witness the offering of flowers upon the altar, the children to lay them there, happy once in the year to be chief in the service of the beautiful Queen of Heaven. For though the image above the altar was blackened by time and defaced by many a scar, the robes were brilliant, and glittered with variously colored jewels of glass; the crown was untarnished, and the little yellow babe in the mother's arms appealed to the strong maternal sentiment which lies deep in the heart of every Mexican woman.

Upon the first day of the feast not one female child of the many who lived within the hacienda limits was absent from the church; and they were so many that the proud mothers, who had spent no little of their time and substance in arraying them, were fain to crowd the aisles and doorways, or stand craning their necks without, hoping to catch a glimpse of the high altar, as the crowd surged to and fro, making way for the tiny representatives of womanhood, who claimed right of entrance from their very powerlessness and innocence. Quaint and ludicrous looked these little creatures, mincing daintily into the church, their wide-spread crinolines expanding skirts stiffly starched, and rustling audibly under brilliant tunics of flowered muslin or purple and green stuffs. These dresses were an exact imitation in material and style of the gala attire of the mothers. The full skirts swept the ground, and over the curiously embroidered linen chemise which formed the bodice was thrown the ever-present reboso, or scarf of shimmering tints. The well-oiled black locks of these miniature *rancheras* were drawn back tightly from the low foreheads, — the long, smooth braids fastened and adorned by knots of bright ribbon, and crowned with flowers of domestic manufacture, their glaring hues and fantastic shapes contrasting strangely with the masses of beauty and fragrance that each child clasped to her bosom. In spite of its incongruities, a fantastic and pleasant sight was offered; and Doña Rita, looking around her with the eye of a devotee, doubted whether any more pleasing could be devised for God or man.

Within the sacred walls of her temple at least, the Church of Rome is consistent in declaring that in her eyes her children are all equal; and upon that spring-time afternoon at Tres Hermanos, among a throng of plebeian children from the village, knelt the daughters of the administrador; and side by side were Doña Rita and a woman from whose contact, as she met her on the court the day before, she had drawn back her skirt, lest it should be polluted by the mere touch of so foul a creature.

Rosario and Chata (as Florentina was so constantly called that her baptismal name was almost unknown) had already laid their wreaths of pink Castillian roses upon the altar, and were demurely telling their beads, when a startling vision passed them.

It was Chinita, literally begarlanded with flowers, — wild-roses, pale and delicate, long tendrils of jessamine, and masses of faint yellow cups of the cactus, and scarlet verbenas, dusty and coarse, yet offering a dazzling contrast of color to the snowy pyramid of lily-shaped blossoms, hacked from the summit of a palm, which she bore proudly upon one shoulder; while from the other hung her blue reboso in the guise of a bag filled with ferns and grasses brought from coverts few others knew of. The flowers made a glorious display as they were laid about the

altar, for there was not room for half upon it. The breath
of the fields and woodlands rushed over the church, almost
overpowering the smell of the incense, and there were
smiles on many faces and wide-eyed glances of admiration
and surprise as Chinita descended to take her place among
the congregation.

Five Mays had come and gone since she had stood under the fateful tree, and given the jet amulet to the cavalier who had so roused and fascinated her imagination;
but whatever may have been its effect upon its new possessor, its loss had certainly wrought no ill upon Chinita.
Though not yet fourteen years of age, she was fast
attaining the development of womanhood, and her mind
as well as person showed a rare precocity even in that
land where the change from childhood to womanhood
seems almost instantaneous. But there was no coyness,
as there was no assumption of womanly ways in this tall,
straight young creature, whose only toil was to carry the
water-jar from the fountain to Florencia's hut, perhaps
twice in the day, — and who did it sometimes laughingly,
sometimes grudgingly as the humor seized her, but always
spilling half the burden with which she left the fountain
before she lifted it from her shoulder and set it in the
hollow worn in the mud floor of the hut, escaping with
a laugh from Florencia's scolding, and hurrying out to her
old pursuits, now grown more various, more daring, more
perplexing, more vexatious to all with whom she came
in contact.

A thousand times had it been upon the lips of Doña
Rita to forbid the entrance in her house of the foundling
to distract the minds of Rosario and Chata by her wild
pranks; but aside from the fact that Doña Rita was of a
constitutionally indolent nature, averse even to the use of
many words and still more to energetic action, the child was
a constant source of interest. She carried into the quiet
rooms a sense of freedom and expansion, as though she
brought with her the breezes and sunlight in which she
delighted to wander. She had too a powerful ally in Doña
Feliz, who kept a watchful eye upon her; and though she
never, like her daughter-in-law or the children, made a pet
and plaything of the waif, yet she was always the first to
notice if she looked less well than usual, or to set Pedro

on his guard if her wanderings were too far afield, or her
absences too long.

Upon this day as Chinita turned from the altar, while
others smiled, a frown contracted the brow of Doña Feliz,
as for the first time perhaps she realized that this gypsy-
like child was in physique a woman. She had chosen to
wear a dress of bright green woollen stuff, — far from becoming to the olive tint of her skin, but by some accident
cut to fit the lithe figure which already outlined, though
imperfectly, the graces of early womanhood. The short
armless jacket was fashioned after the child's own fancy,
and opened over a chemise which was a mass of drawn
work and embroidery; her skirts outspread all others, yet
the flowing drapery could not wholly conceal the small
brown feet which, as the custom was, were stockingless
and cased in heelless slippers of some fine black stuff,
— more an ornament than a protection. But Chinita's
crowning glory were the rows of many-colored worthless
glass beads, mingled with strings of corals and dark and
irregular pearls, that hung around her neck and festooned
the front of her jacket. This dazzling vision, with the inevitable soiled reboso thrown lightly over one shoulder, came
down from the altar and through the aisle of the church,
smiling in supreme content, not because of the glorious
tribute of flowers she had plucked and offered, nor with
pride at her own appearance, gorgeous as she believed it
to be, but because of the delightful effect she supposed
both would leave on her aristocratic playmates; and
much amazed was she as she neared them to see Chata's
expressive nose assume an elevation of unapproachable dignity, while Rosario's indignation took the form of an aggressive pinch, so deftly given that Chinita's shrill interjection
seemed as unaccountable as the glory of her apparel.

Chinita in some consternation sank on her knees, her
green skirt rising in folds around her, reminding Chata
irresistibly of a huge butterfly which she had that very
morning seen settle upon a verdant pomegranate bush.
How she longed to extinguish Chinita's glories as she had
done those of the insect, by a cast of her reboso. There
was no malice in her thought, though perhaps a trifle of
envy, for she too loved brilliant colors. She could not
restrain a titter as she thought what Chinita's vexation

would be ; and with a face glowing with anger and eyes filled with reproach, Pedro's foster-child sailed haughtily past the sisters while the untrained choir were singing hymns of rejoicing, with that inimitable undertone of pathos natural in the voices of the Aztecs, and the censers of incense were still swinging, and left the church, — longing to rush back and to trample under foot the flowers she had so joyously gathered, longing to tear off the fine clothes and adornments she had so proudly donned. She pushed angrily past a peasant boy in tattered cotton garments and coarse sombrero of woven grass, who was the slave of her caprices, who had toiled in her service all day and upon whom she had smiled when she entered the church, yet whom she now thrust aside in rage as she left it, with a "Out of my way, stupid! What art thou staring at? Thou art like blind Tomas, with his eyes open all day long, yet seeing nothing."

"A pretty one thou," cried the boy, angrily. "Dost suppose I am a rabbit, to care for nothing but green? Bah ! thou art uglier in thy gay skirts than in thy old ones of red-and-white flannel ! "

But the girl had not lingered to listen to his taunts. She flew rather than ran to her hut, which on account of the service in the church was deserted. A crowd of ragged urchins who had taken up the cry of her flouted swain, followed her, jeering and hooting, to the door which she slammed in their faces. Not that they bore her any ill will ; but the sight of Chinita in her fine clothes, ruffling and fluttering like an enraged peacock, was irresistibly exciting to the youths whom her lofty disdain usually held in the cowed and submissive state of awe-stricken admiration.

Chinita, scarcely understanding her own miserable disappointment and anger, began to disembarrass herself of her finery, flinging each article from her with contempt, until she stood in the coarse red white-spotted skirt, with a broad band of light green above the hips, — which formed her ordinary apparel. As she stood panting, two great tears rolling down her cheeks and two others as large hanging upon her long, black lashes, she saw the door gently pushed open and before, with an angry exclamation, she could reach it, a little brown head was thrust in.

"Go away!" cried Chinita, imperatively. "Thou hast been told not to come here. Thy mother will have thee whipped, and I shall be glad, and I will laugh! yes, I will laugh and laugh!" and she proceeded to do so sardonically on the instant, gazing down with a glance of contemptuous fury, which for the moment was tragically genuine, upon the little brown countenance lifted to her own somewhat apprehensively, yet with a mischievous daring in the dark eyes that lighted it.

Chinita, with a child's freedom and in the forgetfulness of anger, had used the "thou" of equality in addressing her visitor; yet so natural and irresistible are class distinctions in Mexico, that she held open the door with some deference for the daughter of the administrador to enter, and caught up her scarf to throw over her head and bare shoulders, as was but seemly in the presence of a superior however young. That done, however, they were but two children together, two wilful playmates for the moment at variance.

"Now, then! Be not angry, Chinita!" laughed Chata, looking around her with great satisfaction. "What good fortune that thou art here alone! I slipped by the gate when Pedro was busy talking, and Rosario was making my mother and *mamagrande* to fear dying of laughter by mimicking thee, Chinita; and so they never missed me when I darted away to seek thee, Sanchica."

"And thou hadst better go back," cried Chinita, grimly, more piqued at being the cause of laughter than pleased at Chata's penetration; for in choosing her green gown she had had in her mind the habit of green cloth sent by the Duchess to Sancho Panza's rustic daughter, and had teased and wheedled Pedro into buying her holiday dress of that color, — because when they were reading the story together Chata had called her Sanchica and herself the Duchess, and for many a day they had acted together such a little comedy as even Cervantes never dreamed of, in which they had seemed to live in quite another world than that actually around them. The tale of the "Knight of the Sorrowful Countenance" was a strange text-book for children; yet in it they had contrived to put together the letters learned in the breviary, and with their two heads close bent over the page, these two, as years passed on,

had spelled out first the story, then later an inkling of the
wit, the fancy, the philosophy which lay deep between the
two leathern covers that inclosed the entire secular literature that the house of Don Rafael afforded.

There were, indeed, shelves of quaint volumes in the
darkened rooms into which Chata sometimes peeped when
Doña Feliz left a door ajar ; but so great was her awe that
she would not have disturbed an atom of dust, and scarce
dared to breathe lest the deep stillness of those dusky
rooms should be broken by ghostly voices. But Chinita,
less scrupulous, had more than once, quite unsuspected,
passed what were to her delightful though grewsome hours
in those echoing shades, and with the bare data of a few
names had repeopled them in imagination with those long
dead and gone, as well as with the figure of that stately
Doña Isabel, who still lived in some far-off city, — mourning rebelliously, it was whispered, over the beautiful
daughter shut from her sight by the walls of a convent,
yet who with seemingly pitiless indifference had consigned
the equally beautiful younger Carmen to a loveless marriage ; for the latter had married an elderly widower, and
who could believe it might be from choice?   Chinita
heard perhaps more of these things than any one, for
she was free to run in and out of every hut, as well as
the house of the administrador ; and with her quick intelligence, her lively imagination, and that faculty which with
one drop of Indian blood seems to pervade the entire
being, — the faculty of astute and silent assimilation of
every glance and hint, — she was in her apparent ignorance and childishness storing thoughts and preparing
deductions, which lay as deep from any human eye as
the volcanic fires that in the depths of some vine-clad
mountain may at any moment burst forth, to amaze and
terrify and overwhelm.

But Chinita was brooding over no secret thoughts as
she began to smile, though unwillingly and half wrathfully,
as Chata eagerly declared how well the green dress had
transformed her into a veritable Sanchica, and how stupid
she herself had been not to guess from the first what her
clever playmate had meant ; then she laughed again as she
thought of the billowy green in which Chinita had knelt,
and the half-appeased masquerader was vexed anew, and

sat sullenly on the edge of the adobe shelf that served as a bedstead, and tugged viciously at the knots of ribbon in the rebellious hair which she had vainly striven to confine in seemly tresses. She shook back the wild locks, which once free sprang into a thousand rings and tendrils, and looking at Chata irefully from between them, exclaimed, —

"You laugh at me always! You are a baby; you read in the book, and yet you know nothing. If I were rich like you, I would not be silent and puny and weak as you are. I would be strong and beautiful, and a woman as Rosario is; and I would know everything, — yes, as much as the Padre Comacho, and more; and I would be great and proud, as they say the Señora Doña Isabel is!"

"But," cried Chata, flushing with astonishment and some anger, "how can I be beautiful and strong and like a grown woman at will? My grandmother says it is well I am still a child, while Rosario is almost a woman; and I do not mind being little, no, nor even that my nose turns back to run away, as you say, from my mouth every time I open it; but it is growing more courageous, I know," — and she gave the doubtful member an encouraging pull. "I do not mind all this in the least, while my father and my grandmother love me; but my mother and you and every one else look only at Rosario, and talk only of her —" and her lip trembled.

"But do I talk *to* Rosario?" asked Chinita, much mollified. "Do I ever tell her my dreams, and all the fine things I see and hear, when I wander off in the fields and by the river, and up into the dark cañons of the hills? And," she added in an eager whisper, "shall I ever tell her about the American's ghost when I see him?"

"Bah! you will never see him," ejaculated Chata, contemptuously, though she glanced over her shoulder with a sudden start. "There is no such thing. I asked my grandmother about it yesterday, and she says it is all wicked nonsense. There could have been no American to be murdered, for she remembers nothing about it."

"Oh!" ejaculated Chinita, significantly, and she laughed. "Then it is no use for me to tell you where he is buried. If there was no American, he could not have a grave."

" Yet you have found it!" cried Chata, in intense excitement, for the story, more or less veracious, that had often been told her of the murder of the American years before, and the return of his ghost from time to time to haunt the spot accursed by his unavenged blood, had taken a strong hold upon her imagination. " Oh, Chinita! did you go, as you said you would, among the graves on the hillside? Did you go?"

" Why, yes, I did go," answered Chinita, slowly, winding her arms around her knees, as she leaned from her high perch, her brown face almost touching that of the smaller child, who still stood before her. " But I sha' n't tell you anything more, so you may as well go home. Ah, I think I hear them calling you," and she straightened herself up as if to listen.

"No! no! no!" cried Chata in an agony of impatience, "I will not go till you tell me. I *will* know! Oh, Chinita, if I were but like you, and could run about at will, over the fields and up the hills!" The tears rose to her eyes as she spoke, — poor little captive, in her stolen moment of liberty feeling in her soul the iron of bondage to custom or necessity.

" Well, then," said Chinita, deliberately, prolonging the impatience of her supplicant, while the tears in the dark gray eyes lifted to her own moved her, " I went through the cornfield. I drove Pepé back when he wanted to go with me. Oh, how afraid that big boy is of me! Yes, I went through the corn, — oh, it is so high, so high, I thought it was the very wood where Don Quixote and Sancho Panza met the robbers; but I was not afraid. And then I came to the beanfield, and oh, *niña*! I meant to go again this very day, and bring an armful of the sweet blossoms to Our Lady, and I forgot it!" clasping her hands penitently.

" And well for thee that thou didst," exclaimed Chata, " or a pretty rating my father would have given thee! He says it is enough to make the Blessed Virgin vexed for a year to see the good food-blossoms wasted, when there are millions of flowers God only meant for her and the bees. But, Chinita, I would I were a bee, to make thee cry as I wish! Thou art slower than ever to-day. Tell me, tell me, what didst thou next?"

"Well, did I not tell you I came to the beanfield, — what should I do but go through it?" remonstrated Chinita; "and then I walked under the willows. Ah, if you could only once walk under the willows, *niña*! it is like heaven in the green shade by the clear water, and there are great brakes of rushes, with the birds skimming over them. I saw among them a stork standing on one leg, and he had in his mouth a little striped snake, yellow and scarlet and black, which so wriggled and twisted! Ah, and I saw, besides, little fish in the shallow water, and —"

Chata sighed. She had unconsciously sunk upon the mud floor; her eyes opened wide, as if in imagination she saw all those things of which, though she was set in the very heart of Nature, her bodily eyes had caught no glimpse. How in her heart of hearts the sheltered, cloistered daughter of the administrador envied the wild foster-child of the gate-keeper, who was so free, and from whom the woods and fields could keep no secrets! "Go on!" she whispered, and Chinita said, in a sort of recitative, —

"Yes, I went on and on, not very long by the water's edge, though I loved it, but up the little path through the stones and the thorny cacti. Oh, but they were full of yellow blossoms, and they smelled so sweet; but they were full of prickles too, and as I went up the steep hillside they caught my reboso every minute, and when I stood among the graves my hands were tingling and smarting, and I was half blind and stumbling. I was so tired, oh, so tired! and I sat down and rubbed my hands in the sand. It was very still there; it seemed to me that a little wind was always singing, but perhaps it was the dry grass rustling; but as I bent down to listen, I fell asleep, and when I woke up the sun was no higher in the sky than the width of my hand, and I had no time to look for anything."

"Ah, stupid creature!" cried Chata, after a moment's silent disappointment. "Why did you not tell me so before? I must be missed. I shall be scolded," and in a sudden panic she rose to her feet and turned to the door.

"Stay! stay!" cried Chinita, eager to give her news, as she saw Chata about to fly. "Though I did not look, I found something. Oh, yes, in black letters, so big and clear!"

Chata returned precipitately. "Letters — what letters?" she cried.

"Big black letters, J and U and A and N; and the letters for the American name — how do they say it? Ash — Yes, Ashley — it is not hard — and that he was born in the United States, and murdered here in May, — yes, I forget the figures, but I counted up; it was just fourteen years ago, upon the 13th of this very month. It was all written out upon a little wooden cross, which had fallen face down upon the grave I fell asleep upon. I might have looked for it a hundred years and not have found it, but I had scraped away the sand from it to rub my hands. It is thick and heavy; I could scarcely turn it over to read the words, — but they are there. You may tell Doña Feliz there was an American."

"No, I shall say nothing," said Chata, dreamily. "She likes not to hear of murder or of ghosts. Ah, the poor American! why does his spirit stay here? This is not purgatory. Ah, can it be he cannot rest because he died upon the 13th? — the unlucky number, my mother says."

"Let us make it lucky," said Chinita, daringly. "Let us say thirteen Aves and thirteen Pater Nosters for his soul."

But Chata shook her head doubtfully, and started violently as a servant maid, grimy and ragged like all her clan, and panting with haste, thrust open the door, exclaiming, —

"*Niña* of my soul, your lady mother declares you are dead. Doña Feliz has searched all the house, and is wringing her hands with grief. Don Rafael has seized Pedro by the collar, and is mad with rage because he swears you have not passed the gate; and here I find you, with your white frock all stained with dirt, and that beggar brat filling your ears with her mad tales. The Saints defend us! Sometime the witch will fly off — as she came — no one knows where. But you, *niña*, come, come away!" and the excited woman dragged the truant reluctantly away; while Chinita, thrusting her tongue into her cheek, received the epithets of "beggar brat" and "witch" with a contempt which the gesture only, rather than any words, fluent as she was in plebeian repartee, could at that moment adequately express.

XVI.

Though Chinita as was usual was made the scapegoat for Chata's fault, — Doña Rita averring that the girl possessed an irresistible power for evil over her own innocent children, — Chata on this occasion felt herself most heavily punished, for Don Rafael strengthened his wife's fiat against the dangerous temptress, the gate-keeper's child, by absolutely prohibiting her entrance to his house. Chata wept for her playmate, and for many days Rosario moped and sulked; while Chinita hung disconsolate — as the Peri at the gate of Paradise — about the entrance to the court, finding small solace in the young fawn Pepé had given her, though she twined her arms around it and held its head against her bosom, that its large pensive eyes might seem to join in the appeal of her own. And perhaps the two aided by time and Chata's grief might have conquered; but there was a sudden interruption of the quiet course of life at Tres Hermanos.

One day Chinita found the whole house open to her; there was no one there either to welcome or repulse her save Doña Feliz. Don Rafael, with his wife and children, had obeyed a sudden call, and had hastened to the dying bed of Doña Rita's mother. For the first time in her life Chata had left the hacienda. Rosario had twice before gone with her mother to visit relatives, but for various reasons Chata had remained at home. Doña Rita seemed half inclined to leave her at this time also; but Don Rafael cut the matter short by ordering her few necessaries to be packed, and in a flutter of excitement, perhaps heightened by the frown upon her mother's face, Chata took her seat in the carriage that was to bear her far beyond the circle of hills which had heretofore bounded her vision.

What a pall seemed to fall upon the place when they were all gone! First, a great stillness pervaded the court and corridors where the children's voices were wont to ring; and then hollow, ghostly noises woke the echoes. A second court was now opened which long had been closed, though the fountains played there, and the flower-pots were all rich with bloom. The doors of rooms which before at best had been only left ajar were opened wide; and Doña Feliz, with a few of her most trusty servants, swept out the long accumulated dust, and let the light stream in upon the disused furniture. Chinita had caught glimpses of these things before, indistinct, uncertain, as though they were far memories of a past existence. She and Chata had often talked of them in days when they played at being grand ladies, and in imagination they were rich and beautiful; but when she actually stood in the broad sunshine, and saw the gilt and varnish, the variegated stuffs and great mirrors, the reality seemed a dream, from which she feared to waken. For all these material things appealed to something in the child's nature which it appeared impossible she should have inherited from a long line of plebeian ancestors, — a something that was not a mere gaping admiration for what was bright and beautiful and dazzling by its very height of separation from the poor possibilities of her life, but which one would say had sprung directly from the influences of lavish splendor. There was an impulse toward appropriation and enjoyment in the actual touch of these attributes of an aristocratic life, an instinctive knowledge of the uses of things she had never before seen or heard of, which seemed to come as naturally into her mind as would the art of swimming to a duckling that had passed its first days in the coop with its foster-mother the hen. Nothing surprised her, and the delight she felt was not merely that of novelty, but that of the satisfaction of a long-felt want. Doña Feliz had not forbidden her entrance when she first saw her at the door of Doña Isabel's apartment, but watched her with grave surprise as she wandered through the long rooms, sometimes picking up a fan, a hand-glass, a cup, and unconsciously assuming the very air and walk of a grand lady, — an air so natural that even in her tattered red skirt it never for a moment made her appear grotesque.

Don Rafael returned home in the midst of the work of renovation. He had left his family with the dying mother, forced to return by the exigencies of business, —

but ill pleased to leave them, for the roads were full of bandits, and the country was infested with wandering bands, as dangerous in their professed military character as the openly avowed robbers. They enjoyed immunity in all their depredations and deeds of violence, because they were committed under the standard of the Governor of the State, José Ramirez, — for to his *rôle* of military chieftain the adventurer had added that of politician. In this *rôle* he had hastened the tottering fortunes of President Comonfort to their fall, by seizing in his name a large sum of money belonging to foreign merchants, and with it buying over the troops under his command, — first to declare him military governor, and then to join with enthusiasm the clerical forces, which sprang into being as if by magic, bringing with them money in plenty, and gay uniforms, which put to shame the rags which the Liberals wore and which the resources of the legitimate government were insufficient to replace with more attractive garb. For months the name of José Ramirez had rung through the land in alternate shouts of triumph and joy and howls of execration. The prison doors had been thrown open, and hundreds of convicts had joined his ranks, ready to die for the man who had set them free, — not for gratitude, but in an excess of admiration for a spirit more lawless, more daring, than their own.

Chinita used to stand half aloof, and listen to these things, as wild rumors of them reached the hacienda, a burning pride glowing in her heart as she heard of deeds that made men tremble and stand aghast; and in imagination she saw the tall dark man whom she had made her hero riding through the streets in the full panoply of military splendor, followed by a train of mounted soldiers as gorgeous as himself, — then the blaring band, the gay foot soldiers shouting his name, and that terrible battle-cry of "Religion y Fueros," in which so many infernal deeds were done; and last of all a multitude of half-clad men, women, and boys and girls like herself in ragged garments, not hungry nor wretched, though with all the grime and squalor of poverty upon them. She loathed them in her heart, though she did not consciously separate herself from their kind; but often ran to the covert of the tall corn, or the shade of some tree, and sat down and drew her reboso over her head, laughing softly and breathlessly, for had she not given this man the amulet which gave him a charmed life? Sometimes she heard of attacks made upon him, — how bullets had gone crashing through his carriage windows, how in the very streets of the city, as well as on the battle-field, his horses had been shot under him; but he had never once been hurt. She was a ragged, barefoot girl, but here was something which in her own eyes enwrapped her as with velvet and ermine, — the belief that she had some part in that dazzling career that attracted the gaze, the wonder, the terror of what was to her mind the whole wide world.

Through those hot summer days Pedro saw little of his foster child; and sometimes when he did see her, she would pass by as if he were nothing to her, or would shudder sometimes when he laid his hand with gentle violence upon her arm, and forced her in from the glaring sunshine, in which she often wandered for hours, unconscious of the heat which was burning her skin browner and browner, but painting roses on her cheeks, and filling her eyes with light; and sometimes she would come softly up behind him and throw the brown tangle of her hair over his eyes, almost smothering him in the golden crispness of its ruddy ends, and kiss him wildly between his bushy eyebrows, calling herself his wicked Chinita, his naughty child, until he would draw her on his knee and wipe away her streaming tears with the tenderness but none of the familiarity of a parent, and while he did so, sigh and sigh again, and wonder what these wild moods would lead to.

When Doña Feliz began the renovation of the family apartments Pedro stole in there one day when she chanced to be quite alone, and asked if it was true that Doña Isabel would soon return; it was many years — yes, twelve and more — since she had left them; and the *niña* Carmen, was it true that she was married? And the Señorita Herlinda? "Was it quite certain," and his voice grew low, — "was it quite certain she was in a convent?"

"Did not Don Vicente tell you that?" queried Doña Feliz; "and his sad looks, did they not tell you? Ah, unhappy girl, where should she be but in a convent? Where else in the world should she hide, who was so at feud with life?" She started, remembering herself; but

Pedro was looking at her with impassive stolidity. "Yes, yes," she continued impatiently, "she has chosen her path; she has left the world forever."

"But they say," droned Pedro, monotonously, "that the convents will be opened and all the nuns be made free when the Señor Juarez takes his turn to rule. They say the day he enters the palace the dead men's hands will open, and all their riches escape from their grasp. The silver and gold will be taken from the altars and given to the poor, and the monasteries and nunneries be pulled down, that the people may build their houses with the stones."

Doña Feliz laughed. It was not often any sound of merriment passed her lips, and then not in scorn. "Dreams, dreams, Pedro!" she said. "Are you as foolish as the rest, and think the new law would give all the poor wealth, or even the despoiled their own? Do you think Juarez himself believes it? No, no! he is a sly fox; and while the Church and Comonfort were the lion and bear struggling over the carcass, he strives to glide in and steal the flesh. Do you think he will divide it among you hungry ones? No! these politicians are all alike, and whether with the cry of religion or liberty, fight and plot only for their own aggrandizement, and the poor country is forgotten, as it is drenched by the blood of her sons. There is not one true patriot in all this distracted land."

She spoke rather to herself than Pedro, who shook his head with a sort of grim obstinacy. "I am thinking to go away, Doña Feliz," he said. "You know the Señor Juarez is at liberty, and there will be bloody days soon if Zuloaga does not yield him his rightful place in Mexico. I have a mind to see a few of them. You know I was a good soldier in Santa Anna's time, and as I sit in the gate I hear the sound of the cannon and the rattle of musketry and the voice of my old commander Gonzales, only it comes now from the lips of his son; and I feel I must go."

Doña Feliz looked at him steadily. She knew her countryman well, and though she doubted not that something of the martial spirit of the time was stirring within him, she was equally certain that a second and more potent reason was prompting Pedro to leave Tres Hermanos; but she only said, —

"Then you wish to join Vicente Gonzales? They say he, with all his band, has thrown his fortunes in with those of Juarez. Well, well, perhaps anything was better than that he should be linked with Ramirez. If Vincente is a traitor, it is at least with a noble aim, not for mere plunder. There was something strange, forbidding, terrible, about that man Ramirez. Did you notice his face, Pedro, when he was here?"

Pedro shook his head, returning with pertinacity to his own plans. "You will talk to Don Rafael for me, will you not, Señora?" he said, with a trace of the abject whine in his tone that marked the habit of serfdom, which a few years of nominal freedom had done little to alter, "and with your good leave I will go, and take Chinita with me." He spoke hesitatingly, as though fearful his right would be disputed.

"Take Chinita!" exclaimed Doña Feliz. "What, to a soldiers' camp, to her ruin! You are mad, Pedro. No, she shall remain here with me. I will take her into the house. I will teach her to sew. She shall be my child rather than my servant! .I —" she stopped in extreme agitation, for within the doorway the child stood.

"I will be no one's servant!" she said, proudly drawing herself up; "and as to going to the Indian's camp — ah, I know a better place than that," and she nodded her head significantly. "You shall leave me, Father Pedro, with your Doña Isabel!"

Doña Feliz and Pedro started as if they had been shot.

"I came to tell you she is coming," continued the child. "I was out beyond the granaries, letting my fawn browse on the little hill, and as I was looking toward the gorge I saw a horseman coming, and far behind him was a carriage and many men. Is all ready?" and she glanced around her with the air of a prophetess. "Hark! the courier is in the court now. Doña Isabel will not be long behind him."

Pedro hastened from the room with an exclamation of alarmed amazement. "Go, go!" cried Feliz. "You are too late!" for she knew in her heart that it was in very fear of this visit, and to remove the child from the chance of encountering Doña Isabel, that Pedro had proposed to leave the hacienda; and here was Doña Isabel herself, — for strangely enough, neither of them doubted that what the child had assumed was true. The thoughts of Doña Feliz were inexplicable even to herself. She felt as though she was placed in some vast and gloomy theatre, with the curtain about to rise upon some strange play, which at the will of the actors might become either comedy or tragedy. Though of late she had felt certain that Doña Isabel would return to the hacienda, that very act seemed dramatic, the precursor of inevitable complications.

" Why could she not be content in the new life she had chosen?" muttered Doña Feliz. " What voice has been sounding in her ears, to call her back to resurrect old griefs, to walk among the spectres of long-silent agonies and shame? Foolish, foolish woman! Yet as the magnet attracts iron, so thy hard heart is drawn by these bitter remembrances. Go, go! thou child!" she exclaimed aloud, and almost angrily. " Doña Isabel would be vexed to see thee in her room. Go, and keep thee out of her way!" She gazed after Chinita with a look of perplexity and pain, as with a bound of irresistible excitement the girl sprang out upon the corridor, her laugh rising through the still air as if in notes of defiance. " What said the child?" muttered Doña Feliz. " ' Leave me with your Doña Isabel'?"

XVII.

FROM the city of Guanapila to the hacienda of Tres Hermanos the road runs almost continually through mountain defiles, where on either hand the great masses of bare rocks rise so precipitously that it seems impossible that man or beast should scale them ; and here, where Nature's aspect is most terrible, man is least to be feared. But there are intervals where broad flat ledges hang above the roadway, or where it crosses plateaus shaded by scrub-oak or mesquite and even grassy dells, where after the rains water may be found, offering charming camping-grounds during the noon-tide heat ; and precisely at such places the anxious traveller has need to look to his weapons, and picket his horses and mules in such order that no sudden attack may cause a stampede among them, and that they may, if need offer, form a barricade for their defenders. In those lawless times few persons ventured forth without a military escort, and if possible sought additional security by accompanying the baggage trains which by arrangement with the party for the moment in power enjoyed immunity from attack by roving bands of soldiery, and were too formidable to be successfully assailed by the ordinary cliques of highwaymen. Seldom indeed was there found a person so reckless as to venture forth attended only by the escort his own house afforded ; and daring indeed was the woman who would undertake a two days' journey in such a manner. The least she might expect would be to find her protectors dispersed, perhaps slain, and herself a captive, — held for an exorbitant ransom, and subjected to the hardships of life in the remote recesses of the mountains, and to indignities the very report of which might daunt the most reckless or the bravest.

Yet in spite of all this, a carriage containing a lady and her maid — for such were their relative positions, though both were alike dressed in plain black gowns and the common blue reboso — entered in the early afternoon of a summer's day the narrow gorge that led by circuitous windings through the rocks to the great gorge that formed the entrance to the wide valley of Tres Hermanos, whose entire extent offered to the eye the wondrous fruitfulness so rich and varied in itself, so startling in contrast to the desolation passed to reach it.

The midday halt had been a short one, for it was the rainy season, and progress was necessarily slow over the swollen watercourses and the obstructions of accumulated sands and pebbles, the masses of cactus and branches of trees and shrubs, which had been brought down by recent storms. At times it seemed impossible that the carriage, although drawn by four stout mules, could proceed, and from time to time the servant looked anxiously through the window. But the mistress was equal to all emergencies, herself giving directions to the perplexed driver and his assistant, and though she had been travelling for more than two days over a road usually easily passed in one, allowing no sign or word of weariness or impatience to escape her.

But this carriage and its occupants would have appeared to a passer-by the least important factor in the caravan of which it formed a part; for it was encircled and almost concealed by a band of mounted men, clad in suits of brownish leather, glimpses of the red waist-band glistening with knives and pistols showing from beneath their striped blankets, long knives and lassos hanging at their saddle-bows, rifles in their sinewy right hands, while from beneath their wide hats their keen eyes investigated sharply every jutting rock and peered into the distance with an air of half-defiant, half-fearful expectancy, — for these were men taken from her own estate, who idle retainers as they had been in her great bare house in the city where Doña Isabel Garcia had lived for years in melancholy state, thrilled with clannish fidelity to their mistress and passionate love for their *tierra* to which they were returning, and with that vague delight in the possibility of a fight which arouses in man both chivalrous and brutish daring, as the smell of blood arouses the love of slaughter in the tamest beast.

In front of these rode the conductor of the party clad in a half-military fashion, as became the character he had earned for eccentric daring, the reputation of which perhaps more than actual bravery made him eminently successful in guiding safely the party wise or rich enough to secure his escort. This man was known as Tio Reyes, though his appearance did not justify the honorary title of Uncle, for he was still in the prime of life; but it was applied to him in tones of jesting yet affectionate respect by his followers who had joined the party with him, and adopted by the others to whom he was a stranger, — for at the last moment he had appeared just as they were leaving Guanapila, and with a brief word to the mistress, to which in much surprise and some annoyance she had agreed, had placed himself at their head.

In the rear of those we have described came four or five mules laden with provisions, necessaries for camping, and some private baggage; these were driven by *arrieros* who ran at their sides, for the travelling pace of horses did not exceed that of those trained runners.

The journey, wearisome as it had proved, had so far been made without alarms, and upon nearing the boundaries of Tres Hermanos much of the anxiety though none of the vigilance of the escort subsided; when suddenly upon the glaring sunshine of the day, all the hotter and clearer from the recent rains, rose in the distance a sort of mist, which filled the narrow road and blurred the outline of the towering rocks. The guide paused for a moment and glanced back at the escort. Each hand grasped tighter the ready rifle; at a word the carriage was stopped, the baggage mules were driven up and enclosed within the square hastily formed by the armed men, — for upon that clear day, after the rains, the tramp of many feet was requisite to raise that cloud of dust, and these precautions were but prudent, whether the advancing troop were friends or foes.

Tio Reyes, after disposing his force to his satisfaction, rode forward with his lieutenant to meet the advancing host, which in those few moments seemed to fill the entire range of vision, though at first with confusing indistinctness, as did the sounds that came echoing from rock to rock. The cries of men rose hoarsely above a deep and rumbling undertone, which resolved itself at last into the

lowing of cattle and the bleating of sheep, — harmless and
terrified wayfarers, but driven and preceded by a troop of
undisciplined soldiery, ripe for deeds more tragic than the
plunder of vaqueros and shepherds, who would be more
likely wisely to seek shelter in the crevices of the rocks
than to defy numbers before whom they were helpless.

"Señora of my soul!" cried the servant, catching a
word from one of the men, "we are lost! Virgin of
Succors, pray for us! These are some of the men of his
Excellency the Governor, and you know they stop at
nothing. Ah, what a chance to gain money is this! Once
in the mountains what may they not demand for you?
Ave Maria Sanctissima! Ah, Señora, if you would but
have listened to the Señorita! to me!"

"Silence!" said the lady, in a tone as of one unused
to hear her actions commented upon. "Silence! thou
wilt be safe. If we are captured, thou wilt not be a prize
worth retaining; it will be easy to induce them to take
thee to Guanapila, and obtain a reward from my cousin,
Don Hernando."

"No, no!" cried the woman, brought to her senses by
this quiet scorn and the startling proposition of her mistress. "Could I leave your grace? No, no! imprisonment, starvation, even to be made the wife of one of
those bandits!" and a faint smile curled the damsel's lip,
for she was not ugly, and knew something of the gallantries of Ramirez's followers, — "anything rather than desert my lady! Ay, my life! whom have we here?"

It was Tio Reyes undoubtedly, and with him was a
military stranger, a gallant young fellow, and handsome,
though his hands and face were covered with dust, and
something like a large blood-stain defaced the breast of
his blue coat. "Pardon, Señora," he exclaimed, bowing
most obsequiously and removing his wide hat, disclosing
a young and vivacious countenance, "I am Rodrigo Alva,
your servant, who kisses your feet, captain of this troop of
horse, of the forces of his Excellency Don José Ramirez,
Governor of Guanapila."

"And I am the Señora Doña Isabel Garcia de Garcia,"
responded the lady, with dignified recognition of the young
man's courteous self-introduction; "and as I am unaware
of any cause for detention, I beg to be permitted to pro-

ceed toward my hacienda, which I desire to reach before night closes in."

"It is not my desire to molest ladies," said the captain, gallantly; "and I have besides received express orders to defend your passage and facilitate it in every way."

"I have no acquaintance with Señor Ramirez," said Doña Isabel in surprise; "yet more than once have I been indebted to his courtesy," and she glanced at Tio Reyes. "He it was who sent me this worthy guide. I know not why the Señor Ramirez takes such interest in my personal safety, especially as we are politically opposed;" and she added with a daring which had somewhat of girlish archness, strange from the lips of Doña Isabel, "he has not the name of a man given to gallantries."

"No, rather to gallant deeds," said the young captain, his voice accentuating the distinction. "But you, Doña Isabel, like us who serve him, must be content not to inquire too closely into his motives."

"Whatever they may be," retorted she, in a voice of displeasure, "they are not such as will spare my flocks and herds;" and she frowned as a stray ox, upon whose flank she recognized the well-known brand of Tres Hermanos, bounded by the carriage, from which the escort had gradually withdrawn, and were now exchanging amicable salutations with the more advanced of the host which they would have been equally pleased to fight.

The young man bowed in some confusion. "The men must be fed," he said. "These come from the ranchito del Refugio, Señora, and I regret to say the huts are burned down and the shepherds and vaqueros scattered; one poor fellow was killed in pure wantonness."

"And you dare tell me this!" cried Doña Isabel, in violent indignation, which for the moment overcame her wonted calmness.

"It was but to explain," interrupted Captain Alva, "that we encountered the famous Calvo there. He has succeeded in raising three hundred men or more to march to the assistance of the double-dyed traitor Juarez. Fortunately, but a portion of his troops were with him; the rest have joined Gonzales, — so our work was easy, though the fellows fought well. Three or four were killed, a few wounded, the rest fled to the mountains, and we succeeded in securing the cattle and sheep; and I hope your grace will be consoled in knowing they are destined to feed good patriots."

Doña Isabel waved her hand impatiently. "What matter a few animals?" she said. "But the poor shepherds, — they must be looked to. And the wounded — what of them?"

"*Canalla!*" laughed the captain, carelessly, "one or two are with us here, tied on their saddles. They will do well enough. Others lay down under bushes to shelter their cracked heads. But one there is, Señora, a foreigner, a mere boy, who was in the party by chance they say, just a boy's freak, — but, my faith! he did a man's portion of fighting, and has a wound to end a man's life. He must die if he rides much farther lashed to his horse;" and the young soldier, half a bandit in lawlessness, and in his perplexed notions of honor, perhaps too, scarce free from blood-guiltiness, sighed as he added, "but this is no subject for a lady's ear. Permit, Señora, that my troops and their belongings pass by, and you may then proceed in all peace and safety."

"Thanks, Señor," said Doña Isabel, adding half hesitatingly: "And the wounded youth, — a foreigner, I think you said?"

"By his looks and tongue, English," answered the officer, with his hand to his hat as a parting salute. But Doña Isabel's look stopped him.

"You pity this poor wounded creature," she said, "and I can do no less. You are compelled to travel in haste, and the city — if that is your destination — is far distant."

Doña Isabel spoke as if under some invisible compulsion and as against her will, and paused as if unable to utter the proposal that trembled on her lips; but the voluble young officer, with the eagerness of desire, divined what she would say, and so lauded the appearance and bearing of the wounded prisoner that to her own amazement Doña Isabel found herself making room for him in her carriage, much to the surprise of her maid Petra, who was mounted upon the led horse, which in thought her mistress had at first destined to the use of her unexpected guest.

However, when under the superintendence of Captain Alva and Tío Reyes the youth was transferred from his horse to the carriage, Doña Isabel saw at once that his strength was so nearly spent that even with most careful handling it was doubtful whether he would reach the hacienda alive. She shrank away as his fair young head was laid back upon the dark cushions, and his long limbs were disposed upon blankets and cushions, as much to avoid contact with that frame so evidently of alien mould as to give all the space possible to the almost unconscious sufferer. She scarce looked at him, as with effusive thanks Alva bade her farewell, but forced her eyes, though with no special interest or regret, upon the portion of her flocks that was driven bleating before her carriage, with mechanical kindness closing the window as the horned cattle, bellowing and pawing the dust, followed, and breathing a sigh of relief as the last of the revolutionary force rode by, and the sound of their noisy march grew fainter, and she realized that her own escort had fallen into their places around her carriage, the slow motion of which indicated that her interrupted journey was resumed.

For some time the thoughts of Doña Isabel were necessarily directed to her wounded guest. The wound in the shoulder had been bandaged with such skill and care as could be offered by the self-trained doctor of the rancho, for the nonce become army surgeon; and it would doubtless have done well but for exposure and fatigue, which had induced fever, in which the patient muttered uneasily and even at times became violently excited, looking at Doña Isabel with eyes of inexpressible brilliancy, catching her cool white hands in his own burning ones and calling her in endearing accents names which, though untranslatable by her, were sweet to her ear. Perhaps, they were those of mother or sister, — she almost longed to know. Later, when under her tendance and that of the grooms, who when she motioned for the carriage to be stopped often came to her assistance, he sank into uneasy slumber, she had opportunity to wonder at the impulse that had induced *her* to receive this stranger of a race, that whether American or English, she had long abjured, and to feel once more as she gazed upon his wan features something of the bitter detestation with which she had looked upon Ashley's dead face.

Doña Isabel started; the thought had entered her mind just as they were emerging from the great chasm of rocks which gave entrance to the plain, and she saw once more the Eden from which she had been driven. The house was so far distant still that she caught, across the fields of tall corn, but a mere suggestion of its flat roofs and the square turrets at the corners of the encircling walls; but though more distant still, the tall chimney of the reduction-works rose clearly defined against the sky, — so clearly that she could see where a few bricks had fallen from the cornice, and how a solitary pigeon was circling it in settling to its nest. What a picture of solitariness! Doña Isabel groaned, and covered her face with her hand. It was as she had known it would be. The first objects to meet her gaze were those that could waken the darkest and bitterest memories. Why had she come? Oh that she could retrace the rough path that she had traversed!

The wounded man groaned; he was fainting. "Hasten, hasten!" she cried, "send Anselmo forward; bid them prepare a bed. The road is not so rough; let them drive faster!"

Thus Doña Isabel's words belied the desire of her heart, for she could not by her own wish have approached her home too slowly. This boy was a stranger, not even brought thither by her will, as the other had been; yet as the other had driven her forth, this one was hastening her back. Was it fancy, or did the boy's lips pronounce a name? No, no! it was but her excited imagination. No wonder! Did not the earth and sky, the wide circle of the hills, all cry out to her, "What hast thou done? Where is Herlinda?"

XVIII.

ALTHOUGH Chinita had divined aright when she declared that the carriage she had seen in the distance could be no other than that of Doña Isabel, and the sounds which penetrated from the court announced the arrival of her outrider, she was wrong in supposing that the lady herself would be speedily at hand. There was a long delay in which Doña Feliz had time to recover outwardly from the agitation into which she was thrown, and accustom herself to this verification of her foresight, when upon hearing of the marriage of Carmen she had felt a conviction that Doña Isabel in her loneliness and the unaccustomed lack of interests around her would be irresistibly attracted to the home she had virtually forsworn.

Don Rafael having listened eagerly to the courier's account of the meeting with Ramirez's band, left him to give fuller details to the anxious villagers who gathered around, — many of whom had sons or husbands at that part of the hacienda lands known as the ranchito del Refugio, — and rushed up to Doña Feliz with the news, then down again to the court to mount a horse which had been instantly saddled, and followed by a clerk and servants galloped away to give meet welcome to the lady who had just entered upon her own domains.

Calling the maids, Doña Feliz caused the long-disused beds to be spread with fresh linen, and completed the preparations for this vaguely yet confidently expected arrival. "She had felt it in the air," she said to herself, for she knew nothing of any theory of second sight, nor had ever reasoned, on the other hand, that even the most trivial circumstances of life must work toward some given result, which they instinctively foreshadow to the observant, as the bodily eye makes out the reflection of a material object in a dimmed and besmirched mirror. She bestirred herself as if in a dream, her mind full of Doña Isabel and

the past. Yet like an undercurrent beneath the flood of
her thoughts flowed the idea of the new element that
Doña Isabel was bringing with her. "A *foreigner!*" she
muttered, as if she could scarce believe her words. "Can
it be possible that the hand once stung can dally again
with the scorpion? Ah, no! necessity wears the guise
of heresy, but it is not possible that Doña Isabel can
forget."

She glanced around her; Chinita had disappeared.
Doña Feliz saw her no more until the long-delayed carriage rolled into the court, when she descended to greet
her mistress.

The long summer's day had almost waned, and so dark
was the court that torches of pitch-pine had been stuck
into rude sconces against the pillars, and the face of Doña
Isabel looked wan and ghastly in the lurid and flickering
glare. She could not descend from the carriage until the
wounded youth had been lifted out. Doña Feliz had
never seen but one man so fair. She started as her eyes
fell upon the yellow masses of hair that lay disordered
upon his brow, but pointed to a chamber which a woman
ran to open, and into which the stranger was carried: while
Doña Isabel, cramped and stiff, leaned upon the arm of
Don Rafael, and stepped to the ground. As she did so
she would have fallen but for two strong young hands
which caught hers, and as she involuntarily held them and
steadied herself she turned her eyes upon the face which
was level with her own. Her eyes opened widely, and
with an exclamation of actual horror she threw Chinita
from her with a sudden and violent struggle, and passed
proudly though tremblingly across the court.

Don Rafael and Doña Feliz followed, too astounded to
make one movement to assist their lady's ascent of the
stairs; but when they reached the corridor and heard the
door of the bed-chamber heavily closed, they turned toward
each other, their faces pale in the twilight. "Her thoughts
are serpents to lash her," murmured Doña Feliz; adding
with a sort of national pride, "The Castillian woman may
choose to ignore, but she can never forget or forgive."

Don Rafael shrugged his shoulders. How much with
some races a shrug may signify! His then was one of
dogged resolution. "It is well," it seemed to say; and

he muttered, "As the mistress leads, the servant must follow," while his mother, shaking her head doubtfully, pointed to the court below.

Chinita had rushed furiously away from the carriage and the group of men, who after the first silence of surprise had broken into but half-suppressed laughter, which was soon lost in the babel of greetings that the disappearance of Doña Isabel gave an opportunity for exchanging, and scarcely knowing in her blind rage where she went, had thrown herself upon one of the stone seats that bordered the fountain, and with her small clinched fist was beating the rugged stone. Pedro stood near her, his face as indignant as her own, vainly endeavoring with a voice that shook with anger to soothe her wounded pride, while with one hand he strove to lead her away. She spoke not a word. Suddenly, as the young face of the girl was lifted to the light, Feliz clasped her hands together, and leaned eagerly forward. She motioned to Don Rafael, — she would not break the spell by speech; but unheeding her he left the corridor and walked away, and presently Pedro was obliged to hasten to his duties at the doorway, and the girl and the woman were left alone in the enclosure. Doña Feliz leaned motionless over the railing. Chinita, still beating the stone with her fist, sat upon the edge of the fountain. With her native instinct of propriety, to meet Doña Isabel she had put on her second best skirt — not the green one — and all her necklaces circled her throat. Her hair was closely braided, but curled wilfully round her brow and the nape of her neck. She pulled at it abstractedly in a manner she had when excited. Her face was turned aside, but to Doña Feliz there was something strangely familiar in her attitude, — something which suggested other personalities, but of whom; which recalled the past, but how?

While Chinita still sat there, Doña Isabel came out of her chamber and crossed to the side of Feliz. Her face quivered as her eyes fell on the child, and she laid her nervous white hand upon Feliz's arm. The two women looked at each other, but said not a word; the eyes of the one were full of reproach, those of the other of defiant distrust. When they turned them upon the court again, the girl had moved noiselessly away. Her passion of

9

anger was spent, and with the instinct of the Indian strain in her mixed blood, she had gone to hide herself away in some sheltered corner and brood sullenly upon her wrongs.

As she passed through the many courts, reaching at last that upon which the church opened, she was so absorbed that she did not notice she was closely followed by a man who had been very near when Doña Isabel had repulsed her, and who with a few apparently careless questions had possessed himself of all there was to know of Chinita's history.

"Look you!" said one, "did not Pedro say that a man as black as the devil dropped her into his hands? Who knows but she is the fiend's own child? *Vaya*, she struck me over the face with talons like a cat's only last week."

"And well thou deservedst it," cried the boy called Pepé. But he was laughed down by a shrill majority, for Doña Isabel's unaccountable repulse of her had turned the tide of public opinion strongly against the foundling; and the woman toward whom Tio Reyes — for he it was — now turned for additional particulars, rightly judging that in such matters female memories would prove most explicit, crossed herself as she opined "that the fox knows much, but more he who traps him, and that Pedro who had found the girl could best tell whence she came," — a saying which elicited many nods and exclamations of approval, for Pedro had never been believed quite honest in the matter. A wild story that he had received the babe from the hands of a beautiful and pallid spectre which had once been seen to speak with him in the corridor, and that this was the ghost of some lovely woman he had murdered in those early days when he and Don Leon were comrades in many a wild adventure, had passed into a sort of legend, which if not entirely accepted, certainly was not utterly disbelieved by any one.

"Go thy way! She is the devil's own brat," cried the wife of the man Chinita had once attacked.

"Ay, to be sure!" cried another; "was it not to be remembered how she had struggled and screamed when the good Father Francisco baptized her, and had sputtered and spat out the salt which the good priest had put in her mouth like a very cat. And little good had it done her, for she had never been called by a Christian name."

"Tut! tut!" said the new-comer, "what need of a name has such a pretty maid as that, or of a father or mother either? Though ye women have no mercy, she'll laugh at you all yet. The lads will not be blind, eh Pancho?"

"That they will not!" cried the lad Pepé, throwing a meaning glance at Pancho as if daring him to take up the cudgels in behalf of his old playfellow. "What care I who she is? She's not the first who came into the world by a crooked road; and must all the women hint that it began at the Devil's door because they can't trace it back? Ay, they know enough ways to the same place."

"Well said, young friend!" cried Tio Reyes with a hearty slap on the boy's shoulder. "But, hist! here comes Pedro — with an ill look too in his eye. Ah! I thought so," as the men suddenly became noisily busy with the un-saddling of their horses, and the women slipped away to their household occupations. "Tio Pedro is not a man to be trifled with. But, ah, there goes the girl!" and in a moment of confusion he adroitly left the court with-out being seen, and as has been said followed her steps till, as she crouched behind one of the buttresses of the church, he halted behind another and looked at her keenly, impatient with the uncertain light, eager to approach her before it darkened, yet waiting stoically until she was settled in a sullen crouching attitude, probably for that vigil of silence and hunger in which a ranchero's anger usually expends itself, or crystallizes into a revengeful memory.

After some minutes, during which the girl neither sobbed nor moved, he suddenly bent over and touched her on the shoulder. She was accustomed to such intru-sions, and shook herself sullenly, not even looking up when an unknown voice accosted her. "Hist, thou! I have something for thee."

"I want nothing, not manna from Heaven even."

"'T will prove better than that."

"Then keep it thyself. Thou'rt a stranger. I take neither a blow from a woman nor a gift from a man."

"Ah!" said the man, coming a little nearer and laying

a hand lightly on her shoulder, "if thou wilt have no gift, shall I *tell* thee something?"

The girl shrugged her shoulder uneasily under his hand. "I am not a baby to care for tales," she said contemptuously; yet the man noticed she turned her head slightly toward him.

"Thou art one of a thousand!" he ejaculated admiringly. "Hey now, proud one, suppose I should tell thee who thou art, — what wouldst thou give Tio Reyes for that?"

"Bah!" said the girl, "I have never thought about it." Yet she was conscious that her heart began to beat wildly and her voice sounded faint in her ears. A little picture formed itself before her eyes, of Pepé and Marta and Ranulfo and a score of others, waifs of humanity, and she herself on a height looking down upon them. She had never consciously separated herself from them, — she had never even wished that she, like them, had at least a mother; but presently she was conscious of a new feeling. Yet she laughed as she said, "I was born then like other children, — I had a mother?"

"That had you; but I am not going to sing all that's in the book, *niña*. The wise man talks little and the prudent woman asks few questions, and thus fewer lies are spoken."

"But thou art not my father?" queried Chinita, insolently, yielding to a sudden apprehension that seized her, and turning full upon the stranger.

"God deliver me!" answered he; "badly fared the owl that nourished the young eaglet."

"Tell me who I am!" cried Chinita, in a sudden passion of eagerness clutching the man's arm.

"Tut! tut! tut! that is not my business; and as you will not hear my pretty little tale," — for Chinita thrust him violently aside, — "I will give you but one word of warning and be gone: the old hind pushes at the young fawn, but they both make venison."

Chinita was accustomed to the obscure phraseology and symbolical meanings of the thousand proverbs used by her country people, and she instantly caught the idea the speaker sought to convey; but its very audacity held her silent for some moments. It was only after she had gazed at him long and searchingly that she could stammer, " Doña Isabel — and I — Chinita — the same — of one blood ! "

The man nodded, but put his finger upon his lip. He feared perhaps some wild outburst of surprise or exultation ; but instead she said in an awed whisper, " Is she then my mother ? "

Tio Reyes leaned against the church and burst into irrepressible though silent laughter. " What next will the girl dream of ? " he ejaculated at length, and laughed again.

" What, am I then such a fool ? " asked Chinita, coolly, though with inward rage. " Look you, if you had told me yes, I would not have believed you any more than I believed when Señor Enrique said that she had the young American killed who died so many years ago. Bah ! one thing is as foolish as the other," and she turned away disdainfully.

" What ! " exclaimed the man, eagerly, " do they say that ? Humph ! Well, things as strange as that have happened in her day."

" But that is a lie," cried Chinita, excitedly ; " it was only because Doña Isabel would not interfere to save his son from being shot as murderer and *ladron* that Enrique said so. He went away himself the day after, and he it was who led Calvo to the rancho del Refugio. But what has that to do with us ? " and now first, perhaps because there had been time for the matter to take shape in her mind, she showed an eager and excited curiosity. " Tell me who I am ; you surely have more to tell me than that I was born Garcia ! "

The man stared, then cried, " And is not that enough ? Why, for a word thou canst be as good as Doña Isabel's daughter. With that face of thine she dare not refuse thee anything."

Chinita looked at him as if she would have torn his secret from him. Strange to say, not a suspicion that he was jesting with her entered her mind. Even as she stood there almost in rags, she felt instinctively that she was far removed from him. The one thought that she was a Garcia, one of the family whom she looked upon as the incarnation of wealth and power, overpowered every other emotion, even that of curiosity. She was vexed, baffled that he said no more, yet felt as though she had known all, and had but for a moment forgotten. She even turned away from him with a momentary impulse to rush into the presence of Doña Isabel and assail her with the cry, "Look at me! Why did you thrust me away? I too am a Garcia!"

"Stay!" cried Tio Reyes, as she started from his side. Her wild thoughts had flashed by so rapidly that, quick though he was to read the countenance, he had caught scarce an inkling of what had passed through her mind, and was certain only of the half-dazed dislike with which she looked at him. It irritated and disappointed him.

"What, girl!" he said, "is not this news worth so much as a 'thank you'? Is it nothing to you whether you are the dust of the roadway or a jewel of the mine? Well, I lied to you. Ah! ah! what know I who you are? It was my joke! Tio Reyes always likes a jest with a pretty girl."

"But this is no jest," said Chinita, quick to perceive that the man was already half repentant of his words; "you can better put the ocean into a well, than shut up the truth when it is once out. Ah, I did not need you to tell me I was no beggar's brat, picked up by chance on the plain. I have heard them say that Pedro has rich clothes which I was wrapped in. He has always laughed at me when I have asked about them, but all the same he shall show them to you this very night."

"Chut!" interrupted the man, "what should I know of swaddling clothes? 'T is just a maid's folly to think of such trifles. They would not prove thee a Garcia, any more than the lack of them belies it, or my mere word insures it!"

"That which puzzles me is," said Chinita, gravely, turning her head on one side and looking at him keenly by the dim light, "why you have told me this. Have you been sent with a message from — from those who left me here?"

"No, by my faith," said the man, laughing; "and why do I laugh, think you? Why, you are the first one who ever asked Tio Reyes for a reason. Does anybody who knows me say, 'Why did you take Don Fulano with all his dollars safe through the mountains, and then allow that poor devil De Tal, who had not so much as a four-penny piece, to be shot down like a dog by the wayside?' No, even the village idiot knows Tio Reyes has reasons too great to be tossed from one to another like a ball; and yet you ask me why I have told you the secret I have kept for years, and perhaps expect an answer! No, no! that plum is not ripe enough to fall at the first puff of wind."

" I will tell you one thing, though you tell me nothing," said Chinita, shrewdly, after a pause: " It is not from love to Doña Isabel that you have told me this, nor for love of me either. What good have you done me by telling me I am a Garcia? Why, if I had had the sense of a parrot, I might have known it before." It seemed to her in her excitement as if, indeed, she had always known it.

" A word to the wise is enough," said the man, myste-riously. " Keep your knowledge to yourself, but use it to your advantage. You were sent like a package to Doña Isabel years ago, but stopped by a clumsy mes-senger. She finds you in her path now; let her find something alive under the shabby coverings. God puts many a sweet nut in a rough shell, many a poison in despised weeds!"

"Oh!" cried Chinita, with a wicked little laugh, though even at that moment the chords of kinship thrilled, " I am but a weed to Doña Isabel, eh? Shall I go to her and say, 'Here is a Garcia to be trodden down'?"

She said this with so superb an air of derision that the man who unconsciously all his life had been an inimitable actor in his way, muttered a deep *caramba* of enthusiastic admiration.

"I would by all the saints I could stay here to see how you will goad and sting my grand Señora," he said vindictively. " Ay, remember you are a Garcia, with a hundred old scores to pay off. I have put the cards in your hands, — patience, and shuffle them well!"

"Patience, and shuffle your cards," — those cards simply the knowledge that she was a Garcia, with presumably the wrongs of parents to avenge. The thoughts were not very clear in her mind, but the instincts of resentment of insult and of filial devotion were those which amid so much that is ungenerous, evil, and fierce, ever pervade the breast of the Mexican. She turned again to ask almost imploringly, " My father — my mother — who were they?" when she found she was alone. The stranger had extorted no promise of secrecy, offered no bribe; it was as if he had put a weapon in her hand, knowing that its very preciousness and subtlety would prevent her from revealing whence she had received it, and would indicate the use to which it was to be turned.

Chinita leaned against the buttress and pondered. Strangely enough, she did not for a moment think to seek the man and demand further explanation. As she felt he had divined her character, so she divined his. He had said all he would say. After all, it was enough. At the end of an hour she left that spot, which she never saw after without a thrill of the heart, and walked straight to the doorway where Pedro sat. He was eating his supper mechanically, with a disturbed countenance, which cleared when he saw her.

" They are *tamales de chile*, daughter," he said, pushing toward her the platter, upon which lay some morsels of corn-pastry and pepper-sauce, wrapped in corn-leaves. " Eat, thou must be hungry."

Pedro sighed, for perplexity and vexation had destroyed his own appetite, and thought enviously, as Chinita's white teeth closed on the soft pastry, which was yellow in comparison, " It is a good thing nothing but unrequited love keeps the young from supping, — and that only for a time."

The gate-keeper watched Chinita narrowly as she was eating and drinking atole from the rough earthen jar. There was some change in her he could not understand, quite different from the passion in which he had last seen her, or the languor which would naturally succeed it. She did not talk, and something kept him from referring to the scene in the courtyard; he felt that she would resent it. Two or three times she bent over him and touched his hand caressingly; yet he was not encouraged to smooth her tangled hair, or offer any of those awkward proofs of affection which she was wont to receive and laugh at or return as the humor seized her; neither did he remind her that it was getting late, but at last rose and took from his girdle the key of the postern.

" Put it back, Pedro ! " she said in her softest voice.
" I shall never sleep in the hut with Florencia and the
children again; yet be not afraid, I will not go to the
corridor either. There is room and to spare in yon great
house." She nodded toward the inner court, muttered
a good-night, and before Pedro could recover from his
surprise sufficiently to speak, swiftly crossed the patio
and disappeared.

Pedro looked after her stupefied. He realized that a
great gulf had opened between them; that figuratively
speaking, his foster-child had left him forever. He looked
like one who, holding a pet bird loosely in his hand, had beheld it suddenly escape him, and soar across a wide and
bridgeless chasm. Would it dash itself into atoms against
the opposite cliffs, or perchance reach a safe haven? Such
was the essence of the thoughts for which Pedro framed no
words. " God is great," he muttered at length, " and
knows what He does ; " adding with a sort of heathen and
dogged obstinacy, " but Pedro still is here ; Pedro does
not forget *niña !* " He looked up as if to some invisible
auditor, crossed himself, then wearily threw himself upon
his pallet; but weary as he was, the strong young subject
of his cares was sunk in deep and dreamless sleep long
before he closed his eyes.

XIX.

ONCE within the court, Chinita paused and looked around her cautiously. The doors of the lower rooms stood open, and she might have entered any one of them unnoticed and found a shelter for the night. But she was in no mood for solitude. Indeed it was hard for her to check a certain wild impulse that seized her, as she saw a faint glimmer of light which streamed through a slight opening of a door on the upper corridor, and that urged her to rush at once into the presence of Doña Isabel and claim recognition. To what relationship, and to what rights, she did not ask herself; a positive though undefined certainty that Doña Isabel herself would know, and would be forced to yield her justice, possessed her.

Chinita was now a child neither in stature nor mind, but though so young in years, had reached the first development of her powers with the mingled precocity of the Indian and Spaniard, fostered by a clime that seems the very elixir of passion. She had been maturing rapidly in the last few months, and as she stood that night in the faint starlight, the last trace of childhood seemed to drop visibly from her. She folded her arms on her breast, and sighed deeply, — not for sorrow, but as if she breathed a life that was new to her, and her lungs were oppressed by the weight of a strange and too heavily perfumed atmosphere.

In her absorption Chinita was unconscious that she was observed, — but it chanced that Don Rafael Sanchez and his mother had just left the Señora Doña Isabel, and were passing through the upper corridor to their own apartments. The gallery was wide and they were in the shadow, but a stray gleam of light touched the upturned face of the girl and exhibited it in strong relief within the framing of her waving hair. As they caught sight of it, they involuntarily paused to look at her.

" I do not wonder," whispered Feliz," that such a face is an accusing conscience to Doña Isabel. There is a strange familiarity in every feature ; and what a spirit, too, she has, — one even to glory in strife ! "

Don Rafael nodded. " There has always seemed to me something in that child to mark her as the offspring of a dominant family," he said ; " it is inevitable that she must break the lines an adverse Fate has cast about her. Others such as she stretch out a hand to Vice ; if something better comes to her, who are we to hinder it? "

The brow of Doña Feliz contracted. " Ay, Rafael," she murmured, " what a change a few miserable years have wrought! Once I was a sister to Doña Isabel, and now—"

" You are no traitress," interposed Don Rafael, " and it is by circumstance only that the change has come. Console yourself, dear mother, and remember we are pledged. Though we seem false to her mother, only so can we be true to Herlinda."

He breathed the name so low that even Doña Feliz did not hear it ; she listened rather to the beating of the heart that seemed to repeat without cessation the name of one so loved and lost. " How strange it is, Rafael," she said presently, " that I have such persistent, such mocking dreams, which against my reason, against all precedent, create in me the belief that all is not ended for Herlinda Garcia."

Don Rafael looked at her musingly.

" There is a man called Juarez who has dreams such as yours," he said ; " but they are of the freedom of a race, not of one woman alone. But he is hardly able to work miracles. Yet, mother, this truly is the time of prodigies ; what think you this boy, the young American that Doña Isabel brought hither, calls himself ? "

" I have asked him," she said, " but he did not understand me. Oh, Rafael ! my heart stood still when I saw him first ; yet after all he is not so very like —"

" Yet he has the same name, Mother. It may be but chance ; those Americans are half barbarians as we know, — they forget the saints, and seek to glorify their great men by giving their children as Christian names the surnames of those who have distinguished themselves in

battle or statesmanship. Sometimes, too, a mother proud
of the surname of her own family gives it to her son. It
may have been so with this man. When I gave him pen
and paper, and bade him write his name, it was thus:
'Ashley Ward.'"

The name as spoken by Don Rafael was mispronounced,
would have been hardly recognizable in the ears of him
who owned it; yet to Doña Feliz it was like a trumpet
blast. "Strange! strange! strange!" she repeated again
and again. "Can it be mere chance?"

"That we shall soon know," said Don Rafael. "These
Americans blurt out their affairs to the first comer,
expecting help from every quarter. There is no rain that
falls but that they fancy it is to water their own field.
Nay, mother," as Doña Feliz made a movement toward
the stairway, "go not near the man to-night; he has
fever, and is in need of quiet. Old Selsa is with him, and
he can need no better care. He is safe to remain here
many days; let him rest in peace now. And do you,
mother, try to sleep; you are weary and worn."

With the filial solicitude of a true Mexican, the man,
already middle-aged, took his mother's hand fondly and led
her to the door of her own apartment. There she detained
him long in low and earnest conversation, and when on
leaving her he looked down into the court it was entirely
deserted.

In glancing around her, Chinita's eyes had caught no
glimpse of the figures above, perhaps because they had
been diverted by a faint glimmer of light at one angle of
the courtyard; and remembering that this came from
the room to which the wounded man had been carried, she
darted swiftly and noiselessly toward it, and in a moment
had pushed the door sufficiently ajar to admit of her
entrance, and had passed in. She arrested her footsteps
at the foot of the narrow bed, which extended like a bier
from the wall to the centre of the room. There was not
another article of furniture in the apartment, except a
chair upon which the sick man's coat was thrown; but
Chinita's eyes, accustomed to the vault-like and vacant
suites of square cells that made up the greater part of the
vast building, were struck with no sense of desolation. A
slender jar of water, and a number of earthen utensils of

different forms and shapes, containing medicaments and food, were gathered upon the floor near the bed's head; and on a deep window-ledge was placed a sputtering tallow-candle, which had already half filled with grease the clay sconce in which it was sunk.

As Chinita leaned over the foot of the bed and peered through her unkempt locks at its occupant, he looked up with a start, and presently said something in an appealing tone, which certainly touched her more than the words, could she have understood them, would have done. He had in fact exclaimed in English, with an unmistakable American intonation, "Heavens, what a gypsy! and what can she want here in this miserable jail they have left me in?"

She thought he had perhaps asked for water, so she gave him some, which was not unacceptable, — though it irritated him that after giving him the cup, she took up the candle and held it close to his face while he drank. She was in the mood for new impressions however rather than for kindness, and the sight of a strange face pleased her. Burning with fever though he was, and tossing with all the impatience natural to his condition, he could not but notice the totally unaffected ease with which she made her inspection. He might have been a curly-headed infant instead of a man, so utterly unconcernedly did she look into his dark-blue eyes, and note the broad white brow upon which his damp yellow hair clustered, even touching lightly with her finger the firm white throat bared by the opened collar sufficiently to expose the clumsily arranged dressings on the wounded shoulder, Instantly, with a few deft movements, she made them more comfortable, for which the young man thanked her in a few of the very scanty words of Spanish at his command, — at which she laughed, not ironically, but with a sort of nervous irrelevance, thinking to herself the while, " He is beautiful — bless me, yes! as beautiful as they say the murdered American was! Who knows? this one may come from the same district! It must be but a little place, his country, — there cannot be such a very great world outside the mountains yonder; they touch heaven everywhere. Look now, how white his arms are, and his brow, where the sun has not touched it! and how red his cheeks!

But that must be with the fever." And so half audibly
she made her comments upon the wounded stranger, seemingly entirely unconscious or regardless that there was any
mind or soul within this body she so frankly admired, —
lifting his unwounded arm sometimes, or turning his face
into better view, as she might have done parts of a
mechanism that pleased her.

"Evidently she thinks me wooden," he said with a
gleam of humor in his eyes. "As I am dumb to her, she
believes me also senseless and sightless. Thanks, for
taking away that ill-smelling candle," as with the offending taper in her hand she passed to the other side of
the bed. Then she stopped and laughed, and he remembered that he had seen the old woman who had been left
in charge of him arrange her sheepskins there and throw
herself upon them. Until the young girl had come, old
Selsa's snores had vexed him; since that he had forgotten
them, though now they became audible again. As Chinita
laughed, she placed the candle-stick upon the window-ledge
and looked around her, stretching herself and yawning.
The hour was late for her, the diversion caused by sight
of the blond stranger and the little service she had rendered him had relaxed the tension of her mind, and she
felt herself aweary; the shadows fell dark in every corner
of the room, — there was something grewsome in its aspect
even to Chinita's accustomed eyes. It subdued her wild
and reckless mood, and she scanned the place narrowly
for something upon which she might lie. Presently the
young man saw her glide toward the sleeping nurse, and
deftly, with a half mischievous, half triumphant expression
upon her face, draw out one of the sheepskin mats upon
which the old woman was lying, and taking it to the opposite side of the bed arrange it to her liking upon the
brick floor, and sinking upon it softly and daintily as a
cat might have done, compose herself to sleep.

The candle on the window-sill sputtered and flickered;
old Selsa snored in her corner, seemingly undisturbed
by the abstraction of a part of her bed; the shadows in
the apartment grew longer and longer; the eyelids of
the young girl closed, her regular breathing parted her full
lips. The young man had painfully raised himself upon
one arm, and assured himself of this. He himself was

dropping off into snatches of slumber which promised to become profound, when suddenly with a start he found himself wide awake, and staring at a draped figure which had noiselessly glided into his chamber. Save for the candle it bore he would have thought it a visitant from another world; but his first surprise over, he recognized it as that of a woman. He was conscious that his heart beat wildly; his fever had returned. Where had he seen this pale proud face, these classic features, these dark penetrating eyes? For a moment again he felt as if swinging between heaven and earth, between life and death. Ah! yes, he comprehended, — he had been brought thither in some swaying vehicle, and this woman had been beside him; she perhaps had saved his life.

He murmured a word of thanks, but she did not notice it. "Señor," she said in a voice soft in courtesy, "I pray you forgive me that I had for a little time forgotten my guest. I trust you lack for nothing? Ah! what — alone?" and with a frown, she made a motion as if to awaken the servant Selsa. He understood the gesture though not the words, and stopped her by one as expressive.

"No, no!" he exclaimed. "I too shall sleep; and she is old. I would not awaken her. See, if I need anything a touch of my hand will rouse this girl," — and the young man indicated by a turn of his head and arm the recumbent figure which his visitor had not observed.

With some curiosity she moved to the opposite side of the bed, and bending over lightly removed the fringe of the reboso which shaded the face of the sleeper. Doña Isabel started, and a slight exclamation escaped her lips as she turned hurriedly away, — as hurriedly returning, and shading the candle with her hand, that its light might not fall upon the eyes of the sleeper, she gazed upon the young girl long and earnestly. Unmindful of herself, she suffered the full glare of the candle to illuminate her own countenance; and as he looked upon it, the young American thought it might serve as the very model for the mask of tragedy. Nothing more pitiless, more remorseless, more sombre than its expression could be imagined; yet as she gazed, a flush of shame rose from neck to brow. Her eyes clouded, her breath came with a quick gasp. She stood for a moment clasping the rod at the foot of the bed with her white nervous hand; she looked at the American fixedly, yet she seemed to have no consciousness that she herself was seen; and presently, with the slow movement of a somnambulist, so absorbing was her thought, she turned to the door.

Ashley was watching her intently; suddenly her light was extinguished, and she vanished as if dissolved in air. He was calm enough to remember that she had spoken to him, to know that she could be no phantom of his imagination, and to suppose that upon stepping into the corridor she had extinguished her light, and sped noiselessly along the wall to some other apartment; yet for a long time a feeling of mystery oppressed him, and he could not sleep. A vague consciousness of some strange influence near him kept him feverish, with all his senses on the alert; yet he heard no movement of the woman who crouched within the doorway, leaning against the cold wall, and who during the long silent night passed in review the strange events that had brought her — the Señora Isabel Garcia de Garcia — to guard the slumbers of a foundling, the foster-child of a man so low in station as the gate-keeper of her house.

XX.

Doña Isabel Garcia had been born within the walls of Tres Hermanos, her father having been part owner of the estate, and her mother the daughter of an impoverished gentleman of the neighboring city of Guanapila. Doña Clarita had been a most beautiful woman, whose attractions had been utilized to prop the falling fortunes of her house by her marriage with the elderly but kindly proprietor Don Ignacio Garcia.

At the time of her marriage, Clarita Rodriguez was very young, and with the habits of submission universal among her countrywomen would probably have taken kindly to her fate, never doubting its justice, but that from her balcony she had one day seen a young officer of the city troop ride by in all the magnificence of the military uniform of the period. A dazzling vision of gold lace and braid, clanking spurs and sabre, and of eyes and teeth and smile more dazzling still, haunted her for weeks. Yet that might have passed, but that the vision glided from the eye to the heart, when on one luckless night, at the governor's ball, Pancho Vallé was introduced to her, and they twice were partners in that lover's delirium the slow and voluptuous *danza*. As they moved together in the dreamy measure, a few low words were exchanged, — commonplace perhaps but not harmless, and by one at least never to be forgotten. Afterward an occasional missive penned in most regular characters upon daintily tinted paper came to her hands through some complaisant servant. But Don Ranulfo Rodriguez was too jealous a guardian to suffer many such to escape him, and had been far too wise in his generation to place it in his daughter's power to engage in such dangerous pastime as the production of replies to unwelcome suitors. Like most other girls of her age and position, Clarita had been strenuously prevented from learning to write, and it is doubtful if she ever knew the exact import of Vallé's perfumed

10

missives, although her heart doubtless guessed what her eyes could not decipher.

Whether Vallé's impassioned glances meant all they indicated or not, certain it was that he had not ventured to declare himself to the father as a suitor for the fair Clarita's hand, when Don Ignacio Garcia stepped in and literally carried away the prize. The courtship had been short, the position of the groom unassailable. Clarita shed some tears, but the delighted father declared they were for joy at her good fortune; and they were indeed of so mixed a character — baffled love, wounded pride, and an irrepressible sense of triumph at her unexpected promotion — that she herself scarce cared to analyze them. She danced with Vallé once again on the occasion of her marriage; again a few words were spoken, and the passionate heart of Clarita was pierced with a secret dart, which never ceased to rankle.

Don Ignacio Garcia conducted her immediately to the hacienda, where his jealous nature found no cause for suspicion; and there the little Isabel was born; and on beholding the wealth of maternal affection which the young wife lavished upon her child, the husband forgot the indifference that had sometimes chafed him, and for a few brief months imagined himself beloved. This egotistic delusion was never dispelled, for at its height, upon the second anniversary of their wedding day, when taking part in a bull-chase, Don Ignacio's horse swerved as he urged him to the side of the infuriated animal; a moment's hesitancy was fatal; the horse was ripped open by the powerful horn of the bull, and plunging wildly, fell back upon his luckless rider, whose neck was instantly broken. It was an accident which it seemed incredible could have happened to a man so skilled in horsemanship as was Don Ignacio. The spectators were for a moment dumb with horror and surprise, then with groans and shrieks rushed to the rescue, but only to lift a corpse. Doña Clarita with a wild shriek had fainted as the horse plunged back, and upon regaining her senses, threw herself in an agony of not unremorseful grief upon the body of her husband. It was, however, of that violent character which soon expends itself; and before the funeral obsequies were well over, she began to look around the narrow horizon of Tres

Hermanos, and remember, if not rejoice, that she was free to go beyond it.

Don Gregorio, the cousin of Clarita's husband's, though a mere boy, had been brought up on the estate, and was competent to take charge, and the administrador and clerks were trusty men; so there was no absolute reason why the young widow should remain to guard her interests and those of her child, and it seemed but natural she should return to her father's house, at least during the first months of her sorrow. Thither indeed she went. She had dwelt there before, a dependent child, to be disposed of at her father's will; she returned to it a rich widow, profuse of her favors but tenacious of her rights, one of which all too soon proclaimed itself to be that of choosing for herself a second husband. A month or two after her arrival in the city, Don Pancho Vallé returned from some expedition in which patriotism and personal gain were deftly combined, with the halo of success added to his personal attractions, and was quick to declare an unswerving devotion to the divinity at whose shrine he had worshipped but doubtfully while it remained ungilded by the sun of prosperity. Whether Clarita had learned to read or not, certain it is that Don Pancho's impassioned missives met with a response more satisfactory than pen and ink alone could give, for immediately after the expiration of the year due to the memory of Don Ignacio, she became the wife of the gay soldier.

Don Pancho and his wife were both young, both equally delighted in excitement and luxury; and within an incredibly short time the ample resources which had seemed to them boundless were perceptibly narrowed. To the taste for extravagant living, for gorgeous apparel, for numerous and magnificent horses, shared by them in common, were added a passionate love of gambling, and a scarcely less expensive one for military enterprises of an independent and half guerilla order, on the part of Don Pancho; and thus a few years saw the wife's fortune reduced to an encumbered interest in the lands of Tres Hermanos.

Don Pancho in spite of numerous infidelities still retained his influence over the heart and mind of Clarita; and one night in play against Don Gregorio Garcia—

who, like other caballeros, occasionally engaged in a game or two for pastime — he staked the last acre of her estate, knowing she would refuse him nothing, and lost. For a moment he looked blank, — a most unwonted manifestation of dismay in so practised a gambler, — then laughed and shook hands with his fortunate opponent. There was a laughing group around him, condoling with him banteringly, for Pancho Vallé had never seemed to make any misfortune a serious matter, when a pistol-shot was heard. For a moment no one realized what had happened ; the young officer stood in his gay uniform, smiling still, his gold-mounted pistol in his hand, then fell heavily forward. The ball had passed through his heart. His widow had the satisfaction of seeing by the smile that remained on his handsome countenance that he had died as joyously as he had lived ; not a trace of care showed that aught deeper than mere pique and caprice had moved him. "Angel of my life!" she cried, when her first burst of grief was over, " thou wert beginning to make my heart ache, for I had nothing more to give thee !"

This was her only word of reproach, if reproach it might be called. For love that woman would have yielded even her life, and never have known the hollowness of her idol. Grief did the work that ingratitude and neglect — nay absolute cruelty — would perhaps never have effected, and in a few short months destroyed her life. As she was dying she called her daughter to her. "Isabel," she said, " thou hast wealth, thy brother has nothing ; swear to me by the Virgin and thy patron saint, that thou wilt be as a mother to him, that thou wilt refuse him nothing that thy hand can give ! Money, money, money, is what makes men happy !" That had been the creed her life's experience had taught her. For money her father had sold her ; for that the husband she adored had given her fair words and caresses. "As thou wouldst have thy mother's blessing, promise me that Leon shall never appeal to thee in vain !"

Isabel Garcia was but a child, and the boy Leon but three years younger ; yet as she looked upon her dying mother she solemnly promised to fill her place, to take upon herself the rôle of sacrifice, which her religion taught her was that of motherhood. Poor Clarita ! little had she understood a mother's highest duties, — to warn, to guide, to plead with God for the beloved. The mere yielding of material things, — to clothe herself in sackcloth, that the child might be robed in purple, to walk barefoot that he might ride in state, to hunger that he might be delicately fed, — she had pictured these things to herself as the purest sacrifices, and surely the only ones to appeal to the hearts of such men as she had known ; and the young Isabel entered upon her task with her mother's precepts deeply engraved upon her heart, her mind all uninstructed, awaiting the iron finger of experience to write upon it its lessons.

After their mother's death, the young brother and sister, mere children both, went to live in the house of some elderly relatives, who with generous though not always judicious kindness strove to forget the faults of the father by ignoring them when they became apparent in the boy. The uncle of Isabel, the Friar Francisco, became their tutor, but taught them little beyond the breviary. What could a woman need with more? As for Leon, he took more kindly to the lasso and saddle, to the pistol and sword, than to the book or pen, — and even while still a child in years, more passionately still to the gaming table. Though his elders with a shake of the head remembered his father's fate, and sometimes pushed the boy half laughingly away from the monté table, or of a Sunday afternoon sent him out to the bull-ring for his diversion, where he was a mere spectator, rather than to the cock-pit, where he became a participant, yet the question did not present itself as one at all of questionable morals : every one gambled on a feast day, or at a social game among one's friends. Perhaps of all those by whom he was surrounded, no one felt any serious anxiety for Leon except the young girl who with premature solicitude warned him of the evil, even as she supplied the means to indulge his wayward tastes.

Leon was a brilliant rather than a handsome boy, promising to be well grown ; and his lithe, vigorous figure showed to good advantage in his gay riding-suits, whether of sombre black cloth with silver buttons set closely down the outer seam of the pantaloons and adorning the short round jacket, or in loose *chapareras* of buckskin bound by a scarlet sash and bedizened with leather fringes, — a costume that perhaps served to betray the Indian strain in his blood, which ordinarily was detected only by a slight prominence of the cheek bones and a somewhat furtive expression in the soft dark eyes. At unguarded moments, however, perhaps when he fancied himself unobserved and was practising with his pistol or sabre, those eyes could flash with concentrated fire, so that more than once Isabel had been constrained to call out: "Leon, Leon, you frighten me! You look like the great cat when he pounces upon a harmless little bird and crushes it for the very joy of killing!"

Then Leon would laugh, and the soft, dreamy haze would rise again over the eyes as he would turn upon her. "Ha!" he would say, "you will never be a man, Isabel; you will never understand why I love the sights and sounds that throw you poor women into fainting fits and tears. Ha! Isabel, if I were you I'd not stay in this dull house with a couple of old women to guard me, when you might go to the hacienda and be free as air."

"Nonsense," Isabel would retort; "what could I do there other than here? I could not turn herdsman or vaquero, nor even ride out to the fields to see how the crops were flourishing, nor roam like an Indian through the mountains."

"But *I* would!" Leon would cry enthusiastically; and with his longing ardor for the free life of a country gentleman, with its barbaric luxury and wild sports, he thus first put into the young girl's mind the thought of favoring the suit which her cousin, Don Gregorio Garcia, began to urge.

Don Gregorio had married young, soon after the death of Ignacio Garcia whom he succeeded in the management of the estate of which they had been joint owners; but his wife had died leaving him without an heir, and the first grief assuaged, it was but natural after the passage of years that the widower should weary of his loneliness. There were many reasons why his thoughts should turn to his distant cousin Isabel, for though she was many years younger than himself, such disparity of age was not unusual; the marriage would unite still more closely the family fortunes, and effectually prevent the intrusion of any undesirable stranger; and above all, Isabel was gracious and queenly and beautiful enough to charm the heart even of an anchorite, and Don Gregorio was far from being one. Indeed, in his very early years he had given indications of a partiality for a far more adventurous career than he had finally, by force of circumstances, been led to adopt. Thus he sympathized somewhat with Leon's restless activity, and quite honestly secured the boy's alliance, — no slight advantage in his siege of the heart of Isabel.

This, perhaps more than the good-will of the rest of the family, enabled Don Gregorio to approach so nearly to Isabel's inmost nature that he learned far more of the strength of purpose and capability for passionate devotion possessed by the young untrained girl than any other being had done, and for the first time in his life knew a love far deeper and purer than any passion which mere physical charms could awaken. Such a love appealed to Isabel. She was perhaps constitutionally cold to sexual charms, but eminently susceptible to the sympathetic attrition of an appreciative mind, while her heart could translate far more readily the rational outpourings of friendship than the wild rhapsodies of passion. Thus, although Isabel would have shrunk from a man who in his ardor would have demanded of her affection some sacrifice of the unqualified devotion that she had vowed to her brother, she seemed to find in Don Gregorio one who could understand and applaud the exaggerated devotion to the ideal standard of filial and sisterly duty which she had unconsciously erected upon the few utterly irrational words of a weak and dying woman.

The first four years of Isabel's married life passed uneventfully. Leon was constantly near her, and was the life of the great house, which despite the crowd of retainers that frequented it would without him have proved but a dull dwelling for so young a matron, with no illusions in regard to the staid and kindly husband, who was rather a friend to be consulted and revered than a lover to be adored, — for although Don Gregorio worshipped his beautiful young wife, he was at once too mindful of his own dignity, and too wary of startling Isabel's passionless nature, to manifest or exact romantic and exhaustive

proofs of affection. He used sometimes to mutter to himself: "'The stronger the flame the sooner the wood is
burnt;' better that the substance of love should endure
than be dissipated in smoke!"

Don Gregorio was somewhat of a philosopher; and as
such, as soon as the glamour thrown over him by Leon's
brilliant but inconsequent sallies of wit, and his daring
and dashing manner, was dimmed, and above all as soon
as his unreasoning sympathy with Isabel's predispositions
settled into a calm and sincere desire for her certain happiness and welfare, he began to look with some suspicion
upon traits which had at first attracted him as the natural
outcome of an ardent and generous nature.

Friar Francisco had accompanied the young brother
and sister to the hacienda, partly to minister in the church,
and partly as tutor to Leon; but in the latter capacity he
found little exercise for his talents. Upon one pretext or
another the boy at first evaded and later absolutely refused study; but he joined so heartily in the labors as
well as pleasures of hacienda life,— he was so ready in resource, so untiring in action, so companionable alike to
all classes, that Nature seemed to have fitted him absolutely for the position that he was apparently destined to
fill in life. Yet though he was the prince of rancheros, the
life of the city sometimes seemed to possess an irresistible
attraction for him; and after months perhaps spent among
the employees of the hacienda, in riding with the vaqueros
or in penetrating the recesses of the mountain, even sleeping in the huts of charcoal burners, or in caves with rovers
of still more doubtful reputation, he would suddenly weary
of it all, and followed by a servant or two ride gayly
down to the city to see how the world went there.

At first Don Gregorio had no idea how much those
visits cost Isabel; but as time went on, and rumors
reached them of the boy's extravagant mode of life, Isabel became anxious and Don Gregorio indignant. Some
investigation showed that a troop of young roysterers
who called him captain were maintained in the mountains, and that a thousand wild freaks which had mystified the neighboring villages and haciendas might be
traced to these mad spirits, among whom Don Gregorio shrewdly conjectured might be found many of the

most daring young fellows, both of the higher and lower orders, who had one by one mysteriously disappeared during the few months preceding Leon's eighteenth birthday.

Leon only laughed when taxed with his guerilla following, and although as he managed it it was a somewhat costly amusement, it was not an unusual or an altogether useless one in those days of anarchy; for no one could say how soon the fortunes of war might turn an enemy upon the land and stores of Tres Hermanos, and even Don Gregorio was not displeased to find the most refractory of his retainers placed in a position to defend rather than imperil the interests of the estate. As to the escapades of city life he found them less pardonable, for they consisted chiefly in mad devotion to the gaming-table, which Leon was never content to leave until his varying fortunes turned to disaster and his wild excitement was quelled by the tardy reflection that his sister's generosity would be taxed in thousands to pay the folly of a night.

Before the age of twenty Leon Vallé had run the gamut of the vices and extravagances peculiar to Mexican youths, and large as the resources of Doña Isabel were, he had begun to encroach seriously upon them; for true to her mother's request, she had never refused to supply his demands for money, though of late she had begun to make remonstrances, which were received half incredulously, half sullenly, as though he realized neither their justice nor their necessity. Isabel was now a mother, her daughter Herlinda having been born a year after her marriage, and their son Norberto, the pride and hope of Don Gregorio, three years later; and naturally the young mother longed to consider the interests of her children, which so far as her own property was concerned seemed utterly obliterated and overwhelmed by the mad extravagances of her brother.

Strangely enough, Don Gregorio attempted no interference with his wife's disposal of her income, though it seemed not improbable that at no distant day even the lands would be in jeopardy. Perhaps he foresaw that as her means to gratify his insatiable demands declined, so gradually Leon's strange fascination over his sister would cease; for inevitably his restless spirit would draw him afar to find fresh fields for adventure, since in those days, when the great struggle between Church and State was beginning and foreign complications were forming, such a leader as he might prove to be would find no lack of occasion for daring deeds and reckless followers, nor scarcity of plunder with which to repay the latter.

Whatever were his thoughts, Don Gregorio guarded them well, saying sometimes either to Leon himself, or to some friend who expressed a half horrified conjecture as to where such absolute madness must end, "See you not, 't is foolish to squeeze the orange until one tastes the bitterness of the rind?" He expected some sudden and violent reaction in Isabel's mind and conduct. But though she began to show she realized and suffered, she bore the strain put upon her with royal fortitude. Youth can hope through such adverse circumstances, and it always seemed to her that one who "meant so well" as Leon, must eventually turn from temptation and begin a new and nobler career.

At last what appeared to Isabel the turning point in her brother's destiny was reached. He became violently enamored of the beautiful daughter of a Spaniard, one Señor Fernandez, who of a family too distinguished to be flattered by an alliance with a mere attaché of a wealthy and powerful house, was so poor as to be willing to con-sider it should a suitable provision be made to insure his daughter's future prosperity. The beautiful Dolores was herself favorably inclined toward the gay cavalier, who most ardently pressed his suit, — the more ardently perhaps that he was piqued and indignant that the wary father utterly refused to consider the matter until Don Gregorio or Doña Isabel herself should formally ask the hand of his daughter, presenting at the same time unmistakable assurances of Leon's ability to fulfil the promises he recklessly poured forth.

That Leon had turned from his old evil courses seemed as months passed on an absolute certainty. Not even the administrador himself could be more utterly bound to the wheel of routine than he. To see his changed life, his absolute repugnance even to the sports suitable to his age, was almost piteous; his whole heart and mind seemed set upon atonement for the folly of the past, and in preparation for a life of toil and anxiety in the future. For in examining into her affairs, Doña Isabel found that her income was largely overdrawn; Leon's extravagances, together with heavy losses incurred in the working of the reduction-works, had so far crippled her resources that it was only by stringent effort, and an appeal to Don Gregorio for aid, that she was enabled so to rehabilitate the fortunes of Leon that he could hope to win the prize which was to make or mar his future.

Doña Isabel was as happy as the impatient lover himself when she could place in his hands the deeds of a small but productive estate, famous for the growth of the maguey, from which the sale of pulque and mescal promised a never failing revenue. The money had been raised largely through concessions made by Don Gregorio, and was to be repaid from the income of Isabel's encumbered estate, so that for some years at least it would be out of her power to render Leon any further assistance. Don Gregorio shook his head gravely over the whole matter; yet the fact that the young man was virtually thrown upon the resources provided for him, which certainly without the concentration of all his energies and tact would be altogether insufficient for his maintenance, and also that he had great faith in the energy of character which for the first time appeared diverted into a legitimate channel, inclined him to believe that at last, urged by necessity as well as love, Leon would redeem his past and settle down into the reputable citizen and relative who was to justify and repay the sister's tireless and extraordinary devotion. "Or at least," he said to himself, "Isabel will be satisfied that no more can or should be done; and it is worth a fortune to convince her of that."

Strangely enough, though Isabel had addressed herself with a frenzy of determination to the task of securing a competency for Leon that might enable him to marry and enter upon a life which was to relieve her of the constant drain upon her resources, both material and mental, which for years had been sapping her prosperity and peace, yet as she beheld him ride away toward the town in which his inamorata dwelt to make the final arrangements for his marriage, her heart sank within her; and instead of relief and thankfulness, she felt a frightful pang of apprehension, she knew not why, as if a prophetic voice warned her that her own hand had opened the door to a chamber of horrors, through which the smiling youth would pass and drag her as he went.

Isabel threw herself upon her husband's breast in an agony which he could not comprehend, but which he gently soothed, happy to feel that to him she turned in the first moment of her abandonment,—for indeed she felt that she who had given her substance, her sympathy, her faith, all of which a sister's life is capable, was indeed abandoned, and all for a fresh young face, a word, a smile. Leon was a changed man, but all her devotion had not worked the miracle ; another whose love could be as yet but a fancy had accomplished what years of sacrifice from her had striven for in vain !

There was something of jealousy, but far more of the pain of baffled aspiration in the thought, and through it all that dreadful doubt, that sickening dread as to whether she had done well thus to strip herself of the power to minister to him. It seemed, even against her reason, impossible that Leon could be beyond the pale of her bounty ; she had been so accustomed to plan, to think, to plot for him, that she could not grasp the thought that henceforth he was to live without her, that she was to know him happy, joyous, at ease, and she no longer be the immediate and ministering Providence which made him so.

After the infant Carmen was born, the mother's thoughts turned into other channels. As she looked at this child, the thought for the first time came to her, that some day it might be possible that her children would inherit some material good from her. Their father was a rich man, yet there was a pleasure in the thought that her children, her daughters most especially, would be pleased by a mother's rich gifts, would perhaps from her receive the dower that would make them welcome in the homes of the men they might love. Isabel began to indulge in the maternal hopes and visions of young motherhood, and to feel the security that a still hopeful mind may acquire, after years of secret and harassing cares have passed.

The usual visits of ceremony had passed between the contracting families ; the Señor Fernandez had declared himself satisfied with the generous provisions which had been made for the young couple ; the house was set in order, and an early day named for the wedding. Some days of purest happiness followed the tearful anxiety with which Dolores had awaited the negotiations that were to shape her destiny. An earnest of the future came to her in the present of jewels, with which Leon presaged the marriage gifts which he went to the city of Mexico to choose,—for whether rich or poor, no Mexican bridegroom would fail of a necklet of pearls, or a brooch and earrings of brilliants for his bride; and with his luxurious tastes, it was not to be supposed that Leon Vallé could fail to add to these laces and silks and velvets, fit rather for a princess than for the future wife of a country youth whose only capital was in house and land. Isabel had just heard of these things, and had begun to excuse in her heart these extravagances, which seemed so natural to a youth in love, when a remembrance flashed upon her mind which justified the apprehensions she had felt, and which it seemed incredible should have escaped not only her own but also Don Gregorio's vigilance, — Leon had gone to Mexico in the days of the feast of San Augustin.

Isabel was too jealous of her brother's good name, too eager to shield him from a breath of distrust, to mention the fears that assailed her. She called herself irrational, faithless, unjust, yet she could not rid herself of the dread which seemed to brood above her like a cloud. And so passed the month of June, and July brought Leon Vallé back again, and one glance at his haggard face and bloodshot eyes revealed to Isabel that her fears were realized. He told the tale in a few words and with a hollow laugh.

"You will have to go to Garcia for me now, Isabel," he said. "Your last venture has brought me the old luck, cursed bad luck. A plague upon your money! I thought to double or treble it, and the last cent is gone!"

"And the hacienda of San Lazaro?" queried Isabel, faintly.

"Would you believe it? Gone too! Aranda has had the devil's own luck. 'T was the last of the feast, Isabel. Thousands were changing hands at every table. It seemed a cowardice not to try a stake for a fortune that might be had for the asking. I was a fool, and hesitated till it was too late. Had I only ventured at once! What think you happened to Leoncio Alvarez? He played his hacienda against Esparto's, and lost. He had dared me not five minutes before to the venture. The devil, what a chance I missed! His hacienda was three times the size of San Lazaro! He bore its loss like a man. 'What can one do, friend?' he cried to Esparto; 'it has been thy luck to-day, 't will be mine when we next meet.' Just then his brother Antonio came up. 'What luck, Leoncio?' he said. 'Cursed!' he answered. 'I have played my hacienda against Esparto's here, and lost it.' Antonio shrugged his shoulders and turned away. 'Play mine and get it back,' he suggested, and walked off to the next table. The cards were dealt, and in three minutes Leoncio's hacienda was his own again, thrown like a ball from one hand to the other. It was glorious play!'"

" But this has nothing to do with thee," ventured Isabel.

" No," muttered Leon, moodily; " when *I* ventured my hacienda and lost, there was no Antonio to bid me play his and get it back."

He looked at Isabel with an air of reproach. She had neither look nor word of reproach for him, yet she felt that a mortal blow had been dealt her. And Leon? He had laughed, though she knew that the laugh was that of the mocking fiend Despair which possessed him; and he had bade her go on his behalf to Garcia. She left him in desperation. She knew how utterly fruitless such an appeal would be.

It *was* fruitless. Don Gregorio asked with some scorn in his voice whether Leon thought him as weak as she had been, or as much of a madman as himself when he had dared the chances of the tables at San Augustin. For him, Garcia, to furnish money to the oft-tried scapegrace would be a folly that would merit the inevitable loss it would bring. All of which, though true enough, Don Gregorio repeated with unnecessary vehemence to Leon himself, with the tone of irrepressible satisfaction with which he at last saw humiliated the man who had for so long held such a resistless fascination over his wife.

With wonderful self-restraint Leon replied not a word to the cutting irony with which his brother-in-law referred to the mad ambition and folly which had led to his losses,

and with which Gregorio excused himself from further
assisting in the ruin of the Garcia family, — reminding
the gamester that though he had thrown away the key to
fortune which he had taken from his sister's hand, he had
still youth, a sword, and a subtle mind, any one of which
should be able to provide him a living.

"That is true," replied Leon, with a dangerous light in
his half-closed eyes. "Thanks for the reminder, my
brother. What is the old saying? 'A hungry man dis-
covers more than a thousand wise men.'"

They both laughed. It was not likely that Leon's poverty would ever reach the point of actual want. There
at the hacienda was his home when he cared for it; but
as for money, — why as Don Gregorio had said, the key
to fortune was thrown away, and it seemed unlikely the
unfortunate loser would ever recover it.

Almost on the same day on which Leon Vallé had told
his sister of his fatal hardihood at the feast of San
Augustin, there arrived, with assurances of the profound
respect of Señor Fernandez and his daughter, the jewels
and other rich gifts which Dolores had accepted as the
betrothed of Leon. With deep indignation that his
explanations and protestations had been rejected, but
with a pride which prevented the frantic remonstrances
which rushed to his lips from passing beyond them, Leon
received these proofs of his dismissal, which in a few days
was rendered final by the news that the beautiful Dolores
had married a wealthier and perhaps even more ardent
suitor, whom the insolence and mockery of Fate had provided in the person of the lucky winner of San Lazaro.
Even Don Gregorio felt his heart burn with the natural
chagrin of family pride, and Isabel would have turned
with some sympathy toward the brother of whom, unconsciously to herself, she could no longer make a hero.
Strangely enough, his aspect as a suppliant for her husband's bounty had disrobed him of the glamour through
which she had always beheld him. When she herself was
powerless to minister to him, he was no longer a prince
claiming tribute, but the undignified dependent whom she
blushed to see lounging in sullen idleness in her husband's
house. Yet as has been said, when word of the marriage
of Dolores Fernandez reached them, they would have

given him sympathy; but he had received the news first, and collecting a half-dozen followers had mounted and ridden madly away.

The horses they rode were Don Gregorio's yet Leon had gone without a word of excuse or farewell. Isabel had no opportunity to tell him that she had no more money to give him; and in her distress at supposing him penniless it was an immense relief to her to find that he had retained in his possession the jewels that the father of Dolores had returned to him. He would at least not be without resource. But soon a strange tale reached her. The jewels torn from their settings, the stones in fragments, the whole crushed into an utterly worthless mass, so far as human strength and ingenuity could accomplish it, had been found upon the pillow of the bride. The husband was jealously frantic that her sanctuary had been invaded; the bride was hysterically alarmed, yet flattered at this proof of her lover's passion; and the entire community were for days on the *qui vive* for further developments in this drama of love.

But none came, and soon Leon Vallé's name was heard of as one of the guerrillas of the Texan war, where he fought for — it was not to be said under — Santa Anna; and ere many months his name rang from one end of the republic to the other, — the synonym of gallant daring, which in a less exciting time might have been called ferocious bloodthirstiness.

Isabel quailed as she heard the wild tales told of him; but Don Gregorio shrugged his shoulders and said, "Thank Heaven he turned soldier rather than brigand!" The chief difference between the two in those days was in name; but that meant much in sentiment.

XXI.

Leon Vallé had not parted from his sister in declared hostility, yet months passed before she heard directly from him. But this was not to be wondered at, as letters were necessarily sent by private carriers, and it was not to be expected that in the adventurous excitement of his life he should pause to send a mere salutation over leagues of desolate country.

Meanwhile the prevailing anarchy of the time crept closer and closer to the hacienda limits. Bandits gathered in the mountains and ravaged the outlying villages, driving off flocks of sheep or herds of cattle, lassoing the finest horses, and mocking the futile efforts of the country people to guard their property. The name of one Juan Planillos became a terror in every household; yet one by one the younger men stole away to strengthen the number of his followers and share the wild excitement of the bandit life, rather than to wait patiently at home to be drafted into the ranks of some political chieftain whose career raised little enthusiasm, and whose political creed was as obscure as his origin. "The memory is confused," says an historian, "by the plans and *pronunciamientos* of that time. Men changed ideas at each step, and defended to-day what they had attacked yesterday. Parties triumphed and fell at every turn." The form of government was as changeable as a kaleidoscope, and only the brigand and guerilla seemed immutable. Whatever the politics of the day, their motto was plunder and rapine; and their deeds, so brilliant, so unforeseeable, offered an irresistible attraction to the restless spirits of that revolutionary epoch.

Though Doña Isabel Garcia, like all others, was imbued with the military ardor of the time, the brilliant reputation that her brother was winning in distant fields, though in harmony with her own political opinions, horrified rather than dazzled her. She shuddered as she heard his name

11

mentioned in the same breath with that of the remorseless Valdez, or the crafty and bloody Planillos; yet she was glad to believe his incentive was patriotism rather than plunder, and when at last a messenger from him reached her with the same old cry for "Money! money! money!" she responded with a heaping handful of gold, — all she had been able to accumulate in the few months of his absence. Don Gregorio however, vexed by recent losses and harassed by constant raids from the mountain brigands, sent a refusal that was worded almost like a curse; and ashamed of her brother, annoyed by and yet sympathizing with her husband, Doña Isabel felt her heart sink like lead in her bosom, and for the first time her superb health showed signs of yielding to the severe mental strain to which she had been so long subjected.

June had come again; the rainy season would soon begin, and Don Gregorio, suddenly thinking that the change would benefit his wife, suggested that they should pass some months in the city. The roads were threatened by highwaymen, yet Isabel was glad to go, and even to incur the novelty of danger. Her travelling carriage was luxurious, and with her little girls immediately under her own eye, with an occasional glimpse of the four-year-old Norberto riding proudly at his father's side in the midst of the numerous escort of picked men, she felt an exhilaration both of body and mind to which she had long been a stranger.

The travelling was necessarily slow, for the roads were excessively rough, and the party had at sunset of the first day scarcely left the limits of the hacienda and entered the defile which led to the deeper cañons of the mountains, wherein upon the morrow they anticipated the necessity of exercising a double vigilance. Not a creature had been seen for hours; the mountains with their straggling clumps of cacti and blackened, stunted palms seemed absolutely bereft of animal life, except when occasionally a lizard glided swiftly over a rock, or a snake rustled through the dry and crackling herbage. Caution seemed absurd in such a place where there was scarce a cleft for concealment, yet the party drew nearer together, and the men looked to their arms as the cliffs became closer on either side and so precipitous that it seemed as though a goat could scarcely have scaled them.

They had passed nearly the entire length of this cañon, and the nervous tension that had held the whole party silent and upon the alert was gradually yielding to the glimpse of more open country which lay beyond, and on which they had planned to camp for the night, when suddenly the whole country seemed alive with men. They blocked the way, backward and forward; they hung from the cliffs; they bounded from rock to rock, on foot and on horse, the horses as agile as the men. Amid the tumult one man seemed ubiquitous. All eyes followed him, yet not one caught sight of his face; the striped jorongo thrown over shoulders and face formed an impenetrable disguise, such as the noted guerilla chief of the mountains was wont to wear. Suddenly there was a cry of " Planillos! Planillos! " amid the confusion of angry voices, of curses, and the clanking of sabres and echo of pistol-shots. Don Gregorio found himself driven against the rocks, a sword-point at his throat, a pistol pressed to his temple, his own smoking weapon in his hand.

Immediately the shouts ceased, and before the smoke which had filled the gorge had cleared, the travellers found themselves alone, with two or three dead men obstructing the road. Don Gregorio had barely time to notice them, or the blank faces of his men staring bewildered at one another, when a cry from Doña Isabel recalled him to his senses, and he saw her rushing wildly from group to group. In an instant he was at her side. " Norberto! where is Norberto? " both demanded wildly, and some of the men who had caught the name began to force their horses up the almost inaccessible cliffs, and to gallop up or down the cañon in a confused pursuit of the vanished enemy.

Don Gregorio alone retained his presence of mind; though night was closing in and the horses were wearied by a day's travel, not a moment was lost in dispatching couriers to the city for armed police and to the hacienda for fresh men and horses, and the return to Tres Hermanos was immediately begun. Sometime during the morning hours they were met by a party from the hacienda, and putting himself at the head of his retainers Don Gregorio led them in search of his son, while Doña Isabel in a state bordering upon distraction proceeded to her desolated home.

Her first act was to send a courier to her brother. No one knew the mountains as he did, and in her terrible plight she was certain he would not fail her. But her haste was needless, for information reached him from some other source, and within a few days he was at the head of a party of valiant Garcias, who had hastened from far and near to the rescue of their young kinsman.

In all the country round the abduction of Norberto Garcia was called "the abduction by enchanters," — so sudden had been the attack, so complete the disappearance of the victim. Beyond the immediate scene no trace remained of the act, — it seemed that the very earth must have opened to swallow the perpetrators; and yet day by day proofs of their existence were found in letters left upon the very saddle crossed by the father, or upon the pillow wet with the tears of the mother, demanding ransom which each day became more exorbitant, accompanied by threats more and more ingenious and horrible.

Such seizures, though rare, were by no means unprecedented, and such threats had been proved to be only too likely to be fulfilled. As days went by the agony of the parents became unbearable, and Don Gregorio's early resolution to spend a fortune in the pursuit and punishment of the robbers rather than comply with their demands, and thus lend encouragement to similar outrages, began to yield before the imminent danger to the life of his son; and to Doña Isabel it seemed a cruel mockery that her brother and the young Garcias should urge him to further exertion and postponement of the inevitable moment when he must accede to the imperious demands of the outlaws.

The family were one evening discussing again the momentous and constantly agitated question, when Doña Feliz appeared among them with starting eyes and pallid cheeks, bidding Don Gregorio go to his wife, from whose nerveless hand she had wrested a paper, which Leon seized and opened as the excited woman held it toward him. Don Gregorio turned back at his brother-in-law's exclamation, and beheld upon his outstretched hand a lock of soft brown hair, evidently that of a child. It had been severed from the head by a bloody knife. It was a mute threat, yet they understood it but too well. Every man there sprang to his feet with a groan or an oath. Such a threat they remembered had been sent to the parents the very day before the infant Ranulfo Ortega had been found dead not a hundred yards from his father's door. Did this mean also that the last demand for ransom had been made, and the patience of Norberto's abductors was exhausted?

Don Gregorio clasped his hands over his eyes, and reeled against the wall. Leon sprang to his feet, pale to his lips, his eyes blazing. Julian Garcia picked up the hair which had fallen from Leon's hand; the others stood grouped in horrified expectancy. Doña Feliz stood for a moment looking at them with lofty courage and determination upon her face.

"What," she cried, "is this a time for hesitation? The money must be paid, the child's life saved. Vengeance can wait!" She spoke with a fire that thrilled them, and though they spoke but of the ransom, it was the word "vengeance" that rang in their ears, and steeled Don Gregorio to the terrible task that awaited him.

That night the quaint hiding-places of the vast hacienda were ransacked, and many a hoard of coin was extracted from the deep corners of the walls, and the depths of half-ruinous wells. Doña Isabel saw treasures of whose existence she had never heard before, but had perhaps vaguely suspected; for through the long years of anarchy the Garcias had become expert in secreting such surplus wealth as they desired to keep within reach. Large as was the sum brought to light, it barely sufficed to meet the demands of the robbers; yet it was a question how such a weight of coin was to be conveyed by one person to the spot indicated for the payment of the ransom and delivery of the child, — for it had been urgently insisted upon that but one man should go into the very stronghold of the bandits.

At daybreak, having refused the offer of Leon Vallé to go in his stead, Don Gregorio mounted his horse and set out on his mission. He knew well the place appointed, for he had been in his youth an adventurous mountaineer, and more than once had penetrated the deep gorge into which, late in the afternoon, he descended, bearing with him the gold and silver. As he entered the "Zahuan del Infierno" he shuddered. Not ten days before he had passed

through it, followed by a dozen trusty followers, in search
of his child, and had discovered no trace of him; now
he was alone, weighted with treasure, sufficient sensibly
to retard his movements and render him a rich prize for
the outlaws he had gone to meet. Once he fancied he
heard a step behind him; doubtless he was shadowed by
those who would take his life without a moment's hesitation.
Yet he pressed on, obliged to leave his horse and proceed
on foot, for at times the cliffs were so close together that
a man could barely force his way between them.

Just as the last rays of daylight pierced the gloomy
abyss, at a sudden turn in the narrowest part of the gorge
Don Gregorio saw standing two armed men, placed in such
a position that the head of one overtopped that of the
other, while the features of both were shadowed though
made the more forbidding by heavy black beards, which it
occurred to him later were probably false and worn for
the purpose of disguise. At the feet of the foremost was
placed a child; and though he restrained the cry that rose
to his lips, the tortured father recognized in him his
son, — but so emaciated, so deathly pale, with such
wild, startled eyes, gazing like a hunted creature before
him, yet seeing nothing, that he could scarcely credit
it was the same beautiful, sensitive, highly-strung Norberto who had been wrested from him but a short month
before.

At the sight the father felt an almost irresistible impulse
to precipitate himself upon those fiends who thus dared to
mock him; but even had his hands been free to grasp the
pistol in his belt, to have done so would have been to
bring upon himself certain death. As it was he could but
look with blind rage from the bags of coin he carried to
the brigands who stood like statues, the right hand of the
foremost laid upon the throat of the trembling boy. Even
in that desperate moment Don Gregorio noticed that the
hand was whiter and more slender than the hands of common men are wont to be; the nails were well formed and
well kept, though there was a bruise or mark on the second
one, as though it had met some recent injury. He was not
conscious at the time that he noticed this, but it came to
him afterward. The foremost man did not speak; it was
the other who in a soft voice, as evenly modulated as though

to words of purest courtesy, bade the Señor Garcia welcome, and thanked him for his prompt appearance.

"Let us dispense with compliments," said Don Gregorio, huskily. "Here is the money you have demanded for my child. I know something of the honor of bandits, and as you can gain nothing by falsifying your word, I have chosen to trust in it. Here am I, alone with the gold," and he poured it out on the rock at the child's feet, — "count it if you will;" and he put out his hand and laid it upon the child's shoulder. As he did so his hand touched the brigand's, and both started, glaring like two tigers before they spring; but at that moment Norberto bounded over the scattered heap of coin and into his father's arms.

As he felt that slight form within his grasp the father reeled, and his sight failed him; a voice presently recalled him to his senses, and glancing up he saw the two men still standing motionless, with their pistols levelled upon him and the child.

"The Señor will find it best to withdraw backward," said the bandit; "there is not space here for me to have the honor of passing and leading the way, and it is even too narrow for your grace to turn. You will find your horse at the entrance to the gorge; it has been well cared for. Adios, Señor, and may every felicity attend this fortunate termination of our negotiations."

"I doubt not there will," cried Don Gregorio, though in a voice of perfect politeness, "for I swear to you I will unearth the villains who have tortured and robbed me, and give myself a moment of exquisite joy with every drop of life-blood I slowly wring from them. You have my gold, and I have my child, and now — Vengeance!"

Gregorio Garcia knew so well the peculiar ideas of honor among bandits as well as the spirit of his countrymen that perhaps he was assured that no immediate risk would follow this proclamation. The word "vengeance" rang from cliff to cliff, yet the bandits only smiled mockingly and bowed, waving a hand in token of farewell, as with what haste he might he withdrew. A turn in the gorge soon hid them from his sight, and staggering through the darkness, he hastened on with his precious burden, feeling that Norberto had fainted in his arms.

It was near midnight when Don Gregorio reached the hacienda, and needless is it to attempt to describe the joy of the mother at sight of her child, though Norberto, after one faint cry of recognition, laid his head upon her breast with a long shuddering sigh, which warned her that his strength and courage had been so overtaxed that they were, perhaps, destroyed forever.

As days passed, it seemed evident that the mind of the boy was suffering from the shock. The male relatives who during the absence of Don Gregorio had mostly dispersed to find, manlike, some distraction a-field, returned one by one to embrace him; but he turned from each with unreasoning fear and aversion, unable to distinguish between them and the strangers in whose hands he had been held a prisoner. At some of them he gazed as if fascinated, especially at his Uncle Leon; and when by any chance the latter touched him he would burst into agonizing wails, which ceased only when his father held him closely in his arms, whispering words of affection and encouragement.

Before many days it became evident that Norberto was dying. There was a constant, low, shuddering cry upon his lips, "He will kill me!—he will kill me if I tell!" and the horrified father and mother became convinced that Norberto knew at least one of his captors, and that deadly fear alone prevented him from uttering the name. They entreated him in vain; and one night the end of the tortured life drew near, and Norberto's wailing cry was still.

The family was alone, except for the presence of Leon Vallé and a young cousin, Doctor Genaro Calderon, one of the numerous family connections; and those, with the Padre Francisco and Doña Feliz, were gathered around the bed of the dying child. The father in an agony of grief and vengeful despair stood at the head, and Doña Isabel, ghostlike and haggard from her long suspense and watching, was on her knees at the side, her eyes fixed upon the face of the child, when suddenly he opened his eyes in a wild stare upon Leon Vallé, who stood near the foot of the bed, and faintly, slowly articulated the same agonizing cry, "He will kill me if I tell!"

At that moment, as if by an irresistible impulse, Leon stretched out his hand and placed a finger on the lips of the dying boy. The eyes of Don Gregorio followed it; and then like a thunderbolt hurled through space he threw himself upon his brother-in-law, grappling his throat with a deathlike grasp. He had recognized the bruise upon the second finger of the white hand, — he had recognized the very hand. Recalled .to life by the excitement of the moment, Norberto started up and exclaimed in a loud shrill voice, "Take him away! He cut my hair with his bloody knife! Oh, Uncle Leon, will you kill me?" and fell back in the death agony, — the agony that only the priest witnessed, for even Isabel turned to the mortal combat waged between her husband and her brother.

Don Gregorio was unarmed, but Leon had managed to draw a knife from his belt. The murderous dagger was poised for a blow, when a woman rushed between the combatants; Don Gregorio was flung bleeding upon the bed, Doña Feliz hurled into a corner of the apartment the dagger which she had grasped with her naked hand, and Leon Vallé rushed like a madman from the room. Before he could escape, however, he was seized, pinioned, and thrust like a wild beast into one of the solid stone rooms of the building. Don Gregorio was held by main force from accomplishing his purpose of taking the life of the unnatural bandit ere the bolts were shot upon him. He however gave immediate orders that messengers be despatched in quest of police; but by some misapprehension or intentional delay on the part of the administrador these messengers were detained till dawn, and just as they were about to set forth, a cry went through the house that the prisoner had escaped.

Gregorio Garcia rushed to the room, glanced in with wild, bloodshot eyes, and then with unrestrainable fury, sought out his wife, and grasping her arm cried in a voice as full of horror as of rage, "Traitress! You have set free the murderer of your child!"

She threw herself on her knees at his feet, — he never knew with what purpose, whether to confess her weakness or declare her innocence, — for Doña Feliz cast herself between them.

"It was I who set him free!" she exclaimed. "I love the Garcias too well to suffer them to be made a mockery of by the false mercy of such laws as ours. Think you the idol of the bandits would be sacrificed for such a trifle as a child's life? And you, Gregorio Garcia, would you, this fury passed, avenge your injuries in the blood of your wife's brother, robber and murderer though he be? Leon has sworn to me to hide himself forever from the family he has disgraced, under another name in another land. He has the brand of Cain upon his brow, — God will surely bring his doom upon him!"

Doña Feliz spoke like a prophetess. The superb assurance upon which she had acted, setting aside all rights of man and relegating vengeance to the Lord, did more to reconcile Don Gregorio to the escape of his enemy than all further reflection, decisive though it was in convincing him that in the disordered and anarchical state of the country, the laws would have shielded rather than punished an offender so popular as was Leon Vallé. There was perhaps, too, a comfort in the hidden hope of personal vengeance with which he waited long months to learn the retreat of the man who had done him such foul wrong.

Meanwhile the exact facts of the case were never known abroad; and when at last it was rumored that Leon Vallé had been shot by a rival guerilla chief and hung to a tree placarded as a traitor and robber, there were few to doubt the story, or to make more than a passing comment on the hard necessities of war. There seemed so much poetic justice in it, that Gregorio Garcia, who was near the end of the disease contracted through exposure and mental agony, did not for a moment doubt it, and died almost content. Indeed, the circumstances were so minutely detailed by a servant who had followed Leon in his adventurous career and who dared to face the family in order to prove the death, that even Doña Isabel herself did not question it until long months afterward, when a petty scandal stole through the land. The lady of San Lazaro had disappeared, — whether of her own free will, whether in madness she had strayed, or whether she had been kidnapped, none could conjecture. No demand for ransom came, no tidings were ever heard of the peerlessly beautiful Dolores.

It was after that time that Doña Isabel began to demand tidings of all who came to her door, and a suspicion entered her mind which became a certainty upon the night our story opened, but which no subsequent event had tended to confirm during the years that had passed since then.

This brief relation may serve to explain the strange emotions and experiences that made Doña Isabel what her full womanhood found her, and which with other events of her later life rendered possible and natural the bitter suspense and fear that held her the long night through, a watcher at the door of one who, as others had done, might find a means to pierce her heart and wound her pride, if not to awaken her deep and passionate affections.

XXII.

CHINITA woke with a confused sensation of haste, and in the dim light discovered with a momentary surprise that she was in one of the chambers of the great house. Her first clear remembrance was that there was to be a wedding in the village that day, and that she must hasten to help array the bride, her old playmate Juana, — a girl scarce older than herself, but who as the daughter of the silversmith held some pretentions to superior gentility among the village folk. She wondered that she was not in the hut with Florencia and the children, and raised herself upon one arm to peer through the gloom at the figure upon the bed; then suddenly sprang to her feet with an exclamation. The sight of the wounded man brought to memory the train of events connected with his appearance there. The young man was asleep, but even if he had been awake and in dire need of aid, Chinita would not have paused an instant; for it flashed into her mind that she must see and speak to Tio Reyes before he left. He had told her so little — nothing that she could separate as a tangible fact. She must know more. Surely it was early still, — she never slept after daybreak; he would not yet be gone. Yet in quick apprehension, which burst forth in an irate interjection at her tardy awakening, she ran out into the court.

The morning light was beaming there unmistakably, though no ray of sunlight penetrated it; and not a creature was stirring, and still hopeful the young girl hurried to the outer court. The mingled sounds of the movements of men and horses greeted her ear. Although she was late, Tio Reyes perhaps was still there. Vain hope! One glance around the great court showed her that he whom she sought was gone.

With an angry little cry, which made more than one muleteer turn to look at her with, " What has happened to

thee?" on his lips, Chinita sped across the court, and caught
the arm of Pedro, who was standing dejectedly outside the
great gate. He crossed himself as she appeared, and his
face lighted up, then clouded again as she cried, "Where
are the soldiers? When did they go? Why did no one
awaken me?"

The man pointed with a disdainful gesture across the
plain. Florencia was standing at the door of her hut,
calling in a rage to a neighbor that those worthless vaga-
bonds had robbed her of her last handful of toasted corn;
and Pedro began to explain to Chinita in his slow way that
the good friends of the night before had naturally enough
demanded something from the housewives upon which to
breakfast, and that instead of giving it to them quietly,
and thanking the Virgin that after drinking the soup they
had not taken the pot, the foolish women must needs scold
and bewail, as though soldiers should be saints and live on
air, and as if this was the first raid that ever had been heard
of, instead of a mere frolic, very different from that of the
month before, when the forces of the clergy had carried off
a thousand bushels of maize, without as much as a "God
repay you."

Chinita gazed eagerly toward the east, and presently
burst into passionate tears. The sun, which a moment
before had shown a tiny red disk above the hills, flooded
the plain with light, and dazzled her vision. Through it
she saw some rapidly moving figures. The man she
sought was already miles away. Silently but bitterly she
reproached herself. She had slept like an insensate lump,
and suffered to escape her the man who could have told
her so much, whom she would have *forced* to speak.
She could, as her eyes became accustomed to the light,
distinguish his very figure in the clear atmosphere; and
yet he and all she would have learned were so far away.

"What wouldst thou?" demanded Pedro, gruffly; "the
soldiers have carried off nothing of thine! Heaven fore-
fend! Go to the hut and drink the atolé if there is any left,
and give God the thanks!"

The broad daylight had cleared the mind of Pedro of
all the sentimental fears of the night. The glamour had
passed away; there stood Chinita with the old familiar
ragged clothing upon her, to be talked with, caressed it

might be, certainly scolded with the mock severity of old. Yes, it was the same fiery, uncertain, irascible Chinita, who, clearing her eyes of their unusual tears with a backward sweep of her small brown hand, ran down the hill, — not to the hut where Florencia stood with the water-jar, beckoning her, but in quite another direction, to join the little crowd of sympathizing friends who were gathered at the door of the silversmith.

Pepé was standing there with a gayly caparisoned donkey, destined to bear the *novia* to the village some eight miles distant, where the lazy priest who divided his time between the sinners of that point and Tres Hermanos, had consented to earn a royal fee by uniting two poor peasants in holy matrimony. "It is but for once," Gabriel had hopefully remarked ; "and though one runs in debt for the wedding, one can hold one's head above one's neighbors, to say nothing of dying in peace, if a bull's horn finds its way some unlucky day between one's ribs."

Gabriel was a man who honored the proprieties, and Juana was well pleased with the good fortune that had awarded her to him ; though he was twice her age, and had a squint which made ludicrous his most amorous glances.

"What has happened?" cried Pepé in a disappointed tone, as Chinita darted past him. "Didst thou not say thou wouldst ride with Juana? She has been waiting for thee this half hour. The *novio* will be on his way before her if we tarry longer, and thou knowest what that portends. The impatient lover becomes the husband never appeased! the wife shall wait many a day for him."

"Bah!" returned Chinita, "if Juana were of my mind the *novio* would wait so long that her turn to play at *paciencia* would never arrive."

"Go to!" cried a woman who stood near, "who would have imagined thou wouldst be so envious, Chinita; and thou but a child yet? But thou art one that hast been brought up between cotton, and expectest the soft places all thy life."

"Pshaw!" answered Chinita. "Speak of what thou knowest, Señora Gomesinda ; and thou, Pepé, cease making eyes at me. Thinkest thou I have nothing better to do than to ride after Juana to see her married to yon black giant of a vaquero, who will manage his wife as he does his horses, — with a thong? I tell thee as I tell her, he is not worth the beating she got when he asked for her!"

"Ay, Señora," cried Gomesinda, shrilly, "was ever such talk from the mouth of a modest girl? What could a reasonable father and mother do for a girl when a man asks her in marriage? It is plain she must have played some tricks of our Señora Madre Eva to have beguiled him. Ay, but I remember my mother flailed me black and blue when José asked for me. I warrant you I screamed so hard the whole neighborhood knew she was doing the honorable part by me. Thank Heaven, I knew what was proper as well as another, and if I had given the man a glance from the corner of my eyes, I was willing my shoulders should suffer for it. One may tell of it when one is the mother of ten children."

During this harangue, Chinita had slipped by her, and darted into the hut. She threw her arms around the expectant bride, who dressed in the stiffest of starched skirts, the upper one of which was of flowered pink muslin, stood waiting the finishing touches of her sponsor.

"What, thou art not ready?" cried Juana in a dejected tone, surveying Chinita with disapproving eyes. "Gabriel has twice sent messages that the sun has risen, and that the Señor Priest likes not to be kept long fasting, and thou knowest, as the priest sings the sacristan answers."

"Ay," said Chinita, laughing, "a lesson in patience will be good for both the priest and thy Gabriel; but it will bode thee ill if he learns it at the tavern, as I saw him doing just now. Truly, Juana, thou must go without me. I am in no humor to go so far on thy ambling donkey;" and she drew herself up with an air of hauteur, which did not escape the observant eye of the bride, who said, with a reproachful look, —

"What have I done? Did I ever give thee a sharp word, Chinita?"

For answer, Chinita threw her arms around the girl's neck; for she was really fond of Juana, who had ever been a gentle girl, and had borne her perverse humors with a sort of admiring patience which had flattered and won the heart of the wayward one. Completely mollified, Juana pressed her cheek against Chinita's shoulder, for she had turned her face away, and said, "But thou wilt put on thy finest clothes and sit beside me at the fandango, wilt thou not? And thou wilt help my sponsor to dress me. See! Dost thou think she has done well this time?" and the girl threw her scarf from her head and shoulders, and exhibited her long, well-oiled tresses with an air of conscious vanity.

"Nothing could be better," declared Chinita, heartily, pulling out a loop of the bright red ribbons. "Yes, yes," she added with some effort, "I will stay beside thee all through the feast. Thou hast ever been a good friend of mine, Juana. There, there, they are calling thee;" and she pushed her toward the door, where by this time a noisy crowd had gathered.

Instead of only one donkey, there were five or six standing there, with gay bridles and necklaces of horsehair, brightened with cords of red or blue, and with panniers covered with well-trimmed sheepskins. As the Señora Madrina said, "She who should ride upon them would think herself on cushions of down." On the most luxurious of these rural thrones Juana was raised, and upon the others her mother and a number of her female friends, mostly in pairs, were accommodated; and with many injunctions from the bystanders to hasten, the bridal party were at last dismissed upon their way.

Laughing and chattering, the women dispersed to their huts to grind a fresh stint of maize to replace the tortillas and atolé that had been carried away by the soldiers; but Chinita sat down at the door of the adobe hut thus temporarily deserted, and with a smile of derision upon her lips watched the group of men congregated around the village shop. The bridegroom, a middle-aged man, with a dark face deeply imbrowned by the sun and seamed with scars (for he had been a soldier before he was a vaquero), stood in the midst of them, dressed in a suit of buff leather, gay with embroidery. The embossed leather sheath of his knife showed in his scarlet waist-scarf, and immense spurs clanked on his heels in response to the buttons and chains on the half-opened sides of his riding trousers of goat-skin. He was a picturesque figure — though Chinita's accustomed eyes failed to recognize that — as he stood with his wide, silver-laced hat pushed back upon the mat of black hair that crowned his swarthy countenance, holding high the small glass of mezcal which he was about to drink in favor of the toast some comrade had proposed. Meanwhile, his companions were noisily hilarious, rallying him with impossible prophesies of good fortune, to which he listened with an air of imperturbability which was part of the etiquette of the occasion, — for in all the world can be found no greater slave to his peculiar code of manners than the Mexican ranchero.

The party on donkey-back had almost disappeared upon the horizon before it seemed to occur to the group at the tavern store that any movement was expected from them. More than once the women had stopped in their household tasks to call out a shrill " Go on! go on! By the saints, man, will you keep the priest waiting?" and still Gabriel affected the indifferent, until as if by accident he strolled toward his horse, which stood champing the bit impatiently. Immediately there was a rush of his best friends, and the triumphant one who caught the stirrup and held it as the bridegroom mounted claimed the luck-gift for the good news of the departure, — which was effected at once after a series of pirouettes and caracolling, by Gabriel's putting spurs to his steed and galloping madly away, followed by his friends as quickly as they could throw themselves into their saddles.

The spell of the day before continued still so to rest upon her that Chinita neither joined in the cheer nor the laughter of the women, but turned slowly toward Pedro's hut. The cravings of a healthy appetite subdued for the moment the pride that scorned the lowly home. It was natural to go there for the corn-cake and the draught of atolé or chocolate with which to break her fast. She found the share left for her; but after a mouthful or two it seemed to grow bitter to her taste. She divided it petulantly among the children who clamored around her, and in response to a call from Florencia went to Selsa's hut where they were making tortillas for the wedding feast, arrogantly refusing to help, yet glad of accustomed companionship. Much as she resented old associations, the wrench was too great for her to separate herself from them at once, especially as she had no conception of what could or should take their place. She was like a child upon the banks of a river that separates it from the farther shore which it longs to reach, though dreading to push forth from the land it knows, rough and forlorn though it may be. There was with Chinita a strange sense of clinging to a past which was irrevocably severed from her, of impatience of a problem of the future to be solved, and of lack of will to set herself to its solution, as she went from hut to hut. The fever of her mind expended itself first in seething irony and jests, and later in a wild repentance, which manifested itself in quick embraces of the half offended women, and in practical toil, which effectually promoted the preparations for the feast, and went far to restore her to the good graces of the harassed workers. Indeed, often enough they paused in their labors to listen and laugh, as she stood at the brasiers fanning the glowing charcoal, or watching the tortillas taken from the flat *comal* and piled in heaps upon the fringed and embroidered napkins used on such occasions of ceremony; or went from dish to dish of black beans, or red and fiery chile rich with pork or fowl; or gazed with positive admiration upon the kids and lambs, stuffed with almonds and raisins, forcemeat and olives, and other delicacies, which drawn smoking from the earthen ovens attested the generosity of the administrador toward his favorite vaquero.

Toward noon the bride and her party returned, ambling home upon their donkeys, as humbly as they had gone. Juana was conducted to her future home, and her mother-in-law, welcoming her with distant ceremony, intended to inspire respect, suffered her to touch her cheek with her lips, then led her to the inner room, where lay the apparel for her adornment, — a number of toilets being indispensable upon the occasion, and indicative of the pretensions of the bridegroom who had hired them.

Chinita, in her mingled mood of disdain and levity, had neglected to keep her promise of putting on holiday attire, and stood in some awe and much admiration before the bride as she at last appeared in the little bower or tent that had been raised for her at one side of the hut, facing upon the plaza where the feast was to be held. The little woman — for she was not fully grown — was resplendent in a stiff-flowered brocade of many colors, trimmed with real Spanish lace and bedecked with flowers, and wore a necklace and bracelets of imitation gems set in filagree, fit, as her sponsor proudly declared, for the Blessed Virgin upon the high altar.

Juana threw a glance of reproach upon Chinita; but her new dignity forbade recrimination. A shout presently announced that the bridegroom was in sight. The bride, well-drilled in her part, kept her glance fixed on the ground; and as he swept by her bower Gabriel deigned not a look, but reined in his horse at his own door with a sudden turn of the hand which almost threw the animal on its haunches, and before his stirrup could be seized had thrown himself from his saddle and was shaking hands with his friends, and immediately the feast began.

There was no table set. The fires burned at the corners of the plaza, and the women stood over them, dispensing the fragrant contents of the jars to all comers. Yet in this apparent informality the strictest decorum was observed, and not a mouthful was swallowed or a drink of *pulque* or milky *chia*, without a friendly interchange of courtesies, which rather increased than grew less as the hours flew by.

The proverb is true that at a wedding the bride eats least; and at that of the Mexican peasant the saying becomes a law. Juana was too well drilled in the proprieties to touch a morsel of the delicacies offered her, but wore constantly the air of timid resignation with which she had met the assumed indifference of her spouse, who resolutely avoided casting even a glance in the direction where she held her court, — the women crowding with ever increasing admiration to view her after each change of toilet, as they might have done to examine a gorgeous picture, commenting loudly upon the taste of the dresser and the liberality of the groom. But nothing could be more satisfactory to her than this feigned indifference of her husband. " Is not Gabriel an angel?" she took occasion to ask Chinita, as for the tenth time she was changing her apparel. " Imagine to yourself twelve changes of clothing, and he acts as if the hiring of them were nothing! What a difference between him and Pancho Orteago, who was married at Easter! Four beggarly suits were all he provided for Anita, and not one silk among them ; and he actually was quite close to her again and again, with mouth open, as if he would eat her !

Such an idiot! He would have spoken to her if he had had the chance. I should think she was half dead with mortification! Such foolishness in public! Her mother cried with vexation; and no wonder, with such a slur cast on the family!"

"Yet it has been like a marriage of turtle-doves!" cried Chinita. "Let us see, little woman, if thou wilt say that of thy own six months hence!"

Juana shrugged her shoulders and returned to her seat, with her eyes more coyly cast down, and a dejected mien, which might not have been altogether assumed; for, too earnest in acting her part even to take food in private, she was not unnaturally almost spent with the long and ceremonious state which for perhaps the only time in her life she was called upon to maintain.

By this time, torches of fat pine were blazing at every door-post, and the strumming of harps and guitars and many primitive instruments became incessant. Groups of men, drowsy or hilarious, as the mezcal and pulque they had drunk chanced to affect them, were stretched on the ground, lazily watching and criticising the slow and untiring movements of the fandango; now and then one would spring up, to place himself before some dusky partner, who would raise the song in her shrill monotone, swaying and bending her body in unison with the gliding steps, which seemed as untiring as they were fascinating.

Occasionally the shrill song of the women was enlivened by the snapping of the fingers and thumbs of the men; and more than once, though it had been forbidden, the sharp crack of a pistol-shot indicated the irrepressible excitement of some enthusiastic dancer. As the night wore on, the click of the castanets became more frequent, and the weird and tender refrain of *La paloma* gave place to a bacchanalian chorus. Yet this chorus ever bore an undertone of pathos and sentiment which seemed to render impossible the absolute frenzy and rudeness of mirth that would be apt to characterize such scenes in other lands, — though the element of danger that lurked within began to show itself in scornful glances, and the contemptuous turning of shoulder or head.

The night was chilly and dark, for it was the rainy season, and there was no moon; but the light from scores of torches and from the tripod of burning pitch set in the middle of the plaza illuminated the entire village. The great house was set so high that the lurid glare reached no farther than its gates; yet while its massive façade was in comparative darkness, from its windows the scene of revelry was glowingly distinct, and irresistibly attracted even the indifferent gaze of Doña Isabel.

Late in the evening she stepped into her balcony; Doña Feliz joined her, and they wrapped themselves in their black rebosos, and silently regarded the scene. The dances and sports of the peasantry had been familiar to them from their childhood. A pleasurable excitement thrilled the veins of each as they gazed. This gayety was as far beneath them as the follies of our life may be beneath the pleasures of angels, yet pleased the exalted sense of kindly interest in the affairs of plebeian humanity. They began to murmur to each other something of this feeling, when suddenly both became silent. A single figure had caught the glances of both. It was that of Chinita, who, scornful and cool while the slow *afforados* and *jarabes* were in progress, had yielded to the seductive strains of the waltz, and was drawn from her station at Juana's side by a rual beau from a neighboring village. The two whirled in the mazy dance, presently beginning a series of improvised changes, possible only to the subtle grace of youth under the spell of excitement wrought to its height by music, wine, and amorous flattery. One by one the other couples ceased dancing, the fingers of the musicians flew over their instruments, and the swift feet of Chinita and her partner kept time. Sometimes they swept together around the circle formed by the admiring on-lookers; anon Chinita, lifting her arms to the cadence of the music, waved her swain away, and circled round him like a bird poising for descent, then glided again to his arms; or turning one bare shoulder from which the reboso had fallen, looked back upon him with soft, languorous eyes which challenged pursuit, while she fled with the speed of the wind.

The circle were enraptured, and broke into loud *vivas*, or joined in the words of the air to which the pair were dancing. Pedro stood with the rest, watching with shining eyes; but at his side was a young woman, whose dark brows were drawn together in a spasm of rage. This was Elvira, a young widow, to whom the stranger was plighted, and who in the utter abandonment of her lover to the dance with another younger and fairer than herself, found a fair excuse for the mad jealousy that surged through heart and brain, and convulsed her features. But there was none to notice her; all eyes were bent upon the dancers, when a sudden turn brought them both before the infuriated woman. Seizing a knife from the belt of the unconscious Pedro, she sprang toward Chinita, with intent to wreak the usual vengeance of the jealous country-woman by slashing her across the cheek or mouth, and thus destroying her beauty forever. But quick as a flash Pepé, the derided but faithful, threw himself between them, receiving the blow in his arm; but shouting and gesticulating with pain, he made ridiculous a scene which might have been heroic.

This was no uncommon incident at such gatherings, and roused more laughter than dismay. The dance suddenly ceased. Chinita, panting with exertion, threw herself with a cry for protection upon Pedro, who in rage had involuntarily grasped for the missing knife that had so nearly accomplished so foul a work; and Benito, recalled to his allegiance by this undoubted proof of his Elvira's devotion, turned to her with words of mingled reproach and endearment. Pepé, in spite of his outcry, was quite unnoticed in the general excitement until his sister the bride, forgetting her dignity, forced her way through the crowd and bound her large lace handkerchief over the bleeding wound.

"Thou shalt come home!" said Pedro, resolutely, as Chinita struggled in his grasp, with a half defined intention of assailing the woman who had assaulted her, and who was being led sobbing away by her repentant lover. "What will the Señora think of thee?" he added in a whisper. "She is on her balcony."

Chinita glanced up. She could see nothing against the great blank wall that loomed in the near distance, but a sensation of acute shame overcame her. She suddenly remembered that which in her brief delirium she had forgotten. She turned from the throng as though they had been serpents, and fled up the path to the gate, dashing against it breathless. The postern was open.

She felt for it with her hands and darted through, coming full upon Doña Isabel. Feliz followed her lady, both looking like spectres under the rough stone arch of the vestibule, with its grim garniture of serpents and fierce-eyed wild beasts.

"Wretched girl!" cried Doña Isabel, as Chinita stopped like a deer at bay. "Wretched girl!" grasping her with a grip of steel, yet shaking as with ague. "Hast thou a wound? Is the mark of shame on thy face already? My God! Oh, child! Canst thou not speak?"

"I will kill her!" gasped Chinita, too much excited herself to be surprised by the agitation of Doña Isabel, or to wonder at her presence. "To-morrow I will find her and give her such a blow as she would have given me. What will her Benito care for her then?"

"What is he to thee?" cried Doña Isabel, catching the girl by the wrist, and looking into her eyes, — "he or any such *canalla?* Come thou with me! — with me, I say!" She threw a glance, half inquiring, half defiant, at Feliz, who stood with her eyes cast down, her face strangely white, yet inexpressive. "Come thou with me," she reiterated, scanning the girl from her unkempt shock of tawny curls to her unshod feet. A blush passed over the usually colorless and haughty face of the lady, as she added slowly, "before it is too late."

The girl and the mistress of Tres Hermanos looked at each other searchingly; then Doña Isabel turned and led the way across the court. Chinita followed her with head erect and sparkling eyes. Pedro entered at the instant, but his foster daughter did not hear him; but Feliz, who gave way that the strangely associated lady and girl might pass, looked up, and her eyes met those of the gatekeeper. Pedro approached with his Indian, cat-like silence of movement, and found her standing as if in a dream. The eyes of the man filled with tears. He was too lowly to manifest resentment at the studied reserve he believed Doña Feliz had for years preserved toward him, while still she had made him her tool. He and such as he were made for use. Yet inferior as he was, they had been workers in a common cause, and their common purposes seemed now frustrated at a word.

He bent humbly and touched the fringe of her reboso.

" Have I done well, Doña Feliz?" he queried in a broken voice. "Alas! I can do no more. You see how blood flows to blood, as the brooks turn to the river."

Feliz started. "Strange! strange!" she muttered. She turned upon Pedro a glance of mingled pity and deprecation. She seemed about to say more, but paused. "Thou art a good man, Pedro," she presently whispered. "Thou hast done a greater work than thou guessest. Be content. Thou knowest the child's nature,— Chinita will not suffer with Doña Isabel; but she who thrust from her bosom the dove will perchance warm the adder into life."

"No, no!" cried the man, vehemently. "Cruel, bitter woman! Chinita hath been my child, and though she turn from me I will hear no evil of her. I will live or die for her!" The unwonted outburst ended in a sob, and before he could speak again, Doña Feliz had passed across the court, but — strange condescension! — she had seized his hand and pressed it to her lips, in irresistible homage to a devotion as pure and unselfish as that of the loftiest knight who ever drew sword in the cause of helpless innocence.

Pedro turned to his alcove dazed, stunned. To him it was as if a star should leave its place in heaven to touch the vilest clod upon the highway. A very miracle!

XXIII.

ALTHOUGH Doña Rita had left her home upon a sad errand, and her tears flowed fast when on embracing her mother she beheld upon her countenance the shadow of death, that first startling impression vanquished, she allowed herself to be deceived by the fitful brightness that hovers over the consumptive; and as days passed on she felt a pleased sense of freedom and relaxation, and her return to her early home, which had been undertaken as a pilgrimage, assumed much of the character of an ordinary visit of pleasure.

Doña Rita was a member of a large family, of whom most had married; so that her parents, relieved from cares that had long pressed upon them, were enabled to live in the little town of El Toro with an ease and comfort from which in their narrow circumstances they had necessarily been debarred while the children were dependent. They were, strictly speaking, people of the class known as *medio pelo*, or "the half-clothed order," as far below the aristocrat as above the plebeian; and Rita Farias had been thought to have risen greatly in life when she became the wife of Rafael Sanchez, though he was then but a clerk, the son of the administrador of Tres Hermanos, with no prospect of succeeding soon to his honors. But as the pious neighbors said when they heard of the early death of the bridegroom's father, "God blessed her with both hands," of which one held marriage, and the other death; so Doña Rita was accustomed when she at rare intervals visited her parents to be looked upon with ever increasing respect. Such silken skirts and rebosos as she wore were seldom seen within the quiet precincts of El Toro.

Doña Rita herself was not quite clear upon the point as to whether or not her native place could be considered to rival "the City," as Mexico was called *par excellence*, or even Guadalajara, which she had heard was a labyrinth of palaces; but Rosario who had seen El Toro declared to

Chata that nothing could be finer, and Chata herself was quite convinced of that when opening her eyes suddenly upon the clear moonlight night on which the diligence stopped before the door of the inn, she first looked out upon the plaza.

The two girls shivered a little in their sudden awakening, as, scarcely knowing how, they were lifted from the diligence and stood upon their feet at the door of the inn, with an injunction to watch the basket, the five parcels tied in paper or towels, the drinking-gourd, the bottle of claret, and the young parrot which their mother had brought with her as a suitable gift to her declining relative. With habitual obedience they did as they were bid, more than once rescuing a parcel from the long, skinny claw of a blear-eyed hag, who crouched in the shadow of the wall whining for alms, while at the same time they cast their admiring glances at the really beautiful church upon which the white rays of the moonlight streamed, converting it for the nonce into a symmetrical pile of virgin snow or spotless alabaster. The priest's house, a long low building with numerous barred windows, stood on one side of it, while an angle of the square was formed by a mass of buildings, the frowning walls of which were apparently unpierced by door or window. This was a convent. Later the children learned to know well the gardens it enclosed, and also the taste of the wonderful confections the sweet-faced sisters made. The other buildings seemed poor and small in comparison to those, with the exception of the inn which rose gloomily behind them, a solitary rush-light burning palely in the yawning vestibule, and the torches flaming in the court-yard, where benighted travellers were loudly bargaining for lodgings, — no hope of supper presenting itself at that late hour.

While Rosario and Chata were noticing these things with wide-open eyes but with ill suppressed yawns, Don Rafael and Doña Rita were returning the salutations of the concourse of friends who had come to meet them; and as soon as the children had been embraced in succession by each affectionate cousin or punctilious friend, they were hurried across the plaza upon the side where the shadows lay black as ink, and with a regretful glance at the seeming palaces of marble that rose on either hand were conducted with much kindly help and cheerfulness over the rough cobble-stones along a narrow street of single-storied houses, above the walls of which, as if piercing the roofs, rose at intervals tall slender trees, indicating the well-planted courts within. Reaching the more scattered portions of the town where the moonlight shone clear over open fields and walled gardens and orchards, with low adobe houses scattered among them, they at last entered, somewhat to the disappointment of Chata, a rather pretentious house which fronted directly upon the street. She was consoled upon the following day to find a garden at the back, where a triangle of pink roses of Castile, larkspur, and red geraniums grew, almost choking with their luxuriance the beds of onions and chiles, and rivalling in glory of color the " manta de la Virgin " or convolvulus, which entirely covered the half-ruinous stone-wall — the gaps filled with tuñas and magueys — which divided the cultivated land from the thickets of mesquite and cactus that lay beyond.

In the garden the children spent many hours while their mother sat chatting at the side of the invalid, who rallied wonderfully as she heard the endless tales of her daughter's prosperity ; though like many another *nouveau riche*, Doña Rita had her fancied self-denials to complain of. One of the clerks at the hacienda had a wife whose father had given her a string of pearls as large as cherries upon her wedding day, while she the wife of the administrador was left to blush over the shabby necklace — not a bead of which was bigger than a pea — which Rafael had gone in debt to give her on her wedding day, and which until the advent of the fortunate Doña Gomesinda she had thought most beautiful ; and then too her dearest friend had a daughter who would inherit a fine house of three rooms or more in that very town, and money and jewels fit for a *hacendado's* daughter ; and it was quite possible that she would marry — who could tell? it might even be an attorney or an official, — while with two to endow (and it was well known that Rafael loved to enjoy as he went), Heaven only knew to what her own flesh and blood were doomed ! There was Rosario for example, — and her own grand-mother, who would not be prejudiced, could judge if there was a prettier or more daintily-bred girl in the whole town, — what chance was there that an officer or an attorney, or indeed any one but a clerk, a ranchero, or a poor shop-keeper, should pretend to their alliance when they could give so poor a dower with their daughter? Doña Rita's eyes filled with tears, and decidedly she was obliged to compress her lips very tightly to prevent herself from uttering further complaint; for since Rosario had with true Mexican precocity burst into the full glory of young womanhood, this had become a very real grievance to her mother, but one of which, with the awe of the promoted as well as trained daughter and wife, she had seldom ventured to hint of either to Doña Feliz or Don Rafael.

As Rosario had outgrown her sister in physique, so had she also in womanly dignity and apparent force of intellect. At least she thought of matters, and even to her admiring mother and female relatives began to give weighty opinions upon affairs which either wearied Chata or interested her little. The grandfather, old Don José Maria, used to sit under a fig-tree watching with disapproving eyes as Chata darted hither and thither chasing a butterfly or ruby-throated humming-bird, or with her lap full of flowers or neglected sewing pored over some entrancing book lent her by the village priest (he was a man whose ideas, had he not been the Santo Padre, would have been the last that should have been tolerated in the bringing up of sedate and simple maidens) ; and those same eyes lighted with pride as they fell on Rosario, beating eggs to a froth to mix with honey and almonds for her grandfather's delectation, or bending over a brasier of ruddy charcoal watching anxiously the cooking of the *dulce*, of which already more successes than failures showed her a born artist. Then again sometimes, when Don José came in the cool of the evening from the plaza where he had been to buy his jar of pulque or his handful of garlic, he could see his favorite sitting demurely in the upper balcony with her head bent over her needle, listening it is true to that *maldito libro*, " that pernicious book," which Chata was reading, but as far as he could see doing no other harm, unless the very fact of a young and pretty girl looking into the street was a harm in itself, — but *Maria Purissima!* one must not be too rigorous with one's own flesh and blood: like others before him and more who will come after, Don José Maria forgot in tenderness to the grandchildren the discipline he had thought absolutely necessary with the preceding generation.

Chata, too, thought it delightful to sit on the balcony and peer through the wooden railing at the long stretch of sand which led far away where the houses dwindled into a few half-ruinous hovels, where children and dogs throve as well as the bristling cacti. On Sunday mornings very early, as the mother and daughters came from Mass along that road, they used to be covered with dust thrown up by the scores of plodding donkeys who wended their way to the plaza laden with charcoal and vegetables, eggs and screaming fowls. Doña Rita and her daughters would cover their faces with their rebosos, and trip daintily by, scarcely appeased by the admiring salutations and apologies of the drivers, who pulling off their rough straw hats apostrophized the dust and the scorching sun and the clumsy donkey, " by your license be the name spoken ! "

Sometimes more distinguished wayfarers passed over the road and turned into the inn, or rode on to the barracks which lay quite at the opposite extremity of the little town ; for it happened that a company of soldiers were quartered there. They were for the most part well clad in a gay uniform of red and blue, and every man had a profusion of stripes on his sleeves or lace on his cap. No one knew and no one asked whether they were Mochos or Puros, Conservatives or Liberals, — for the nonce they were Ramirez's men. This General had been a Liberal the month before, and was suspected of favoring the clergy at this time. Who could tell ? Who knew what he might be on the morrow ? In the night all cats are gray ; in times of perplexity all soldiers are patriots. The ragged urchins of El Toro threw up their hats for the soldiers of Ramirez, and the discreet householders leaned from their balconies every evening to hear the little band play, and to exult for a brief quarter of an hour in the mild excitement inseparable from a garrison town.

Chata and Chinita had delighted in the distant music, and had caught glimpses of the soldiers, as disenchanting as those of the rude grimy structures they had in the moonlight imagined to be marble palaces ; they had gazed up and down the dusty street and watched the noisy ragged urchins play "Toro" with a big-horned, long-haired, decrepit goat, with crowds of half naked elfin-faced girls as spectators, until they were actually beginning to weary of the attractions of the town and long for home, — when one day the beat of a drum was heard and a squad of soldiers went filing past, with a young officer riding at their head, who threw a glance so killing at the balcony where the young girls stood that, whether intended to reach her or not, it pierced the heart of Rosario on the instant.

Chata had also noticed the young officer (a slender under-sized young fellow, with a swarthy lean face and keen black eyes, shaded by a profusely decorated sombrero), but merely as a part of the mimic pageant, — a prominent part, for the trappings of his horse, as well as his own dress, were covered by that profusion of ornament affected by gallants whose capital was invested in the adornment of the person with which they hoped to conquer fortune; for in those days there were numberless roystering adventurers, who to a modicum of valor united a vanity and assurance which provided many a rich girl with a dashing and fickle husband, and his country with a soldier as false to Mexico as to his Doña Fulana.

It was just after this that evening after evening Rosario would lean pensively over the balcony rail, resisting Chata's entreaties to come to the garden where there was no dust to stifle them, and where the dew would soon begin to fall upon the larkspurs and roses, and already the wide white cups of the *gloria mundo* were beginning to fill with perfume. The dew would chill her, the perfume sicken her, Rosario said. Chata remonstrated; Rosario smirked and smiled. Chata grew vexed; she thought the smile in mockery of her. She need not have lost her sweet temper, — Rosario was thinking of a far different person. The young captain was walking slowly down the opposite side of the street; he had just laid his hand on his heart. It was on him Rosario smiled.

Doña Rita, discreetest of mothers, was not one to leave her daughters to their own devices unwatched. It was she who always accompanied them in their walks or to Mass; yet curiously enough the young captain found means to slip a tiny note into Rosario's ready hand, as she knelt on the grimy stone floor of the church. Obviously, Doña Rita could not be in two places at once, and she usually knelt behind Chata, who needed perhaps some maternal supervision at her devotions; and it came about that the space behind Rosario was occupied by some stranger. It was Don José Maria who first noticed that quite as a matter of course that stranger grew to be the Captain Don Fernando Ruiz; and quite accidentally it happened that thereafter the mother and daughters went to an earlier Mass. Don José Maria was not so early a riser as Don Fernando was; so he was not there, while the young soldier was in his usual place.

Chata was perhaps a stupid little creature, — Rosario it is quite certain would never have done such a silly thing; but one day when Don Fernando had pressed a note into the hand which was nearest to him, and which in the confusion of dispersal happened to be that of the smaller sister, she gave it in some indignation to her mother. It was full of violent protestations of affection, and entreated the life of his life to give her lover hope; it was signed her " agonized yet adoring Fernando."

Doña Rita showed herself capable of great self-control; she said sadly that she would not ask which had been guilty of attracting such impassioned admiration, but she assured the girls she was heart-broken. When she reached the house, after first carefully closing the door that her father might not hear, she rated them both soundly. Chata did not think it strange they should both be thought guilty; she assumed that Rosario was as innocent as herself. Doña Rita, giving Rosario the note to read, that she might learn for herself the daring and presumption of which man is capable, forgot in her indignation to reclaim it. An hour afterward Chata saw Rosario read it over in secret, and was scandalized to see her kiss it; and late that day, as they stood as usual on the balcony (the little mother, as Chata remarked, was so forgiving!), she caught Rosario's hand spasmodically as Fernando passed by, but the girl released it with some impatience and slyly kissed the tips of her fingers, — and Chata, with a pang of awakening, realized that her sister had not been and was not so innocent of coquetry as she had assumed, and thenceforth suffered indescribable tortures between her sense of loyalty to her sister and duty to her mother.

Rosario's ideal of truth was in accordance with that which surrounded her; to be silent when speech was undesirable, to equivocate pleasantly where plain speaking would be harsh, to tell a lie gracefully where truth would offend, — this was her natural creed, which she had never questioned. But Chata, unknown to herself, had never accepted it; her soul was like certain material objects which resist the dyes that other substances at once absorb. It was not enough for her to give the truth when it was asked, — it was a torture, an unnatural crime, to her to withhold it. She would not indeed have done so in this case, had not Rosario in a manner put her upon her honor the very next day.

The washerwoman had been there, and Rosario, who was an embryo housewife, had been deputed to attend her, and Chata, who had gladly escaped the duty, ran to the bedroom when she saw the servant depart to congratulate her sister on the dispatch she had made; when Rosario closing the door mysteriously, cried: "Look! look what he has sent me! Is it not beautiful, charming, divine?" and she held up to the light her hand, on the first finger of which glittered a ring.

Truth to tell, Chata was dazzled; at that moment her own insignificance and the womanliness and beauty of Rosario were more than ever apparent. She gazed at Rosario with greater admiration than on the ring, beautiful though it was. Here was a sister just her own age, yet a woman with an actual lover! Oh!

"What will our mother say?" she began in an awed voice, when Rosario, her womanly dignity gone, began to spring up and down, screaming yet laughing, "*Ay, Dios mio!*" throwing her hand over her shoulder and slipping it into the loose neck of her dress. "Oh, my life! the creature is down my back! it is crawling now on my shoulder! No, no, grandfather," for Don José Maria had entered, "it is Chata who will help me. No, my mother! Ay, it is gone now! I would not have you frightened, it was but one of those bright little beetles that live on the roses;" and she contemptuously tossed something out of the window, and Chata saw with speechless wonder that the ring which had been on her finger was gone. The bauble at least had slipped into a secure hiding-place, and Chata really could not determine whether the beetle had ever existed or no.

An air of delightful mystery began to pervade not only the house but the quiet street all the way from the plaza, which Don Fernando Ruiz crossed at intervals in the long, dull, sultry days. It became quite a diversion to the initiated to watch what clever turns and doublings he would make, and with what assumed indifference he would linger by the fruit-stand at the corner, where old Antonina sold tuñas or a few poor figs and lumps of roasted cassava root. She made quite a fortune from the young captain, who seemed bent on dazzling her bleared eyes; for every day, and sometimes three or four times in a day, he appeared resplendent in uniform of blue and red, or a riding suit of buckskin embroidered in silver, or perhaps, when his mood was sombre, in black hung with silver buttons, and more than once in a suit of velvet and embossed leather, with buttons of gold set with brilliants, and riding a horse with accoutrements so splendid that Doña Rita declared he must be as rich as the Marquis of Carabas himself, and without any apparent consistency embraced Rosario with tears.

Truth to tell, Doña Rita was a match-maker born, and though her talents had lain dormant during the years she had spent at the hacienda, they had not declined; and it was natural that she should find a quiet exultation in exerting them in favor of her daughter, for young though Rosario was, her precocity and the custom of the country and period rendered it perfectly natural that marriage should present itself in her immediate future.

A vision of it rose before the impassioned girl like a star, though there was a period of clouds and mourning when her grandmother died, and Chata, sobbing in the garden or moving sadly about the darkened rooms, wondered that Rosario could smile over those pink notes she was always stealing into corners to pore over. During the nine days that her mother remained within doors receiving visits of condolence, the notes indeed were the aliment upon which Rosario's fancy fed; for Doña Rita, though the little drama of courtship had undoubtedly made less absorbing to her the tragedy of illness and death, was too strict an observer of the proprieties to allow her maternal affection to betray her at such a time into permitting even a shutter to be left ajar, or to suffer her daughter to approach a window to satisfy herself by a momentary peep as to whether the love-lorn captain was on his accustomed beat or no. It was a time however when without offence the veriest stranger might leave a card and word of sympathy, and this he never failed to do from day to day. Doña Rita would glance at the bit of cardboard with an affectation of indifference, but it would always shortly disappear from the table, and with the cruel sarcasm of childish intolerance Chata would suggest to Rosario its suitability for baking the little puffs of sugar and almonds upon, which she was so deft at compounding.

At last the *novena* of grief was ended, and taking her aged father's arm Doña Rita dutifully led him into the street to breathe the air. Rosario knew that at that hour the captain was on duty at the barracks, but nevertheless could not resist the opportunity of stepping into the balcony and gazing upon the scene from which she had been so long debarred. A neighbor across the way greeted her with a significant smile ; and somewhat piqued, Rosario drew back, half closed the shutters with a hesitating hand, and then dropping on the floor in the long ray of sunlight that streamed through the aperture, set herself to the ever entrancing task of re-reading her lover's letters.

As she sat there opening them one by one and after perusal leaving them unfolded in her lap, she became so absorbed that she did not notice the passage of time until a footstep sounded behind her, and glancing up she saw with trepidation that her grandfather was ushering in a tall and imposing stranger, whose military garb made her heart beat madly, for a wild thought of Fernando Ruiz flashed through her mind. Her confusion was not lessened by perceiving that the visitor was a man of more advanced age and infinitely greater assumption of rank. The tell-tale letters were in her lap, though involuntarily she had dropped her reboso over them ; but she dared not rise lest they should drop in a shower around her, and she equally feared the anger of her grandfather and the condemnatory surprise of the visitor.

"I pray you enter the house, Señor ! Pass in, sir, pass in !" she heard her grandfather say in his smoothest tones.

" My daughter will be here almost immediately; but she stopped at the convent for a moment to buy a blessed candle to place before the altar of Our Lady of Succors. She will be honored indeed by this visit. Take care, Señor, the room is somewhat dark, but I will open a shutter. *Valgame Dios*, what have we here?" as he caught sight of the bent figure sitting in the narrow streak of sunshine. "*Caramba, niña*, rise! rise, I say! seest thou not the Señor General?"

" Ay, but I have the cramp in my poor foot, my grandfather," cried Rosario in a voice of lamentation, vainly endeavoring under cover of the reboso to make some disposal of the letters which rustled alarmingly. " *No, Señores*, by Blessed Mary my patroness, let me alone!" she cried, as both her grandfather and the stranger attempted to help her, — the latter with a faint gleam of amusement in his eyes, the former with genuine consternation depicted on his face. " Ay, Chata," for by this time her sister had appeared. " Oh, but my back is broken! it is worse than when you struck me with the stick when you were trying to knock the peaches from the tree. Oh! ah! no, it is impossible for me to rise!"

In dire affright Chata knelt before her. " Oh, what shall I do?" she cried, in remorse at the remembrance of an escapade that had been almost forgotten, and in sudden fear that it might have been the cause of her sister's present distress. " Oh, my life! I thought it was your poor foot!" and she began rubbing one small slippered member, while Rosario eagerly whispered, " Stupid one, hide me these letters!" and the mystified Chata felt her sister's hand with a mass of fluttering papers thrust under her arm, covered with the ever useful reboso.

Involuntarily the hapless confidant pressed them to her side, and at the same moment Rosario limped from the room, inwardly raging at making so poor a figure before the General, while Chata, standing for a moment abashed, was about to follow, when a voice which bewildered her by its strange yet familiar accent said gayly, " And you, my fair Señorita, have you never a twinge of the same disorder that afflicts your sister?" and he glanced meaningly at a pink envelope, which had fallen at her feet, — at the same time covering it with his foot that it might not attract the suspicious eye of the old man, who with profuse apologies for the informality of the reception was assuring the visitor that until that moment never had there been a healthier damsel than his granddaughter Rosario, adding with a sigh, "But the Devil robs with one hand and pinches with the other."

Chata trembled and blushed painfully as she raised her eyes timidly to the General's, while with a sense of the grotesque she was conscious of wondering whether he, like herself, was thinking her grandfather had suggested no complimentary agency in her grandmother's removal to another sphere. But at the instant all present perplexities vanished in the surprise with which she recognized the face which she had seen but for a few brief hours years before, — the face of the man of whom Chinita had never grown weary of talking. "The Señor General Ramirez," she said in a low voice, with some awe. She was more than ever bewildered by the look he had fixed upon her. She shrank back, barely dropping her hand for a moment upon that he extended toward her. She was actually inclined to be frightened, his eyes were so brilliant, his smile so eager. The foolish thought struck her that had not her grandfather been there, this strange imperious man would surely have taken her in his arms, would have kissed her! She hurried from the room to find Rosario waiting for her at the end of the corridor, alternately smothering her laughter in the folds of her dress, and angrily chafing at her sister's delay.

"Your horrid letters!" cried Chata, thrusting them into her hands. "Here, take them, read them, laugh over them or cry, or kiss them if you will! I hope I shall never see a love-letter again in my life. He saw them, — the Señor General. I know he did. Oh, what shame!"

"Pshaw!" interrupted Rosario. "What does it matter? He will think none the worse of me. Without doubt he is come on the part of Fernando to ask for me. How proud and happy my mother will be, and how she will rail at me! It will not be difficult for me to cry as I ought, for I am mad with vexation to have appeared such a fool when I should have been so dignified. Why, the Señor will think me a child still! Does he not look like

some one we know, Chata? And yet we can never have
seen him before."

"Yes," returned Chata, "we have seen him. He is the
General José Ramirez."

"Ah, my heart!" ejaculated Rosario, dramatically.
"What a misfortune! My father hates the General
Ramirez because he once had some horses driven away
from the hacienda; and besides he is a good Christian
and fights for the Church! Ay, unlucky Fernando, to
have chosen such a messenger! But thank Heaven, it
is my mother who will first hear him! Ah, there she
comes!" and in irrepressible excitement Rosario grasped
her sister's hand. "Oh, child!" she added sentimentally,
"you too may be asked in marriage some day!" and she
sighed with an air of vastly superior experience, while
Chata revolved in her mind what her playfellow Chinita
would say when she told her of this unexpected meeting
with the hero whom she fancied she had rendered invincible by the gift of the amulet.

Like most children of her country Chata wore a scapulary.
It had lain upon her breast ever since she could remember.
She drew it out and looked at it. Some day she thought
she would open it; now she only made the sign of the
cross, as she replaced it. Rosario in nervous unrest had
left her. The cool of the evening had come; the perfume
of the flowers stole in at the open window, and the breeze
soothed the unusual agitation of her mind. Glad to be
alone, yet anxious and perplexed, she stepped into the
garden. More than once as she walked down the alley
she stopped, her heart palpitating violently. She fancied
she heard her name called, or that Ramirez would step
from the shadow of a tree to encounter her. It was an
unnatural and unchildlike mood quite new to her. It
seemed to her that her grandfather's unnecessary mention
of the Devil's name might have incited that enemy of
innocence to annoy her, and she whispered an *Ave*.

There was a large cluster of bananas just behind the
house. Chata sat down there to watch the fantastic clouds
which hovered where the sun had set. In her absorption
in the glowing scene she was unconscious that any sound
disturbed the silence around her. It was indeed but a low
indistinct hum, scarcely recognizable as the sound of

human voices. Had she noticed them, she would have remembered that she was within a foot or two of a window which was screened from sight by the foliage, and would have withdrawn from possible discovery; but as it was, she remained there an unconscious trespasser. The first distinct sound that reached her ear at once startled and impressed her, for it was the deep voice of Ramirez uttering her own name.

"Chata, yes it was Chata I said," he affirmed dictatorially. "Why attempt dissimulation with you, Señora? I am in no humor for trifling. Will Doña Isabel provide a dowry for your daughter? It is my fancy that Ruiz should marry the little one, and I can make or mar him. So far the boy has blundered, but if he once turns his eyes on the pretty face of Chata, he will not find the mistake irremediable."

Chata could not credit the evidence of her senses, and remained as if rooted to the spot. She presently heard her mother sobbing: "This is an unheard of thing! A young man pays court to one child, — perhaps she is not insensible to his advances, — and his patron comes to me to bid me give him another, whom he has not perhaps even glanced at. Oh, it is too much! too much!"

"I have already told you," said Ramirez, coldly, "that Ruiz is poor. His father was my father's servant, and is mine; more than once he has saved my life at the risk of his own. Years ago he rendered me a service that I swore to repay in a certain manner. More than once of late I have been reminded of my promise, and the marriage of Fernando with your daughter would render its fulfilment impossible."

"By my patron saint!" cried Doña Rita, "it is strange indeed that a poor little country girl should interfere with the projects of a man as great as yourself. But even if that is possible, why bid me give him Chata?" — adding with asperity, "have I not done enough? No, no! I will not, I cannot make my Rosario a sacrifice!"

"*Caramba!*" cried Ramirez, laughing, "is it so dreadful a thing that she should wait until the next lover comes, — he will be sure to come, Señora, — and that she should have a double dower to make her fairer in his eyes? for I tell you Ruiz will ask no dowry from you with the little one. Come, come, Señora, I am not used to reasoning and pleading, yet I am not cruel. The child has been yours too long for me to tear her from your arms. It was a cunning device of Doña Isabel to hide her from me. Ah, it is not the first trick she has served me, and, like the others, she will find it turn to my advantage!"

"As Heaven is my witness," ejaculated Doña Rita, in a voice of intense impulse and fear, "never have I breathed to mortal the secret which you seem to know! Who are you, sir? What have you to do with the child?" Suddenly, she uttered a horrified shriek. Chata, who had started from her seat with dilated eyes and lips parted, gasping for breath, heard her mother spring to her feet, and rush toward the door; heard also Ramirez follow her and apparently draw her back, remonstrating in low tones. Then she realized no more.. Perhaps she fainted, though to herself there appeared no interruption of consciousness. Though she did not notice the stars come out, she beheld them at last looking down upon her, as if they heard the questions that were repeating themselves again and again in her mind. Whose child was she; who was the man who claimed the right to shape her destiny? That she was not the child of Rafael Sanchez and his wife she felt certain. Doña Rita had not denied the insinuation.

The child—all childish thoughts suddenly crushed by the overwhelming revelation she had surprised—remained in the same spot, unconscious of the passage of time, until she heard her sister—no, Rosario—calling her in anxious yet irritated tones: "Where art thou, Chata? Chata, the supper is ready; the grandfather is angry that thou art so long in the garden! Oh, here thou art!"

The two girls encountered each other in the dusk. Rosario threw her arms around the truant. "How cold thou art!" she said. "Hast thou seen a ghost here alone? Bless me! one would think the General Ramirez had brought the plague with him. My mother has shut herself up, and when I went to her door to beg her to tell me whether she was ill, she answered me, 'The world is all ill. Go dress saints, my child, it is all that is left to thee!' What could she have meant? Can it be after all that the General did not come from Fernando?"

Rosario stopped to wipe a tear from the corners of her eyes. Evidently she was more perplexed than dismayed. She was too young to fear the mischances and mishaps of love. Her words recalled to Chata's mind the fate that was decreed to her, — to which she had given no second thought, in her discovery that she was not the child of those she called father and mother. Friendless, homeless, nameless, — yes, she reflected bitterly, that she had *never* been known by a Christian name, — she felt as though the solid earth had opened beneath her, and she was clinging desperately to some tiny twig or bough to prevent herself from being engulfed forever. She clung hysterically to Rosario, who had begun to laugh nervously. And so old Don José Maria found them, and querulously bade them go into the house; nothing but ill fortune would befall maidens who wandered alone in the dark; did they not know that the Devil stood always at the elbow of a woman after the sun set? With which second-hand and scurrilous wisdom the old philosopher ushered them into the dimly lighted dining-room. Doña Rita was there, and as the girls entered lifted her eyes, which were heavy with weeping, and for the first time in her life Chata saw in them aversion, — yes, actual fear and dislike.

The child sighed deeply, and sat down at a shaded corner. No one noticed that she ate nothing. The old man was sleepy, Doña Rita was occupied with Rosario, who grew more and more depressed. From her mother's very kindness her daughter foreboded little good from the tidings she could give her.

XXIV.

For many succeeding days Chata seemed to herself to be struggling to awaken from a torturing dream. The household was very quiet. Doña Rita and Rosario went gloomily to work to set the house in order and prepare for departure; they talked together in low tones, and sometimes one or the other would sigh in echo to poor old Don José Maria, who was contemplating a lonely widowhood, though a kindly cousin had consented to take charge of his domestic affairs, — a kindness which was taken exceedingly ill by the two elderly servants. It was natural enough that the atmosphere around her should be charged with gloom, and as natural that to Chata it should seem a part of the evil dream from which she longed to emerge. At times she thought desperately that she would rush to Doña Rita and beg her to tell her all; but she shrank from dispelling the illusion of her life, from losing the father and mother whom she had believed her own. Her father! — was it possible he could be other than Don Rafael? No, no, no! she loved him, he loved her; he was her own, her very own, — even Rosario did not love and cling to him as she did. And if by word or deed he was deposed from that relationship who would take his place?

The unhappy girl shuddered from head to foot; her very heart seemed to become ice. Who, if all she had heard was true, could be her father but this man, General José Ramirez, — the bloody guerilla, the unscrupulous robber? He had not, it was true, declared so in as many words; it would kill her to hear them — she would not hear them. And so in a sort of dumb frenzy she resisted the temptation to disclose what she had heard; and with a miserable conviction that she was the object of suspicion and dislike, and feeling herself a hypocrite and impostor, she lived from day to day, nursing in her heart such repressed misery as perhaps only a sensitive and uncomprehended child can feel.

Chata was at the point in life where the intuitions of womanhood begin to encroach upon the credulity and frankness of immaturity. A year earlier it is likely she would have gone to Rosario at once with her surprising discovery; but now she unconsciously felt that she was — however unwillingly — her rival. She needed no instruction by word or experience to tell her that Rosario would feel no sympathy with the stranger who had shared as a sister in the love of father, mother, and friends, and who it was purposed should be given to the man whom she had herself won. Strangely enough the remembrance of this only occurred to Chata at intervals, and simply in connection with Rosario. Her mind was so engrossed by the sense of desolation and the agonizing fear of the General Ramirez, that the thought of Ruiz seldom presented itself to her; and the possibility of his being in any way made to affect her life seemed so absolutely incredible that even the sight of him brought no blush to her cheek nor a thrill of interest, either of dislike or latent kindness, to her bosom.

The bewildered and suffering girl did not realize that there was any change in her manner. Sometimes she wondered that she could sleep all night, that she could laugh, yes even talk, so wildly at times that Don José Maria sniffed impatiently, and muttered that it was hard an old man could not take his sorrow in quiet, — as if it was some sort of soothing potion, which to be healthful must be lingered over. But the truth was that the dull, heavy, unrefreshing sleep which came to the child took the place of food to her, besides following naturally upon the physical exhaustion consequent on incessant thought and movement; her sharp, penetrating laugh and inconsequent babble were the outbursts of mental excitement that otherwise must have found vent in passionate cries and tears.

Chata, it is true, had suddenly become invested with a new interest to Doña Rita, who, while events flowed smoothly on, accepted without question the prevailing opinions and sentiments of those surrounding her. She had honestly thought she loved her foster daughter as her own, and that her welfare was as dear to her as that of her own child; but now, without reasoning on the matter, without a throb of anguish in contemplating the fate which Ramirez might will for her, she saw in the girl but a rival who, once knowing them, might well approve and glory in the designs that threatened the pride and affections of Rosario.

Doña Rita dared not repeat to her daughter the substance of her interview with Ramirez; and even had she been at liberty to do so, her satisfaction in being the possessor of an actual secret would have led her to assume, as she did now, mild airs of superior wisdom, — which were perhaps as effectual as words could have been in assuring Rosario that the opposition which the General Ramirez had urged against his subaltern's engagement was more serious than the ordinary interest of a patron would have induced him to make; and for a week or more her affectations of despair, her abundant tears and hopeless sighs, were sufficient to justify her mother's exaggerated tenderness, — a tenderness which Chata contrasted bitterly with the indifference that permitted her own suffering to pass unnoticed.

The secret fear of Chata's heart was that she might meet Ramirez, might even be called upon to speak with him. The thought of either filled her with a frenzy of dread. Had it been possible she would have fled from the town. Oh, if she could but have hoped to find her way to the hacienda alone, even though she dared not make herself known to Doña Feliz and the administrador! Oh, was it possible that they could be cold, suspicious, as Doña Rita was? The thought was an impiety, yet it returned to her again and again, and her dread of meeting Don Rafael became — from vastly differing causes — almost as strong as that with which she imagined herself enduring the mocking and triumphant scrutiny of Ramirez. In her desolation the memory of Chinita rose before her. Oh, to steal with her into the hut and lean her head upon the breast of that poor waif, who must in her woman's consciousness be feeling something of the misery that day by day was becoming more agonizing and unendurable to Chata! The similarity of lot so unexpectedly revealed to her seemed to explain the irresistible attraction which

the foundling — who had apparently been so far removed from her by caste and circumstance — had always
possessed for her. At the thought, a tint of crimson
suffused her neck and face. How could she know but
that in the obscurity of Chinita's life as the adopted child
of a poor gate-keeper, even the foundling had perhaps
less to blush for than the supposed daughter of the
administrador?

Doña Rita had talked much during the early part of
her visit of the family affairs of the important personages
whom her husband served. Chata had heard the talk
with more entertainment than interest; but she was of a
reflecting and acute mind, and she began now to weave
theories and form conclusions which sometimes startled,
sometimes horrified her. Had she but caught the name
that had brought the shriek from Doña Rita's lips the evening the General Ramirez had talked with her! But without that clew her speculations were idle, and she tortured
herself in vain, yet with unconscious dissimulation hid her
wild and bitter thoughts beneath an exterior that to the
ordinary observer appeared one of thoughtless rather than
feigned and hysterical levity.

In the fear of meeting the General — though the temptation often came upon her to fly from the house lest he
might enter it — Chata avoided going into the streets, and
but that she feared it might prove a deadly sin she would
even have made an excuse of illness to remain from Mass.
But this might not be, though no temptation of a week-day
feast would draw her forth. And thus it happened that
she and Doña Rita were alone when the General Ramirez
for the second time visited the house.

Rosario by chance had accompanied her grandfather on
a visit. She had gone in the best of spirits; for she had
shown Chata a note from Ruiz, in which he declared that
though forbidden to ask for her until in the course of the
revolution he had acquired a competency, or her father
should lose his unjust prejudices against the Church party,
he should ever remain true to her, and should live only in
the hope of calling her his own. For the first time Chata
had embraced Rosario with a genuine sympathy with this
love which seemed so true and yet so hopeless, and had
watched her turn the corner leading to the plaza, when

she was suddenly aroused from a melancholy — which was actual repose compared to the state of excitement that had long possessed her — by the sound of a quick, imperious knock upon the street door; and glancing down, she saw the General Ramirez impatiently flicking his boot with the small cane he carried, and glancing up and down the street as if suspicious rather than desirous of observation. He had not seen her she was sure. Quick as thought she ran through the room, and passing through the window pushed open a door which led to the parapeted flat roof of the back building, and crouching behind a low brick wall prayed breathlessly to the Virgin for protection. It was a solitary place, where only a servant came sometimes to place a tub of water to be heated in the noonday sun, or to hang some household article for speedy drying. It was not likely, even were she wanted, they would think to look for her there. She was out of hearing, away from all the ordinary sounds of the house; no voice could reach her there, — not even that voice whose accents she could never forget, which had made her desolate.

As the time passed on and the stillness grew oppressive, and the sunbeams, which had at first annoyed and distracted her, stole to the wall and at last receded altogether, a sense of bitter forlornness and weariness overcame her; and ceasing from the vain repetitions of *Aves* and *Pater nosters*, Chata clasped her hands over her face, and resting it upon her knees burst into heartrending sobs.

Her passion did not continue long; it was perhaps too severe. It was arrested as by a blow, — by the sudden bang of a heavy door. She lifted her head and listened. Was it fancy, or did she hear the rattle of musketry? It was an unfamiliar sound, and yet she recognized it. What had happened? Was an enemy entering the town? Had the garrison revolted? Accounts of such events were too frequent to make these conjectures other than natural even to Chata's unwarlike mind. She hastily rose, pushed aside the bolt of the heavy door, and stepping into the corridor found herself face to face with Doña Rita.

" Ah, you are here! " that lady exclaimed in a hurried

and abstracted manner, far different from that which she would usually have worn at the discovery of such a misdemeanor. "I have been seeking you everywhere,—I could not send a servant. And now something has happened in the street, and he has rushed away without seeing you,—the Señor General Ramirez, I mean."

"I know whom you mean!" cried Chata. "Oh, my mother, why should I see him?" Then with wild passion she threw herself at Doña Rita's feet, and buried her face in her skirts and the flowing ends of her reboso. "Oh, tell me that it was not true—what I heard! I was in the garden the other evening as you talked! Oh, my mother, my mother!"

Doña Rita looked down at her in startled surprise, but almost instantly an expression of relief rose to her countenance. "Rise, child, rise!" she said in a low, not ungentle voice; yet there was an inexpressible lack of maternal solicitude in it, which struck to the heart of the suffering child. "Listen; be reasonable; have I not ever been kind to thee? I do not blame thee even now that thou art forced to repay me so ill; it is not thy fault."

"But you shall not be repaid so ill!" exclaimed Chata. "I will be your child forever. Oh, it is not possible that he—this strange man, who frightens me—would dare take me from you?"

"Bless me, *niña*, you are a strange one! If you but knew it, you have rare good fortune. A handsome lover and a rich dowry are not to be had every day for the asking. But you show a proper spirit, and one I should have expected after the good training you have had. Heaven knows what would have been the result had you been given to Doña Isabel, and allowed to run at large like most of the children of Our Blessed Lady. Yet it was a cruel trick my mother-in-law played me, and Rafael too! Well, well, it shall be brought home to him some day. Listen! was not that the sound of cannon? and my child abroad! Ave Maria Sanctissima!"

"Mother, be not afraid!" said Chata, desperately. "She and my grandfather will not yet have left Doña Francisca's, and that you know is quite away from the plaza or the barracks; they have only to cross the gardens and be home in a 'God speed us!' But as for me,

I am in more fright and misery than if a thousand guns
were levelled upon me. Do you not see, I know only
that I am not your child! Who am I? What is to become of me?"

"The last seems settled already," returned Doña Rita,
with an accent of chagrin which was almost spiteful;
"and the long and short of it is, child, that you were
sent to Doña Isabel, but that my mother-in-law had the
fancy you would be safer with me; and I, like a ten-
der-hearted simpleton, did not object to humoring her
whim, thinking at the same time I was doing a person
whom I loved a service she would know how to appre-
ciate, — and now when the time has come for recompense,
instead of gain, comes loss. There is nothing in this
world but vexation and disappointment."

"I cannot understand anything of this," said Chata,
with a deep sigh. She had risen to her feet, and was
looking pitifully at Doña Rita, who walked up and down
the corridor, listening to the distant and irregular firing, and interrupting her discourse with interjections and
doubts as to the safety of her daughter. "But when I
see my father, Don Rafael, I will ask him, or Doña
Feliz, — yes, Doña Feliz always loved me."

"Ay, but you must ask nothing," almost screamed
Doña Rita, running to Chata and seizing her by the
shoulders. "They will think it was I who betrayed the
secret; they will never forgive me. Oh, I should lead a
dog's life! You are not old enough to know how cruel an
angry husband or a baffled mother-in-law can be. And
poor Rosario —"

"What can it matter to Rosario?" interrupted Chata.
"Were you not lamenting that her dowry would be so
small? Will it not be double now that I shall not inno-
cently rob her?"

"Yes, yes," whispered Doña Rita, eagerly. "The General Ramirez promised me this very day that when you,
Chata, married Ruiz, he would make a gift to Rosario of all
my husband may bestow on you, and that as much more
should be given her on her wedding day, provided that the
secret of your birth be kept. It is useless to ask me his
reasons. He gave me none. I cannot guess them any
more than I can surmise why Doña Isabel would not re-

ceive you, and therefore you were thrust into my arms. Heavens, what a reverberation! the whole house shakes!"

"It is nothing," cried Chata, "but the slamming of a door. I hear the voices of Don José Maria and Rosario. Stay!" she added, grasping Doña Rita as she was about to run down the stairs. "I warn you that I will know all the truth. Your poor reasons shall not keep me from demanding it. Doña Feliz shall not refuse me!"

"Doña Feliz will do as she wills!" retorted Doña Rita. "But this I tell you, child, that the moment Ramirez knows that those who once crossed his plans are warned against him, you will be spirited away. Ramirez has his own purposes, and is not to be thwarted. He is already angry against Rafael and Doña Feliz for their attempted and long successful deception. He is a man of great and mysterious power, and knows not the meaning of the word forgive; and as sure as you stand there, if you disobey his commands sent you through me he will separate you at once from your home and friends, and bring ruin upon those who have cared for you."

Doña Rita spoke with that impressive eloquence and fire which upon occasion seems at the command of every Mexican. She stood with one foot on the corridor floor, the other upon the stair, which she was about to descend, and she had turned half-way round, stretching out her hands, and lifting her dark and anxious eyes to encounter and fix the gaze of Chata. Below, in the stone entrance-way, stood Rosario, volubly describing to a servant the dangers she and her grandfather had encountered. For the moment Doña Rita appeared in Chata's eyes like some timorous yet desperate animal standing between her and her young. "My Rosario, my poor child," said the mother in a low voice, "is her life to be blasted by you? Ramirez is in two minds now. One is to resent the frustration of his will, and be the mortal enemy of those who have sheltered you; the other to applaud and reward them. Upon your discretion all depends."

"But I shall go mad if I have only this to think upon," exclaimed Chata. "Who, who can tell me anything to make this dreadful revelation endurable, if not Don Rafael or Doña Feliz? Ah, yes, there is — there is the General."

"Surely!" replied Doña Rita. "Yes, my life, I am

coming"—to Rosario. "Yes, Chata, could I have found you to-day, you would have known all. Ask him what you like—it will please him. Oh, he is most considerate. Did he not show that by taking me into his confidence? Yes, yes, you are right; insist upon knowing all from him, and you shall tell me: who could understand, or sympathize so well? But as you love me and value the safety of Rafael, not a word to him or Doña Feliz. — Rosario! what an impatient one! What is there to see? If there is commotion in the street, keep back from the windows. Ay, who would have thought the troops would pass this way? God save us, we shall be killed! the whole town will be destroyed! The street is alive with soldiers. Bar the doors! close the shutters! Oh, what horror! Is it Comonfort returned? Is it a *pronunciamiento?* What new alarm is this?" Ejaculating these last sentences Doña Rita hurried downstairs and rushed from room to room, directing the bewildered servants and chiding Rosario, who, attracted by the sound of music and the trampling of men and horses, strove to peep through a crack in the shutters.

Chata, standing where she had been left at the head of the stairs, heard it all as though in a dream. She said over and over to herself, "It is the General I will ask. Yes, yes, I will have the courage! No word of mine shall bring danger on my father. Oh, why do I say 'my father'? Yes, I will say so; he is mine until he turns me away! Oh, what shall I do? Oh, Sanctissima Maria, help thy child! May I not say to Don Rafael, 'Here is thy poor little child; she will be the daughter of no other'? Oh, I know he would cling to me, fight for me; but that Doña Rita says would be ruin! Ah, I know the soldier is cruel and false, even if he is my father; he has been so to me—" She stopped suddenly, as though blasphemy had escaped her. Though she would not believe in her heart the testimony which her reason could not disallow, she was struck dumb by the mere possibility of filial disrespect and with the actual abhorrence which she felt in her bosom toward the man whom she instinctively feared.

As if to flee from her thoughts, she rushed into a room that faced upon the street, and with an impulse such as leads the desperate man to throw himself into a vortex of seething water, or into the thickest of battle, as her ear caught the sounds of commotion, she threw open the shutters and stepped out upon the balcony.

A scene of confusion met her eye, in which men on horseback and on foot seemed mingled indiscriminately, each individual struggling in an attempt to secure a personal advantage. Ranks were broken and scattered. Men and officers alike were for the most part un-uniformed, and to the uninitiated it was impossible to distinguish the adherents of one party from those of another, save by the wild cries of " *Religion y Fueros!* Long live Liberty! Long live Juarez!"

The name of Juarez had begun to be a familiar one in all ears; and even though it possessed not the magic of later years, the voices that uttered it thrilled with an intensity of purpose which seemed to infuse the word with life, — to make it a watchword for great and noble aspirations and deeds, not the mere echo of a name, a party cry to be shouted with frenzy to-day and execrated to-morrow.

It was impossible to tell what chance had forced the combatants upon that straggling highway. The struggle had begun at the barracks, when a party of horse had surprised the garrison, pouncing upon it from the hills like hawks upon their prey, and by the sheer force of surprise, rather than any superiority of numbers or courage, throwing it into a confusion which in spite of the efforts of the young officers speedily resulted in a panic. The soldiers who had been drilling before the town prison, — which had done duty as a fort, — after a feeble and confused attempt to defend its doors, had been driven into the plaza; and when Ramirez reached this, it was to find his own guns turned upon him. His servant had been leading his charger up and down the street, awaiting him; and catching a glimpse of his master as he hurried past an alley in which the groom had taken refuge, he called in mingled devotion and affright, —

"For God's sake, Señor! here is the black. Mount him for your life! another moment and we should have been discovered! Everybody knows Choolooke, and my life would not have been worth a cent had they caught sight of him. My faith, I like not these surprises! This

way, Señor! Around by the church there is an alley unguarded. They are fighting like ten thousand devils in
the plaza. It is madness to go there!"

Ramirez sprang into the saddle with a laugh, though his
lips were white and his eyes blazing with rage. It was a
new experience to him to be thus caught napping, — his
scouts must have played him false. His horse snorted
and bounded under him. In another moment he was in
the midst of the mêlée, and an electric shock seemed to
pass through friends and foes alike. There were wild
shrieks at sight of him. The exultant invaders echoed
with some dismay the name of Ramirez, the battle-cry
with which his followers made an attempt to rally, seizing
arms from the hands of their opponents, or using the pistols which had remained forgotten in their belts.

For a few moments the plaza appeared to be a veritable
battle-ground, though there was far more noise and confusion than actual fighting done. Ramirez knew with
infinite rage and shame that he would probably be forced
to yield the town, rather by strategy than superior numbers. It would have been an actual pleasure to him at
the moment to have seen his followers falling in their
blood, rather than flying disarmed, — even though they
should rally later and take a terrible revenge upon the
enemy. For an instant his presence stemmed the current
of retreat, but for an instant only. There had been a
secret dissatisfaction in his ranks, which the sight of
the well-known face of a popular leader, together with
panic, rapidly fermented into a *pronunciamiento ;* and
even as Ramirez, waving his sword above his head, entered
the street of the Orchards, he was saluted with the shout,
"Down with Ramirez! Down with the Clergy! Long
live Juarez! Long live Gonzales!" and through the dust
and smoke he caught sight of Vicente Gonzales, almost
unrecognizable under the grime of the hurried march and
the heat of excitement and success.

The two were so close together they could have touched
each other. One of those hand-to-hand encounters which
the history of Mexico proves were not infrequent even at
that date seemed inevitable, as they turned toward each
other with the fury of personal hatred added to partisan
animosity.

But at the moment when the two fiery steeds would
have clashed together, a woman threw herself before
Ramirez and caught his arm, calling aloud his name.
With that wonderful power of the bridle-hand possessed
by the horsemen of Mexico, Gonzales drew back his
charger and gazed full at his opponent, whom force more
potent than a blow seemed to arrest. The crowd surged
in ; Ramirez's horse was forced back. The woman
had fallen in the mêlée ; and with a curse upon her the
guerilla chieftain was swept onward in the current of
retreat.

Chata from the balcony had witnessed this incident in
the distance. She shrieked as the woman fell. An officer
who was speeding past looked up, — it was Fernando Ruiz.
"Coward !" she involuntarily cried, "to leave your General ! " She realized how impossible, having lost the first
moment of vantage, would be an attempt to control the
undisciplined and flying rabble when even the officers had
succumbed to panic ; and for the first time her sympathies
woke for Ramirez.

Yielding to the necessity of the moment the General
had put spurs to his horse. The bullets flew past him as
he sped over the highway ; yet he glanced up as he passed
the house, — he even drew rein for an instant in alarmed
surprise.

"Go in ! go in !" he cried. "What ! wilt thou be
killed in mere wantonness? Go in, I tell thee ! Are *both*
to be killed before my eyes to-day?" Chata sprang
through the open window in affright, obedient rather to
his stern yet imploring gesture than to his words. He
glanced back, fired a pistol toward a pair of Liberal
soldiers who had rapidly gained upon him, and without
the change of a muscle upon his set face, as one of them
pitched headlong from his plunging steed, continued his
flight and disappeared in the low bushes.

With horror Chata watched the death agony of the
wounded soldier. His comrade had not thought it worth
while to linger ; there might be booty or sport elsewhere.
All the church bells were being rung for the victory by
this time. The half hour's fight was over ; the fort had
been taken, the garrison routed, a *pronunciamiento* successful ; the town had changed its politics. A few dead

men were lying in the streets, a few wounded were bathing or plastering their bleeding heads or limbs; the closed houses were opening again; the street merchants were setting forth their wares; and one of the thousand phases of the revolution had passed.

The next day the Liberal soldiers were lounging about the streets; the boys were shouting, "Long live Gonzales!" as they went by, as they had shouted before, "Long live Ramirez!" A tranquil gayety pervaded the place. No one would have known its peace had ever been disturbed.

So lovely was the afternoon, and the distant sounds of the band playing in the plaza were so inspiring, that Doña Rita and her two charges sallied forth to visit the convent. They had often been there before. Rosario thought it dull to wait while her mother chatted at the grating with the soft-voiced nuns, but Chata watched them with awe. There was one whose pale face used to peer out wistfully through the semi-darkness; her voice and her large dark eyes, it seemed to Chata, were always softened by tears. She longed to touch the white hand which she sometimes saw raised to the sensitive lips, as if to check some ill-considered word.

Upon this day some rays of light piercing the barred window of the corridor rendered the features of the nun unusually distinct. A sense of bewilderment stole over Chata as she gazed upon them. Where had she seen them before? Who was this Sister Veronica?

The short time allowed for the interview expired; the attendant nun gave her hand to Doña Rita to kiss in token of dismissal, and turned away. As the Sister Veronica extended her hand in turn, Doña Rita caught it eagerly: "Forgive me! Forgive me! Oh, I had thought so ill of you," she said earnestly; "yet to think ill of you seemed to make my own life noble. Forgive me, Señorita Herlinda, that I ever thought you anything but a true and spotless saint!"

The eyes of the nun opened wide. "Forgive, forgive? I have nothing to forgive; why should not you — ay, all the world — condemn me?" she whispered hoarsely. "Oh, Rita, that face! that face!"

At that instant the slide was drawn and the white face and eager eyes of the nun disappeared.

Chata turned to look behind her where the nun had apparently directed her gaze. A woman was crouching on the door-sill. She was not old, though over her wonderful Spanish beauty some power of devastation seemed to have swept. She was carelessly but richly dressed, the disorder of her person seemingly according with that of her manner, — perhaps of her intellect; for though evidently a lady by birth, she lay in the sun, her head uncovered, her shawl thrown back from her shoulders, her hair, which was of a peculiar reddish brown, half uncoiled, twining like little serpents around her throat.

She glanced carelessly up as Doña Rita and the young girls passed her. Chata saw with surprise that one side of her face was bruised, and there was a deep scratch on her arm. Where had she seen before the glint of that shining hair? It flashed over her in a moment. This was the woman who had thrown herself upon Ramirez!

Chata involuntarily paused, but Doña Rita caught her hand and drew her away. She had motioned Rosario on before. Her very garments had rustled with disdain as she passed the prostrate woman.

"Such as these one can at least be certain of," she said sententiously. It was not a pleasant thing to own one's self mistaken. Chata detected chagrin in the tone of her voice: was she piqued that she had misjudged Sister Veronica? Then she remembered with a start what the new interest of the moment had driven from her mind, — the name by which her mother had addressed the nun: it was of the Señorita Herlinda that her mother had asked pardon!

A feeling of awe crept over her. She had seen Doña Isabel's beautiful and sainted daughter, around whose name hung so much romance and mystery. And oh the sadness of that face! the wistfulness of those eyes! the appealing agony of that voice!

When they reached the house the door was ajar; there was a mild excitement within. A familiar voice saluted their ears. Doña Rita clutched Chata's arm and whispered, "Not a word, I command thee!" and with a glance of mingled entreaty and menace followed Rosario to greet Don Rafael with exclamations of welcome and delight.

Chata took with icy fingers the hand he extended at sight of her and bent over it with tears and kisses. "My father, my own father!" she whispered. Even had she been at liberty to do so, she would not for the world have broken the spell of those words.

"My patron saint!" cried Don Rafael, regarding her with puzzled fondness, "what has come to the child?" He caught her on his arm and held her from him. Her eyelids lowered, her color rose beneath his gaze. Presently he released her and turned away. He had not kissed her. Had he forgotten? Had some new, deep feeling withheld him? Chata felt cold and faint; he too had muttered under his breath, "That face! that face!" and *he* had spoken those words of *her*.

XXV.

For many days following the unexpected event which closed the feast of Juana's marriage, an old proverb went the rounds of the gossips of Tres Hermanos: "She who would handle the wild-cat should wear steel gloves." Doña Isabel had heard it perhaps, though it was not likely to reach her ears then: and assuredly she had reason to remember it.

Perhaps when Chinita crossed the court and followed Doña Isabel upstairs to her own room, dazzling visions flitted before her of being clasped in the embrace of her patroness, and being called by the name which to her was sovereign. But nothing of the sort occurred. Doña Isabel threw herself into a chair as if exhausted, and bent her face upon her hands, leaving the child standing so long regarding her in silence that at length her impatient spirit rose in rebellion, and she said, "The Señora surely brought me here for something more than to stand like a drowsy hen waiting for morning."

Doña Isabel raised her head at these words, which though impatient did not strike her as impertinent, — she was too well acquainted with the characteristic speech of her inferiors, rich in quaint phrases and figures drawn from familiar objects, — and regarding the girl with that curious mixture of admiration and repulsion which never entirely disappeared, she replied, —

"Thou art a proud child. Humility would better become thee. Hast thou no other name than Chinita, which I hear all call thee?"

"I was baptized like any other Christian," cried Chinita, indignantly. "And as for surname," she added recklessly, "if I am not Garcia, you Señora, will tell me!"

Doña Isabel's lips compressed; no effort of her will could prevent the falling of her eyelids, — an actual fear of the girl seized her; yet she was fascinated. She said not a word, and presently Chinita began to laugh in a low, triumphant tone, which was to Doña Isabel like the mocking of a thousand devils.

"Hush, hush!" she said violently at length. "You distract, you madden me!"

She caught up a candle, took the girl's hand and drew her impetuously into the corridor. She tried several doors, and opened the first that yielded. It was not until they stood within the room that Doña Isabel knew it was that (long deserted, half unconsciously avoided) of Herlinda. She started, and clasped her hand over her heart. Then as if scorning her weakness, pointed to the bed, and without a word turned from the room.

With a sense of wild exultation Chinita saw she was to sleep in a bed, like a woman of quality; in the very bed of the daughter, whose name, like that of a saint, was spoken with bated breath by the vulgar, and was perhaps too sacred for utterance by those who had loved her.

The little structure of brass, with its mattresses and pillows, its linen and lace, was unpretentious enough, but Chinita walked around it and eyed it almost in awe, as if it had been the throne of a princess. The candle was beginning to flicker in its socket when she at last lay down, adjusting her head to the unaccustomed pressure of the pillows with some difficulty, saying to herself with an impatient smile, "What a poor creature I am! Even the things I have longed for hurt more than please me to learn to use. But there must be still greater things to conform to, and I shall do it. Oh, yes, Sanchita thought she could ride in a coach, and be taken for a lady as well as another; and I who was born a lady must forget I have been ever a Sanchita. It should not be hard!"

Chinita had slept far better upon the preceding night upon a sheepskin. Her excitement and the unusual comfort of the bed kept her wakeful; and at early dawn she was up, peeping into the wardrobe, where long-disused dresses and other garments were hanging. She took down one of bright silk and put it on, and thought how exactly it fitted her. She could scarcely see herself in the dim mirror, and she went to the door to open it for the admission of more light, and with a momentary fright found herself a prisoner.

She decided in a moment that Doña Isabel had no intention of detaining her beyond the sleeping hours, yet a feverish impulse seized her to escape at once. That any one should hold her at a moment's disadvantage was intolerable to her. Without thinking of the dress she had on, she glanced around her eagerly for means of egress. The window was barred, but there was a door that opened into an adjoining chamber, into which she passed hastily, finding the door that opened on the corridor actually ajar. As her way was open, she was in no hurry to depart, but stood balancing herself on one foot, holding by one hand to the door-post, and with the other pushing back her hair that she might see clearly into the court.

Not a creature was astir; the very bird that was in a cage hanging near her stood silently on his perch, with his head on one side, gazing through the bars as if in pensive wonderment at the silence.

Chinita had a feeling that the world had been transformed with her; she was half terrified, yet amused, and longed for some one to speak to. Could she speak the old words, the accustomed sounds? Was she indeed Chinita and not another? Had Rosario or Chata been under the same roof, she would have been tempted to run to them at once with the query; but there was no one who would know what she meant if she put such a question to them. They would only laugh and stare and pass on. Ah, there was one who could not pass on! At a bound she was on the stairs, and in a minute stood at the door of the stranger's room. It was open; he liked the air. Early as it was, Selsa had left him; so without let or hindrance Chinita seated herself at the foot of the bed, and with expressive pantomime began to inquire into the state of the wounded shoulder.

The young man looked at her in amaze. This was the strangest of the strange visitors he had had. At first he did not recognize her in the incongruous dress; but a glance at the elfin face and the mop of curls recalled to his mind the name Chinita, and he held out his hand with a gesture of welcome and surprise, and even found words in his meagre stock of Spanish to ask her where she had been.

"I have been in my home," she answered with a great show of dignity. "Do you not see, I am a lady, a grand lady?"

She had risen and spread out the silken dress with her hands. The young man caught one of the locks of her hair, and pulled it teasingly, "*No comprendo*, I don't understand. Tell me where is your mother? Where is your *padre?*"

Such a mixture of languages should have been unintelligible, but Chinita understood very well, and with a sudden prompting of the spirit of mischief which was never far from her, replied, "*Padre mio muerto! Americano guero, como Ud.! Oh, si Americano!*"

"What!" cried the young man in English, "Your father dead! An American? Fair like me?" He had clutched the lock of hair so tightly, as he rose in his bed in his excitement, that her head was quite near him. "Are you quite sure? Can it be possible?" adding, with sudden remembrance that intelligent though she was it was impossible she should understand his foreign tongue, and angry as he saw her at his vehemence, it was unlikely she should care to divine his meaning, "*Niña bonita*, pretty child, pardon me! Your father an *Americano?* Well, that is wonderful! I *Americano*,—I, Ashley Ward. *Pardona mi!*"

Chinita was not to be at once appeased; but she saw with inward delight that he was much impressed by her claim jestingly set forth to American parentage, and there was something in the sound of his name that recalled to her mind the man who had been murdered so many years ago. She began with a thousand gestures, which made somewhat intelligible her voluble Spanish, to give an account of him. The young man listened with intense excitement, anathematizing his ignorance of the language in which she spoke, yet convinced that chance had led him to the very spot which he had had it in his mind to seek. In the interest of her narration, Chinita forgot the assertion she had made; but her listener more than once supposed that she alluded to it, and looked intently upon her face to catch a glimpse of some expression that should remind him even of the race to which the man of whom she spoke had belonged. But there was nothing. The features, expression, color, were those of a Mexican of mixed Spanish and Indian types, with nothing individual other than a weird beauty and vivacity, and the peculiar hair which had suggested the name that even Doña Isabel did not seek to disassociate from her. For at the moment when the interest of her narrative was at its height, and Ashley Ward had risen on his pillows and was following her every gesture with mute and rapt attention, the lady of the mansion entered, calling breathlessly, "Chinita! Chinita!" suddenly arresting her steps, as she caught the concluding words: "And so he was killed! And they say it was not a man, but the Devil who did it. But for my part I don't believe it, for the ghost of the American can be seen under the tree or at the old reduction-works any night; and it's not likely Señor Satan would give so much liberty to a soul he seemed so anxious to get."

Chinita had finished her sentence with a certain defiance, for she felt guilty before Doña Isabel, — not so much for being found in the room of the wounded guest, as because of her borrowed attire. But Doña Isabel did not seem to notice that. "Thou art wrong to come here," she said; "thou art wrong to talk like a scullery-maid of things thou dost not understand. What did I hear thee say of an American as I came in?"

"Did I say American?" retorted Chinita with a laugh at the thought of the jest she had made, for the idea of falsehood did not occur to her. "Ah, yes! I told him the American was my father! He would have believed me even had I said Señor San Gabriel. Oh, it is a grand diversion to see his eyes open with wonder! Selsa says he is dumb and deaf and understands nothing, but there is not a word I say that he does not understand quickly enough; and he knows — " But she ceased suddenly, for Doña Isabel was deadly white. She had turned to the American almost fiercely, and demanded hoarsely, "What has this child told you? What tale has she poured into your ears, wild, improbable, — the dreams of a child, filled with the superstitious tales of the common people? What have you heard? What have you believed?"

Ashley Ward looked at her in some surprise at her

vehemence. Her gestures did not translate to him the
purport of words which had not even a familiar sound.
After a moment he shook his head, and said slowly : " *No
comprendo !* I do not understand Spanish."

Doña Isabel breathed freely ; her rigid face relaxed ;
she almost smiled. " Foolish child," she said to Chinita ;
" he does not understand our language. Come, thou
shalt have chocolate with me. I am not angry, though
thou art a runaway."

Chinita seldom afterward found Doña Isabel so gracious when she had committed a fault ; but she discovered
at night, when she was left in her room alone, that that
particular escapade was not to be repeated. The door
which led to the adjoining room was locked, as well as that
which opened upon the corridor. She shook the bars of
the window in impotent rage. She opened her mouth to
scream, to wake the echoes with the name of Pedro, but
at a second thought refrained, and went and lay quietly
down like a baffled animal reserving its strength for the
time when its prey should be near. She did not sleep.
She had done nothing to tire her, and also she had
dropped into slumber more than once during the day in
the silence of Doña Isabel's room, where she had sat
watching her, as she opened drawers and boxes, and as if
by stealth moved various articles to a large trunk, turning
from it with affected carelessness when Doña Feliz or any
servant entered.

Chinita was living over again in her mind the long monotonous day, feeling as if a thunder-clap or some con-
vulsion of Nature must break upon the feverish stillness,
when she heard a tap at her window. The sash was
already raised, but she sprang noiselessly from the bed
and across the floor, and thrust her hand through the bars,
for she divined that Pedro had called her.

" It is but for a moment, *niña*," he whispered, almost
humbly, as he kissed her hand. " But tell me, art thou
happy ; art thou content ? "

" Why should I not be happy ? " she asked. " I have
worn a silk gown all day long, and have eaten and drunk
things so dainty a humming-bird might sip them ; and
Doña Isabel has dared not say no to me, — though she
does not love me, Pedro, and I love not her."

"Then thou wilt come again to poor Pedro, who does love thee?" queried the gatekeeper in a tremulous and doubting voice.

She withdrew her hand, tossing her head scornfully. "No," she said. "You know how the black cat strayed once into the hut, and though Florencia drove him away, and would strike and frighten him if he stole as much as a morsel of dried beef, he would come back and curl himself under the bench, and lie there upon the cold floor, though he might have gone to the granaries and had his fill of fat mice, and plenty of straw to lie on. Well, Pedro, I am the black cat, and I will stay in Doña Isabel's house because it is my humor, and I cannot tell why, and there is an end of it."

Pedro sighed; but presently he said in his slow way, "Well, well! God is God, — may he care for thee! Pedro can be of no more use to thee; the guitar that does n't accord with the voice is best hung upon the wall. Farewell, Chinita; God grant thee so much good that thou needst not remember thy old friends."

Chinita laughed. "Thou art vexed, Pedro; but I love thee, and I would love thee more if thou wouldst tell me the name of my father or my mother." Pedro shook his head. "Oh, I am sure thou dost not know; thou couldst not have kept a secret all these years!" She looked at him sharply, but he was not the man to begin unwary defences, which might to a keen eye expose the weakest spots in his armor. He stood for some moments quite silent. Chinita saw by the moonlight that his face had lines upon it she had never seen before. Her conscience smote her, yet she could not say she was sorry for the fate which had parted them, — for it did not occur to her any more than to him that he might question the act of Doña Isabel, and refuse to yield the child he had sheltered from its birth.

"What secret should the tool have?" he asked at length bitterly. "It is taken up and laid by as the master wills. Years ago I used to think I was a man, but since then I have been but a dog to watch and to guard; but the watch is over, and the dog may be a man again. That would please you, would it not? There is better work than to sit at a gate and see the soldiers come and go, and never hear so much as the echo of a shot; or as much as know why there is a smell of blood always in the air, and men are dragged away to death. Gonzales told me the struggle is for liberty; I can do no more for you, and I will go and see. Who knows what I may find beyond there? Who knows what news I may bring to you?"

The face usually so stoical in its expression was lighted as if by an inward fire. For the first time Chinita knew that this man too had his ambitions, the stronger that they had been repressed for years. Would he join the next band of soldiers or bandits that came that way? The thought struck her comically, like a touch of the mock heroic; yet it thrilled her. She would have liked to be a soldier herself. She would have chosen to be a boy to go with him; and yet she was glad they were to part, if that indeed was his meaning, — that her foster father would no longer sit at the gate.

He had touched her hand and bent to kiss it humbly, as he might have saluted Doña Isabel herself. Then he thrust a long narrow package through the bars, muttered softly, " *Adios,*" and stole noiselessly away.

Though Chinita saw him at his old place on the morrow, she understood that an eternal farewell had been made to their old relations and their old life. All that remained of them was contained in the package of trinkets he had brought her, — the coral beads, the few irregular pearls, the many-hued reboso, and the ribbons she had prized and which in his simplicity he had thought she would regret. Indeed, she had recognized them with a thrill of delight; nothing half so bright or costly had been offered her in the new life she had imagined would be so rich and brilliant. Yet she clung to it as hers of right, the more firmly after turning over and over, again and again, the dainty swaddling clothes, which she had never seen before, but which she knew Pedro had yielded to her as the sole possessions with which she had come to him, — possessions useless in themselves, but invaluable to her as proofs that she came from no plebeian stock. She wondered if her mother had arrayed her in them to cast her out, — and though she was of no gentle mould, her mind revolted from the thought. Then, had her father disowned her; or had an enemy filched her from her cradle, and unwilling

to be guilty of her blood, left her in the first hands he
had encountered? She ran over in her mind all the tales
she had heard of mysterious disappearances, — and they
were not a few, — but none would fit the case; and surely
a hue-and-cry would have been made at the abduction of a
rich man's infant.

Chinita wrapped up the clothes and hid them away in
impatient despair. Once she thought of taking them to
Doña Isabel; but what would be gained by that? That
her protectress knew the secret of her birth she was convinced, not by any course of reasoning, but by the simple
fact that she had assumed the charge of her as her right.
The girl did not know how baseless are apt to be the
caprices of a great lady.

The days passed wearily to the eager child. They
would have been intolerable — for she was always alone
or with Doña Isabel, who gave her no certain status as
equal or inferior, and with whom she was feverishly defiant, or seized with sudden tremors of awe or actual fear—
but that she knew Don Rafael had gone to bring his family
home. She longed to pour her secret thoughts into the
ears of Chata, to show the infant clothes and hear her
comments and suggestions. It appeared to her that Chata
would certainly penetrate the gloom, and in her sweet simplicity throw some light upon the mystery which enveloped
her. Besides, the wilful girl exulted in the anticipation
of dazzling the eyes of Rosario and Doña Rita by her
connection with Doña Isabel. She was shrewd enough
to see it had greatly increased her importance in the estimation of the servants and employees. Even Don
Rafael, before he went away, had seized an opportunity
to ask her whether she was content, and afterward had
never failed to bow to her with grave politeness when
they met.

Once a strange thought had been set in the child's mind:
it returned and vexed her again and again. Doña Feliz
had come into the room when in an unusual mood of devotion Chinita had knelt to pray before the image of the
Virgin, before which, though she did not know it, had been
poured forth so many bitter cries. Feliz started as she
saw her, and Chinita rose to her feet.

"Do not rise," said Doña Feliz; "learn, child, to pray.

Many amens must perforce reach Heaven; it is well to begin thy task young."

"What task?" Chinita queried. "I shall have something more to do than to pray all my life. That is for saints and nuns; and even Pedro would not take me for a saint."

"But thou couldst still be a nun," said Doña Feliz, with a peculiar smile; "and why shouldst thou not be?"

"Why not?" ejaculated Chinita. "Because I will not!" Then seized with a sudden terror, she cried, "Is that why Doña Isabel has taken me from Pedro? Is it to shut me up to pray for her and the wicked brother she loved so much? Selsa told me she had set her own daughter to free his soul from purgatory, and is not that enough? I'll not do it. My knees ache when I kneel; I yawn, I fall asleep. I cannot bear to be forever in one place. It is to go away, to see strange sights, to wear silk and lace every day, as the *niña* Herlinda must have done, — see, here are some of her dresses still, — it is for this, and because I was born for such things, that I stay with Doña Isabel; it is not to pray. I care not to pray, nor sing hymns, nor dress saints. I will go to her and tell her so!"

Doña Feliz caught the arm of the excited child. "I am your friend," she said. "Speak not a word of what I have said. Perhaps it was a foolish thought; but many more beautiful than you have entered convents, and perhaps have been happy."

"Is the Señorita Herlinda happy?" asked Chinita, her excitement calmed by the thought of another. "Selsa told me once, — it was the night Antonita saw the ghost of the American, when she came back from the mountain, — Selsa told me a witch had laid a spell upon her the day he was murdered, — a witch who loved the foreigner; and that the *niña* Herlinda drooped and withered and would have died, but that a fever carried away the evil woman before she could read her into her grave."

"The witch!" ejaculated Doña Feliz, mystified. This was a superstition of which she had heard nothing. "Who was the witch?"

"How can I tell?" answered Chinita. "Chata knows more of her than I. It is to her old Selsa told her tales; she is never cross to Chata. But after the American was killed I know the witch used to read and read and read

15

strange words to the poor *niña*, and she grew paler and paler, and more and more sad."

"And the witch died?" queried Feliz, thinking of Mademoiselle La Croix.

"Yes, in a good hour," answered Chinita, energetically. "But I forgot; you must know it all, Doña Feliz. Tell me," — with her old gossiping habit, — "tell me, did the Señorita love the American? Was it for him she pined away; or because she was bewitched; or was it because the Señora would not let her marry the Señor Gonzales, but would send her to the convent to pray for the wicked Don Leon?"

"*Quien sabe?* Who knows?" answered Doña Feliz, in the non-committal phrase a Mexican finds so convenient. "It is not for us to chatter of the Señorita Herlinda. Peace be with her! and have a care how you mention her name to Doña Isabel." Her brow contracted as she thought how many conjectures, how much gossip of which she had known nothing, had been busy with events she had believed quite passed from remembrance.

XXVI

ASHLEY WARD had been, an involuntary though perhaps not entirely an unwilling guest, at Tres Hermanos a month or more before it dawned upon him that he was not a perfectly welcome one. Throughout his illness, which had been prolonged by the peculiar nursing and diet to which he had been for the first time in his life subjected, he had, though left almost entirely to the care of Selsa, been provided with luxuries and delicacies that even his imperfect knowledge of the country and situation enabled him to know were rare and costly, and most difficult to obtain. Doña Isabel Garcia was like a princess in her quiet dignity and in her gifts ; and like a princess too, he grew to think, in the punctiliousness with which, every day, she sent to inquire after his health, and the infrequency with which she entered to express a hope that he lacked nothing. She never touched his hand, seldom indeed turned her eyes upon him when she spoke, and never smiled ; and when she left him he inwardly raged, and vowed he would leave the hacienda on the morrow, even though he should die from the exertion. But his wound was slow in healing ; the fever had sapped his strength ; he was alone, and no opportunity of securing escort presented itself. He was virtually a prisoner. And besides, after these periods of vexation he would fall into a fit of musing, which would end in the resolve never to leave Tres Hermanos until certain doubts were set at rest, which from day to day grew more and more perplexing.

The nurse, Selsa, was more communicative than the Indian peasant woman is apt to be. She had been employed constantly in and about the great house in positions of some trust, and had lost that awe of superiors, which held the mere common people dumb. In a sense, indeed, she felt herself one of the family, privileged to use gentle insistence with the sick, even against their aristocratic wills, and to be present, though eyes and ears were to be as blind and deaf as the walls around her, while matters of family polity were at least hinted at, if not openly discussed. She had in fact been to the house of Garcia "the confidential servant," without which no Mexican household is complete, — one of those peculiar beings who however false, cruel, deceitful, and thievish with the world in general is silent as the grave, devoted even unto death, true as the lode-star, to the person or family which she serves.

There was something in the personality of this wrinkled crone, growing out of these relations, which early impressed the young American; and gradually he grew to feel that he was face to face with an oracle, had he but the magic to unseal her lips, as the witch-like Chinita had had to change her air of vexed though friendly equality into unobtrusive yet unmistakable deference. Other servants who came and went spoke with some envy and spite of the sudden elevation of the gatekeeper's foster-child. But Selsa, sitting in the doorway of the sick man's room, combing out her long black locks, — for that, though she never succeeded in smoothing them, was her favorite occupation, — would glance askance at Ward and say, —

"Be silent! the Señora knows what she does. Go now! she has a heart like any other Christian. What was to become of the girl, now that Pedro will be leaving for the wars? Would you have Don 'Guardo think we are barbarians here, who would leave the innocents to be devoured like lambs by the coyotes?"

Don 'Guardo was the name Selsa had evolved from Ward, which she had perhaps believed to be the foreign contraction of Eduardo; and as Ashley, with boyish enthusiasm easily acquiring the limited vocabulary of those around him, began to relieve the monotony of his convalescence by listening to their conversations, and asking some idle questions, he found himself answering to the convenient appellation and alluding to himself by it, until it became as familiar to his ears as his own baptismal name, and certainly conveyed far more friendliness to him than the formal Señor Ward, which Don Rafael and his mother rendered with infinite stumbling over the unattainable W.

There was a subdued excitement throughout the hacienda upon the day that Don 'Guardo first appeared at the great gateway. Pedro was sitting there in the dull, dejected manner suggestive of loss, or waiting, or both ; and it was only when Florencia, with an exclamation, twitched his sleeve that he looked up.

"*Maria Sanctissima!*" he stammered, staggering to his feet. Ashley stood in the dim light in the rear of the deep vestibule, with his hand on Pepé's shoulder, — for the boy had been called to attend him, — but with a sudden faintness he had paused to rest against the stone wall hung with serpents. Ashley was a handsome youth, but in Pedro's eyes a thousand times more startling than the most hideous snake or savage beast. So had he seen John Ashley stand a hundred times or more, not pale and trembling, but full of life and joy. Was this his sad ghost, come with reproachful eyes to haunt him?

"It is the Señor American," said Florencia. "My life! how pale he looks! Go, go, Pepito! bring him hither before the carriage of my Señora drives in ; here it is at the very gate."

Pedro instantly recovered his usual stoicism. "Wait, Señor!" he said, "you are well placed where you are. The carriage can pass and not throw an atom of dust on you." And at that moment the feet of the horses and the rattle of wheels were heard on the stone paving, and the hacienda carriage was driven rapidly into the courtyard. As it passed, Ashley caught a glimpse of Doña Isabel — how pale and statuesque! — and beside her a creature radiant in triumph, who nodded to Pedro as she passed ; her smile seeming to say, "Behold me!" Hers was not an ignoble pride, but the wild exultation of an eaglet that had been chained to earth, and for the first time had tried its wings in the empyrean. That morning Doña Isabel had said, "Chinita, thou shalt go with me ;" and though the lady's brows had risen a little when with unconscious audacity the girl had taken the seat beside her, and not that opposite, where Doña Feliz was wont to sit, she said nothing. "The child is pale," she thought, "and needs the air ; there is no one to heed that she sits beside me."

It would be hard to tell what were the thoughts of Chinita ; they were a sudden delirium after the intense quiet of the semi-imprisonment, which she had borne with stoical fortitude for the sake of a dimly seen future of power. In this enforced quiet, day by day, her ambitions were shaping

themselves; the dominant passion of her being was seeking a point from which she might have advantage over all
the narrow field within the range of her mental vision.
As yet her aspirations knew no name; they were mere
vague, impatient longings, or rather impatient spurning of
the old ignoble conditions of life. To ride in a carriage
was an intoxication to her, because the low-born peasant
went afoot. She chafed in a very thraldom of inaction
because the high-born toiled not. She loved the rustle of
a gaudy silk, while her hand shrank from the contact of
the stiff and rustling fabric, because such attire was only
for the rich and great. As undefined as had been the joy
with which she had heard she was a Garcia, was still the
delight of each fresh conquest that she made. No eager
virtuoso groping in the dark among undescribed treasures
could be more ignorant yet more wildly anticipative of the
glories the daylight should discover than she of what the
future should reveal.

From where Don 'Guardo and his attendant stood, they
could see Doña Isabel and Chinita as they descended from
the carriage. Doña Isabel, without glancing around, ascended the stairs to her own apartment. Chinita followed
a step or two behind, then turned and paused. Her quick
eye scanned the little group that had gathered in the court.
Ashley Ward himself was startled by the change that had
passed over her since he had seen her last. What had
been elfish in her wild abandonment of bearing had become a subtle grace of manner, which gave piquancy to a
hauteur that counterfeited the dignity of inherent nobleness. "The gypsy has borrowed the air of a queen!"
was the thought of the American. He felt Pepé quiver
beneath his hand, and looking at him saw a sullen fire
in his dark, slumberous eyes, though his lips were white
and his dusky face ashen as if a chill had seized him.
The girl had overlooked him and all the plebeian crowd,
and her eyes rested in a triumphant challenge on Ashley.
She smiled, and a ray of sunlight darted down and reddened the crisp and straggling tendrils of her hair. The
smile or the sunlight dazzled him; he leaned heavier on
Pepé's shoulder. She reminded him of a Medusa idealized, of incarnate passion surrounded by the halo of
radiant youth.

Ashley was roused by a sudden movement of Pepé, who had for the moment forgotten his station, and impetuously thrown himself upon a bench in an attitude of impotent grief and rage ; then he sprang to his feet, and again placed his shoulder under Ashley's hand. Once more he was the mere stock and stick ; but Ashley had discovered in him the soul and heart of a man.

" Poor fool ! " he thought, with a sort of anger mingled with his pity ; " here is a touch of the tragic in this little comedy, which the wily little peasant is inspired to play so daintily. She appears to have bewitched me with the rest ; I can't keep the thought of her, or rather of her words, out of my head, — and yet I have only a word to build a whole fabric of theory upon."

These thoughts had passed through his mind in an instant, — the instant in which Chinita had lightly run up the stone steps after Doña Isabel, and in which Ashley and Pepé had reached the broad gateway of the hacienda. Ashley sank upon the stone bench where Pedro was wont to sit, and Pepé leaned sullenly against the rough wall. Both looked in silence over the village, across the fields, the narrow line of cottonwood trees and yellow mud which marked the bed of a torrent in the rainy season and a waste of desolation in the long drought, and onward still to the gray and barren mountains whose distant peaks of purple pierced the deep blue of the cloudless sky. The scene to Pepé was as old as his years, too familiar to distract for a moment his tortured mind ; but Ashley beheld it in a sort of rapture. Perhaps any glimpse of the outer world would have charmed him after his unwonted imprisonment ; but the fertility of the valley, this gem set in the broad expanse of bare and sterile Mexico, was a revelation to him of that wonderful productiveness and beauty which in his journeyings he had often heard of but had never encountered, until at last he had believed that the horrors of war, in its years of duration, had swept over the land and blasted it. But here was one spot at least that had escaped, — such a spot as he had pictured for months, and sought in vain.

For a time he gazed upon it in simple admiration, then at first almost unconsciously began to look about him for certain landmarks. Yes, here at his back was the great pile of buildings; here on the sandy slope in front, the village of adobe thatched with knife-grass; there along the line of the watercourse, the few straggling huts of the miners and laborers; there away to the right, the low walls of the reduction-works with its tall brick chimney, and in its rear the gaping cleft of the mountain which marked the entrance to the mine. All now was silent and deserted; yet for a moment he seemed to look upon it with other eyes, and to see the trains of laden mules filing in and out of the wide gateways, and to trace the black smoke rising in a column to the cloudless sky. "This must be the place!" he inwardly exclaimed; and drawing from his breast-pocket a flat case of papers, he selected from them a torn and yellow letter, and read it slowly over, ever and anon raising his eyes to identify some point in the description, which a hand as young, more firm, more resolute than his own, had in an hour of leisure so accurately written years before. The date of the missive was gone, and with it the name of this new place in which the writer seemed to have found an earthly paradise, — "not wanting," as he said at the close of the letter, "an Eve to be at once the gem of this perfect setting, and the inaccessible star to which poor mortals may raise longing eyes, but may never hope to win."

Ashley smiled as he read the words. Who could this divinity have been? But for other letters that had been put into his hands he would have thought the paragraph mere bathos, boyish gush, and sentiment; but it was a prelude to what might prove a strange and fateful series of events. Somewhere here his cousin had years ago lived and loved and been done to death; and his mission was to trace the sequence of these events, and to learn whether or no with John Ashley had passed away all possible influence upon the fortunes of his own life.

Until within a few months such questions had never occurred to him. The John Ashley whom he had dimly remembered had been murdered years before; and so had ended an adventurous career, which had been his own choice, or perhaps his evil destiny. To Ward, as to others, that had been the sum and substance of the tragedy which had thrown a gloom for a time over all the family, and had stricken a proud mother to the heart. She had

suffered years in silence, the name of her wayward son
never passing her lips ; her young daughter had grown up
with no knowledge of her brother but his name. It was
she who after the mother's death had found these letters,
and entreated her cousin to seek the fatal spot of John
Ashley's death, — surely there must be somewhere records
that would give the exact location, — and to make inquiries
for the wife, and for the possible child, of whom he wrote in
his last short letter, full of passionate appeal to his mother
in behalf of the young creature who for him had forfeited
the confidence, perhaps the love, of her own. "Herlinda!
Herlinda! Herlinda!" was the burden of the letter. "The
name rings in my ears," Mary Ashley had said. "How
could my mother have been deaf to it? She thought
of those people as barbarous, false, cruel, treacherous.
But what matters that to me, if there is among them one
who has my brother's blood, or one who loved him?"

"The marriage laws of those countries are strange,"
Ward had ventured to say. "Perhaps your mother
feared complications which could but bring disgrace and
misery."

"I do not fear them," said Mary Ashley, proudly. "It
is a wild country for a woman to go to, but if you will not
investigate this matter, I will brave any inconvenience,
any danger, to do so. I cannot live with this tantalizing
fear in my heart."

The idea that tormented Mary seemed at best that of a
mere possibility to Ashley, — the possibility of an event
which, as the mother had seen, might if proved bring far
more pain than joy, especially at this late date; yet it
worked upon his mind gradually, as it had upon Mary's
suddenly, — perhaps the more surely because he personally
profited by the supposition that his cousin had died unwed.
By his aunt's will he had been left the share in her property that John would have inherited, on condition that
neither he nor any legitimate heir should appear to claim it.

People shrugged their shoulders and smiled pityingly.
"Poor soul, had she then doubted her son's death?"

The news had reached Mrs. Ashley in an irregular way ;
the war had supervened, and particulars had been few and
far from exact. But later, through some business house,
inquiries had been made and some few books and almost

worthless articles of clothing had been obtained from an alcalde, who swore they had been the dead man's sole effects. Certainly the proofs had been irregular but sufficient. What could one expect from such a lawless set of uncivilized renegades, who knew nothing of civil or international law, and were bent on the sole task of exterminating one another? They smiled at the condition in the will, and pitied the poor woman who could thus hope against hope. Ashley Ward himself, the orphan nephew whom his aunt had loved with a jealous devotion, which at times wearied him by its suspicions and exactions, at first smiled also. But when Mary brought to him the fragments of three old letters to read, just as his mind was filled with plans for a career which the possession of ample wealth and leisure seemed to justify, and which in poverty he could never have dared aspire to, he grew thoughtful, moody at times, — then suddenly his own impetuous, generous self again.

" I will go to Mexico, Mary," he said, " and bring you word of your brother's life there. No doubts shall shake their spectre fingers at me in my prosperity, nor torment your loving and anxious soul."

" Good, true cousin! " was all she answered. She perhaps did not realize what effect upon the prospects of Ashley the results of this journey might possibly have; they dawned upon her little by little as the days went by and no news came of him.

The daring traveller had been obliged to enter Mexico at some obscure point. The Liberal government under Juarez was installed at Vera Cruz; the Conservatives held the City of Mexico; and the length and breadth of the country was in a state of riot and ferment, torn and devastated by roving bands who changed their politics as readily as their encampments. Ashley's journey through the Republic was like a passage over smouldering coals between two fires, and constant address and fearlessness were required to avoid collision with either faction, — his ignorance of the language and causes of contention perhaps serving him a good turn in making natural the indifference and absolute impartiality which he could never so successfully have assumed had his sympathies been ever so slightly biassed.

In the distracted state of the country it was almost a hopeless task to endeavor to trace the movements of an alien who had lived in it but a short time, and that years before. If any record had been made of the exact place and mode of John Ashley's death, it certainly had been unofficial, and retained no place in the archives of either the Mexican or American government.

Ashley Ward was at first appalled by the unexpected difficulties that he encountered. Inquiries brought to his knowledge the existence of several haciendas bearing the name of Los Tres Hermanos; and these he successively visited, reserving to the last that which lay in the most isolated and mountain-begirt district, — a point which it seemed impossible could, amid wild and sterile surroundings, offer the panorama of beauty and fertility which the pen of his cousin had described. He would perhaps have abandoned his search, at least for that unpropitious time, but for a re-perusal of the first letter which contained neither news nor descriptions of importance, but in which was mentioned the fact that the writer had been offered employment by the family of Garcia. The owners of the distant hacienda of Tres Hermanos, Ashley Ward discovered, were called Garcia, — a name too common, however, to be any proof of identity, yet which seemed to make it worth his while to spend another month or more of precious time in the search, which in another country, with records of average exactness, would perhaps have been performed in one or two days.

The trip had been made as quickly as the excessively bad state of the roads at the rainy season would allow, and with but few divergences and delays; and the boundaries of the estate had been already passed when the young American and his servant were, in a merry rather than a savage humor, detained or rather actually captured by the redoubtable Calvo, who to amuse the leisure that hung rather heavily upon his hands invited the young American to ride in his company. In his broken but expressive English, the freebooter uttered such courteous phrases that the young man was quite unconscious that he was in fact a prisoner, and passed a not uninteresting day in exchanging political opinions, local and international, with the dashing chieftain, — who, while apparently absorbed in the novelty and pleasure of listening to the conversation of his involuntary guest, was mentally preparing the speech in which he should convey to him on the morrow the terms of ransom for himself and servant, — a likely fellow whom Calvo had more than half a mind to add to the number of his followers.

But the servant himself had no illusions as to the glory of fighting or the chances of booty, and sometime during the night in which they were encamped at the *ranchito* of El Refugio managed to elude the lax watchfulness of the troop, who had made a merry meal on freshly killed lambs and such other modest viands as Doña Isabel Garcia's trembling shepherds could furnish, and without so much as a word of warning to the American had escaped, — bearing with him the small bag of necessaries of which he had charge, a pair of silver-mounted pistols, and a sum of money which Ward had been assured would in case of attack and capture be more secure in the possession of this " loyal and honest man " than in his own.

Ashley had barely had time to realize the defection of his servant, to suspect his actual position as a prisoner in the hands of the courteous but mercenary and implacable Calvo, and wrathfully to regret the ignorant trustfulness with which he had divided with the much lauded servant the risk of transporting his funds, retaining in his own hands perhaps not enough to meet the rapacious demands of his captors, when suddenly his meditations were interrupted by cries of confusion, shouts, the crack of rifles, the whizzing of balls, challenges and defiant yells, the shrieks of women, and the groans and appeals of the helpless shepherds, — followed by the sight of huts ablaze, of frightened flocks wildly bleating and rushing blindly under the very feet of the horses, which trampled them down, while their keepers, as bewildered as they, fell victims to the mad zeal and excitement of the opposing troops who had so unexpectedly met on that isolated spot.

It was conjectured that the missing servant had in his flight to the mountains accidentally come upon the soldiers of the Clergy, and to turn attention from himself had betrayed the proximity of the Liberals. A hurried march in the early morning hours had proved the truth of the ser-

vant's information ; and the surprise and some advantage
in numbers — for the Captain Alva had spoken with a trace
of the usual exaggeration of the speech of his countrymen,
in describing the enemy as numbering three hundred —
turned the chances in favor of the attacking party ; although Calvo at first seemed inclined to contest the matter
obstinately, and Ward, with an involuntary feeling of
fealty to his host (though he had already some inkling of
his intentions in regard to himself) had ranged himself
upon his side. He soon saw with indignation, however,
that the defence of the poor villagers held no part in
Calvo's thoughts. To frustrate some movement of the
enemy, he actually ordered the firing of a hut in which
women and children had taken refuge ; and it was while
defending the humble spot from Puro and Mocho alike,
that Ward received the wound which disabled him, —
that covered with blows from muskets and swords he
fell, and trampled beneath the feet of the now flying and
pursuing soldiers, for a few horrible moments believed
himself doomed to die in a senseless mêlée, in which his
only interest had been to protect the weak, but in which
he recognized no inherent principle of right. Later he
saw in those apparently senseless broils the throes and
struggles of an undisciplined and purblind nation toward
the attainment of a dimly seen ideal of justice and freedom, and learned the truth that these people, who seemed
so lightly swayed by the mere love of adventure, held
within their breasts the divine spark that distinguishes
man from the brute, — the deathless fire of patriotism.
They too could suffer, bear imprisonment, famine, even
death, for freedom.

But these were none of Ashley Ward's reflections as he
found himself laid apart from three or four dead men, who
had been hurriedly thrown together for burial, and after
being subjected to a hasty examination — which resulted
in the abstraction of his remaining funds, his watch and
other valuables, and the binding up of his wound — lifted
to the back of a raw-boned troop-horse, and forced to join
the march of the triumphant guerillas. He would have
preferred to be left to the care of the houseless and destitute shepherds ; but Captain Alva, whether with the hope
of some ultimate benefit from the capture of the foreigner

or not it is impossible to tell, professed himself horrified at the barbarity of deserting him, — and, as we have seen later, in apprehension of his death from exposure to the sun, and the fever that seized him, availed himself of the opportunity of evading the responsibility of the death of an American upon his hands, by delivering him to the care of Doña Isabel Garcia.

And so, still weak, and destitute of money until he could arrange for a supply from the City of Mexico, but full of hope, confident that he had reached his goal, and that a few discreet inquiries would give him the information he sought, and perhaps allay forever the doubts that tormented his sensitive conscience, Ashley Ward drew a deep breath of satisfaction as he sat at the hacienda gate; and in an animated mood, which supplemented his insufficient Spanish, addressed himself to the reticent and gloomy Pedro, startling him from his usual stoicism by the exclamation, "And you, my man, can you tell me of the American your foster-child spoke of? There is not so much happens here that you can have forgotten."

Had Ashley known anything of the instincts and customs of the genuine ranchero, he would have begun his investigations in a far more guarded manner. That a certain Don Juan had met a bloody death there years before, he already knew; that this had been his cousin, he surmised; that the gatekeeper should know more of the domestic life of an employee of the hacienda than the owner herself, or even the administrador, was a natural conclusion. But had Ashley Ward wished to seal the lips of the suspicious and astute gatekeeper, he could not have chosen a more effective manner of accomplishing it. As well touch the horns of a snail and expect that it would not withdraw into its shell, as to question this man directly and hope to learn aught of value.

Pedro looked at the inquirer from under the shadow of his bushy eyebrows and wide hat; and though his heart bounded, his face became a very mask of rustic stupidity as he answered, "Your grace has had much fever with your wound. Heaven and all the saints be thanked that you are young and healthy, and will soon be as strong as ever."

"Um!" ejaculated Ward, for the moment disconcerted.

" Yes, I have had fever, but that has nothing to do with
the American. He was a living man fourteen or fifteen
years ago, if there be any truth in what your — young
mistress told me." He hesitated how to designate the
girl, whose status and relations seemed so strangely
undefined.

Pedro's eyes for a moment lightened. Pepé laughed
ironically, yet he would have turned like a wild beast on
another who had done so.

" Who speaks much, speaks to his undoing," quoth
Pedro, gruffly, and turned away; yet he eyed the young
American furtively, with an inborn hostility to his race,
an unreasoning belief that in the guise of such fair tempters lurked the demon who would destroy unwary damsels body and soul, yet with an almost irresistible desire
to unburden his soul of the weight that had so long
oppressed it, to cry aloud, " I can tell you all you would
know, — how the American lived, how he died, how the
child he never saw lives after him. Is it her you seek?
And why?"

Pedro clenched his hands with a gasp. He remembered
that the natural instincts of kindred had changed to bitterness against Herlinda's child. She had been cast out, disowned, deserted. Who was this stranger, this foreigner,
that he should be more just, more generous, toward the
doubtful offspring of one who had died years before? How
should he even guess such a child to be in existence?
No, he could not guess it. What a mad thought had
darted through his own brain! Pedro actually laughed
at his own perplexed imaginings. What! the secret of
Herlinda, which had been kept so inscrutably, in danger
from this idle news-seeker? Preposterous! yet an odd
conceit entered the gatekeeper's mind: " The blind man
dreamed that he saw, and dreamed what he desired."
This groping youth had come far to inquire into the fate
of a man long dead, — it must be because it would bring
him profit, for it did not for a moment occur to Pedro
that the questions asked were from mere idle curiosity,
— and would it be possible anything should escape him?
" Well, what God wills, the saints themselves cannot
hinder."

Pedro sat down upon the stone bench opposite, in an

affectation of sullen obstinacy. Ashley was weary and chagrined, and in silence looked over the landscape with an increasing sense of recognition. Pepé stood in the same lounging attitude, patiently waiting. One might have thought him carved of wood against the stone wall, yet of the three men he it was whose passions were fiercest, whose thoughts like unbridled coursers followed one another in mad confusion. His mind was full of Chinita! Chinita! Chinita! her beauty, her insolent grace, — the memory of her pretty, haughty ways when she had been but a barefoot, ragged peasant like himself, and the contemplation of the hopeless height to which she had risen. Never before had he been conscious that he had aspired. Now, bruised, torn, wounded as if by a fall into hopeless depths, he saw her image swimming before his disordered vision ; he thought of her as a princess, a goddess, yet he laughed when he heard her named as mistress.

Such was the mood in which Pepé presently listened to the disconnected dialogue between Pedro and the guest, who was hampered by a language strange to him, and by suspicious caution on the part of the gatekeeper. For the first time in his life, Pepé was struck by a peculiarity in Pedro with which he had always been acquainted ; namely, his unwillingness to speak of the tragedy, which to other minds had seemed no more horrible than scores of others that had occurred in the neighborhood and were common subjects of conversation. As he listened, Pepé became conscious that Pedro was detracting from the interest of the tale rather than adding to it ; and when the young American at last said inquiringly, " And the cause of this murder was never known? There was no woman — " he was startled that Pedro answered not with the old jest, " Was there ever an evil but that a woman was at the root of it?" but rose and strode rapidly away.

" There *was* a woman," muttered Ward, looking after him, "and the gatekeeper knew her. I have found the man who can tell me of Herlinda."

He spoke in English, but Pepé the eager listener caught the name "Herlinda." Five minutes later, when Ward turned to speak to the youth, he found him with his hands clasped, stretched out before him, his eyes staring into vacancy.

"Idiot!" was the half contemptuous, half pitying comment of the American.   Little guessed he that the conversation that had seemed to result in so little to him had offered both a suggestion and an inspiration to the peasant, — the very key to the problem which he had himself come so far and dared so much to solve.

16

XXVII.

Upon the following day, Ashley Ward went again to the gateway, — not merely to breathe the fresh air and enjoy the view, but irresistibly attracted by the remembrance of the taciturn warder. The more he reflected upon the emotion the man had shown when his eyes first rested upon him, a stranger, as he had entered the vestibule; the more he thought upon the guarded replies to the questions he had asked concerning the young American who had been there years before, — the more convinced he became that there had been a mystery which had led to his kinsman's death, and that Pedro, if he would, could divulge it.

Was it possible the man himself was the assassin? The perplexed youth began to sound Pepé cautiously as to the reputation Pedro had borne. But the young fellow was absorbed in other matters, of which Ashley rightly conjectured Chinita was the vital point, and was wandering and curt in his answers. Yet he seemed to feel that Ashley divined, if he did not comprehend, his pain, and so attached himself to him and followed him about, much as might a wounded dog some stranger who had spoken to him with an accent of pity in his voice.

So when Ashley went to the gateway, it was Pepé's arm that aided him, though with the impatience of a young man he protested against this need of a crutch, and had actually walked steadily enough across the court, under the gaze of Doña Feliz and Chinita, who happened to be in the window; but he had been glad to clutch at Pepé as they entered the vestibule. The lad was not trembling then, but erect and flushed: Chinita had smiled upon him as he passed.

Pedro was standing in the gateway, shading his eyes with his hand, and gazing toward the cañon which opened behind the reduction-works. He did not notice Ashley and Pepé, but presently began to mutter: "Yes, it is they. Don Rafael has had a lucky journey. Go thou, Chinita, and tell Doña Feliz the master and her daughter-in-law and children will be here for the noon dinner."

Pepé laughed derisively. "You forget, Pedro," he said; "it is the *niña* Chinita, and the Señorita Chinita now; even if she heard, she is scarce likely to run at your bidding. But are you sure the Señor Administrador comes there? If so, I will myself go and tell them."

"Go then, go!" cried Pedro, impatiently. "I am not blind, though old usage sometimes misleads me, and I talk like a dotard. Yes, yes. There comes the carriage down the cañon, and Don Rafael himself on his gray, and Gabriel and Panchito; I can almost distinguish their very faces."

So could Ashley, for the air was brilliantly clear, and the travellers had yielded to the inspiring influences natural at the sight of home, and allowed their horses to break into a mad pace, far different from the methodic gait of ordinary travel.

Pepé, in spite of repressed excitement, had gone at his usual lounging and listless pace to inform Doña Feliz of the approach of her son, and a little group of villagers had assembled around Pedro, when a lithe, active young figure brushed by them and leaped upon the stone bench at Ashley's side. He glanced up, and to his surprise saw Chinita, her hair flying, her eyes bright with anticipation. Putting her finger upon her lip as he was about to speak, as if to enjoin silence, she pressed herself close to the wall. There was a long narrow niche where she stood, and it received almost her entire figure. No one but Ashley and Pepé, who came with haste behind her, had noticed her.

"Hush! hush!" she whispered. "Chata will look for me here, — here where I used to stand. Ay, Pepé, you were a good lad to warn me in time, so I could slip away. Doña Isabel will never miss me, — she is at her prayers; and Doña Feliz is wild with joy that her son comes home again."

The excited girl had spoken in the softest of voices, yet Pedro heard her. But the rest of the gathering crowd were craning their necks and straining their eyes in the direction in which the approaching travellers were to be seen.

Pepé looked up at the ardent and gypsy-like young creature, as though she were a saint, and Ashley with a glance of genuine admiration and sympathy. He knew not whom she was thus eager to welcome, but it thrilled and surprised him that she should manifest such lively affection. Both the young men instinctively drew near as if to shield her, and stood one on either side, almost hiding her.

"That is right; but you will stand away and let her see me when the carriage drives by," she whispered, placing a hand on Pepé's shoulder. "*Dios mio*, how my heart beats! She will cry with joy when she sees me, with silk skirts and all so fine. And Doña Rita and the *niña* Rosario, — how they will open wide their eyes!" And she broke into a low laugh, which to Ashley's ears was too full of a sort of malicious triumph to be merry.

The time of waiting seemed long; it was indeed far longer than Chinita had counted upon. "They will miss me from the house; they will look for me here!" she whispered again and again in an agony of impatience.

Strangely enough, the adults of the gaping throng, who were intent on watching the approach of the travellers, had not noticed her; but three or four children arrayed themselves in a wondering row, pointing their fingers at her with ejaculations of "Look! look!" but were checked from uttering more by Pepé's warning frowns and Chinita's own imploring gestures.

Ashley was beginning to realize that there must be much that was absurd in the scene. Surely, never was so strange a background made for a group of gossiping peasants as this of the eager-eyed and beautiful girl, leaning from her niche in the massive stone-wall between the two young men — the one the type of aristocratic refinement and delicacy; the other of swarthy, ignorant, half-tamed savagery — who served as caryatids, upon whom she leaned alternately in her excitement, seeming herself to partake of the nature of each.

The carriage with its group of outriders now rapidly approached. "Ah! ah!" exclaimed Chinita, "the horses are plunging at the tree where the American was murdered. They say the creatures can always see him there, Señor.

Ah, now they have passed; they come gayly, they come straight. It is not only the Señor Administrador and the servants, there are strangers too. I am glad! I am happy! I love to see new faces!"

"Be silent!" whispered Pepé, hurriedly; "all the world will hear if you sing so loud. *Carrhi!* the soldier sees you!"

It was true; though the villagers had been too intent upon welcoming the new-comers to heed Chinita, and the carriage flashed by so rapidly the inmates could have caught but a glimpse of color against the cold gray wall, a stranger in a travel-stained uniform started as his eyes fell upon her, and checked his horse so suddenly that it reared.

"The Virgin of our native land!" he muttered in a sort of patriotic and admiring wonder. "Ah, what a beautiful creature!" he added, as the girl he had for a moment classed as a saint sprang from her niche to the bench and thence to the ground, and darted through the crowd to the inner court, — where by this time the carriage had stopped and its inmates were descending.

Ashley sank upon the bench with a sudden access of weariness. Pedro, oblivious of his vicinity, crouched rather than sat beside him. The gatekeeper's nerves doubtless were weak. The carriage that had driven into the court was the same in which Herlinda Garcia had departed years before; as it dashed by him he could have sworn he saw her face framed in the window. He had seen, as had Chinita, the sad and gentle countenance of Chata. Grief reveals strange likenesses.

When Chinita reached the carriage door, she found it blocked by the descending travellers and those who welcomed them. Doña Rita was so slow in carefully placing her feet from step to step, and paused so often to answer salutations, that there was ample time for the young officer to reach the spot and extend a hand to Rosario who followed her. Her blushes and coy smiles; the air with which she drew back and with which, with a little shriek, she pulled her dress over her tiny foot lest it might be seen; the soft glances which she threw from beneath her long lashes, — formed a pretty piece of by-play, quite intelligible to all beholders, but for that time certainly quite thrown away upon the stranger.

Ten minutes before, to have held for a few brief minutes
the tips of Rosario's fingers would have been to him
ecstasy. Now he was scarcely conscious that they were
within his own, and his eyes were fixed upon Chinita as
she stood breathlessly waiting for Chata. Never in his
life, he thought, had he seen such a face. The changeable
yet ever radiant expression was like the dazzle of warm
sunshine through scented leaves ; the shimmer of rebellious
hair was a divine halo, though the sparkle of the dusky
eyes declared a daring soul more fit for earthly adventure
than ethereal joys.

Rosario's eyes followed his gaze. She had heard the
strange tale of Doña Isabel's intervention in the fate of
the waif. She had wondered whether the high-born lady
could have seen anything in the girl's face that attracted
her ; and that moment more decidedly than ever she answered "No," yet realized that here was a face to bewitch men. She tossed her head and passed on. Doña
Feliz stopped her to embrace her, and meanwhile the two
early playmates met.

"Life of my soul!" cried Chinita. "How I have
longed for you! Did you not see me perched in the
niche of the wall? Ay, how Doña Isabel would frown
if she knew!"

"I saw only the tall, fair man," answered Chata in a
low voice. She was pale and trembled : "I thought first
it was the ghost of the American. Oh God, what a
shock!"

Chinita laughed merrily. "What! a coward still, and
with the old stories we used to tell still first in your mind?
Ah, I have tales to tell now will be worth your hearing."
She bent low and added in a whisper, "Have they not
told you? I have the place of the Señorita Herlinda
now! I have her room. I think sometimes she must
be dead, and I have risen in her stead. Do I look like
a ghost, Chata?"

"Hush, hush!" entreated Chata. "Oh Chinita, I wish
I never had gone away. Oh, how shall I live now? How
can I bear it?"

At that moment Doña Feliz approached, and evading
her proffered embrace the young girl bent her head on
the arm of the woman and burst into tears. Chinita stood

confounded; the light and joyousness died out of her face; a certain half-savage look of inquiry came over it. She turned abruptly to the young officer, —

"What have they done to her?" she demanded.

"Chinita," said a cold, impassive voice, "this gentleman is a stranger to you. It is not seemly that you stand here questioning him;" and with an imperious wave of her hand, Doña Isabel seemed actually to force the two apart.

Almost unconsciously the young man drew back, bowing low, and Chinita turned to the staircase; yet as she obeyed the movement of Doña Isabel's hand a furious rage possessed her. As she stepped upon the ·first stair, some demon prompted her to wind her arm around Chata's neck and raise her tear-stained face.

"I am going to the Señorita Herlinda's room," she said. "I am there in her place; and — " here she stopped, laughed, and threw a glance over her shoulder — " there is the American!"

Her last words had been prompted by a glimpse of Ashley Ward as he crossed the court. He caught the appellation, and bowed and smiled. Chinita ran up the stairs, and Doña Isabel stood rigid with a face like death. Her eyes were resting however on Chata's countenance.

The young girl had shrunk within Doña Feliz's protecting arm. Had Doña Isabel turned her eyes upon the woman's defiant yet apprehensive face, it might have been a revelation to her; but she looked at Don Rafael.

"Your daughter has a strange face and strange ways for a ranchero's daughter," she said, with an attempt at irony; but it failed. Her face worked painfully as she added, "She reminds me of those I would forget. We have strange fancies as we grow old."

A laugh sounded from the window above. She started and looked up, then dropped her head again and turned slowly away.

Chata gazed after her awestruck, though she knew not why. Her manner was so different from that of the proud and haughty dame she had pictured. Don Rafael looked from Doña Isabel to his mother. Both these women, it seemed to him, had grown wonderfully aged since they had met, but a month or so before. There was a subtile

antagonism between them — these two who loved each
other, as only such deep intense natures can — which
tore and harried them far more than actual hate could
have done.

"What hast thou, my life?" Doña Feliz whispered to
Chata. "Art thou not happy? Have strange tales been
told thee?" and she looked keenly at her daughter-in-law,
who had smiled and courtesied in vain as Doña Isabel
went by.

"My mother," said Doña Rita in her softest voice,
"the child is weary; she must rest. Heed not this silly
child, Don Fernando. Thank Heaven, Rosario is not so
fanciful!"

But Don Fernando was not thinking of Rosario, or
of Chata either for that matter, but of how he had slunk
away from his chief to prosecute a love-affair that he had
believed no power could make less than a matter of life or
death to him; and how in a moment it had become lighter
than air. The boyish perversity with which he had determined, even at the risk of offending his patron, to continue
his courtship of Rosario Sanchez, trusting to fate or her
father's generosity to make marriage with her possible,
faded from his mind like a dream, and with it her image;
and in its place rose the arch mocking face of the "little
saint of the Wall." Proved she angel or demon, he felt
that she was henceforth the genius of his destiny. He
was a vain and profligate adventurer; but all the same
the arrow had found his heart, not as a thousand times
before to inflict a passing scratch, but to bury itself in
its inmost core.

All had taken place in a few short moments. While the
horses were being unharnessed and led away; while the
villagers were still crowding around the carriage, and Doña
Rita's baskets and packages were being lifted out; while
a few words of greeting were exchanged, — emotions and
passions had sprung into being that were to make the
seemingly prosaic household a very vortex of conflicting
elements.

The young American, who thought himself but a looker-
on, was also not unmoved. Like Doña Isabel, he said
within himself, "That young girl has a strange face and
strange ways for the daughter of a Mexican. And yet

what know I of Mexicans or their ways? This is a strange atmosphere, and fills my brain with strange fancies. Perhaps out of them all I shall evolve some reality. May the Fates grant me again such a chance as I had to-day of speaking to the wild gypsy Chinita! Nothing has happened here, I can well believe, that she cannot tell me of. But after the escapade of to-day, she will hardly escape the vigilance of her duenna again. Ah, here comes the young soldier — too travel-stained to be as dashing as is his custom, no doubt. He looks a gay bird with sadly bedraggled feathers."

Pepé apparently approved of him as little, as he passed by to the room assigned him. The peasant did not cease from lounging against the wall or bare his head as an inferior should.

"Insolent barbarian!" muttered Don Fernando, in a revival of his usual contempt for the peasantry, as the swarthy young fellow scowled at him, he neither guessed nor cared why. What could such a vagabond have to do with the Señora Garcia's *protégée?* He would serve when the time came, to make one, in the independent troop he, Fernando, would raise: such worms as he were only fit to serve men. There were wild rumors afloat of the wonderful fortune of that phœnix Benito Juarez. What if he, Ruiz, should join his standard? There was a strange fire and exultation in the young man's veins. He had been tied to a resistless fate long enough, — he would break his trammels, and by one daring act free himself forever from control, from tutelage, from Ramirez.

"Señor Don Rafael!" cried a hoarse voice at break of day. "Rise, your grace! for strange things have happened while we have slept! Ay, Señor, if the demon himself has not carried away Pedro the gatekeeper, who can tell us how he has gone?"

"Gone!" echoed the voice of Don Rafael from within.

"Gone, Señor, and left not even so much as his shadow; yet the doors are locked, and not even in the postern is there so much as a crack, nor the key in the lock. The muleteers, who were to be upon the road at cock-crow, have waited until both they and their beasts are cramped with standing, and all to no purpose."

"Is this true?" exclaimed Don Rafael, presently appearing with a *serape* thrown over his shoulders, and shivering in the morning air. "Ay, man, thou hast a tongue like a woman's. And Pedro, thou sayest, is gone?"

The man drew one hand sharply across the other, as who should say, "vanished!" though his lips ejaculated, "Gone, Señor; and who is to open the door now that it is shut? And who could shut the door upon Pedro but Satan himself?"

"Who, indeed?" said Don Rafael, gravely. "Think you so bulky a fellow could creep through the keyhole of the postern and take the key with him? By good fortune, he brought me the key of the great door as usual, and here it is. If the Devil hath carried away one gatekeeper on his shoulders, it is but fair he should send me another; and thou, Felipe, shall be the man."

Felipe stared a moment; then with a transient change of expression which might be of intelligence, or simply a vague smile at his own good fortune, extended his hand for the keys; and suddenly mute with the weight of his unexpected promotion trudged down the stone stairs, across the silent inner court and the outer one, where by this time the household servants were exchanging exclamations of wonder and alarm with the impatient muleteers. Felipe unlocked the wide doors, threw them open with a clang, sank into Pedro's place upon the stone bench, and thereafter reigned in his stead.

The wonder of Pedro's disappearance grew greater and ever greater, until the boy Pepé said sulkily he had been played a shabby trick. Had not he said to Pedro the night before, when the Señor Don Rafael had told them that the General Vicente Gonzales was in El Toro, that for a word he himself would go to him there; and doubtless Pedro had stolen away alone, like the surly fox that he was. But the saints be praised, the road was open to one man as well as another.

"Hush!" said one in a warning tone; "though Pedro may have a fancy for a cleft head or broken bones, must we all cry for the same? Go to thou Pepé! thou art scarce old enough to leave the shade of thy mother's reboso. Did I not see thee sucking thy thumb but last Saint John's day?"

There was a roar of laughter, and though Pepé raged, no one heeded his wrath; the talk was all of Pedro. That he had gone to be a soldier was universally believed; that Don Rafael, and not the Devil, had aided his going was not for a moment thought of. The women crossed themselves, and the men spat on the floor emphatically, — yet there had been more mysteries than that in the life of Pedro.

Florencia, who was distraught at her uncle's disappearance, and tore her hair and bewailed herself as a bereaved niece should, found her way to Chinita to pour out her griefs and fears; although since the change in the young girl's position they had by common consent ignored their former relations, — Florencia, because of the wide social gulf fixed between the great house and the hovels around it; Chinita, from pure indifference. She was too full of her new life to think of the old, or of the persons connected with it.

It was so early that she was still not fully dressed, and the chocolate wherewith to break her fast stood untouched upon the table, when the sound of some one sobbing at the door brought a tone of sorrow into thoughts which had simply been vexed before.

Chinita had risen in an ill humor. Doña Rita and Rosario, and even Chata herself, had failed to show any surprise at her position. True, Don Rafael had warned them of it ; but at least something more than a kindly indifference might have greeted her, — if only a glance of envy from Rosario. What wonderful things had they all seen, that they had no thoughts to spare for her? Bah! Rosario had neither eyes nor thoughts for any one but the young officer with the red neck-tie. Well, they should see! But what of Doña Rita, — and Chata too? Why, Chinita hardly knew her. Was she also thinking but of herself, like the others? That was a change in Chata, and one that ill-suited her.

Chinita had slept badly for thinking of these things ; and truth to tell, when her mind was ill at ease the softness of the bed troubled her. She had dreamed of snakes, of three snakes who had lifted their heads out of water to hiss at her. Here was the first one. Certainly she had not dreamed of snakes for nothing. Well, to be sure, here was Florencia, whom she had almost forgotten, come with some trouble! She felt a little flutter of gratification, and unconsciously assumed the air of a *patrona,* as she said, —

"Ah, is it then Florencia? And what ails thee ; and how can I help thee? What, has Tomasito broken the newest water-jar, or by better fortune his neck? Or has Terecita choked herself with a dry bean?"

"God has not desired to do me such favors," returned Florencia, piously and with a flood of tears. "No, rather than my children should become little angels, he prefers that they shall be friendless upon the earth. *Ay de mi!* what is a father, what is a husband (and you know the very driveller of a man I have), what is any one to an uncle who was a gatekeeper of Tres Hermanos? — a veritable treasure of silver, a spring of refreshing! Was there ever a time Florencia asked a shilling of Pedro in vain?"

At another time Chinita would have laughed at this pious exaggeration ; now it filled her with inexpressible alarm.

"What! is my god-father dead?" she cried, wringing her hands and for the moment relapsing into the demonstrative gestures and cries of her plebeian training. "*Ay Dios*, Florencia, it cannot be! Answer me, stupid one! Is thy mouth as full as thy eyes that thou canst not answer?"

"Is chocolate served to the poor at day-break?" cried Florencia in an injured tone, and with a glance at the dainty breakfast; and then at an impatient word from Chinita she explained how Pedro had departed in the night, though the hacienda doors were locked upon the inside, and conjectured that if he had not been spirited away by the Devil, he had gone to join the Liberal General Gonzales, — there could be no other alternative. She had heard Señor Don Rafael talking to him till late in the night of how Gonzales had beaten the General Ramirez at El Toro, and was still there trying to strengthen his forces, while those of the Clergy had disappeared, no one knew where, but surely to gather men and means to recover the lost position.

Chinita's eyes flashed. She knew nothing of politics, but she thrilled at the name of Ramirez. She laughed scornfully that Pedro should throw his puny strength into the force against him. Still she said, "God keep him;" and jested away Florencia's fears.

"Bah! What should happen to my god-father?" she said. "And thou knowest thou wilt want for nothing. Hark thou! there is nothing to cry for that thy uncle is gone. Has he not often told us of the dollars he made in the wars?"

"I fear me he is likely rather to receive hard blows than hard dollars now," answered Florencia, disconsolately, — an expression of expectancy, however, relieving her doleful countenance, as she added, "Ah, Chinita of my soul, thou wert ever the kerchief to wipe away my tears."

Chinita laughed. "Thou used to say I was a prickly pear to draw tears, rather than a kerchief to dry them," she presently said, pushing her chocolate toward Florencia, and thrusting into her hand the little twists of bread.

"There, take them; I would a thousand times rather

have a thick cake and a drink of white gruel. One is not
always in the humor for sweets;" and she tugged viciously
at the hair she tried vainly to smooth, — she was always
at feud with it because it was not longer. But at last she
confined it in two short tresses, tying each with a red
ribbon; and then suddenly dropping on her knees before
Florencia, placed her hands palm downward upon the
floor, and looking up in the woman's face with a laugh
exclaimed, as a tinge of red deepened the olive of her
complexion, "And what of the American, Florencia? Is
he like him thou sayest the Señorita Herlinda loved?"

"Ave Maria Purissima!" cried the startled woman.
"The saints forbid that I should say such a thing of a
Garcia, and she dedicated to the Madonna!" But recovering herself, "Certainly this American is like the other.
Is not one cactus like another that grows on the same
mountain? Should a white-blooded American be like a
cavalier of blue-blood, or like an Indian of the villages?
Yet both, one and the other, are we not Mexicans?" and
she uttered the words as one might say, "Are we not
gods?"

"That is very true," commented Chinita, gravely; "and
yet they are not frights, these Americans. Why should
not the Señorita Herlinda have loved one if it pleased
her? Listen, Florencia; I will tell thee a dream I had
one night. When one's bed is too soft, one dreams
dreams."

Florencia looked at the girl with an admiring glance.
How amiable she could be, this Chinita, when she
chose. "Little puss! little puss!" she murmured,
giving her the pet name Pedro had used, when in her
kittenish moods one had never known whether she would
scratch or fondle one with soft purrings, begun and ended
in a moment. "Little puss! thou wert ever good to thy
Florencia."

"Thou art a flatterer!" ejaculated Chinita, half-inclined
to withhold her confidence, yet longing for a listener. "Ay,
Florencia, thou knowest not what it is to sit for hours in
the gloom within four walls. Ah, what thoughts come
into one's head! When I ran about the village, the wind
blew the thoughts about as it did my hair; but now my
brains are like cobwebs, and when a thought touches them

it clings like dust, and so they grow thicker and heavier until my very skull aches;" and she pressed her head with her hands, and heaved a deep sigh.

"But to think is not to dream," said Florencia, in some disappointment, for she had a child's love for the marvellous, and did not understand Chinita's abstractions, — unstudied and simple though they were.

"But dreams come from thoughts," answered Chinita; "and what should I think of here but of mysteries, — such as why the Señora should keep me with her, though she loves me not; why she walks the floor and counts her beads, and when she forgets I am in the room murmurs over and over the name of Herlinda; why she looks before her sometimes, as you used to tell me the woman looked who saw the ghost of the American, — and that is always when she chances to meet this Don 'Guardo whom she will not speak of, or suffer Doña Feliz to invite to our table, though he stays here so long. And after I have asked so many things, I set myself to the answer. Oh, you would wonder at what I say to myself of all these things, — and then sometimes come dreams to tell me I am right."

Florencia looked at the door vaguely, — she was thinking perhaps she had better go.

"Yes, yes," continued Chinita, as if to herself, "I am growing perhaps like the owl, — I, who in the broad sunlight saw nothing, have discovered many things here in the dark. Well, well, Florencia, one thought came to me on a vexed night when I could not sleep. I had been talking to Doña Feliz that day. I know not why, but I am with Doña Feliz like the young fox my god-father tamed, — when I touched him with my hand he was pleased, yet he bristled and longed to bite. Good! we had talked that day. Yes, — it was of the nuns, and she said the Señora might desire I should be one; and I was angry, and said I would not be shut up to pray as the Señorita Herlinda had been; and then Doña Feliz bade me be silent and ponder what she had said. And after she went away it was not of myself I thought, but of the Señorita Herlinda; and in the midst of my thoughts I saw the American pass the court, and Doña Isabel, who was near, turned herself away, as if an adder had darted upon her."

Florencia looked up with a mute inquiry or fascination in

her gaze. Chinita, in a sort of monotone, followed the thread of her thoughts.

"When I went to sleep at last, I dreamed that I, though still Chinita, was Herlinda, and that the American who was lying wounded in the room below came up the stairs, and tapped lightly at my window. I stepped softly and looked out at him through the grating. Ah, it was this Don 'Guardo, yet so different, as a man is different from his reflection in a glass; and I did not wonder to see him there. I put my hand out and touched him, and was happy. And as I stood at the bars, — I myself, and yet the *niña* Herlinda, — the man of my dream said, as a husband says to his wife, 'Open, my life;' and when I opened the door he led in by the hand a little child, — I knew it to be his child, though it had not blue eyes nor the yellow hair. Well, I stood there, and stood there, and strove to speak and could not; and the vision of the man and of the child faded, and the thought that I was still Herlinda faded too, and the dream was ended."

She ceased speaking, and looked at Florencia with a vague yet searching gaze.

"By my faith, a strange dream!" murmured Florencia, disquieted. "You should have lighted a blessed candle when you woke, and passed it before you three times, saying an *Ave* each time. Santa Inez! I would rather see the ghost of the American than dream such a dream!"

"Coward! it frightened me not," continued the girl. "And I did not seem to wake, though I knew that I, Chinita, lay in the bed, and that my head sank deep in the soft pillow, and that I could not or would not raise it; and the meaning of the dream crept into my mind, as the light creeps into a dark room. Yes, I felt as I used to when I saw the little green blades shoot up in the spring, and I could think how the corn would grow, and the leaves would wave, and the maize would lie in the silk and the yellow sheath; and so I had thought of what I had heard, — of the love of Herlinda for the American, and what might have come of it."

"Hush!" interrupted Florencia with a scared look. "You said you dreamed of a child. Did you see its face?"

"No," answered Chinita, slowly. "But what need that I should see it?"

The two had risen as if by one impulse, and looked into each other's eyes. The woman was awed as much by the penetration and daring of the young girl's mind as by the thought that for the first time arose within her.

She cast her thoughts back. She had been young when the American was murdered, when the Señorita Herlinda had left the hacienda never to return, when the child had been found at the gate; yet she wondered that she had been so blind to what now appeared so plain, and that all alike — the wise and simple, the old and young — had been so utterly dazzled by the glamor that surrounded the family of Garcia that no suspicion of dishonor might attach to its women, or of cowardice to its men. Surely none other than Herlinda Garcia would have escaped the lynx-eyed Selsa, or a score of other scandal-loving women! Curiously enough, while a feeling of detraction for the nun, whom she had long been used to canonize in her thoughts, stole into her mind, a sensation of traditional reverence for the Garcia arose for the young girl before her. Florencia's ideas of morality were perhaps vague on all points; they certainly did not reach that of aspersion of the innocent fruit of another's fault.

" Ay, *niña*," the woman said at last with a gasp, " it is not every one who drinks red wine that is happy. Thanks to God, the peasant woman who carries a burden in her arms too soon needs only to suckle it under her scarf, like any mother, and needs not to close upon herself the doors of a convent. Santa Maria! who would have thought such things of the *niña* Herlinda?"

" Be silent!" cried Chinita, with a tardy repentance of her confidence. "How do I know that I am not the worst of evil thinkers, and a fool, a very fool? Look thou, Florencia, it is thou who shall discover the truth for me. Pedro is gone; perhaps he never knew it. The Tio Reyes must know; but where is he? Yet I *must* know. Oh, I could bear the truth from Feliz, from Doña Isabel; but they are as silent and as sorrowful as the image of the Madre Dolores. It is thou, Florencia, who must help me. Oh, it will be but a diversion for thee. Thou shalt talk of thy Tio Pedro, and of the day I was dropped in his hand, and of the days that went before. Thou canst talk now of the murder of the American, and of the Señorita Her-

17

linda too, and there will be no Pedro to chide thee. And see, — " as the woman began some faint objection, — " I have all the pretty things Pedro gave me, and money too ; yes, more than thou wouldst think. And thou shalt never miss thy uncle ; thou shalt have them all, if thou wilt but talk to the old women of things that happened here before the time of the great sickness. But, Florencia, thou must tell them nothing. Oh, if I could only run again in and out of the village huts as I used to do ! "

Florencia looked at the excited girl with a nod of intelligence. " Have no fear," she said ; " it is not possible that Florencia knows not how to manage her own tongue, though no one knows better than thyself it was ever a quiet one. But it shall wag now, and not like the dog's tail, in mere idleness."

Chinita laughed, then glancing around her warily, drew from her bosom a small gold coin. She had evidently prepared herself for a chance meeting with Florencia.

"Take it," she said, " and go. Thou hast been here too long already ; and," she added with the flush of red again tingeing her face, " talk and gossip when the American is near. He must be sad, — it will cheer him to hear the voices, even if he understands but little ; and if by chance he speaks to thee, why ! thou shalt tell me what he says."

Florencia had experienced one great surprise that morning, and here was another ; the first had awed, the second delighted her. Like all her race she had the instincts of secrecy and intrigue, and suddenly the opportunity to practise both were offered her. She looked at Chinita with a glance of infinite cunning in her soft dark eyes ; but the young girl would not meet her gaze. "Go, go!" she said impatiently; " you have been here too long. The Señora is coming — or is it Doña Feliz? Go! go, I say!"

It was neither Doña Isabel nor Feliz, but only Chata, who entered with a preoccupied air, scarcely noticing the woman who passed her on the threshold. She did not speak, however, until Florencia had reluctantly passed out of hearing ; and then she cried eagerly, " Chinita ! Chinita ! who is the stranger who stood with thee at the doorway? God bless us ! I thought I saw the ghost of the American we used to talk of; and but now I met him below in the court. Who is he? What is he here for?"

"That remains to be seen," answered Chinita, with an uneasy laugh. Her hasty confidence in Florencia troubled her, and closed her lips toward the friend for whom she had hitherto longed. "At least the stranger is no ghost; yet how can we know that the man who was murdered here so many years before was anything to him?"

"But I do know," insisted Chata. "I had gone to the arbor, thinking thou mightest be there, to break my fast. I was standing in the centre, with my eyes turned toward this room, thinking I should see thee leave it, and thinking too of the *niña* Herlinda,— O Chinita! she is still so beautiful,— when I heard a step behind me. It was a strange step, and I turned quickly and saw the American looking at me as if he too believed he saw a ghost. Was it not strange, Chinita? We looked at each other quite steadily for many moments, then he said, —

"'Pardon me, you are then the daughter of the administrador? You came here yesterday?'

"I could scarcely make out his words, yet I understood what he said, and I seemed to know that he had taken me for another, — perhaps for thee, Chinita; and then again he said, 'Pardon me! Pardon me!' and we still continued to look at each other; and I did not think how bold I must appear until the other stranger, the young officer who loves Rosario, stepped out of the room they have given him. I heard his spurs clank on the pavement, and then I fled away to thee. But for the fright, I should not have dared to come hither, Chinita. All yesterday my grandmother kept me from thee. She said now thou art the child of Doña Isabel, and that without leave I must not go to thee."

"Chata, thou hast a poor spirit!" exclaimed Chinita, with some severity, — though she remembered with impatient anger that Doña Isabel had kept her in the garden at her side, on pretence of showing her the strings of irregular pearls, which she should some day arrange in even strands. Doña Isabel had made no promise, but Chinita could almost see them in the future bedecking her own neck and arms. She had been beguiled,

even as Chata had been commanded, to keep apart from
her old playmate.

"There is a mystery in it all!" she exclaimed.
"Though I am here with Doña Isabel, I know not who I
am. It is intolerable! Sometimes I fear I am but her
plaything, with no more right to her notice than had the
fawn I found on the river bank and petted, till it died from
very heartbreak because it longed so for the mountains
and its kind. And so I long, Chata. Ah, thou knowest
not what it is to be a nameless wretch, to be tossed from
hand to hand, and have no share in the game but the
dizzy whirling through the air. Pshaw! I would rather
be dashed to pieces against the first wall than go through
life with nothing but favor to rely on. I want a name, a
place, a right. I will have them: even you, who are the
daughter of the administrador, have those; and I— Well,
I will not be simply *Chinita*, whom Doña Isabel makes
a lady to-day, who was a child of the Madonna yesterday,
and may be a beggar to-morrow."

Chata had been leaning on the arm and pressing her
head against the shoulder of Chinita. She raised it now
with a sharp low cry, and turned away. Little guessed the
impetuous, ambitious foundling how her words tortured
and taunted the other, who longed to cry out, "I too
am no one! I too am a stray, a waif, and if I know my
father, know him only as a terror, — a horror." Her
promise to Doña Rita silenced her. She felt there was
but one person in the world to whom she would break her
promise, — the pale, sweet-faced nun of the convent of El
Toro. In her passionate, bitter mood Chinita chilled and
silenced her. She did not even tell her that as she hastened from the arbor the American had caught the end of
her flying reboso, as if by an irresistible impulse, and
cried: "I am Ashley Ward! Ashley! Ashley! remember
the name!"

Remember it! it seemed to Chata as if she had always
known the man as well as the name, which had ever before
been to her the symbol of the dead rather than of the living. That she should have seen the Señorita Herlinda,
whom she had always known to be alive, seemed more
wonderful, more incredible to her mind, than that the
young man should have risen before her to claim the

name of the murdered foreigner. Now that he had come, she seemed all her life to have been expecting him. She did not see him again for days, but all that time the expression of his eyes haunted her. She could not fathom it. She did not guess it had been but a reflection of the surprise, yet conviction, in her own.

Chata did not again transgress the commands of Doña Feliz; nor did she remain long enough with Chinita in her first visit to be tempted into further confidence. Indeed, they parted with something like a quarrel, as they had been used to do in their childhood's days. Rosario's name had been mentioned, and Chinita had with some scorn commented both on her sentimental air and the indifference of her lover.

"Did he love her at El Toro?" she asked with the laugh that was so mocking. "He stood for an hour, you say, at the corner of the street waiting for a glance from her; he wrote verses by day and sang them by night beneath her window? Well, he stood from noon till night yesterday with his eyes turned upward, — one would have thought he had never gazed at anything lower than the sky; yet it was only for a glimpse of *my* face, and a single glance from my eyes dazzled and blinded him. Thank Heaven, he dare not tune a guitar beneath my windows for fear of Doña Isabel, or I should be tormented with all the old rhymes changed from Rosario to Chinita. Ah, there are likings and likings, and this pretty soldier is one who would try them all!"

"Chinita," cried Chata in indignation, "you are false, you are cruel! Rosario has done nothing to you that you should torment her. I understand nothing of such things as Rosario does; though I am her age, she seems to be a woman while I am still a child. But she says she loves Fernando, and for love a woman's heart may break."

Chata was thinking of the pale, sad nun; but Chinita threw herself into a chair and broke into a peal of laughter. It rang through the silent house, and startled Doña Isabel in the further chamber. She started nervously and clasped her hands over her ears.

"What a strange child it is." she murmured, "Ah, I should have loved her if—" She glanced at a note she had just written. It was addressed to Vicente Gonzales, and promised him a thousand mounted soldiers.

Doña Isabel made no idle promises, and she had counted well the cost when she had thus irrevocably committed herself to the cause of the Liberals. She had watched for years the course of events, and none saw more clearly than she that the time for passiveness had gone. On every hand there must necessarily be sacrifice. "That which goes not in sighs, must in tears," she said sententiously. "I like not the Indian Juarez, yet his policy promises deliverance from the vampire that for generations has grown strong and ever stronger, as it has drained the very life of the nation."

The knowledge that Gonzales was in El Toro enjoying the prestige of an accidental victory, but with a force entirely insufficient to meet that which Ramirez might at any day bring against him, had been the immediate cause of her action. To reward Pedro with a service which should at once remove him from her sight and fill his mind with new and absorbing interests, were the reasons why he had been chosen to ride from rancho to rancho secretly inciting the men to join the standard, which was to be raised upon the morrow.

"Ah, this Ruiz is a poor tool!" muttered Doña Isabel, "yet for that reason may be the more readily bought. He loves the daughter of my administrador, and will do much to gain my good word. Rafael says he is a brave soldier, if a false one; and there will be those with him who will guard against treachery. He shall fulfil his empty offer to lead a thousand men to Gonzales, and claim of Rafael the reward he sighs for. Ah, there is the child's laugh again, — I could almost fancy it in mockery of me! Ah, this of patriot is a new *rôle* for me, and tries my nerves. Well, Chinita shall laugh while she can: if it is for long, it will prove her none of the blood of Garcia. Was there ever a happy woman among them?"

While Doña Isabel pondered thus, Chata in deep indignation had turned from her whilom friend. She had been brought up among a people who in matters of love held man excused and woman guilty in all cases of inconstancy. "Farewell!" she exclaimed, "I will come no more to you who are so cruel. Doña Isabel was right to part us; she has changed your heart as she has your fortune. Ah!" she added bitterly, "all the world is changed to me, and why not you?"

The grieved and imbittered girl went out so quickly that Chinita's answer did not reach her. As she passed through the corridor Chata glanced down. The young officer stood there, as Chinita had described. He would catch the first glimpse of her as she left her room. Chata flushed in anger, yet tears of pity rose to her eyes. She was still a child, yet her heart foretold what might be the agony of woman's slighted love.

Even so soon Chinita was laughing no longer; she had crouched forward and sat with her face bent almost to her knees. "What have I done?" she asked herself. "It is early morning still, and I have told a secret to a fool, and offended her I should have trusted!"

She had eaten nothing; the excitement under which she had acted suddenly expired, and she burst into sobs and tears. Doña Feliz coming in a few minutes later, found her on her knees before the little image of her patron saint, passionately vowing the gift of a silver *Christo* in return for the boon she craved.

"Go to the corridor, my child," said Feliz pityingly. The girl was a problem to her, which every day seemed more difficult of solution. "You look weary and ill; but console yourself, — Pedro is safe. You will see the good foster-father again, be assured."

Chinita looked at her in astonishment. She had for the time forgotten Pedro's very existence. Doña Feliz discerned at once that she had credited the girl with a sensibility to which she was a stranger. Five minutes later she was quite certain of it, as Chinita sat on the corridor, apparently equally unconscious of the impassioned glances of Ruiz, or those of the invisible but infuriate Rosario, drawing the threads of some dainty linen and singing, —

Sale la Linda,
Sale la fea,
Sale el enano,
Con su galea.

" The beauty comes out,
The ugly one too;
Then comes the dwarf,
With a gay halloo."

As unstudied and inconsequent as the meaningless words of the song seemed the actions of the singer, but Feliz shook her head, and met Doña Isabel with a face that was even more serious than its wont. The problem became to her mind each day more complicated. Would the result be bitterness, and that grief most dreaded by the proud heart of Doña Isabel Garcia, — the grief and bitterness of shame?

XXIX.

FLORENCIA fulfilled her mission well, — recalling skilfully to the minds of the elder gossips the events and doubts of years agone, and those suspicions, light as air, which had once before menaced the fair name and fame of her who later had been revered as a saint under the name of Sister Veronica.

It was natural after the excitement of Pedro's disappearance had subsided that reminiscences of events in which he had figured should, in default of some new interest, rise to the stagnant surface of hacienda life, and be re-colored and adorned with suggestions probable or improbable, and that the favorite topic should be torn to shreds in its dissection, while the motive power of its appearance should in the excitement of discussion be utterly lost sight of. Florencia herself, in the interest of tracing the sequence of events, and in hearing attributed to the characters that had figured in her girlhood traits and deeds of which she had heard little or nothing at that bygone time, almost forgot that she was talking with a purpose, and therefore perhaps had a truly unprejudiced account to give to Chinita, — when she could again see her, for Doña Isabel had become a wary duenna, and the girl had had no opportunity of learning anything that might have thrown light upon the theory she had formed of her birth and parentage.

In his insufficient knowledge of the language, Ashley Ward let much of the gossip of the women who chatted about him as they performed their daily tasks pass entirely unheeded, while he pondered upon the very subjects which with more or less directness were discussed. But one morning he caught the name of Herlinda, and thenceforth all his senses were alert. Great was his surprise when he discovered this to be the name of a daughter of Doña Isabel who had been a beautiful girl when the

American was killed, and thenceforward his mind became preternaturally keen; so that he divined the meanings of words he had never heard before, — gestures, glances, the very inflection of a tone, became revelations to him.

Hitherto, without cogitating upon the matter, Ward had naturally assumed from hearing no reference to another that the newly married Carmen was the only child of Doña Isabel. Now he learned the tragical fate of Norberto and the existence of the elder and more beautiful daughter Herlinda, the cloistered nun; and she was for the time the theme of endless reminiscences and conjectures. Her winsome childhood; her early gayety and incomparable beauty; the open love of Gonzales; the suspected mutual attachment of the young American and the daring child, who with her mother's pride had failed to inherit her mother's strength of will; the murder of John Ashley; the time of the great sickness; the death of Mademoiselle La Croix; the effect of the shock and horror upon the mind and appearance of Herlinda; the scarcely whispered, faint, yet not wholly disproved suspicions which had floated over the name and fame of the daughter of a house too absolute in its ascendency and power to be lightly attacked; her removal from the hacienda; her strange rejection of the suit of one who had always been dear to her, and to whom her mother, in accordance with good and seemly usage, had pledged her; her renunciation of the world she had loved, and entrance to a convent, which she had held in horror, — all these circumstances were discussed from a dozen points of view.

And all he heard confirmed in Ashley's mind the belief that the woman whom his cousin had loved was traced; that whether she had been actually a wife or no, she, Herlinda Garcia, the daughter of a woman whom it would be a mortal offence to approach upon such a subject, was the possible mother of a child which he could scarcely refuse to believe existed, — though here a new perplexity confronted him as (like the young officer, whom he regarded with a half-contemptuous amusement that should have prevented him from following any example set by so love-lorn a cavalier) he began to seek occasion for observing Chinita with an intensity that made her doubly the object of the jealous and ireful dislike of Rosario and her mother. To his alert and dispassionate mind circumstances pointed to this girl as the possible link between the families of Ashley and Garcia, though the most minute and patient observation only seemed to make absurd the supposition that American blood mingled in the fiery tide which filled her veins, colored her rich beauty, and vivified the scornful and stoical yet ambitious spirit, which as by a spell at the same moment repelled yet charmed both himself and the haughty Doña Isabel. What was the secret of the foundling's influence? He cared not to analyze either his own mind or the irresistible fascination of Chinita; but that the girl, though not positively beautiful, and unmistakably repellent in her caustic yet stoical discontent and ambitious unrest, possessed a bewitching and bewildering grace far different from any he had ever beheld in woman, of whatever race or kindred, impressed him daily more and more deeply, while — But stubborn facts made speculation and efforts at inquiry alike futile.

As days passed on, a certain friendship sprang up between Ward and Don Rafael. They talked for hours over the political situation, — Ashley straining ear and mind to comprehend the administrador's smooth and impressive utterances, and Don Rafael with grave politeness listening without a smile or gesture of amusement to the hesitating and often utterly incomprehensible attempts of the young American to deliver his opinions, or to make minute inquiry into reasons and events which often horrified as well as puzzled him. Don Rafael had the air of simplicity and candor which is so infinitely attractive to the stranger, and which presented so great a contrast to the lofty coldness of Doña Isabel and the grave and melancholy reticence of Feliz. Their demeanor left the baffling and depressing conviction that there was an infinity that they might reveal were but the right chord touched; while that of Don Rafael was satisfying in its cordiality, even while no response fulfilled the expectation that his fluent and kindly frankness appeared to encourage.

As soon as the state of his wound permitted, Ashley joined the administrador in his early morning rides to the fields and pastures, and learned much of the workings of a great hacienda. These rides were confined to the im-

mediate neighborhood of the great house, and four or six
armed men were invariably in attendance, — for, as Don
Rafael explained with a smile, the administrador of the
rich hacienda of Tres Hermanos was invested with the dignity of its possessors, his personal insignificance being
absorbed in the state of those he represented ; so that his
person bore a fictitious value, and if seized by an enemy,
either personal or political, would doubtless be held at a
prince's ransom, which the honor as well as the interest of
his employers would force them to pay.

In the course of these rides they not infrequently approached the deserted reduction-works, and it was upon
the first occasion that this happened that Don Rafael
questioned the young American as to his relationship to
the last director ; and upon learning it, rehearsed with
deep feeling the story of his murder, pointing out the very
tree under which the bloody tragedy was enacted.

Ashley watched his countenance narrowly as he talked.
His words, whose meaning might have been obscure to
the foreigner, were rendered dramatic by the deep pathos
of his tone and the expressive force of his gestures ; even
the men who rode behind drew near as his voice rose on
the stillness of the air in a tale so foreign to the peace and
beauty of the scene. As they skirted the low adobe wall
and looked over upon the stagnant masses of mineral clay,
the piles of broken ores, the adobe sheds and stables
crumbling under rain and sun, Ashley was ready to credit
the whispered words with which Don Rafael ended his
narration ; "Señor, it is said in the silent night, when
the moon is at its full, phantoms of its old life revivify
this deserted spot, and that its massive gates open at
the call of a ghostly rider, who wears the form of that
poor youth who after his last midnight ride came back
feet foremost, recumbent, silent, from the tryst he had
sallied forth to keep."

"And did you know the woman ?" gasped rather than
demanded Ashley Ward.

"Did *I* know the woman ?" answered Don Rafael. "*I*
know the woman ? I was a stranger, and, truth to tell, no
friend of Americans ; a faithful husband withal, and was
it likely, though he had them, this stranger would have
shared secrets of a doubtful nature with me ?   When

I said a 'tryst' I used it for want of a better word. What attraction should a man so refined, so engrossed in his affairs as this busy foreigner, find in the humble and rustic beauties of the village? For my part, I find it impossible to imagine such coarseness in a man so little likely to be governed by a base passion as Ashley appeared. You know your own people better than I can ; what say you?"

"I say the same!" answered Ward, eagerly, with a keen glance at the sensitive dark face of the administrador. "Yet I know that my cousin loved ; that he claimed to be married ; that the lady—"

He paused,—some of the men were within hearing, listening like Don Rafael himself with rapt faces. That of Don Rafael lighted for a moment with an incredulous smile. "Ah, then there *was* a woman?" he said. "That might be ; but a marriage? Ah, Señor, if there had been that, all the world would have known it. You know but little of our laws if you suppose such a contract could be here secretly and legally made. If he claimed such to be the case, he was vilely deceived, or himself was—"

He stopped at the word, as if fearing to offend.

To urge the matter further seemed to Ashley worse than useless. He had learned enough of marriage laws in Mexico to feel that to mention the name of Herlinda Garcia in connection with that of Ashley was to cast upon it a slur such as could but bring upon him the resentment, and perhaps the revenge, of the family to which he was probably indebted for his very life, and certainly for a hospitality that merited respect for its liberality if not gratitude for its warmth.

"I shall never learn the truth," he thought; "and why indeed should I seek it? My aunt was wise in her generation. Though ignorant of the possibilities or impossibilities of Mexican society and character, she wisely refrained from problems which its keenness and honor ignored or left unsolved. I will go back again in content to my houses and lands, to my silver and gold. I am despoiling no legitimate heir ; and to imagine the existence of any other is an offence either to my cousin's intelligence or honor, as well as to the chastity of a woman whom even in thought I must be a villain to asperse. Let but a momentary quiet come that I may be able to

obtain the requisite funds, and I will abandon this senseless quest, and leave my murdered cousin to rest in
peace in his forgotten grave, in this land of violence and
mysteries."

This was the resolve of one hour, — to be broken in the
next, as the sight of a girl's face or the sound of her
voice, like a disturbing conscience, assured him that in
absence the doubt, or rather the tantalizing certainty,
would each day torment him more and more, and so make
enjoyment of his wealth even more impossible than it had
been when Mary's sensitive imaginings had urged him
upon his Quixotic errand.

Trivial and even ridiculous things often divert minds
most harassed and burdened, and exert an influence when
great and weighty matters would benumb or torture. It
would have been impossible for Ashley Ward, in the em-
barrassment of his situation (for his funds in the City of
Mexico were entirely cut off by its investment by the Liberals) and in the perplexity of his thoughts, to have
entered with enjoyment upon any festivity or pleasure
requiring exertion either of body or mind; but he was,
quite unconsciously to himself, in the mood idly to view
the little comedy which was enacted more and more freely
before his eyes, — just as in seasons of deepest grief
and anxiety one may seek mechanical employment for
the eye and relief for the brain in the perusal of a tale
so light that neither the strain of a nerve or a thought,
nor the excitement of pleasure or pain, shall awaken
emotion or burden memory.

Fernando Ruiz was too wily a youth, too courteous, too
kind, to throw off at once the semblance of devotion to a
goddess who had lured him to a shrine that held a divinity
whose charms, in his inconstant sight, so far surpassed
her own that he could not choose but transfer his worship,
even were it but to be disdained and rejected. In the
decorous visits he made to Doña Rita and when they met
at table, he would still sigh and cast despairing glances at
the bridling Rosario, who but that she intercepted others
more fervent still, directed toward the upper end of the
board where Doña Isabel and Chinita sat in lonely state,
would have believed quite true the tale with which her
mother strove to console her, — using such feeble prevari-

cation as is usual in Mexican families when ill news is to be ultimately communicated, in the fond hope of softening a blow which doubt and procrastination can but cause to be the more nervously dreaded. But well was Rosario convinced that though Ruiz held daily conferences with her father, and even once or more was honored by a few moments' speech with Doña Isabel, it was not of her or of love that they spoke ; and with a philosophic determination to replace with a more faithful lover the fickle admirer whom she could cease to love but would never forgive, the piqued, but lightly wounded damsel began to turn a shoulder upon the recreant soldier and her smiles upon the stranger.

Ward was perhaps singularly free from vanity, or too much absorbed to notice the honor paid him ; but with a sense of angry surprise he became aware that Chinita no longer ignored the existence of the persistent languisher, who at early morning paced the court in trim riding-suit of leather, a gay serape thrown negligently over his left shoulder, his wide-brimmed hat poised at the angle whence he could see the door of her room open, and Chinita rival the sun in dazzling his enchanted eyes. At noon he stood in the self-same spot in gay uniform, from which by some miraculous process all stain and grime had disappeared ; and not infrequently at evening he reappeared in the holiday dress of some clerk, who for the time had lent his jacket of black velvet trimmed with silver buttons, or his riding-suit of stamped leather and waist-scarf of scarlet silk, well pleased to fancy he was represented by the lithe young officer, who filled them with a grace that made them thenceforth of treble value in the owner's eyes.

This masquerade might have continued indefinitely, — for Ruiz wearied no sooner of changing fine clothes than of descanting to Ashley of his sudden but undying passion for the young Chinita, whose fortunes he conceived, as the favored of Doña Isabel Garcia, would be as brilliant as her charms, — but that first, one by one, then in twos and threes, in tens and dozens, men flocked into the adjacent villages ; and though reluctant to be torn from gentler pursuits, yet proud to form and command a regiment, the young adventurer was set the task of bringing order out of the wild and discordant elements, — a task for

which the training of his life, and his peculiar knowledge
of the material with which he had to work, more fitted
him than any especial talent, however brilliant, in the
conduct of ordinary military affairs would have done.

The young officer's vanity was flattered, for in some
occult way the responsibility of the spontaneous rally was
thrown upon his shoulders, and he became the central
figure in a movement which within a few days assumed a
picturesque and imposing character. He himself assumed
that the magic of his name had called from their rocky
lairs these mountain banditti, these sturdy vaqueros, these
apathetic but resolute rancheros who trooped in, bringing
with them rusty carbines and shotguns, and sometimes
polished Henry and Sharp's rifles, which the enterprise of
speculative Americans had introduced into the country.
There was no choice of weapons, but every one brought
something, — a silver-mounted pistol, worthless as pretentious, or a strong and formidable short-sword, or
glittering curved sabre, forged in some mountain or
village smithy.

It seemed too that by mere force of will money came into the captain's hands, and that clothing, horses, and provisions were thus brought forth from the stores and fields
of Tres Hermanos ; that plans were laid, and adverse
possibilities provided against, a way marked out and
guides provided ; and that he suddenly found himself at
the head of a force more fully equipped than any he had
before beheld, — men eager for adventure and battle, and
clamorous to be led to join the forces of Gonzales, who
while the cause with which he sympathized was meeting
bloody reverses around the City of Mexico in which the
Clerical forces were concentrated, was daily attracting in
the interior formidable additions to the numbers of the
Liberals. The tales of Conservative despotism and barbarity, which later investigations proved to have been well
founded, aided much in influencing the masses to seek
a change of evils, even where hopeless of any lasting
benefit from the new condition of affairs which it was
proposed to inaugurate.

A people who had for generations found in changes of
government simply fresh despotisms and encroachments
were not likely to be as enthusiastic in discussion as mad

for action, — for crushing and destroying the old, and seizing upon all available booty, not as necessary to the success of their cause, but as a despoilment of the enemy. And upon this principle it within a few days happened that Tres Hermanos presented more the appearance of a forced than a voluntary contributor to the military necessities of the time. Not only the common soldiers but those who were to lead them, — most of them men as skilled in ordering the sacking of a hacienda as in defending a mountain pass or assaulting some unwary town, — had poured in and filled every vacant nook in the village huts, and occupied the long-deserted reduction-works and the ruinous huts along the watercourse, and overran the courts and yards of the great house itself.

The great conical storehouses of small grains and corn were opened and the mill invaded by the soldiers, who under the half-reluctant directions of the skilled workmen kept the somewhat primitive machinery in constant motion, — varying their employment by breaking the half-wild horses brought in from the wide pastures and talking love to the village girls, who in all their lives had never before beheld a holiday-making half so delightful.

The long-closed church too was thrown open, and a priest from the next village was busied all day long shriving the sins of those whom he shrewdly suspected were ready to raise the standard of revolt against the temporal rule of the Church, whose ghostly powers had overshadowed earth with the terrors of its supernatural dominion.

Ruiz had gained a certain fame, more as a reflection from that of the man with whom he had been associated than from any daring episodes in his own career; and he actually possessed a military training that ordinarily well filled the place of innate genius, and at other times counterfeited it. He had impressed Don Rafael as a man well suited, if hedged with precautions, to lead the forces that his representations induced Doña Isabel to send to the relief of her favorite Gonzales. A leader of more positive aspirations and declared opinions than Ruiz manifested, would not so happily have welded and moulded men of such diverse and conflicting elements, — men who, accustomed to the freedom of guerilla warfare, were more

18

ready to be led by the glitter than the substance of authority. A man of straw, who though answering a purpose for the time could create no diversion of devotion to his own person in detriment to the supremacy of Gonzales, was sought and found in Ruiz. He was indeed the simple tool of Doña Isabel Garcia, manipulated by her administrador, yet so skilfully that he came to think himself the moving power which from an isolated farmhouse had within a few days changed Los Tres Hermanos into a military camp.

In proportion with the importance of the position into which Ruiz was forced his love and daring grew, and he remembered that many men of family as obscure, and certainly of less tact and talent than he, had crowned their fortunes by marriage with beautiful daughters of rich houses ; and he even began to reflect with some dissatisfaction upon Chinita's doubtful status, although a few days before he had despaired of rising to a height where he might dare so much as touch the hand of Doña Isabel's favored *protégée.*

These changes of feeling were watched from day to day with amusement by Ashley Ward, and with rage by Pepé, as with despair he saw himself fading completely from the horizon of Chinita's life, and a new and dazzling star rising upon her view. More than once Ashley Ward saw him nervously fingering the knife in his belt, as the unconscious Ruiz stood by the fountain in the moonlight and strummed the strings of a bandoline, and in the shrill tenor which seems the natural vehicle of such weird strains sang the *paloma,* "the Dove," or *Te amo,* "I love thee," — sounds pleasing in any female ear, though doubtless, thought Doña Isabel, intended to reach the heart of one particular fair one ; at which she smiled as she imagined this to be the pretty brown Rosario, while the tender notes in reality appealed not quite in vain to the girl who with a remarkable semblance of patience shared the seclusion of her own life.

Once only had Chinita rebelled, and that was when, instead of her usual ramble in the garden with Feliz or Doña Isabel herself, she had asked to be driven through the village, past the reduction-works, that she might see the preparations of which the distant sounds reached her.

She would not be appeased at Doña Isabel's refusal, even by the suggestion that she should stand upon the balcony of the central window, whence she could overlook the scene for miles;. and so contrary was her humor that Doña Isabel was glad to agree to her sudden fancy that her old playfellow Pepé should be allowed to describe to her what he had seen. "Men see more than women," the wilful girl exclaimed; "he will tell me something more than of the chickens that are stolen, and the number of tortillas that are eaten. Ay, Dios! I would I were a man myself, to be a soldier!"

So toward evening a message brought by Doña Feliz herself startled the sullen Pepé. Ashley Ward watched the youth with some curiosity as he sauntered across the court and ascended the stone stairs. Pepé's dress that day was in a Saturday's state of grime, and at best consisted of a shabby suit of yellow buckskin, from which the metal buttons had mostly dropped, and which gaped at the armholes as widely as at the waistband; and his leathern sandals and sombrero of woven grass showed signs of age, corresponding to that of the ragged blanket he wore with such an air that he might have been taken for the very king of idle loungers.

Doña Isabel glanced up at him as he muttered the customary salutation, uncovering his shock of black hair and inclining his head to her, while his black eyes furtively sought Chinita. There was nothing in his appearance for the most careful duenna to fear, and although Doña Isabel remembered that a few weeks ago those two had been equals, they now seemed as widely sundered as the poles; and knowing the prolixity with which the ordinary ranchero usually approached and gave his views upon any subject, she withdrew to the lower end of the gallery, where she might count her beads or con her thoughts undisturbed. The murmur of voices reached her with sufficient distinctness for her to know that the usual process of minute questioning and tantalizing indefiniteness of answer was in progress; and at length, soothed by the warm still air, the low song of a bird in the orange-tree which exhaled a sweet and heavy odor, and the habitual absorption of her own reflections, she failed to notice that the murmur of the voices grew less and less distinct, and indeed blended faintly with the low medley of sounds peculiar to the coming eveningtide.

"Pepé," Chinita was saying then, in a tone a little above a whisper, "tell me, is it true that this Don Fernando Ruiz, who for love of Rosario, and to please Don Rafael and Doña Isabel, is to lead these recruits to join Don Gonzales, — tell me, is it true that he was the associate of that Ramirez who was here so many years ago?"

"It is likely," answered Pepé, sullenly. "I have heard that he is Ramirez's godson; and what more likely," he added in an undertone, "than that the Devil should stand sponsor for an imp of his own blackness?"

"In that case," said Chinita, sharply, "it is impossible Ruiz has pronounced against him. Who ever heard of a godchild drawing sword against his sponsor? It should be against his father 'or brother rather. Go to, Pepé, you and I know nothing of Puro or Mocho. Bah! they know not the difference one from the other themselves; but we do know Ramirez and Gonzales, and it is the first that I love. What are you frowning at, Pepé? Oh! oh! oh! you are jealous, as you used to be of Pancho and Juan and Gabriel! What an idea! Ha! ha! ha!"

"Why do you laugh so loudly?" asked Doña Isabel across the corridor, not displeased to see her merry.

"Because he was telling me how the Tia Gomesinda broke the jar over the shoulders of the brave recruit who drained it of her last boiling of corn gruel," answered Chinita, readily. "But excuse me, Señora, I will not disturb you again;" and she turned with a conciliatory smile toward Pepé, who was regarding her with an expression of malignant idolatry, — if such an extravagant phrase may be coined, to indicate a love which was capable of destroying, but never of renouncing, its object.

"Thou art more unmannerly and more easily vexed than when thou usedst to follow me through the corn and bean fields, bending under the loads of wild fruit and flowers I piled upon thee, and then throwing them down some stony ravine because of one sharp word I would give thee. How canst thou expect ever to be aught but a poor ranchero, with a temper so unreasonable?"

"And what if I were as patient as Saint Stephen himself, what would it matter? Thou wouldst not love me,"

answered the young man. " And what care I whether I
am poor or rich, ranchero or soldier? It is all one now
that thou art with Doña Isabel. Why, if thou wert her
child she could not be more choice of thee. Those who
ate from the same plate and drank from the same bowl
with thee are less than the dogs who followed thee ; " and
he would have kicked, had it been near enough, the cur
which had been Pedro's, and which like many others had
the undisputed right to the corridor, and with patient
obstinacy chose to lie at Chinita's door.

The young girl looked up with a tantalizing smile. She
had been used to these speeches of covert jealousy, which
she feigned to take as the envy of an ill-mannered ranchero.
" Pshaw ! " she said gazing at him through her half-closed
lids, and yet from beneath the long lashes that veiled them
casting a languorous though wholly unstudied glance,
which dazzled and thrilled him, " ' friends, bacon, and
wine should be old ! ' What friend like an old friend?
He is better than a new-found relation. It is he who
will do a bidding and ask no reason for it ; it is he — "

" What can I do for thee?" whispered Pepé, hoarsely.
" Tell me, and thou shalt see whether I am a friend or no ;
and then Chinita thou wilt — "

" Sh-h ! " interrupted Chinita, her finger again on her
lip. " What does it matter to me who wins or loses in
these senseless battles? Yet I wonder thou art not with
Pedro ; I would not have him sick or wounded, and alone,"
and her eyes filled with tears. Pepé moved from foot to
foot, and rubbed his shoulder against the wall uneasily.
There was a covert reproach in her tone which he resented, and yet it pleased him too that she should be
troubled : if Pedro were remembered, he could not himself
be wholly forgotten.

" It is not my fault," he muttered : " he stole away in
the night. Some say after all he has not gone to Gonzales,
and that the men who are gathered here may find themselves led to Ramirez. At any rate this Ruiz — who you
say loves Rosario, but who sighs like a furnace when his
eye lights on you, and who has worn away the post of his
door writing verses to your praise with the point of his
rapier — should be but little to be trusted."

" Ah ! " ejaculated Chinita, " I do not think thou lovest

him, Pepito. Thou wouldst not that he should do me a favor instead of thyself?"

"I would see him choked first with the wine in which he drinks a toast to thine eyes," answered Pepé, hotly. "Señor Don 'Guardo and I are in the same mind about that; but it is not that he thinks thee a beauty," he added hastily.

Chinita flushed and tossed her head proudly. "What matters it what Don 'Guardo thinks?" she said. "There could be nothing but ill luck in the favor of a man like that. Hast thou shown him the grave of the other American? Ah, thou must know where to find it. Didst thou think I did not see thee following me behind the tuñas and bushes the day I found it after I had bidden thee go back? Thou wert like Negrito there. Come here, Negrito; thou art lean and black, but I love thee;" and she stooped to pat the slinking cur. "Ah, ah! Pepito, it would be a good jest if thou wouldst show Don 'Guardo the American's grave, and tell him Chinita bids him beware of the same fortune."

"He would think thee a gypsy more than ever, and a saucy one," answered Pepé. "But I know this is not the favor thou wouldst ask of me. Thou art thinking ever of Ramirez, who bewitched thee. Ask it of the Captain Ruiz rather than me. I would die for thee, but I see not how I can serve thee by turning traitor."

Chinita started up angrily. "Am I a false-hearted wretch to ask it of thee?" she cried furiously, though in a low voice. "Ramirez fights for the side of right. Is it his fault if the Clergy are right to-day and the Liberals to-morrow? Were not he and Gonzales upon the same side when they were here years ago? Were not his men crying '*Dios y Libertad!*' when they passed here six months ago? And suppose the cry is changed. Bah! with Doña Isabel's men he would be of Doña Isabel's opinion! What does it matter to him? He is a man to fight, not to sit down like Don Rafael and the major-domo, old Don Tomas, and talk, talk, talk!"

"That is very well," said Pepé, staidly; "but why do you not tell this all to Doña Isabel? Or listen, now: to please thee I will seek Pedro, — I warrant me he is not so far away, — and I will tell him how thou wouldst have

Ramirez rather than Gonzales to lead th troops; if it
matters not to him, *cierto* it will not to me! But I tell
thee frankly I would be of those who would pull down
rather than build up churches. I see no gain to be had
in fighting for the Señores the bishops, who have so much
already that the poor man can have nothing but leave
to fast while the priests revel in plenty. Go to, Chinita!
thou hast heard Pedro talk of freedom as much as I have.
If Don Benito Juarez and Don Vicente and the rest of
them gain the day, I — why I might be an alcalde myself,
or a general; and then — well, anything thou wilt!"

Chinita laughed and nodded at him. "It is the Señor
Ramirez who could bring about all that," she said with
conviction; "and, Pepé, though thou dost not love the
Captain Ruiz, thou shalt take him that message from Chinita. Yes, yes! go thy way quietly to Pedro, and if there
is treason, Ruiz shall work it. So the General Ramirez
shall be brought over to our side, and Ruiz shall be the
only man who will be blamed, if Doña Isabel is vexed."

Pepé shook his head doubtfully. His views were no
clearer than Chinita's, but they were not additionally obscured by an unreasoning enthusiasm for a self-created
hero. Doña Isabel was rising from her chair; the rattle
of the wood upon the bricks startled the two speakers.

"How goes it with thy sister Juana?" asked Chinita,
lightly. "She told me once she loved Gabriel because,
though he was old and ugly, he would do more to please
her than all the young and handsome lovers. Are they
happy, do you think, or has he beaten her already, as I
said he would?"

Pepé looked at her keenly and with an expression of wild
hope from behind the wide hat he was holding in both
hands before his face, in awkward preparation for departure. Would Chinita too marry the man who would please
her? And after all it was but a little thing, — just a hint to
the man whose admiration she jeered at.

"Thou canst go now, Pepé," said Doña Isabel, approaching. "I am sure the Señorita has heard enough of
the wild doings of these mad soldiers. Thank Heaven,
they leave us soon! Ah, now that I think of it, thou
mayst say to the Señor Americano that Captain Ruiz told
me to-day he would gladly give him safe escort as far upon

their way as their roads may lie together ; and — but I forgot, such messages are not for thee. I will send them by the Señor Administrador."

Pepé muttered his adieus and bowed himself away in some confusion. Chinita looked after him meaningly ; he caught her glance and then the motion of her lips. His heart beat wildly ; they formed the refrain of a popular song,—

"Adios, my dearest love ! "

Pepé reached the court quite dizzy. Ashley Ward and Captain Ruiz were both waiting for him. His excitement had reached a crisis. He seized Ruiz by the arm. "If you would please her," he hissed in his ear, "find Ramirez, and let him, and not Gonzales, lead the troops."

"You are drunk ! " answered Ruiz ; yet he clutched the youth by the arm, and led him into his room.

Pepé came to his senses with the shock as he sank upon a stone bench against the cold, hard wall. Presently he gave a brief account of Chinita's desires and reasons. Ruiz listened without a smile. Childish and unprincipled as they were, they were not more so than scores he had heard discussed in the course of the years of anarchy in which he had entered upon manhood. Find Ramirez, pledge him to the Liberal cause, leave it to him to gain such an ascendency over the troops that they would themselves proclaim him their leader ! It was an easy task. It set him thinking, and Pepé slunk away to hope, to doubt, to despair, to hope again.

"Adios, my dearest love ! " —

just the refrain of a song, yet it pursued and bewildered him. For less, stronger men than Pepé the ranchero have committed unimaginable crimes.

The next morning when they met in the court, Captain Ruiz stopped Pepé. "Tell her her wishes are law to me !" he said. "If she but love me, I — "

"*Caramba!*" cried Pepé, savagely. "Am I an old woman or a priest that I should carry your messages? She love you ! she would needs have been born to lead apes, to love you." And Pepé flung himself off in a rage, while the astounded Ruiz gazed after him in open-mouthed amazement.

" By my life, he loves her himself!" he muttered vacantly. "Señor Don 'Guardo, heard you ever such presumption? The bare-skin beggar loves the favorite — what shall we say? — niece of Doña Isabel!"

" Let us say you are both fools!" said Don 'Guardo in good round English and with a sudden rage, the motive of which was to himself inexplicable; and the discomfited captain bowed, not doubting that his own expression of disgust had been echoed.

"*Caramba!* a woman so beautiful gazed at by every beggar, like an image of the Virgin of Remedios carried in procession! I swear I will not forget thee, Pepito, and will keep a close eye on thee, now I know thou hast been tampered with!" continued Ruiz, hotly. "A word to the General Gonzales will be enough if he is of my mind!"

That day, in spite of Doña Isabel's diligence, a pink note found its way to Chinita. "Good!" she said after reading it, " My General Ramirez will have the men; the Señor Gonzales will be helped, and Doña Isabel will do a double good. This is not so bad a subject, — this Ruiz; and his eyes are as black and large as those of Ramirez himself. All is well. All things will come right at last. Ah, if only what Don Rafael told Feliz one night should come true, and the convents are opened, then — "

She paused. It seemed too utterly impossible even to dream of. She looked again at her first love-letter; a twinge of remorse seized her as she thought of Rosario. She laughed, but she tore the paper into infinitesimal shreds.

What was the writer thinking? "Onward! I have gone too far to turn back even at the word of Chinita. A promise will gain her love, but the essential thing is the good-will of Doña Isabel. ' A pearl is all the better for a golden setting!' No treaties then with Ramirez. Though he is my godfather, I need not his patronage. Doña Isabel, a straight path, and Juarez! Forward! Ruiz, fortune favors you!"

XXX.

A few days later the troops had left Tres Hermanos, and Ashley Ward stood in the silent graveyard on the mountain side, pushing back with his foot the loose sand his tread had disturbed, as it threatened again and again to cover the rude wooden cross upon which his eyes were fixed. It bore the name of his murdered cousin, faint yet distinct, preserved by the sand, for the wind had soon prostrated it after Chinita's shallow replanting. The words seemed to Ashley to call to him aloud from the dust of his kinsman; in the hot sunshine their spell was as potent as though a ghostly voice had spoken at midnight. For the first time, something more intense than the desire to satisfy conscience by proving that he wronged no rightful heir in entering upon property which would have been John Ashley's had he lived, arose in his mind. The absolute reality of his cousin's death for the first time seemed to become an overwhelming conviction; and with it came memories of the young and daring man whom he had in childhood held in wondering admiration. And as he stood within sight of the spot where the brilliant young life had ended in a bloody tragedy, a deep wave of sorrow surged over his soul, and from its depths, as from the loose sands of the wind-levelled grave, appeared to rise a cry for vengeance.

Though not till now had Chinita's charge that he be taken to the American's grave been carried out, the message from Doña Isabel, which Pepé had not failed to deliver, had reached him some days before, and had been supplemented by a visit from Don Rafael. Although a certain fascination had inclined Ashley to linger still at Tres Hermanos, he had so little hope of adding to the information he had already gained of his cousin's life, — there seemed so little possibility that the marriage which John Ashley had intimated had taken place, could ever have been more than a mere sentimental dedication of the lovers one to the other, in which they deemed themselves man and wife in the sight of God, but which in the sight of man was a mere illicit connection, to be condemned or ignored, — that he had not dared to present himself before the haughty mother of the one Herlinda whom he suspected to have been the object of his cousin's passion, and to insult her with questions or insinuations that would cast a doubt upon her daughter's purity and a stain upon the fame of the house of Garcia, which even the blood of John Ashley and his own added thereto would be insufficient to wash away.

The young man had decided then to accept the order of dismissal, so delicately conveyed in the intimation that by accepting the escort of the troops as far as they might proceed toward Guanapila, he would not only reach a point whence in all probability he might in safety proceed to that city, but that he would thus render a favor to Doña Isabel, who was minded by the same opportunity to withdraw from the hacienda, — her presence there being liable to act as a lure to either party, who might after seizing her person levy a ransom upon the family which even their large resources would be severely strained to meet.

Although the fiction was maintained that her assistance of the Liberal cause was involuntary, it was readily surmised that Doña Isabel Garcia was in reality seeking to avoid the vengeance of the Conservatives, while their forces were so demoralized and scattered that she might hope to reach Guanapila, which was then occupied by a patriot guard, before the tide of the war should turn and bring the army of the Church again to the fore *en masse*, — collected by the clarion cry of fanaticism, and lavishly rewarded from the hoards of silver and gold drawn from the vaults into which for generations had been drained the prosperity and the very life-blood of the peasantry.

Ashley Ward had been struck with admiration of the woman who thus dared the dangers of the road, — to which she had been no stranger. He had felt something of the chivalrous enthusiasm of a knight of old, as he joined the irregular band which by daylight had gathered upon the sandy plain before the straggling village. The soldiers had fallen into march with something like order, with Ruiz

at their head, — for once with an anxious face, for he felt
that the die was cast, and that he had raised up for himself an enemy whom it would be mad temerity to face,
and hopeless to attempt to conciliate. The baggage-mules
were driven by the leathern-clad muleteers, who even thus
early had begun their profane adjurations to the nimble-
footed beasts, that listened with quivering ears thrown
back in obstinate surprise at every unwonted silence. The
women who had come from other villages had laughed
and chided their unruly infants, as they arranged and re-
arranged their baskets of maize and vegetables upon the
panniers of their donkeys, if they were fortunate enough
to possess any, or upon their own shoulders if they
were to walk; and those who were for the first time leaving their birthplace to follow the fortunes of husband or
sweetheart, had burst into loud lamentations. Ashley had
been glad to find these changed to laughter, however,
before they were well past the broken wall of the reduction-works; which they skirted, entering upon the bridle-
path which led across the hill, where the rough heaps of
sand showed through the scattered cacti, and where, by
the rude wooden crosses, he now for the first time learned
lay the village graveyard.

Pepé had ridden sullenly by his side. He had been
sent back with a sharp reprimand from the station he had
taken among the mounted servants who surrounded the
carriage of Doña Isabel, Ruiz in petty tyranny refusing
him so honorable a place. A glance from Chinita had
been the deepest reproof of all; and as he pondered upon
it, certain words which she had uttered, and which he
had hitherto forgotten, had come into his mind. As they
neared the graveyard his eye caught Ward's, and suddenly
laying his hand upon the bridle of the American's horse,
he had muttered, —

" Señor, she thinks I have forgotten all her wishes; but
there is not even one so foolish that I scorn it. Turn aside
but for a moment, Señor, — here where the adobe has
fallen, your horse can scramble through the wall. Follow
me, they will not miss us before we can reach our places
again. *Caramba!* Don Fernando watches me as a cat
watches a mouse. Here, Señor, — never mind the women.
Stupids! how they herd their donkeys together, when

they might have the whole hillside to pick their own paths on! Patience! Let us wait a little, Señor! Ah," he reflected, as they remained silent and motionless, "there is the spot. I have never forgotten it since I followed her through the rushes down there by the stream, and scratched my face in the tuñas, darting behind them that she should not see me. I was not half so tired as Chinita was though, when she sat down to rub sand upon her smarting hands, and fell asleep with the sun beating upon her head. I wonder if she ever thought it was I who covered her face with her ragged reboso, — she wears one of silk now, as clean and soft as a dove's breast, — or that I lay behind the big pipes of the flowering organ-plant as she turned over the fallen cross which her hand struck against, and read the name and age of the American who had been murdered years before? Who ever would have thought — for I hated her then if I did follow her, as she maddens me now with her soft eyes and her mocking smile — that I should be bringing here the man who perhaps is just the handsome, woman-maddening demon they say that other was, and at her will too? *Ave Maria Purissima!* what God wills the very saints themselves may not say No to, — much less a poor peasant like Pepé Ortiz."

These thoughts, perhaps scarcely in the order in which they are set down, passed through the mind of Pepé, as lingering until the straggling procession had passed, he emerged from the shade of such an organ-plant as had once sheltered him years ago, and taking his bearings with unerring eyes, beckoned to Ashley, — who had waited within touch of his hand, and whose heart had begun to beat suffocatingly, though he knew that it was utterly improbable that anything more important than the mound that covered the body of his cousin would meet his eye, — and led the way to the most wind-swept and desolate portion of that paupers' acre, and presently stooping where the ground was sunken rather than heaped, turned with some effort the half-buried cross, and exposed to Ashley's view the name from which his own had been derived.

The young man gazed at it in a sort of fascination, actually spelling the letters over and over. He felt as if a part of himself must be buried there. His eyes burned; the glaring sunshine leaped and quivered above the ill-carved letters, distorting and confounding them. His heart beat violently; every sense but that of hearing seemed to fail him, and every sound upon the air became a weird, mysterious voice, — blood crying unto its kindred blood.

This deep emotion fixed the indifferent and wandering eye of Pepé, who, holding the bridles of the horses, stood near, impatient to be gone, yet intending to watch out of sight the last stragglers; for it was with a double purpose he had turned aside to point out the grave of the American, — first, perhaps, to gratify the seemingly jesting wish of Chinita; and then to seize the opportunity to turn his fleet steed into the narrow bridle-path which led to mountain villages, where he shrewdly suspected Pedro might be found, or at least be heard of. He had promised to carry the message of Chinita to Pedro, and would have set forth upon the very night she had charged him with it, but until mounted by Ruiz's command had found it impossible to provide himself with a horse, without which it was hopeless for him to attempt his quest. To escape the discipline of the ranks, he had induced Ashley to retain him as his servant, feeling no scruple at his intended abandonment. As his eye rested upon the pale and excited countenance of Ashley, Chinita's words, with which she had bade him taunt him, flashed into his mind; yet he forbore to utter them, saying presently in a tone of concern, —

"Let us go now, Señor, it is growing hot. It is almost noon, and you are faint. Let us ride on, and I will point out the way that you must take when we have crossed the face of the hill. Then comes a slight descent, Señor, and upon the little plain that lies between that and the cañon of the Water-pots will the troop stop for the nooning. This has been a rapid march. Doña Isabel will feel all the safer when she is once on the highway. But as for us, Señor, we must part company. You will find a better servant; I should but ill serve your grace. You know yourself I am but a stupid fellow, and it is only the patience of your grace that has been equal to my ignorance."

Ashley heard neither the excuses of Pepé nor his own

praises, but with a gesture at once commanding and entreating the servant to leave him, said: " Pepé, I had
forgotten. There is something which will keep me still at
Tres Hermanos. The Señora Doña Isabel must pardon
me. Go! go to your duty, as I must to mine. God! how
could I have forgotten it? Oh John, John! does time and
distance make men so unnatural? Is it possible I could
leave the place where you were so foully murdered, without
knowing why or by whom? Who killed him, and why
was the deadly and secret blow struck? Ah, that involves
the question of the very mystery I came here to fathom,
and which I was turning my back upon; for I am convinced that it is here, and not by following Doña Isabel
Garcia, that it may be solved. She is too resolute, too
astute; nothing is to be forced or beguiled from her lips!
But now that the spell of her presence is removed, I may
learn everything from these people, who with all their cunning and clannish devotion can surely be influenced by
reasons such as I can give."

" Who would have guessed the sight of a grave would
so stir the blood?" soliloquized Pepé. " Can it be that
Chinita — But no, she was more in jest than earnest; she
always laughed at the *niña* Chata for her sorrow for the
foreigner. — Well, all must die!" he said aloud. " Believe
me, Señor, after all these years a knife-thrust is a little
matter to inquire into. *Caramba!* Chinita herself would
tell you that to turn back on a journey because of the dead
is an omen of evil; 't was not for that she would have
me show you the grave of your countryman, — God rest
him!"

Ashley looked at him keenly. " Ah," he said, " it is
then no accident that you have brought me here? God!
what a mystery! Pepé, tell Chinita I know her thoughts,
and that I never will rest till I prove them right or
wrong. She is a strange creature, and likely to prove
an enigma to more men than myself. Poor lad, she is
not for you to dream of."

" I will not see her again till I can tell her that which
shall please her," said Pepé. " Look you, Señor, she is
one who will have the world turn to suit her."

" A wilful girl," thought Ashley, with judicial disapproval. " She has all the craftiness and deceit of the Indian

and the pride and passion of a Spaniard; yet what if I should follow her? No, no! mere circumstance and conjecture shall not turn me! — *Adios*, Pepé," he said aloud, " and beware! It is Doña Isabel you serve, and not the young girl who has bewitched you."

Pepé smiled vaguely; his glance roved over the landscape. "Her heart is virgin honey in a cup of alabaster!" he murmured. Ashley was becoming accustomed to the poetic expressions of these unlettered rancheros, and with some impatience took in his own hand the bridle-rein of his horse, and reminding Pepé that it was nearly noon, and that he would be missed should he longer delay, bade him mount and hasten with messages of excuse to Doña Isabel for his own sudden return to Tres Hermanos.

With the customary apparent submission of a peasant, Pepé prepared to obey. He was in fact anxious to set forth as soon as he could be certain that no straggler was near to mark his movements. The troops and their followers had disappeared. "The Señor Don 'Guardo should leave this solitary spot on the instant," he said with genuine concern; " in these days of revolution, one can never say what dangerous people may be wandering abroad."

" I have nothing to fear from them," answered Ashley, " unless it should be that they might attempt to rob me of the horse Doña Isabel has lent me. Well, for its sake, I will be prudent; though in truth the sight of a ghost in this desolate spot of sunken graves would seem more probable than that any living being should pass here. Now, then, good-by, Pepé."

" Until our next meeting, Señor! " replied Pepé, gravely lifting his hat. He had attached himself to Ashley, and it seemed to him an evil omen that they should part at a grave. and he thus attempted to console himself by the pretence that it was but for a little while. " For a short time Señor, and God keep you! "

Ashley shook his hand warmly. The ranchero drew his hat over his eyes, adjusted his scrape so that his face was almost hidden, and dropping into that utterly ungraceful posture into which the skilled horseman of Mexico relapses when he suffers his steed to take his own way and pace across a wearisome stretch of country, he turned his horse's head toward the bridle-path they had left, and slowly receded from Ashley's gaze. Once however beyond the crest of the hill, the rider's eye brightened, his figure straightened ; a distant sound of voices reached his keen ear, — it was so remote that but for the rarity of the atmosphere it would have failed to reach him. Bending his head, he listened intently for a moment ; then raising it he gazed searchingly on every hand, rode for a short distance to the right, guided his nimble-footed beast down the cleft sides of a deep ravine and along the dry bottom of a rock-strewn path, which rapid floods had in some past time cut in their fierce descent from the steep sides of the frowning mountains, and so gradually gained the dark and solitary defiles that led directly to those eyries of bandit mountaineers, who under the guise of shepherds, charcoal-burners, and goat-herds had been, as Pepé well knew, the chosen comrades of Pedro Gomez and his mates in the boyhood days of that Don Leon whose wild deeds were still the theme of many a tale, and like the story of his death became more mythical with every repetition.

Pepé rode steadily on for hours, picturing to himself his meeting with Pedro should he find him, or the quiet exultation of Chinita when she should hear that he had deserted the troops, or of the return of Don 'Guardo to the hacienda. In his heart he was not displeased that the American should be separated from Chinita, though it left her the more completely to the gallant care of Ruiz. He had comprehended instantly the emotion which had seized upon Ashley at his kinsman's grave, — the instinct for revenge. He said to himself that those Americans, after all, were people of sensibility, and he felt a certain satisfaction that he had been the instrument of calling into action a sentiment that did the foreigner so much credit.

Meanwhile the heat of noon passed, and Ashley's horse stood with patient dejection in the shadow of the huge cactus to which he had been tethered, not even taking advantage of the freedom allowed by the length of the rope, so little temptation to browse was offered by the sparse and coarse tufts of herbage which struggled into existence here and there. The time wore on, and an occasional stamp attested his disapprobation of a master who lay prone upon the ground under a mesquite tree

19

when the sun shone hottest, and who when the cool breeze of afternoon swept over the silent spot, stood long and still beside the grave he had not sought, and yet felt infinite reluctance to leave.

It was a foolish thought, but as he gazed across the broad valley to the great square of buildings set among the fields, the youth imagined how indeed the dead man might at times steal forth to visit again those fertile scenes where he had lived and loved. As he stood there, Ashley could see the people like pigmies passing in and out the great gateway, or going from hut to hut in the village. There was one figure — it seemed that of a woman — which his eye sought from time to time, as it appeared and disappeared in the corn and bean fields, and at last came out on the open road that lay between them and the reduction-works. He was becoming quite fascinated by its hesitating yet persistent progress, when he was startled by a sound; and glancing up, he saw a man leaning upon the crumbling wall and regarding him with a gaze so bewildered, so fixed, that involuntarily he moved a step toward him.

The stranger started, as if some frightful spell had been broken. Ashley saw that he crossed himself, and muttered some invocation; yet that he had not the look of a nervous man or a coward, but rather of a somnambulist pacing the earth under the impulse of some horrible dream. The man was not ill-looking, — no, decidedly not; and though his skin was deeply browned as if from much exposure, and his cheek bones were prominent, giving his face a certain cast below the eyes that was plebeian or Indian in character, the eyes themselves were dilated and brilliant, and the straight nose and pointed beard gave him the air of a Spanish cavalier, though he wore the broad sombrero and serape of a common soldier of the rural order. Perhaps on ordinary occasions even a more practised eye than that of Ashley Ward would have accepted the stranger for what he purported to be; but the American with an extraordinary feeling of repulsion little accounted for by the mere sense of intrusion caused by the man's unexpected appearance, at once leaped to the conclusion that his dress — though he had no appearance of strangeness in it — was virtually a disguise, and that instead of a soldier of the ranks, the man before him was of no ordinary position or character.

The new-comer seemed to have risen out of the ground, so stealthily had he approached. It would have been quite possible for him, tall as he was, to have skirted the wall without observation from any one within the enclosure. But undoubtedly he had taken no precaution in that solitary place, which except at funeral times was shunned as the haunt of ghosts and ill-omened birds and reptiles, and thus had come unexpectedly upon the motionless figure of the tall young man clothed in a plain riding-suit of black, with bright conspicuous locks at the moment uncovered, and fair-skinned face of a characteristic American type, — all unremarkable in themselves but associated in the mind of the observer with one whom he had seen but twice or thrice, and this on the mad night when the moon had shone down upon a victim quivering in the death-agony above which he had exulted.

The two men held each the other's gaze in silence for a full minute, both unmindful of the common courtesy usual in such chance encounters in solitary places. Then recovering from the superstitious awe which had overpowered him, the Mexican stepped over the broken wall. Ashley noticed as he did so that heavy silver spurs were on his heels, and that the fringed sides of his leathern trousers were stained as though with hard riding, and that, as if from habit, rather than any purpose of menace, his nervous hand closed upon the pistol in his scarlet band, as with a few long strides he reached the spot on which Ashley stood with that air of defiance which a sudden intrusion upon a solitude however secure naturally arouses in a man who is neither a coward nor an adept in the self-command that is perhaps the most perfect substitute for invincible courage.

" Señor," said the Mexican, " your pistols are on your saddle. You are right; this is an evil habit to wear them so readily at one's side. Pardon me if in my surprise I assumed an attitude of menace; but these are troublous times. One scarcely expects to find a cavalier alone in such a place." He looked around him with a smile, which did not hinder a quiver of the lip expressing an excitement which his commonplace words denied.

Ashley regarded the speaker with ever-increasing repugnance. It was true his pistols hung from the saddle, but there was a small knife in his belt, and his hand wandered to it stealthily as he answered : " Señor, I make no inquiry why you are here, and on foot, — which you must acknowledge might well cause some curiosity in this place ; but in all courtesy I trust your errand is a happier one than mine. Whatever it is, I will not intrude upon it longer than will suffice to plant this cross." And with an air of perfect security, yet with his knife in hand, he bent to the work, which the other regarded with an almost incredulous gaze, — the preservation of a grave or its tokens being a sort of sentimentality to which by tradition and training he was a stranger ; and to see it exhibited for the first time in this God's acre of laborers, almost sufficed to dissipate the impression the unexpected encounter had made upon him. As Ashley quietly pursued his work, the new-comer had an opportunity to look at him narrowly. After all, this one was like many another American ! Yet there was something in the young man's appearance that brought the sweat to the brow of the soldier ; he pushed back his hat, and breathed hard. As he did so, Ashley braced the cross against his knee. The action brought the letters into clear and direct view. The eyes of the Mexican rested upon them. He fell back a step or two in superstitious awe, involuntarily exclaiming :

"*Cristo!* was *he* buried here? And who are you?"

Ashley glanced up. There was a revelation to him in the questioner's disordered and ashy countenance. He dropped the cross, sprang over the grave, and seized the stranger by the right arm. "Who are you who ask?" he cried. "What do you know of the man who is buried there?"

" My faith ! you are a brave man to put such questions !" retorted the new-comer, wrenching himself free. Ashley had spoken in English, but the violence of his act had interpreted his words. "Take your pistols and defend yourself, if you are here for vengeance. Kill him? Yes ; I killed him as I would a dog. Faith, I thought it was his accursed ghost that had risen to challenge me !"

" I am his cousin ! Assassin, give me reasons for your deed !" cried Ashley, furiously, yet with a remembrance that to every criminal should be allowed some chance of justification.

But the Mexican seemed little inclined to profit by it.

" Reasons ! " cried he. " Yes, such reasons as I gave him when I thrust the knife into his heart." He raised his pistol and fired. The shot passed so close to Ashley's temple that he heard it whiz through the air. In the same instant the two men clinched. The horse, which during the controversy had plunged and reared madly, broke away, and careering over the graves galloped wildly down the hillside. A fresh horse with its rider at the same instant dashed into the enclosure, and a voice cried, " For God's sake my General ! what adventure is this? Mount! mount! there is no time to be lost ! "

The combatants at the sound of a third voice had involuntarily paused. Had the knife in the hand of the American been in that of the Mexican it would have sheathed itself in his opponent's heart ; but Ashley, less ready in its use, arrested his hand midway. His passion half spent, the scarcely healed wound throbbing in his shoulder, his strength exhausted, he had much ado to keep himself from staggering.

" A touch of my sabre would finish him," said the newcomer coolly, as he reined in his restive horse, and put his hand on the long weapon swinging from his saddle. But the soldier stopped him.

" No killing in cold blood," he exclaimed. " 'T is a madman, but his fury is over. What brings you here, Reyes? Were you not to wait at the rendezvous ? "

" Wait ! " he retorted, " this is no time to wait ! We are already a day too late. A thousand men are on the road before us, my General ! We let them pass us this morning as we lingered on the opposite side of the mountain in the Devil's gate ! "

" And the troops are there still ? " cried the other furiously. " Where is Choolooke ? Did you not think to bring me a horse ? Back to the Zahuan, man ! We must begin the march this very night. I know Ruiz ; he will yield in a moment at sight of me ! "

" Not he ! " answered Reyes. " He has a new patroness ; Doña Isabel herself is with him."

" Isabel ! " cried the officer with an oath. " Ah, then,

Tres Hermanos is partisan at last! *Carrhi!* my lady Isabel shall find what she has begun shall be soon ended!" He put a small silver whistle to his lips and blew a shrill blast, which was answered by a neigh. A black horse lifted its head and looked over the wall with a gaze of almost human intelligence.

"He followed me at a word," exclaimed Reyes, " and stood by the wall like a statue when I bade him. Never was there such another horse as your black Choolooke, my General. Even the stampede of that unbroken brute that was tethered here could not startle him."

" Ay, I discipline horses better than I do men, — eh, Choolooke?" The horse with its jingling accoutrements had cantered into the enclosure, and with one bound his owner was in the saddle.

All had passed in the few minutes in which Ashley was recovering breath, and in utter bewilderment endeavoring to gain some insight into the meaning of this rapid transformation scene, of which he himself had formed a part. As his late opponent sprang into the saddle, he could have fancied he heard the sound of the bugle, so alert were the man's movements, so soldierly his bearing. But in the midst of his involuntary admiration he did not forget the extraordinary relations in which they stood to each other. He threw himself before the horse at the imminent risk of being trampled down. " Your name!" he cried. " By your own admission you are my cousin's murderer. We must meet again! I am Ashley Ward; and you?"

" Out of the way!" cried the rider, checking his horse by a dexterous turn of his hand. " My name? Ah, yes! Tell them there," and he nodded in the direction of the hacienda, " they will soon have reason never to forget it !" He hesitated; plunged the spurs into his already impatient steed, and dashed furiously away, followed by Reyes; then rose in his stirrups to shout back in defiance the name — " Ramirez!"

XXXI.

Ramirez! Ashley's heart bounded, his brain throbbed dizzily yet acutely. Here was no obscure assassin, who once escaping him would perhaps be lost forever.

The name was on every lip with those of Juarez, Ortega, Degollado, Miramon, and a score of other popular chieftains who of one party or another, or of independent factions, attracted to themselves a host of followers, more by their own personal magnetism than for the sake of any principles they represented. In that time of anarchy any head that rose above the common herd led enthusiastic multitudes, who followed a nod and applauded to the echo even one deed of daring. But Ramirez held his prestige by no such recent and uncertain tenure; throughout the long years of revolution he had been a central figure in the bloody drama. Even his recent defeat at El Toro and his subsequent disappearance had added but a fresh glamor of mystery to his adventurous career, without detracting from the almost superstitious awe with which he was regarded. It was believed that he would reappear when and where least expected. Ashley Ward had smiled covertly at the strange and daring escapades attributed to this man. He had become in his mind a figure of romance; and here in the broad day he had risen before him, the self-denounced murderer of John Ashley, — and as suddenly as he had come, so had he escaped him.

Thinking no more of the cross, which had fallen upon the ground, hiding beneath it the name that had been so long preserved for so strange a purpose, Ashley Ward turned from the sunken graves and striding across the mounds, scarred and broken by the sacrilegious tread of the horses' feet, stood for a moment upon the broken wall, scanning the country in his excitement for some sign of the desperate men who but a few moments before had urged their restive steeds up the steep path and disappeared over the crest of the hill. He saw his own recreant steed galloping toward the hacienda walls, keeping the high-road, on past the reduction-works and the long stretch of open country beyond, and plunging and rearing at the fatal mesquite-tree. The superstitious vaqueros had instinctively imbued their animals with the same irrational terrors in which they had themselves been trained. Yet no sight of ghost or smell of blood lingered there to rouse memory or vengeance. Their waiting-place had been that long-forgotten grave upon the desolate hillside.

Ashley leaped from the wall and rapidly began the descent to the valley. The sun was still high in the heavens, for the scene we have recorded had passed in less than a brief quarter of an hour. As he walked on, gradually falling into a more natural pace, the whole matter took definite form and coherence in his mind. That which had been so unexpected, so unnatural, seemed to be the event to which his whole journey to Mexico, all his wanderings, his strange and wearisome experiences, had inevitably and naturally tended. And then arose a point beyond. His work at Tres Hermanos seemed ended; the primal cause of his being there was forgotten. The definite thought now in his mind was to reach the hacienda, provide himself anew with horse, guide, and arms, and follow on the path which Ramirez had chosen, and upon which he would sooner or later re-appear, decoyed by the rich booty that Doña Isabel had intrusted to the weak and presumably faithless Ruiz. Could he reach and warn her in time?

Ashley's scarce-healed wound was throbbing painfully, the way was long, the heat intense; yet he pressed on resolutely, though at last he staggered as he went. He sat down to rest awhile among the dry rushes of the spent watercourse, under a straggling cottonwood-tree, the few poor leaves of which scarcely sufficed to shade him from the fierce rays of the sun. A fever heat was in his veins; wild theories and speculations passed through his brain, — some of them, perhaps, not far from being keys to the mystery of that tragedy which that day for the first time had become to his mind other than a vague and gloomy fantasy. Now, like the murderer himself, it was real, absorbing, appalling.

The young man rose and again pressed on. After the descent to the long rude wall of the reduction-works, he skirted it slowly, thinking as he went how changed the aspect of the place must be since his cousin had ridden forth to his death. How proudly John had written, and almost vauntingly, of the prosperity his management had inaugurated, of the crowds of laden animals that passed in and out of the wide gates, of the men who led their slow, laborious lives among those primitive mills and wide floors of trodden ores.

Ashley glanced at the great square mass of walls and towers of Tres Hermanos, glistening in the distance. To his weary eye it looked far away; yet doubtless he thought it had been but the ride of a few eager minutes to the lover, as he went at midnight to cast a glance at the walls that circled his mistress, or to rein his horse beneath her window that he might win a word or glance from her who whispered from above. These, Ashley had heard, were lovers' ways in Mexico; he did not know that no maiden of Tres Hermanos ever occupied one of the few apartments whose windows opened toward the outer air. Yet as he debated the matter with himself, it became more and more probable to him that John Ashley had upon the fatal night been actually within the walls of the hacienda, and been stealthily followed thence by his treacherous rival, — for what, he thought, even to a Spaniard, could justify so foul a murder but the falseness of his mistress, the triumph of a hated rival? Pedro's taciturnity and gloom Ashley construed as proofs of his complicity in the crime. Even then Ramirez had been a chieftain of renown, and Pedro in his youth had been a soldier, a free rider, of whom strange tales were told. Was it not probable that he had opened the gate at a comrade's bidding, — or, more likely still, had bidden him wait beneath the tree where the favored lover was wont to mount his horse, and so take him unawares? Ashley remembered that such, it had been said, had been the manner of his cousin's taking off. He had been slain with the swiftness and sureness of a secret and unhesitating avenger.

The ardent youth railed at the mocking chances that had combined to suffer Ramirez to escape him in the unpremeditated struggle in which they had clinched with a deadly enmity. In such a struggle he could have found himself the victor without remorse, or could have died without regret; but it was not in his nature to follow a man for blood. Yet neither could he shut his ears to that cry for vengeance, for justice, which seemed ringing through the sultry stillness, — the more importunate as the possibilities of their attainment shaped themselves in his mind.

That this must be a personal matter between himself and Ramirez was clear. At any time it would probably have been useless for an alien to have denounced so popular and influential a man as the proud and daring *revolucionario*. To attempt his arrest for a murder committed years before and probably in rivalry for a lady's favor, would be but to throw a new mystery about him, and add a fresh legend of romance to those which already made him rather a character of ideal chivalry than of mere vulgar, every-day lawlessness and semi-barbarity. Though the brilliant adventurer was now under a temporary cloud, one threat of attack from law would make him again a popular idol; indeed it was likely that a *pronunciamiento* in his favor would be the immediate result, and that in falling into his hands the American would lose, if not his life, at least all opportunity either of obtaining the satisfaction of the law for his cousin's death, or of investigating further those doubts and probabilities which he had forgotten, but which now came upon him with redoubled force.

The excited Ashley planned in his mind to refresh himself upon reaching the hacienda, and demanding horse and guide to set forth upon that very night, hoping to rejoin the force at daybreak. It was useless, he reflected, to waste further time in idle questionings. It was to Doña Isabel herself he would appeal, and warning her of the danger that threatened her from the bandit chieftain, induce her to make common cause with him against one who for years must have been their common enemy. Impossible was it for him to solve the mystery of the relations in which the several actors in this strange drama in which he was so unexpectedly taking part, stood either to one another, or to himself. There was but one fact certain; by that alone he could connect himself with beings who seemed almost of another world,

— the one undoubted fact of the discovery of John Ashley's murderer.

Ashley's ready apprehension of the public mind had been helped by what he knew to be the actual state of affairs in the ranks to which Doña Isabel had intrusted the safety of her person, trusting to the resources which were at her command, and to the present ascendency of Gonzales, to bind those soldiers of fortune to the cause she had espoused. Perhaps none knew better than she the elements that an alluring chance of gain or a transient enthusiasm had drawn together; but she could not know how near the fire lay to the straw, and how at her very side were those who in the name of patriotism — or, like Chinita, for a personal sentiment as unexplainable as it was imaginative and ardent — would sacrifice her dearest plans, and think it a grand and noble deed to raise the ubiquitous and dashing Ramirez upon the fall of the slow and cautious Gonzales. Ashley had imperfectly comprehended the scheme or its bearings; he had little understood, and felt but little interest in, those strange complexities and personalities of Mexican politics; but now a sudden party zeal and horror of treason seized him. Where was Pedro Gomez, who, having played traitor once, might do so a hundred times more? Where was Pepé? Had he rejoined the troops, or had the detour to the graveyard been but a clever plan for eluding them? Were these, and perhaps Ruiz too, the tools of Ramirez? Yet the latter had appeared to have ridden far; the news of the gathering and departure of the troops had appeared to have astounded as much as it had enraged him. Who had carried the news to Reyes?

The way was long and the youth's excitement waning; his recent illness and still aching wound began to declare their effects. In his full vigor Ashley Ward would have found the walk under the glaring sunshine — which, though no longer vertical, was fierce and blinding as it neared the western hilltops — more than he would have chosen for an afternoon's stroll. Weak as he was, and becoming painfully conscious that he had fasted since morning, he was glad to lean sometimes against the high adobe wall and measure with his eye the slowly decreasing distance. It was a landmark on his way when he caught sight of the

heavy gate set in the wall of the reduction-works; he
knew then just how much farther he must go. He had no
thought of actually approaching it, but he noticed with
surprise that one heavy valve was slightly ajar; and with
that sudden collapse which is apt to assail the overtasked
frame at the unexpected sight of an open door, however
meagre the entertainment it may suggest, he dragged
himself onward with the natural belief that he should find
within some servant or attaché of the great house. But
when he reached the gate and looked through the narrow
aperture, a perfect stillness reigned within. No horse
stamped in the courtyard; no spurred heel rang on the
pavement.   Great cacti were pushing their gaunt and
prickly branches into the narrow space, as if stretching
longing arms out into the wide world from which they had
been so long shut in.

With some effort Ashley thrust back the strong and
aggressive barrier, and forced his way in. Rank grass,
which was at that season yellow and matted, had grown up
between the cobble-stones, and raised them in little heaps,
over which the lizards ran.   One -- fiery red — stopped as
Ashley's boot-heel woke the echoes, and turned a wondering ear, then glided swiftly on.

Between the main building and the offices there was a
small arched lobby, through which one entered the great
court, upon which piles of broken ores and the long dried
masses were spread.   In this lobby in the olden time the
workmen had been stopped by the watchman or gate-
keeper and searched, — a proceeding to which they daily
submitted with indifference, holding their arms on high
while the practised searcher ran his hands over their thin
and scanty garments, shook out the coarse serape and
tattered sombrero, peered among the rows of glistening
teeth and under the tongue, for those fragments of rich
ore or amalgam which in spite of all precautions, or by the
connivance of the searcher, reached the outer world, netting in the aggregate a considerable surplus to the income
of the laborers, which found its way to the gambling tables,
or was spent in the adornment of their wives, — as was
proved by the great decline in the village of the manufacture of filagree ornaments of quaint and delicate designs
upon the closing of the Garcia mining-works.

Ashley, with a feeling of curiosity or a sense of impending action, which renewed his strength as a tonic might have done, noticed that the door upon the side of the lobby that opened into the main building or living rooms was also ajar. He glanced in, but except where the long ray of light stole in through the aperture, which his person partially obscured, all was so dim that he saw only imperfectly a few scattered articles of furniture, — and they appeared to be so old and battered that they were scarce worth the protection which the great padlock and rusty key, hanging from a staple in the door, indicated had been afforded them.

With a feeling of awe, Ashley remembered that his cousin must have lived, and perhaps had lain dead, in that room. With nervous energy he thrust open the door, and the light streamed in. He started as his eyes fell upon the floor. It was of large square bricks, thickly spread with the dust of many years, but impressed with footprints so blurred that, dazzled as his eyes were, he could not tell whether they were those of man, woman, or child. They seemed mysterious, ghostly. There was no sound of human presence. His heart beat as it had not done in all the excitement of that day.

"I am here! I have been waiting as you bade me," said a low, frightened voice. The words came so unexpectedly that Ashley scarce understood them. He stepped forward and glanced around searchingly. In the further corner of the room a female figure was in the act of rising from a low seat on which it had crouched. The face was half-averted, the dark reboso was drawn over it with the left hand, the right was outstretched as if in supplicating, almost compulsory, welcome.

"Good God!" — "*Dios mio!*" The ejaculations were simultaneous; the girl sank to the floor, the young man involuntarily drew back.

"Señorita!" he exclaimed in a voice of incredulity, "Señorita, you here and alone?"

"*Maria Sanctissima!* not the General Ramirez!" he heard her moan; yet in the fright and confusion there seemed an accent of relief. "Don 'Guardo! Oh, what has brought you here? Oh, Señor, believe me — "

"Do not distress yourself to explain, Señorita," interrupted Ashley, coldly. "Rise, I beg, and I will go at once; but that you may not waste more time in waiting, I will tell you that the man you speak of will not be here to-day. And," he added, with an intensity that startled even himself, "if there is justice in heaven or upon earth, never again shall he fulfil a lover's tryst upon a spot that by any other than a demon would be shunned as a scene of gentle dalliance, if not abhorred as the theatre of a crime that should have blasted his whole life!"

The girl threw back her head-covering and looked up in uncomprehending amaze. As her gaze caught Ashley's both colored, both averted their eyes in confusion. Ashley recoiled before hers, so childlike, so honest.

"Chata!" he murmured; "Chata!" involuntarily extending toward her his hand in deprecation, in entreaty, in protection. She clasped it as a frightened child might, and clinging to it rose to her feet, swaying a little and bending low, not with weakness, but with shame.

"I dared not disobey him," she murmured at last. "I dared not disobey."

Ashley dropped her hand, — almost flung it from him.

The girl's face crimsoned; she opened her lips, hesitated, then clasping her hands together, cried, "It is not as you think. Oh, rather than the truth, would to God it were! I am not the child of Don Rafael and Doña Rita! José Ramirez is my father!"

XXXII.

"José Ramirez is my father!"

Had her words been a thunderbolt hurled at Ashley's feet, they could not have astounded him more. The daughter of Ramirez!

"I do not believe it! I cannot believe it!" he exclaimed, with no thought for courteous words. "Oh, that is a tale for a jealous lover! but I am not one. Anything, anything rather than that, Señorita, would serve to explain the reason of your presence here!"

"Why have I spoken?" cried the young girl with tears. "Why have I broken my promise, and only to be disbelieved and scorned? O, Señor, I know not what it was in you that wrung the words from me! Did he not command me to be silent till he gave me leave to speak? He is my father, yet I have disobeyed his first command. In the letter the woman brought me, two days after he left El Toro, and in which he commanded me to meet him here upon this day, he enjoined secrecy again and again; and yet I forgot. Miserable girl that I am!"

Ashley had lived among Mexicans long enough to learn something of their ideas of filial duty. No matter how vile, how cruel, how debased the parent may be, the duty of the child is perfect obedience and respect; the petted infant in its most wilful moments ceases its passionate cries to kiss the father's hand; the young man deprives himself, his wife and children, to minister to his aged parents; he who cannot or will not work, esteems it a pious act to become a bandit upon the highway rather than that his father or mother shall look to him for food or even for luxuries in vain, — and thus he comprehended the remorse of this conscience-stricken child, as the conviction rushed over him that her belief might indeed be true. There was that in the contour of her face which resembled that of Ramirez more markedly than the mere

general type that in her babyhood had given her that resemblance to Rosario, which daily grew less, and indeed
had never been apparent to Ashley; though in her face he
had traced resemblances which had puzzled and bewildered
him, and which as he gazed upon her now became still
more confusing.

As they had been conversing, Ashley and Chata had
gradually drawn near to the door, where the light fell full
upon the agitated girl. Yes, in the square brows, the
heavily fringed lids resting upon the olive cheeks, —
too broad beneath the eyes for beauty, but singularly
delicate about the mouth and chin, — so far she resembled
Ramirez; or was it but a common Aztec type? The
mouth itself, sensitive, refined, — which should have parted
but for laughter, — quivered with emotion, and the large
gray eyes she lifted to Ashley's were singularly grave
and earnest. Where had he seen such a mouth, such eyes?
The contrasts and combinations in the face confused him.
Never had he seen its counterpart, yet fancy might under
other circumstances have led him upon wild theories.
That face familiar, yet strange, had haunted him since
he had first seen it. Vainly he had sought in his memory for some picture, some dream, with which to connect
it. Now, though he had seen Ramirez, though Chata
declared herself his child, the same feeling of uncertainty,
of tantalizing familiarity yet strangeness, remained; the
association of one with the other did not even momen-
tarily satisfy him. He was not conscious that the face
appealed to his imagination rather than to his memory,
or that it had always awakened an interest different from
that with which he had looked upon others. Certainly
its beauty had not delighted him; even as he looked at
her now, the witching, glowing, ever-changing countenance
of Chinita rose before him. "Strange! strange!" he
murmured. "What can be the mystery that from the
first has seemed to hover around you, to separate you
from the rest?"

"Ah, yes!" she said humbly. "I have realized that
myself. Oh, for a long, long time I have felt as a stranger
among them all, — they so good, so true; and I — O
God, who am I? Ah, I used to pity Chinita, but they
have given her her proper place. It must have been a

worthy one, or Doña Isabel would not have made her her child. But when they separate me from Don Rafael what shall I be?"

"Do not think of it. He — this Ramirez — is gone, perhaps never to return," said Ashley, soothingly. "And if not, why should you go with him? Appeal to Don Rafael, to Doña Feliz."

"Doña Rita has told me already that would be worse than useless," replied Chata. "Don Rafael and Doña Feliz have already interfered in his plans for me ; to thwart him further would be to make him their deadly enemy. Oh, you know not, Señor, what men like Don José Ramirez will do ; and yet he is my father!"

Her voice failed in an agony of terror and shame. Ashley's words died on his lips. Here was a grief he could hardly understand, against which he could offer no advice to one whose education and mind were so different from his own. What could he say to her to lessen the burden of her grief? Surely not, as he would have done to Chinita, that she should strive to content herself in a destiny which would raise her from an obscure station to wealth, — for the revolutionary chieftain, he supposed, had never-failing resources, — and to a certain dignity, as the daughter of a popular hero. He could have imagined Chinita as glorying in such a position, and Rosario as reigning with a thousand airs and graces in the miniature court around her ; but here was a child, a very child, shrinking from the possible contact with cruel and conscience-hardened adventurers, and stricken to the heart by the thought of losing the heritage of an honest name.

Presently Chata spoke again, as though to speak to this stranger in whom she had involuntarily confided was, in spite of her self-reproach, to lay her long repression, her doubts and fears, before a shrine. Almost incoherently, in the rapid utterance of overwhelming excitement, she poured forth the story of the interview of Ramirez and Doña Rita which she had overheard in the garden at El Toro. In her earnestness she did not even omit the project which had been discussed for uniting her future with that of Ruiz. Ashley's teeth became set and his lips pressed each other as he listened. Here indeed was confirmation of the villain's claim ; and yet — and yet —

20

"It cannot be!" he interrupted. "I cannot believe it. You say yourself, your very being recoils from him — ah, it must be for some deep cause you hate him so! And I too — I hate him. Did I not tell you I have a long arrear of wrong to settle, and —"

"You!" she ejaculated wonderingly. "What wrong can he have done to you? Was it he who robbed and wounded you?"

"No, no!" he answered. "Those were but the chances of travel. There is something far greater than that; but while you believe him to be your father, I will not talk to you of avenging myself. I should be a brute indeed to add a feather's weight to your trouble. Do not think of that again; but believe me, there is some mystery neither of us understands. The truth may be far from what you think it. I will demand it of Don Rafael, of Doña Feliz — they must know."

She was looking at him wonderingly, almost in awe, with those large, clear, gray eyes, which seemed to have in them the reflection of a purer, calmer sky than the intense and fiery one beneath which she was born. As he looked at her, her very dress seemed a disguise, so entirely did she seem disassociated from the scenes in which he found her.

"Ah," she said hopelessly, clasping her hands, "you do not know my people as I do. I have not asked Don Rafael or Doña Feliz to tell me the secret of my birth. They have concealed it for some weighty reason, and until the time comes when they judge it right for me to know, I might plead with them in vain. By going to them I should but lose their love, and become the object of their suspicion and doubt. Oh, I could not endure that, I would not endure it! Doña Rita is changed, is cold, distrustful; and why should I by useless haste bring their anger upon her? No, no, Señor, I beg, I entreat you, say nothing to Don Rafael. Let me be in peace as long as I may. My father has not come to-day; perhaps he has forgotten me!"

"You reason wildly," said Ashley. "I cannot understand these strange duplicities; yet I know it is quite true I should gain nothing by direct questioning. What have I ever gained? No, it is to Doña Isabel I will go, and to Ramirez himself. But promise me, Chata," he added earnestly, " promise me, by all you hold most sacred, never to leave the hacienda to meet him or any messenger of his. Promise for your own sake, and I swear I will leave no measure untried to free you from this strange bondage."

He had expressed himself with difficulty throughout, but she caught his meaning eagerly. "Oh, if I dared to promise!" she murmured. "But it is the duty of the child to obey. Besides, he would tell me the truth; even this very day I thought I should have known the wretched story, — oh, I am sure it is a wretched one! Well, I have a respite, — a little respite. Go, Señor; you have been kind, — be kind still by being silent. I must go; the sun will soon set. Ah, unfortunate that I am, the men will be coming in from the fields, the women will be at their doors, — how shall I ever return without being seen?"

Here was indeed a difficulty. The strictly nurtured girl had never in her life been outside the precincts of the village alone; that she then should be, and with a young man, would occasion endless gossip. The two involuntary culprits looked at each other with blank faces, — Ashley in absolute dismay, for he had heard of the strict requirements of Mexican customs and etiquette, and knew to what cruel innuendo this young girl had exposed herself. He realized then for the first time how great her courage had been in venturing forth in obedience to the command of Ramirez.

"Chata, Chata! for God's sake," he cried, "go at once! I will remain. Your mad freak will be pardoned this time, when they see you are alone."

"Alone!" she echoed, a crimson flush suffusing her face as she fully realized the significance of his words, and saw that with a sudden faintness he leaned against the wall, spent with excitement and fatigue.

"Yes, yes," he said wearily, "none will know I am here. The night will soon pass; in the morning I will wander in to one of the huts. They will fancy I was lost on the mountain. None will think — you will be safe."

"I *am* safe," said the girl with sudden resolution. "Would a woman of your own country leave you to hunger and shiver through all the night in a desolate place

like this? Ah," she added with a long-drawn breath and
a tremor, " even ghosts are here."

Ashley smiled. " I do not fear them," he said. " I
fear but for you. Go! go at once! And yet before you
go, promise! — promise me never to run these risks again;
never in any place to meet Ramirez! "

In his earnestness he clasped her hand and gazed
eagerly into her limpid eyes. " I promise, yes, I promise," she said hurriedly. " But I will not leave you, —
weak, fasting, fainting! "

She looked up at him with the angelic pity in her face
that innocent children feel before they have learned distrust. Ashley read the perfect trust, the perfect guileless-
ness, of her tender nature. Rather, he thought, would he
die than cast a cloud upon her name; and what, after all,
would matter the privations of a few hours? That he must
not be seen in the neighborhood for some time after her
unusual wanderings was a foregone conclusion. How
should he combat her resolution? Truly, this gentle girl
had deep springs of action within her. For duty and
right she could be a very heroine.

As these thoughts passed through his mind, a sudden
breeze stole through the open gate and reached the lobby;
there was a faint smell of cactus flowers, and a rustle of
the dry grass. The effect was weird and ghostly. A
shadow fell between them. Had the sun plunged down
beneath the western hills? They glanced up and started
apart, — Doña Feliz was before them.

The ordinarily grave and self-possessed woman was for
a moment the most agitated of the three. She gasped for
breath. She had been walking fast, but it was not that
alone which caused the earth apparently to reel beneath
her. She had found Chata, whose disappearance from the
hacienda she had discovered at the moment when a cry
had run through the house that the horse of the young
American had returned riderless; that the youth had
doubtless met an evil fate. She had found them both, —
and together!

She pressed her hands over her eyes as though to shut
out some horrid vision; a moan broke from her lips, —
then she caught Chata in her arms and glared at Ashley
with concentrated anguish and fury. Had one guilty

thought possessed him, or had he meditated a doubtful act, her glance would have covered him with confusion. As it was, he read in her expressive face and gesture a volume of deep and terrible significance, far different from that which an anxious duenna ordinarily casts upon the imagined trifler with the affections of her charge. Nothing of that assumption of virtuous indignation, yet of flattered satisfaction, which in the midst of remonstrance gives indication of a certain sympathy and inclination to condone the offence in consideration of its cause, was apparent. Doña Feliz evidently had in her mind no lover's venial follies. This meeting was to her a tragedy, — the very culmination of woes.

Ashley read something of this in her expression and gesture, and hastened to reassure her, by giving a partial account of the reasons of his return. The anxious guardian of innocence would perhaps have thought his turning aside at the instance of Pepé to view his cousin's grave, his lingering there, the departure of the servant, the flight of his horse, all a fabrication, but for the meeting with his cousin's murderer, which the young man recounted with startling brevity and force, unconsciously regaining in the recital much of the excitement and deep indignation which had thrilled him at the time of the encounter, and which had gradually subsided amid the new complications that Chata's words had opened before him.

Involuntarily Ashley refrained from any allusion to the fact that the young girl had ventured forth to meet this man Ramirez ; and acute though she was, it did not suggest itself to Doña Feliz, who seemed lost in wonder at the almost miraculous chance which after so many years had brought into contact the secret murderer and him whose mission it seemed to avenge the innocent blood. In his recital, Ashley had not mentioned the name of the self-confessed assassin. Doña Feliz did not ask it, — perhaps she inferred that it remained unknown to him, — yet Ashley was certain his identity was no problem to her. Had she guessed the secret all these years? Had she screened the guilty and fostered the innocent, at the same time?

Deep as was her interest in his tale, full as was her acceptance of the fact that the meeting of Ashley Ward and Chata was purely accidental, Doña Feliz did not exhibit a tithe of that horror and dismay which was depicted upon the countenance of Chata, who listened breathlessly, — her lips apart, her hair pushed back, her startled eyes opened wide. Ashley would gladly have recalled his words as he looked at her. Every particle of color had faded from her face.

In her absorption in Ashley's words, Doña Feliz had ceased to regard or even remember the young girl, who suddenly recalled herself to that lady's mind.

" Doña Feliz," she murmured in an agonized and pleading voice, " when my mother forsook me, why did you not suffer me to die? Oh why, why did I live to hear such horrors, to know such wretchedness as this? "

As if in a frenzy, before either thought to stop her, or found words with which to answer or recall her, she ran out from the lobby, — her small figure passing unimpeded through the cactus-guarded gateway, — and fled across the plain toward the hacienda. She was young and strong, — excitement lent wings to her feet. Doña Feliz and Ashley standing together in the gateway looked at each other in amazement. The girl continued her flight until she reached the outskirts of the village. There a horseman stopped her. Even at that distance they recognized Don Rafael, and saw that Chata clung to him passionately when he dismounted.

" She is safe !" murmured Doña Feliz. " Rafael will know how to account for her presence with him."

" Yes," thought Ashley ; " these Mexicans fortunately know how to coin a plausible tale as well for a good cause as for a bad one."

They saw that Don Rafael, placing Chata on his horse before him, had turned in the direction of the hacienda, and was signalling to the vaqueros lingering in uncertainty at the gate.

" They will be here in a few moments, Señor," said Doña Feliz, calmly. " We must lock the gates and conceal the keys. You must be found outside of, not within, these walls."

Ashley assented, and within a few moments, and in silence, their necessary task was accomplished. Doña Feliz then led the way toward the village, walking rapidly

as though impelled by the agitation of her thoughts or a
desire to escape question. Ashley kept pace with her
with some effort, though the chill which had come with
the grayness of evening over the landscape revived and
strengthened him. The breeze was whistling in the tall
corn in the fields as they passed them; the cattle were
lowing in the yards; the distant sound of horses' feet was
beginning to be heard; the riders like gray columns were
seen approaching. Ashley laid his hand upon the arm of
Doña Feliz. She turned and looked at him. His face
was to her a volume of reproach and question. Her voice
broke forth in a great sob.

"Ashley! Ashley!" she exclaimed, "do you not comprehend that a vow stronger than death controls me?
Ask me nothing, but follow the indications which the good
God — Fate — Providence — has given you. The time
may come — for strange things are happening in our land
— when I may be free once more. Now I may only watch
and wait and pray. Ah! what hard tasks for a woman
such as I am! But I have vowed; I cannot retract!"

"You are wrong!" cried Ashley. "How strange that
a woman of so much intelligence, of a conscience so pure,
can suffer herself to be led by the spurious customs and
traditions that pride and priestcraft together have fastened
upon her people! But your very reticence, Doña Feliz,
confirms my beliefs. I will go as you recommend, as my
own judgment urged me, to follow the clew I have so unexpectedly obtained. Do not think that a vulgar and
wolfish desire for vengeance alone actuates me; but justice must be done. Even for Chata's sake, this man must
not be suffered to continue his course unchecked." He
would have added more, but Gabriel and Pancho, the
vaqueros, came galloping up with *vivas* and cries of
welcome.

"Praised be our Holy Mother, and all the saints!"
exclaimed one. "Don Rafael told us you were safe.
Who would have thought the Señora and the *niña* Chatita
would have found you no farther away than deaf and blind
Refugio's? Ay, Doña Feliz, without seeking, finds more
than will a dozen unlucky ones, though they have specta-
cles and lanterns to aid them. In the name of reason,
Don 'Guardo, how happened your nag to throw you and

gallop back thus? He is manageable enough with any of
us —" and there was a suspicion of irony in the solicitude,
of the horseman, which did not escape Ashley as he
answered, —

"To-morrow you shall have the whole tale. These
roads of yours are no place for a man to linger on alone.
But for the present, remember I have a wound not too
well healed, and am more anxious for supper than for recounting adventures."

"Ah! ah! he was stopped on the road by banditti, —
and has escaped." The vaqueros regarded Ashley with
vastly increased respect. Their numbers were augmented
as they neared the hacienda; and when the party reached
the gates, wild rumors of Ashley's prowess were already
flying from mouth to mouth.

Ashley did not present an imposing figure as he passed
in between the crowds of admiring women; but he served
to turn their thoughts from the unprecedented appearance
of Chata, which was but unsatisfactorily explained by Don
Rafael's ready fiction that she and Doña Feliz had been
piously visiting at the hut of old Refugio, and that upon
the arrival of Ashley there, the young girl had hastened
to meet her father, and give him news of the American's
safety.

"Doña Feliz is even too careful of her grandchildren,"
said some of the more liberal. "What harm would have
come to the maiden from a walk of a few minutes, or a few
words spoken, with an honorable young man such as he
seems to be? Now, if it were Don Alonzo, or that gay
young Captain Ruiz, for example!"

Rosario, who had been leaning over the balcony as Ashley arrived, heard something of what was said, and smiled.
She was not at all ready to believe that Chata's walk had
extended only as far as the hut of blind Refugio; and that
it had not been made in company with Doña Feliz she was
quite certain. But she had no time just then to interest
herself in Chata's affairs, — her own were far too engrossing; for the new clerk whom Carmen, at Doña Isabel's
request, had sent from Guanapila, evidently was much
more intent upon studying the charms of Rosario than his
new duties, and in seeking favor in her eyes than in those
of the administrador himself. The new clerk was· Don

Alonzo, and Don Alonzo was a handsome fellow, with the face of an angel, Doña Rita said, — a contrast indeed to that little brown monkey Captain Ruiz; and Rosario smiled coyly, and did not gainsay her.

The next morning at an unusually early hour this same Don Alonzo tapped on Ashley's door. "Pardon, Señor," he said, "but the horses and servants are ready, and I have orders myself to accompany you beyond the boundaries of Tres Hermanos."

The announcement was not a surprise. Ashley had arranged his departure with Don Rafael upon the preceding evening. He dressed hastily, and while partaking of his cup of chocolate, glanced often around him, in expectation of the appearance of Don Rafael or his mother; but in vain. The American could no longer hope to learn at a parting moment what each had chosen to withhold. Irrationally, and against all likelihood, he ventured to hope that Chata might steal forth for a farewell word. He laughed at himself afterward for the thought, saying that the air of intrigue had begun to affect his own brain.

Sooner than was usual, even in that land of early movement, Don Alonzo warned him it was growing late. It was not too late or early for Rosario to wave her little brown hand from her mother's window in token of adieu. Ashley did not see it, but he for whom it was intended did. So with more foreboding and reluctance than he could have imagined possible but a few hours before, Ashley once more rode forth from Tres Hermanos, — this time with a definite object, from which he felt there could be no turning back, no possible end but his own death or the downfall of a man to whom but yesterday he had been utterly indifferent, but who to-day was inseparable from all his thoughts, his passions, his purposes, — Ramirez the *revolucionario*, the declared murderer of John Ashley, the declared father of the young girl who seemed the very incarnation of honor and sensibility, of tenderness and purity.

THE departure of Ashley Ward from Tres Hermanos was not so entirely disregarded as he had supposed. It was not Rosario only, who left her chamber at daybreak. Scarcely had she disappeared in the gloom of Doña Isabel's apartments on her way to the favorite balcony, when her father stepped out upon the corridor, starting as his eyes fell upon Doña Feliz, who, seemingly with the spirit of unrest that pervaded the household, at the same moment emerged from her room. With a muttered salutation each abandoned the original intention of exchanging a farewell word with the departing guest; and arresting their steps at the balustrade, they leaned over and listened intently to the sounds of the early exit. The light was still so uncertain that though Don Rafael noticed, he did not wonder at, the gray tinge upon his mother's face; it seemed only in harmony with the prevailing darkness.

The rains of the past season had been insufficient, and a murky though almost inpalpable mist, felt rather than seen, brooded over the silent landscape. It was scarcely oppressive enough to affect the young men who rode forth stirring the sluggish air, nor the eager horses lifting their heads to fill their lungs with the breath of morning, and expelling it again with a force that agitated the stillness with a sound like a blow upon water; yet it weighed inexpressibly both upon the body and mind of Don Rafael. As he had come to the corridor with a certainty in his mind that he should meet his mother, he had purposed to question her as to the actual occurrences of the day before, for the connection of Chata with the return of Ashley Ward remained entirely unexplained. That his mother was satisfied that it was not a mere vulgar *rendezvous* into which she had been tempted, he was assured by her manner toward both the young man and the recreant girl; indeed, it appeared that she had scarcely noticed an incident which in that place, and at the age of Chata, was sufficient to array against a young girl the suspicions of the most trusting and generous of matrons. Yet Don Rafael could imagine no possible inducement but the voice of a lover that could have called her forth alone from the great house, — for that Chata had gone alone, he knew as well as did his keen-eyed daughter Rosario.

The last gray figure had long since disappeared from the outer court, into which they looked as into a distant and narrow vista; the clank of the horses' hoofs upon the paving had changed to the thud upon the roadway, then ceased altogether to be heard; and Don Rafael turning his eyes upon his mother's face, had opened his lips to question her, — when with a thrill of surprise, which became terror even before the momentary utterance was repeated, he heard her laugh that strange, unmirthful, hollow laugh that indicates a mind diseased, while she said whisperingly, —

"He is gone. Yes! yes! I unbarred the door, and Pedro picked the lock so cleverly and noiselessly that the very watchman asleep across the threshold did not hear him. Ah, I knew Gregorio would be quiet enough by daylight; but Leon was awake, wide awake. For all your tears, Isabel, he would not have gone but for me; he swore he would kill Don Gregorio for the blow he gave him. Why did you say you loved at last as a woman should the husband who was your brother's foe to death, and that you sent him freedom that he might seek a death more worthy of his villany than by the sword of an outraged father, or the executioner's bullet? They were bitter words, and you knew they were false, — for even with your child lying dead through his persecution, you loved him still. And when he would not stir because of your taunts, but swore he would meet his fate and shame the callous heart whose love had been as weak as her sacrifice was forced and incomplete, what was there for you to do but to throw yourself on your knees before him, and entreat him for his mother's sake to be gone? Even then he would have stayed but for me. 'What!' I cried, 'to shame your sister, you will give another victory to the husband of Dolores?'

"Ah, it is not tears that conquer such a man as Leon!

In a moment he had sprung to his feet; he had thrust Isabel aside, and me too, — yes, that was nothing. Pedro held his horse, but Leon glared at him as he sprang into the saddle. 'But for you, I should have given the last blow at midnight,' he cried. 'It shall be thine some day, when thy master's account has been closed!' and with that he was gone. Yes, he is gone. Not a sound of the horse as he gallops! Gone, and none too soon! the morning is come," — and she uttered again that sound called a laugh.

"Mother, what hast thou?" cried Don Rafael, clasping her arm, and noticing for the first time the deep hollows beneath her brilliant eyes, and the wide circles that made more appalling their unnatural glare. "Mother, thou art dreaming! thy hand burns, and thy temples. Maria Sanctissima! dost thou not know me?"

"Know thee? — yes. Why, thou art Rafael," she answered, letting her eyes drop for a moment on his scared and anxious face. "Why should I not know thee? Had ever woman a better son? Yes, yes, he is safe; let Don Gregorio wake when he will, Leon is away. Ah, at the last he was not so cruel, — eh, Isabel? Why should you moan and wring your hands because he vowed never again but by his death should his name shame you? Ah! Ah! Ah! well, they say he died, shot and hanged to a tree as a miscreant should be. Do you believe it, Isabel? Yet why not? God of my soul! is it only the son of Pancho Valle that can be pitiless? Only — " so she muttered on, in a low monotonous voice, pacing the corridor with an uncertain step, varying from the halting motion of one about to fall, to the impetuous haste with which she fancied herself urging again the unwilling flight of the sullen and revengeful youth, whom she too, with the perversity of woman's heart, had loved as sincerely as she had condemned.

Don Rafael followed her in a perturbation of surprise and terror, which drove from his mind all other thoughts save those that his remembrance of former plague-stricken seasons forced upon his mind. Fever was in the air, and his mother was the first victim! The rainy season, which in most years cleared the black watercourses and the village itself of the accumulations of nine dry and almost torrid months, had failed to do its accustomed work. No rush-

ing torrents had cleared the watercourses; but instead of
proving the friend of humanity water had become its
enemy, by mingling scantily with the foul elements that
had gathered during the long period of drouth, and which
exhaled the subtle miasma which even the pure air of
that elevated region was powerless to render innoxious.
Don Rafael absolutely wrung his hands before the evil
he foresaw, and which neither experience nor intelligence
had led him to combat with any sanitary precautions.
That the fever should from time to time decimate the
hacienda appeared to his mind one of the inevitable
calamities of life, no more to be avoided than the spring
floods or the blasting lightning or the outburst of volcanic fires. But had all these forces combined assailed
him at once, his consternation could not have been
greater than to witness in his mother the delirium which
testified to the dreaded typhoid. As has been intimated,
his love for his mother was of no common order; without being weak in judgment or irresolute in character,
he had been accustomed to share with her his every
thought, and their sentiments and aims were ever in
such perfect accord that a dissentient word had never
arisen between them.

As Don Rafael followed his mother in her erratic and
excited movements, scarcely conscious of what he did, or
of anything except that with each moment her talk grew
more distracted, while her thoughts were persistently
fixed upon the events and woes and passions of by-gone
years, a door at the end of the corridor was timidly
pushed open, and Chata's face peeped anxiously out.
Had Don Rafael's thoughts been free, he would have
wondered that the girl was fully dressed at such an
early hour; but he did not even heed the explanation
she hurriedly gave as she advanced to meet him.

"I would not have left my grandmother alone, but she
forbade me to come," she said. "Oh, I could not sleep.
I thought the morning would never dawn. I went to her
with the first light, but she would not listen to me. She
bade me leave her; and I thought it was because she
was angry, but it was this! Oh, Father, is it a sickness?
See, she does not know me? *Mama grande*, it is I; it is
your Chata."

" Be silent ! " exclaimed Don Rafael, the more sharply because of his extreme alarm. " Fly, Chata ! fly to thy mother, thy sister ! Call old Selsa, any one who has sense and knows what remedies to bring. Why do you stare? Do you think my mother is mad? It is the fever. It is not for nothing that the rains have been delayed so long. Pitying Saints, as I rode by the ditches last week they were black as pitch and foul as a vulture's quarry. Run ! I will lead her to her room. Ay, ay, Mother, thou art strong, and not so old yet," — and with the tenderness of a child and the devotion of a lover the son guided the steps of the delirious yet gentle woman, who, half-conscious of her state, half-resentful of care, suffered herself to be led into the chamber she had quitted in apparent health but a brief quarter of an hour before.

Apparent health only, for she had passed an utterly sleepless night, strangely excited by the events of the day, yet unable to fix her mind upon them. Chata, upon her return to the hacienda, had sought her own chamber ; and in the press of other thoughts Doña Feliz had failed to follow and to question her upon the strange escapade, which the whole character and bearing of the young girl combined to render utterly inexplicable, — for she had no data by which to connect it with the appearance of Ramirez at the cemetery, and she absolved Ashley Ward from any pre-arrangement with the young girl as completely as though they had been found a thousand miles asunder. As was natural, suspicions of some precocious love, of which some one of the many volatile and dashing youth that had lately gathered at the hacienda was the object, haunted the mind of Doña Feliz ; but she rejected them with disdain, promising herself upon the early morning to demand the truth, not doubting she should learn it. Even while awake to the importance of the incident, and inwardly debating it, she was conscious that the remembrance of it, as well as of Ashley and his strange participation in the life-drama in which she had enacted so forced and painful a part, constantly strove to elude her, and was recalled with an effort that with every hour grew greater and less effective ; while all the events and actors of long ago passed in endless review before her, — Doña Isabel in her matronly girlhood, soothing and bribing with tender words and lavish gifts her wilful half-brother; Don Gregorio; the dying Norberto; the scowling and furious abductor; then Herlinda and John Ashley. The pale procession, spectral yet real, voiceless yet each repeating with irresistible eloquence the tale of his love, his guilt or anguish, passed before her, thrusting aside, as often as they re-appeared, the forms of those who at this new and critical point had appeared upon the scene.

As the night passed, she was perfectly aware of this tantalizing inability to command her thoughts; and as again and again she set herself to follow the probable course and effect of Ashley Ward's intervention in the fate of the man who to her seemed gifted with demoniacal powers for evil, and an absolute invulnerability to human vengeance, or as she began in mind to question Chata, the persons both of the young man and the girl seemed to fade from before her, and the voices that should have replied, were those which had been familiar years before, — oftenest that of Herlinda in wild repetition of her unhappy love, and agonized entreaties for the babe she was but to embrace and forever relinquish. Through it all Doña Feliz had retained the thought of Ashley's departure; and with some vague thought that the sight of him would calm her fevered brain, she instinctively strove to accomplish the resolve with which she had begun the night. And thus her last conscious act before the positive delirium of the fever seized her, had been to look, with the half-fearful gaze of one who invokes· yet dreads the vengeance of heaven, upon him who seemed to her morbid and superstitious mind fraught with a mission to avenge and right the innocent, — both the living and the dead.

Don Rafael, in consternation, had recognized at once the serious character of his mother's illness. As he called aloud for help, and Chata with white and affrighted face hastened to obey his command, Rosario, followed by her mother in some confusion, appeared from the farther corridor. Too much bewildered and alarmed to wonder at seeing his daughter also dressed and abroad at such an hour, her father exclaimed in impatience at the voluble reproaches of Doña Rita, who, pushing Rosario from the side of Doña Feliz, bade her cease from such tempting of Providence, affirming that for her own sins she (Doña

Rita) must have been burdened with the plague of so reckless a child, and praying her in the name of the Holy Babe to fly from infection lest she should break her mother's heart by her premature decease.   To all of which Rosario submitted with a sobbing declaration that she was already faint and ill, whereupon Doña Rita hastily retreated to her own room, dragging Rosario with her; and in spite of his hurriedly formed resolution to the contrary, Don Rafael was forced to confide his mother to the care of Chata and of the servants, who, subservient to the slightest wish even of this inexperienced girl, were however absolutely useless without the guiding presence of a superior.

XXXIV.

The hilltops were flooded with sunshine when the party from Tres Hermanos reached them; the atmosphere was so clear, that looking back over the broad valley, spread with fields of maize and beans, and the half-tropical luxuriance of fruit and flower, Ashley could distinguish every break and fret on the massive front of the great house, and recognized with a feeling almost of awe the tall, slender figure standing upon the centre balcony. She waved her hand in token of God-speed. Strange, inscrutable woman! She had bidden him go forth as the minister of fate, she had furnished him with servants, horses, money, arms, — yet had spoken no word. Ashley felt as though he were an enchanted knight in an enchanted land!

The traveller bade adieu to Don Alonzo in sight of his cousin's grave; then, followed by his two servants, rode rapidly onward in the direction taken the day before by the troops and Doña Isabel, by Ramirez and Reyes, — indifferent which he first should encounter, confident that sooner or later the full significance of the impulse that had led him upon his Quixotic journey to Mexico would be revealed. The little cloud no bigger than a man's hand had grown so great as to overshadow his earth and heavens. He rode on as in a dream. The day passed, the night came, and the party was still alone. The guide had mistaken the way. That night they encamped but a league from the village of Las Passas. Ashley slept neither better nor worse for that; there was no voice to tell him it could be more to him or his than a score of other villages which lay in the recesses of these wild mountains. The next day he left it to the right, and set his face toward El Toro.

Meanwhile the march of the troops had been as rapid as the nature of the country, broken by deep ravines and at first offering a tortuous ascent to the table-lands, would allow. To Chinita, though the slow movement of the car-

21

riage was irksome and irritating, and the clouds of dust that rose from beneath the tread of the horses obscured the sights which in their novelty delighted and filled her with exultation of a new and expanding life, the hours passed as though winged by enchantment. In the joyous clamor of the camp followers and the scarcely less restrained hilarity of the troops, in the tramp of the horses, the clanking of arms, there was a subtile music that aroused all the energies of her adventurous spirit, and imbued her with an animation which like a flame within a crystal vase seemed visibly to fill and surround her whole being with strength and beauty.

Had the country passed over been as dull and uninteresting as it was in fact wild and picturesque, the effect of movement and change would have been still the same to her; for hers was a mind to be affected by the various phases of humanity rather than of inanimate nature. The landscape in truth offered to her view little of novelty, for in her childhood she had wandered where she listed, and her lithe young limbs had been as untiring as her curiosity. The succeeding cañons and hills, the slopes and cactus-planted valleys, were but counterparts of those which she had explored on every side of the plain on which Tres Hermanos stood. With ready tact she avoided recalling her unwatched, untended childhood to the mind of Doña Isabel, who received with a distaste which seemed of the nature of regretful shame any allusion to the life from which the girl who now called her *Tia* (aunt) had been rescued.

The use of this appellation had been brought about by Ruiz, in his evident uncertainty as to how the apparent relationship between his patroness and her *protégée* should be defined. He had tentatively alluded to Doña Isabel as the godmother of Chinita, a designation which some conscientious scruple led her to reject. The word *Tia* is used by Mexicans as a term of respect toward an elder as often as in actual acknowledgment of relationship; and when with some daring Chinita one day applied it to Doña Isabel, in answering some remark of the young captain, the lady allowed it to pass unchallenged; and gradually "*mi Tia* Isabel" took the place of the formal "Señora," which hitherto had helped to keep their intercourse as reserved and cold as when Chinita still stood at the gate at Pedro's side, and Doña Isabel had furtively glanced at her glowing beauty, and felt the hand of remorse pressing upon her heart.

The haughty lady felt it still; and that it was which made her lenient to a score of faults in this young girl that in her own children would have been deemed almost unpardonable. She did not admit that she loved her, — it is doubtful if she really did, — yet she strove by all the arts of which the long repression of her nature made her capable to win the heart of the girl, who she saw with suspicious intuition beheld in her one who had wronged her, and was even now withholding her birthright. Doña Isabel bestowed rich presents, but never a caress; perhaps Chinita would have spurned the last as lightly as she received the first. Ruiz, admitted to a certain intimacy by the necessities of the time, was impressed by the entire absence of any sense of obligation with which the young girl took her place with Doña Isabel, as if she had never known one more humble, while there was something in the cold and stately manner of Doña Isabel which seemed to shrink before the imperious force of character of her young companion.

It was at their first halt that Doña Isabel had, with unexpected hospitality, sent to invite Ruiz to share their midday meal; and, evidently with some effort, at the same time she bade the servant extend the invitation to the young American. Ruiz presented himself with due acknowledgments, but Ashley was nowhere to be found: he and his servant Pepé had disappeared from the ranks. No one remembered having seen them since they ascended the face of the hill of the graveyard; doubtless, it was surmised, the young man had grown weary, and had unceremoniously returned to Tres Hermanos.

Doña Isabel's face clouded. Upon the next day she had hoped to part company with her unwelcome guest forever; and now, — part of her purpose in leaving the hacienda was already frustrated. Ruiz was scarcely less disquieted; a glance at Chinita's triumphant countenance confirmed his apprehensions. Pepé, at least, had not returned to the hacienda, he was assured. The officer had had it in his mind to have the servant strictly watched; but it had not occurred to him that upon the first day he would attempt to evade him and fulfil Chinita's wild project of summoning Ramirez. He inwardly cursed his own folly and the duplicity of Ashley, whom he hitherto had not for a moment supposed in sympathy with the plot. He and the young American had even laughed at it together as the foolish dream of an imaginative girl. Now to the suspicious officer's apprehensions was added a burning jealousy. For Chinita's sake the American had doubtless made her cause his own; and with such an ally, Ruiz reflected, it was not impossible that he might see himself confronted by the man who he knew well never forgave a slight, never left unrevenged an injury.

The manner of Ruiz was so grave and abstracted that day, that Doña Isabel was inclined to credit him with far more depth and earnestness than as the reputed suitor of Rosario, or the airy and flippant recreant follower of the notorious Ramirez, she had attributed to him. Ruiz had the art of involuntarily suiting his demeanor and conversation to those in whose company he was thrown. There was no conscious hypocrisy in this, for the desire to please was natural to him, and often served him in good stead in the absence of genuine feeling, and even under the sting of wounded self-love held him silent, and masked his resentment. Many a time in his life-long intercourse with Ramirez had he chafed under the General's haughty patronage and made no sign; and it was only when he found himself thwarted in what was for the moment his strongest passion, that he began to question the designs of the chieftain to whom he owed all the fortune which birth or talents combine to make possible to other men.

Ruiz was the son of Tio Reyes, a life-long follower of Ramirez, for whom the chieftain had been sponsor, and toward whom he had with minute conscientiousness directed every worldly advantage which his means and position rendered possible. To Ramirez, Ruiz — who was known by the name of his mother (a not uncommon custom where her family renders the cognomen more honorable than that of the father)—owed the chance which had made him a soldier of fortune instead of a laborer in the village where his brothers and sisters plodded and toiled, in absolute ignorance of the father who had forsaken them.

Ruiz's knowledge of this strengthened his resolution to

ignore the past, and suffer no ill-timed revelations to interfere with his determination to win at one step love and
fortune by gaining the hand of the *protégée* of Doña Isabel,
— a purpose he was certain Ramirez would oppose, for in
a moment of confidence the General had intimated that
it was to a daughter of his own, in accordance with a
promise made long years before to Reyes, that the
young man was to be united; it was for this destiny his
future had been shaped, his fortunes moulded.

At any previous time the ambition of Ruiz would have
been fully satisfied; his whole desire would have been to
meet this promised bride, and by his marriage strengthen
the interest which the caprice or affection of Ramirez alone
caused to be centred upon him, and which, though often
burdensome and tyrannous, was apparently the young
man's sole passport to success. Even when in pique and
half-timorous defiance he took advantage of his separation
from Ramirez to follow Rosario to Tres Hermanos, it was
with no fixed resolution to tempt fortune alone. His short-
lived passion and his independence and anger would have
died together, had not his love for Chinita and the unexpected opportunities thrust upon him opened before him a
prospect of advancement and triumph far above his wildest
dreams, and completed his treason to his early patron,
without teaching him the lesson of truth either to the new
cause or to the mistress to which he was sworn.

In the eyes of Doña Isabel Ruiz was but the hireling
whose faith was purchased for Gonzales; in those of Chinita, the devoted follower of Ramirez; in his own — well,
time and circumstance would decide.

Like thousands of others who took part in the strife that
rent and decimated Mexico, Ruiz had but little conception
of the points at issue. He had simply followed the lead
of the popular chieftain to whom circumstances had attached him. He had learned by observation that wealth
flowed from the coffers of the clergy into the hands of
Ramirez, who scattered it lavishly to all about him, —
dissipating the greater part in luxurious living in cities,
and the maintenance of hordes of followers in towns and
cañons of the mountains, and with ready superstition returning much to the source whence it came, for never a
follower of his kept child unchristened or burial Mass

unsaid for want of means to purchase the services of a
priest.

Ramirez had appeared to the young imagination of Ruiz
absolute and ubiquitous.   There were few daring deeds
done that he had not shared in ; scarce a town been seized
and its merchants arrested until the forced loans demanded
from them were paid, scarce a train of wagons laden with
silver stopped, scarce a *pronunciamiento* with its excitement and rapid exchange of power and property effected,
that he had taken no part in.   He had been found wherever
fighting or plunder were.   He had taken a bloody part in
the repulse of the Liberals at the City of Mexico, where
the names of Zuloaga the President and of Miramon alike
were made infamous.   He had shared in the futile attacks
upon Vera Cruz, where Juarez at the head of the Provisional Government maintained with stubborn tenacity,
with a handful of followers, the most important stronghold
upon the seaboard, promulgating those unprecedented resolutions and decrees which revealed to the minds of the
people that of which they had never hitherto dreamed, —
namely, the separation of Church and State ; the suppression of the monasteries, which like vampires had for
generations drained the resources and absorbed the intellect of the people ; and the secularization of those immense treasures which, donated by the faithful to feed the
hungry and the sick, train the orphans, maintain the glory
and worship of God, had become the means of oppression
and bloodshed, and were the thews and sinews of the civil
war, in which the clergy strove to maintain the abuses of
the past and forge fresh chains for the future.

In a country where the dogmas of Catholicism were as
the oracles of God, where every heart was bound either
by the truths or the superstitions of Rome, or in most
cases by both inseparably, the magnitude of the task
assumed by the astute and resolute Juarez was almost
beyond the comprehension of those bred in the lands which
have never groaned beneath the yoke of ecclesiastical
tyranny.   Any premature act, any unguarded word, might
become the cause of offence ; and yet it was no time for
hesitation or timorous questioning.

Juarez knew the time and the temper of his countrymen ; and environed though he was, virtually imprisoned

in one small town upon the seashore, his influence reached
to the most remote districts of the interior. And although
the armies of the clergy swept the country from sea to sea,
in obscure fastnesses rose daring bands in tens and twenties and hundreds, who promulgating the new promises of
liberty sent forth by Juarez, maintained them with a tenacity of purpose that made defeat impossible. Worsted in
one quarter, they arose in another, employing with unscrupulous daring every means that cunning or audacity could
bring within their power,— claiming the excuse of necessity
for those acts of rapine and cruelty in the satisfaction of
personal enmities, the warfare upon the women and children, and the thousand barbarous deeds which make the
history of that time a continual record of horrors. Had
example been necessary, they would have found it in the
career of the opposing forces ; but in truth it was a time
when the attributes of patriot and plunderer, soldier and
bandit, became inextricably confused ; so that, perhaps as
completely to himself as to others, the average actor in that
bloody drama became a baffling and unsatisfying enigma.

Such was the mental condition of Ruiz, though it did
not occur to him to define it. Attached to the clerical
party by long association, and by the uninterrupted prosperity which he had shared with Ramirez, — who since
separating himself from Gonzales had followed an independent career, in which he had found the highest bidders
for his services among the crafty leaders of the old régime
(who to their rich gifts added the indulgences of the
Church, to which no soul however blood-stained and conscienceless could remain indifferent),— when Ruiz declared
himself to Don Rafael a convert to the Liberal cause, it
was but as a precautionary measure recommended by
Doña Rita ; and it was only when he saw in Doña Isabel
a patroness more powerful than the one he had abandoned,
added to his resolution to make himself independent of
the man who had hitherto controlled as well as defended
him, that he in reality inclined to the faction which day
by day seemed gathering strength, and likely to become
the dominant power.

But though his political views thus shaped themselves
to meet Doña Isabel's, Ruiz was no more faithful to her
purposes than to those of Chinita. To abandon Gonzales

to his fate at El Toro, — for he did not doubt that Ramirez would return with overwhelming numbers to the destruction of its insufficient garrison, — and at the same time to win the confidence of Doña Isabel and that of the troops under his command, thereafter seizing the first opportunity of having himself proclaimed their permanent leader and marching to join Juarez, whose cause was becoming strengthened day by day by fresh accessions from the interior, became his dream. Thus he hoped to blind Chinita by an apparent inability rather than disinclination to further her designs, mislead Doña Isabel, and secure for himself a position which should render it not absurd or incredible that he should aspire to the hand of a *protégée* of the Garcias, and to the dower which he shrewdly suspected he might of right demand.

All these plans were not perfected in a day, and the defection of Ashley Ward and his servant seriously interfered in the ambitious captain's calculations; but he allowed no trace of uneasiness to appear in those rare intervals when he found an opportunity to exchange a few words with the impatient Chinita.

Unconsciously also, Doña Isabel herself aided to establish a bond of confidence between them. When the long irregular column, with banners flying, driving before it the lowing cattle, whose numbers grew less after each night's slaughter, and followed by the motley line of women and children with the rude equipage of the camp, would be fairly in motion after the confusion of the early start, Ruiz would rein his prancing steed at the side of the carriage and deferentially place himself at the orders of the ladies. On these occasions his manner was one of perfect respect to both, of entire concurrence in the dictates and desires of Doña Isabel, and of half-indifferent, half-amused rejection of the immature and inconsequent conjectures and opinions of the girl, for whose beauty he exhibited a timid but irresistible recognition, which flattered while it disarmed the suspicious mind of Doña Isabel. She believed him still the ardent admirer of Rosario, — a thing which, she reflected, was under the circumstances - most fortunate.

In the freshness and animation of those morning hours conversation became natural and easy, and the events and names which were upon every tongue furnished food for abundant reminiscence and comment. Doña Isabel was eloquent in praise of Gonzales, who to his success at El Toro had added others in the neighborhood, which together with the occupation of Guanapila had made the entire district the undisputed territory of Liberalism. Ruiz assented to her enthusiasm with an ardor which seemed but natural in a youth who having separated himself from one powerful patron, should desire to place himself beneath the protection of another; and a comparison of the two, which should explain his defection from the first, followed in natural course; and with carefully chosen words, whose meaning held a subtile relation to the thoughts and predilections of his two auditors, he spoke of the intrepid and unscrupulous Ramirez.

More than once Doña Isabel, in the midst of his talk, sank back in the carriage lost in deep and painful thought, as the wild and terrible deeds in which that lawless man had figured recalled to her mind the horrors of her youth. Deeds such as these might have been planned and executed by the boy who had once been the pride, as he was afterward the bane, of her life, had he lived; but he was dead. Yes, thank God! though her heart had bled inwardly for long years; he had made no sign since the tale of his end came — he was dead!

While she was thus lost in thought, Chinita listened with glowing cheek and eyes. Ruiz knew of the meeting with Ramirez to which she looked back with such peculiar and unwearying fascination; and discerning in her admiration of his former leader an unfailing means of rousing in her a personal attraction which in her passionate nature might become an absorbing love, he carefully refrained from giving her any hint of his real sentiments toward her hero, and spared no covert word, no mute eloquence of his dark and expressive eyes, to increase an enthusiasm which had already led her into such strange defiance of the plans of Doña Isabel. To reinstate her hero in the power from which he had fallen became Chinita's dream, the aspiration of her soul.

On the fifth night of their journey it chanced that they entered a village, where Doña Isabel and her servants were enabled to find a shelter, which after the restricted

and insufficient accommodation of tents seemed absolutely
luxurious, primitive and rude though it was. Doña Isabel
wearied with travel, and depressed with anxiety at the
unaccountable delay of Gonzales, who she had supposed
would have hastened to take command of the troops that
her energy and bounty had provided, had early retired to
the room assigned her. Chinita had reluctantly accompanied her, for a fandango was in progress in the great
kitchen, the charcoal brasiers flaming red against the dark
walls of yellow-washed adobe, and shining upon the
bronzed faces of a group of swarthy men, who strummed
upon stringed instruments of various shapes and sizes;
while another group of mingled men and women went
through the rhythmic motions of the dance, with which the
young girl, gazing from her cell-like retreat across the
court, had long been so familiar.

Chinita had never danced since the night that she had
fled from the wedding *fiesta* into the waiting arms of Doña
Isabel. She had thought of the scene and its pleasures
only with anger and disgust; and yet as she looked into
the red glare and watched the swaying figures, she longed
to rush in and throw herself among them. To her, as
to Doña Isabel, the time of suspense was growing unbearably long; she was mad for action. Unreasonably, she
felt that there among their caste she might find Pedro,
Pepé, — some one who would do her bidding, who would
not dare put her off as Ruiz was doing with tantalizing
promises.

Chinita knew that instead of following the most direct
paths as Doña Isabel had commanded, the route on various pretexts had been changed, — she supposed to make
communication with Ramirez possible. She had no reason
to doubt the good faith of Ruiz, yet she was impatient and
miserable. A straggler upon the road had given them the
news that Ramirez had been seen upon the hills with a
forlorn and ill-armed troop, which bore evidence of the
ill fortune which the defeat at El Toro had inaugurated.
She had conceived a violent and unreasonable antagonism
to Gonzales, who from his whilom associate had become
the successful opponent and rival of the man whom by the
childish gift of an amulet she had fancied herself endowing with invincible good fortune. Even as she grew older,

her faith in the magic powers of a charm which had been the creation of a wizard, and had been blessed by Holy Church, scarcely grew less; and the remembrance of it undoubtedly strengthened the fealty so strangely sworn. Besides, a purpose had arisen in her mind of appealing to Ramirez to establish her position in the house of Garcia, by wresting from Doña Isabel an acknowledgment which would give her rights and a certain status (though clouded it might be) where now she was but the recipient of favors, — the peasant born raised to a dignity which was a mere scoff and jest to the ready wit of the sarcastic and epigrammatic rancheros. Chinita knew them well. Were not their gifts and prejudices her own?

Musing thus, the girl glanced from the barred window where she stood back through the gloom of the apartment to the bed where Doña Isabel was lying, — already asleep. The yellow light of a candle just touched the lady's pale face; it was contracted with that habitual expression of pain which the darkness of night permitted to the proud and suffering woman, but which in the day, or under the eye of even the most unobservant, she banished resolutely, though its shadow rested ever uncomprehended, unpitied.

There was something in the lassitude of Doña Isabel's figure, the hopeless grief upon the countenance, which for the first time suggested to Chinita the possibility that emotions deeper than that pride of birth which was as great in degree in herself, though neither as pure in principle nor bounded by the conventionalities of caste, had actuated the deeds and embittered the life of her who to the eye had been so absolute, so unassailable. With a feeling of awe Chinita took a step toward the sleeper, when a sound drew her glance to the court. Into the motley throng of lounging soldiers and *arrieros*, with their mules feeding and stamping around them, two belated travellers forced their way. It was the voice of one of them that had startled the watcher, and claimed instantly all her thoughts, setting her heart beating stiflingly as she sprang to the lattice and pressed her face eagerly against the iron bars.

The red light from the kitchen was augmented by the flame of a smoking torch, as a servant came forward to take the horse of the foremost rider. When he leaped lightly from his saddle, pushing back his broad hat, Chinita recognized the American, while a woman ran across the court and clasped the arm of the other as he alighted: it was Juana, the wife of Gabriel.

"Hist! hist!" said the man in a low voice, "no crying nor screaming. The Señor and I are here on business that would please your captain but little. By good fortune he is camped to-night at the outskirts of the village, and dare not leave his post. Tell me, Juana,—and not a word to Gabriel when thou seest him,—where is Chinita?"

Before Juana could gather her wits to reply, a hand was thrust through the bars almost at the speaker's shoulder; but it was Ashley who first saw it. He took it for an instant in his own, and bent over it. "I must speak with you, Chinita," he said; "join me in the corridor as soon as the house is quiet. I have much to say."

It was not the voice of a lover that spoke, but it thrilled her as that of a prophet. "Speak low," she answered, breathlessly, "Doña Isabel sleeps close by; but I will escape,—yes, I will come to you. Is not Juana with you? She must take my place here. The door is locked; the key is in the hand of Doña Isabel. But I will have it, trust me; the Señora sleeps heavily."

The girl's face glowed with excitement; she was ready for any adventure, the more daring the more welcome. Ashley Ward looked at her with a strange pride and admiration: this was a nature that no shame could crush, no outward fate dismay!

Chinita, standing at the grating, feeling an almost unrestrainable desire to burst into wild laughter and tears, was for some time utterly silent, waiting the hour when, the revelry over, sleep would fall upon the house. Ashley drew into the shade of the corridor. The inn was but a caravansary; there was none to notice who came or went. In the laughing, chattering crowd he was virtually alone. The thoughts that came to him as the fires faded, as the noisy revellers strolled one by one to their sleeping-places, and the pale light of the stars shining down upon that strange scene showed Pepé wrapped in his blanket, standing sentinel at his side, were indescribable. A phantasmagoria seemed to glide before him, in which Mary, his cousin, the ordinary places, scenes, and associates of his youth, Ramirez, Chata, all the strange actors in this drama, in new and ill-comprehended scenes, passed by; and in the midst the door of a chamber cautiously opened, and the girl of the siren face, which the very voice of fate had seemed to bid him seek in this far land, stepped eagerly and lightly forth to meet him.

In an angle of the corridor, where from sunrise to
sunset a woman usually sat, selling cigarettes and small
glasses of *chia* to the passers-by, stood a low *banquito*,
which was in fact only a superfluous adobe jutting out
from the massive wall. Ashley withdrew his foot from this
rude stool and greeted Chinita ceremoniously, and yet
with an air of protecting authority, inviting her by a gesture to be seated, saying, " So you will be less likely to
be seen by any chance comer. But from necessity, I
would not have asked you to speak to me here."

The girl looked at him with a little quiver of laughter rippling her mouth, though her eyes were anxious. Evidently she was troubled with no sense of impropriety, and
the thought of having eluded Doña Isabel diverted her.
Instead of obeying Ashley's invitation, she darted to
Pepé's side, caught a fold of his blanket in her hand, and
drew it from his half-covered face.

" Ah, Pepito, and is it thou?" she cried breathlessly.
" What news dost thou bring me? Hast thou then seen
my godfather, and what does he say of the Señor General?
Does he not think the plan a good one?"

Pepé shuffled uneasily to regain possession of the blanket, answering pettishly and in a stifled voice, " Is the
servant to talk when the master stands by with the words
ready? Go now, Chinita, you knew better than that
when Florencia used to pull your ears for a saucy one!"

The girl pouted, turning to Ashley with a lowering
face. She felt instinctively that what had been to her a
matter of simple expediency, a means of securing the fortunes of a man who was in her imagination all that was
noble and great, might have a meaner aspect to this
stranger, who would perhaps think she had meant harm
to Doña Isabel. Why had Pepé dragged this American
into the matter at all? Idiot! Ruiz had said nothing but

evil would come of it; and here was the stranger standing so straight and silent to be questioned, — and looking at her, too, with a sort of pity in the curious gaze he turned upon her. She felt half inclined to turn back to the room whence she had come; yet she said somewhat mockingly,

"It is you, Señor, who must speak, though it was the servant I sent on my errand; but perhaps you have seen Pedro and asked him my questions?"

"You had better sit down, Chinita," answered Ashley, severely. "I should not be here to-night if it were not to tell you things hard for you to listen to, and only to learn of matters of life or death should you have consented to come. Heavens! what a strange perversity of fate that you of all others should be anxious for the welfare, infatuated with the character, of — Ramirez!"

He spoke the name as though it were a curse, and the ready flame leaped into Chinita's eyes and cheek.

"Ah, then," she said, in a low but intense and penetrating tone, "you have come to tell me, like the others, that he is a brigand and a wretch! It is false! He is too brave, too daring, too noble for such cowardly spirits as yours to understand! Pepé, thou wert a craven. Stupid, it was Pedro I bade thee go to, not to this pale American, who has lost all his blood through a single wound!"

Ashley smiled faintly, vexed to find himself stung by a girl's unreasoning passion, but interposed quietly, "We lose time, Señorita, which is prudent neither for you nor for me. I beg you will listen to what I have to say. You will agree with me then that this is no hour to talk of my courage or the lack of it."

He had stepped between her and Pepé, to whom with a strange perversity she turned as if to show her disdain for the foreigner, whose every word had a tone of reproach. A mere suggestion that the proprieties which Doña Feliz and Doña Isabel had attempted to graft upon the rude stalk of her untrained, unguarded childhood had some other meaning than an elder's caprices, touched Chinita's mind: a young man could know nothing of woman's freaks and prejudices; she felt the hot blood rising to her cheek as she encountered his quiet gaze. All at once the court and corridor seemed to become wonderfully dark and still. A slight shudder ran through her frame; she drew back from the American and sat down where he had directed her, 'drawing her reboso close around her.

" Señor," she said, quite humbly, " I am listening."

Ashley did not speak at once, though Pepé seemed to urge him to do so by a motion of the head, which betokened readiness to confirm his speech; and when he began, it was at a point entirely unexpected by either listener.

" Señorita," he said, " is it not true that when you think of an American, you have in your mind a pale-faced, mysterious, unresisting youth, gliding spectre-like about the hacienda walls, tempting by a love-song the bloody steel of some dark and daring desperado? In a word, is it not the vision — distorted, insufficient, faint — of my murdered cousin, John Ashley, that comes before you?"

The young girl started. " Yes! yes!" she said hurriedly, not knowing what she said. " At least, once I thought like that. I had not seen an American then; I did not know — "

" And the first American you have known has had the benefit of the preconception," interrupted Ashley, grimly. " Well, it is something to know the secret of a contemptuous indifference which has always been so frankly expressed." This comment was in English, and though Chinita watched the motion of his lips, their silence could not have given her better opportunity to recover her confused and startled thoughts.

" Then it is true," she said. " You are of the family of the poor American, who was killed like a rabbit by a hawk. Why, they say that he could not have even clapped his hand on his belt, though a *man* from very instinct would draw a knife on his enemy, even in his last gasp. Is it not so, Pepito? I used to tell Chata that, when she would shed her soft tears of pity for him. Well, I could not cry, but I have watched at the mesquite-tree for the coming of his ghost a thousand times; yet I never saw it, — and it was I who found his grave."

" And it was you who bade Pepé show it me," interrupted Ashley; " and perhaps not as a mere jest as he thought." She nodded, looking up at him vaguely and keenly. " You thought perhaps I had come these many miles from my own country to find it?" he added. " Well, that was scarcely so; it had not presented itself to me as possible that the obscure grave of a murdered foreigner should be remembered still, and that his name should be found above it. No, I came for proofs of John Ashley's life, not of his death. It was not even to trace his murderer or to avenge him that I came."

She looked incredulous. "Why then should you come?" she asked. "Had you a vow? If I had known and loved the dead man, it would have been to kill the man who struck him in secret that I would have come. But it is as Captain Ruiz says, — the blood of an American runs so slowly it cools his heart, while ours is a burning torrent that causes the soul to leap and the hand to smite at a word."

Ashley realized that impatient contempt of him was struggling with a feeling to which, with sudden apprehension of its importance, she dared not give utterance; or perhaps the idea that had long been shaping itself was for the moment obscured, but yet in the darkness and confusion was growing to an overwhelming certainty in her mind. Chinita had risen to her feet, but suddenly she sat down, covering her face with a hand which Ashley saw in the dim light shook with suppressed excitement. Her attitude was that of a listener; and in a low voice he told her of his boyhood, of the days when he had come in from school and stood at the shoulder of his grown cousin, — the young man with the silky shadow just darkening his upper lip, and with the clear frank eyes of a boy, who looked so eagerly forward into the active life of manhood, restive under the restraints and cautions that hampered him, until at last he broke away, and was no more seen, nor scarcely heard of, until the news of his early and violent death came to cast an unending gloom over the household, which before had been captious, foreboding, but ever loving, ever secretly proud of the bold, irrepressible spirit it could not chain to its standard of decorum, or tame to walk in the narrow path of uneventful and passionless existence. The years of his own youth he passed lightly by; there was nothing in them for comment until he came to the time of his aunt's death, his inheritance of the fortune that should have been John Ashley's, the reading of those few letters which had given

22

to Mary Ashley such strange dreams, and which in the re-reading had filled his mind with thoughts of the same possibilities that racked her own. He spoke of them briefly in a single sentence: "We found by his letters that he believed himself married; it was to find the woman he had loved, or any trace of her, that I came."

Chinita sat so still one might have doubted if she heard; but that very stillness convinced Ashley that she listened with an absorbing interest, too great for questioning. She could but wait breathlessly for what was to come.

"After long and vexatious wanderings I was taken wounded to Tres Hermanos," continued the young man. "There, when my hope was almost exhausted, I heard the name that had been in my mind so long,—heard it only to make inquiries which ended in confusion, and threatened to involve me in endless complications; so at last I was glad to suffer myself to be convinced that my conjectures were the mere vagaries of an overburdened fancy, a too scrupulous conscience, and to turn my face homeward, determined that thereafter I would live my life, and take in peace the goods fortune sent me. In such a mind I rode with the troop across the plain and up the desolate hillside, along which the scattered graves of the poor lay, the mounds scarce noticeable among the rocks and cacti. Pepé remembered your jesting command; it would give him an opportunity to withdraw from the troops unheeded. He invited me to go with him to see something that would interest me. When I saw the grave, my heart began to beat; when I read the name upon the fallen cross, the blood rushed into my eyes and suffocated me; every drop in my heart accused me! There lay my cousin murdered, and in looking for a possible claimant to his name, I had forgotten him! I had forgotten that his death was still unatoned for, the murderer undiscovered, unsought, unpunished."

Chinita dropped her hand from her face and looked up, her eyes glowing, her lips apart, her bosom rising and falling with the quick breath that came and went. Here were words she could understand; here was a spirit that touched her own.

"And then, then, then?" she muttered; and Pepé

leaned out from the wall, like a gaunt shadow, to hear the narration, as if every word was too significant to allow a single one to escape him. "Then?"

"Then," resumed Ashley, "I seemed chained to the spot. I could not tear myself away, though reason told me that to stay there was useless; to hasten forward and demand the truth from those I had hitherto shrunk from offending, the only course open to me. Reason as I would, I could not force myself to leave the spot. After a time, yielding to necessity and to my command, Pepé left me. I was alone for hours with the dead. My mind was full of him; I heard his voice; I looked into the eyes which death had closed for so many unregarded years. I saw before me that face which I had so long forgotten; but my fancy pictured him never as in life, gay, happy, resolute, but pale, bloody, corpse-like, stretching out dead hands to me and speaking with the soundless voice of those we dream of. Who remembers the tone of a voice, silent forever? Yet it echoes in our heart; it awakens our joys, our griefs, our fears; it is more powerful, more terrible, than any living voice. And so upon that day was the voice of the dead John Ashley to me. As I listened to it, I swore never to leave Mexico until the mystery of his death, as well as that of his life, was open to me; until I had called to account the villain who had cut him off so secretly, so vilely.

"While I was full of the thought, and the whole world around me seemed to stretch on every side silent, void, waiting for me to choose whither I would go, in what direction I would set out to seek the nameless object of the new absorbing passion, which seemed more vital, more essential to my being than the air I breathed, I felt a presence near me. I looked up, — a man was leaning over the wall. I instantly conjectured he was not the mere peasant his dress indicated. A sense of mysterious connection between his life and mine seized upon me; it strengthened as he crossed the wall and strode toward me over the sunken graves. He came as though under a spell; I looked upon him as if under the fascination of a serpent-like gaze. I recoiled, yet for worlds I would not have turned from him. His eyes fell upon the cross; the expression of his face, the words that sprang from his lips, —

vague though they were, — sped to my brain with an electric thrill. I knew the man before me was John Ashley's
murderer."

Chinita had risen. She stretched out her hand and
touched the hilt of the knife in Ashley's belt. It was the
action of a moment, yet it was a question that the quick
beating of her heart and the panting breath made at the
instant impossible from her lips. Ashley answered it by
a brief account of the combat and its interruption.

As he ended, she drew a deep breath of relief. It did
not occur to him that it could be for any other than himself. It flattered and pleased him, for an instant he realized how deeply, as having in it something of the tender
unreasoning fears of gentle womanhood. Yet the readiness with which she had comprehended his passion for
revenge, while it justified him, had set her in a harsh and
cruel aspect, which made her lithe, dark beauty forbidding, unrelenting, tiger-like. Yet this strange young
creature, he thought, at once so foreign to him, and
still so near, concealed after all, under the surface of incomprehensible moods and half barbaric customs, those
attributes of gentleness, those instincts of justness, which
amidst the perplexing differences of national manners
and standards of good and evil may be distinguished.
and understood by every mind. At that moment Ashley
felt her to be less an alien than he had ever been able
before to consider her. She was not only beautiful, bewitching, but in part, at least, comprehensible.

Chinita stood silent for many moments; she had not
even started when he spoke the name Ramirez. The personality of the man of whom he had spoken had been a
foregone conclusion in her mind.

"It was the amulet I gave him that saved him," she
said simply; and Ashley stared at her blankly, not comprehending the meaning of her words, but only that the
relief she had experienced had been rather for the aggressor than for him. Had he then been mistaken? Was
she an entire stranger to the thought which so permeated
his own mind that he had imagined it must be present in
hers?

"Yes, the amulet that I gave him must have all the virtues Pedro told me of," she said musingly. "So it was

the General Ramirez who killed the American? *Dios mio!* he must have had good cause; yet it angers me. Ah! it is well I have time to think what cause he must have had!"

"Cause!" ejaculated Ashley, "cause!"

The girl nodded her head in an argumentative way. In the dim light Ashley could read the struggle in her mind, — indignation at the deed, dismay at its consequences, battling with attempted justification of the perpetrator. "By my patron saint!" she exclaimed at length, "it was the woman who was to blame. Why did she torture him? He must have loved her; and what was there in the American to make her false to Ramirez? Strange she should have preferred another to him!"

"For God's sake say no more!" cried Ashley, with actual horror in his voice. "I forgot that this tale has no deeper significance to you than any other; that the American is to you simply an American, and Ramirez the hero of your own countrymen, by whose desperate deeds your imagination is dazzled, and for whom, even in the midst of horror, you find excuse, admiration, justification. To you he seems but a jealous lover, taking just revenge upon a successful rival."

Chinita spoke not a word, but bent her head as though his words were an accusation. Her face, in the dim light, was so impassive it was impossible for Ashley to conjecture what was passing in her mind. Did she remember that he had said he had come to seek a child, and was it possible that the mystery of her own birth had not suggested to her that she might have an interest in the ghastly deed of Ramirez far deeper than would make natural or possible to her the excuse of jealousy in the perpetrator? He had learned something of the reticence and self-restraint of these people since he had come among them; yet was it possible this young girl could suspend judgment in such a cause until her own relation to it was fully ascertained? Were prejudice, education, sentiment, so much stronger than the voice of Nature? Did no instinct cry in her heart, denouncing this man, of whom she had made a hero, — no womanly pity hover over his victim? What a ready apprehension she had shown of Ashley's own desire for vengeance! Was that simply because it was the pas-

sion strongest in her own soul, and so gave to her ready
excuse even for murder?

Under the moonlight it seemed to him that the young
girl's face grew hard as marble. No, she was not one to
yield her faith lightly. This deed, which had filled the
mind of Chata with dismay, and intensified a thousand-fold
the horror in which she held the character of the man whom
she believed it sin not to reverence and love, would in no
wise shake the faith and admiration of this stronger soul,
who could condone it with the thought that a woman
had played the murderer false.

"Yet with all this, Señor," she said at length, looking
up, "if you have no more to tell me, I see not why this
should turn me against the Señor General. For you it is
different — oh, quite different; but for me, —" She paused
suddenly, and Ashley saw that the hand which hung at
her side was clenched till the nails marked her flesh.

Yes, the deed itself was nothing, — a trifle, at most, —
but in its relation to her, how great, how terrible, it might
become!

Ashley was not deceived. He felt that by a word he might
fan into a resistless flame the fire that lay smouldering in
that resolute heart, — a word which would be no surprise
to her, which would but confirm the conviction against
which, in loyalty to Ramirez, she struggled with even a
certain anger against the persistent suspicion that made
the legendary and unheroic figure of the American a mute
denouncer, more powerful, more persuasive, than the living man who had revealed the author of the tragedy
which through all her life had been so dark a mystery.
It seemed to Ashley that she held her breath to listen to
his next words; but he could be as hard as she was herself
to this girl, whose heart seemed incapable of feeling aught
but a personal injury, or any passion but revenge.

"Señorita," he said, "I went back to the hacienda.
My horse had fled; there was nothing else for me to do, if
I would find means to follow this man who had suddenly
become my debtor in all the dues of outraged kinship.
My object was to obtain money, a horse and guide, and
to regain the troop as quickly as should be possible; to
denounce this murderer to Doña Isabel, and reveal the
plot against her interests which had appeared to me so

weak, so absolutely absurd, but which now assumed an
importance commensurate with my detestation of him
whom it was designed to serve. But with further thought
my resolution changed. If all her agents were false,
— Pedro, Ruiz, as well as you, whom I know to be "
(Chinita winced), — " and Pepé should be successful in
inducing Pedro to play into the hands of Ramirez, what
power could Doña Isabel employ to prevent that change
of leadership which it was more than probable the troops
— indifferent to the cause, eager only for action and
booty — would accept with acclamations? Clearly, my
only course was to proceed to El Toro and arouse the
too confident Gonzales, who in incomprehensible inactivity
was awaiting the promised succor, — incomprehensible if
the emissaries of Doña Isabel had reached him; for, as I
knew, not one word in reply had been returned.

"I had much to ask of Doña Isabel Garcia, — questions
which had burned upon my lips before; but reflection
told me I was no more ready to ask them now than I had
been; that her pride might be still as obdurate. No, there
were months before me in which by gradual assault I
might acquire all the knowledge I would in vain endeavor
to gain by sudden force. I was confident that if by no
stratagem or treason Ramirez ultimately could place himself at the head of these troops, he would be found in the
field against them. I learned that he hated Gonzales as a
personal, no less than a political, foe. Gonzales then was
the man for me to follow. In serving Doña Isabel against
the machinations of those she had so blindly trusted, I
should serve myself; keep in view the mocking fiend
whose downfall I had sworn, and perchance satisfy myself in regard to the still importunate doubts which had
led to my presence amid these strange scenes.

" I had intended to leave the hacienda upon the very
night of my return, but on my way — Well, that is nothing to the purpose; I reached it exhausted. But the
early morning found me in the saddle. My strength revived with every step toward El Toro. Once we caught
sight of the long line of the hacienda troop crossing the
open plain. We had passed through cañons and byways,
and were far in advance of them. More than once in the
mountains we heard the name of Ramirez, and made wide

detours of hamlets where men were gathering in twos and threes and sixes, — ragged, unkempt, unarmed for the most part, but full of enthusiasm in their leader, and confident of booty and glory. Without doubt, the reverse of Ramirez at El Toro would not remain unavenged. I realized the spell of that potent name, the very echo of which seemed to be as eloquent as the living voice of most men, chieftains and leaders though they might be."

Chinita's eyes glistened; she raised herself with a proud gesture, as if the involuntary tribute to the genius of the adventurer was a personal commendation.

"Though we avoided the villages," continued Ashley, "I did not hesitate to question the few passengers we met upon the roads. These were chiefly wandering traders, stooping under their burdens of clay-ware or charcoal, adherents of no particular party, and reticent or the opposite, as their natural impulses or the supposed necessities of the time prompted. These I plied in vain for news of Pedro, of Pepé, or even of the noted Ramirez himself. Each and every one seemed to have passed, and left not even a memory behind; though from these very ranchos and hamlets I knew Doña Isabel's troops had been drawn, and that the followers of Ramirez were daily drawing more, — forcing those they could not persuade, laughing at the protestations of the women, and feeding the adventurous ardor of the men with tales of daring exploits and promises of plunder. All this we heard, and knew the whole country was in a ferment, yet passed through it undetected, on our own part unable to catch a glimpse or hear a word of the covert from which Ramirez directed and inspired the movement. Travelling rapidly, we entered upon the third day a deep gorge, which cut the foothills of the very mountain that overshadowed the towers of the convent town toward which I was journeying. Still a painful stretch of twelve hours, of an almost pathless labyrinth of rock and sand, I was told, lay before us; and early in the evening I ordered a halt, intending to set forth before the day broke. One of my servants spoke of a spring which he knew of; and though the season was so dry that we had little hope of discovering it, we decided to push on, although at every step the horses seemed to protest against the effort, — for they had been ridden mercilessly, without change and almost without food or rest. As we neared the spot where we hoped to find water, the aspect of the country seemed to grow even more forbidding.

"'The dry season has swallowed it,' said the servant dejectedly, after a careful survey of the locality. 'There is nothing here but sand, — a dry welcome for our thirsty beasts;' and at a signal from me he threw himself from the saddle, and tethering his panting horse, clambered up the gorge to gather a handful of dry grease-wood with which to light a fire. Meanwhile, his fellow busied himself in unpacking the few articles we had brought, and I threw myself on the ground against a rock, feeling myself more secure in that wild and secluded pass than I had done since I left the hacienda.

"The place was very still. Although it was yet daylight in the world without, the whole gorge was in shadow. The crackling of the herbage under the horses' feet, or a low word occasionally spoken by the men, was all that broke the stillness. I suppose from thought I was gradually falling into slumber, when the sound of horses galloping, of men laughing and shouting, broke upon the air. I started to my feet and seized my arms, calling for the men; but they had disappeared; the three horses were rearing and plunging. I caught and succeeded in mounting my own; but as the cavalcade drew near, I realized that its members were so numerous and in such mad humor that it would be worse than folly for me to approach them. One of my men had recovered from his panic, and stole up to me with blanched face and wide-staring eyes. I pointed to the horses, and with wonderful dexterity he bounded into the saddle of one, and caught the bridle of the other. In as little time as it takes me to tell it, we gained the shelter of the rock. Calmed by a few low words, the horses stood motionless, and from our covert we saw the company of lawless soldiery go by.

"Ramirez was at their head; and by a cord at his bridle-rein was tied a man, who vainly strove to keep pace with the gallop of his horse. At almost every step he fell, and was struck by the hoofs of the foremost horses, whose riders leaning down brought him again to his feet with blows from the flat sides of their swords. There were perhaps thirty ruffians engaged in this brutal sport; and after them ran a man at such a pace as only an Indian could maintain, even for moments, wringing his hands and praying and crying, — alternately a prayer and a curse. And in him, more by his voice, gasping and hoarse though it was, than by sight, I recognized Pepé Ortiz."

Chinita would have screamed, but the ready hand of the peasant closed over her mouth. "The man! the man tied to the horse's rein!" she gasped, when he released her.

"I could not see his face, and he had no breath to cry out," said Ashley. "They passed so closely, I could have shot Ramirez like a dog. But I seemed paralyzed by horror. It did for me what perhaps a moment's reflection would have done had I been capable of it, — it saved me from suicide. To have moved then would have been certain death. I could not comprehend the mad jests of those around the victim; but a moment after they passed I heard a sound which to all ears conveys the same meaning, — a pistol shot, — and the voice of Ramirez crying, —

"'*Caramba!* the next fall would have killed him, and the dog should die only by my hand. There! I have paid the debt I owed thee, — thou knowest for what. It should have been paid thee like the other villain's years ago. Would that I had dragged him at my horse's rein as I have thee!'

"The man fell; a soldier, with a laugh, cut the rope; all swept on with shouts and laughter, — Ramirez the quietest among them. In a few minutes they were far up the gorge. One glance had satisfied Ramirez that his shot had reached its aim.

"None seemed to remember the panting wretch behind. I had reached the prostrate body as soon as he, and together we raised it up. Under the mask of bruises and blood and the dust of the roadway, I recognized the man I had been seeking, — Pedro Gomez."

Pepé caught Chinita on his outstretched arm, — she had staggered as though struck by a heavy blow. Ashley sprang to her side in remorse, — he had spared her nothing in the recital: but she had not fainted. She raised herself slowly, and lifting her arms above her head, wrung her hands in speechless agony.

The man who had been murdered years before had been a shadow, a myth, in her mind. He became at that supreme moment a living presence, joining with, blent with, the martyred Pedro in denunciation of the man whom she had raised in her admiration to a pinnacle of glory. The idol of years crashed to the earth, in semblance of a demon, — and with it fell the stoicism and pride that had encased as in bands of steel the softer emotions of her nature.

"Murdered! murdered both!" she moaned at length. "Was it not enough he should bereave me even before I came into the world, but that he should so vilely slay the only creature who has loved me? Oh, my God!" she added, shuddering, "why have I been so cursed as to have given one thought to such a wretch? Oh! forgive, forgive, forgive!"

XXXVI.

To whom was that vain cry addressed? Ashley questioned not, but clasping in his the icy hands which strove to smite and beat each other, spoke such words of soothing as came readiest in the stranger tongue he found so inadequate. He realized that it was not to him Chinita directed that wail of self-abasement and remorse; and he also apprehended somewhat of the wild joy that would have been his, had she involuntarily turned to him in the anguish of her desolation. But she was scarcely conscious of his presence, and in her frenzy — terrible to witness, though it was not loud — even Pepé's rough accents were unheeded.

"*Niña* of my soul!" he said earnestly, "Pedro is not dead. No, it is not a lie I tell thee! Who would lie to thee in such an hour as this? I have come to tell thee that he lives; 't was he himself who sent me."

"He himself!". she echoed at last, turning her wild, tearless eyes upon Pepé's face. "Ah, it is because thou art here that I know he is dead, else thou wouldst not dare to leave him!"

"And by my faith, it is not of my own will I am here!" answered Pepé, bluntly. "Señor Don 'Guardo, you can tell her that."

"I can in truth," replied Ashley, who seeing that the peasant's words were received by her but as mere attempts to defer the evil moment when the inevitable assurance of the death of her foster-father must be given her, — so well did she know the customs and manners of her country people, ever prone to useless prevarication, even in their deepest sorrow, — hastened to describe to her the few scant means they had found in his extremity to recall the exhausted Pedro to the life that had apparently been thrust and beaten and driven from him forever.

The ball of the pistol had but grazed the cheek of the tortured man; the blood and dust had deceived the accustomed eyes of Ramirez, as it had deceived their own. The greater danger arose from the frightful condition of laceration and fatigue to which the mad race through the stony cañon had reduced him. ,

In a few words Pepé told the tale. He and Pedro had met but the day before, and it was while hastening to El Toro to apprize Gonzales of the plot that Pepé, in the petition of Chinita, had revealed to the indignant Pedro, that they had encountered face to face the irate chieftain and his followers. Pepé understood little of the cause that led to their being seized, dragged from their horses, and threatened with instant death. Both alike protested innocence of any scheme to baffle or injure the mountain chieftain; but he understood too well the ease with which a foe too weak to fight could assume the aspect of a friend. At the worst, however, Pepé imagined they might be forced to turn back on their way to spend a few unwilling hours among the bandit followers, until chance should give them opportunity to escape. But Ramirez's memory was keen as it was vengeful. Suddenly he bent and gazed searchingly into the face of the elder prisoner.

"Ah!" he exclaimed, with an oath, "I know thee! Thou art Pedro Gomez."

Pedro, who till this moment had bent his head to avoid the gaze of his captors, raised it swiftly with an ejaculation of amazement. A red handkerchief bound the brows of Ramirez; his face was swarthy and grimed with hard riding.

"Ah, and thou knowest me, too!" Ramirez cried. "Thou hast called me a devil more than once in thy lifetime; and now I will prove thy word true. Hereafter thou wilt have no further chance for that, or for opening the gate to the man who would make my—" He gnashed his teeth in speechless rage, and with his sword struck the keeper across the face.

The action spoke louder than words. Some one, in ready comprehension of the leader's mood, threw a lasso, and catching the prisoner across the breast began to mimic the wild shouts of a bull-fighter. But Ramirez was in no humor for pastime.

"On! on!" he cried. "'Tis nearly sunset. Let us see how far on our way this fellow can accompany us till then; and then by a vow I made to my patron San Leonidas, more than a score of years ago, he shall die. *Caramba!* did ever man play Ramirez false, and he forget to pay him his dues?"

Pepé, amid the shouts and laughter of the band, heard these words with a wild sense of terror; but it was only when he beheld Pedro struggling at the side of the plunging horse, that he realized that the gate-keeper was to be dragged to his death. He had heard of Ramirez's wild jests, and imagined that this might be one, until he beheld the cortège speeding forward, urging the unhappy Pedro before them with blows and jeers, or exhibiting their wonderful horsemanship in evading his prostrate body, — which, however, more than once, as he fell, sounded under the thud of the horses' feet.

Pepé could have escaped at any moment, for in the concentration of attention upon Pedro his companion had been utterly forgotten; but he followed madly, expostulating, entreating, cursing, while his breath allowed; and then was swept onward in the whirl, seemingly almost unconscious, till he heard the shot that ended the mad scene, and found himself staggering over the body of the bleeding Pedro.

The sight of Ashley, as unexpected as it was reassuring, as though an angel had arisen, saved the wretched youth from utter collapse of mind and body. But for the new excitement he would have fallen prone, and had he ever regained consciousness it would have been to find his comrade dead. But under the impulse of Ashley's energetic action and sustaining words, he even helped to raise the victim, in whom, lacerated though he was, Ashley soon discovered a feeble flutter of the heart.

"We took him to the shelter of the rock," said Ashley, who had by signs hastened Pepé's conclusion of the account, which, related in his own profuse manner, was far more agonizing than the brief outline here given, "and found that his extraordinary powers of endurance, though strained to the uttermost, had stood him in wonderful stead. An arm was broken, and every muscle so wrenched and strained that when he regained his consciousness the resolute will, which during the progress of the torture had withheld him from uttering protest or groan, utterly gave way, and he screamed in agony. Happily his persecutors were too far distant to be recalled by those unrestrainable cries of returning consciousness. Even while we poured brandy down his throat, and rubbed and stretched his limbs, it seemed as though it would have been a thousand times more charitable to suffer him to die than to recall him to such agony. When he regained full consciousness, however, the cries ceased, — not because the pain was less, but that the will regained its mastery. "As his eyes fell upon me, he gazed at me a moment as upon an apparition. So wild was his look, I thought he was going mad.

"'Don Juan! here! here!' he muttered hoarsely. 'Are we in hell together? But, no!' he sprang up, then fell back with a groan. 'I shall live to warn her yet. Oh God, that the child should entreat me to turn traitor for him! But she shall not fall into his accursed hands. Never! never! Ah, Pepé, thou art here; hasten, hasten! tell her she is the child of John Ashley, the man Ramirez murdered. What though I die? She will be saved! Go! go! I pray you!'

Chinita started. Ward anticipated some outburst of emotion, but the glance she flashed back at him indicated simply keen intelligence; the springs of feeling remained untouched. With an effort Ward continued: —

"My recreant servant had returned. It was Stefano, whom you know well. He is a coward, but ready in resource, and with a kindly heart. He knew the country well, and told us of a cave he once had slept in, and led us to it unerringly. To our surprise we found there a scanty supply of toasted corn, left by some wandering tenant, and a quantity of water, still fresh enough to show that the cave had not long been empty. There was a remnant of a woman's dress in one corner, — heaven knows how brought there, — and this we used to bind the pistol wound; while Stefano used the best means available in setting the broken arm. These rancheros are possessed of strange accomplishments, — I don't believe a surgeon could have done it with more skill.

"During the course of our passage through the dusk, bearing as best we could our groaning burden, Pedro's hallucination that I was John Ashley merged into recogni-

tion. It was but little I could do for him, but it filled him
with gratitude. 'You are a good Christian,' he ejaculated
again and again ; and once in the night, when the others
slept, he muttered ' *Niña, niña* Herlinda, forgive me ! I
am dying. You bade me protect the child ! Ah, even in
life it has not been possible ! Is she not in the hands you
bade me defend her from ? '

" These sentences, murmured at intervals, kept me
waking while all others slept, hanging over him with
entreaties to disburden his mind of the secret which
weighed so heavily upon him that it seemed under it
he could neither live nor die.

" ' Tell me at least,' I said, ' who is this man called
Ramirez, whom I saw this evening wreak upon you so
terrible a revenge ? How comes it that you are so hated
by the man for whom your foster-daughter is plotting ?
Have you not been his follower in by-gone days ? Surely
it is not Chinita who has set such enmity between you ! '

" ' No, no ! it began before she was born,' answered
Pedro shudderingly, his pale countenance becoming more
ghastly still. ' Oh, Lady of Sorrows ! ' he continued, as if
forgetful of my presence, ' was it not enough that the child
should fall again into the power of Doña Isabel, — she who
tore it from its mother's breast to cast it among the beggars who feed with the dogs at her gates, — but that her
father's murderer, her mother's destroyer, should wield
this devil's witchcraft over her ? My God, who will defend her ? Who will rescue her ? ' "

Chinita raised her head, her nostrils quivering, the veins
upon her neck and temples swollen and palpitating.

" ' Tell her the truth,' I said ! ' Then she will be her
own defender ; and I — you know me ; for what other purpose am I here but to shield her ? Yes, Pedro, the secret
you have kept so long is mine as well as yours. John
Ashley, my cousin, died because he dared love a woman
named Herlinda ; and that Herlinda was the daughter of
Doña Isabel Garcia.' " A look of indiscribable hauteur
and triumph passed over Chinita's rigid face, while Ashley
continued, —

" Pedro stared at me in wild dismay, ' *Niña, niña !* ' he
muttered, piteously, ' I have not betrayed thee ; and Doña
Isabel, though you have taken the child from me which

you thrust upon me in such mockery, have I not borne the torture meekly? No, even to this man, so like the other that he needed not to tell his name and kin, I have told nothing to shame you!'

"His words sprang from his lips in spite of the will that would have kept them back; for a time he was like a man under the influence of a maddening draught. Striving to calm him by the assurance that I would never use the knowledge he might give me to dishonor the family to which his whole life had been devoted, I drew from him little by little his strange tale. It concerns neither you nor me, Chinita, until in recompense for secret service done her in the cause of her wretched brother Leon, Doña Isabel Garcia made Pedro gate-keeper at Tres Hermanos. There my unfortunate cousin gained his good offices in his secret meetings with the young Herlinda. The man seems in truth to have been conscious of no serious offence against Doña Isabel in lending his aid to the tender intercourse of the young lovers, although he was cognizant of her plans regarding the marriage of Herlinda and Gonzales. My cousin claimed the right to visit his wife; and Pedro took his gold and was silent, if not convinced.

"'Ah, how joyously Ashley left his wife — for the last time,' Pedro exclaimed at length, ceasing to expect my questions and taking the tone of narrative. 'Yes, Don Juan called Herlinda always his wife: what was the keeper of the gate to demand, — the word of a priest forsooth, rather than that of the man whom his mistress loved? Ah! Doña Isabel I knew would ask all, or the young Gonzales. One cannot do worse than put his hand in a boiling pot, and wherefore do that when it hangs over his neighbor's fire? Yes, never had Ashley seemed more confident, more gay. "I shall not again need to waken thee at midnight to let me pass like a thief who leaves a bribe," he said; "to-morrow I shall be free to come and go as I will."

"'Alas!' the remorseful Pedro continued, 'as my eyes followed the young American, I thought any woman might be pardoned for loving him: had he not beguiled my own heart? for I swear I loved him. Yet I wondered at the courage of the *Niña* Herlinda, — she who had seemed so timid, so yielding to her mother's every wish. *Caramba!*

23

it is true, — "There is nothing too strong for love or death." I laughed as Ashley stepped forth, to think how youth in its folly can baffle caution, when a voice behind me echoed the sound. The blood froze in my veins, so overpowering was the very presence near me even before it touched me. Almighty powers! when I looked up, the man in the peasant's dress, whom only a few hours before I had admitted as a stranger within the walls, hurled himself upon me; but the blaze in his eyes could burn only from the fierce and terrible rage of the evil spirit of that house. It was Leon Vallé who dashed me down and rushed out into the night.'"

Chinita uttered an exclamation; then repeating the name, "Leon! Leon Vallé," listened with bated breath, while Ashley continued in the words of Pedro: —

"'I knew at the moment that Ashley was lost. Not a thousand prayers, nor the swiftest aid my cries could have gained him, would have saved him. I waited, scarce daring to breathe; with strained ears I listened. Would the murderer, his first work accomplished, return? I knew then he held my life forfeit; yet had he returned, I should have opened the gate to him. Ah, you know not the power of that man! As it was in Leon Vallé then, so it is now in Ramirez. God, what power in those terrible eyes! I felt it then, I felt it to-day. What resistance was possible? The morning came. I was still alive, but the people came to me crying of the dead. What need had I to ask the name? In the midst of the tumult a terrible shriek rang on my ears. I thought my brain was turning. There was but one thought that steadied it, — confession, confession to Doña Isabel.

"'As soon as it was possible I sought her presence. I cannot tell you what passed; I only know the words I would have spoken died on my lips. Whether Doña Isabel had known of it or not, I could not determine; but that the love of Herlinda Garcia and the young American was to die with him, and that the terrible vengeance which had been worked for her was not to be in vain, seared itself upon my mind. The preservation of that secret was to atone for my sins, and not confession. Never to mortal was my knowledge to be breathed. This was the penitence laid upon me. And so, despairing, I left her. What was the immortal soul of a poor peasant in comparison to the honor of the family of Garcia?

" ' It was well! Why should a servant gainsay his mistress? So months went on, Señor. Within and around the hacienda people were dying. They told me the *niña* Herlinda herself was pining, — some whispered for the American ; but a terror seized even on the boldest, and the American's name ceased to be heard, and that of the young Gonzales took its place. The gossips were content to blame any name unchid for her wan cheeks and sunken eyes. But I knew that no man had scorned her love, and that no living man had aught to answer for had she loved too well. I had not seen her for weeks and weeks ; but one night a creature so pale and wan I thought it her ghost, accosted me. Strange, strange the mission that brought her. It was to entreat my protection —that of the worthless Pedro — for the child which in secret and in banishment she was about to bring into the world.

" ' Well! well! I promised all she asked. I should have done so even had I thought it possible the dire need she pleaded would be hers. Oh! I had heard strange and fearful tales of deeds that have been wrought within the walls of these great and solitary haciendas ; but that Doña Isabel would stoop to crime, and that I should find it in my power to save a child which she would strive to sacrifice, I could not believe. Trouble, I thought, had made Herlinda mad. But she was mad only with the frenzy of a prophetess.

" ' With terrible forebodings I saw her taken from her home. Day and night I thought of her, and my heart was like ice ; but one day, when worn out with watching and expectancy I sat at the gate, I fell into a doze, and in my dream heard the voice of Herlinda calling me. It changed to that of a man. I woke with a start, and a child was dropped into my hands. Strange and wonderful must have been the means by which the hunted and distracted Herlinda had evaded the mother she feared! Who had been her friends, Señor? The wonder is with me still. I saw the face of her messenger but for a moment, yet it has haunted me. Yes, more than once, when I have thought of new faces that have passed before me, I have said, "Such an one was like the man; why was I blind to it when he stood before me?"' Pedro started up, and clasped my arm so powerfully that I shrank. 'Señor!' he cried, 'As God lives, I saw such a face to-day! It was that of the man who rode behind. him they call Ramirez.'

"'Reyes!' I ejaculated. 'Reyes!' What strange sport made the messenger of Herlinda the follower of Ramirez? I—"

Ashley paused, for Chinita echoed the name with an intense surprise far greater than his own. She clasped her hands to her temples, as though fearing the mad bewilderment of her thoughts was crazing her. "Tell me no more," she said faintly. "Do I not know the unnatural wretch that I have been? But what of Pedro? Why did you leave him? How dared you leave him? You!" She turned upon Pepé, accusingly. "He lives, you say, and yet you are here!"

"No less would content him," interposed Ashley, while Pepé muttered an inarticulate remonstrance. "It was Pepé you had sent upon your errand; it was Pepé whom Pedro would dispatch with his answer."

"Ay!" said Pepé, grumblingly, "and with you I must remain. I am sworn to that, whether you like it or loathe it."

"I," said Ashley, "have ridden thus far out of the direct path I would have taken to El Toro, to warn you of the character of the man you have made your hero; to tell you I believe you to be the daughter of my cousin, to offer you the home and the fortune that would have been his."

He spoke unhesitatingly, yet a strange sense of bewilderment swept over him. He was conscious that it was no fear of material loss that troubled him, though not for an instant did he dream of using the advantage of the law against this defenceless girl; but that this strange impulsive creature should be of the same blood as he, as the calm and gentle Mary; that she should come into their life with her wayward passions, her erratic genius, her weird beauty, — was a thing incomprehensible, almost terrible. Yet the blood leaped stronger in the young man's veins as he beheld her; and his heart bounded as he said,

"Yes, I must go; for I have certain news that the enemy is massing his forces for attack. I go to warn Gonzales; but I shall return to claim you as my cousin's child. Meanwhile, be silent — patient. Pedro prays you keep the secret of your birth. He believes as firmly as ever that only thus can you be safe. And for that mother's sake I pray you be silent. Right may be won for you, and her good name be still left untainted. There may be a mystery still to be unravelled."

"I will be silent; I will wait," Chinita said in a cold, hollow voice.

Ashley noticed that she had no word of sympathy for him, no recognition of the endeavors that had led to her discovery. Apparently the thought that he was aught to her was as far from her mind as any grief had ever been for that other American, — as far indeed as such was at that moment. For, strangely, Ashley seemed to penetrate the inmost shrine of her thought; and still the figures around which centred her love, her hopes, her passions were only those of Pedro, of Ramirez, of Doña Isabel.

"I will be silent," she repeated. "Ah, it will be easier now! Yes, hasten to El Toro, bring Gonzales; he will be a surer, safer leader than Ruiz — though I will turn him again to my will. Yes, yes, more than once I have thought Ruiz wavering, uncertain! Now at a word I will make him what before he has only affected to others to be, — the undying enemy of Ramirez!"

Ashley was silent. He would have had this girl passive, supine, womanly; yet from the very necessity of warning her, he had been forced to arouse in her this vindictive wrath against the man who had done her unwittingly such foul wrong.

"Listen!" he said hurriedly, after a pause. "It is Pedro who implores, who commands, that until he gives you leave, nothing of what I have told you shall pass your lips. I might have had your promise before I would speak. See, the stars are shining that must see me on my way. Give me two promises before we part, — one that you will be silent; the other that Pepé shall be continually within your sight or call. For this he was sent from the side of the suffering, perhaps dying, Pedro. He would have you safe, — safe from Ramirez."

"And I will kill you before you shall fall into his hands," interposed Pepé, grimly.

Chinita smiled with cynical bitterness, and said indifferently, "I promise. Yes, I promise. Ah, yes, Señor, you will see I have been silent when you come again. And now I will go back. What if the Señora Doña Isabel should wake and find me missing? — the child she loves so well!"

She waved her hand, and stepped backward through the darkness. At the door of the chamber where Doña Isabel lay, she seemed to vanish into air, so swift, so silent, was her going.

Ashley gazed after her long in silence, — so long that another spectral figure stole through the doorway, and with noiseless steps reached Pepé's side. "The Señora slept like the dead," Juana whispered; "but not for a thousand hard dollars would I lie in Chinita's place again, while she forgets time in lover's chat. I wonder at thee, Pepé! thou hast not a man's heart in thee. I thought thou lovedst her thyself!"

"Fool!" said Pepé, sulkily, and turned away; while Juana, ill paid for her devotion, sought a corner of the corridor in which to sink to sleep.

"Strange, incomprehensible creature!" muttered Ashley at length. "What emotions, what thoughts are hers? At least it is certain that the fascination of Ramirez is dissolved, — horror, hatred perhaps, has taken its place. She is safe. And now Pepé, my horse; I must take the road. And if it be true that Juarez is at hand, even Ramirez himself may tremble; the combined forces of Gonzales and Ruiz will hold him at bay, and keep an open road for the intrepid Liberal to the capital."

It was scarcely two hours past midnight, though his interview with Chinita had lasted long, when Ashley cautiously emerged from the inn, and took his way toward the open country. The troops lay at the east end of the town; but giving the watchword to the few sentinels who challenged him, he avoided them, and soon found himself in the vast solitude of the night. He had taken the precaution to procure a fresh horse, and for some leagues the way lay across a level country, so he made such speed as brought him by dawn within sight of the mountain upon

which Pedro lay, — but on a side many miles nearer El
Toro, his destination, where Gonzales, with his insufficient
garrison, was anxiously awaiting the reinforcements without which he could neither dare to advance, nor hope to
maintain his position in case of attack.

As Ashley glanced toward the ragged and solitary cliffs
where like a hunted animal the man was lying, he remembered that after the first horror was passed, Chinita had
spoken no more of her foster-father, had asked no question as to what hands were set to tend him, nor in what
direction lay the cave in which he was sheltered. Such
queries would have been useless, — she could do nothing; yet it would have been but natural that she should
have made them. Even if the gate-keeper's care of her
neglected infancy was forgotten, or accepted as a matter
of course, and though her mind was absorbed by thoughts
of her own history and her wrongs, yet his very connection with them should have made him an object of interest
if not of tenderness.

"Heavens!" murmured Ashley, "can it be that this
strange creature, as different in her instincts as in her appearance and education, is of the same blood as Mary?
A bewildering charge shall I take to her, if Doña Isabel
still, to save the reputation of her daughter, lays no claim
to this beautiful girl, and denies her such scanty justice as
she can give! For a daughter of an Ashley must not be
left to the sport of chance, — neither to be sold to the first
who bargains for her beauty; nor, worse still, to be consigned to a convent, as the unhappy Herlinda was." He
reasoned calmly, yet his heart and temples beat hotly.
"Let me think. If this Gonzales but proves a man of
honor, I may gain some aid from him; he, at least, may
know in which convent this woman — whom he also loved
— is immured. By the way, he is a fanatic upon this new
scheme of Juarez, of secularizing the property of the clergy.
Ah, in event of the success of the Liberal arms, that might
work countless and unimagined changes!"

The thought was full of suggestion. Ashley gave rein
to his horse, and dashed forward with fresh vigor. Afterward he scarce remembered how the day passed; but its
close found him, spent and weary, alighting at the door of
the inn of El Toro.

Almost at the same moment, far on the other side of the mountain, two travellers, so wrapped in long striped blankets and covered by wide sombreros as to be almost indistinguishable, the man from the woman, drew rein before a mass of cactus and gray rock; and while the one gazed furtively around, vainly seeking a sign of human contiguity, the other dismounted, and bending to a mere crevice in the rock gave a long, low whistle, then turned to help his companion, saying, " That will bring Stefano. Chinita, thou wilt see that, though a coward, he is no fool, and has cared well for thy foster-father. Said I not so? Ah, here he comes."

Chinita was cramped by long riding, and was fain to cling to her guide. She looked around her with a shudder. The wild solitude of the place was terrible. She feared to move, lest she should find herself face to face with death. Her head swam, the world turned black before her eyes; and in the midst a strange hand touched her own. A low laugh sounded on her ear, — it was that of a woman.

" Santa Maria ! " she heard Pepé exclaim. " It is the Virgin of Guadalupe herself. It is then that we are too late to serve the poor *padron !* "

The low laugh sounded again, — there was in it more of madness than sanctity. Chinita, with superstitious fear and desperation, sought to wrench her hand from the hot clasp in which it was held. The close air of the entrance of the cave closed round her, as with persistent force she was drawn within; and with a scream of terror she fell fainting, overcome by the excitement and exertion of many hours, and by the unexpected apparition which had greeted her.

The illness which attacked Doña Feliz upon the morning that Ashley Ward set forth from Tres Hermanos, was the first indication of an epidemic similar in character and force to that which had devastated the hacienda fifteen years before. Reminiscences of the time of the great sickness became the absorbing topic of conversation, until the care of the dying and the burial of the dead silenced all voices, and turned all thoughts to the overwhelming cares of the present.

At first with unspeakable remorse Chata attributed the illness of Doña Feliz to her unwonted exertion in walking to the reduction-works through the fierce sunshine, and to her grief and shame in discovering her, whom she believed to be her granddaughter, there in conversation with a stranger, — from whom a modest maiden would have shrunk in decent coyness, if not in fear. Chata's heart burned with grief and remorse. She longed to throw herself upon her knees, and pour out her soul before the woman she held in such love and reverence that the thought of her distrust and displeasure was like a mortal wound in her heart. Yet she was forced to be silent, before the unconsciousness and delirium which for days and weeks overpowered the body and mind of the strong, though no longer youthful, woman.

It was some consolation to the distressed maiden that she was called upon, almost alone, to bear the labor and responsibility of the care of Doña Feliz. Don Rafael was almost helpless before his mother's peril; the servants were terrified and incompetent. Soon Chata, in the incessant toil, almost ceased to think of the trials and perplexities of her own life, save to cry bitterly to herself that had she never known before that Doña Rita was not her own mother, the difference in her bearing at that crisis toward Rosario and herself would have betrayed the truth.

"Even Don Rafael," she thought, "though he loves me, is content that I, rather than his own child, should risk the danger of the infected atmosphere."

But in truth the alarmed and harassed man was capable of but little reflection or discrimination as to the actions of those about him. He gave no heed to the selfishness of his wife or Rosario, while he found Chata ever at Doña Feliz's side, tireless, calm, unmurmuring, ministering with a rare ability, which even natural tact and long experience seldom combine to produce in such perfection, to the needs and comfort of the ever delirious patient. He grew speedily to have a perfect trust and faith in this ministering child; and though once, when for a little while his mother was silent, and the servants had fallen asleep, he opened his lips to question her, there was something in the imploring yet innocent gaze of those clear gray eyes before which he shrank, as Ashley Ward had done, powerless to utter a word that should indicate distrust.

"Perhaps my mother knows, — yes, doubtless she knew," he said to himself, with a faint attempt to justify his silence. "*Caramba!* a man must have a black heart himself who could doubt the whiteness of so pure a soul!"

Almost hourly his perturbation of mind was increased by the report of some fresh name upon the list of the sick. With a faith as profound as their own in the decoctions of herbs and roots used by the village quacks, and a superstitious respect for the alleged virtues of blessed relics and candles, and even for amulets of less sacred renown, he went from hut to hut, endeavoring to propitiate the favor of Heaven by charitable deeds, — thus perhaps gaining for himself a more personal affection than the mere clannish regard which he in a measure shared with the actual proprietors of the vast estate, but which was not strong enough to insure him against the wit or malice of the dependent yet utterly indifferent and irresponsible host he attempted to govern. A doctor had been sent for, and also a priest; but neither appeared, — the priest perhaps because the last one, who had but lately left there, had given accounts of Doña Isabel's proceedings little likely to be acceptable to the Church. This added to the perplexities of Don Rafael.

In the midst of them he was one day accosted by

Tomas, the husband of Florencia, who in tones of genuine distress, which for the time gave pathos to his usual drunken whine, bewailed the sickness of his wife, and related how, spurning his care, she called vainly upon her Uncle Pedro (not a day's luck had befallen them since he had left them), and upon the Señorita Chinita (praying his grace's pardon for mentioning one whom the Señora Doña Isabel herself had chosen to be a lady), to come and give her a cup of cold water, — as if he, Tomas, himself had not spilled over her a jar of honeyed *pulque* in the vain effort to pour a draught down her parched throat. It was plain to see that the woman was doomed, and that it was for her the corpse-candles had been lighted.

"The corpse-candles!" echoed Don Rafael, — for he well knew the popular superstition at Tres Hermanos, that when the burial lights were to burn in the great house, their spectral counterfeits were first seen in the ancient dwelling where the spirits of the early possessors of the hacienda still guarded treasures, which awaited some daring and fortunate claimant in a descendant who should combine their faith with a tenacity of purpose and an untiring energy worthy the riches that had eluded their own weak and inconstant efforts. Had indeed the conclave of shades gathered to welcome another unsuccessful toiler among them? Don Rafael shuddered and crossed himself, and wondered that there was no news of Doña Isabel. He gave Tomas a silver piece, and told him that it was not for Florencia, or even for his own mother, that the corpse-lights of the Garcias would burn blue, and sent him away comforted.

An hour later, through the medium of the fiery liquors distilled from the agave, Tomas had so far strengthened his courage that he forgot the corpse-lights altogether, until he saw them again at midnight glimmering in the distance, not only behind the hacienda walls, but fitfully in the darkness of the middle distance. He crossed himself, as he fancied he caught at intervals glimpses of spectral bearers. His comrade on the watch jested at the fears that he opined transformed the soft brilliancy of the large and brilliant firefly into the light of ghostly candles; and Tomas was content to yield to the soporific charm of the mescal, rather than contest the matter with his drowsy comrade, — who, with a regularity which custom made invariable, at certain intervals awoke and emitted the shrill whistle that proclaimed that the sleepers of Tres Hermanos were safe beneath his vigilant care.

Just at dawn the man straightened himself suddenly before the rampart against which he had been leaning, gazed over the landscape with keen apprehension, and uttered a faint cry of consternation. The sandy line between the hacienda gates and the village had become a living one. Whence had the figures stolen? There they stood motionless, horse and man. The watchman stooped and shook his unconscious comrade. "Mother of Jesus!" he cried; "your corpse-lights were in the hands of living men. They are here! they are here! Ah, they are knocking upon the doors! That fool Felipe is turning the key in the lock! Up! Up!" At the same moment his whistle sounded shrilly, and the crack of his rifle upon the air woke the slumbering tenants of the assaulted house.

Too late! the unwary gatekeeper was surprised; the heavy doors were forced open, the courts in an instant were full of armed men, and Don Rafael, half dressed, staggering from his scarce tried slumbers, was seized by a half-dozen soldiers, while a voice he well knew, though it came as if from the dead, and knew to be that of a man who was as inflexible in act as unscrupulous in purpose, exclaimed, —

"How now, Don Rafael? Doña Isabel Garcia has at last showed her true colors. It is for Gonzales and the Liberals the men and treasure of Tres Hermanos have been accumulating! What, nothing for her Mother the Church? Ah, it is the old story, — nothing for those of her own household!"

The unwelcome intruder glanced around him with the air of one familiar with, yet inimical to, his surroundings; he laughed as he dropped the point of his sword upon the brick pave, and his spurred heel rang upon the stone step. Yet a close observer might have noticed a false note in the light and scornful tone, as though some poignant memory troubled his present purpose; and it was with a half evasive though still a threatening glance, that he lifted his eyes to encounter those of the administrador, who stood a disordered and helpless but resolute prisoner upon the steps above him.

At the sound of voices and the tramp of men, Chata had run hastily out from the room of Doña Feliz, whose illness had approached a crisis. The press of men prevented her from reaching Don Rafael, who imperatively signed to her to retreat. Still she would have dared much to reach him; but catching a glimpse of the triumphant countenance of the man at the foot of the stairs, she drew back, covered her face with her hands and fled precipitately, — in fear for herself perhaps, but more with an instinctive feeling that her presence endangered rather than helped her foster-father. That the General José Ramirez had entered Tres Hermanos in a mood to seize any pretext to assume toward it and its people the *rôle* of an injured and desperate man, was to be seen at a glance. The very soldiers had already divined as much, and were leading their horses and mules to drink at the fountain, and invading the arbor and lower rooms; the sound of their jests and laughter was mingling with the crash of the great flower-pots, carelessly pushed from their stands, and the sharp crack of jars of the quaint black and gilded ware of Guadalajara, which ornamented the corridors.

Chata re-entered the room of the sick woman, with pallid face and lips, and eyes expanding with a terror such as the mere sight of the imminent destruction of material things alone could not have occasioned. Terrible had been the tales she had heard of houses laid waste and property destroyed; yet even when the horrors seemed about to be repeated around her, she felt that she could have endured them bravely as among the chances of war had not this invasion brought to her an intensely dreaded and peculiar danger. She passed the group of alarmed and excited women who gathered at the bedside, uttering exclamations of terror, and kneeling at the head of the couch she clasped in her own the hand of the unconscious Doña Feliz.

"Grandmother, my dearest!" she murmered in a low voice, yet full of agony; "surely he will not tear me from thee! Oh, rather may I die with thee!"

"Oh, by the saints," cried the voice of Doña Rita in her ear, "for my child's sake, Chata, rise and fly to him!

It is thou only who canst save us. What did I tell thee in El Toro? Doña Isabel has ruined us! but for her fool-hardiness in sending aid to Gonzales all might have been well; but that has brought the wrath of Ramirez upon Rafael!" She turned toward her prostrate mother-in-law, with something very like fury, clenching her hand and crying, "Ah! ah! your clever deception will not seem so happy a one when you wake to find it has killed your son! That is what you deserve! You deceived even me. Do you think had I known, I would for all the favor promised me have played mother to the brat of Leon Vallé?"

The women ceased their cries to listen to this frantic outburst, which though but Greek to them, had a sound of mystery, which for the moment deadened their ears to the increasing tumult without. "Leon Vallé!" said one in an awe-struck voice, — "that was the Señora's wicked brother."

"Leon Vallé!" echoed Chata, a new light dawning upon her. "Maria Sanctissima, can it be?"

"What more natural?" cried Doña Rita, testily. "Was he ever weary of extorting some proof of Doña Isabel's devotion? But *Dios mio*, there was to be an end of her infatuation! Had he not killed her child? What better chance for vengeance was she to find than to conceal, destroy, every trace of his, when with devilish mockery he thrust it upon her? But then he might have known it was like thrusting the lamb into the jaws of the wolf. On my faith, girl, it maddens me to see you standing there motionless, when it is as if the legions of Satanas himself were loose. Go! go! I say, to soothe him. En-treat him to restrain his troops. The house will be sacked. Who knows what horrors may follow!"

"I will not go to him," said Chata, slowly, a red spot burning upon either cheek, her eyes dark with horror. "If he is indeed the man you say, will he not defend the home of his sister? If I am his child, will he not claim me? If he does, I must submit; but go to him — No! To save the hacienda — what has Doña Isabel done for me? To save my life — no!"

XXXVIII.

In the few moments during which this scene had passed, the administrador at a sign from the General had been half forced — though he made no attempt at resistance — to the lower corridor. Thence he followed his captor to a dining-room, where a servant with terrified alacrity was already bringing in cups of chocolate for the breakfast, while a woman with a tray of small loaves of sweet-bread in her hands dropped it incontinently at sight of the dreaded Ramirez. He laughed, throwing himself into a chair, and looking around him with the furtive glance with which men involuntarily regard places or persons connected with memories distasteful or horrifying. There was an image of the Virgin of Guadalupe at one end of the apartment, with a small lamp burning before it. He crossed himself, and muttered an *Ave* as he looked at it; then pointed to a second chair and the cups of chocolate.

" It is early, Don Rafael," he said lightly, " but I have a soldier's appetite, which the fresh air has sharpened, — and you know the saying, that a stomach at rest makes an active brain; so accompany me, I entreat, in breaking the morning fast, and then let us to business." And with a show of indifference, which imposed far better upon his followers, who made an interested throng around the door, than upon Don Rafael, he tasted the chocolate he had drawn to his side.

The administrador remained standing, though the two soldiers, who had each held an arm, released their grasp and stepped back. Disconcerted by the thought that in his dishabille he could scarcely present a dignified figure, Don Rafael still maintained his composure sufficiently to refuse the proffered refreshment with the air of a man who questions the right of another to play the part of host, — assuming, in fact, toward the intruder rather the attitude of personal than of political hostility.

Ramirez divined this, and his face darkened. " You know me, Don Rafael," he said in a low tone, " and that I am a man to take no denials."

" Yes," answered the administrador, shortly, " I know you. The saints must have blinded me that I was so easily deceived upon your last visit; but you had always the power to mask your face at will."

" Bah! every man has a dozen countenances at his command, if he but know how to summon them," replied Ramirez, carelessly, " and a touch of art to fix their coloring, and twist the eyebrows or moustache. Why, even your mother was deceived! Where is she now? Ah! that woman was like Isabel herself; I swear she would have killed me, even when she seemed to love me most. It is the way of women, like serpents, to twine and sting at the same moment."

" My mother is dying," said Don Rafael, lifting his eyes for a moment upon the face of the image of Mary. " Yet living or dying, it is not for a man to hear another speak lightly of his mother. But this is nothing to the purpose."

" Nothing," replied the other, accepting the rebuke; " and I have no time to lose." He seemed to forget the chocolate, pushing the cup from him, and turning as if to rise from the chair. " Look you, Rafael, what money did Isabel leave with you? Not half her resources went in that mad freak of raising a troop for Gonzales."

Perhaps Don Rafael had expected the question, for his countenance remained imperturbable. " There are horses and cattle and corn and men, still," he answered. " The administrador of Tres Hermanos can do nothing to defend them; but the money, — by Heaven and the Holy Virgin, its hiding-place is known only to him, and he will die before you shall have another dollar to add to those which have cost so much blood and so many tears!"

Ramirez's eyes flashed; yet the look of astonishment which he threw upon the small, half-clothed man was as full of admiration as though he had been a king clad in royal robes. But even a king would not have thwarted Ramirez with impunity.

" You know me," he reiterated in the same intonation with which he had before spoken the words, allowing a

long, dark, intimidating gaze to rest upon the face of Don
Rafael.

" Yes, I know you," was the answer as before. " Yes,
I know you; and it is for that reason I have said that
never a dollar belonging to the woman you have so foully
wronged shall pass into your hands. Thank Heaven that
she is not here to be tempted! Thank God that while the
identity of Ramirez with the bane and curse of the house
of Garcia has been shaping itself in my mind, no hint of
the truth has been in hers! "

" I do not believe it! " cried Ramirez, violently. " She
hates me! for the sake of that puling boy and her dotard
husband she hates me still! ' The bane of the house of
Garcia,' said you. Why, what man among them has a
name beyond his own door-stone but me? And the
women! Ah, ah! What saint would have saved the
fame of the women of the house of Garcia had it not
been for me?"

Don Rafael glanced around him warningly, — the room
was full of strange faces, beginning to light with wondering curiosity at this strange conversation, so different in
substance from that usual between the guerilla and his
victims. This was no place in which to talk of women;
yet Don Rafael himself desired to avoid a private interview with this man, while Ramirez on his part assumed an
ostentatious air of having nothing to conceal, — nothing
that he might be ashamed his followers should learn. He
knew, in fact, that at that crisis, surrounded as he was by
the most unscrupulous and desperate characters, the prestige of his mad career might be advantageously heightened
rather than diminished, if he would keep his ascendency.
Don Rafael read his thought, and lest in very hardihood
his opponent should be led to accusations or revelations it
would be impossible for him to leave unanswered, he began
one of those long and desultory conversations that, while
apparently frank and unstudied, are triumphs in the art of
avoiding or concealing the real subject at issue.

Ramirez, well as he knew the tricks of the genuine
ranchero, whether of the higher or lower grade, was himself for a time deceived, — for, with far less than his
usual astuteness, he allowed himself to lapse into occasional denunciations, and to make demands of the admin-

24

istrador that increased the curiosity and interest of his listeners. These did not in any degree shake the constancy of Don Rafael, who, with the thought that the crisis of his life was approaching, crossed his arms upon his breast and fortified his courage with the remembrance of the vows by which he had pledged himself, and the less heroic satisfaction that he promised himself then in thwarting the plans of a man whose will had been as triumphant as it was insatiable.

Meanwhile, the tumult in the house increased. A wild rumor had spread that the General José Ramirez was by right the master of the place and all it contained. Some said he was the lover, others the brother, of Doña Isabel. At last, even the name by which he had been known there began to be shouted, though the sound of it was less popular than that by which he had won his way later to fame. Still, it gave a certain authority for license where there had been before a show of restraint; and a speedy assault was made upon the store-rooms and granaries, and even upon the inner chambers and courts, which contained nothing but furniture and ornaments, — useless to soldiers on the march, or even as booty for their wives and followers.

Ramirez listened to the tumult without attempting to interfere. Evidently his object was to break the resolution of Sanchez by an exhibition of the destructive and unscrupulous character of his followers. But Don Rafael never winced except once, when the cry of a woman pierced the apartment.

Ramirez heard it also. "Ah! it came from the kitchens, from some scullery-maid," he commented after a moment. "Now, Don Rafael, you see and hear for yourself what a crew of devils I have with me, — just the riff-raff of the mountains, whom that cursed Pedro failed to wile away from me. *Caramba!* never was a surprise greater. It would not have happened but that like a fool I lingered near El Toro waiting for a chance to pounce upon Gonzales. Never let a private vengeance sway the judgment," he added sententiously. "A thousand devils! It seems as if the hacienda were tumbling about our ears! - Yet at a word I can stop it. Where is the money?"

"If the din never ceases till I reveal that," answered

Don Rafael, doggedly, " you will never have your revenge on Gonzales; for what I have sworn I have sworn. The flocks and herds I can't defend; and what are a few hundred beeves or horses? But the money; no, by God! if Doña Isabel herself should command it, I would not suffer that another coin should touch your bloody hand!"

Ramirez started up with an oath. Involuntarily he glanced at his hand. It would not have surprised him to have seen it literally red, — and, strangely enough, the blood gushing from the fatal wound he had dealt the American, just from the arms of Herlinda, rather than that of his nephew or Don Gregorio, was that which presented itself to his mind. He walked the room in a new and undefinable excitement. The sight of Don Rafael, to whom the destruction of the property that was precious as his life seemed as nothing to the pleasure of baffling the man he abhorred of the money he believed absolutely necessary to his success in leading troops to encounter the well-reinforced and well-equipped Gonzales, revealed to him the hatred and horror in which he was held. Doubtless that of the servant was but a mere reflection of that of Doña Isabel.

Well, let them hate him with reason; let the wild mountaineers take their own sport unchecked. He heard one of the clerks, flying rather than running through the corridor, exclaim that Don Rafael must come, or there would be a famine in the place before the next harvest; that the great storehouses of maize had been forced open, and the contents scattered throughout the village for horses and men to tread under their feet; and that the very oxen and sheep were revelling in the abundance, liable to destroy themselves by very excess, even if the soldiers should fail to drive them before them.

Ramirez and the administrador glanced at each other. They had not spoken for many minutes, each feeling the other implacable, yet each perhaps believing that the wanton destruction would appeal to the other's weaker or better nature. Ramirez grew crimson, almost black, with inward rage, — rage as great with those who were wreaking destruction on his sister's house, as with this insignificant yet determined man who withstood it. Don Rafael was white as death, his lips blue, his eyes strained; again the cry of a woman sounded on the air! It came from above.

He started toward the door. A dozen hands seized him. Ramirez turned upon him with his drawn sword.

"Where is my daughter?" he demanded in a voice of fury. "I will find a way to force the gold from you, but first my daughter, — where is she?"

"Your daughter?" echoed Don Rafael in a tone of such absolute amazement that even Ramirez was for a second distracted from his rage.

"Yes, my daughter! She whom you have aided Isabel to hide from me all these years. Faith, it was a pretty trick, — an eye for an eye, with a vengeance. But after all it was a petty plot, and soon fathomed. You were less jealous of flesh and blood than of this cursed gold, and gave me the first inkling of her whereabouts yourself."

"I?" exclaimed the administrador; "I? What know I of a child of yours?"

"Ah, that is what you must satisfy me of. Where is she, — the Chata, whom you nodded and hinted about so mysteriously in your cups so many years ago?"

Don Rafael — if it were possible — turned a shade whiter than before; his form seemed to shrink, his heart sank with guilty shame and absolute terror. How well he remembered those few words, which, though so indirect and apparently unimportant, he had thought of with remorse a thousand times. And to what a terrible, though utterly unforeseen, conclusion they had led this man! He lifted his hands above his head.

"By the Blessed Mother, I swear," he said, "that I know not what you mean! I know nothing of a child of yours!"

Ramirez looked at him contemptuously. "You will tell me next that the child your wife denies is yours," he said.

In effect it had been upon the lips of Don Rafael to claim Chata as his daughter, as he had done a thousand times before. Was she not his before all the world? Had she not been from the very moment the eyes of his wife had rested upon her? But she had betrayed the confidence to which she had been but partially admitted, — Rita! He hesitated, and Ramirez seized the advantage.

"You dare not!" he exclaimed. "Your wife has confessed all: it will never do to trust a woman with a secret

in company of a man who cares to learn it, though very
perversity might keep her silent with a world of women."
The sight of the discomfiture of Don Rafael had restored
to Ramirez some portion of good nature. "The screeching has ceased," he added. "Yet I am a fond father. I
would assure myself of my child's safety. Where is the
girl? I must and will see her, if but to tell her why I
played her false last week. Where is my daughter?"

Don Rafael's face, which throughout this interview had
retained its pallor, crimsoned with excess of agitation.
The mystery of Chata's visit to the hacienda was revealed.
Had she met this man? Did she know — did she believe?
He remembered her changed aspect, her silence, her tears.
Ramirez stood watching him with impatience, yet triumph.
The crimson flush convicted the administrador. Don
Rafael strove in vain to steady the glance of his suffused
and burning eyes, to still the throbbing of his temples,
while he sought to command the most impressive and
convincing words in which to answer and forever silence
this mad assumption. But none presented themselves.
The group around listened breathlessly, more excited
than Ramirez himself. They looked silently from face
to face of the two men who were engaged in this singular
dispute. Inside the room one might have heard a feather
float through the air, so deep was the silence; and at last,
in despair of finding imposing words, the administrador
uttered the simple denial, "Chata is not your child."

Most of the men drew back for the moment convinced.
Not so Ramirez. "It is false!" he cried. "I have your
own maudlin hint, and your wife's positive confession, that
the girl is neither hers nor yours."

Don Rafael grew pale again. There was that in his
face which would have augured ill to Doña Rita had she
seen it; but he said with an effort, "I will not give my
wife the lie. The child is neither mine nor hers!"

"Then whose — whose but mine?" demanded Ramirez
fiercely.

Don Rafael paused a moment as before. In an instant
he had recalled the circumstances that had attended the
adoption of the child. Rita had been young, placable,
easily pleased with a gift: the fewer confidants the better; it was ever the duty of a Mexican wife to obey un-

questioningly, — she had been obedient then; it had not
been necessary that she should know more than it had
been wise to tell. Don Rafael drew a deep breath of
relief. Ramirez and the group around him watched him
narrowly.

" Declare then ! " queried Ramirez at last, " whose
daughter is she if not mine ? "

" I will not say," answered Don Rafael ; " but I do
swear she is not yours. Stay," he added, struck with
an idea. " What reason have you for thinking she is
yours ? "

" Reason ! " echoed Ramirez scornfully ; " because fifteen years ago, more or less, — perhaps you have reason
here to remember well that year, — I sent my child here,
to Doña Isabel : it was a whim of mine that she should
have tender nurture and decent training. I was a fool to
trust a woman's love. Of course Isabel remembered her
own bantling, though I had even some foolish thought
that the little one I sent might console her, — most women
have hearts for baby wants and fancies that sicken men.
Of course for her it was a chance for revenge too good to
be lost. I have been in two minds ever since I knew how
she scorned my trust whether to be angry or pleased with
you for aiding her purpose. But let it pass ; yield the
child and the money quietly and " — he looked over his
shoulder with an impatient frown — " that infernal tumult
and destruction shall cease. If not — "

" I will yield neither the girl nor the money ; " replied
Don Rafael. " They are neither of them mine nor yours ;
but I have possession of both, and will keep them. —
Surely Rita has both girls in the secret recess, as we have
always planned in such a case as this," he thought, with a
qualm at the remembrance of his wife's treason, as revealed
by Ramirez. " Surely at such a time she will protect a
young damsel, even though she be not her own child."

Ramirez looked at him with a lowering brow, repeating
again, " If not mine, whose child is she ? By Heaven, I
know she is mine ! There could not be on all the earth a
creature in whom Doña Isabel or Feliz or yourself could
have so deep an interest as to trouble yourself for life
with his child. It is incredible, impossible. Unless she
is — " He paused on the name, looked round him,

clinched his hands, advanced to Don Rafael, and gazed searchingly into his face.

Don Rafael did not flinch. Ramirez burst into a laugh. " I would have killed you had you dared even to have looked askance," he said. " *Caramba!* the women of the Garcias may be fools or devils,— they have shown the spirit of both; but if a man should ever kill another because of one of them, it would be for his daring, not in revenge of his triumph."

Did these words indicate a tardy repentance, a conviction that Herlinda had been indiscreet but innocent ? Don Rafael had no time to discuss the question with himself; but he had such new insight into the mind of Ramirez that he was warned from giving any fresh cause of offence. Had he had no previous reasons, it would have been a sufficient one for him to keep inviolate the secret which he had sworn to preserve to his life's end. In his present humor, the man with whom he had to deal would in his baffled and vengeful rage have spared neither the name nor fame of even his own mother, had occasion offered to tempt him to blacken it. Don Rafael believed the women of his household as well as the money safe in the hiding places he had constructed for them, — the first known to Doña Feliz and Doña Rita, the second to himself alone. To any fate that might befall himself he looked with stoical courage if not indifference. Leaning against the wall, he crossed his arms defiantly and awaited events.

XXXIX.

At high noon a terrible and heartrending wail of anguish sounded through the house, penetrating with dismal insistence through the clamor of the soldiery and the thousand indescribable noises of the animals, which had been hastily collected, and which added the element of mere brute bewilderment to the scarcely more reasonably restrained terror of the people.

Ramirez had recognized the obstinate defiance of the administrador. More than once before he had dealt with others as tenacious of the interests of those they served. He had no time to lose in vain persuasions, and had himself conducted the search throughout the vast building, of which he believed he knew every nook and corner. But he had to his amazement and chagrin found neither treasure nor any member of the family of the administrador save the apparently dying Doña Feliz. After a fruitless endeavor to recall her to consciousness, he left her with a curse, and returning to her son, assaulted him with menaces, alternated with fair promises, — the one as little regarded as the other.

Upon one subject only would Don Rafael permit himself to speak; and to that Ramirez, in his rage, refused to listen. The suggestion that his daughter, if indeed he had a reason to seek one there, might prove to be Chinita, the foster-daughter of Pedro Gomez, he received with utter contempt. He remembered her well, he said; an imp as black as Pedro himself, — black as he must be now, scorching in Hades. That little demon was none of his, while Chata had the very face of his mother, — the face of an angel. Ah! ah! that was indeed a daring jest, that Isabel should strive to palm off upon him the brat of her doorkeeper! Once long before, like the witch she was, the girl had stopped him and thrust into his hand an amulet, — he drew it from his pocket, and cast it from him. By the way, now Pedro was dead, if Rafael still believed her worth a thought, he had better see in such a day as this that she had some other protector. She must be nearly a woman now!

Ramirez fell into greater rage when he learned that Doña Isabel had taken charge of this despised waif. He swore that it was in mockery of himself; and Don Rafael soon perceiving that every word he uttered was construed as an attempt to deceive, and fearing that at some time it might bring evil upon the girl to whom, whether she were the daughter of Ramirez or no, he certainly desired no harm, the administrador became utterly silent, in his heart commending the prudence of Rita in following this time with exactness his instructions, and condoning the treason of which by the assurances of Ramirez he had been forced to believe her guilty.

In truth, although at first the alarmed and not too scrupulous woman had urged Chata to secure the safety of herself and her child by claiming the protection of Ramirez, as time passed and he made no movement toward such recognition she began to distrust the effect it might produce upon the renowned guerilla. He and his soldiers were there for plunder and rapine, not paternal sentiment. As the cries of the women-servants and villagers reached her, the resolution to seek safety in concealment seized her. Though still far from wishing to conceal Chata from Ramirez, to whom the accidental sight of her might recall some sense of mercy or tenderness, she feared both him and her husband too greatly to dare leave her to the chance of insult from the licentious soldiery. But Chata absolutely refused to leave Doña Feliz, from whose side even the servants had fled; and it was her scream that had penetrated to the rooms below, when, by the friendly force of Don Alonzo, she was immured with Doña Rita and Rosario in the secret recess, which Don Rafael had constructed with a vague apprehension of such an emergency.

It chanced that this recess, which was in the immensely thick outer wall of the great house, was dimly lighted and ventilated by a loop-hole so small as to be barely visible from without, but which opened funnel-like toward the inside of the apartment. Through this loop-hole these three women, whose voices were quite inaudible to those either

within or without the building, heard confusedly the village
cries, and caught uncertain glimpses of the space outside the
hacienda gates. After what seemed hours of incarceration, during which Rosario had fretted and slept, and
Doña Rita had alternately chided and lamented, while
Chata entreated to be released that she might return to
the side of Doña Feliz, they saw with anxious surprise a
crowd gathering upon the sandy slope; not of the soldiery alone, but the people of the hacienda, — clerks, workmen, women who were wringing their hands and uttering
sharp cries of terror and entreaty, which ended in that
deep wail, which seemed to signify some agonizing
catastrophe.

Doña Rita was the first to divine what was happening.
"Maria Purissima!" she cried. "Is it possible Rafael
is as mad as the administrador of Los Chalcos, — that
he has refused some demand? Does he not remember
how Ramirez caused that poor foolish one to be hanged
without mercy! O my husband, my husband! Oh!
has he no thought for me, for his child, that he will sacrifice his life for Doña Isabel? How will she thank him?
Whoever thinks twice of the foolhardy obstinacy of an
administrador?"

Chata sprang to her feet. "Give me the key!" she
cried. "Let me go! Now if Ramirez is my father, he
shall prove it! Would he deny his daughter the life of her
foster-father? Give me the key!"

"No, no!" screamed Doña Rita, "the place is full
of ruffians. Ramirez himself is a tiger! I—" but Chata
had wrenched the key from her numbed and shaking
hands, and thrusting it in the lock had turned the grating wards.

When she rushed into the corridors they were empty, —
there was a sight to behold elsewhere. On she flew, not
noticing that Doña Rita and Rosario followed, and that
their shrieks rose with hers, as in a minute or less they
reached the outer court, and strove to penetrate the throng
that filled it and extended to the village beyond.

Within the high arch of the doorway, clear against the
deep blue of the mid-day sky, swayed the figure of a man,
— of Rafael Sanchez. Below, sword in hand, stood Ramirez and two panting laborers who that instant had

accomplished his decree. Around them were gathered scores of armed men, evil-eyed, with the ferocity of brutes in their faces; and Ramirez stood pre-eminent, a very demon.

The crowd parted like water before the shrieks of the three women. In a moment Chata reached the side of Ramirez, and grasped his sword. "Spare him! spare him!" she demanded rather than entreated. "If I am your daughter, cut the rope! Spare him, and do as you like with me; else I swear I will die with him rather than be known as your child!"

The women were on their knees, — not Doña Rita and Rosario alone, but all those of the village. Sobs and entreaties filled the air. Ramirez threw a glance of triumphant admiration upon Chata, and put one arm around her, while he raised the other, pointing with a nod to the swaying figure.

A man sprang to cut the rope, and the administrador fell into the dozen arms stretched out to receive him. Chata saw with infinite joy that he was not dead. He threw up his arms, gasped, opened wide-staring eyes. A moment later, she was hurried away. Half-fainting though she was, she was glad to escape that embrace from which she dared not shrink.

"Ah, Rafael, you are conquered, — I have the girl! And now where is the gold?" she heard Ramirez exclaim, and saw the gesture of defiance with which the scarce conscious victim answered this demand.

An hour later Chata was riding by the side of the baffled Ramirez. She knew not whether her foster-father was living or dead, and dared not ask; but stifling her sobs, looked back through a mist of tears upon the desolated hacienda. It was incredible even to her horrified and longing gaze, the terrible devastation that had been worked in a few short hours. Seemingly to complete its ruin, a thunder-cloud, which had been lurking over the valley, discharged its contents over the devoted house. Upon the hills the sun shone; Chata was safe from the fury of the storm. And yet she felt as though the very wrath of heaven had burst over her.

"*Caramba*, Chatita! thou wilt make a soldier's daughter yet!" Ramirez was exclaiming. "By my faith, I am proud of thee!" In spite of the unattained gold, he pressed on in rare good humor. His fury, like the storm, was quickly expended. "And by our Lady of Glory I am glad that you came in time to save that obstinate fool, Rafael. He has, after all is said, served me a good turn in aiding Isabel to put what she meant for a shabby trick upon me. *Caramba!* It was clever of her. I should never have discovered it but for a slip of the tongue on Rafael's part which no one else would have noticed, and but for thy wonderful likeness to my mother, — the angels give her good rest!"

Chata could not be grateful for this favor of nature; it seemed to her indeed the bitterest spite that could have been wreaked upon her. She turned her eyes upon the face of Ramirez with a questioning glance, which startled him: those gray eyes, limpid and clear as they were, were far different from the large, languorous, black ones of his mother, — yet not unfamiliar. Where had he seen such before? The inquiry was not worth a special effort of memory. Enough that the eyes were beautiful. The very softness and appeal in their expression held a peculiar charm for this fierce, hard spirit. He had begun a denunciation of the revenge practised against him by his sister, but he abruptly paused. What if this young creature knew nothing of those wild deeds of bygone years? Why shock her tender and immature mind by the recital of such episodes as she would view but at their darkest? For the first time in his life he felt the impossibility of impressing his hearer with the daring rather than the villany of his deeds, and rode beside her in silence, furtively watching her face, which with wonderful control, indicating a latent strength of character, she suffered to reveal none of the horror or fear with which he inspired her, but only the natural grief with which she had been separated from the home of her childhood.

Indeed, the thought of Doña Feliz was the dominant one in Chata's mind, and prevented any serious grief or alarm as to her own situation. The question of her own safety or future position troubled her little. It was the fact of her separation from the beloved and stricken friend, who was so dependent upon her care, and her absolute horror of the murderer of the American, — for as such Ramirez

ever figured in her thoughts, — which rendered it so difficult a task for her to retain her self-possession and answer
with calmness the few questions or remarks that were from
time to time addressed to her.

Chata soon perceived that as the day wore on, and she
began to exhibit signs of fatigue from the hurried march
and the heat, her presence caused far more anxiety than
triumph to her captor. "The old folly!" he muttered
from time to time, — "to act without counting the cost.
I doubt whether there is a decent woman among this
drove of camp-followers. If I had but thought to bring
one from the hacienda! In fact, it was a fool's act to bring
the child at all, with such work before me as I have!"

Chata caught these broken sentences with a wild hope
that he might decree her return to Tres Hermanos. Willingly would she have risked going alone on foot if necessary. But the sun set, the shades of evening closed in,
and the hurried march was still pursued, until, when she
was ready to faint with fatigue, the General ordered a
halt, and lifting her from the saddle, placed her upon a
pile of blankets; while a half-dozen men set to work
with practised hands to build a little hut or tent of mesquite and manzanita boughs to shelter her from the
night air.

As the weary girl sat near the tent fire, endeavoring to
eat the food of which she stood in much need, but for which
she could not force an appetite, she found herself the centre
of a wild horde of perhaps nearly five hundred persons, of
whom a fifth were women and children, who were busy at
the fires preparing the evening meal while the men were
staking horses, or patrolling the circle of the camp, keeping within bounds the hard-driven and panting cattle and
sheep, whose distressing lowing and bleating at intervals
filled the air. Apparently there was an entire lack of discipline, the unreasoning enthusiasm of the moment and the
personal magnetism of the renowned leader serving to
hold the unruly elements subservient to the necessities
of the occasion, and obedient to his slightest mandate.
The majority of the troops were of the most wild and
even savage appearance; for, as their leader had said, they
were the riff-raff, the scourings of the mountain villages and remote farms. Chata was not unaccustomed to

the sight of such individuals, but in mass the impression they made upon her was of concentrated evil. The trace of gentler feeling that each face or person might have revealed on scrutiny was lost in the prevailing ferocity of expression and accoutrement. The clash of arms, the jingle of spurs, the hoarse voices made her shudder no less than the sullen faces, the gleaming eyes, and the sinewy and powerful frames.

Strangely enough, as her eyes followed Ramirez, a sense of his complete harmony with his surroundings seemed in the girl's mind to condone the wild deeds of which he had figured as the hero. She realized for the first time the fascination that unlimited power over such elements must exercise over a mind given to daring, and uncontrolled by any moral principle. She thought of Chinita, and how her adventurous spirit would have exulted in such an adventure as this. As she gazed into the fire the very face of that fearless, enigmatic young nature seemed to rise before her, beautiful, passionate, yet with that capacity of endurance, which in a man might become cruelty, that capricious changeableness, which one moment dissolved in tears, and the next shone in a smile. So real was the vision that Chata started, and found herself gazing affrightedly into the face of Ramirez, who was regarding her with the expression of mingled affection, triumph, and vexation which had not left his countenance since he had set her upon Doña Rita's favorite horse at the door of the hacienda.

"I have a notable project in my mind for you," he said abruptly. "You know that I am the Governor of Guanapila."

"Yes," she said timidly; "but I thought—" she hesitated, fearing to offend.

"Ah, you thought I was beaten and barred out. They will find I am neither one nor the other. The gate is shut but not bolted, and it will be hard if I find not a way to creep in. It is impossible for me to keep you with me on the march. You must be with some woman."

"Oh, I would rather be with you. Indeed I will give no trouble! I will be brave!" she exclaimed, instinctively shrinking from the thought of contact with such women as she saw around her.

He smiled with gratification, his egotistic nature flattered by the thought that he was gaining her confidence; but his face darkened as she added with hesitation, " I had hoped — I thought perhaps you were taking me to my mother."

" It is not of your mother I was thinking," he said ambiguously, " when I spoke of Guanapila, but of my niece Carmen de Velasquez. She knows that the General Ramirez once sent an escort with her mother to Tres Hermanos, and levied upon her husband for a loan of ten thousand dollars when he might have had five times as much, — for the old fellow she has married is rich, and does honor to the financial acumen of the fair Carmen, and we will see whether she has a just appreciation of the favors I am supposed to have rendered her. There, go to your tent and sleep in peace; in three days you shall be safe within the house of Velasquez in Guanapila."

It cannot be said that Chata slept in peace; yet the prospect was reassuring, and enabled her to bear with resignation the fatigues and excitements of the following days, and the loneliness and terrors of the nights. The General slept before the opening of her tent. Upon the fourth night he awoke her, and handed her a torn and shabby reboso and a skirt of coarse red cloth, with instructions to put them on. She did so with some repugnance, though the clothing she left was not better; and at a call stepped out into the starlight. The young Captain Alva preceded her in silence outside the limits of the camp, where two horses were in waiting, held by a man whom at the first startled glance she failed to recognize. It would have horrified her beyond control had she known that in his size and air and dress he was the image of the ranchero who had entered Tres Hermanos on the night of the murder, years before. She uttered a cry of relief as Ramirez greeted her.

" Ah, is it not a perfect disguise? " he said. " Why, I might go into El Toro itself with impunity ! Mount, child, and keep close at my side ! "

In a minute or less, with the assistance of Alva, Chata was ready for the start, — her courage rising with the sense of mystery and daring under which Ramirez seemed to glow and expand. He paused to give his last commands to Alva, of which she heard only the concluding words: "Reyes should be here by daylight. Keep him at all hazards, for he must sound Ruiz before another day passes. *Caramba!* I cannot believe that fellow has failed me; but whether or no, the end will be the same, — except that I swear if Ruiz prove false, were he twice my godson he shall not escape my vengeance."

The General pulled his hat over his eyes, waved his hand, struck the spurs into his horse, and led the way at a swift canter. Chata until within the last few days had never ridden on horseback; but she was singularly free from fear or awkwardness, and with ease, though in silence, kept at his side.

"Chata," Ramirez once said abruptly, turning his dark and piercing eyes upon her, "I am risking much for your sake. Remember that you are my daughter. Be faithful to me, obey my bidding, and I will cherish you as the apple of my eye. It may depend upon you whether the troops of Doña Isabel follow my lead or that of Gonzales. You will know my meaning later; but I swear to you, as I have done by Ruiz, my vengeance shall rest upon whomsoever balks me, — yes, if it is even you, the new-found daughter whom I love."

Chata trembled. Though his words were an enigma, they indicated that her *rôle* was not to be an utterly passive one. Her companion awaited no answer, and Chata did not attempt to make one. They rode on at ever increasing speed as the night advanced. Just at daybreak they reached a hut, which was placed at the mouth of a cañon. There they left their horses, and an old woman appeared with a crate of turkeys in each hand, one of which she gave to the disguised chieftain, the other to the wondering Chata.

An hour later they were in the streets of Guanapila, and before they had broken their fast Chata sat overcome with fatigue and dismay upon the stone stairs that led to the corridor of a palatial residence. The ranchero, as the servants supposed him, had gone to speak with the lady of the mansion. It was a long time before he re-appeared; and when he did, a beautiful woman preceded him. She was very pale, and there was in her eyes an incredulous and startled expression, which changed to pity as her gaze fell upon Chata, — who, looking up, thought of the pale and lovely face she had seen but once, and knew she must be in the presence of Carmen, the sister of the nun of El Toro.

Ramirez whispered a word in the ear of the bewildered girl, it might be of warning or of farewell; but her senses failed her, — she neither saw nor heard more.

"Go, go!" cried the mistress of the house. "For God's sake go, before there is any one to wonder. Whether your tale be true or false, she has the face of a Garcia, and a loveliness and sweetness of her own. I will guard her as though she were my child. Go, go! and the saints grant you a safe passage. I will not betray your confidence. Ah, she has fainted! I will manage that; it shall be my pretext for charity."

Ramirez kissed the hand of the unconscious Chata, and turned away. For once he had executed an act of extreme self-denial, yet amid it all his crafty mind foresaw how he might use it to his advantage.

The exit from the city was readily effected, but Ramirez did not proceed many miles unrecognized after mounting his horse at the hut where he had left it. The man who spoke his name unhesitatingly, though in a cautious voice, was Reyes. He gave the General unwelcome tidings. Gonzales had joined forces with those of Tres Hermanos. He had risked the attack and occupation of El Toro, and it was conjectured would attempt the march to the Capital itself, round which the audacious Juarez was from his stronghold in Vera Cruz directing the concentration of the Liberal forces.

Ramirez ground his teeth in rage. "I have been delayed and hampered by that girl," he cried. "Could I but have gone straight to Ruiz, he would not have dared defy me. As it is —"

"As it is," interrupted Reyes, "all is not yet lost. I have still to see Ruiz, — he is not my son if it is impossible to convince him upon which hot plate the cake is best toasted."

The conference of the two men lasted but a few moments. They had been so accustomed in their long intercourse to treat of subjects of which one was as well informed as the other, and upon the course to be taken

25

at the present time they were so well agreed, that they parted with no attempt at explanation, but simply after a few words of instruction had been given by Ramirez to the other.

"Tell him," the chief said finally, "I am ready to fulfil my word; and if Ruiz be anxious to see her, let him risk as much for love as I have done. She is at the house of Doña Carmen Velasquez in Guanapila; and tell him as surely as he is my godson and your son he shall be shot as a traitor if he fails me in this affair. Good-by for a time; good news or bad news, my blood is up for a desperate venture now. It cannot be that after all these years luck is turning against me at last."

"It did that years ago when you stabbed the American," thought Reyes as they parted; "it was that that weighted the scale. That accursed foreigner who is here to avenge him has upset all our plans for misleading Gonzales. With both together Ramirez has fearful odds against him, which even with the help of Ruiz and his men he may find it hard to combat. But how in heaven's name has the General his daughter with him? *Caramba!* I have often wondered how he would relish that drunken freak of mine! Faith, I did not care to try his temper to-night by many questions. Well, who would have thought he would have kept in the same mind for so many years! To think of his striving to give her the family training at this late date! Ah, ah, ah! it is more likely to mar than to make her. If Fernando is of my mind he will wait in such a matter for no pruning and training, but pluck the flower while it is within his reach, thorns and all."

With which poetic simile, Tio Reyes rode on well pleased on his errand to the young Ruiz, while Ramirez, proceeding rapidly in the opposite direction, regained within the hour his enthusiastic but disorderly horde.

VAIN would be the attempt to describe the consternation of Doña Isabel when she awoke at early dawn, and felt about her that peculiar stillness — a stillness that seems absolutely tangible — which indicates the abstraction of the element of humanity from the associations about us, and is especially impressive when that loss is utterly unexpected.

It was not yet daylight, and it was by this peculiar stillness, and not by sight, that Doña Isabel learned with a deadly feeling of dismay at her heart, that she was alone. For a moment she lay silent, then raising herself on her elbow sought to peer through the gloom, while with faltering voice she uttered the name "Chinita."

There was no answer. She would have been inexpressibly surprised had there been; and yet refusing to be convinced, she arose from her bed and made her way to that of Chinita. Had the girl been there, in the infinite relief and excitement of the moment the lady must have clasped her in her arms with kisses and tears; as it was, after passing her hands wildly over the empty couch, she sank upon it with a deep and bitter moan, feeling anew, and with the intensified agony of remembrance, the shock with which she had heard the cry of Herlinda, — "My husband! My husband!" What but a like betrayal could in that place and time have drawn a young girl from her chamber? Alas! alas!

The thoughts of Doña Isabel flew to Ruiz; a thousand trifles, unheeded before, crowded her remembrance as confirmation of some secret understanding between him and Chinita. If she had noticed them at all it was to think with a smile that they had reference to Rosario. How had she been so blind! She sprang to her feet and hastily dressed herself with some undefined intention of seeking him in his quarters, and demanding an explanation of him if he were to be found, or of confirming her worst fears if he had fled. All her old distrust of him, which he had so skilfully lulled, returned with overwhelming force, and in her unfounded suspicion she included the more just one of treason to her purposes to the cause of liberty and to Gonzales, and with irresistible certainty became convinced that the delays and detours which Ruiz had made had been expedients of traitorous policy. In the few moments needed for the completion of her toilet, a terrible fear took possession of her. For the first time that night she had been separated from the main body of the troops, — what if she were abandoned! Nothing seemed more likely. Only the great self-possession that she habitually practised prevented her from rushing out — yes, even into the streets of the village — to satisfy herself that the rude encampment remained unbroken.

Yet with all this raging excitement of grief and doubt within her, she presently stepped out upon the corridor with that stately calmness which she ever wore before the world, were it represented by but the meanest peasant. Day had scarcely broken, yet there was a sound of movement unusual in so small a place. To the excited mind of Doña Isabel it appeared that like herself the people all must be searching wildly for the girl who had so strangely escaped her. She went to the inn door and looked out. The camp-women were wandering through the streets already, chaffering and bargaining with the vendors of milk and bread and vegetables. In the distance she saw the soldiers preparing for the march. Three or four officers were lounging down the narrow street. To her infinite surprise and relief she saw among them Ruiz. He hastened his steps and joined her with an air of consternation, which even in her excitement she noticed had in it a subdued suggestion of apprehension as of one detected in some doubtful act.

In a few words Doña Isabel apprised him of the disappearance of Chinita. It was impossible that it could be concealed; it was absolutely necessary that search should be made. Ruiz listened with an emotion greater even than hers. "Good heavens. Señora!" he cried, "we are undone. Ramirez must be at hand. In some way she has learned his whereabouts; she has fled to him!"

Doña Isabel thought Ruiz had suddenly gone mad. " Fled to Ramirez ! " she cried. " Impossible ! What can she know of the man? What object can she have in seeking him? "

Instinctively the lady had led the way back to the room she had left. Ruiz followed her, in the utter demoralization of his mind at the unexpected tidings, pouring out incoherent explanations of the designs that Chinita had cherished, and unconsciously revealing much of the duplicity of the part he had himself acted. With an acuteness of mind perhaps intensified by the keen emotion with which she listened to the unexpected accusations against the young girl, Doña Isabel conjectured at once that the speaker had played a double part; and it was a not improbable solution of the mystery of Chinita's disappearance, that in discovering this the young girl had resolved to precipitate a crisis in the fate of the man who exercised so unaccountable a fascination over her.

Yet with whom had she fled? Had Ramirez himself stolen into the inn and borne her away? The face of Ruiz blanched at this suggestion. Had the girl learned what was indeed a fact, that upon that very day the troops of Doña Isabel Garcia were by their officers to protest against a further attempt to reach Gonzales, and declaring Ruiz their chosen and permanent leader were at once to take up the march to join the forces of General Ortega, a newly arisen and popular Liberal chieftain who was a personal and implacable enemy of Ramirez, — thus leaving El Toro to its fate? Had Chinita indeed gone with such news to Ramirez? Ruiz felt that his doom was sealed, for he rightly conjectured that the excitement of Chinita's disappearance had already dampened the ardor in his behalf which he had found it a slow and almost impossible task to awaken among the troops. Indeed, that it had been roused at all was owing to the discontent which had arisen through the cleverly concealed tactics he had used in contriving so long and monotonous a march to the aid of a man but little known or admired, and from the general belief in the love of the beautiful *protégée* of Doña Isabel for the young aspirant for fame. In her hand the favor of Doña Isabel was supposed to lie. Eager for action, eager for booty, brought to a point where they were almost within sound of the bugles of General Ortega, who was making his hurried and triumphant march to the capital, it had been decided that upon that very morning a *pronunciamento* should be made, which, while involving no change of politics, should compel the consent of Doña Isabel to the apparently spontaneous outburst of patriotism upon the part of her troops, and confirm Ruiz in the command that she had temporarily confided to him.

Ruiz had so cunningly planned every detail that he doubted not that not only Doña Isabel, but Chinita as well, would be convinced of his entire ignorance of the *coup*, and that the girl's ambition, and perhaps a somewhat malicious satisfaction in the reversal of the plans of Doña Isabel, would lead her to an acceptance of the apparently unavoidable forfeiture of her own desires.

To this end the ambitious young officer had been patiently working since the day he had found himself at the head of the troops of Tres Hermanos. He had been amazed at his own success. Everything had seemed to contribute to it. Not even the triumph of seeing himself actually attracting the good-will, if not the love, of Chinita had been denied him; and now at the moment least expected, at the most critical juncture, she had failed him. It was impossible for him to assume his usual self-sufficient air as he re-issued from the apartment of Doña Isabel, — an air that imposed on the majority of observers as that of a man conscious of power, rather than as a disguise of incompetency. His crest-fallen bearing as he gave the necessary orders for scouts to be sent out in search of those who in the night must have left the ill-guarded town was evident to the most careless eye, and did much to increase the feeling of distrust and coldness that was already beginning to supplant the ill-considered ardor of a few hours before.

The scouts had been despatched; and the main body of the troops waited for marching orders, which were long delayed. Ruiz, closeted with the men who had been most amenable to his reasoning, urged openly the arguments that he had but covertly suggested before. That exhausted apathy which following an exploded project is far more hopeless than that which, merely unignited,

precedes its agitation, resisted all his efforts at revival.
The officers, like the soldiers, listlessly waited to hear
what would happen next, absolutely indifferent to Ruiz,
and concerned for the moment in a mere matter of gossip,
— the escapade of a young girl.

Toward noon some of the messengers returned. Most
of them had nothing to report, but the vaquero Gabriel,
the husband of Juana, as soon as he could escape the
questioning of Ruiz, disappeared. An hour later he
entered the apartment of Doña Isabel.

"What news, Gabriel, what news?" the lady cried
excitedly. "Did you come upon any trace of — of the
child; of those who have stolen her away?"

The vaquero shook his head, and Doña Isabel groaned.
Those few hours had wrought a terrible change in her
appearance. She was not young and able to meet shocks
of disaster as she had been when they had shaken her
in by-gone years.

"I found no trace of them, my Señora," said the man,
slowly. "Perhaps my eyes are not as keen as they were,
and they say when one thinks much one sees little. Since
I am married I find one must think. A woman gives one
abundance for thought. She grinds care for a man more
surely than corn for his bread."

Doña Isabel looked up at him quickly. She knew that
this oracular sentence had some bearing on the subject
that absorbed her thoughts. "Speak," she said. "What
has your wife to do with this?"

"She was the playmate of the young Señorita," he
suggested.

"True, but what of that?"

"She would be likely to be in her confidence, — at least
where there was no other to trust."

Doña Isabel started, looking at him with fixed attention.

"The thought came to me as I rode out of the town,
— it came back to me again and again. After hours of
vain search I suffered myself to be convinced. I came
back and taxed Juana with knowing with whom, and when
and where, her friend had gone."

"Well?" ejaculated Doña Isabel, in extreme agitation.

"She denied it. By all the saints she denied it; but I

had a saint she had forgotten to commend herself to." He smiled significantly.

Doña Isabel understood the arguments used by rancheros to refractory wives too well to doubt what his grim jest meant. At another time she would have indignantly dismissed from her presence the man who admitted laying a hand in castigation upon his wife; now she merely by an imperative gesture urged him to finish what he had to communicate.

"It was as I thought," he said coolly. "Two men talked with her last night. The one was Juana's brother, Pepé; the other was the Señor Americano your grace knows of."

Doña Isabel sank back in her chair as if struck by a sharp weapon. "The American! the American!" she repeated again and again. She felt as though a hand had been thrust from the grave to torture her. The superstitious dread which had been planted in her breast by the first glimpse of the face of Ashley Ward, and which had perhaps led her irresistibly to a course that the resolution of years would under ordinary circumstances have rendered impossible to a nature as tenacious as was her own, became a horrible certainty. Evil fate in the guise of the American appeared to pursue her. Whatever the purpose with which he had lured Chinita from her side, it could but be productive of woe for her. Would the tale of her daughter's shame and her own apparent heartlessness be told throughout the land? Had this pale and seemingly spiritless young man resolved on such a vengeance of his cousin's fancied wrongs? Or — worse still — was this but a repetition of the old, old tale of passion and folly? Doña Isabel covered her face with her hand and groaned again.

Gabriel had called his wife to the room, and she came with eyes red with weeping, and told the tale that seemed to her best. Fearful of bringing the vengeance of the Señora upon Pepé, should she avow that he had left the inn alone with Chinita, she declared he had but accompanied the American, whom she boldly affirmed had set out for the coast, with the young girl, intending to set sail for the wild country whence he had come.

Doña Isabel and Gabriel both knew too well the inventive genius of their countrywomen literally to believe all she said; yet as hour after hour passed by and no news of the fugitives was heard, and no trace of them in spite of the most untiring search was found, they were at length led to conclude — the one with despair — that Juana's words were true, and that the brief connection of the beautiful foster-child of Pedro Gomez with the lady of Tres Hermanos was ended forever.

Never perhaps did so marked a change occur in the discipline and carriage of any body of troops, from a cause apparently so slight, as that which followed the flight of Chinita. Of the visit of the American nothing was publicly known, but the wildest rumors of her probable action ran like wildfire through the ranks, the name of Ramirez coupled with her own being on every tongue. So potent was the fame of the guerilla chieftain and the fascination of Chinita, that a word from her at that excited moment would have acted like fire on straw, and set a blaze to the smouldering insubordination and disappointed energies of the baffled and impatient recruits, who had entered upon the service from love of adventure and booty rather than with any fixed convictions or an intelligent conception of the interests at stake.

Doña Isabel wore before the world the same impassive face as ever, but at night the demon powers of remorse and intolerable anxiety wrought cruel havoc with its beauty. It was impossible too for her to conceal utterly the suspicion and distrust with which Ruiz inspired her ; and the influence which through Chinita mainly he had for a brief period acquired, both over Doña Isabel and the troops, and which at best had been looked upon as a privilege he should yield later with his authority to Gonzales, began to wane rapidly. Dissatisfaction and mutinous threatenings were manifested on every hand, and the position of Ruiz but for the presence of Doña Isabel would have been absolutely untenable ; and a crisis was evidently imminent, when the long desired leader suddenly appeared to relieve the tension of the situation, and to awaken a frenzy of enthusiasm for the cause, which had been at the point of abandonment.

It was with intense relief that Ruiz himself greeted the appearance of Gonzales, unexpected though it was, and incomprehensible the means by which he had obtained information that had led him so completely to alter his plans. That the American was concerned in the matter Ruiz did not doubt, though he could imagine no clew to his motives, the conviction being still in the mind of the baffled officer of Chinita's indifference to Ashley, and of her flight to Ramirez.

It was with amazement and alarm that Gonzales witnessed the ravages of time and care upon the once beautiful and stately Doña Isabel. The very excess of joy with which she welcomed him seemed weak and pitiful. He had been detained long upon the way from El Toro by a series of petty annoyances, such as the bad state of the roads and a succession of trifling skirmishes with the enemy, resulting in burdening the march with the care of the wounded; and thus the loss of Chinita had become to Doña Isabel by the time of his arrival an assured fact. With tears of anguish she told him of the ingratitude of the child she loved, though she carefully concealed the fact that she supposed her to be other than one of the class of people from whom she had taken her; and with this explanation only Gonzales could not enter fully into her grief, or accept the fact that the loss of her *protégée* was indeed the entire cause of her anguish. Had she not mourned for years as he had the living entombment of her daughter Herlinda? Had not the sight of him revived in her mind the keenness of her woe?

Doña Isabel was ill both in body and in mind; worn out with anxiety and the fatigues of travel, the reaction occasioned by the appearance of Gonzales was doubtless too great for her enfeebled powers. To his extreme embarrassment and anxiety he found himself charged with the unexpected responsibility of the care of a lady of much social consequence, and one personally extremely dear to him, who was stricken with an illness that demanded the most efficient attendance and complete isolation from disturbing influences. Added to the present necessity of gaining the confidence of the disorganized troops, and of continuing the march with the most unrelaxing vigilance, the situation thus became most onerous to the young commander, — not the less so because of the presence of a man he had thwarted and displaced, and whom it was necessary to keep in view and perhaps conciliate.

Upon the next night after the arrival of Gonzales, when Ruiz with seeming cordiality though with relief and rage contending in his mind had yielded his command, he strode to the outskirts of the camp, and smoking or rather forgetting to smoke a cigarette, mentally reviewed with bitter disappointment the perplexing and conflicting events that had led to so utter an overthrowal of his carefully concocted schemes. With the rapidity and excitement of his thoughts, his pace increased as though he was striving to tread down his mortification while he was preparing therefor a speedy and certain revenge.

The thought of this was chiefly directed toward Chinita. But for her flight Ruiz doubted not his position would have been so firmly assured that he would have been enabled to carry out his schemes. Thus he had hoped to find himself at the head of a force which in the event of final victory would have recommended him to the highest honors in the gift of Juarez, or at any rate assured him against the vengeance of Ramirez. To treachery time had added actual hatred of the man who had befriended him, and whose evil deeds, while he professed to abhor them, he would have rejoiced to have courage and address to imitate, and of whom he still held a superstitious dread, which had once been absolute awe.

It maddened the recreant follower of Ramirez to think of Chinita in the power of such a man. That day the last wild escapade of the lawless adventurer, the torture of Pedro, had in some way reached the ears of Ruiz and destroyed a lingering hope he had cherished that the girl, proud and hard though he believed her, had in some impulse of affection gone to her foster-father, — a thought that he had not even hinted to Doña Isabel, for with petty spite he refrained from uttering that which he imagined might give relief to her long agony. He imagined how Chinita, who doubtless had seen through his double dealing, would make it contemptible by her scorn, and ridiculous with her irony; and how Ramirez would, after listening to her account of him rise his sworn enemy: Ruiz had witnessed such scenes. No; return to Ramirez was impossible. Besides, that chieftain's ultimate defeat was certain: the Liberal cause was strengthening every hour. Ramirez must have lost his former keenness to

follow thus a losing venture. Ruiz began to console himself by thoughts of how, though only in a subordinate part,
he should assist in the discomfiture of the proud general
and that of the girl who loved him, — for the ignoble youth
was incapable of believing hers to be the love of a mere
unreasoning child, though to a purer heart her words would
have a thousand times declared her enthusiasm to be but
a fanatical admiration, untouched by a tinge of passion.
The maddening jealousy that had raged in the heart of
Ruiz since he had learned of the flight of Chinita, and had
rendered him incapable of a sustained effort to renew the
ambitious projects so fatally shaken, now flamed up with
cruel intensity; and yet he loved her. At that moment
he would have liked to throttle her, yet would have recalled her to life with words of passionate love and burning kisses.

As he pondered, he struck his breast with his clinched
hand. "*Caramba!*" he muttered, "is all lost? Is there
no way to overset this miserable favorite of the Señora?
Maria Sanctissima! who is that?" His hand like a flash
passed to his pistol.

"Hist!" said a voice. "It is I, Fernando. I have not
a moment to spare. I have tried to gain a way to thee for
an hour or more. I know all that has passed. Fool!
thou shouldst have raised the battle-cry for Ramirez before this Gonzales reached thee; there were men with
thee who would have sustained thee well!"

"Bah! a man has opinions," answered Ruiz, coolly,
recognizing the voice; "and if Ramirez still chooses to
fight for the priests, that is no argument for my being as
mad. I tell you plainly, Father, I am tired of playing a
boy's part; you will hear of me yet as something more
than the lieutenant of Gonzales."

"Big words, big words," laughed Tio Reyes. "Now
listen to that which I have to say to you;" and leaning
from his saddle in a few concise words he delivered the
message of Ramirez, adding a few paternal injunctions
as to the conduct Ruiz should in future observe.

"Up to this time nothing is lost," he continued; "in
truth had you acted in good faith, no course could have
been better save this last step, — but that may easily be recalled. Ramirez will soon be prepared to attack Gonzales

in force ; his mind was set on regaining El Toro, but that
can be deferred. 'When the loaf is cut the crumbs may be
soon eaten !' Be you prepared to pass over to your rightful commander at the last moment with all your men. The
rest of the troop will follow like sheep. Bah ! what is the
name of Gonzales to that of Ramirez ! With the forces
we could then combine, what might we not attempt ! I
promise you in the name of Ramirez, on his honor as a
soldier and his faith as your godfather, a free pardon for
all that has passed. *Caramba,* man ! I can't imagine
how you could have been so mad. I have seen the girl
who has bewitched you, and by my faith I thought her
nothing more than any other brown chit, save that her eyes
were darker and bigger than most, and her tongue sharper
than a man cares to find between his wife's lips ! What,
you hesitate? You believe Ramirez at the bottom of a pit,
and the pit dry? Fool ! He has treasure you know nothing of ; and as for men, did the mountain villages ever
fail him ? — and you know how many may be counted on
here. *Caramba,* try them ! Tell them he has sacked
Tres Hermanos."

" I know it," said Ruiz, thoughtfully, " and doubtless the
booty was great ! "

Reyes shrugged his shoulders but did not contradict
him, reiterating again and again the assurances of the
favor of Ramirez in the event of Ruiz's acceptance of his
proposals, and on the contrary the chief's determination to
wreak an awful vengeance upon his god-child should he
prove obdurate and attempt to carry to injurious lengths
the treacherous intrigues which he had designed against
his benefactor.

Ruiz vehemently denied his guilt, yet hesitated to make
promises which, whether kept or broken, might make still
more dubious his future position. Reyes read his mind,
and at length said coolly, —

" The fact is, you have been bred a servant of Ramirez.
When I swore the service of my life to him, yours went
with it. You are the one creature in the world he has never
met with a frown or given a harsh word to ; but do you think
he will spare you for that? No ; if you should fall into his
hands as a traitor, which sooner or later you would be sure
to do, you would be shot ! Yes, like a dog, — " and the

speaker spat on the ground to emphasize his contempt. " But if you are reasonable he will forget all that has passed, — more than I would do in his place I can tell you ; ay, he will even give you his daughter."

" His daughter ! " echoed Ruiz with a sneer.

" On my soul, you must be hard to please," cried his father. " For the girl's sake I was sorry enough he killed the fool of a gatekeeper five days ago. For all her proud ways, she loved him like a child, — more than she will love Ramirez though he is her father, when she hears of this mad deed."

Ruiz sprang to his side. "What do you mean?" he cried, seizing his arm. " Is Chinita the daughter of Ramirez? Is she with him? Is she indeed the girl who has been promised to me for these years and years? *Por Dios*, what would I not do for her? What would I not dare? But I do not believe it. Ramirez knows I love her ; this is but a deception. Ah, I know him too well ! "

Reyes laughed. " He told me if you were not satisfied you might go and see for yourself. Faith, he had no thought you loved her already. I met him on the road as he came back from leaving her. Does that surprise you? He is a careful father ; she is in the house of the Señora's daughter, Doña Carmen."

Ruiz seemed stunned. Reyes saw that his point was gained, and uttered but a few words more, which elicited only the response, — " Ramirez's daughter? Wonderful, wonderful ! And after all, she will be mine. Heavens ! how can I live a day longer without seeing her? Commend me to the Señor General. You know, my father, my heart is good, though my brain may have erred ! Tell me, has she said but one good word for me? She — "

" Enough ! " cried Reyes, laughing the more. " I have not seen her, I tell thee ; and if thou wouldst know what she thinks, find a pretext and see her at Doña Carmen's house. It was a strange freak of the General's to take her there, but a happy one. Thou shalt not be molested on the way, I promise thee. But I have no further time for talking. Adios ! thou art the only man I have ever seen whom love has brought to his right senses. It will be well if thou art as sane a year after the wedding ! "

The two men embraced, in the fashion of the country,

and with an ardor on the part of Ruiz that he seldom affected.

"*Caramba!* the father is a man of a thousand," he muttered to himself as he watched him disappear, guiding his horse so deftly that not a sound broke the silence of the night. "Virgin of consolation!" he continued, as he walked slowly back to his quarters. "This is like a dream. Plague upon it! That is the fault of my father; he is always in haste. I would have asked him a thousand questions, had he given me but a quarter of an hour. But it is of Chinita herself I will ask them. Surely she must have shown some favor toward me, or my godfather would not recommend me to her with such confidence. *Santo Niño*, show me some way to make it possible to steal into Guanapila and exchange a word with her!"

The curiosity of the young man as much as his love prompted the latter aspiration. His suspicion of the identity of Ramirez with the brother of Doña Isabel, the Leon Vallé so long supposed dead, returned to him with force; but he longed to know whether the secret of her birth had been conveyed to Chinita, and how her flight had been contrived. He pictured her then like a bird in a cage beating herself against the iron bars of Doña Carmen's windows. That was not what she had hoped for when she had talked to him of Ramirez. If she had tolerated him before, would he not now be doubly dear, as one who should liberate her from the natural restraints of a maiden's life?

Ruiz forgot his fancied wrongs in an intoxication of delight. Constant pondering upon the question how he should manage to evade the vigilance and suspicions of Gonzales and effect a visit to Guanapila kept him preoccupied, yet feverishly alert, until the increased indisposition of Doña Isabel brought about what appeared to him a special interposition in his behalf, and in pleading for the aid of "Our Lady of the Impossible" he promised her in pious gratitude a candle of enormous proportions.

To reach a point where he might leave his generous but failing friend had become the most earnest desire of Gonzales. But its fulfilment had seemed an impossibility, for from the time he assumed command of the troops almost hourly news had been brought to him of gatherings of bands of Conservatives, which promised to offer formidable resistance to any movement he might make; and until Doña Isabel was safely disposed of, he desired at almost any risk to avoid an open collision.

The march had slowly proceeded, and so constantly had Gonzales been occupied, and so serious became the condition of Doña Isabel, that there was but little conversation between them, and somewhat to his impatience that on her part had been limited to a few brief sentences of warning against Ruiz and constant inquiries for Chinita, and entreaties that search should be made for her in every direction.

Gonzales, as far as was possible, had obeyed these inopportune requests; but the anxiety and grief that prompted them seemed to him strained and unnatural, though he could not doubt after due inquiry made that the lost girl was of remarkable beauty and of an original and fascinating character. Still, his knowledge of the class whence he supposed her sprung had made quite credible to him the generally accepted theory of her flight. Yet he started when Doña Isabel had mentioned the American as her probable companion or instigator, adding in a low voice, "Twice an American has robbed him." What did she mean? His cheek flushed as he remembered that it had been said that for love of the murdered Ashley, Herlinda had taken the veil. And had Doña Isabel dreamed that he would find consolation after so many years in this beautiful peasant girl whom she had raised from the dust? Gonzales silently resented the insinuation. Yet none the less the suggestion of the complicity of the American in her disappearance haunted and vexed him. He did not tell Doña Isabel that to Ward he owed the definite news of the approach of reinforcements, and that he had virtually left him in charge of El Toro, and that the commission from Juarez for which the foreigner had applied had already doubtless reached him. Had he betrayed this young girl, — the *protégée* of Doña Isabel, — in spite of his zeal in his service the American should have much to answer for to him. A few weeks would decide all. He preferred to wait patiently the development of affairs, and refrained from perplexing further the mind of Doña Isabel.

Meanwhile the condition of the lady had become rapidly worse. Perhaps she had brought from Tres Hermanos the germs of the disease that during these very days was working such terrible havoc there; perhaps the long days and nights of exertion, anxiety, and grief had produced it, — but certain it is that as the position of Gonzales became more critical, so the imminent danger of Doña Isabel increased. A desperate evil commands a desperate remedy. So it was at length decided that an effort should be made to convey the lady to the city of Guanapila, to the house of her daughter Doña Carmen; and Ruiz, in the utter impossibility that Gonzales found of personally conducting the party, was permitted to execute the delicate and important trust.

With an apparent readiness of resource and disregard of danger, which commended him greatly to the perplexed General, Ruiz himself had proposed the measure.

Taking the precaution to send with him men from Tres Hermanos only, and such as he knew to be warmly devoted to their mistress, Gonzales acceded to the plans of the wily young officer, and despatched him upon the important and seemingly dangerous mission.

After the separation of the detailed party from the main body, skirmishing parties began upon the latter frequent and harassing attacks, and the suspicions of Gonzales were again aroused by the impunity which Ruiz enjoyed, yet alternated with fears for his ultimate safety. He could scarcely believe that knowing it to be in their power to secure so rich a prize as Doña Isabel, the hungry forces of the clergy would suffer her to escape, unless indeed Ruiz was himself as false as he had once suspected. Again and again he reproached himself for yielding to the apparent frankness and loyalty of the man he had at first distrusted, and with an anxiety which grew into actual torture he awaited the outcome of the action which circumstances against his will and judgment had forced upon him.

Ruiz, unmolested, made his way as rapidly as the condition of his charge permitted toward Guanapila. He comprehended well the circumstances which were distracting the mind of Gonzales. These constant though petty attacks he knew from information sent by Reyes were destined to weaken the prestige of Gonzales by a series of petty misadventures, after which his destruction by the desertion of Ruiz, followed by the mass of the disaffected, might, it was conjectured, be readily accomplished. It seemed the simplest matter in the world to effect, and had been instantly agreed to by Ruiz in the hasty conference with his father. Yet further reflection gave him an unaccountable antipathy to the course he was to pursue. It cannot be said that a lingering trace of honor influenced him, or any genuine disapproval of the character or convictions of Ramirez, for Ruiz was in the widest sense a man to be bought and sold, a creature influenced by every turn of advantage; but in spite of all that had passed between him and Reyes, he doubted the good faith of Ramirez. The good fortune that was to give him Chinita at so slight a cost seemed to him incredible. Did the girl love him, and had she owned as much? Or was she to be fooled into acquiescence in the plans of Ramirez by the chimera of his parental power? No; he knew Chinita too well to believe she would marry against her own desire, even to gratify a parent who exerted over her the extraordinary ascendency that she had instinctively acknowledged in Ramirez. Ruiz was, moreover, impressed with a belief in the ultimate disaster of the Conservative cause. For Chinita's sake he would risk involvement in the ruin he foresaw, hoping that by some spar he himself might float; but unless assured of her good-will, — the thoughts of the young conspirator carried him no further, unless vaguely to conjecture the extent of power which he might thereafter exert over the fortunes of Doña Isabel, through his connection with her mysterious *protégée*.

With ill-concealed impatience, and hopes and emotions which every hour grew more dazzling and overpowering, Ruiz at length found himself in the house of Doña Carmen, and in her presence and that of her young companion. With inexpressible amazement, instead of her he sought he found himself face to face with Chata, the supposed daughter of Don Rafael.

The confusion and excitement of the arrival gave almost instantly an opportunity for him to pour into the ear of the young girl the burning questions which rushed to his lips. In the necessity in which she found herself to attend instantly the wants of her mother, Doña Carmen left the young soldier and her charge alone together. Breathlessly demanding of Chata news of Chinita, Ruiz revealed to the astounded girl the separation of her playmate from Doña Isabel, the mystery of her flight, and the extraordinary purposes which the young girl had cherished in relation to Ramirez. In every word too he betrayed his own love for her he denounced, and the raging jealousy which possessed him.

Chata in her extreme agitation, forgetting the promises she had made, revealed her own connection with Ramirez, in describing in a few brief sentences the scenes which had taken place at Tres Hermanos, and especially the means by which she had saved Don Rafael. She could not comprehend the rage and disgust with which Ruiz flung himself from her when she announced herself to be the daughter of Ramirez, but a moment later it flashed upon her that she had heard herself named as the destined bride of this man who so openly despised her. Had he too known of the destiny awarded him? She turned from him with a burning blush, and without a word they parted. She remembered afterward that she might perhaps have sent news to the hacienda, — to her foster-father Don Rafael, to Doña Feliz did she still live; but her one chance had gone, and her semi-imprisonment began anew. Doña Carmen was not again betrayed into a momentary forgetfulness of her charge.

Ruiz turned from the house with a thousand conflicting emotions. The encounter with Chata had produced in his mind an absolute fury of resentment, as he reflected that this was the girl whom Ramirez had promised him as his wife, — in his boyhood jestingly; in his manhood as a reward, an incentive. Heavens! what was this puny creature in comparison with Chinita? And Chinita was perhaps at that very moment with Ramirez, — perhaps even laughing with him over the weakness and discomfiture of the youth they had combined to deceive! With blind and insensate rage, Ruiz believed himself the victim of a conspiracy between Ramirez and his own father to substitute this girl for the peerless creature that he loved, and who doubtless was at that moment in the camp of her triumphant lover. They had thought to entrap him into furthering their designs, deeming it impossible that he should enter Guanapila and discover the trick that was to be played upon him.

Ruiz did not for a moment conceive it possible that Ramirez had known nothing of his love for Chinita, or that his father had himself been ignorant of the identity of the girl whom Ramirez had claimed as his daughter, or that Reyes had drawn a false conclusion from his own hasty questions.

In this mood Ruiz was presently met by old acquaintances, before whom he was forced to mask his excitement ; and moreover they were in festive humor, which prevented them from being observant or critical. The town, but imperfectly garrisoned, had for some time held an anxious and harassed populace, prognosticating nothing but invasion and the levy of forced loans ; but it chanced that on that day a guest had arrived, who by the mere magic of his presence, unattractive and unimpressive as was his bearing, inspired confidence and hope. Benito Juarez himself had made one of those secret incursions for which he was famed, and had reached Guanapila with the purpose of conferring with such officers of his party as had ventured to meet him. There were but few, and Ruiz was honored by an invitation to represent Gonzales. The deference paid him as a delegate from so important a leader, in command of so considerable a force, raised to its highest pitch the absolute fury of resentment that convulsed the desperate lover ; and at the banquet that followed the conference, the wine and flattering notice of the Liberal President completed the overthrow of the little caution that he had hitherto maintained in his speech and demeanor.

The toasts drunk were loud and frequent, and the name of Ramirez was the most deeply execrated. Many of the young men indulged in extravagant boasts and declarations as to the deeds they would accomplish in the near future, scorning the prowess of the man at whose very name they were accustomed to tremble. Some one spoke with a laugh of a beautiful girl who had been seen in his company but a few days before. It was not until afterward that Ruiz reflected that the spy had probably caught a glimpse of Chata on her way from Tres Hermanos. At the moment his mind was full of Chinita, and rising impetuously, in a torrent of fiery words he broke into denunciation and invective, telling the tale of Pedro's martyrdom as he had heard it, and vowing that as Ramirez had slain the poor peasant, so he himself would accomplish the defeat and death of the "mountain wolf." "I promise you, Señores," he concluded, "that when you next hear of Fernando Ruiz you shall have cause to remember the vow I have here made. Ramirez is doomed!"

The stoical man at the head of the table smiled faintly at the storm of applause that followed this speech, and as Ruiz a few minutes later took his departure Juarez muttered to his neighbor, "That young fellow will bear watching. He has either a tremendous personal wrong to avenge, or he is striving to mislead us. I know him to be the godson of this very Ramirez, whom he thunders against. A Mexican may turn against, may even murder, his own father; but his godfather, — he must be a renegade indeed to attempt his destruction!" His neighbor assented.

When the words of Ruiz were reported to Ramirez, — as reported they were a few days later, — he smiled as grimly as Benito Juarez himself had done. "The cockerel crows loud," he said. "He was always a blusterer. Well, we shall see; a week at latest will decide all that. Bah! if the fellow but had in him the blood of his father! — but with the name of his mother he must have taken a braggart's tongue. It will be well for him if he does not weary my patience in the end. But for my promise to Reyes —"

He frowned darkly. Had Ruiz seen the face of his godfather then he might have repented his boast. As it was, his own mad words served as a spur urging him to the inevitable future. He returned to the camp of Gonzales unmolested, and was received with intense relief, with thanks and praises, yet wore thereafter a dark and vengeful face.

THE arrival of Doña Isabel at the house of her daughter brought a change into the life of Chata that might have been considered even more dreary and oppressive than the semi-imprisonment to which she had thus far been subjected, though she was spoken of as an honored guest. In fact this change was most welcome to the young girl; for while it afforded her even less freedom of movement, it gave a sufficient reason for her seclusion, as also occupation both to body and mind.

What had been the nature of the communication that Ramirez had made to Doña Carmen, Chata knew not, but it had evidently impressed that lady with a deep sense of responsibility. In those days there were even in the quietest times no regular mails into the country districts, and this gave a ready pretext to Doña Carmen for resisting all attempts to communicate with the household at Tres Hermanos. The highways, infested as they were by roving bands of soldiers and banditti, were indeed scarcely safe for the transmission of even peaceful intelligence; and thus none reached Guanapila from the hacienda, and Chata, and in a lesser degree Doña Carmen herself, endured a painful uncertainty as to the condition of Don Rafael and of Doña Feliz and others whom Chata had left stricken with the dreaded fever. Day by day she had awaited news; day by day she had hoped for the appearance of Doña Isabel and Chinita, — while Doña Carmen, after listening with astonishment and some manifestations of displeasure to the account Chata gave of the departure of her mother from Tres Hermanos under the escort of troops destined to the relief of Gonzales, gave the opinion that the destination she would seek would be El Toro rather than Guanapila.

" My sister the religious is at present there," she said; and Chata with glowing face. and lips that trembled at the memory, told her of the chance glimpse she had once caught of the beautiful and saintly nun.

Doña Carmen's eyes filled with tears, and she silently embraced the girl; the little incident drew Chata nearer to her heart. "Ah, child," she would say, "I never have known, I never could conjecture, why our beautiful Herlinda chose so sad a life, — it must be sad to be shut away from this fair world, from sweet companionship, from love. Yes, Herlinda might have chosen from among a score of the handsomest and noblest of cavaliers. And then our mother, — how she loved her! one might see it through all her sternness. I never knew the truth, yet I am sure a great and terrible sorrow caused Herlinda to enter a convent. She had no inherent fitness, no liking natural or acquired, for such a life."

Doña Carmen was not accustomed to speak thus freely of family affairs. She had much of the characteristic reticence of the Garcias. Chata met many of the younger members from time to time. They were too well bred to show any curiosity concerning her; but among the servants of the household and of others, there was much gossip as to how and why she had come, and what relationship she bore to the husband of Doña Carmen, who, kind and amiable man that he was, seemed to take peculiar pleasure in her companionship. But the arrival of Doña Isabel in an apparently dying condition turned all thoughts into a new channel.

From the first, Chata had entreated to be allowed to take her part in nursing the stricken lady, but had been gently refused. Thereafter, the husband of Doña Carmen used often to see their young guest gliding restlessly about the house vainly seeking some distraction for her anxious thoughts. He did not know the secret pain that tormented her. He would gladly have facilitated her return if he could to that Don Rafael from whom in a mad freak the mountain chieftain had stolen her; yet there were circumstances, — there were reasons for not offending one so powerful. Who knew? Guanapila was of course under Liberal rule to-day, but what would it be to-morrow? The cautious man shrugged his shoulders and said something of this to Chata, who smiled and thought him good to care, yet wondered with all his goodness and his years,

— the years that had not brought in their train any additional attractiveness to his person, — that Doña Carmen loved him. Was it as she had heard, that his riches had beguiled one already passing rich?

Since she had left El Toro, Chata had become a woman. Change of scene had given impetus to the somewhat retarded development of her physique, and mental anxiety had stimulated her mind and given to it an intuitive appreciation of causes and events that is generally gained by innocent and unsuspicious natures, such as hers, only after long experience.

Thus she comprehended fully, as she would not have done a few months before, the gravity of the step Chinita had taken in separating herself from Doña Isabel. Ruiz had not spared the woman he loved in the few brief sentences he had passionately uttered : love was with him but a devouring flame, ready to destroy its object either in the struggle of attainment or in the fury of baffled desire. Chata blushed even in secret when she remembered the aspersions he had cast upon the friend of her childhood. She knew the innate purity of the girl's mind, though it had been developed amid surroundings which might well have tainted it. She knew her pride : even when she was but the barefoot foster-child of Pedro the gatekeeper, Chinita had held Pepé and his mates as far apart from her as the dogs that followed them or the mules they tended. Dogs and mules she liked well and made serve her needs, as also she did the lads. Chata did not doubt that Pepé now as ever had proved himself the slave of Chinita's will. Perhaps it was to Tres Hermanos she had gone. Although knowing as she did the fascination that Ramirez had always exerted over the girl's mind, she could not but fear that led not by reckless passion but by a spirit of devotion at which Ruiz had sneered, yet in which Chata herself recognized the peculiar strength and determination of Chinita's character, the impulsive creature might actually have sought an entrance to the camp to urge the plan that she conceived was to further the glory of the Church and the interest of him whom she had made the hero of her imagination. That Ashley Ward was in any way concerned in the disappearance of Chinita, either as a principal or an accessory, Chata indignantly refused to believe. Her heart beat suffocatingly as she thought of him. No, no! he was not a man to entice a girl to her ruin.

And as days went by news reached Chata that strength-ened this conviction. The American was engaged in deeds of a far different character. In his way he was beginning to fill the minds and occupy the conversation of people as much as Ramirez had ever done. They gave him a new name, as those at the hacienda had done; but Conservatives and Liberals alike wondered at and exagger-ated his exploits, until Ashley had won a reputation for reckless bravado quite foreign to his true character, — which was exhibiting itself in the most careful and nice calculations of chances, the whole tending toward the fulfilment of the task to which he had dedicated himself; namely, the downfall of the unpunished and unrepentant murderer of John Ashley.

Chata recognized this, and was filled with emotions per-haps more conflicting, more strange, than had ever be-fore met in the breast of so young a girl. They held her thoughts by day and night. Oh that she had never left Ramirez! Oh that she could speak but for a few moments with Ashley! But she was powerless; and meanwhile what was the fate of Chinita? What that impending over the man she was in duty bound to warn, — to love if it were possible?

But before these reflections had reached this point, an employment that prevented them from becoming utterly overwhelming was afforded her. Chata no longer wandered aimlessly about the house, but kept the strict seclusion of Doña Isabel's apartment, to which she had been hastily summoned one night by Doña Carmen herself.

" My mother talks so strangely," she had said in a low voice, pressing her hands to her white and frightened face. " No, I cannot comprehend what she says; but I cannot have the servants about her. They might imagine un-speakable things. Oh, what tales and rumors they might set afloat! No, no! I will not have them here, with their suspicions and evil thoughts. But you, — you are inno-cent and frank; you will not torture into strange meanings the mutterings of a diseased imagination."

" No, no!" answered Chata, reassuringly. " It was the same with Doña Feliz. Sometimes she talked so strangely.

so sadly, one was forced to weep, and then again to laugh; yes, in all my trouble I laughed. But I will not now, Doña Carmen; only let me be useful. Doña Isabel did not seem to like me when she was at the hacienda, so I kept as much as possible out of her sight. She said my face was not such as Don Rafael's daughter should have; and after all," she added sadly, " she was right."

What passed in that sick chamber through those long days and nights Doña Carmen and Chata never repeated, even to each other. Perhaps they could not, all was so disconnected, so improbable, and through all her delirium the patient held so great a restraint over her utterances. Sometimes one escaped her that startled and commanded attention; but the next invariably contradicted it, and it was impossible to form a connected theory even had Chata tried. But that great sorrows, events to cause constant and secret care and remorse, had taken place in the life of Doña Isabel, and that they concerned Chinita closely, was abundantly clear. What pathetic appeals, what wild ravings, in which the names of those who had lived in the past, — of her husband, her mother, her brother, and of Herlinda, — were constantly mingled with those of the American and Chinita. And friends or servants followed each other in endless yet confusing succession; yet of them all the name of Chinita was the most frequent. The present grief combined all others; in Chinita seemed centred the agonies and loves of her lifetime.

Chata listened with a sort of envy. Ah, if it had been given to her to raise such a passion of feeling! She found herself from day to day leaning with infinite tenderness over this woman, who had seemed so cold, but whose heart was now revealed as a very volcano of repressed and seething emotions. She was grateful and deeply touched that Doña Isabel in her delirium clung to her fondly, calling her " Mother," or " Quina," which Doña Carmen told her was the name of a cousin she had dearly loved. Even after she had recognized her when the delirium was past as the daughter of Don Rafael, she seemed pleased to have her there; though she said querulously, " It is strange you are only a little country girl. But Feliz has good blood in her; it has been transmitted to you, — there is nothing of Rita, nothing of Rafael himself."

After that she made no further comment; but her eyes often followed the movements of Chata with a puzzled expression painful to see. One day after she had become convalescent, Doña Carmen spoke of this. "Whom does she remind you of?" she asked lightly.

"I cannot tell; I do not know," Doña Isabel answered wearily. "Perhaps it is of Chinita. Oh! I can think of nothing but Chinita. Are they still looking for her, as I have prayed, — as I have commanded?"

"Mother," said Doña Carmen, solemnly, "who is Chinita? Why should you care so much?"

The face of Doña Isabel grew rigid. "Shall I tell you what you have uttered in your delirium?" continued Doña Carmen, looking fixedly into her mother's eyes. "Shall I ask you if you spoke the truth, or if what I have gathered — here a word, there a word — is but a dreadful fancy? Mother, Mother! if it is the truth, no wonder that the fate of this girl is on your soul! No wonder Herlinda —"

She paused affrighted. In her excitement she had said far more than she had intended. What if her mother in her delicate condition should sink beneath this cruel attack, — should faint, should die? Carmen threw herself down beside the couch with a prayer for forgiveness.

Doña Isabel in the first surprise had clasped her hands over her heart. Slowly the pale hue of life returned to her face. "Carmen," she whispered faintly, "speak! speak! After all these years, accusation — even from my own child — is more bearable than silence. O my God, I meant well! — it was for Herlinda's sake. Yet what remorse, what agony I have suffered!"

The two women sank into each other's arms. There had ever been a barrier of reserve between them, — in a moment it was swept away. Doña Isabel poured out her heart. It was Carmen who withheld what might have been revealed; a conviction seized her that there was much in this strange family mystery yet undeclared, and of which Doña Isabel knew nothing; and that her mother's mind was in no condition to be perplexed by further doubts and complications. She left the room and went to her husband.

"Chulita my beautiful one," he said anxiously, as she was about to leave him an hour later, "thou wilt do nothing rash? Yet I will not forbid thee. In truth, but that robberies and abductions are so common upon the roads, I would go with thee myself."

"Not for the world!" exclaimed Doña Carmen in genuine consternation. "They would seize thee and carry thee into the mountains. But as for me, — I promise thee no robber shall think me worth a second thought. But hold thee ready, — the desire may come to her at a moment's thought, and I would not leave thee without warning; I would not have thee unprepared."

XLIII.

WITH the same unreasoning fury with which he had denounced Ramirez at the banquet, Ruiz had returned to the camp of Gonzales; and through a cleverly managed correspondence with Ramirez — in which however he dared not mention the name of Chinita, lest he should awaken in the astute mind of the General a suspicion that his godson conjectured the deception which was to be played upon him — Ruiz gradually drew from the chief data through which to propose such movements to Gonzales as procured for him as a strategist the respect and admiration of that commander, which well might have satisfied a laudable ambition.

Meanwhile Ramirez himself, though surrounded by no despicable force, which was daily augmented by accessions from the mountains or from the ranks of less popular leaders of either party, was for the first time in his life oppressed by a vague melancholy, — which, with some impatience, he ascribed to the forced separation from the child whose purity and innocence had so irresistibly attracted him. There were times when he thought with what horror such a record as his would be viewed by that gentle and upright nature; and a positive dread came upon him of her ever knowing the one incident that had been so vividly recalled to him by the appearance of the avenger upon the grave of the man he had murdered years before, — one crime among many he had almost forgotten. He said to himself that an evil spell had been upon him ever since the day when he had foolishly thrown away the charm the elf-like child had given him. His emissaries had brought him word time and again of the miscarriage of his best-laid plans. Who had betrayed them?

Ramirez knew too well who had frustrated them. - The American who had escaped his knife at the cemetery seemed ubiquitous since obtaining the commission which authorized him to wage war against his cousin's murderer.

Not content with defending El Toro with unexampled bravery, he appeared at every point where an advantage was to be gained. "*Carrhi!*" Ramirez said to himself, "I shall be forced to give that fellow a thrust of my dagger in secret, since he appears to be impervious to ball and proof against the chances of open warfare. He or I must fall. There's not room in all Mexico for him and me."

Whether there was room or not, it seemed destined that they should remain in it together, though not without constant collision. Gonzales became to the mind of Ramirez far less formidable than this yellow-haired foreigner, who with a mere handful of followers so constantly harassed and baffled him. Like most men of his class, the mountain chieftain was intensely superstitious, and one night in the moonlight he saw, or fancied he saw, a female form glide before him into the chapparal. He caught but a glimpse of the face, but it had reminded him of Herlinda, for whom he had done the deed that, so late, seemed to have brought upon him a threatened retribution. As he searched the bushes for the woman, whom he could not discover, he shuddered as he remembered the expression of her eyes, — as of a wronged creature who had loved and now hated. He had seen such an expression in a woman's eyes before. More than ever after this strange occurrence the thought of Ashley Ward tormented him; the young man's face haunted him; and curiously enough other faces also began to peer upon him, — faces of women he had wronged, of men who with good cause bore him deadly hatred, or of others whom, like the American, or the gatekeeper, he had murdered.

Ramirez grew strangely taciturn and nervous. Not even the letters of Ruiz aroused him. In his heart he distrusted his godson, as he did all men but Reyes, all women but Chata. Had she been near, he thought, he would have talked to her and cast off his fancies; but in her absence they grew upon him. One day he could have sworn he saw clearly not only the face but the figure of Pedro Gomez; and upon another, that of the woman he had loved long years before. Bah! they were fantasies. He wondered whether he too would be seized with the fever, which was still raging at Tres Hermanos, and of which they said its lady was dying at her daughter's house in Guanapila. Was this weakness of nerve the presage of what was to come?

At last battle was joined with Gonzales as had been planned. The day turned in favor of Ramirez; even the gallant assistance of Ward availed little against the desperate courage of the mountain troops. The genius and valor of their leader were manifested with a vigor that declared they had been but shaken, not broken. Until the arrival of Ward it had even appeared that the forces actually under the command of Ramirez would have been sufficient to effect a victory; but Ward's appearance speedily turned the tide in favor of Gonzales, and with some impatience Ramirez gave the signal that was to hasten the promised action of Ruiz.

But at the critical moment the expected ally failed him. With a vindictive fury which was demoniacal in its exhibition, Ruiz threw himself against his old commander. The carnage was terrible in that part of the field; and when the fray was ended, the demoralization of Ramirez's troops was complete, — yet he himself had escaped.

That such should be the case seemed to Ashley Ward incredible, as later he walked over the field seeking among the slain the man against whom he had begun a private warfare, which to his own surprise had, with further investigation of the principles involved, rapidly attained in his mind the dignity of a struggle for liberty that even dwarfed the incentive of personal revenge, although it was impossible that this should be wholly forgotten or ignored.

Gonzales marched into El Toro amid the clanging of bells and shouts of rejoicing; for though that was a convent town, the people of the lower class were mad *Juaristas,* who did good service under Ward when troops were scarce. The triumph had however not been gained without much loss upon the Liberal side; and among the missing was the young officer who in the eyes of Gonzales — and to the astonishment of Ward — had so ably vindicated his character as a stanch adherent in the day of battle. Pepé too, the right-hand man of Ward, was gone.

In very truth, at the last moment the most important and useful calculation of Ruiz had failed. He saw Ramirez, by his orders, surrounded by desperate men; it seemed inevitable that he must be stricken down, — when a party led by Reyes broke through to his assistance, and in the fury of the onslaught Ruiz himself was swept from his horse and hurried away, and to his consternation found himself a prisoner dragged onward in the irresistible impetus of flight.

They were miles distant from the scene of battle when the fugitives at last paused; and here for the first time Ramirez knew of the special prisoner that had been made. When his eyes fell upon the youth, a frown which darkened as with a palpable cloud his already rigid and pitiless face, overspread the countenance of Ramirez and made it absolutely terrible. Even to fallen angels the crime of ingratitude may seem the one damnable offence. In Ruiz, remembering the love and favor he had shown him, Ramirez held it so to be. This insignificant boy had compassed his ruin; his life seemed too poor a forfeit to condone the offence. The baffled, desperate, outraged chieftain cursed the fate which had cast the treacherous favorite into his power. But the terrible blackness of his face still deepened, as he gazed.

A lasso had been drawn tightly around the waist of Ruiz. His face was cut and bleeding; the gold lace and epaulettes had been torn from his coat; his uncovered hair was filled with dust, and his face reeking with sweat. He raised his bloodshot eyes appealingly. He knew the man before him, — the man, worthless and unscrupulous though he was, who had been kind to him, whom he had betrayed, and whose death he had attempted to compass. Ruiz did not attempt to speak, but fell on his knees and raised his bound hands. Ramirez gazed at him a moment in silence, then without the quiver of a muscle in his impassive face uttered the sentence, " Let him be shot at once!"

Shot at *once*, — from that terrible mandate there was no appeal. There was not one there to utter a word in the traitor's behalf, but only a moan from the dust to which he had sunk. Reyes was not there; probably the result would have been the same had he been. The soldiers raised the young officer and stood him against a tree.

At the last moment that strange indifference to death,

27

which among his countrymen so often counterfeits courage, caused Ruiz to straighten his figure and raise his
head ; and in the insolence of despair he said to Ramirez,
with a glance of malignant contempt, "Had you fallen
into my hands I would have shot you with my own pistol
an hour ago."

Perhaps the still proud youth hoped by this speech to
escape the ignominy of execution by a file of common
soldiers. If so he was mistaken. Ramirez gave the signal ; the balls whizzed through the air and found their
way to their destined aim. Ruiz fell without a groan.
Ramirez himself, though still with an impassive face, to
the astonishment of all stooped and stretched the limbs
and crossed the hands of the young man upon his breast.
There was a spot of blood upon the face, and the chief
wiped it away as tenderly as a mother might lave the face
of her dead infant ; and yet but a few moments before he
had commanded this youth to a violent death, and according to the creed he held, his soul to purgatory without
benefit of clergy.

Forgetting to give the expected order for the execution of the other prisoners, Ramirez turned away. In
another moment he had placed himself at the head of the
party and continued the retreat. "At the next halt it can
be done as well," remarked the lieutenant, philosophically.
"There are plenty of horses ; bind the prisoners well and
bring them along."

And thus for that day at least Pepé Ortiz among others
knew he had escaped a fate of which the very idea — with
the remembrance of Ruiz to intensify its horror — made
his tongue cleave to the roof of his mouth and his knees
quiver with terror. Yet the day came when he, like the
traitor whose end he had witnessed, straightened himself
against a tree, and with apparent coolness awaited the
mandate of Ramirez that was to consign him to eternity ;
naught but a miracle it seemed could save him. He
only begged a cigarette of a soldier, remarking that they
might be scarce where he was going, — secretly hoping
thus to hide the quiver of the lips which belied the bravado of his words.

Shortly after this time, Chata to her surprise received
by the hand of an Indian fruitseller a brief note from

Ramirez. At the first reading its contents seemed hard and indifferent. He spoke with an almost savage irony of those who were driving him back like a wolf to his mountain lairs. "I know of fastnesses, if I care to seek them, where no foot but mine has ever trod, and where this accursed American who is hunting me down like fate could never hope to follow me," he wrote. "But it shall never be said that Ramirez fled from man or spirit, were it Satan himself. After all, a man may not escape from him who is destined to bring death to him. Ruiz was marked to die by me. I loved him, yet his fate is accomplished."

Chata shuddered. It seemed incredible that save by accident such a thing could happen, so sacred is esteemed by Mexicans the tie between sponsor and godchild; and the tone of the letter impressed her as that of a desperate man who was ready for unheard-of deeds. Had Ramirez in truth deliberately destroyed the man whom for years he had associated in his every hope and plan, to whom he had promised the hand of his child? Deep indeed must have been the villany that had merited such an end. The sigh of relief which Chata involuntarily breathed, that she was free from the possible accomplishment of the destiny that had been marked out for her, was perhaps as sympathetic as any caused by the death of Fernando Ruiz.

A reperusal of the letter gave to Chata's mind an impression of the longing, the stinging regret, the remorse which the words had been designed to conceal rather than display. The pride, the fierceness, the unconquerable will of the writer pervaded them; yet the wail of a lost spirit crying for the one good that it had known, and now believed forfeited forever, seemed to echo through her soul. "He loves me," she thought remorsefully. "He believes himself doomed to die, and that he will see me no more. Oh! if it were possible I would go to him. Oh, if I dared tell Doña Isabel! — but no, she would keep me from him; she would mock my pain with the cry that this was but the just recompense of the evil he had brought upon her long ago. She believes her brother dead; why torture her by telling her my miserable history?"

Chata showed the letter to Doña Carmen, and she it was who called the girl's attention to some chance mention of the name of the place where Ramirez said he might be able to remain some days, even if closely pressed, for the people there were secretly sworn to his support. Day after day wild rumors flew through the city of the pursuit of Ramirez, his capture, his death, only to be contradicted upon the next. They did not seriously agitate Chata, for not once was the name of the place he called his stronghold mentioned.

One night the anxious girl had a vivid dream. She dreamed she saw the chieftain and Chinita lying dead, — the one on one side of a village street, the other on the opposite. The people were rushing wildly about screaming and gesticulating madly, while Doña Isabel, followed by women clothed in black like herself, was in frenzy passing from one to the other, uttering that low wail that seems the very key-note of woe.

Chata woke with a stifled scream. The wind was blowing shrilly through the trees and seemed to bring to her a voice, which said, "Wake! oh wake, Chata! I have dreamed of her." The voice sounded close to her ear. It came from Doña Isabel, who leaning over the dreamer's bed was repeating again and again the words, "I shall find her. I have dreamed of her."

Chata raised herself upon the pillows and caught the lady's wasted hand. "Yes, yes," continued Doña Isabel, "I have dreamed of Chinita and of another, — one I loved long years ago. I saw them together in Las Parras. It is a revelation! Why have I not thought of it before? No other place would be so fitting. I shall find her. I am going now, now! My carriage, my horses, my men must be here; I will call them. Tell my daughter when she wakes; she will understand."

Doña Isabel turned to leave the room, her excitement supplementing her returning strength; but Chata detained her. "I too will go," she cried. "Nothing shall prevent me. Doña Carmen will not stop us, — she knows; she dare not forbid me. I will tell her now. She will know what is best for us. The carriage is still here, but — "

Chata hastened from the room and wakened Doña Carmen. "Ah," said the daughter to herself, "the thought is come, and the hour." She hastily wrote a line to her husband, who was absent at a hacienda he owned near the city; provided herself with some rolls of gold, and presently entered her mother's room dressed in a somewhat soiled cotton gown, and with her reboso over her arm. Doña Isabel, who in the excitement of her thoughts was walking hither and thither, taking up and putting down articles of apparel, looked at her daughter blankly. Why, she thought, had a servant come at that hour?

"See, I am ready," cried Carmen, cheerfully. "The diligence is to leave the city for the first time to-day. We shall pass through the country quite safely. Who would stop such poor creatures as we appear to be?"

Doña Isabel looked at her daughter gratefully, — her mind had been running helplessly upon carriages and mounted escorts and all the paraphernalia of travel, which require so much time and thought to prepare. "True, true!" she said, "that will be best, oh much the best!" In feverish haste she prepared herself for the journey as Carmen had done, arraying herself in a plain dark dress and reboso. But her daughter noticed that she did not think of the expenses of the journey, and herself silently assumed the direction of the little party.

Doña Carmen led the way from her own house so quietly that only the doorkeeper to whom she gave a few directions, which he doubtless in his amazement straightway forgot, was awakened. The three ladies were so humbly dressed that they attracted but little notice at the diligence house, and being hastily motioned to the poorest seats in the coach were soon on their way. Covering their faces with their rebosos, they did not so much as speak to one another.

Some ten leagues from the city the diligence was stopped by a half-dozen armed men. The male passengers were ordered to lie down upon their faces, and were despoiled of all their money and valuables. Chata to her extreme disgust — which fortunately was disguised by her alarm — received an amicable expression of approval from one of the bandits, which was abruptly checked by the remark of the captain that this was no time for fooling, as there was a rival band but a half-mile farther on. The elder women escaped remark. Happily, the other band did not present itself, and the three ladies told their beads in devout thankfulness.

That night the travellers remained at a miserable hut, which served as an inn, feeling a certain protection in the presence of an aged priest, who chanced to be awaiting there an opportunity to proceed upon a long-interrupted journey; and upon the following morning he formed one of the travelling party. Beyond bestowing upon them his blessing, he said nothing to them, — although somewhat to her discomfort Doña Carmen noticed that he often turned an inquiring gaze upon them. Early in the afternoon the diligence stopped at a miserable village, the nearest point at which, in the interrupted arrangements of travel, it approached Las Parras; and having deposited Doña Isabel's party and the priest, diverged toward the north.

Doña Isabel looked around her helplessly, saying, "It is nearly eight leagues to Las Parras. I have often been here, — I know the road well. We shall never reach there!"

"You will see, Mother, you will see," answered Doña Carmen, cheerfully; and greatly to the astonishment of the priest and the women who stood near, she drew forth a half-dozen ounces of gold, and held them up. "See." she said in her clear patrician voice, "you are good people here; we are not afraid to trust you," — her quick eye had shown her there was not an able-bodied man in the almost ruinous place. "We are not so poor as we look, and I will give you all this for three, four —" she glanced at the priest — "horses, donkeys, or mules, be they ever so poor, upon which we can go our way."

The women laughed stupidly, and looked at one another and then at the gold. Evidently if there was a beast of burden in the village it was securely hidden, and though the money tempted them they were afraid.

"No, no," said one at length. "Three weeks ago the Señores Liberales drove off our last cow, and the week after the Señores Conservadores slaughtered the turkeys, and —"

"But we want neither cows nor turkeys," interrupted Carmen, impatiently.

"Quite true; but the Señorita would have horses," answered the matron imperturbably; "and yesterday the General Ramirez was here —"

She paused as though it were unnecessary to say more

of the fate of their horses; and Doña Isabel, starting up impetuously, hurriedly questioned the assembled gossips. Upon the subject of the visit of Ramirez the villagers were eloquent. He and his followers had reached there spent with fatigue and long fasting. In a few moments the place had been sacked of all its poor provision; there had not been enough to give one poor ration to the half-dozen prisoners who were with them. They would have been shot—yes, upon the very spot upon which their graces were standing—but for the prayers of a young girl, who seemed to be the lieutenant's wife; at least she was in his care,—and Ramirez had admitted it could be done as well at the next halt. She herself gave a drink of water to the poor lads for the love of God, and also a tortilla to one among them that she knew,—poor Pepé Ortiz; but he was too weak to swallow it, and had given it to another less wretched than he.

Chata began to cry softly, while Doña Isabel demanded a description of the young girl who had been of the party. This was vague enough; but insufficient as it was it made the thought of further delay impossible,—and the eloquence and gold of Doña Carmen, to which was added the authority of the priest, presently induced the villagers to produce four sorry beasts, upon which with some difficulty the party were secured, for no saddles or panniers were to be had. It was almost sunset when, following the old stage-road, the already wearied travellers set out upon their long and possibly perilous ride.

The women of the village stood for a long time with arms akimbo, looking after the departing travellers. They had divided the money among themselves,—they felt rich and could afford to be pitiful. "The poor Señora has perhaps lost a daughter," said one—"doubtless the fair girl who rode with the lieutenant. The Holy Mother protect her, for the man was in two minds about taking her farther; but the Señor General swore he would run his sabre through him if he cast her off to starve in such a hole. To starve, eh! One who has never lived in my birthplace cannot know how well the pigs fatten here when the tunas are ripe."

"Pshaw! girls are fools, and not worth breaking one's head for," said a second, whose only son kept her rich, when well-laden travellers were plenty. "Where go they now? They are turning toward Las Parras. They will miss the soldiers, or I am no prophet."

"As a prophet one may give thee a thousand lashes, for thou art ever at fault," laughed a third. "But what matters it to us where they go? The road is open to them as to another. They should not go far wrong with a holy little priest to guide them."

XLIV.

Upon the very morning that Doña Isabel and her companion left Guanapila, news which might perhaps have changed their movements had they heard of it flew like wildfire over the city. The convents throughout Mexico had been simultaneously opened under a decree of the Liberal government, and thousands of women dedicated to a cloistered life were thus set free to choose anew their destiny.

Women who for half a century, perhaps, had lived apart from life and love were returned to die amid the turmoils of a home where love for them had ceased, or to pass over seas to seclusion in strange lands. Others, in whom voices as of demons were but just then ceasing to tempt the memory with whispers of the world and its alluring joys, saw those joys actually within their reach, and with dismay sought to turn their eyes away, and prayed for strength to brave the perils of the deep, and bear the homesickness that in a strange country would torment the soul of the cloistered nun as surely as if she had been free to gaze upon the valleys and mountains of the native land she was about to leave forever. Younger women, those to whom the early years of seclusion had brought but disenchantment, were cruelly roused from the stupor of habit which was succeeding pain and presaging content, and with secret regret now clung to the vows they fain would have cast aside forever, or in a few — a very few — cases became that shunned and despised creature, a recreant nun. That night was the signal for horror and tears throughout the land. A wail arose from thousands of families, about to catch a glimpse of their consecrated dear ones, and then to know them banished forever. Such uprooting of ties, such griefs, such domestic woes, are inevitable in all great national or social revolutions.

A certain secrecy had been observed in the preparations for and execution of this stroke of policy, which had indeed been threatened and openly urged as a political necessity, but which in spite of the exile of the archbishops and the suppression of, monasteries had been thought — even by those who acknowledged its probable benefits to the nation — too daring a measure ever to be carried into effect. It had been thought a dream of the arch-iconoclast Juarez. But he was a man whose dreams were apt to come true ; and so it happened upon this summer night, striking admiration and consternation to the hearts of Liberals and Conservatives alike, for there was scarce a family of either party throughout Mexico that was not represented in the vast religious houses which abounded in every town. Into these, overcoming their superstitious scruples, the populace for the first time now penetrated, and learned something of the surroundings and consequent life of those whom for centuries they had supported as saints, dedicated to prayer and fasting for the sins of the people. To their disenchantment and surprise, the people found many of these gloomy piles filled with wide and beautiful chambers, where flowers and musical instruments stood side by side with the altar and *prie Dieu*, and parlors and refectories which opened upon gardens planted with the choicest and most luxuriant shrubs and flowers. There were kitchens too where the choice conserves were made which sometimes found a way to the outer world, and where doubtless other savory dishes were prepared for the saintly sisterhoods. In many of these retreats each nun had her servant, who came and went at her command, and life — if one may judge from the inanimate things and the low whispers that sometimes reached the outer air — was made a soft and sensuous prelude to the celestial harmony of eternity.

But there were others — and they were many — where the utmost austerity pictured by the devout secular mind was practised ; where entered the poor daughter, or she whom the priests perceived had a true vocation, or a deep and agonizing grief, which would keep her faithful to the vows of poverty, of devotion, and obedience. There were none of those amiable daughters of rich families too bountifully supplied with girls, and for whom a dowry to the

Church provided a safe and pleasant home, whence they might easily glide through this life into another, — where female angels would never be esteemed too plentiful, — but where were only the poor, the sorrowful, the despairing; and the well-filled vaults beneath the gloomy chapels attested how rich a harvest death had gleaned in those dreary abodes of penance.

For many days the officers in command at various points had been in possession of orders, — which it is to be conjectured were in many cases transmitted to the abbesses of the principal nunneries, that they might take advantage of this notice by quietly disbanding their sisterhoods and sending each member to her own family, or in communities to the United States or some transatlantic land. But the opportunity for moral martyrdom was not to be destroyed by a mere concession to convenience, and not in a single case was the knowledge acted upon, — except perhaps that in a few convents upon the designated night the nuns refrained from repairing to their dormitories, but prepared for exit, awaited the mandate praying in the lighted chapels; and where this occurred, the mothers superior afterward acquired reputations of special sanctity for the supposed spirit of prophecy which had moved them. But in the majority of these establishments, so absolute was the belief that the threatened invasion would never be attempted, or if attempted would bring upon the intruders the instant vengeance of the Almighty, that no change was made in usual habits, and an outward composure was maintained, which we may believe among the initiated at least disguised many a beating heart filled with genuine horror, or with a wild guilty anticipation from which it shrank in remorse. The world! the world! With a turn of the lock, with scarce more than a step, they would be in it; and then — then!

Guanapila was not, strictly speaking, a convent city. The few small retreats within it were vacated with so little commotion that, except in the houses to which the sisters were removed, nothing was known of the measure until the following morning. But in the much smaller town of El Toro there were whole streets lined on either side with high, massive, and windowless walls which were the façades of vast cloisters. It was with feelings of intense though repressed excitement that Vicente Gonzales placed himself at the head of a small force which was to demand entrance to those formidable but peaceful structures, while the mass of the troops remained at the citadel, ready upon a signal to enforce his authority, whether questioned by Church or people. It was true the populace had declared itself Liberal in sentiment ever since the defeat of Ramirez had left them under the guns of the *Juaristas;* but bred as they had been under the very shadow of these colossal monuments of the Church it was not unlikely that when their sanctity was threatened, the momentary conversion of the citizens to patriotism might yield to zeal in the defence of institutions that had appeared to them as unassailable as the very heavens.

Vicente Gonzales might readily have sent another to fulfil the dubious task before him, — in fact in most cases men of dignity unconnected with the army were chosen as peaceful ambassadors of the power that held the sword; but the hour had arrived for which this man had prayed and fought, — for which he would have prayed and fought had no individual suffering added sharpness to the sting of the thorn that for so long had tormented his nation. He himself, he resolved, would execute the decree that should sweep this great incubus from the land. Perchance among the released he might find one whom he had never consciously for one moment forgotten; he might see her, if but for a moment, as she passed in the throng. He had never ceased to see the yearning, despairing, yet resolute expression upon the young face of Herlinda Garcia, as amid clouds of incense it faded from his sight behind the iron bars that separated her and her sister nuns from the body of the church whence he had witnessed her living entombment. That was in a city far away; most likely she was there now. Yet there was a chance, — a mere chance!

Strangely enough, Ashley Ward had never spoken the name of Herlinda to Gonzales; nor had either mentioned that of Chinita — an inexplicable yet differing motive holding both silent. The rapid events of the war, which had given full occupation to body and mind, had prevented discussion of domestic matters, and there was something in the reticence of Gonzales that forbade aught but deeply serious investigation; and for the present Ward was unprepared to attempt this. They were friends; but there were deeps in the nature of each that the other made no attempt to fathom. Upon this night Ward knew the mind of Gonzales perhaps better than did the man himself; and throughout the unwonted scenes of which he was a mere passive spectator, to him the most engrossing were the emotions that betrayed themselves upon the countenance of the commanding officer.

As Ashley and Gonzales left their quarters together, behind them followed closely a man in a sergeant's uniform, who halted painfully, and across whose face was a livid scar. To those who had heard nothing of the torture he had undergone, Pedro Gomez would have been scarcely recognizable, — for besides the disfiguring scar, there was an expression of vengeful and ferocious daring where before had been but dogged obstinacy and a certain rough kindliness; and to those who had believed him dead, his appearance would have brought a superstitious horror as that of one escaped from the torments of the damned.

Besides these three, several officers and other gentlemen, with a small guard of soldiers, passed out of the citadel afoot, and at a short interval were followed by all the available carriages of the town. What occurred thereafter may perhaps be best described by a translation of the chronicles of the time: —

" One night — one terrible night — a long and unusual sound, a prolonged rumble, was heard in the streets. It seemed shortly as if all the carriages in the city had become mad, now rushing hither, now thither, waking from sleep the peaceful neighborhood; so that each person demanded of the other, ' What is this? ' ' What has happened? ' and no one could answer with certainty the other.'

" While the people wondered, the carriages stopped at the doors of the nunneries, and the gentlemen charged with the commission demanded entrance, and intimated to the nuns the order to leave their cells and refrain from reuniting in cloister.

" ' But, gentlemen, for God's love! '

" ' How can this be? '

" ' His will be done ! '

" ' But where can we go?   Oh, what iniquity ! '

" Such were the phrases that broke the startled stillness of the cloisters, But the commissioners were deaf to all appeals, merely rubbing their hands and saying, —

" ' Let us go.   Let us go on, Señoritas !   We have no time to lose ! '

" Truly the time was limited, — that night only, for perchance by day the gentlemen commissioners would have had a distaste to penetrate the convents ; or perhaps only by night can certain mischievous deeds be carried to the desired exit.

" It is said that some naughty novices upon hearing themselves called señoritas forgot for an instant their grief, and smiled.   There did not lack also of those who had entered the category of grave mothers who did the same ! And after all, was not this a venial and excusable fault? Should not a girl, beautiful and fragrant as a jasmine, become tired of hearing herself addressed every hour and every day in the year as ' Little Mother,' ' My Reverend Mother,' ' How is your Reverence?' . . .

" This was an event which each one was obliged to accept as she would, but none the less surely.   ' Came it from God?   Came it from Satan?'   By either it may have come ; but is it not true that Satan is — ourselves? "

The party headed by Gonzales asked themselves no such questions as these, but cautiously, swiftly, and effectively did the work, which history might criticise.   No time was allowed the nuns for preparation.   Even from the richest convents few articles were carried away as the nuns dispersed.   Perhaps more previous preparation than was suspected or afterward acknowledged had been made ; certain it is that the most magnificent and valuable jewels had disappeared from the vestments of the virgins and saints upon the altars.   But as quickly as might be the weeping and lamenting sisters were placed in carriages and conveyed to houses ready to receive them ; though many in the confusion wandered out into the darkness and rain afoot, and gave a pathetic chapter to the tale of bloodless martyrdom.   As one by one the convents were vacated, the party passed on ; until the smallest and dreariest of those retreats, that which nestled beneath the shadow of the parish church, was reached.

Throughout the work Gonzales had spoken only to give the necessary orders. The measure that in itself had been so dear to his soul was now in its actual execution repugnant to him, — the tears, the sighs, the long processions of black-robed and wailing women distressed his heart, and filled him with shame and anger. As all this continued, his face darkened and a profound melancholy oppressed him. It was raining dismally. In other towns doubtless the same scenes were being enacted. He turned faint, his eyes filled as with blood. Even Ashley Ward, amid the intense interests of the scenes around him, — the views of those grand interiors lighted by the candles borne by the retiring nuns, and the red glare of the soldier's torches, — felt the influence of the deep sadness of this solemn exodus. The clouds of incense sickened him, and through them the glorified Madonnas, the bleeding Christs upon the altars, the troops of black-robed nuns themselves, seemed alike beings of another world, into which he had stepped unbidden. The light shone upon rows and rows of white faces, which looked forth from their wrappings like faces of dead saints. He seemed to see each individual one. He was excited to the utmost; the blood pulsed hotly through every vein, yet a sense of keen disappointment chilled his heart, and unconsciously to himself something of what he read upon the faces of Gonzales and Pedro was reflected upon his own. A profound quiet and solemnity fell upon the party, as they passed the vestibule and penetrated the dim recesses of the Convent of the Martyrs.

There the nuns were all gathered in the chapel, praying and waiting, and the wail of the Miserere stole from the great organ through the dim arches and bare cells. In that place there was nothing of beauty, of grace, of sensuous luxury. The stern austerities of an asceticism scarce surpassed in mediæval days was found behind those massive and windowless walls, which shut out the light, material and moral, of the nineteenth century.

As the men entered the chapel, the nuns fell upon their knees and covered their faces, — all except the abbess, who remained standing to hear the mandate of expulsion.

"Blessed be God!" responded her deep, pathetic voice, "Blessed be God in all his works! Sisters, let us go hence;" and taking up the woful strains when the organ ceased, with each nun adding to them the weird beauty of her voice, the abbess led the way to the portal, and the sisterhood passed into the bleak darkness of the unfamiliar street.

By this time the wind was blowing, — a summer's wind, yet it pierced the bodies upon which for years no air of heaven had blown, — and it was raining heavily. Fortunately many vehicles had gathered at the curb, and ere long the banished nuns were under shelter; and the work of the night was accomplished.

Ashley Ward, with other officers and gentlemen, had busied himself in bestowing the poor ladies as rapidly and commodiously as possible in the carriages, and as the last one turned the corner of the great building, the soldiers fell into line at the word of command; and in a few moments he found himself alone. He discovered this when he turned to speak to Gonzales. He was nowhere to be seen, and Ashley remembered that when he had last seen him it was at the chapel door, watching with pale and anxious countenance the exit of the nuns.

Gonzales had been suffering from a recent wound. Had the fatigue and exposure, and that deadly sickness of crushed and dying hope overcome him? Ashley caught up a torch, which was sputtering and about to expire on the dripping pave, fanned for a moment its flame, and then made his way back into the forsaken building.

He found Gonzales standing on the spot where he had parted from him, and before him stood a man with a flickering torch. Both were in an attitude of extreme dejection; both started as Ashley's footsteps broke the stillness. Pedro — for the second man was he — led the way into the outer darkness, and Gonzales, having in his hand the heavy key which had been delivered by the abbess, turned to lock the abandoned house. He paused and looked to the right and left. The street was utterly forsaken; the rain came in gusts, and it was with much ado that Pedro, turning hither and thither, kept alive the flame of the torch.

Once as he turned, the light fell full upon the face and

figure of Ward; and at the instant an exclamation of incredulous joy, followed by a groan, fell upon their ears. Gonzales dropped the key, and it rang sharply upon the stones at his feet.

"There is a woman here!" he ejaculated breathlessly. Something in the tones had drawn the blood from his heart. "Here! here! a light, Pedro, in God's name!"

The senses of Pedro were even more acute than those of Gonzales and Ward. Not only had he heard the voice, but he knew whose it was, and whence it had come. His torch flashed upon an alcove of the deep wall; and there ensconced they saw the sombre and meanly clad figure of a nun. She had covered her face; her form shook violently.

"Señorita," said Gonzales, recovering himself and respectfully approaching the woman, "forgive us that you are left behind. We thought all had been provided for — all."

"It is I who would have it so, — I who promised myself I would escape," answered the nun, brokenly, yet with an almost fierce intensity. "Have I not prayed and wept for this hour? Could I let it pass? No, no! I lingered — I fled — I could not, would not, go with them. They would have dragged me with them across the seas — away — away from her, — my child! my child!"

She uttered the last words almost in a scream, yet her gaze followed Ward. "Who is he? who is he?" she asked in a feverish whisper. "It is not my murdered angel, — my love, my husband, — it is not he; and yet so like! Oh my God, is it because thou hast forgiven me that thou bringest this vision before me?"

Gonzales started back; gazed eagerly, rapturously at the nun; then rushed to clasp the coarse folds of her drapery. Pedro dropped at her feet. Ward alone uttered her name, — "Herlinda!"

Gonzales bent over her hand, uttering inarticulate words of greeting. She scarcely seemed to hear them. "Vicente, is it thou?" she said faintly. "But he, who is he? — the man of the yellow hair, with the face that at prayer and at penance, asleep and awake, has ever haunted me?"

Herlinda stepped nearer to Ward. Her lips were parted, her eyes aflame; never in all his life before and never

28

again saw he a woman so beautiful as this one in the unsightly garb, so coarse it grazed the skin where it touched it. "No wonder," he thought, "my cousin loved her; he could have done no other, even had he known he was doomed to die for her!"

Ah! the unhappy daughter of the haughty Garcias was far more beautiful that night than ever John Ashley had beheld her. Suffering first had refined, and now the divine inspiration of hope illumined those perfect features. Ashley Ward comprehended this; but Gonzales with horror recalled her words, and thought her mad. "*Maria Sanctissima!*" she cried as the light flashed full on the American, "I am forgiven, that I behold the living likeness of his face."

Ward bent before her, inexpressibly touched. He would have spoken, but at this instant her eyes fell upon the kneeling man at her feet. "It is Pedro,—yes, it is Pedro," Herlinda said in a low voice. "Perhaps he knows of her,—yet, my God, he dares not look at me!"

"Niña, Niña!"

"Speak, Pedro, speak! thou must know of her. Tell me, was Feliz faithful? Is my child well, happy?"

"Merciful God, she is indeed mad!" interjected Gonzales. "O Herlinda, know you not you never were married, never had a child?"

Herlinda turned on him a glance of mingled entreaty and impatience, then raised her eyes piteously toward heaven. "They said I was not married," she moaned brokenly; "but oh, I had a child,—and they took her from me. Oh, if I could have died!"

Gonzales turned from her with a groan. How bitter was the revelation! Married! It could not have been! And a child? Ah! he knew then why a convent had been her doom.

In a broken voice Pedro began to speak. Ashley, with the red glare of the torch he held falling full upon him, seemed to Gonzales a mocking witness of the shame and woe which from Herlinda were reflected upon him, the man who loved her, had ever loved her; yet he felt instinctively that the American had a right to hear, to judge, as well as he. Ah, it was an American who—"An American!" he gasped, and his hand touched the hilt of his sword.

"Niña, Niña!" Pedro was saying. "They brought the child to me. Oh, the sweet child, with its soft, dark eyes, — oh, the child with its ruddy curls! and I remembered all that you had said, my Señorita. I watched over it, I cherished it, it was my own!"

"Thine! thine!" cried the nun clasping her hands, and in her excitement even thrusting him from her. "It could not be! Oh Feliz, Feliz! thou couldst not be so false!"

The tone of incredulity, of horror, in which she spoke pierced Pedro to the quick; yet he answered humbly, "I thought to please you, Niña, to keep her from those you distrusted; and she was happy, oh quite happy, all through her little childhood. You know one can be quite happy playing in the free air."

The released nun burst into sudden tears. "Happy in the free air! Oh yes, yes!" she cried. "Oh, if all these years I could have begged even from door to door with my child, even with the brand of shame upon me! Oh the suffering, the suffering of these long, long desolate years!"

Gonzales stepped to her side, and placed her arm within his own. "Thou shalt be desolate no more, Herlinda," he said, "thou betrayed angel of purity!"

"Betrayed, no!" cried Ashley Ward, looking up. "Deceived perhaps they both were, but the man who was slain as her betrayer believed himself her husband, as she believed herself his wife, — as I believe now she most truly was. Thank God I am here to champion their cause and that of their child!"

Gonzales left Herlinda a moment to embrace Ward in his southern fashion; then supporting her again listened to what Pedro had to say.

The mother's face grew whiter and whiter as the tale proceeded. "That, *that* my child!" she murmured at intervals, and her head sank lower and lower upon her breast. Even Gonzales and Ward heard with amazement the story of Chinita's appearance at the cave where Pedro had lain wounded. "What!" one cried, "has she not been all this time in the house of Doña Carmen? Did you not tell us that in a strange freak of impatience she had hastened there?"

"It was you, Señores, who affirmed it must be she,

when you heard of the young girl who had been taken there, from the Indian whom you captured as a spy of Ramirez," answered Pedro, with the humble cunning of the true ranchero ; "and why should your servant contradict you, when Chinita herself had commanded otherwise — "

"And where in God's name is she now?" demanded Ward. "You know who I am. You know all this time I could not have rested tranquil had I thought — "

" Have no anxiety, Señor," answered the man with his old sullenness. "And I swear to you, Niña, she is safe, quite safe. She is with a woman who can guard her well. She is gone to seek the man who murdered her father. Ah, Niña, your daughter has the blood of the Garcia ; she will avenge you ! "

Herlinda sank with a moan. Ashley would have raised her, but Gonzales motioned him back. There was a house at a little distance where a widow and her daughters dwelt, and thither he bore her.

It was then at the middle hour between midnight and dawn ; and long before light, after a hurried consultation, the three men met again before the widow's door. All arrangements had been made for the brief transfer of the command of the troops. Gonzales, Ashley, and Pedro acted as outriders for a strong military coach drawn by four fleet mules. Into this stepped Herlinda and the widow, both dressed as respectable gentlewomen ; and before the people of El Toro wakened from their deep sleep that followed the excitement of the early night, the travellers were far upon the road, and though the way was long and rough were gaining fast upon the diligence which bore Doña Isabel, her daughter, and Chata.

XLV.

On the evening when Doña Isabel and her companions
set forth from the village upon their toilsome pilgrimage
to Las Parras, two women leaned against the gate-posts
at the entrance to the garden where the mistress of Tres
Hermanos and the mother of the administrador had parted
so many years before, and looked wearily along the silent
road. One would not have been surprised to hear that
during all these years no other mortal had approached the
place, for the air of neglect it had worn then had deepened
into that of utter abandonment. It looked not merely disused, but actually shunned. The gate had fallen from its
hinges and lay broken upon the rank coarse grass and
weeds, which thrusting themselves between the bars filled
the paths. Thick clumps of cacti and stunted uncultivated fruit and flowers, with manzanita and other common
shrubs of the country, had outgrown and outrooted the
feebler growths, and almost hid the low front of the solid
but dismantled building, upon which the iron-ribbed shutters hung forlornly like broken armor on a battered image.

The sun and wind and rains had done their work unchecked in all these years, aided by the revolution, which
had torn and scathed whatever had attracted its greedy
hand and then passed on, leaving desolation to continue
or repair the work of destruction. The vines, which had
at first served as a graceful drapery, hung so heavily on
every porch and wooden projection of the house that they
had broken down the frail supports, and added to the
general appearance of riot and disorder; while their
matted masses offered a defiant obstruction to any adventurous comer. Yet these women had forced a way into
the dark and mouldy rooms, and found a certain pleasure
and security in their seemingly impenetrable and forbidding aspect.

"We have been here three days," said the younger,
who even in the declining light one might see was a mere

girl, while her companion, though small, was old in face
and figure, — not with the dignity of actual age, but with
a sort of lithe grace and abandon, which comes from years
of free and careless action. "We have been three days
waiting, yet he has not come! You may be mistaken.
How can you reckon upon what a man like Ramirez will
do? He is not like a blind man, always led by his dog
upon the same round."

"Necessity and habit are the dogs that lead him," said
the woman with a slight laugh. "Fortune is against him ;
he has been beaten from every stronghold. I know this
is the hole he will creep into at last."

"And the people here, they would save him?" said
Chinita, musingly. "He has ever spared them, ever protected them, that he might have a safe refuge in time of
need. Here, here, but for us he would be safe? — but for
us, Dolores?"

"Ah, he is not the first who does not find even nests
where he hoped to find birds," answered the woman called
Dolores. "To-day he is laughing at the little troop of
Liberals patrolling these hills ; he will make a way between them. Yes, you will see ; here, here, upon this
very road, we shall see him flash by like a meteor, and
then be lost. But my eyes can trace him ; my hand will
be able to point the way he has gone."

The woman had unwittingly conjured up a vision that
thrilled the imagination of the listener. "Oh!" she cried
with a sudden gesture of repulsion and weariness, "I am
sick of this mean and miserable life. Would to God I
had gone to him as I vowed to do. Do not tell me he
would have laughed at my rage! No, no! a man could
not laugh at the girl who accused him of the murder of
her father ; who stood before him to remind him of all
his secret and unnatural crimes! Ah, I cannot endure
this silent, creeping enmity. Three times already by
our means he has been tracked and driven from his
stronghold ; once but for Pepé he would have been
killed, — Ruiz himself would have killed him!"

"Fox against tiger!" cried Dolores, contemptuously.
"Bah! the idiot might have known that with the smell
of blood in the air, not even the shadow of the cross
would save him if he fell into the hands of Ramirez ;

yet he rushed on his fate. And for Ramirez there waits for him a doom more just than death on the battlefield, — though you, who warned Pepé to save him, are but a faint-hearted weakling."

"Would you have him die without knowing the revenge that followed him?" cried Chinita. "What would death alone be to such a man as he? It was you, yourself, who first urged Pepé to leave us, — not that he might kill, but if need were save, Ramirez."

"It is true," answered Dolores, mollified; yet she fixed upon Chinita a long and penetrating gaze, which seemed to read her very soul. "But you are a strange, strange creature, — a peasant for all your pride. He is still more a grand gentleman to stare at with fear than a murderer and robber to you."

Chinita's face turned white. The reproach of the woman stung her, yet she felt it was just. "Oh, if I were a man!" she presently muttered; "oh, if I were a man!"

"Yes, the way would have been short then," said Dolores. "Just a knife-thrust, and the debt would have been paid. But the revenge of women can be a thousand times more deep, more sweet, if one has the patience to wait."

"Patience!" exclaimed Chinita in that shrill, metallic voice that indicates a mental tension so violent and long continued that every chord of the nervous system vibrates painfully at a word. "Have I not had patience? Have I not waited at your bidding until I seem to live in a frenzy of fear lest he should escape, and never hear, never see me, never know who I am? And what have I gained? Ruiz is dead; Pepé perhaps is dead. Ah, if I had spoken! Had Ramirez known that I live, it might have saved them both!"

The woman's answering laugh had more of scorn than mirth in it. "Be quiet, child!" she said. "You are young. You think Ramirez has a conscience, and that you would have roused it to torment him. Pshaw! I will arm you with a better weapon; a little patience — perhaps to-morrow — and you will see!"

"Mysteries! always mysteries!" exclaimed Chinita, with increased impatience. "*Santa Maria!* why do you not push back that black kerchief from your brows?

Have you the mark of a jealous woman's knife across
your forehead? Is your hair white, or — or — " She
paused, with a horrid suspicion flashing through her mind.
Was this woman, with whom she had daily and nightly
associated for weeks, a victim of that species of leprosy
known as the " painted "? Was some dread trace of it to
be seen upon that constantly covered head? Dolores with
careless grace had raised and clasped her hands above
the unsightly kerchief. The bared arms were clear and
fair ; only the deep-lined face they encircled looked old,
but care, not disease, had marked it. She looked at
Chinita through the growing dusk with an inscrutable expression in her almond-shaped and beautiful eyes. They
were eyes that still might fascinate at will. Chinita drew a
little nearer to her, and sighed deeply. There was a sense
of guilt upon the girl's mind since she had heard of the
death of Ruiz ; a sickening apprehension, too, for the fate
of Pepé Ortiz.

Dolores read her thoughts. She dropped one hand
from her head upon the young girl's shoulder. There
seemed something magnetic in the touch. Chinita, though
she would rather have resisted, yielded to it, — like a nettle grasped in a strong hand. " Silly one," said the
woman soothingly, " fret not yourself for Ruiz. Ramirez
knew him better than did you. He had had long years to
con the lesson in. It is well for the weak defenceless
creatures of the earth that these wild beasts attack and
destroy one another ! "

Chinita looked unconvinced. In spite of doubts, she
had had a certain pride and solace in the belief that Ruiz
would prove true to Ramirez, — true through his love for
her. She had purposely left him ignorant of the change
in her own views and feelings in regard to Ramirez that
he might be free to act upon his own impulses and convictions. She knew not what she would have had him do,
yet all the same he had disappointed her. She had no
clews to the motives of Ruiz, other than those Dolores
suggested to her, and there was an uncertainty and vagueness overhanging him which made him in her eyes a victim
to his love for her, and a fresh cause for accusation of the
man who seemed destined utterly to bereave and despoil
her. Strangely enough, in her wildest excitement Chinita

had never formulated for herself any definite mode of action when she should see Ramirez, — as see him, accuse, defy him she would ! There had been a conviction in her mind that in her the ghosts of the innocent he had slain, the shame, — which with strange perversity he had shrunk from when it menaced his family pride in the person of Herlinda Garcia, — the contempt and hatred of his wronged sister, would all rise to confront and overwhelm him. That which should follow, time, circumstance would determine ; but that the wild fever of her passion would be satisfied she would not doubt. She had longed with an ever increasing excitement to find herself before Ramirez, and to pour forth her wrongs in burning words. Yet this woman Dolores, with a fascination even greater than the unconscious one that Ramirez himself had exerted over her, had withheld her from her purpose, had even led her to gain the secrets of the chieftain's plans from his most trusted confidants, — the young girl reddened with shame and anger, yet with flattered vanity, when she remembered that the sight of her beauty had been more potent than the gold of Dolores. Chinita had not guessed that she had been purposely employed to act the part of a spy, and had resented deeply the fact that her discoveries had more than once been transmitted to Gonzales, and that her revenge was supposed to be gratified by the consequent defeat which had overcome Ramirez. Her longing was for a more dramatic, more direct revenge. Pedro and Dolores could plot and scheme for the silent overthrow of him who had wronged them ; they gloried in their astuteness that made him an unsuspicious victim, while Chinita writhed under it, and only the promise that in Las Parras she should accuse Ramirez face to face had made endurable to her the life of secret intrigue and absolute disguise and constant change that she had led for weeks. The element of peril, it is true, had stimulated her adventurous spirit ; but she would fain have been in the midst, not hovering a ready fugitive upon the edge of the fray.

When weeks before Chinita had, after her faintness, opened her eyes in the low, rocky cave in which Pedro lay, it had been to find him an almost unrecognizable mass of wounds and bruises, lying on a sheepskin pallet, gazing at her with wide-distended eyes, and ejaculating

in tones of dismay, mingled with incredulous delight,
" What have I done? Oh God! is it possible that she
has come to me,—the miserable, dying Pedro?"

" Yes, yes, Pedro, I am here!" she cried staggering
to her feet. " Ah, the American thought I had forgotten
thee; but thou wert in my heart all the time that he
talked. Ah, though I am of other blood, it is thou that
hast saved me! They would have thrust me out to die.
I will cling to thee while thou livest; I will avenge thee
when thou diest!"

" Hush!" muttered Pedro faintly, as she stooped and
kissed his hand, bedewing it with her tears. " Ah, I
shall not die, now you have come. Did I not tell you,"
he asked, turning to a figure beside Chinita, " that I
should live if I could know she loved me?"

" And this is the girl you have nurtured?" asked the
stifled voice of a woman. She was not as tall as Chinita,
and she held a candle up close to the face of the girl to
look at her. Chinita was spent with fatigue; moreover
there were tears on her face, and she resented the inspection, pushing away the woman's hand rudely. Yet
it was not that of a servant, nor of a woman of the lower
class. Even in the excitement of the moment Chinita
was conscious of wondering who and what this person
was. How came she there in the cave among these
fugitives?

" But for her I should have been dead already," Pedro
was saying. " She has wondrous skill and knowledge of
surgery and herbs. But," he added, in a low, apologetic
voice, " she knows all. I have talked in my delirium. I
could not help it. You will pardon me,—if I die you will
pardon me?"

" I have nothing to pardon!" cried Chinita. " What!
you think because my mother lives I would hide her name?
No, no! I have endured enough for her cowardice and the
shame of Doña Isabel. No, no! let me but see Ramirez,
— this Leon Vallé, — and though it be before all the world,
I will declare who I am. The American, Ashley Ward,
says he will claim me as his cousin. Pepé must ride and
tell him I am here, and we will have vengeance together
for the cruel deeds of Ramirez. You shall be avenged,
Pedro, you shall be avenged!"

The sick man's eyes glistened. As she spoke, Chinita's face had glowed with an unrelenting and cruel intensity of purpose. The woman at her side had never once removed her eyes from her. No one was noticing her; had they done so, they would have beheld an extraordinary series of changes pass over her dark but mobile face, — suspicion, delight, doubt, alarm, conviction. · Suddenly she seized Chinita's hand, and pressed it to her heart; it was beating so tumultuously that the young girl drew back startled. The woman thrust her hands under the loose folds of the black kerchief that draped her head with a sombre yet Oriental grace, then withdrawing them caught a stray lock of Chinita's hair, and burst into a long, low, triumphant laugh.

Chinita drew herself away, alarmed and offended. Pepé had come in; and looking at her anxiously he said, "Nina, do not mind her. Esteban tells me she is a mad woman; yet she does no harm. She does not know what she talks of, and one moment denies what she has said at another. It would not be strange if she should tell you some dreadful tale, and afterward laugh, and say grief had made her mad!"

"And so it has," cried the woman. "Ah yes, I have been mad; but that is past. Yes, yes. Life of my soul," turning to Chinita, "how beautiful thou art! And the hair, it is a miracle! In all the world there should be no other with such hair. Thou hast had good fortune, Pedro, to bring up such a child. She is an angel. Ah, it is as if I had seen her all my life! And thou hast a spirit to match thy face," she added turning again to Chinita. "Thou canst not brook a wrong. Well, well! we will make common cause; and some day — soon, soon we will stand together before Leon Vallé with such a tale, such a revenge, that even he will sink before it. To think that after all these years, I shall turn against him the dagger with which he has pierced me!"

"Who are you? What do you know of me?" cried Chinita, shuddering, though she understood that the weapon of which the stranger spoke was no material tool. "Why should you join with me, or I with you? No, no; when Pedro is able, we will go away, you your way, and I mine!"

"Our ways lie together!" cried the woman, excitedly. "The one without the other would fail. Oh! you think me mad, but I am not. I could tell you things, — but no, I will wait; perhaps thou hast not even heard of me. Ah! how many years is it since I disappeared from the world, that I have been forgotten?"

Pedro raised himself upon his elbow painfully, and gazed at her with a long and eager scrutiny. "I know you now," he said, "though I never saw you but once, and then you were beautiful as the Holy Madonna on the high altar at Pueblo."

"Yes," she interrupted; "I am Dolores, whom Vallé loved. Ah, you think that strange, because my beauty is gone, and I am old, and like a witch, living in this murky cave! Where else should I go — I, whom he stole away and betrayed, and despoiled and forsook?"

"But you are rich," said Pepé in wonder, and in a tone that seemed to condone the rest.

"Rich!" she said scornfully. "Rich! yes, for such needs as mine. Rich! he used to give me jewels a queen might have been proud of. He thought I wasted, lost, destroyed them, as he would have done, but I kept them, — kept them for my child. Ah, I knew she would be beautiful, would be worthy of the rarest and costliest I could give her. Ah, I would give her jewels! such jewels as would buy her love, were she as capricious, as hard, as Ramirez himself."

Chinita drew back from her, with a certain hauteur, a certain loathing upon her face. "I have heard of you," she said coldly. "You chose your lot. If you have wrongs, they can be nothing to mine. See" — and she pointed to Pedro — "what Ramirez has done but now; while but for his murderous knife my father would have lived, and my mother would not have been obliged to hide her disgraced head in a convent, and I should not have been left a pauper at the gate of my mother's house."

"There can be no wrongs greater than these?" said the woman half interrogatively, half affirmatively. "Yet listen! He stole me away from my husband; I swear I did not go willingly, though I loved him, — oh my God, how I loved him! For him I died to the world. I forsook the father who was dear to me as life. I lived a life of infamy, hiding in obscure villages, in mountain huts, in caves when need were. I bore him children; but they died, — all died as though there was a curse upon them. That angered him; then he grew cold, then false and cruel. One day a captive was brought into the camp for ransom, — a captive he himself had made. He sent to me to look at the man and to set a price upon his head. I went, as he told me, in gay attire, with jewels blazing on my arms and neck, a diadem upon my head. When the prisoner looked up and saw me, with the price of my shame as he thought upon me, he staggered, gasped, and fell down dead. He was my father. My senses fled, yet when another child was born they returned to me. She was strong and beautiful. I clasped my treasure; but my heart burned against her father. I swore I would leave him, that I would hide the child where he never should discover her. Fool! fool! that I was! When I woke next day, for in my weakness I slept, the babe was gone, — dead they told me; gone too the pretty clothing I had made, the little trinkets I had placed about her neck. But the blessed prayers I had bought from the holy nuns of La Piedad were not in vain! No, no! wretch, demon, that he was!"

Chinita's heart beat suffocatingly. "What! you think the child was still living?" she said.

"I know it! I know it!" cried Dolores. "I feel it here, — here in my heart, which beats for her. And sometime, when I find that child, if I do find her, think you she will love me? Think you she will hate her father as I do? Think you she will avenge my wrongs and hers?"

"But if he loved her," said Chinita; "if he meant to separate her from — from such a woman as you had been! Oh, I know you have suffered, that you have reason for vengeance; but—" she cried hysterically, striking her hands together, terribly moved, she knew not why. The strange woman broke into sobs, piteous to hear. Chinita clasped her hands. "But you would not have her — your child — his child — hate the man you loved?"

"Hate him!" echoed Dolores. "I would have her hate him with such hate as she would bear toward the fiends of hell. I would have her know him as you know him, — the insatiable monster who wrecked the happiness of

a sister too fond, even when most foully wronged, to seize
the vengeance that was within her grasp. Ah, Doña
Isabel it was who set him free to murder, to betray, to
wrench the child from its maddened mother, and cast it
out by the first rude and careless hand that would do his
will! My God! were you his child could you have pity?
Would you not feel your wrongs, — the wrongs of the
mother who bore you?"

Dolores spoke with the wild excitement of one who for
years had brooded on this theme. Chinita herself seemed
to be struggling with some fantasy of a disordered brain.
The woman actually glared upon her, as if on her reply
hung her destiny. Overcome by the unexpected demand
upon her sympathy, — a demand that the peculiar circumstances of her life made irresistibly impressive, —
Chinita shrank with horror at the tumult of emotion which
revealed to her mind the possibilities of her own passionate nature.

"Tell me no more! Ask me no more!" she cried.
"Ah, if I were his daughter! But no, I am the daughter
of Herlinda Garcia, and of the man he murdered in secret.
Yes, I will seek Ramirez out. I — I — O God! I know
not what I will do, but I will have justice! revenge!
revenge!"

The girl ended with a scream, and fell down, burying
her head on Pedro's shoulder. The wounded man, his
ghastly face pressed close against her twining hair, looked
appealingly to the excited woman who stood over them.
There was scorn, rage, intense offence upon her face; but
slowly they died out, and she turned away with the weary
air of one in whom some periodic excess of passion or
madness had wrought its work and brought its consequent
exhaustion. A half hour later she brought the girl some
food, wonderfully dainty for the place and its resources,
and gently fed and soothed her. Pepé and Pedro looked
on wonderingly. All that had been said had passed so
quickly that they had not realized that aught of consequence had happened; but in the quiescent attitude of
Chinita, and the strange calm that had fallen upon the excited and erratic woman, they instinctively felt that a new
phase of life had begun for them. A new spirit was in
future to lead and rule them; and it dwelt in the frame of

this half-crazed woman, who had declared herself mistress of the cave. The men thenceforth seemed led by a spell; and to the same spell Chinita gradually succumbed.

This had been the first meeting of Chinita with the woman who stood talking with her nearly two months later at the garden gate of Las Parras. They had left the cave weeks before, — Pepé and Pedro, the latter still bruised and maimed, to join the troops of Gonzales; and Chinita, unable to resist the influence of Dolores, followed rebelliously with swift and unerring movement the fortunes of Ramirez. By what arguments Pedro had been won to consent to separate from his foster-child, and to maintain silence concerning her to Ashley, can be but guessed; though certain it is that Chinita on her part reminded him of the promise he had made Herlinda to protect her child from Doña Isabel, to whose care she justly suspected Ashley Ward would strive to return her. Meanwhile Dolores adroitly fostered in the girl's mind that hope of a peculiar and swift revenge, which was to satisfy at once the many wrongs that in those diverse lives were clamorous for justice; while an intense anticipation urged the gatekeeper to hasten without delay to join the Liberal army, — the anticipation of that event which presented to his mind such wondrous possibilities. The convents once opened, would Herlinda claim her child? Would she by some strange miracle confront Leon Vallé and her proud mother with the proof of that which Ashley Ward had in spite of adverse law and custom declared still possible, — the proof of her marriage with the American who had been slain without accusation, without the possibility of defence?

Pedro could not reason; he could but doggedly wait, and guard with silent fidelity and ferocity the charge that had been given him. That a superior intelligence, an undeclared authority potent as an armed power, had for a time wrested Chinita from him, made him only the more tenacious when once again he held her in his grasp. His foster-child while in the mountains with the woman whose life was bound in the same interests, the same mysteries, as her own, was safe from the possibilities of removal from his cognizance.

Pedro was asked no questions which he cared not to

answer, when he presented himself among the Liberal forces. Ashley, tranquil in the belief that Chinita was with Doña Carmen in Guanapila, avoided more than casual mention of her name ; and Pedro jealously guarded his secret, and patiently waited the moment he superstitiously believed would come, — the moment which, when it did come, gave him the sharpest sting he had ever known in his stoical existence ; when Herlinda Garcia cried in uncontrollable horror and dismay, "What! you, — *you* have brought up my child? She was given to *you!*"

On the journey from El Toro there was but one thought in the mind of him who had served with such blind faithfulness. For the first time a doubt tormented him. "Would the beautiful, uncontrollable idol of his heart satisfy the longing — the years of longing — of the woman who freed from her bonds was hastening to claim her daughter and acknowledge her before the world?" As the hours passed, Pedro shunned the eyes of Herlinda, though they looked upon him with a grateful affection that should have been at once an invitation to confidence and a recompense of his long fidelity. Yet with the remembrance of Chinita ever before him, the glance of Herlinda seemed that of accusation and reproof. Her words rang like a knell in his heart. He, who knew the vices and virtues of the two castes which he and the still beautiful woman represented, knew that like oil and water they were irreconcilable, and understood the full significance of that involuntary cry, "What! *you*, — *you* have brought up *my* child?"

XLVI.

A LEAGUE or less from the village of Las Parras there
stood — and perhaps still stands — a small chapel, built,
no one knows in fulfilment of what pious vow, at the
entrance to a mountain pass of the roughest and most
dangerous sort alike from the forces of Nature and of
humanity. Likely enough some rich hidalgo, escaping
from brigands, raised here the humble pile, and vowed
that the lamp should ever burn before the Virgin and
her blessed Child. But through the long years of war,
as a pious ranchera had said in holy horror, the blessed
Babe had remained in darkness. But some time after midnight, one rainy night, a sudden flash of flame lighted up
not only the dingy altar but the whole of the small mouldy
interior of the chapel, and a scene was revealed which a
passing monk might have viewed with reverence, so nearly
must it have copied one that may have been common
enough when Joseph and Mary journeyed to Jerusalem,
eighteen hundred years and more ago.

This thought indeed entered the mind of a man who
riding through the drizzling rain caught a glimpse of the
unusual light through the unguarded doorway, and reining
his horse gazed curiously in. At first the place seemed to
him full of women and jaded beasts ; then he saw there
were but four of each, and that one of the human creatures
was a man, — a priest. The women, — good heavens ! they
were the Señora Doña Isabel Garcia, and the girl whom
he had once seen under circumstances almost as extraordinary, — she whom he knew as the daughter of Ramirez
and the foster-child of Don Rafael. Of the other woman
he scarcely thought, yet he instinctively guessed she was
Doña Carmen. Ashley Ward looked round in bewilderment. Only that day some definite account of what had
occurred at Tres Hermanos had reached him, told by a
man who had been with the administrador and his mother

29

in their vain endeavors to trace the girl who had been so boldly spirited away. The search had been long delayed because of the illness of Doña Feliz; but once begun, it had been prosecuted with untiring zeal. Not a village, scarce a hut throughout that region had been unvisited, yet all in vain.

Ashley had heard the tale with deepest sympathy. Oh inconceivable obtuseness! that it had not once occurred to him or to Gonzales that the girl of whom they had heard as sojourning with Doña Carmen, and whom he had believed to be Chinita, might prove to be her vanished playmate, — simply because the remembrance of the house of Doña Carmen had slipped from their minds when their supposed knowledge of the movements of Chinita made Doña Carmen's young guest no longer an object of interest to them, simply because the means adopted by Ramirez for the security of Chata would never have suggested themselves to minds less daring, less original than his own. Ashley Ward turned from the doorway dazed. The presence of these personages in such a place, at such a time, seemed unreal, bewildering, ominous.

Upon the heavy sand the horse that Ashley rode had made so little noise that it had not roused the miserable travellers as they cowered wet and shivering around the sputtering fire, upon which the priest with unhesitating hands threw some dry portion of a wooden railing and the broad cover of a sacred book of music. Vain sacrifice! for being of parchment it but curled and blackened, yet would not burn any more than would the bare stone floor upon which the welcome embers lay.

Turning back a few paces Ward encountered the carriage he had accompanied thither. With bowed heads, endeavoring thus to shelter their faces from the mist, General Gonzales and the servant Pedro rode, one on either side of the heavy travelling carriage. Just as Ward appeared they caught sight of the light. The coachman and his helper, half dead as they were from want of sleep, saw it too, and all the mules were stopped as though transfixed. The men began to mumble prayers, crossing themselves with unction. Gonzales, following his habit of caution as well as the motion of Ward, rode softly forward to reconnoitre.

Before the occupants of the carriage had time to question the meaning of the stoppage, Gonzales had returned. His face was white with excitement as he dismounted and opened the door of the vehicle.

"Señorita," he said in a voice that shook from suppressed emotion, " a wonderful thing has happened!"

Herlinda leaned eagerly forward. She caught the gleam of the light and the grim outline of the chapel against the leaden sky. "Is my child — Leon, my uncle — here?" she gasped.

"No, no! that would not be so strange; we may perhaps at any moment encounter them. But your mother, your sister, — they are in yonder church, drenched, wretched; travellers seemingly more anxious, more eager than ourselves. From a word I heard, they too seek — your child."

Gonzales spoke the last two words with evident difficulty and repugnance. Herlinda did not notice that. She scarce had heard more than the words, " Your mother, your sister." In trembling haste she descended from the carriage. Instinctively she clasped the arm of Ashley Ward to support her through the inequalities of the roadway; and followed by Gonzales and Pedro, who had dismounted, she sped with surprising fleetness to the open door of the chapel.

At the sound of approaching footsteps, those within sprang to their feet in terror. Even the brutes hurtled together within the very rail of the altar, leaving free the space between the fire and the low arch beneath which the intruders stood. The women stood panting, their hands clasped upon their hearts, their lips parted, their eyes staring wildly. Doña Isabel was foremost. She first saw as in a vision her daughter, whom she believed still within convent walls, supported by the arm of the American. She sank upon her knees; her tongue clave to the roof of her mouth.

"Mother," said Herlinda in a voice which gave conviction of the reality of her presence, " I am no ghost. The convents have been opened, — I am free. Where is my daughter? You took her from me, — give her back to me. My child! my child!"

She advanced into the chapel with a gesture so earnest,

so impassioned, that it seemed that of concentrated power and anguish combined.

Doña Isabel bowed her head on her hand. Under the red light of the fire her form seemed to shrink and wither. "Have mercy! oh, Herlinda, have mercy!" she moaned. "Your child is not here. I am seeking her, oh with what grief, what anguish! Ah, my God, it is true, — all, all that you can say to me!" She raised her eyes and they fell upon Gonzales. "I thought to save your honor and mine. That there still might be love and joy for you, I gave the child to Feliz to do with as she would. I did not think, I could not think —"

"Cruel, cruel mother!" cried Herlinda, "and false Feliz! Oh, what reproaches will be bitter enough, sharp enough, to heap upon her! She promised me she would love my child, care for it, protect it, — yes, even from you, unnatural mother that you were! Yet together you have degraded, perhaps brought about the ruin of, my child! I have been shut in from all the world, — and yet I am not the weak girl I was. No, the heart and brain of a woman grow even in utter darkness. You had no right to thrust my child away. No, she was mine, — come disgrace, come scorn, what would, she was mine. You tore her from me, — give her back to me!"

While this extraordinary scene took place, Chata with indescribable emotion recognized the pale impulsive face of the nun of El Toro, — so pale still, so worn, yet so strangely young, and lighted by the intense and resolute spirit of a wronged and noble woman.

"Yes, give me back my child!" reiterated Herlinda. "Ah, Mother, I read your heart; I know now better than I did then your motives for utterly ignoring, utterly denying my connection with the American. Your brother killed him: it was to shelter him, Leon Vallé, as much as to hide what you believed my shame, that you tore my baby from me. You resolved that there should be neither wonder nor question that could incriminate your idol. Oh, a sister's love, a sister's sacrifice is beautiful; but where in all the world before has it been stronger, more prescient than that of the mother for her child?"

Doña Isabel raised her hands above her head as though to ward off some crushing blow. Carmen rushed forward and caught her sister's hand. "Herlinda," she cried, "say no more. I am your sister — I am Carmen! Oh, I have always known there was a mystery; yet I have loved you, believed you true, believed you pure. You were almost a child, — you knew not the evil!"

"I was not a child!" returned Herlinda, proudly, yet clasping her sister with a grateful joy. "For all my trusting love I would not have stooped to sin. I was married. Yes," she added defiantly, "though all the world deny it, I was married. God grant that I may one day stand before my husband's murderer, — oh, with that word I will overwhelm him. What! he, the ravisher, the assassin, think to avenge *my* honor!"

The form of the excited woman dilated as she spoke. Through the dim chapel her voice pealed with a ring of purity and truth, more clear than the tone of silver bells. There was a clamor of answering voices. Even the priest started forward, but Chata caught his flowing gown and whispered him in broken accents, —

"Oh, for the pity of God hide me. Let her not see me! Oh, this is too terrible, too terrible!" She shook with dread. "Madre Sanctissima, it will kill me if her eyes fall upon me! I am the daughter of the man she seeks. O Virgin of Succors, pity me!"

The burly person of the priest supported and sheltered the stricken and trembling girl. "Courage, courage!" he whispered. "Thou shalt plead for him. For thy sake she will forego the claims of justice, — she will forgive!" He naturally attributed her emotion to apprehensions for her father's fate. "Yes, even I will plead with her."

But in the brief space of this interference there had been a movement at the door, and a strange voice was heard. Gonzales — who throughout had stood just back of Herlinda, chafing that he was not at her side, for he would have championed her before the world — disappeared for a moment; then returning, strode forward to the fire and raised Doña Isabel with a not unkindly though imperious hand.

"Señora," he said, "I have this moment heard news of Ramirez, brought by an escaped prisoner, one of your own men, Pepé Ortiz by name. As we suspected, the defeated and desperate chief is on his way to, perhaps has entered, Las Parras. There is no time to be lost. With him — accusing him, for such was her mad purpose — we may find your daughter's child. Oh, would to God," he added with fervor, " I had known this horrible blight upon Herlinda's young life! I would have sheltered, I would have sustained her. I would have appealed to Rome."

Doña Isabel looked at Gonzales in a dazed way, slightly swaying as she stood. "Thou wert ever noble, ever true," she said dreamily. "Thou lovedst her. But Leon? She spoke of Leon. Then it is true! He did indeed murder the American. But he is dead; he is dead."

The mind of the poor lady seemed wandering. She stood looking about her with an awful smile. Gonzales saw that she did not connect the name of Ramirez with her brother. Illness, exertion, and the intense emotions of that hour had made it impossible for her to receive any fresh impressions, or even to recall those that perhaps had once faintly suggested themselves and had faded. She was conscious of but one thought, one hope. " Herlinda's child, Herlinda's child!" she repeated again and again. " O God, to find, to give back the child!"

The agonized woman would have clasped the hand of Gonzales appealingly, but he had turned and led Herlinda from the place. Chata, gliding toward Doña Isabel, drew the arm of the suffering lady around her neck, and murmuring fond words, thus stood supporting her. And thus some moments later Ashley Ward found them. The young girl seemed in his eyes the very embodiment of Tenderness supporting Despair.

Ashley took her hand. "Oh, Chata!" he said, "what a fearful error this has been! And Chinita, where shall we find her? Poor girl, poor girl! God grant she has not found that man; the horrible fascination he held over her might prove more fatal than her newly-sworn hatred. Come, come, let us hasten. It is at least certain that Ramirez is at this moment in Las Parras."

" Chinita!" cried Chata, her heart sickening. " What, is Chinita the child of Doña Herlinda? I love her, but oh she — the Señorita Herlinda! No, no, it cannot be!"

Ashley smiled drearily. " The eagle is sometimes found in a dove's nest," he said. " Ah, with such a mother what a glorious woman that strange defiant creature might

have become! But what powers for good have been debased in those low associations among which she was
thrown!"

The young man stopped, remembering Doña Isabel;
but she had moved away. She was already at the door.
Gonzales, who was returning for her, led her silently to
the carriage. The widow who had been with Herlinda
had dismounted and joined Chata and the priest, as they
issued from the gloomy chapel. The poor woman looked
confused and wretched; it was a comfort to her to hear
the muttered benediction of the friar.

Chata mounted the sorry beast on which she had come,
despite the remonstrance of Ashley. "No, no, I cannot
bear the accusing gaze of the Señorita Herlinda," she
protested. "You, Don 'Guardo, know who I am. My
place is at Leon Vallé's side, not here. O God, would
that it were not so!"

The rain had ceased. There was a streak of dawn in
the sky. The road lay like a pale yellow serpent, which
grew brighter as they followed its sinuous twinings among
the hills. There was a slight accident, which detained the
carriage; but Chata, accompanied by Pepé, — who had recognized her with amazement, and who gave her a brief
account of all that had happened in the life of Chinita
since they had parted, — hastened on as speedily as was
possible to her jaded beast. Just at the dawn she found
herself entering the straggling town; and suddenly the
mass of verdure beyond a broken wall which they were
skirting, and over which she was gazing with eyes as
heavy as the dripping herbage, sparkled as with a thousand diamonds. The sun had risen; and facing it — his
eyes so dazzled that the figures upon the roadway were to
him like the scattered trees, mere black, shapeless masses
— was the object of her dread, yet also at that moment
of her fondest anguish bloody and travel-stained with the
marks of battle and flight upon him, the wreck of what
she had last seen him.

Filial duty and womanly pity supplied the place of that
love which she could not conjure even then, and with a
cry she drew rein at the prostrate gate; and to the amazement of Pepé, who knew nothing of the relations between
the young girl and the defeated chieftain, she sprang to

the ground and rushed to the embrace of the hunted man. Looking back she saw the others approaching, and sought to repel them by an entreating gesture. Her voice was heard in warning; but Ramirez heeded it no more than he did the sound of wheels and the tread of horses on the roadway. He had known of late such strange vicissitudes and such unaccountable experiences, which had been so unforeseen, often so disastrous yet fleeting, that they seemed the phantasmagoria of a frightful dream. These noises, these figures, were but the same to his stunned senses. But this girl in his arms, who called him father, — she was real flesh and blood, and thrilling with life. He clung to her with rapture; and as he would have done in a dream, he saw her there without surprise, — only with a vague bewilderment, a fear that she too would fade away. No! She clung to him with tears, as though seeking to protect him from some menaced danger.

Ah, he understood: this man who had reached them was the American who had accused him at the grave of him whom he had murdered. Great God! Had beings of this world and the other combined against him? There was Pedro, or his ghost; there too was Herlinda! Yes, though it was years since he had seen her, and then only for a moment in her lover's arms, he knew her instantly.

Ramirez recoiled before her glance. His arms fell from Chata. The released nun, who had not known that the young girl had been of their company, thrust her aside, then caught her hand and looked searchingly into her face. Her own face quivered as she looked. It grew whiter and whiter still, as Chata raised her eyes and returned the gaze.

"I saw you from the convent grate — at El Toro," said Herlinda, breathlessly.

Carmen's face brightened like that of one who solves a joyful mystery. Chata sighed deeply.

"Chata," cried Ashley, who divined what must be in the mind of Herlinda, "speak! Tell the Señorita that you are not her daughter. Her suspense is terrible!"

But Chata could not utter a word. Ramirez broke into a laugh. He himself heard that betrayal of his overstrained nerves with a shudder. He would not have

laughed had his will served. Why should he laugh?
Then the shame, he thought, of this poor Herlinda had
been complete. She had a child ; she had come to the
avenger of her shame hoping to find the lost proof of her
frailty. Even his sister Doña Isabel was crying wofully,
" Oh Leon, Leon, is it thou? Art thou the Ramirez my
poor Chinita loved? Oh, in pity give her back to me! I
will forgive all — yes, even Norberto's death — if thou
wilt give Herlinda her child."

" You are all mad ! " cried Ramirez, recalled to himself.
" What know I of Herlinda's child, or even that she ex-
ists? I only know that this is mine," he laid his hand
upon Chata, — " she of whom you thought to cheat me.
Ah, had I known there was another infant to claim your
secret love," he added mockingly, " I could have better
disposed of my own ! "

While the unrepentant brother of Doña Isabel was saying this, Pedro in gruff and surly accents was reminding
him of the girl who had stopped him upon the road years
before, and had given him an amulet. Yes, the impatient listener remembered her ; he had heard her name, —
Chinita ; that was the girl of whom Rafael had spoken,
she who had been the foundling of the gatekeeper. A
vision of the unkempt, witch-like creature who had startled
his horse, as she stood under that accursed mesquite-tree,
rose before him. Was that Herlinda's child? She stood
still with her hand upon Chata, gazing upon her incredulously. Ramirez threw it off in sudden passion.

" Uncle Leon," said Herlinda humbly, hopelessly, " you
killed my husband. Oh, I would forgive you that, could
you give me my child ! Oh, when I saw this girl here — "
she dropped her face into her hands and wept.

" Shame on you ! " cried Ramirez. The sight of
woman's tears irritated him, and Herlinda's assertion of
her marriage made blacker still a deed whose silent,
stealthy consummation had ever been to him a secret
cause of shame. " What though I killed your lover, was
it not to avenge the honor of the Garcias ? "

" The honor of those you had disgraced ! " cried the
outraged woman scornfully, — " of her whose life you had
crushed ! No, your hand was ready for murder, your
heart delighted in blood, — and so you killed my love,

without a word of warning; and because in your vile, cruel heart you could believe no woman pure, no man just, you thus brought in an instant desolation and ruin upon me!" Ramirez shrank before the indignant pathos of her voice. "Ah," she added, "all, all this I would forgive — O God, have I not prayed to thee and thy saints for grace to forgive? — if I could but behold my child. They tell me she has followed you, — one says because of the strange infatuation your mad career presents to her; another, that she may avenge her wrongs, her father's murder. I warn you! beware! such a girl is not to be scorned."

"I know nothing of her," cried Ramirez, vehemently. "Here is your mother — Pedro; they have known the girl, they should render you an account of her. As for me, there is a man here who upon the grave of him I killed declared himself his avenger: it is to him I will answer for that deed."

Ashley Ward involuntarily drew his sword, eager for the offered combat; but Pedro and Gonzales threw themselves between the two men. "This is neither the time nor the place," exclaimed Gonzales; while Herlinda cried, "Do not touch my uncle for your life! My mother, my mother!"

Doña Isabel had indeed thrown herself upon her knees before the priest, and frantically implored his interposition. As he raised her he was seen to speak; but no one heard his words, for shrill female voices in altercation added to the confusion of the moment, and every eye was turned in the direction whence they came.

"Let me go! let me go! I will hear no more! I will wait no longer! He will escape. Oh, it is not with such weak words I will speak!"

Two female figures issued panting from the covert, — it seemed that the elder woman had striven to hold the other back, but the younger had triumphed. Doña Isabel uttered a cry of infinite gratitude and joy. Chata caught and held the girl as she came. "Chinita! thank God," she cried, "you are here!"

Pedro in an ecstasy seized the robe of Herlinda. "There, there," he cried, "is your child! your beautiful child!"

" Yes ! " cried Chinita in mad excitement which only burning words could relieve. Not then could she pause for fond greetings or reverent tears ; the sight of Ramirez seemed at once to fire yet absorb her wildest passions. She sprang toward him, as one may suppose the lion's whelp faces a tiger that in some fierce struggle has filled the air with the scent of blood. The very aroma arouses and maddens its kindred nature. With an outburst of eloquence which like arrows tipped with venom seemed to sting and paralyze the object upon which they were directed, she assailed Ramirez with the story of his crimes ; and separated from the picturesque and daring events that had accompanied and disguised them, and told with dramatic eloquence and vivid anger, they thrilled every listener with shuddering abhorrence and dismay. Blackest of all, she pictured the murder of John Ashley. Ramirez himself seemed visibly to shrink and wither before her scathing words, while Herlinda pressed her hands over her ears, entreating her to cease. The agonized woman could not endure the vivid rendition, for the girl unconsciously acted out, as she conceived, the scene of midnight murder.

From the moment of Chinita's appearance, Ramirez had seemed overwhelmed as by the sight of some unearthly being ; and while she spoke his eyes riveted themselves upon her, his jaw fell, his countenance took the hue of death. Suddenly the girl burst into wild sobs and tears. Her rage was spent. " Go, go ! " she said, — " you who have cursed my life, you who killed my father, you who condemned my mother to a convent and me to a beggar's life ; for was it strange they cast me out, hoping I should die ? And so I should have done but for Pedro — Fiend, to pursue him with devilish tortures after so many years ! Oh ! that it was which brought my hate upon you. Ah, I had loved you from a child, — not with a woman's fancy, but as though the thought of you were the very soul that was born with me. Of you I thought, for you I prayed — was it not so, Chata ? It was I who gave you the amulet they said would insure life and fortune. I planned and schemed to give you wealth and power. Ah, even when I knew the cursed wrong you had done me, I could not believe, I could not realize ; that murdered man had been dead so long he seemed of another world, another time, — he seemed nothing to me. But the torture of Pedro, — ah, that was real, that was of my life; it maddened me. Ah! ah! ah! it brought your downfall. You have wondered how your skill, your well-laid plans, your valor, all have failed you. It was because of me! because of us!"

Chinita turned and indicated her companion with a gesture of her hand. She saw then what had riveted the gaze of Ramirez, and rather than her words had held each witness dumb. Dolores—her face kindled into fictitious youth, her beautiful eyes gleaming with a flame that seemed to scathe — had drawn from her brows the kerchief she had worn. The act had revealed a wondrous mass of brown hair, with the russet tinge of the chestnut, gleaming in the sunlight with threads and spirals of gold. The two heads, that of Chinita and of the woman, seemed to have been modelled the one from the other, so exact was their form, and so similar the texture and color and peculiar growth of the marvellous wealth of curls that crowned them both.

Chinita drew back with dilated eyes, speechless with the overwhelming horror of conviction. Chata would have clasped her in her arms, but she drew herself away. In the woman whose wild laugh rang upon the air Chata recognized the one who had thrown herself before the horse of Ramirez, and who had lain a bruised and shameful figure upon the convent steps at El Toro.

There was a moment of profound silence. Even the sultry air seemed waiting, as though for the thunderclap that follows the lightning flash.

"Ah, Leon Vallé! you know now who accuses you," cried the woman. "Oh, is not this a sweet revenge, to curse you by the lips of your own child, — the child you robbed me of? What! you thought *that* your child!" she pointed with ineffable contempt to Chata, who in the overwhelming excitement of the moment clung to the pallid and trembling Herlinda. "Bah! what is she to the beautiful being I bore you,— into whose soul was infused the idolatrous love that had been wrested from my heart, the love that had been my ruin? Ah, such love dies hard! It lived again in her, — it lived in her heart for *you*. Because of it I dared not claim her, though I knew her the moment my eyes fell upon her, — yes, as you know her now. In whom but in our child could be reproduced this wonderful wealth of hair you used to call the siren's dower? In whom but in our child could reappear your own face, glorified, masked, by woman's softness? Ah, Doña Isabel and this Pedro were deceived; they thought it was the beauty of Herlinda that they saw. But I knew it to be yours. Ah, in all these weeks I have taught your child how to hate you; I have plucked out that root of love; I have made more real the fancied wrongs of which she has accused you. Trifles! trifles! trifles all! — the murder of a supposed father, the torture of an old man, the death of a base lover, — yes, that Ruiz to whom from her birth you destined her. But I, — I cry to you give back my innocence! give back my ruined life! give back my father, who by your act was killed as surely as though your hand had struck the blow! give me the young years of my daughter's life, those she squandered a beggar at your sister's gate! Ah, you cannot, you cannot! But I, — I can avenge my wrongs and hers."

Quick as a flash the infuriate woman levelled a pistol. Quick as an answering flash Chinita threw herself before her and sprang to her father's breast. A second shot following so quickly on the first that they seemed as one, a cry of agony, a scream of madness, the cries of women, the hoarse voices of men, made the garden a pandemonium of hideous sounds. The desperate woman, whose bullet had touched its mark harmlessly to Ramirez through the slender form of Chinita, fled madly. Ramirez, scarce conscious whether the blood which streamed over him was that of his daughter or his own, bore the wounded girl through the throng that pressed him, wildly calling upon his child, — alas, alas! his but for the brief span during which her warm young blood should leap from the deadly puncture in her breast!

Herlinda, the first to regain self-control even amid the intense revulsion of feeling through which she had almost instantaneously passed, tore into shreds some portion of her garments and strove to stanch the wound; but in vain. Chinita, with a smile which succeeded her first wild cry and stare of horror, motioned her away. She pressed her own fingers on the wound, raising her head from the arm of Ramirez to say, "I saved you, I saved you! just as I used to think I would do. Ah, I could not hate you, — no, no! though I tried. And she could not root out my love, — it lives here still." She pressed her hand still tighter on the wound. "My father! my father!"

The face of the hardened man contracted in agony. He turned toward Doña Isabel and Herlinda with a heart-rending cry. "You are avenged, — both, both, avenged! O my God! You never can have known such agony as this. Oh wretched man that I am, to see the sum of all my crimes cancelled by this terrible reprisal!"

The hand of the dying girl fell from its place. Chata knelt and placed her own with desperate energy against the fatal wound. Chinita smiled and faintly kissed her. "My dream has come true," she said. "Ah, when they pity me you will say, 'She always longed to die for him.' Tell them it was best that I should die, I loved him so. Death wipes out every wrong. He is my father!"

Ramirez groaned. Great drops of sweat stood on his brow. He strove still to support her; but Gonzales on the one side and Ashley on the other bore her weight.

By this time the garden was full of people. A man forced his way through the throng.

"Reyes! Reyes!" cried Ramirez, "Villain, did you not as I commanded give my child to Isabel, my sister; or was yours the accursed hand that brought her to this pass?"

Reyes gazed at the dying girl in horror. A suspicion of the misapprehension under which Ramirez had acted, and which had confirmed Ruiz in his treachery, had haunted him for days, since in a remote village he had met the administrador of Tres Hermanos and heard from him the tale of the carrying away of Chata. He had hastened toward Las Parras with Don Rafael and his mother, bent on warning Ramirez and confessing the wild carelessness with which he had disposed of the child who had been confided to him, and who he had supposed until his meeting with Chinita had indirectly reached the person to whom she was destined. It had not been possible for him — a man in whom the paternal instinct had never dwelt — to imagine it the one virtue in the callous, fierce, and unscrupulous Ramirez. But with this bleeding, dying figure in his arms Ramirez seemed transformed. Reyes fell on his knees.

"Ah, had you but told me the whole truth!" sighed the dying girl. "A Garcia you said! Ah, I should have been prouder to be *his* daughter than a thousand times Garcia!"

She turned her head, and her eyes fell on Ashley's face and rested there. A soft, strange illumination animated her own, as though from some inward light just kindled. "Adios! Adios!" she murmured. "Ah, you were noble, generous! yet you thought I did not feel, that I did not understand. Ah, could I live, you should see! But this is best; you will never need trouble now for Chinita. No, no, no! do not grieve — Ah, that might make me weak! I would not — find it — hard — to die."

She looked at him long and fixedly, — perhaps to her as to Ashley a secret as sacred as it was precious, was then revealed. A blueness crept around her mouth, a glaze over her beautiful eyes. "No wonder that she loved the American!" she whispered at length, — dreamily, as though her mind wandered to the past. The words sank like lead in Ashley's heart, to be forgotten never, never!

After a moment the lips of the dying girl moved in prayer. The priest, who had from time to time endeavored to control an emotion which seemed a personal rather than a merely sympathetic grief, bent over her, and all present fell on their knees. Chinita whispered in his ear a few words, and received absolution with a smile of perfect peace. Then began the solemn litany for the departing soul; Chinita was evidently sinking rapidly.

Pedro had fallen on his knees before her, in grief too deep for words. Pepé from behind him gazed into her glazing eyes with stoical despair. Suddenly she smiled, and laying her arm over Pedro's shoulder, extended her blood-stained hand, looking at Pepé with the pretty, winning, disdainful smile of old, and said faintly, though proudly, "I am the daughter of the Señor General. Lead me, Pepé, — lead me. I am tired!"

And thus with her arm around him who had been so blindly faithful, and with her hand in that of the peasant youth who through life had been her adoring slave, with one long sigh, which left her lips smiling as it passed, Chinita fell asleep, — resting forever from the passion and turmoil of life.

"Peace, peace, peace!" reiterated the solemn voice of the priest, in assurance, in warning, in invocation. It penetrated hearts to which the very word had seemed a mockery. The hardest, the most reprobate, the haughtiest, the most sorrowful, repeated it with a sob. Ramirez on his knees, crushed to the earth, heard it as the cry of a despairing angel. Where for him could peace be found?

XLVII.

WHEN Pedro Gomez rose from his knees he held in his hand a little square reliquary of faded blue. The string from which it had hung had been pierced by the fatal bullet, and it had dropped unheeded from Chinita's neck.

Reverent hands bore the corpse into the desolate house; while Ramirez, or Leon Vallé, — for by his true name he was ever after called, — rising at the entreaty of his sister, stood like one bereft of sense or movement. Suddenly he laid his hand upon the gatekeeper's arm and muttered hoarsely, "Kill me Pedro! See, I have no sword. If thou wilt not for vengeance, do it for love. You loved her, — for her sake end my misery!"

Pedro laid the reliquary in his hand. "If it should not be true?" he said doggedly of the faded silk. "Oh, was it for this I bore so many years the mocking silence of Doña Feliz and my mistress? No, no! it cannot be. Open this. 'T was on her bosom when she came into my hands. The niña Herlinda promised me a token. It will be found there, — there in the blessed reliquary. Fool that I was to think it had nothing to declare to me. Ah, how your hands shake! Well, 't is but a moment's work."

The gatekeeper ripped the sewed edges with his dagger's point quickly, desperately, as though he were profaning a sacred thing, — then blankly looked at the worthless trifles on his palm. Just a tiny curl of brown and gold, and the eye-tooth of some animal, a fancied charm against infantile diseases, both wrapped in a paper scrawled with a faintly-written prayer.

Pedro was convinced. Till then he had clung to the belief that had given to his clownish life the elements of heroism, of love and sacrifice. Chinita the beautiful, the beloved, was dead — dead; but to his soul there came a bereavement far more terrible than that of death. He raised his glazing eyes appealingly, hopelessly. Ah, there was Doña Feliz, — she whom all these years he had accused as the hard, unpitying witness of the degradation of Herlinda's child! and of her Doña Isabel with sobs was entreating brokenly in God's name some news of the charge she had received years before. Pedro listened with a jealous eagerness, which the involuntary cry of Chata, interrupting for a moment the answering voice of Doña Feliz, made intolerable. "Mother of God!" he cried at length, "it was Doña Feliz then who guarded Herlinda's child!"

"O false, cruel Feliz! why did you deceive me?" cried Doña Isabel. "Why did you suffer me to believe the gatekeeper's foundling was of my own flesh and blood? Ah, God, so she was! It was the beauty of my mother that deceived me; it was repeated in the offspring of Leon, as it could never be in that of the American. Ah, it was for that I loved Chinita with such passionate tenderness and remorse! Oh, why did you suffer it? Why give me no warning? And now Chinita is dead, and my daughter cries to me for her child, and I cannot answer her."

"Did I not warn you at this gate?" responded Doña Feliz, "that the day would come when you would bitterly repent the words you uttered; when you bade me take and hide the babe even from your knowledge, — never to mention her whether living or dead, that to you it might be as though she had never existed? Have I not obeyed your mandate? Ay, even when my heart bled because I saw the agony, the delusion under which you labored, I have suffered with you, but I have been faithful."

Doña Isabel bent her head in speechless woe. For her there might not be even the poor consolation of reproach. Yet she murmured, "In pity, where is Herlinda's child?"

"She is here. Thank God she is here!" replied Doña Feliz, — this girl whom you have believed to be the daughter of my son. "Weeks ago your brother, Leon Vallé, reft her from us, believing her his own. Only by revealing the secret we had sworn to keep could Rafael have saved her. Ah, God knows! Perhaps at the last moment, when hastening from the strong room she threw herself into the power of the ravisher that she might save her foster-father from death, then perhaps his will might have failed; but he was speechless. I have been ill; yes, near to death," — her haggard face, her sunken eyes, her wasted figure attested that, — " yet we sought her far and near. Until last night we had no tidings. A rough soldier listened in the inn to the tale we everywhere proclaimed. He came to me secretly; ' Señora,' he said, ' the girl you seek is perhaps in the house of Doña Carmen. Ramirez himself is deceived.' This was the first stage of our route to Guanapila. We need go no farther; for standing there, Herlinda, with Carmen, is your child."

Doña Feliz broke into sobs, sinking weak as a child into the arms of Don Rafael. " The struggle is over," she said to him; " our task is accomplished, the long dissimulation is ended ! "

Herlinda and Chata had not needed the conclusion of the brief words of Doña Feliz; they had clasped each other in a rapturous embrace. But the sobs of the distressed lady recalled them from their joy, and hastening to her side they poured out in fervent gratitude such words as seemed to repay to her sensitive heart its long years of devotion as truly as though each word had been a priceless jewel.

" Ah ! " said Doña Feliz, " all, all is nothing to merit the happiness of this hour. It is the poor Pedro, he whose matchless devotion mocked my poor work, who is worthy of such words as these. Ah, my heart bled for him, but I could not, dared not speak."

" Oh foolish unreasoning girl that I was so to bind you ! " cried Herlinda. She turned to speak to Pedro, but he was nowhere to be seen. There was a movement among the villagers, who, repulsed from the windows of the house by the soldiers, began to disperse, when the voice of the priest stopped them.

" Listen, friends," he said. " This has been a dread and fearful hour, an hour to try the souls of men. I am old, yet never have I known such anguish as this day has brought to me. Some sixteen years ago, a stranger in this land, ignorant of its language and customs, I came to this village with a young American whom I met. He was a handsome youth and won my heart, — a warm, Irish heart that often led me contrary to my judgment. The American told me that here his love was staying. I laughed at him for fixing his heart upon some brown-skinned, dark-eyed peasant girl. He did not contradict me, but bade me be ready in the early morning to wed him to the lovely object of his youthful passion. I remonstrated, yet was glad to serve him. Though no priest lived here, the little church was open; the people were glad of the opportunity to hear Mass. Just before it began, John Ashley and Herlinda Garcia were married. As she for a moment loosened the reboso she wore to make the necessary responses, I caught a glimpse of a face that led me to suspect it was no simple peasant who stood before me. Yet it was only in after years, when the requirements of the law and the customs unalterable as law among the different castes existing in your land became known to me, that I remembered with disquiet the marriage I had celebrated here. I was a missionary among the tribes of Northern Indians, doing good work. I strove to assure myself that, irregular as I knew the marriage to be, — contracted in secret, unknown to and probably against the consent of the young girl's parents, in a language unintelligible to the few witnesses, — the parties were probably living in amity, satisfied, as surely God and man might be, with a marriage which only the quibbles of the law made disputable. Yet I could not be at ease; a voice seemed calling me hither. Alas, alas! I came but to witness the consummation of the tragedy begun years, years ago, — a tragedy, the direct outcome of my fatal error. But I will atone. I will go — would to God in penance it might be upon my knees — to the Holy Father in Rome, and pray him to ratify the marriage. Doña Herlinda Garcia, pure in name as in deed, shall give a spotless name to the child of her virtuous love!"

The old monk ceased; tremblingly he wiped away his tears. "Pardon, pardon!" he murmured to Herlinda. "Oh my daughter, how you have suffered! But daughter, the certificate I gave, — had you not the paper? That, however subject to cavil, would have declared your purity."

"Ah, a paper!" cried Herlinda. "I have thought of it a thousand times. It was in English. I thought it was a blessed prayer, though John told me to treasure it as my life; that was why I sewed it in the reliquary I placed about my baby's neck."

With a cry Chata drew forth the tiny bag, almost the counterpart of that poor Chinita had worn, and the sight of which had confirmed the mistake of Pedro, — on such slight things hangs fate! She thought of how often she and Chinita had compared them when children, laughingly proposing to exchange or open them, yet ever shrinking from tampering with them in superstitious awe. Pedro, who had returned, snatched it from her hand, — the act irresistible. As he opened it with his dagger's point, a filigree earring fell into his palm. He groaned and turned away.

Herlinda caught from his hand a tattered paper. "Read, read!" she cried to Ashley. "See that he was noble, true as you have said! He was my husband!"

The proof attested by the signature of the long dead Mademoiselle La Croix, and that of the living priest, was of the simplest, the most efficient, and all these years had been preserved by the piety or superstition of the child to whom it had been confided, and who, had she but known it, had so vital an interest in its discovery. Chata gazed at the paper in blank amaze. Around her were men and women giving thanks to God and his saints. At the knees of Herlinda was her uncle Leon Vallé and Doña Isabel her mother.

Ashley Ward was the first to break the spell. He took Herlinda's hand. "Remember, here is a man who never doubted you," he said.

"And here one who would have died for you!" said Gonzales.

In a single phrase each had expressed the loyalty of the nation he represented, — Ashley, that of faith in man's honor and woman's chastity; Gonzales, the tenacious love that distrust might change to jealous madness, but which it could never destroy.

Within a few hours a sad and solemn funeral cortége set forth from Las Parras, bearing all that was mortal of the beautiful Chinita. Not far from the limits of the town Ashley and Gonzales came upon a startling and awful sight, — a woman lay dead upon the road, her garments sodden, her beautiful hair defiled by the mud of the highway. She had fallen face downward. As though some evil omen warned him, Leon Vallé hastening from the rear anticipated them in raising the corpse.

It was that of the maddened Dolores. It had needed no weapon to reach her heart; despair and agony had summoned to her destruction the swift and fatal malady that had killed her father. Those who saw her, he who pressed her wildly to his breast and bade her live, accusing himself not her, called it a broken heart. As her child had said, " Death wipes out every wrong." Only remorse, pity, love survive.

They buried them both — the two of that sad name Dolores — in the hacienda church. But one lies in a nameless grave, and the other is marked by one that recalls a vision of a beautiful girl, to whom a happier destiny should have brought the joys of life, and whose proud spirit should have conquered its cares; yet its perplexities, its conflicting passions, had made the pilgrimage so hard, so set with thorns, that she had been content — yes, thankful — to end it there: " CHINITA."

In so short a life the unfortunate girl could not have wandered far from heaven; yet for years there was one on earth who spent upon each day long hours of prayer and fasting at the tomb of her brother's child, — to the memory and the name of Chinita uniting that of Leon, and embracing both in the undying love which looked beyond the grave for its perfection and its reward. At evening would come one older, but more peaceful than the mourner, to lead her home; and hand in hand, the two would pass out into the soft and tranquil air. Thus Doña Isabel and Feliz renewed with tears the friendship of their youth; and thus — ended the ambitions, the passions, the impetuous pride, sources of such strange and grievous perplexities — they await together in peaceful gloom the light of a perfect day.

The two men looked at each other. "Why disturb the Señora Doña Isabel with such matters? The American is dead. The ranchero can be nothing to her," said Don Rafael, sententiously. "He who gives testimony unasked brings suspicion upon himself. No, no! leave the matter to his countrymen; they have a consul here who has nothing to do but inquire into such matters."

"True, true! and one might as well hope to find again the wildbird escaped from its cage, as to see that Juan Planillos! God save us! if he was indeed the true Juan Planillos!" and the mystified major-domo actually turned pale at the thought. "They say he is more devil than man; that would explain how he got out of the hacienda, for Pedro Gomez swears he let no man pass, either out or in."

Don Rafael had his own private opinion about that, and of whom the disguised visitor might be. Yet why should he have attacked the American? Had Ashley too been within the walls, — and for what purpose? These questions were full of deep and startling import, and again impressing upon his subordinate that endless trouble might be avoided by a discreet silence, he walked thoughtfully away, those vague suspicions and conjectures taking definite shape in his mind. He went to the gate with some design of warily questioning Pedro, but the man was not there; for once, friend or foe might go in or out unnoticed. But it was a day of disorder, and Don Rafael could readily divine the excuse for the gate-keeper's neglect of duty. Remembering that he had not broken his fast that day, he went to his own rooms for the morning chocolate; and from thence he presently saw Pedro emerge from the opposite court, and with bowed head and reluctant steps repair to his wonted post. Don Rafael Sanchez knew his countrymen, especially those of the lower class, too well to hasten to him and ply him with inquiries as he longed to do. He knew too well the value of patience, and more than once had found it golden. Rita, his young wife, had come to him, and through her tears and ejaculations was relating the account of the murder the servants had brought to her, which was as wild and improbable as the reality had been, though not more ghastly, when a servant entered with a hasty message from Doña Isabel.

IV.

WHILE the discovery of the murder had caused this wild excitement outside the walls of the hacienda, a far different scene was being enacted within. Mademoiselle La Croix, the governess of the two sisters Herlinda and Carmen Garcia, had arisen early, leaving her youngest charge asleep, and, hurriedly donning her dressing-gown, hastened to the adjoining apartment, where Herlinda was enjoying that deep sleep which comes to young and healthy natures with the dawn, rounding and completing the hours of perfect rest, which youthful activity both of body and mind so imperatively demands.

A beautiful girl, between fifteen and sixteen, in her perfect development of figure, as well as in the pure olive tints of her complexion, revealing her Castilian descent, — Herlinda Garcia lay upon the white pillows shaded by a canopy of lace, one arm thrown above her head, the other, bare to the elbow, thrown across a bosom that rose and fell with each breath she drew, with the regularity of perfect content. Yet she opened her eyes with a start, and uttered an exclamation of alarm, as Mademoiselle La Croix lightly touched her, saying half petulantly, as she turned away, "Oh, Mademoiselle, why have you wakened me? I was so happy just then! I was dreaming of John!"

She spoke the English name with an indescribable accent of tenderness, but Mademoiselle La Croix repeated it after her almost sharply.

"John! yes," she said, "it is no wonder he is always in your thoughts; as for me, Heaven knows what will happen to me! I am sure, had I known—" and the Frenchwoman paused, to wipe a tear from her eye.

"Ah, yes, it was thoughtless, cruel of us!" interrupted Herlinda, penitently, yet scarcely able to repress a smile as her glance fell upon the gayly flowered dressing-gown which formed an incongruous wrapping for the thin, bony figure of the governess; "but, dear Mademoiselle, nothing worse than a dismissal can happen to you, and you know John has promised —"

The governess drew herself up with portentous dignity. "Mademoiselle wanders from the point," she interrupted; "it is of herself only I was thinking. This state of affairs must be brought to a close," she added solemnly, after a pause. "At all risks, Herlinda, John must claim you."

"So he knows, so I tell him," answered Herlinda, suddenly wide awake, and ceasing the pretty yawns and stretchings with which she had endeavored to banish her drowsiness. "Oh, Mademoiselle," a shade of apprehension passing over her face, "I have done wrong, very wrong. My mother will never forgive me!"

"Absurd!" ejaculated the governess. "Doña Isabel, like every one else in the world, must submit to the inevitable."

"So John said; but, Mademoiselle, neither you nor John know my mother, nor my people. She will never forgive: in her place, I would never forgive!"

"And yet you dared!" cried Mademoiselle La Croix, looking at the young girl with new admiration at the courage which stimulated her own. "Truly, you Mexicans are a strange people, so generous in many things, so blind and obstinate in others. Well, well! you shall find, Herlinda, I too can be brave. If I were a coward, I should say, wait until I am safely away; but I am no coward," added the little woman, drawing her figure to its full height and expanding her nostrils, — "I am ready to face the storm with you."

"Yes, yes!" said the young girl, hurriedly and abstractedly. "What," she added, rising in her bed, and grasping the bronze pillar at the head, "what is that I hear? What a confusion of voices!" She turned deadly pale, and her white-robed figure shook beneath the long loose tresses of her coal-black hair. "My God! Mademoiselle, I hear his name!"

The governess too grew pale, though she began incoherently to reassure the young lady, who remained kneeling in the bed as if petrified, her hands clasped to her breast, her eyes strained, listening intently, as through the thick walls came the dull murmur of many voices. Like waves they seemed to surge and beat against the solid stones, and the vague roar formed itself into the words, " Don Juan ! Ashley ! "

Although a moment's reflection would have reminded her that a hundred other events, rather than that of his death, might have brought the people there to call upon the name of their master, one of those flashes of intuition which appear magnetic revealed to Herlinda the awful truth, even before it was borne to her outward ear by the shrill voice of a woman, crying through the corridor, " God of my life ! Don Juan is killed ! murdered ! murdered ! " She even stopped to knock upon the door and reiterate the words, in the half-horrified, half-pleasurable excitement the vulgar often feel in communicating dreadful and unexpected news ; but a wild shriek from within suddenly checked her outcry, and chilled her blood.

" Fool that I am ! I should have remembered," she muttered. " Paqua told me there was certainly love between those two ; she saw the glance he threw on the young Señorita in church one day. But that was months ago, and she certainly is to marry Don Vicente."

At that moment a middle-aged, plainly-dressed woman, with the blue and white reboso so commonly worn thrown over her head, entered the corridor. Her figure was so commanding, the glance of her eyes so impressive, that even in her haste she lost none of her habitual dignity. The woman turned away, glad to escape with the reproof, " Cease your clamor, Refugio ! What ! is your news so pressing that you must needs frighten your young mistress with it ? Go, go ! Doña Isabel will be little likely to be pleased with your zeal."

The woman hastened away, and Doña Feliz, waiting until she had disappeared, laid her hand upon the door of Herlinda's chamber, which like those of many sleeping apartments in the house opened directly upon the upper corridor, its massive thickness and strength being looked upon as more than sufficient to repel any danger which could in the wildest probability reach it from the well guarded interior of the fort-like building.

As Doña Feliz touched the latch, the door was opened by the affrighted governess, who had anticipated the entrance of Doña Isabel. The respite unnerved her, and she threw herself half fainting in a chair, as Herlinda seized the new-comer by the shoulders, gasping forth, "Feliz, Feliz, tell me! tell me it is not true! He is not dead! dead! dead!" her voice rising to a shriek.

"Hush! hush, Herlinda! O God, my child, what can this be to thee?" Doña Feliz shuddered as she spoke. She glanced at the closed window; the walls she knew to be a yard in thickness, yet she wished them double, lest a sound of these wild ravings should escape.

"Feliz, you dare not tell me!—then it is true! he is murdered! lost, lost to me forever!" The young girl slipped like water through the arms that would have clasped her, crouching upon the floor, wringing her hands, tearless, voiceless, after her last despairing words. Feliz attempted to raise her, but in vain.

Carmen, aroused by the sounds of distress, appeared in the doorway which connected the two rooms. "Back! go back!" cried Doña Feliz, and the child frightened and whimpering, withdrew. Feliz turned to the governess, — the deep dejection of her attitude struck her; and at that moment Doña Isabel appeared.

"Herlinda," she began, "this is sad news; but remember—" she paused, looked with stern disapprobation, then her superb self-possession giving way, she rushed to her daughter and clasped her arm. "Rise! rise!" she cried; "this excess of emotion shames you and me. This is folly. Rise, I say! He could never have been anything, child, to thee!"

Herlinda did not move, she did not even look up. She had always feared her mother; had trembled at her slightest word of blame; had been like wax under her hand. Yet now she was as marble; her hands had dropped on her lap; she was rigid to the touch; only the deep moans that burst from her white lips proved that she lived.

The attitude was expressive of such utter despair that it was of itself a revelation; and presently the moans formed themselves into words: "My God! my God! I am undone! he is dead! he is dead!"

The words bore a terrible significance to the listeners. Doña Isabel turned her eyes upon Feliz, and read upon her face the thought that had forced its way to her own mind. Her face paled; she dropped her daughter's arm and drew back. The act itself was an accusation. Perhaps the girl felt it so. She suddenly wrung her hands distractedly, and sprang to her feet, exclaiming, "My husband! my husband! Let me go to him! he cannot be dead! he is not dead!"

The words "My husband" fell like a thunderbolt among them. Herlinda had rushed to the door, but Doña Feliz caught her in her strong arms, and forced her back. "Tell us what you mean!" she ejaculated; while the frightened governess plucked her by the sleeve, reiterating again and again, "Pardon! pardon! entreat your mother's pardon!"

But the terrible turn affairs had taken had driven the thought of pardon, or the need of it, from her mind. "I tell you I am his wife! Ah, you think that cannot be, but it is true; the Irish priest married us four months ago in Las Parras. Let me go, Feliz, let me go! I am his wife!"

"This is madness!" interrupted Doña Isabel, in a voice of such preternatural calmness that her daughter turned as if awestricken to look at her. "Unhappy girl, you cannot have been that man's wife. You have been betrayed! Child! child! the house of Garcia is disgraced!"

A chill fell upon the governess, yet she spoke sharply, almost pertly: "Not disgraced by Herlinda, Madame. She was indeed married to John Ashley, in the parish church of Las Parras, by the missionary priest, Father Maganley."

The long, slow glance of incredulity changing into deepest scorn which Doña Isabel turned upon the governess seemed to scorch, to wither her. She actually cowered beneath it, faltering forth entreaties for pardon, rather, be it said to her honor, for the unhappy Herlinda than for herself. Meanwhile, with lightning rapidity, the events of the last few months passed through the mind of Doña Isabel. Yes, yes, it had been possible; there had been opportunity for this base work. Her eyes clouded, her breast heaved; had she held a weapon in her hand, the intense passion that possessed her might have sought a method more powerful than words in finding for itself expression. As it was, she turned away, sick at heart, her brain afire. Doña Feliz had placed a strong, firm hand over Herlinda's lips. "It is useless," she said in a voice like Fate. "You will never see him again."

Herlinda comprehended that those words but expressed the unspoken fiat of her mother. She shuddered and groaned. "Mother! mother!" she said faintly, "he loved me. I loved him so, mother! Mother, I have spoken the truth; Mademoiselle will tell you all; I was indeed his wife."

Doña Isabel would not trust herself to look at her daughter. She dared not, so strong at that moment was her resentment of her daring, so deep the shame of its consequences. "Vile woman!" she said to the governess, in low, penetrating tones of concentrated passion; "you who have avowed yourself the accomplice of yon dead villain, tell me all. Let me know whether you were simply treacherously ignorant, or treacherously base. Silence, Herlinda! nor dare in my presence shed one tear for the wretch who betrayed you."

But her commands were unheeded. The present anguish overcame the habits and fears of a whole life, — as, alas! a passionate love had once before done. But then she had been under the domination of her lover, and had been separated from the mother, whose very shadow would have deterred and prevented her. Now, even the deep severity of that mother's voice fell on unheeding ears. Though tears came not, piteous groans, mingled with the name of her love, burst from the heart of the wretched girl, who leaned like a broken lily upon the breast of Doña Feliz, who from the moment that Herlinda had declared herself a wife gazed upon her with looks of deep compassion, alternating with those of anxious curiosity toward Doña Isabel, whose every glance she had learned to interpret. She was a woman of great intelligence, yet it appeared to her as though Doña Isabel, who was queen and absolute mistress on her own domain, had but to speak the word and set her daughter in any position she might claim. The supremacy of the Garcias was her creed, — that by which she had lived; was it to be contradicted now?

"Tell me all," reiterated Doña Isabel, in the concentrated voice of deep and terrible passion, as the cowering governess vainly strove to frame words that might least offend. "How did this treachery occur? Where and how did you give that fellow opportunity to compass his base designs?"

Herlinda started; she would have spoken, but Doña Feliz restrained her by the strong pressure of her arm; and the faltering voice of the governess attempted some explanation and justification of an event, which, almost unparalleled in Mexico, could not have been foreseen perhaps even by the jealous care of the most anxious mother.

"This is all I have to tell," she stammered. "You remember you sent us to Las Parras six months ago, just after you had refused your daughter's hand to John Ashley, and promised it to Vicente Gonzales. We remained there in exile nearly two months. Herlinda was wretched. What was there to console or enliven her in that miserable village? Separated from her sister, from you, Madame, whom she deeply loved even while she feared, what had she to do but nurse her grief and despair, which grew daily stronger on the food of tears and solitude? At first she was too proud to speak to me of that which caused her sleepless nights and unhappy days. But my looks must have expressed the pity I felt. She threw herself into my arms one day, and sobbed out her sad tale upon my bosom. She had spoken to this Ashley but a few times, and then in your presence, Madame; but in your country the eye seems the messenger of love. She declared that she could not live, she would not, were she separated from John Ashley; that the day of her marriage with Vicente Gonzales should be the day of her death."

"To the point," interrupted Doña Isabel in an icy tone. "I had heard all this. Even in John Ashley's very presence Herlinda had forgotten her dignity and mine. This is not what I would know."

"But it leads to it, Madame," cried the governess, deprecatingly, "for while I was in the state of mingled pity and perplexity caused by Herlinda's words, a message was brought to me that John Ashley was at the door. I went to speak to him. Yielding to his entreaties, I even allowed him to see Herlinda. How could I guess it was to urge a course which only the most remarkable combination of events could have made possible?"

"Intrigante," muttered Doña Isabel, bitterly.

"You," continued the governess, piqued and emboldened by the adjective, "angered by the sight of him as you passed the reduction-works, had yourself invented a pretext for sending him to San Marcos. You could not well dismiss him altogether from a position he filled so well. He might, you thought, reveal the reason."

"Deal not with my motives," interrupted the lady haughtily. "It is true I sent him to San Marcos. And what then?"

"Then, by chance, he learned what here no servant had dared to tell him, — the name of the village to which Herlinda had been sent, so near your own hacienda, too, that he had never once suspected it. And there he met a countryman. These English, Irish, Americans, — they are all bound together by a common language; and he, this poor priest, entirely ignorant of Spanish, coldly received even by his clerical brethren, was glad to spend a few days in a trip with Ashley; and as they rode together over the thirty leagues of mountain and valley between San Marcos and Las Parras, he formed a great liking for the pleasant youth, and beyond gently rallying him, made no opposition to staying over a night in the village, and joining him in holy matrimony to the woman of his choice, whom he imagined to be a poor but pretty peasant, so modest were our surroundings."

Doña Isabel's face darkened. "Hasten! hasten!" she muttered. "I see it all; deluded, unhappy girl."

"Unhappy, yes!" cried the governess. "Prophetic were the tears that coursed over her cheeks, as she went with me to the chapel in the early morning, and there in the presence of a few peasants who had never seen her before, or failed to recognize her under the dingy reboso she wore, was married to the young American."

"Ignorant imbeciles!" ejaculated Doña Isabel, but so low that no one distinctly caught her words. "And this *marriage* as you call it, in what language was it performed?"

"Oh, in English," answered Mademoiselle La Croix, readily. "The priest knew no other. Immediately after the ceremony the bell sounded, the groom and bride separated, the people streamed in, and Holy Mass was celebrated, thus consecrating the marriage. Reassure yourself,

Doña Isabel, all was right; the good priest gave a certificate in due form, which doubtless will be found among
John Ashley's papers."

In spite of the stony yet furious gaze with which Doña
Isabel had listened to these particulars, the governess had
gathered confidence as she proceeded, and ended with a
feeling that the most jealous doubter must be convinced,
the most inveterate opponent silenced.

But far otherwise was the effect of her narrative upon
Doña Isabel; she had been deceived by her own daughter,
befooled by her hirelings. Her keen intelligence declared
to her at once the fatal irregularity of the ceremony. It
indeed vindicated the purity of Herlinda, but could it save
her from dishonor? Thoughts of vague yet terrible meaning tormented her. The horrors of a past day returned
with fresh complications to menace and torture her; and
even had it been possible at that moment for her by one
word to prove her daughter the honorable widow of John
Ashley, it would have caused her a thousand pangs to have
uttered it; and could one single word have brought him to
life, she would have condemned herself to perpetual dumb-
ness. A frenzy of shame and baffled intents possessed her.
But her thoughts were not of these. She knew that this marriage as it stood was void; it met the requirements of neither
Church nor State. Yet — yet — yet — there were possibilities: her family were powerful, her wealth was great.

Doña Feliz watched her with deep, inquiring eyes. Her
child stood there, a voiceless pleader, her utter abandonment of grief appealing to the heart of the mother; but
between them was an impregnable wall of pride and a
cloud of possibilities which confused and distracted her.
She came to no determination, made no resolve, but clasping her hands over her eyes, stood as if a gulf had opened
in her path, — from which she could not turn, and over
which she dared not pass. Slowly, at last, she dropped
her arms, resumed her usual aspect of composure, and
passed from the room. For some moments the little
group she had left remained motionless. A profound stillness reigned throughout the house. Time itself seemed
arrested, and the one word breathed through the silence
seemed to describe the whole world to those within the
walls, — "dead! dead! dead!"

V.

As Doña Isabel Garcia turned from her daughter's apartment, she stepped into a corridor flooded with the dazzling sunshine of a perfect morning, and as she passed on in her long black dress, the heavily beamed roof interposing between her uncovered head and the clear and shining blue of the sky, there was something almost terrible in the stony gaze with which she met the glance of the woman-servant who hurried after her to know if she would as usual break her fast in the little arbor near the fountain. It terrified the woman, who drew back with a muttered "Pardon, Señora!" as the lady swept by her, and entered her own chamber.

The volcano of feeling which surged within her burst forth, not in sobs and cries, not in passionate interjections, but in the tones of absolute horror in which she uttered the two names that had severally been to her the dearest upon earth, — "Leon!" and "Herlinda!" and which at that moment were equally synonymous of all most terrible, most dreaded, and were the most powerful factors amid the love, the honor, the pride, the passions and prejudices which controlled her being.

For a time she stood in the centre of her apartment, striking unconsciously with her clenched hand upon her breast blows that at another time would have been keenly felt, but the swelling emotions within rendered her insensible to mere bodily pain. Indeed, as the moments passed it brought a certain relief; and as her walking to and fro brought her at last in front of the window which opened upon the broad prospect to the west, she paused, and looked long and fixedly toward the reduction-works, as if her vision could penetrate the stone walls, and read the mind which had perished with the man who lay murdered within them.

As she stood thus, she presently became aware that a sound which she had heard without heeding, — as one ignores passing vibrations upon the air, that bring no special echo of the life of which we are active, conscious parts, — was persistently striving to make itself heard; and with an effort she turned to the door, upon which fell another timid knock, and bade the suppliant enter; for the very echo of his knocking proclaimed a suppliant. She started as her eyes fell upon the haggard face of Pedro the gate-keeper.

He entered almost stealthily, closing the door softly behind him. "Señora," he whispered, coming up to her quite closely, extending his hands in a deprecating way, "Señora, by the golden keys of my patron, I swear to you I was powerless. Don Juan told me he had your Grace's own authority; he told me they were married!"

Doña Isabel started. In the same sentence the man had so skilfully mingled truth and falsehood that even she was deceived. By representing to his mistress that Ashley had used her name to gain entrance to the hacienda, he had hoped to divert her anger from himself, — and what matter though it fell unjustly upon the dead man? But in fact the second phrase of the sentence, "He told me they were married," was what struck most keenly upon the ear of Doña Isabel, and chilled her very blood. How much, then, did this servant know? How far was she in his power? Until that moment she had not known — had not suspected — that the murdered man and the murderer had been within the walls of the hacienda buildings. This knowledge but confirmed her intuitions! Partly to learn facts which might guide her, and partly to gain time, she looked with her coldest, most petrifying gaze upon the man, and asked him what he meant, and bade him tell her all, even as he would confess to the priest, for so only he might hope to escape her most severe displeasure.

As she spoke, she had glided behind him and slipped the bolt of the door, and stood before the solid slab of unpolished but time-darkened cedar, a very monument of wrath. Pedro trembled more than ever, but was not for that the less consistent in his tale of mingled truth and falsehood. He had begun it with the name "The Señorita Herlinda," but Doña Isabel stopped him with a portentous frown.

" Her name," she said, " my daughter's name need not
be mentioned. She knows nothing of the woman John
Ashley came here to see, if there is one ; the Señorita
Herlinda has nothing to do with her, nor with your tale.
Proceed."

Pedro, not so deeply versed in the dissimulation of the
higher class as was Doña Isabel in that of the lower,
looked at her a moment in utter incredulity. He learned
nothing from her impassive face, but with the quickwitted-
ness of his race divined that one of the many dark-eyed
damsels who served in the house was to be considered
the cause of Ashley's midnight visits. In that light, his
own breach of trust seemed more venial. Unconsciously,
he shaped his story to that end, and even took to himself
a sort of comfort in feigning to believe, what in his heart
he knew to be an assumption — whether merely verbal
or actual he knew not — of Doña Isabel.

The arguments by which he had been induced by Ashley to open the doors of the hacienda for his midnight
admittance he would have dwelt on at some length, but
Doña Isabel stopped him. " Tell me only of what happened last night," she said ; and in a low whisper he
obeyed, shuddering as he spoke of the man whom he
had admitted under the guise of a peasant, and who had
rushed out to encounter the devoted American, as a madman or wild beast might rush upon its prey.

At his description, eloquent in its brevity, Doña Isabel
for a moment lost her calmness ; her face dropped upon
her hands ; her figure shrank together.

" Pedro ! " she murmured, " Pedro ! you knew him?
You are certain? " she continued in a low, eager voice.

" Certain, Señora ! Should I be likely to be mistaken?
I, who have held him upon my knees a thousand times ;
who first taught him to ride ; who saw him when — "

Doña Isabel stopped the enumeration with a gesture.
She paused a moment in deep thought ; then she extended
her hand, and the man bent over it, not daring to touch it,
but reverently, as if it were that of a queen or a saint.

" Silence, Pedro ! " she said. " Silence ! One word,
and the law would be upon him, — though God knows
there should be no law to avenge these false Americans,
who respect neither authority nor hospitality, and would

take our very country from us. Pedro, this deed must not bring fresh disaster; 't was a mistake; but as you live, as I pardon you the share you bore in it, keep silence!"

The words were not an entreaty; they were a command. Doña Isabel understood too well the ascendency which as lords of the soil the Garcias held over all who had been born and bred on their estates, to take the false step of lessening it by any act of weakness. She comprehended that that very ascendency had led him to open the gates to the declared husband of Herlinda — ay! as to her lover he would have opened them. It was the *house* of Garcia he served, as represented by the individual possessing the dominant influence of the hour. As occasion offered, he and his associates would have favored the interests of any member in affairs of love, believing the intrigue the natural pleasure of youth, and conceiving it presumption to impugn the actions of one of the seigneurial family.

Doña Isabel became, at this time, when the terrible consequences of his levity overpowered him, the controlling power, and with absolute genius in a few words, admitting nothing, explaining nothing, offering no reward, she made the conscience-stricken man the keeper of the honor of the powerful house of which he was but the veriest minion.

Within the hour, while the people still thronged the walls of the reduction-works, Doña Feliz left the great house. The few who witnessed her departure were accustomed to the peremptory commands of the Señora Doña Isabel and the instant obedience of her confidential servant, and had as little speculation in their minds as in the gaze with which they followed the carriage and its outriders, — yet murmured a few words of pity for those who, after the horror of the tragedy, would lose the sombre splendor of the rites which must necessarily follow.

Upon the next day, John Ashley, carried in procession by the entire population of men, women, and children of Tres Hermanos, excepting only the immediate family of Doña Isabel and Pedro the gate-keeper, was borne across the wide valley, up the bleak hillside, and laid in a corner of the low-walled, unkempt graveyard, among the lowly dead of the *plebe*.

Not a sound escaped Herlinda, as from the windows of her mother's room she watched the funeral procession. She had intuitively guessed the time it would issue from the gates of the reduction-works, and her mother placed no restraint upon her movements. Through the clear atmosphere of the May day she could perfectly distinguish the form, ay the very features of her beloved, as he lay stretched upon a wide board surrounded by flowering boughs, his fair curls resting upon the greenery, his hands clasped upon his breast.

To steady their steps perhaps, rather than from any religious custom, the people sang one of those minor airs peculiar to the country, and which are at once so sad and shrill that the piercing wail reached even so far as the great house, — a weird accompaniment to the swaying of the ghostly white lengths of candles borne in scores of hands, and the pale flames of which burned colorless in the brilliant sunshine.

Strangely impressive, even to an indifferent eye, might well have been that scene; the slow march of Death and Woe across the smiling fields, blotting the clear radiance of the cloudless sky, and awesome then even to a careless ear that wail of agony. Mademòiselle La Croix burst into tears and threw herself upon the floor. Doña Isabel, deadly pale, covered her eyes with a hand as cold and white as snow. Herlinda sank upon her knees with parted lips and straining eyes to watch the form upborne before that dark and sinuous procession; but when it became lost to view amid the throng which encircled the open grave, she fell prone to the floor with such a moan as only woe itself can utter, — a moan that seemed the outburst of a maddened brain and a bursting heart.

That night instead of lamentation the sounds of festivity began to be heard, and days of revelry among the peasants followed the hours of horror and gloom which had for a brief period prevailed. In the midst of them Doña Feliz returned to the hacienda. Wherever her journey had led her it had outwardly been unimportant, and drew but little comment from the men who had attended her, and was speedily forgotten. She herself gave no description of it, nor volunteered any information as to its object or result. Even to Doña Isabel, who raised inquiring eyes to the face of her emissary as she entered her private room, she said, briefly, "No, there is no record; absolutely none."

Doña Isabel sank back in her chair with a deep-drawn breath as if some mighty tension, both of mind and body, had suddenly relaxed. She had herself sought in vain through the papers of Ashley for proofs of the alleged marriage with Herlinda, and Feliz had scanned the public records with vigilant eyes. Part of these records had in some *pronunciamiento* been destroyed by fire, but the book containing those of the date she sought was intact. The names of John Ashley and Herlinda Garcia did not appear therein; the marriage, if marriage there had been, was unrecorded, and as secret as it was illegal. Conscience was satisfied, and Doña Isabel was content to be passive. Why bring danger upon one still infinitely dear to her? The heart of Doña Isabel turned cold at the thought. Why rouse a scandal which could so easily be avoided? Why strive to legalize a marriage which could but bring ridicule upon herself, and shame and contempt upon Herlinda?

That day, for the first time in many, Doña Isabel could force a smile to her lip; for even for policy it had not been possible for her to smile before. She was by nature neither cold nor cruel, but she had been brought up in the midst of petty intrigues, of violent passions and narrow prejudices; and while she had scorned them, they had moulded her mind, — as the constant wearing of rock upon rock forms the hollow in the one, and rounds the jagged surface of the other. What would have been monstrous to her youth became natural to her middle age. She had suffered and striven. Was it not the common lot of woman? What more natural than that her daughter should do the same? And what more natural than that the mother should raise her who had fallen? — for fallen indeed, in spite of the ceremony of marriage, would the world think Herlinda. But why should the world know? She pitied her daughter, even as a woman pities another in travail; yet she looked to the future, she shrank from the complexities of the present; and so silently, relent-

lessly, shaping her course, ignoring circumstance, she, like
a goddess making a law unto herself, thus unflinchingly
ordered the destiny of her child. Could she herself have
divined the various motives that influenced her? Nay,
no more perhaps than the circumstances which will be
developed in this tale may make clear the love, the
woman's purity, the high-born lady's pride, that all combined to bid her ignore the marriage, which, though irregular, had evidently been made in good faith; and for
which, in spite of open malice or secret innuendo, the
power and influence of her family could have won the
Pope's sanction, and so silenced the cavillings if not the
gossip of the world.

AND thus in that remote hacienda — a little world in itself, with all the mingled elements of wealth and poverty, and all those subtile differences of caste and character which form society, in circles small as well as great — began a drama, which to the initiated was of deep and absorbing interest. To the common mind despair and agony can have no existence if they do not declare themselves in groans and tears, and to such Herlinda's deep pallor and her silence revealed nothing; but there were a few who watched in solemn apprehension, feeling hers to be like the intense and sulphurous calm with which Nature awaits the coming of the tempest.

But there were indeed few who saw in her any change other than the events and anxieties of the time rendered natural. At first indeed there had been whispers in corners, and half-pitying, half-fearful shrugs and glances; but almost from the day of Ashley's burial a new and fearful cause of public interest drew attention from Herlinda, from her pallor and her wide-eyed gaze of horror, to the consideration of a more personal anxiety.

The common people declared that from the night of the murder, death, unsatisfied with one victim, had hovered over the hacienda. The rains which should have fallen after the long dry winter, with cleansing and copious force, flooding the ravines and carrying away the accumulated impurities of months, had but moistened and stirred the infected mud of the stagnant water-courses and set loose the fevers which lingered in their depths. Years afterward the peasants dated many a widowhood and orphanage from those plague-stricken weeks. There was one death or more in every hut, and even the great house did not escape its quota of victims. One after another, members of the families of the clerks and officers succumbed, — the major-domo of the courts among the first, and then Mademoiselle La Croix, who indeed, it was afterward observed, had from the first sickened and fallen into a dejection, from which it was almost impossible she should rally. The governess was the object of the most devoted care even from the usually cold and stately Doña Isabel, while the panic-stricken Herlinda, careless of her own danger, bent over her with agonized and fruitless efforts to recall the waning life, or soothe the parting and remorseful soul.

But in all that terrible time this was the only event that seemed to touch or rouse her; for the rest, one might have thought those dreadful days but the ordinary calendar of Herlinda's life. Indeed, it is to be supposed that they suited so well the desolation of her spirit, and that they presented so congruous a setting to her melancholy, that it became merged and absorbed as it were in her surroundings, and so was unperceived, save as the fitting humor of a time when ease and mirth would have been an insult to the general woe.

Doña Isabel had announced her intention of replacing the director of the reduction-works; but time went on, and in the general consternation produced by the epidemic nothing was done. There was much sickness at the works; many of the most experienced hands died; and one day when the clerk in charge was at the crisis of the fever, the men who were not incapacitated from illness went by common consent to the *tienda* to stupefy themselves with fiery native brandy; and Doña Isabel, who was fearlessly passing from one poor hovel to another, aiding the village doctress and the priest in their offices, ordered the mules to be taken from the *tortas*, and the stamps to be stopped. Thus, as the masses half mixed lay upon the floors, they gradually dried and hardened; and as the great stone wheels ceased to turn in the beds of broken ores, so for years upon years they remained, and the works at Tres Hermanos gradually fell into ruin, — a fit haunt for the ghost which, as years went by, was said to haunt their shades. But this was long afterward, when the memory of the handsome and hapless youth had become almost as a myth, mingled with the thousand tales of blood which the fluctuating fortunes of years of international and civil war made as common as they were terrible.

This fertile spot until now had been singularly free from the terror and disorder that had affected the greater

part of the country; and though sharing the excitement of party feeling, the actual demands of strife had
never invaded it.   But quick upon the typhoid, when
the peasants who had been spared began to think of
repairing their half-ruined hovels, many of them were
summoned away with scant ceremony. Don Julian Garcia
appeared at the hacienda, his uniform glittering with gold
braid, buttons, and lace, the trappings of his horse more
gorgeous even than his own dress. He was raising a
troop to join his old commander, Santa Anna, who had
returned in triumph to the land from which he had been
banished, to lead the arms of his countrymen against the
foreign foe, which already had begun its victorious march
within the sacred borders of their country. In a word,
the American War had begun, and involved all factions
in one common cause, giving a rallying cry to leaders of
every party, to which even the most ignorant among the
people responded with intuitive and unquestioning ardor.

Don Julian was uncertain in his politics, but not in his
hatreds. He heard the tale of the murder of the American with complacency; the taking off of one of the heretics seemed to him natural enough, — it was scarcely
worth a second thought, certainly not a pause in his
work of collecting troops. If Isabel, he commented, had
writhed under wounded patriotism as he had done, the
American would never have had an opportunity of finding
so honorable a service in which to die. Evidently the
grudge of some bold patriot, this. What would you?
Mexicans were neither sticks nor stones!

Herlinda heard and trembled; a faint hope, a half-
formed resolve, had wakened in her breast when she had
heard of the arrival of Don Julian. He was a distant
cousin, a man of some influence in the family. She remembered him as more frank and genial than others of
her kindred. An impulse to break the seal of silence
came over her, as she heard his voice ringing through the
courts and the clank of his spurs upon the stairs; but it
was checked by the first distinct utterance of his lips,
which, like all that followed, was a denunciation of the
perfidious, the insatiable, the licentious and heretical Americans. For the first time, to the indifference with which
she had regarded the desirability of establishing her posi-

tion as the acknowledged wife of Ashley was added a sensation of fear. What had been in her mind an undefined and incomplete idea of the anger and scorn which the knowledge of her daring would cause among her family connections, became now a terrifying dread as the impetuous but unrepented act assumed the proportions of treason. The words which at the first opportunity she would have spoken died upon her lips, and she became once more hopeless, impassive, unresisting, cold, waiting what time and fate should bring.

And time passed on unflinchingly, and fate was unrelenting. Carmen, after a slight attack of fever, had been sent to some relative in Guanapila, and there she still remained. Doña Isabel's household consisted only of herself, Herlinda, and the aged priest her cousin Don Francisco de Sales, who though in his dotage still at long intervals read Mass in the chapel, baptized infants, and muttered prayers over the dying or dead, not the less sincere because he who breathed them himself stood so far within the shadow of the tomb. The old man was kindly in his senility, and spent long hours dozing in the chair of the confessional, while penitents whispered in his ear their faults and sins, for which they never failed to obtain absolution, little imagining that the placid mind of the old man, even when by chance he was awake, dwelt far more upon the scenes of his youth than the follies and wickednesses of the present. Sometimes he babbled harmlessly of days long past, even of sights and doings far from clerical; but the priestly habit was second nature, and even if he heeded the confidences reposed in him, in his weakest moments they never escaped his lips. To him Herlinda was free to go and disburden her mind, complying with the regulations of her Church, and seeking relief to her troubled soul. To him, too, Doña Isabel resorted; and these two women with their tales of woe, which as often as repeated escaped his memory, roused faintly within his heart an echo of the pain which he uneasily and confusedly remembered dwelt in the world, from which he was gliding into the peace beyond.

Sometimes at the table, or as he sat with them in the corridor, — the priest in the sunshine, they in the shade, — he looked at them with puzzled inquiry in his gaze, which changed to mild satisfaction at some caress or fond word ; for this gentle old man was tenderly beloved, with a sort of superstitious reverence. Even Doña Isabel attributed a special sanctity to his blessing, looking upon him as an automaton of the Church, which without consciousness of its own would — certain springs of emotion being touched — respond with admonition or blessing, fraught with all the authority of the Supreme Power. Doña Isabel, as a devout Romanist, had ever been scrupulous in the observances of her Church, submitting to the spiritual functions of the clergy absolutely, while she detested and openly protested against their licentiousness and greed, as also their pernicious interference in worldly affairs. Therefore throughout her life, and especially during her widowhood, she had studiously avoided the more popular clergy, and had sought the oracle of duty through some clod of humanity, who, though dull, should be at least free from vices, — choosing by preference one of her own family to be the repository of her secrets and the judge of her motives and actions. Unconsciously to herself, while outwardly and even to her own conscience fulfilling the requirements of her Church, she had interpreted them by her own will, which, in justice let it be said, had often proved a wise and loyal one ; in a word, Doña Isabel Garcia, with exceptional powers within her grasp, had skilfully and astutely freed herself from those trammels which might at the present crisis have forced her into a diametrically opposite course from that which she had determined to pursue, or would at least have forced her to acknowledge to her own mind the doubtful nature of deeds that she now suffered herself to look upon as meritorious. For years, unconsciously, her will had imbued the judgments of her spiritual adviser, as the Padre Francisco was called, and it was not to be supposed that she should cavil now, when with complacent alacrity he echoed yea to her yea, and nay to her nay, — and as she left him, sank back into his chair with a faint wonder at her tale, to forget it in his next slumber, or until recalled to him by the anguished outpourings of Herlinda, for whom he found no words of guidance other than those which throughout his life he had given to young maidens in distress, the commendable ones, "Do as your mother

directs ; " though, as he listened to her words, the tears
would pour down his cheeks, and pitying phrases fall from
his trembling lips. Poor Herlinda would be comforted
for a moment by his simple human sympathy, — even
weeping perhaps, for at such times the blessed relief of
tears was given her, — yet found in her darkness no
light, either human or divine.

Had Mademoiselle La Croix lived, Herlinda would doubtless have received from her the impetus to throw herself
upon the pity and protection of her cousin Don Julian,
which in spite of his prejudices he could scarcely have refused ; for the governess, though she was at first stunned
and terrified by the knowledge of the invalidity of the
marriage, was no coward, and would have braved much
to reinstate the girl she had through compassion — and,
she had with a pang been obliged to own, through cupidity — aided to bring into a false position. But she had
scarcely recovered her bewildered senses, the more bewildered by the incomprehensible calm of Doña Isabel, when
she was attacked by the fever, — to which she succumbed
a month before the appearance of the doughty warrior,
whose blustering fierceness would not have appalled her or
deterred her from urging Herlinda to lay before him the
matter, whose vital importance the stunned young creature failed to comprehend.

Later it burst upon her, but it was then too late, —
Don Julian had marched away with his troops. She was
alone, — no help, no counsellor near. Alone? Ah, no !
there were human creatures near, who could behold and
suspect and shake the head. Herlinda awoke to the
shame of her position, as a bird in a net, striving to fly,
first learns its danger. O God ! where should she fly?
Were these careless, laughing women as unconscious as
they seemed? Where might she hide herself from these
languid, soft eyes, which suddenly might become hard and
cruel with intelligence? Herlinda drew her reboso around
her, and with flushing cheek traversed the shadiest corridors in her necessary passages from room to room, her
eyes, large with apprehension, burning beneath her down-
cast lids. Every day she grew more restless, more beautiful. She walked for hours in the walled garden, which
the servants never entered. They began to whisper, for-

getting the gossip of months before, that the chances of war were secretly stealing the gayety and buoyancy of Herlinda's youth, by keeping from her side the playmate of her childhood, her lover Vicente Gonzales. Feliz smiled when a garrulous servant spoke thus one day, but ten minutes later entered the room of Doña Isabel.

The next morning it was known that the Señorita Herlinda was to have change, was to go to the capital, that Mecca of all Mexicans. Doña Isabel and Feliz were to accompany her. The clerks and overseers wondered, and shook their heads wisely. They had heard wild tales of the political factions which rendered the city unsafe to woman as to man; Santa Anna's brief dictatorship had ended in trouble. Still, in that remote district nothing was known with certainty, and these bucolic minds were not given to many conjectures upon the motives or movements of their superiors. If anything could arouse surprise, it was the fact that the ladies were not to travel by private carriage, as had been the custom of the Garcias from time immemorial, attended by a numerous escort of armed rancheros; but being driven to the nearest post where the public diligence was to be met, were to proceed by it most unostentatiously upon their way. This aroused far more discussion than the fact of the journey itself; though it was unanimously agreed that if Doña Isabel could force herself to depart from the accustomed dignity of the family, and indeed preserve a slight incognito upon the road, her chances of making the journey in safety would be greatly increased.

Her resolve once made it was acted upon instantly, no time being allowed for news of her departure to spread abroad and to give the bandits who infested the road opportunity to plan the *plajio*, or carrying off, of so rich a prize as Doña Isabel Garcia and her daughter would have proved. And thus, early one November morning, — when the whole earth was covered with the fresh greenness called into growth by the rainy season which had just passed, and the azure of a cloudless sky hung its perfect arch above the valley, seeming to rest upon the crown-like circlet of the surrounding hills, — Herlinda passed through the crowd of dependents who, as usual on such occasions, gathered at the gates to see the travellers off. Doña

Isabel, who was with her, was affable, smiling and nodding to the men, and murmuring farewell words to the
nearest women; but Herlinda was silent, and it was
not until she was seated in the carriage that she threw
back the reboso which she had drawn to her very eyes,
revealing her face, which was deadly pale. As she
gazed lingeringly around, half sadly, half haughtily,
with the proud curve of the lip (though it quivered)
which made all the more striking her general resemblance
to her beautiful mother, a thrill, they knew not of what
or why, ran through the throng. For a moment there was
a profound silence, in the midst of which the aged priest
raised his hand in blessing. Suddenly a flash of memory,
a gleam of inspiration, came over him; he turned aside the
hand of Doña Isabel, which had been extended in farewell,
and laid his own upon the bowed head of her daughter.
" Fear not, my daughter," he said, " thou art blessed.
Though I shall see thee no more, my blessing, and the
blessing of God, shall be with thee."

The old man turned away, leaning heavily upon Doña
Rita, the wife of the administrador, who led him tenderly
away, and a few minutes later he was sitting smiling at
her side, while without were heard the farewell cries of
the women. "May God go with you, Niña! May you
soon return! Adios, Niña! more beautiful than our
patron saint! Adios, and joy be with thee!" And in
the midst of such good wishes, as Herlinda still leaned
from the window, a smile upon her lip, her hand waving
a farewell, the carriage drove away and the people dispersed; leaving Pedro, the gate-keeper, standing motionless in the shadow of the great door-post, his eyes riveted
on the sands at his feet, but seeing still the glance of
agony, of warning, of entreaty, which had darted from
Herlinda's eyes, and seemed to scorch his own.

VII.

Upon the death of Mademoiselle La Croix, or rather perhaps from the time of her return to the hacienda after her ineffectual quest, Doña Feliz had virtually become the duenna of Herlinda. Not that such an office was formally recognized or required in the seclusion of Tres Hermanos, but it was nevertheless true that Herlinda had seldom found herself alone, even in the walled garden. Though she paced its narrow paths without companionship, she had been aware that her mother or Doña Feliz lingered near; and it was this consciousness that had steeled her outwardly, and forced her to restrain the passionate despair that under other circumstances would have burst forth to relieve the tension of mind and brain. When she at last roused from the apathy of despair, her days became periods of speechless agony, but sometimes at night, when she had believed that Feliz — who, since Carmen's departure, had occupied the adjacent room — was asleep, for a few brief moments she had yielded to the demands of her grief, and given way to sobs and tears, to throw herself finally prostrate before the little altar, where she kept the lamp constantly burning before the Mother of Sorrows. Thence Feliz at times had raised her, and led her to her bed, — chill, unresisting, more dead than alive, yet putting aside the arm that would have supported her, and by mute gestures entreating to be left to her misery.

Fortunately for her reason, there were times when in utter exhaustion Herlinda had slept heavily and awoke refreshed, — and this had occurred a night or two after she had learned, by a few decisive words from her mother, of her imminent removal from Tres Hermanos. She had retired early, and awoke to find the soft and brilliant moonlight flooding her chamber. Every article in the room was visible; their shadows fell black upon the tiled floor, and the lamp before the altar burned pale. A profound stillness reigned. Herlinda raised herself on her pillow, and looked around her. The scene was weird and ghostly, and she presently became aware that she was utterly alone. She listened intently, — not the echo of a breath from the next room. Her heart leaped; for a moment its pulsations perplexed her; another, and she had moved noiselessly from her bed and crossed the room. She glanced into that adjoining. That too was flooded in moonlight, which shone full upon the bed. Yes, it was empty. Doña Feliz had doubtless been called to some sick person; she had left Herlinda sleeping, thinking that at that hour of the night there could be no danger in leaving her for a brief half hour alone.

In an instant these thoughts darted through Herlinda's mind, followed by a project that of late she had much dwelt upon, but had believed impossible of realization. With trembling hands she took from her wardrobe a dress of some soft dark stuff, and a black and gray reboso, and put them on. Without pausing a moment for thought that might deter her, she glided from the room, crossed the corridor, and descended the stairs, taking the same direction in which Ashley had gone to his death. She paused too at the gate, to do as he had done; for she touched the sleeping Pedro lightly upon the shoulder, at the same instant uttering his name.

The man started from his sleep affrighted, — too much affrighted to cry out; for like most haciendas, Tres Hermanos had its ghost. From time to time the apparition of a weeping woman was seen by those about to die. Had she come to him now? His tongue clove to the roof of his mouth; he shook in every limb. The moonlight shone full in the court, but the archway was in shade: who or what was this that stood beside him, extending a white arm from its dark robes, and touching him with one slight finger? A repetition of his name restored him to his senses, and he staggered to his feet, muttering, "Señorita! My Señorita, for God's sake why are you here? You will be seen! You will be recognized!"

" ' In the night all cats are gray,' " she answered, with one of those proverbs as natural to the lips of a Mexican as the breath they draw. " No one would distinguish me in this light from any of the servants; but still my words

4

must be brief, for my absence from my room may be discovered. Pedro, I have a work to do; it has been in my mind all this time. You, you can help me!"

She clasped her hands; he thought she looked at the door, and the idea darted into his mind that she contemplated escape, or that she had a mad desire to throw herself upon her lover's grave and die there.

"Niña! Niña, of my life!" he said imploringly, using the form of address one might employ to a child, or some dearly loved elder, still dependent. "Go back to your chamber, I beg and implore! How can I do anything for you? How can Pedro, so worthless, so vile, do anything?"

The adjectives he applied to himself were sincere enough, for Pedro had never ceased to reproach himself for his share in the tragedy which, in spite of Doña Isabel's words, he had never really ceased to believe concerned Herlinda, though he had striven for his own peace of mind, as well as in loyalty to the Garcias, to affect a contrary opinion, until this moment, when his young mistress's appearance and appeal rendered self-deception no longer possible. Again and again he reiterated, "What can the miserable Pedro do for you?"

Apparently with an instinct of concealment, Herlinda had crouched upon the stones, and as the man stood before her she raised her face and gazed at him with her dark eyes. How large they looked in the uncertain light! how the young face quivered and was convulsed, as her lips parted! Pedro, with an inward shrinking, expected her to demand of him the name of Ashley's murderer; but the thought of vengeance, if it ever crossed her mind, was far from it at that moment. "Yes, yes, there is perhaps something you can do for me," she said. "Men are able to do so much, while we poor women can only fold our hands, and wait and suffer. I thought differently once, though. John used to laugh at what he called our idle ways; he said women were made to act as well as men. But what can I do? What could any woman do in my place? Nothing! nothing! nothing!"

Pedro was silent. He knew well how powerless, what a mere chattel or toy, was a young woman of his people. It seemed, too, quite natural and right to him. In this particular case the mother was acting with incompar-

able severity, but she was within her right. Even while
he pitied the child, it did not enter his mind to counsel
her to combat her mother's will. He only repeated mechanically, " What can I do? What would you have your
servant do? "

" Not so hard a thing," she said with a sob in her voice ;
" even a woman, had I one for my friend, could do this
thing for me ; and yet it is all I have to ask in the world.
Just a little pity for my child, Pedro! " She rose to her
feet suddenly, and spoke rapidly. " Pedro, they say that
I was not truly married ; they say my beautiful, golden-
haired husband, my angel of light, deceived me. It is
false, Pedro! all false! But they say the world will not
believe me, and so I must go away ; and my child, like an
offspring of shame, must be born in secret, and I must
submit. It will be taken from me, and I must submit.
There is no help! no help! "

She spoke in a kind of frenzy, and her excitement communicated itself to Pedro. He understood, far better than
she could, the motives of Doña Isabel; he did not condemn her, neither did he attempt to justify her to her
daughter. He only muttered again in his stoical way,
" What can I do? "

Herlinda accepted the words as they were meant, as an
offer of devotion, of service. " Pedro, you can do much,"
she said rapidly. " You can watch over my child.
Years hence, when I come to ask it, you can give me
news of it. Ah, they think when they take my child from
me, it will be as dead to me ; but Pedro," she added in an
eager whisper, " I have found what they will do. Never
mind how I learned it. They will bring my child here, —
here, where only the peasants will ask a few useless questions, where there will be no person of influence to interfere. Yes, it will be brought here, and — forgotten! But
Pedro, promise me you will watch for it, you will protect
it. Promise! promise! promise! "

Pedro was startled, but not incredulous. This would
not be the first child that had been found at the hacienda
doors, left to the charity of the señoras ; more than one
half-grown boy, of whose parents no one knew anything,
loitered in the courts, and even the maid who served Doña
Isabel was a foundling of this class.

"But how shall I know," he stammered, after he had satisfied her with the promise she desired. "True enough, it may be brought here, but how shall I know?"

Herlinda scarcely heeded his words. She was busy in taking a small reliquary from her neck. It was square, made of pale blue silk, and in no way remarkable. "See, I will put this around its neck," she said. "No one will dare remove a reliquary. There is a bit of the true cross in it. It will keep evil away; it will bring good fortune. The first day I wore it I met John; and" she added, nervously fingering the jewel at her ear, "take this, Pedro. The other I will put in the reliquary, with a prayer to San Federigo. When you see the strange child that will come here, look for these signs, and as you hope for mercy hereafter, guard the child that bears them."

She had placed in his hand a flat earring of quaint filagree work, one of the marvels of rude and almost barbaric workmanship that the untaught goldsmiths of the haciendas produce. Pedro would have returned it to her, swearing by all he held sacred to do her will; but some sound had startled her. She slipped the reliquary into her bosom, drew her scarf around her, and glided away. He saw her pass the small doorway like a spectre. He could scarcely believe that she had been there at all, that she had actually spoken to him. He crossed himself as he lost sight of her, and looked in a dazed way at the earring in his palm.

"Would to God," he muttered, "I had told Doña Isabel all the truth, as I meant to, when I went to her from the dead man's side. Why did I not tell her plainly I knew her daughter Herlinda to be the woman Ashley had come here to meet, — would she have dared then to say she was not his wife? Fool that I was! I myself doubted. What, doubt that sweet angel! Beast! imbecile!" and Pedro flung his striped blanket from him with a gesture of disgust. "And now, what would be the use, though I should trumpet abroad the whole matter? No, my hour has passed. Doña Isabel must work her will; I will not fail her, for only by being true can I serve her daughter. But who knows? — Herlinda may be deceived; her fears may have turned her brain. Yet all the same I will keep this token;" and he looked

at the earring reverently, then placed it in his wallet.
Two days later, when she left Tres Hermanos and he saw
its fellow in Herlinda's ear, he caught the momentary
glance in her dark eye, and stood transfixed.

Pedro Gomez hitherto had been a careless, idle, rollick-
ing fellow; thenceforward he became grave, watchful, and
crafty, — the change which, had there been keen observers
near, all might have noticed in the outward man being as
nothing to that from the specious fellow whom Ashley had
found it an easy matter to bribe, to the conscience-stricken
man who stood at the gates of the great hacienda of the
Garcias, cognizant of its conflicting interests, and sworn
to guard them; his crafty mind inclining to Doña Isabel
and the cause she represented, his heart yearning over the
erring daughter.

VIII.

Though Herlinda Garcia had forced a smile to her lips as she left, perhaps forever, the house where she was born, as the carriage was driven rapidly across the fertile valley her eyes remained fixed with melancholy, even despairing, intensity upon the walls wherein she had learned in her brief experience of life much that combines to make up the sum of woman's wretchedness.

Herlinda had ever been an imaginative child, even before she had attained the age of seven years, at which she had been taught to consider herself a reasoning, responsible being; she had been conscious of vague feelings and desires, which had in a measure separated her from her family and the people who surrounded her, and had set her in sullen opposition to the aimless and inane occupations which served to while away days that her eager nature longed to fill with action. Though she had not been conscious of any especial direction into which she would have thrown her energies, she had been most keenly conscious that she possessed them, and early rebelled against the petty tasks that curbed and strove to stifle them, — such tasks as the embroidering of capes and stoles, or drawing of threads from fine linen, to be replaced with intricate stitches of needle-work, to form the decoration of altar cloths, or the garments of the waxen Lady of Sorrows above the altar in the chapel, or of the Virgin of Guadalupe in the great *sala*, — as she did also against the endless repetition of prayers, for which she needlessly turned the leaves of her well-thumbed breviary. How she had longed for freedom to run with the peasant children over the fields! How many hours she had hung over the iron railing of her mother's balcony, and gazed upon the far hills, and wondered what sort of world lay in the blue beyond them.

Sometimes Herlinda had attempted to talk to Vicente Gonzales of these things when he came from the city, privileged as the son of an old friend, and the scion of a wealthy and influential family, to form an early intimacy with the pretty child, whom later he would meet but in her mother's presence with all the restrictions of Spanish etiquette. She had always liked the proud, handsome boy, but he was far slower in mental development than she, and could only laugh at her fancies. And so as they grew older, and he in secret grew more fond, she had become indifferent, restlessly longing for an expansion of her contracted and aimless existence, yet finding no promise in the prospects of war and political strife which began to allure Gonzales, and in which she could not hope to take part, — and to sit a spectator was not in the nature of Herlinda. Her mother delighted to watch the fray, to counsel and direct. It was perhaps this trait in Doña Isabel's character that, while it had awakened her daughter's admiration, had chafed and fretted her, checking the natural expression of her lively and energetic spirit, even as the cold and stately dignity of her manner repressed the affections which lay ardent within her, waiting but the magnetic touch of a responsive nature.

Such an one had not . been found within her home ; all were cold, preoccupied, absorbed in the every-day affairs of life. Sometimes, when by chance Herlinda had caught a glimpse of the repressed inner nature of Doña Feliz, the mother of the administrador, she had felt for a moment drawn toward her ; but although all her life she had lived beneath the same roof with her, there had occurred no special circumstance to draw them into intimacy, or in any way lessen the barrier that difference in age and position raised between them, — for perhaps in no part of the world are the subtle differences of caste so clearly recognized and so closely observed as in those little worlds, the Mexican *haciendas de campo*.

Sometimes, in her unhappiest moods, when her unrest had become actual pain and resolved itself into a vague but real feeling of grief, Herlinda had thought of her father, in her heart striving to idealize what was but an uncertain memory of an elderly, formal-mannered man, handsome according to the type of his race, — sharp-featured, eagle-eyed, but small of stature, with small effeminate hands which Herlinda could remember she used to kiss, in the respectful salutation with which she had been taught to greet him. He had died when Herlinda was eight years old, just after the second daughter, Carmen, was born; and though Doña Isabel seldom mentioned him, it was understood that she had loved him deeply, and for his sake lived the life of semi-isolation which her age, her beauty, her talents, and wealth seemed to combine to render an unnatural choice. As she grew older, Herlinda began to wonder, and sometimes repine, at this utter separation from the world of which in a hurried visit to the city of Guanapila she had once caught a glimpse. Especially was this the case after the arrival of Mademoiselle La Croix, who was lost in wonder that any one should voluntarily resign herself to exile even in so lovely a spot; and although she opened for Herlinda a new world in the studies to which she directed her, they had been rather of an imaginative than a logical kind, and stimulated those faculties which should rather have been repressed, while personally the governess had answered no need in the frank yet repressed and struggling nature of her pupil.

These had been the conditions under which Herlinda had met John Ashley, and we know with what result. As the tiny stream rushes into the river and is carried away by its force, their waters mingling indistinguishably, so the mind, the very soul of Herlinda had felt the power of that perfect sympathy which, in the few short words uttered in the pauses of a dance (for they had first met at Guanapila) and the expressive glances of his eyes, she believed herself to have found in the mind and heart of the alien,—a man in her mother's employ, one whom ordinarily she would have treated with perfect politeness, but would have thought of as set as far apart from her own life as though they were beings of a separate order of creation. The fact that he was a handsome young man would primarily have had no effect upon Herlinda, though undoubtedly it served to render to her mind more natural and delightful the ascendency which, in spite of all obstacles, he rapidly gained over her entire nature.

Needless is it for us to analyze the mind and character of Ashley. It is certain he loved Herlinda passionately, and in the opposition of Doña Isabel to his suit saw but irrational prejudice and mediæval tyranny. His entire freedom from sordid motives, and his fears of the consequences of delay, — knowing as he did of the desired engagement between Herlinda and the young Vicente Gonzales, — justified to his mind a course which the canons of honor would have forbidden, but of the legality of which he certainly had had no question, the intricacies and delicacies of marriage laws having engaged no share in the attention of a somewhat adventurous youth.

This very heedlessness and activity of John Ashley's nature had formed an especial charm to Herlinda; she would have shrunk from and pondered over a more cautious nature, — perhaps would have ended in loving, but she never would have cast aside all the traditions of her youth. All her life she had been like a bird in the cage. For a brief space she had seen the wide expanse of the sky opening above her, she had fluttered upward; but death had struck her down to darkness, — death, which had pierced the strong and loving one who would have guided and protected her! She moaned, and turned her face to the corner of the carriage. An arm stole around her; it was that of Doña Feliz.

THE pale dawn, creeping over the hills behind which the sun was still hidden, revealing to the accustomed sight of Doña Feliz a narrow, irregular street of adobe hovels; a tiny church with a square tower, where the swallows were sleepily chirping; around and behind, stray trees and patches of gardens; upon the waste of sand, where cacti and dusty sagebrush grew, up to the hills where the pines began, a road of yellow sand, winding like a sinuous serpent over all; two or three early loiterers, with eyes turned toward the diligence, which thus early was making its way from the night's resting place toward the distant city, — such was the scene upon which the trusted servant and friend of the Garcias looked on a morning early in November. She was standing in the low gateway that gave entrance to a garden overgrown with weeds and vines. These vines spread from the fig and orange trees, and half covered the ruinous walls of a house which had once, where the surroundings were so humble, ranked as an elegant mansion, and which indeed had served in years gone by as a temporary retreat, small but attractive, for such of the family of Garcia as desired a few days' retirement from their accustomed pursuits. Here the ladies had wandered amid the flowers, and sat under the arbors where the purple grapes clustered, and honeysuckle and jessamine mingled their rich odors; and the gentlemen had smoked their cigarettes in luxurious ease, or sallied forth to shoot the golden plover in its season, or hunt the deer amid the surrounding hills. This had in fact been a *quinta*, or pleasure resort, but since the days of revolutions and bandits it had been utterly abandoned to the rats and owls, or to the nominal care of the ragged brood who huddled together in the half-ruinous kitchen; and here the romance of Herlinda's life had been enacted.

When Doña Isabel Garcia had desired to send her daughter from the hacienda of Tres Hermanos, in order to remove her from the neighborhood of Ashley and give her the benefit of change, she had at first been sadly perplexed where to send her. Should she go to her relatives in the city, it was possible that her dejected mien and unguarded words might give them a suspicion of the truth, — and Doña Isabel detested gossip, particularly family gossip; besides, she looked upon Herlinda's marriage with Vicente Gonzales as certain, and dreaded lest the faintest rumor of the young girl's attachment should reach his ears, and awaken in him the slumbering demon of jealousy, — which, though it might rouse the young soldier as a lover to fresh ardor only, might incite him later as her husband to a tyranny which the mind of Herlinda was ill disposed to bear. In this dilemma the house at Las Parras had occurred to her. Once in her own girlhood she had visited the place, and she remembered it as a most charming sylvan retreat; and although she knew it to be situated in the outskirts of a small hamlet scarce worthy of the name of village, and that it had been abandoned for years, its isolation and abandonment at that juncture precisely constituted its attractions; and thither, under the care of Don Rafael the administrador and of Mademoiselle La Croix, Herlinda had been sent. Precautions had been taken to baffle the inquiries of Ashley as to their route and destination, which, as has been said, an accident revealed to him just when his mind was most strongly excited by the mystery which his disposition and training, as well as his love, led him passionately to resent. Hither, too, when a new and still more important need had risen, Herlinda had been brought.

Doña Isabel had been unaffectedly shocked, when, after a tortuous journey by diligence in order to evade conjecture as to their destination, they had at nightfall arrived at this deserted mansion, and had passed through the narrow door-way set in the high stone-wall that surrounded the garden, and had looked upon its tangled masses of half tropic vegetation, and entered the ruin, to find that only three or four small rooms opening upon the vineyard were habitable. But in these few rooms they and their secret were safe, — safe as if buried in the caves of the earth. Herlinda looked around her for familiar faces, but all she saw were strange to her. Doña Isabel had guarded against recognition of Herlinda, and even her own identity was disguised. To the women and the old man who performed the work of the kitchen and went the necessary errands, but who were rigidly excluded from the private rooms, she was known only as a friend of Doña Isabel Garcia, — one Doña Carlota, whose family name awoke no interest or inquiry.

After satisfying her hungry anxiety to catch a glimpse of the servants, and finding them strangers, Herlinda made no further effort to encounter them. She was very ill after arrival, and it is doubtful whether the attendants — dull, apathetic creatures — ever saw her face plainly from the day she entered the house until that of which we speak, when Doña Feliz stood in the low doorway in the garden wall, and looked toward the diligence which appeared indistinctly, a moving monster in the distance. She glanced back occasionally, half impatiently, half sorrowfully, to the house. Through the open door of it presently glided Doña Isabel. Her head was bent, her olive cheeks were deadly pale, and she shivered as with cold as she stepped out into the dusk of early morning, — or rather late night, for it was an hour when not a creature around the place was stirring, not even the birds; a wide-eyed cat stared at her as she passed down the narrow walk, and she shrank even from its gaze. She held something under her black reboso, which upon reaching Feliz she passed to her with averted eyes.

"Take it," she said; "Herlinda is asleep. We trust you, Feliz. I in my shame, she in her despair, we give this child to you, never to ask it of you again, never to know whether it lives or dies."

The passionless composure with which she said these words, the absolute freedom from any tone of vindictiveness, gave to them the accent of perfect trust. There was nothing of cruelty, nothing of hesitancy in the tone or words or manner with which Doña Isabel Garcia laid in the arms of Feliz a new-born sleeping infant, and thus separated herself and her family from the fate which with absolute confidence she placed in the hands of the statuesque, cold-faced woman who stood there to receive it.

But with the child in her arms a great change swept over the face of Feliz. One could not have told at a glance whether it was loathing and resentment, or an agony of pity, that convulsed her features, or all combined. "My words are all said," she murmured. "Herlinda is, you say, resigned. Oh, Doña Isabel, Doña Isabel, you will rue this hour! I do your will; do not you blame or accuse me in the future!"

The diligence had driven through the village. To the astonishment of the idlers it stopped before the wall that circled the half-ruined *quinta;* a woman stepped through the doorway, and was helped to her seat. She had evidently been expected by the driver. They would have been still more surprised had they also seen the lady who waved a white hand at parting, and who turned back into the garden with a deep-drawn sigh of relief, followed by a groan that seemed to rend and distort the lips through which it came, and which she vainly strove to keep from trembling as she entered the house, and answered the call of her awakened daughter.

What can I say of the scene that followed? What that will awaken pity, unstained with blame, for that poor creature, so powerless in that land that her sisters, in others more blessed, perhaps, find it impossible to put themselves in imagination in her place even for a single moment? But the captive slave can writhe; woman, the pampered toy, may weep: and where woman was both (for even in Mexico a new era is dawning on her), she could struggle and despair and die,—but, as Herlinda knew too well, in youth at least she could not assert her womanhood, and make or mar her own destiny. In such a land, in such a cause, what champion would arise to beat down the iron laws of custom which manacled and crushed her? Not one!

X.

ONE day Pedro Gomez, half-sleeping half-meditating as he sat on the stone bench beneath the hanging serpents that garnished the vestibule of Tres Hermanos, thought he saw a ghost upon the stairs which led from one corner of the wide court into which he had glanced, to the corridor of the upper floor. An apparition of Doña Feliz, he thought, had passed up them; and with ready superstition he decided in his own mind that some evil had befallen her in her journeyings. He was so disturbed by this idea that a few moments later, as her son Don Rafael passed through the vestibule, he ventured to stop him and tell him what he had seen; whereat Don Rafael burst into a loud laugh.

"What, do you not know," he said, "that my mother has returned? Ah, I remember you were at Mass this morning. She came over from the post-house on donkey-back. A wonderful woman is my mother; but she knew we had need of her, and she came none too soon. I opened the door to her myself;" and Don Rafael hastened to his own apartments, where it was understood Doña Rita his wife hourly awaited the pangs of mother-hood, and left Pedro gazing after him in open-mouthed astonishment.

In the first place nothing had been heard of the probability of the return of Doña Feliz; in the second, the manner of her return was unprecedented. She was a woman of some consequence at the hacienda. It was an almost incredible thing that under any circumstances she should arrive unexpectedly at the diligence post, and ride a league upon a donkey's back like the wife of a laborer. And thirdly it was a miracle that he Pedro had himself gone to Mass that morning, — he could not remember how it had come about, — and that discovering his absence from the gate Don Rafael had himself performed his functions, and had not soundly rated him for his unseasonable devotion; for Don Rafael was not a man to confound the claims of spiritual and secular duties.

Pedro Gomez did not put the matter to himself in precisely these words; nevertheless it haunted and puzzled him, and kept him in an unusual state of abstraction,—which perhaps accounted for the fact that later in the day, just at high-noon, when the men were afield and the women busy in their huts, and Pedro had ample leisure for his siesta, he was suddenly aroused by a voice that seemed to fall from the skies. Springing to his feet, he almost struck against a powerful black horse, which was reined in the doorway; and dazzled by the sun, and confused by the unexpected encounter, he gazed stupidly into the face of a man who was bending toward him, his broad hat pushed back from a mass of coal-black hair, his white teeth exposed by the laugh that lighted up his whole face as he exclaimed,—

"Here, brother! here is a good handful for thee! I found it on the road yonder. *Caramba!* my horse nearly stepped on it! Do people in these parts scatter such seeds about? I fancy the crop would be but a poor one if they did, and I saw a good growth of little ones in the village yonder. Well, well! I have no use for such treasure; I freely bestow it on thee,"—and with a dexterous movement the stranger placed a bundle, wrapped in a tattered scarf, in the hands of the astounded Pedro, and without waiting question or thanks, whichever he might have expected, put spurs to his horse and galloped across the dusty plain.

Twice that day had Pedro Gomez been left, as he would have said, open-mouthed. Almost unconscious of what he did, he stood there watching the cloud of dust in which the horse and rider disappeared, until he felt himself pulled by the sleeve, and a sharp voice asked, "In the name of the Blessed, Tio, what have you there? Ay, Holy Babe! it is a child!"

A faint cry from the bundle confirmed these words; a tiny pink fist thrust out gave assurance to the eyes.

Pedro Gomez, strong man as he was, trembled in every limb, and sank on a seat breathless; but even in his agitation he resisted the efforts of his niece to unwrap the child.

"Let it be," he said; "I will myself look at this gift which the Saints have sent me."

With trembling hands he undid its wrappings. The babe was crying lustily; red, grimacing, struggling, it was still a pretty child, — a girl only a few days old. Around its neck, under the little dress of white linen, was a silken cord. Pedro drew it forth, certain of what he should find. Florencia pounced upon the blue reliquary eagerly. "Let us open it," she said; "perhaps we shall find something to tell us where the babe comes from, and whose it is."

"Nonsense!" said Pedro, decidedly; "what should we find in it but scraps of paper scribbled with prayers? And who would open a reliquary?"

Florencia looked down abashed, for she was a good daughter of the Church, and had been taught to reverence such things.

"No, no, girl! run to the village and bring a woman who can nourish this starving creature;" and as the girl flew to execute her commission, Pedro completed his examination of the child.

It was clothed in linen, finer than rancheros use even in their gala attire, and the red flannel with white spots, called *bayeta*, was of the softest to be procured; but beyond this there was nothing to indicate the class to which the child belonged. Upon a slip of paper pinned to its bosom was written the name *Maria Dolores* (what more natural than that such a child should bear the name, and be placed under the protection of the Mother of Sorrows?), and upon the reverse was "Señora Doña Isabel Garcia." Was this to commend the waif to the care or attention of that powerful lady? Pedro rather chose to think it a warning against her. "What! place the bird before the hawk?" With a grim smile he thrust the paper into his bosom. Doña Isabel was he knew not where, — later would be time enough to think of her; meanwhile, here were all the women and children, all the old men, and halt and lame of the village, trooping up to see this waif, which in such an unusual manner had been dropped into the gate-keeper's horny palms.

Some of the women laughed; all the men joked Pedro when they saw the child, though a yellow nimbus of hair around its head and the fineness of its clothing puzzled them.

Pedro had hastily thrust the slip of paper into his breast, scarce knowing why he did so; for though some instinct as powerful as if it were a living voice that spoke, urged him to secrete the child, to rush away with it into the fastnesses of the mountains, rather than to render it to Doña Isabel, he did not doubt for a moment that she herself had provided for its mysterious appearance at the hacienda, that it might be received as a waif, and cared for by Doña Feliz as her representative.

These thoughts flashed through his mind, and he heard again Herlinda's despairing cry: "Watch for my child! Protect it! protect it!" Was it possible that she had actually known that this disposition would be made of her child? Involuntarily his arms closed around it, and he clasped it to his broad breast, looking defiantly around.

"Tush, Pedro, give it to me!" cried one stout matron, longing to take the little creature to her motherly breast. "What know you of nursing infants? A drop of mother's milk would be more welcome to it than all thy dry hugs. Ah, here comes the Señor Administrador," and the crowd opened to admit the passage of Don Rafael, who attracted by the commotion had hastened to the spot in no small anger, ordering the crowd to disperse; but he was greeted with an incomprehensible chorus of which he only heard the one word "baby," and exclaimed in indignation, —

"And is this the way to show your delight, when the poor woman is at the point of death perhaps? Get you gone, and it will be time enough to make this hubbub when it comes."

The women burst out laughing, the men grinned from ear to ear, and the children fell into ecstasies of delight. Don Rafael was naturally thinking of the expected addition to his own family, and was enraged at what he supposed to be a premature manifestation of sympathy. Pedro alone was grave, and stepping back pointed to the infant, which was now quiet upon the bosom of Refugio, her volunteer nurse. "This is the child they speak of, Señor," he said, and in a few words related the manner in which it had been delivered to him.

5

If he had expected to see any consciousness or confusion upon the face of Don Rafael, he must certainly have been disappointed, for there was simply the frankest and most perfect amazement, as he turned to the woman who had stepped out a little from the crowd and held the infant toward him. He saw at a glance that it was no Indian child,—the whiteness of its skin, the fineness of its garments, above all the yellow nimbus of hair, already curling in tiny rings around the little head, struck him with wonder. He crossed himself, and ejaculated a pious " Heaven help us ! " and touched the child's cheek with the tip of his finger, and turned its face from its nurse's dusky breast in a very genuine amaze, which Pedro watched jealously. The child cried sleepily, and nestled under the reboso which the woman drew over it, hushing it in her arms, murmuring caressingly, as her own child tugged at her skirts,—" There, there, sleep little one, sleep ! nothing shall harm thee ; sleep, *Chinita,* sleep ! "

But the little waif—whose soft curls had suggested the pet name—was not yet to slumber ; for at that moment Doña Feliz appeared. Pedro noticed as she crossed the courtyard that she was extremely pale. Some of the women rushed toward her with voluble accounts of the beauty of the child and the fineness of its garments. She smiled wearily, and turned from them to look at the foundling. A flush spread over her face as she examined it, not reddening but deepening its clear olive tint. She looked at Rafael searchingly, at Pedro questioningly. He muttered over his thrice-told tale. " Was there no word, no paper ? " she said, but waited for no answer. " This is no plebeian child, Rafael. What shall we do with it ? Doña Isabel is not here, perhaps will not be here for years ! "

There was a buzz of astonishment, for this was the first intimation of Doña Isabel's intended length of absence. In the midst of it Pedro had taken the sleeping child from Refugio's somewhat reluctant arm, and wrapping it in a scarf taken from his niece's shoulders, had laid it on the sheepskin in the alcove in which he usually slept. This tacit appropriation perhaps settled the fate of the infant ; still Doña Feliz looked at her son uneasily, and he rubbed his hands in perplexity. " Of all the days in the year for a babe like this to be left here," he said, " when, the Saints willing, I am to have one of my own! No, no, mother, Rita would never consent."

"Consent to what?" she answered almost testily. "What! Because this foundling chances to be white, would you have your wife adopt it as her own, when after so many years of prayer Heaven has sent her a child? No, no, Rafael, it would be madness!"

"There is no need," interpolated Pedro, with a half-savage eagerness, and with a look which, strangely combined of indignation and relief, should have struck dumb the woman who thus to the mind of the gate-keeper was revealed as the incarnation of deceit,—" there is no need. I will keep the child; 'without father or mother or a dog to bark for me,' who can care for it better? Here are Refugio and Teresa and Florencia will nurse it for me. It will want for nothing." A chorus of voices answered him : " We will all be its mother."—" Give it to me when it cries, and I will nurse it." — " The Saints will reward thee, Pedro!"—in the midst of which, in answer to a call from above, Doña Feliz hastened away, saying, " Nothing could be better for the present. Come, Rafael, you are wanted. I will write to Doña Isabel, Pedro; she will doubtless do something when you are tired of it. There is, for example, the asylum at Guanapila."

Pedro gazed after her blankly. In spite of that momentary flush on the face, Doña Feliz had seemed as open as the day. He never ceased thereafter to look upon her in indignant admiration and fear. Her slightest word was like a spell upon him. Pedro was of a mind to propitiate demons, rather than worship angels. There was something to his mind demoniacal in this Doña Feliz.

Half an hour after she had ascended the stairs, and the idlers had dispersed to chatter over this event, leaving the new-found babe to its needed slumber, the woman who acted the part of midwife to Doña Rita ran down to the gate where Pedro and his niece were standing, to tell them that there was a babe, a girl, born to the wife of the administrador. A boy, who was lounging near, rushed off to ring the church bell, for this was a long-wished-for event; but before the first stroke fell on the air,

the voice of Doña Feliz was heard from the window:
"Silence! Silence! there are two. No bells, no bells!"

Two! Doña Rita still in peril! The midwife rushed
back to her post. The door was locked, and there was a
momentary delay in opening it. "Where have you been,"
said Doña Feliz severely, "almost a half an hour away?"

The woman stared at her in amaze,—the time had
flown! Yes, there was the evidence,—a second infant in
the lap of Doña Feliz, puny, wizened. She dressed it
quickly, asking no assistance, ordering the woman sharply
to the side of Doña Rita.

"A thousand pities," said Don Rafael as he looked at
it, "that it is not a boy!" Then as the thought struck
him, he laughed softly: "Ay, perhaps it is for luck, —
instead of the three kings, who always bring death, we
have the three *Murias*."

Doña Rita had heard something of the foundling, and
smiled faintly. "Thank God they were not all born of
one mother," she said. "Ay! give me my first-born
here;" and with the tiny creature resting upon her arm,
and the second presently lying near, Doña Rita sank to
sleep.

THOUGH the three Marias, as Don Rafael had called them, thus entered upon life, or at least into that of the hacienda of Tres Hermanos, almost simultaneously, except at their baptism they found nothing in common. On that occasion, a few days later than that of which we have written, the aged priest, in the name of the Trinity, severally blessed Florentina, Rosario, and Dolores, — each name as was customary being joined to that of the virgin Queen of Heaven; but as they left the church their paths separated as widely as their stations differed. Dolores, for whom in vain—were it designed to subdue or chasten her—was chosen so sad a name, was taken to the dusky little hut, a few rods from the gate, that was, when he chose to claim it, Pedro's home, and there cared for by his niece Florencia with an uncertain and somewhat fractious tenderness, and nourished at the breast of whomsoever happened to be at hand. She passed through babyhood, losing her prettiness with the golden tinge of her hair, and as she grew older looking with wide-opened eyes out from a tangle of dark elf-locks, which explained the survival of her baby pet-name Chinita, or "little curly one."

Meanwhile the two children at the great house were seldom seen below stairs, so cherished and guarded was their infancy. Rosario grew a sturdy, robust little creature, with straight shining brown hair, drawn back, as soon as its length would permit, from her clear olive temples, in two tight braids, leaving prominent the straight dark eye-brows that defined her low forehead. Long curling lashes shaded her large black eyes,—true Mexican eyes, in which the vivacity of the Spaniard and the dreamy indolence of the Aztec mingled, producing in youth a bewitching expression perhaps unequalled in any other admixture of races. She had, too, the full cheeks, of which later in life the bones would be proved too high, and the slightly prominent formation of jaw, where the lips, too full for beauty, closed over perfect teeth of dazzling whiteness. Rosario was indeed a beauty, according to the standard of her country; and Florentina so closely followed the same type, that she should have been the same, but there was a certain lack of vividness in her coloring which beside her sister gave her prettiness the appearance of a dimly reflected light. Rosario was strong, vivid, dominant; Florentina, sweet, unobtrusive, spirituelle,—though they had no such fine word at Tres Hermanos for a quality they recognized, but could not classify; and so it came about, as time went on, and Rosario romped and played and was scolded and kissed, reproved and admired, that Florentina grew like a fragrant plant in the corner of a garden, which receives, it is true, its due meed of dew and sunshine, but is unnoticed, either for praise or blame, except when some chance passer-by breathes its sweet perfume, and glances down in wonder, as sometimes strangers did at Florentina. In the family, ignoring the fine name they had chosen for her, they called her little " snub-nose,"—Chata,—not reproachfully, but with the caressing accent which renders the nicknames of the Spanish untranslatable in any other tongue.

So time passed on until the children were four years old. The little Chinita made her home at the gateway rather than at the hut with Florencia, who by this time had married and had children of her own, and indeed felt no slight jealousy at the open preference her uncle showed for his foundling. For Pedro was a man of no vices, and his food and clothing cost him little; so in some by-corner a goodly hoard of sixpences and dollars was accumulating, doubtless, for the ultimate benefit of the tiny witch who clambered on his knees, pulled his hair, and ate the choicest bits from his basin unreproved; who thrust out her foot or her tongue at any of the rancheros who spoke to her, or with equally little reason fondled and kissed them; and who at the sight of the administrador or clerk or Doña Feliz, shrank beneath Pedro's striped blanket, peeping out from its folds with half-terrified, half-defiant eyes, which softened into admiration as Doña Rita and her children passed by.

They also in their turn used to look at her with wonder, she was so different from the score or more of half-naked, brown little figures that lolled on the sand or in the doorways of the huts, or crept in to Mass to stare at them with wide-opened black eyes. They used to pass these very conscious of their stiffly-starched pink skirts, their shining rebosos, and thin little slippers of colored satin. But though this wild little elf crouching by Pedro's side was as dirty and as unkempt as the other ranchero children, they vaguely felt that she was a creature to talk to, to play with, not to dazzle with Sunday finery, — for even so young do minds begin to reason.

As for Chinita, after the rare occasions when she saw the children of the administrador, she tormented Pedro with questions. "What sort of a hut did they live in? What did they eat? Where did their pretty pink dresses come from?"

This last question Pedro answered by sending by the first woman who went to the next village for a wonderful flowered muslin, in which to her immense delight Chinita for a day glittered like a rainbow, but which the dust and grime soon reduced to a level with the more sombre tatters in which she usually appeared. When these were at their worst, Doña Feliz sometimes stopped a moment to look at her and throw a reproving glance at Pedro ; but she never spoke to him of the child either for good or ill.

One day, however, — it was the day, they remembered afterward, on which the Padre Francisco celebrated Mass for the last time, — the two little girls accompanied by their mother and followed by their nurse went to the church in new frocks of deep purple, most wonderful to see. Chinita could not keep her eyes off them, though Rosario frowned majestically, drawing her black eyebrows together and even slyly shaking a finger half covered with little rings of tinsel and bright-colored stones. But the other child, the little Chata, covertly smiled at her as she half guiltily turned her gaze from the saint before whose shrine she was kneeling ; and that smile had so much of kindliness, curiosity, invitation in it that Chinita on the instant formed a desperate resolution, and determined at once to carry it through.

Now, it had happened that from her earliest infancy

Pedro had forbidden her to be taken, or later to go, into the court upon which the apartments of the administrador opened. Everywhere else, — even into the stables where the horses and mules, for all Pedro's confidence, might have kicked or trodden her; to the courtyard where the duck-pond was; to the kitchen, where more than once she had stumbled over a pot of boiling black beans — anywhere, everywhere, might she go except to the small court which lay just back of the principal and most extensive one. How often had Chinita crossed the first, and in the very act of peeping through the doorway of the second had been snatched back by Pedro and carried kicking and scream- ing, tugging at his black hair and beard, back to the snake- hung vestibule to be terrified by some grim tale into sub- mission; or on occasion had even been shut up in the hut to nurse Florencia's baby, — if nursing it could be called, where the heavy, fat lump of infant mortality was set upon the ragged skirt of the other rebellious infant, to pin her to her mother earth. Florencia perhaps resented this mode of punishment more than either of the victims, for they be- gan with screams and generally ended by amicably falling asleep, — the straight coarse locks of the little Indian min- gling with the brown curls, still tinged with gold and red- dened at the tips by the sun, of the fairer-skinned girl.

Upon this day, Chinita in her small mind resolved there should be no loitering at the doorway; and scarcely had the two demure little maidens passed into the inner court and followed their mother up the stairway, when she darted in and looked eagerly around. There was nothing terrible there at all, — an open door upon the lower floor showing the brick floor of a dining-room, where a long table set for a meal stood, and a boy was moving about in sandalled feet making ready for the mid-day dinner. There was a great earthen jar of water sunk a little in the floor of a far cor- ner, and some chairs scattered about. A picture of the Virgin of Guadalupe, under which was a small vessel of holy water, met her eyes as she glanced in. She turned away disappointed and went to another door, that of a sit- ting-room, as bare and uninviting as the dining-room, but with an altar at one end, above which stood a figure of Mary with the infant Jesus in her arms. Even the saints in the church were not so gorgeous as this. Chinita gazed in admiration and delight; if she could have taken the waxen babe from the mother's arms she would have sat down then and there in utter absorption and forgetfulness. As it was, she crossed herself and ran out among the flower-pots in the courtyard and anxiously looked up. Yes, there leaning over the railings of the corridor were those she sought. At sight of her Rosario screamed with delight, her budding aristocratic scruples yielding at once to the charms of novelty. Chata waved her hand and smiled, both running eagerly to descend the stairs and grasp their new play-fellow.

" What is your name?" asked both in a breath. "Why are you always with Pedro, at the gate? Who is your mother, and why have you got such funny hair? Who combs it for you? Does n't it hurt?"

Chinita answered this last question with a rueful grimace, at the same time putting one dirty little finger on Rosario's coral necklace, — a liberty which that damsel resented with a sharp slap, which was instantly returned with interest, much to Rosario's surprise and Chata's dismay.

At the cry which Rosario uttered, following it up with sobs and lamentations, both Doña Feliz and Doña Rita appeared. Rosario flew to her mother. "Oh, the naughty cat! the bad, wicked girl! she scratched me! she slapped me!" she cried, between her sobs.

Chata followed her sister, still keeping Chinita's hand, which she had caught in the fray. "Poor Rosario! poor little sister," she said pityingly; "but, *Mamacita*, just look where Rosa slapped the poor pretty Chinita," and she softly smoothed the cheek which Chinita sullenly strove to turn away.

" Why, it is that wretched little foundling of Pedro's!" cried Doña Rita, indignantly, as she wiped Rosario's streaming cheeks. "Get you gone, you fierce little tigress! Chata, let go her hand; she will scratch you, she may bite you next."

" Oh, no," cooed Chata, quite in the ear of the ragged little fury beside her; while Doña Feliz, who had been silent, placed her fingers under the chin of the little waif, and lifted her face to her gaze. "Be not angry at a children's quarrel," she said; "they will be all the better friends for it later."

"But I don't wish them to be friends," cried Doña Rita, — though the absolute separation of classes rendered intimate association possible and common between them which neither detracted from the dignity of the one caste, nor was likely to arouse emulation in the other. "What a wild, savage little fox! No, no, my lamb, she shall not come near thee again!"

But the mother's lamb was of another mind, for suddenly she stopped crying, pulled the new-comer's ragged skirt, and said, "Come along, I'll show you my little fishes;" and in another moment, to Doña Rita's amazement and Doña Feliz's quiet amusement, the three children were leaning together, chatting and laughing, over the edge of the stone basin in the centre of the court.

In the midst of their play, a sudden fancy seized Doña Feliz. Catching up a towel that lay at hand, she half-playfully, half-commandingly caught the elf-like child and washed her face. What a smooth soft skin, what delicately pencilled brows appeared! how red was the bow of that perfect little mouth! Doña Rita sighed for very envy; Doña Feliz held the little face in her hands, and looked at it intently. But Chinita, already rebellious at the water and towel, absolutely resented this; and in spite of the cries of the children she broke away and ran from the courtyard, arriving breathless at the knees of Pedro, to cover herself with the grimy folds of his blanket.

Little by little he drew from her what had passed, comforting her though he made no audible comment; and an hour later Doña Feliz, catching sight of the child, wondered how it had been possible for her to get her face so dirty in so short a time, though a suspicion of the truth soon caused her to smile gravely. While Chinita had been telling her adventures, Pedro had drawn his grimy fingers tenderly over her cheeks, in this way at once resenting Doña Feliz's interference, curiosity, interest, whatever it was, and manifesting his sympathy with the aggrieved one. Nor did he scold the child for her intrusion to the court, or forbid her to go again; and when after some days of hesitation, anger, and irresistible attraction she found her way thither, she wore on her neck a string of coral beads which made Rosario cry out with envy, and which Chata regarded with wide-eyed and solemn admiration.

XII

THE acquaintance thus unpromisingly begun among the three children grew apace. At first, Chinita's visits were as infrequent as Pedro's watchfulness and Doña Rita's antipathy to the foundling could render them, although neither openly interfered, — Pedro, for reasons best known to himself, and Doña Rita out of respect to her mother-in-law, who she saw, in her undemonstrative and quiet way, seemed inclined to regard the child with an interest differing from that with which she favored the children of the herdsmen and laborers. Doña Feliz seldom gave Chinita anything, even in the way of sweets, with which on special festival days she sometimes regaled the others; but in the chill days of the rainy season, or when the norther blew, she it was who chid her if she ran barefooted across the courts, or left her shoulders and head uncovered, and who set all the children to string wonderful beads of amber and red and yellow, placing the painted gourd which contained them close to the brasier of glowing coals, so that the shivering little creature might benefit by its warmth.

Not that the waif was neglected, according to the customs of Pedro's people, — indeed he was lavish to her of all sorts of rural finery. But where all children ran barefoot, where none wore more clothing than a chemise, a skirt, and the inevitable reboso (a long striped scarf of flexible cotton), and in a clime where this was usually more than sufficient for protection, it did not occur either to Florencia or Pedro to provide more against those few bitter days, when it seemed quite natural to shiver, perhaps grow ill, and to mutter against the bad weather; and so, very often the child he would have given his life to shelter had run a thousand risks of wind and weather, which custom had inured her to, and a robust constitution defied.

Still Chinita was glad of shelter and warmth, though like others, she bore the lack of them stoically, and at first

in the bad weather went to the administrador's for such
comforts, as much as from the attraction which Rosario's
spiteful fondness and Chata's soft friendliness offered;
while so it chanced that she was suffered to go and come as
the dogs did, sometimes caressed, sometimes greeted with
a sharp word, often enough unnoticed except by Chata,
who looked for the visit each day, never forgetting to save
in anticipation a tiny bit of the preserved fruit she had been
given at dinner, or a handful of nuts. These offerings of
affection often proved efficacious in soothing the irritation
caused by Rosario's uncertain moods. Yet it was to
Rosario that this perverse little creature attached herself;
with her she romped, and chased butterflies in the garden;
with her she laughed and quarrelled; and Chata looked on
the two with a precocious benignity pretty to see, leaning
often upon Doña Feliz's lap, and, with a quaint little way
she had, smoothing down with one little finger the tip of
her tiny nose which obstinately turned skyward, giving
just the suggestion of sauciness to features which otherwise
would have been inanely uncharacteristic.

Doña Rita was of opinion that all that was necessary in
the education of girls was to teach them to hem so neatly
that the stitches should not show in the finest cambric,
and to make conserves of various sorts, — adding, by way
of accomplishment, instruction in the drawing of threads
and the working of insertions in many and quaint designs,
or the modelling of fruits and figures in wax, to be used
in the wonderful mimic representation of the scene of the
birth of the Saviour made at Christmas. But Doña Feliz
held more liberal views, and much as she esteemed accomplishments, considered them of inferior value to the arts of
reading and writing, which she had herself acquired with
infinite difficulty, at the pain of disobedience to well-
beloved parents.

Reading and writing, according to Feliz's father, were
inventions of the arch-enemy, dangerous to men, and fatal
to the weaker sex. What could a woman use writing for,
asked he, but to correspond with lovers, — when she should
only know of the existence of such beings when one was
presented as her future husband, by a wise and discreet
father. What could a woman desire to read but her
prayers? — and those she should know by heart. In vain,

therefore, had been Feliz's appeal to be taught to read and write. At last she and the Señorita Isabel had puzzled out the forbidden lore together, both copying portions of stolen letters, or the crabbed manuscripts in which special prayers to patron saints were written, thus acquiring an exquisite caligraphy, and learning the meanings of words as they noticed them appear and reappear in the copies of prayers they knew by heart. By a similar process the art of reading printing was acquired, — all in secret, all with trembling and fear. Isabel, much assisted by Feliz, who was older and had sooner begun her task, had successfully concealed her knowledge until it could be revealed with safety; and great was the indignation and surprise of Feliz's father, when on her wedding day the bride took up the pen and signed her marriage contract, instead of affixing the decorous cross which had been expected of her, — while the groom, too, was perhaps not over pleased to find himself the husband of a wife of such high acquirements.

But these acquirements, added to her natural penetration, had been powerful factors in the life of Doña Feliz. Her husband had been weak and inefficient, yet had through her tact retained throughout his life the management of the Garcia estates ; in which he had been succeeded by his son, a man of more character, which perhaps the preponderating influence of his mother as much overshadowed as it had sustained and lent a deceptive brilliancy to that of his father, who, like many a man who goes to his grave respected and admired, had shone from a reflected light as unsuspected and unappreciated as it was unobtrusive and unfaltering.

Doña Feliz had all her life, in her quiet, self-assured way, ruled in her household, — in her husband's time because he had accepted her opinions and acted upon them, unconscious that they were not his own ; while now by her son she was deferred to from the habitual respect a Mexican yields to his mother, and from the steadfast admiration with which from infancy he had recognized her talents. Thus, it is not an exaggeration to say that Don Rafael, whatever might have been his temptations to do otherwise, invariably identified himself in thought as well as act with the mother to whom he felt he owed all that was strong or fortunate or to be desired, not only in his station, but in mind or person. Therefore it was not to be expected that he would interfere when Doña Rita complained to him that his mother made Rosario cry by keeping her poring over the mysteries of the alphabet, and that Chata inked her fingers and frocks over vain endeavors to form the bow-letters at a required angle, and that both would be better employed with the needle. And indeed Don Rafael thought it a pretty sight, when he came upon his mother seated in her low chair, with the two sisters before her, Rosario's mouth forming a fluted circle as she ejaculated " Oh ! " in a desperate attempt at " O," and Chata following the lines painfully with one fat forefinger, her eyes almost touching the book, — no dainty primer with prettily colored pictures, but a certain red-bound volume of " Letters of a Mother," containing advice and admonition as alarming as the long and abstruse words in which they were conveyed.

With all her inattention and impatience, Rosario learned her tasks with a rapidity which roused the pride of her mother's heart ; but Chata, in those early years, stumbled wofully on the road to learning. At lesson-time Chinita, not a whit less grimy than of old, used to hasten to crouch down behind her victimized little patroness, and sometimes whisper impatiently in her ear, sometimes give her a sly tweak of the hair, when her impatience grew beyond bounds, and at others vociferate the word with startling force and suddenness ; until one day it occurred to Doña Feliz, who had made no effort to teach her anything, and had often been oblivious of her very presence, that this little elf-locked rancherita was her aptest pupil. That day, when the others unwillingly seated themselves to their copy-books, she watched the gate-keeper's child, and saw her write the words she had set for her little pupils upon the brick floor with a piece of charcoal taken from the kitchen, then covertly wipe them off with the hem of her skirt.

Doña Feliz was touched. Here was a child of five doing what she herself at fifteen had painfully acquired. She did not pause to think that what with her had been the result of deep thought, was here but parrot-like though effective imitation. She took away the charcoal from the child's blackened fingers, bade her stand at the table, and gave her pen and ink.

After the lesson Chinita flew rather than ran across the court, leaving Rosario and Chata astounded and offended that she would not play, and thrust into Pedro's hand a piece of dirty paper covered with cabalistic characters. She had already confided to him that she could read, and had even once spelled out to him a scrap of printed paper which had come in his way, amazing him by her knowledge; but now that she could write, a veritable superstitious awe of this elfish child befell him.

That evening Pedro stole into the church, and lighted two long candles before the image of the Virgin. Were they an offering of thanks for a miracle performed, or a bribe against evil? The man went back to his post thoughtful, his breast swelling with pride, his head bowed in apprehension. He never had heard that those the gods love die young, yet something of such a fear oppressed him, — though as he found Chinita in flagrant disgrace with Florencia because she had drunk the last drop of thin corngruel which the woman had saved for her uncle's supper, he had reasonable ground for believing that the healthful perversity of her animal spirits and moral nature might counteract the malefic effect of mental precocity; and as he was thirsty that night, so might have been interpreted the muttered " A dry joke this ! " with which he looked into the empty jar, and swallowed his tough tortillas and goatmilk cheese.

" Ay ! but Florencia is cross to poor Chinita," whispered this astute little damsel, seizing the opportunity to creep up behind him when he was not looking, of stealing a brown arm around his neck, and interposing her shock of curls between his mouth and the morsel he destined for it. " Who has poor Chinita to love her but Pedro, good Pedro ? " And so Pedro's anger was charmed away, even as he thought evil might be turned from his wilful charge by the faint glow of the two feeble candles he had lighted. Were her coaxing ways as evanescent, as little to be relied on, as their flicker ? Ay, Chinita !

XIII.

These few years of which the flight has been thus briefly noted, had wrought a subtle change in the appearance of Tres Hermanos as well as in the life of its inhabitants. Gradually there came over it that almost indescribable suggestion of absenteeism which falls upon a dwelling when there is death within, and which is wholly different from the careless untidiness of a house temporarily closed. True, there was movement still at Tres Hermanos, — people came and went, the fields were tilled, the herds of horses roamed upon the hillside, the cattle lowed in the pastures, the village wore its accustomed appearance of squalid plenty, the children played at every doorway, the same numbers of heavily-laden mules passed in at the house-gates, the granaries were as richly stored, — and yet, even to the casual observer, there was a lack. At first, one would attribute it wholly to the pile of deserted buildings to the west. No smoke ever issued from the tall stack of the reduction-works; the lizards ran unmolested upon the walls, which already had crumbled in a place or two, affording entrance to a few adventurous goats, which browsed upon the herbage that sprang up in the court, and even around the great stones in the reduction-sheds. But turning the eyes from these, there was something desolate in the appearance of the great house itself. The upper windows opening upon the country were always closed, dust gathered in the balcony where Doña Isabel had been wont to stand, and a rose, which had long striven against neglect, waved its slender tendrils disconsolately in the evening breeze. Some one pathetically calls a closed window the dropped eyelid of a house; and so seemed those barred shutters of cedar, upon which beat the last rays of the setting sun.

The great event of the American War had despoiled Tres Hermanos of many of its young men. Others had from time to time been drawn into the broils that followed, and which had been augmented by the dictatorship of Santa Anna; yet the estate itself had escaped invasion. Its great storehouses of grain remained intact, its fields were untrodden by the horses of soldiery either hostile or friendly; but a change menaced it, — a hoarse murmur as of the sea seemed to gather and break against the bulwark of mountains that environed it. News of the great events of the day penetrated the remote valley, and with them vague apprehensions and disquiet. Even the laborers in the fields felt the oppression of the storm which was raging without, and which threatened to break upon them. Their hearts quaked; they knew not what an hour might bring forth. For the first time they realized that the great events which had been transpiring, and were still in progress beyond their cordon of hills, meant more to them than food for gossip, or an attraction to some idle boy to whom army life meant a frolic and freedom from work.

These events had followed one another in such rapid succession, and were seemingly so contradictory, that to the onlooker they appeared irrational, childish, even traitorous. But in truth they were the vague, blind outstretchings of a people groping for self-government, for a liberty and peace which they were both by nature and training as yet unprepared to enjoy. The thraldom of Spain had left them madly impatient of fetters, yet they clung to the stake to which they had been chained. Were the prop called King or President, an individual rather than abstruse principles was demanded to uphold them. This it was which in the chaos that followed the war with the United States led them to recall the man whom they had exiled, — the man who had failed them in their greatest need, yet whose unaccountable ascendency over the minds of the masses led them to turn to him again as a deliverer, and whose triumphant march through the land intensified a thousand times the prevailing misery. As one of the historians of Mexico says of Santa Anna, —

" On his lips had been heard the words of brotherhood and reconciliation. The majority had believed in them, because they thought that in the solitude of exile the experience of years and the spectacle of his afflicted country must have purified and instructed the man. It is impossible to say whether

6

his was hypocrisy or a flash of good faith; but certain it is he deceived those who believed, and silenced those who had no faith in his words, and none can imagine the days of distress and mourning which followed.

"His term of office was to last a year; his promises were to redeem his nation from the yoke of slavery, to announce a code of wise and just measures which should insure its happiness and prosperity. A hopeless task, perhaps, in the midst of a nation distracted by years of foreign and civil wars; but at least an attempt was possible. But when once the sweets of power were tasted, all sense of honor and patriotism was lost in the intoxication of personal ambition. Beguiled by promises of protection of their interests, so often and so violently assailed by the Liberal and Conservative parties, the clergy and their adherents in all parts of the Republic secured the passage of an Act which declared him perpetual ruler, with the title of Serene Highness, with his will as his only law, and his caprices his only standard."

Those not lost in the inconceivable stupor which the deadly upas in their midst cast far and near, opened wide eyes of amaze. A trumpet cry rang through the land! Liberals and Conservatives, even the less bigoted of the clerical party, sprang to arms. The entire nation, grieving and reduced to misery by the loss of ninety thousand men who had been dragged from their homes to support the pomp and power of the tyrant, to become a prey upon the land, and upon the helpless families of whom they should naturally have been the support, had refused long to be dazzled by the spectacle of military pomp, or to be beguiled by the *fiestas* and processions which in every town and village made the administration one that appeared a prolonged carnival and madness. These continued insults to the public misery; the daily proscriptions of men who dared to raise the voice or write a line against the Dictator or his senseless policy; the oppressions of the army; the cold, cruel, implacable espionage which made life unendurable, — these wrought quickly their inevitable consequences among a people accustomed to disorder and revolutions, and who in their blind, irrational way longed for liberty. Disgust and detestation of the dictatorship became general. As suddenly as it had sprung into being it was met and crushed. Rebellions sprang up on every hand; the populace rose in mass; the statues of Santa Anna were thrown down in the streets, his portraits stoned;

the houses of his adherents were sacked, their carriages destroyed. The popular fury culminated in the practical measure of the promulgation of the plan of Ayutla, which condemned to perpetual exile the ambitious demagogue who had disappointed and betrayed all parties, mocking with cruel levity his country's woes, and which declared for the establishment of a Republic based upon the broadest platform of civil rights. Gomez Farias gave form to this act; but Ignacio Comonfort became its soul when he proclaimed it in Acapulco, and in the almost inaccessible recesses of the South raised the standard of a rebellion, which rapidly extending throughout the land hurled from its pedestal the idol of clay, that for a brief moment had been taken for gold, to place in its stead a new favorite.

Then another exile returned to his country, heralded by neither trumpets nor acclamations. Calm, astute, watchful, he took his place amid the revolutionary forces; but without seeming effort, from a follower he became a leader. His was the brain that was to develop from the imperfect plan of Ayutla liberties more daring and precious than men had learned to dream of to that hour. Comonfort the last President was the figure toward which all eyes turned; but behind him stood the quiet, insignificant Indian, successful general now, Benito Juarez, shaping the destinies of those who ignored or despised him.

Comonfort was daring, impulsive, utterly devoid of physical fear; a man of action, prone to plunge into difficulties, yet ready to compromise where he could not fight, antagonistic to the temporal power of the Church, yet superstitiously bound by its traditions, he was at once the initiator and the enemy of reform. Finding himself in triumphant opposition to the clergy, he recklessly attacked their most cherished institutions; to open a passage for his troops he threw down their finest convent; to pay his soldiery he levied upon their treasures. Yet he trembled before their denunciations, — upon one day sending the bishop into exile; on the next, he cowered before the meanest priest who threatened him with the Virgin's ire. The terrors of excommunication unnerved him. Scared by his own audacity; unable to quell the storm he had roused; viewing with dismay the reaction that his ill-considered boldness had created in the minds of a people dominated by ghostly fears, even while they groaned under the material oppressions of priestcraft; led beyond his depth by unscrupulous counsellors, or by those who like Juarez had ideas beyond the epoch in which he lived, — Comonfort, while he maintained a kingly state, looked forth upon the new aspect of distraction which his country wore, and vainly sought a method of compromise to evoke order from chaos. He who had dared all physical dangers shrank before a revolution of sentiment. His vacillating demeanor — above all his conciliations of the clergy whom he had so short a time before defied — awoke distrust on every hand.

Such was the political aspect, so far as known at Tres Hermanos, upon the eve when the first straggling band of soldiery crossed the peaceful valley, and its doors opened to receive the first of those armed guests, which in the near future were to become so numerous and so dreaded.

In one far corner of the great house there was a little balcony with its high iron railing; and behind it, scarce reaching to its top, stood two children on tip-toe, looking with wide eyes upon the glory of the purpling mountains, and then with mundane curiosity dropping them upon the more homely attractions within hearing as well as sight. And upon that special afternoon in October these chanced to be of a somewhat unusual character; for across the plain rode one of those predatory bands, which in those wild days sprang up like magic even in the most isolated regions, — the arid mountains and the fertile plains alike furnishing their quota of material, which blindly, ignorantly, but for that none the less furiously, became sacrifices to the ambition of a score or more contesting chiefs. Yet amid the cupidity, unscrupulousness, and barbarity of these chiefs still lingered the spirit of liberty, which though drenched in blood, and bound down by ecclesiastical as well as military despotism, was yet to rise triumphant, perhaps after its years of long struggle stronger, purer, holier than the world before had known it.

But license rather than liberty seemed to animate those wild spirits who, invigorated after a long day's march by the sight of a halting place, urged their steeds with wild shouts and blows with the flat side of their sabres, as well as with applications from their clanking spurs, across the plain, where scattered at intervals might be seen the laggards of the party, chiefly women, on mule or donkey back, with their cooking implements hanging from the panniers upon which they squatted in security and comfort, nursing their babies or quieting the more fractious older children, as the animals they rode paced quietly on or broke into a jog-trot at their own wills.

It was a cause of great excitement and delight to the children in the balcony to see the soldiers — most of them still arrayed in their ranchero dress of buff leather, but some of them resplendent in blue-and-red cloth, with stripes of gilt upon their arms and caps — stop at the huts along the principal street or lane of the village, and laughingly take possession, bidding Trinita and Francisca and Florencia, and the rest of them, to go or stay as it pleased them. Some of the women were frightened and began to cry and bewail, but others found acquaintances among the new arrivals; and there was much laughing and talking, in the midst of which two personages who appeared to be the leaders of the party, and who were followed by a dozen or more companions and servants, rode up to the hacienda gates, and one, scarcely pausing for an answer from the astonished Pedro whom he saluted by name, rode into the courtyard, whither he was followed by the gate-keeper, who with stoical calm yet evident amazement saluted him as Don Vicente; and holding his stirrup as he dismounted added in a low voice, —

"The Saints defend us, Don Vicente! The sight of you is like rain in May, — it will bless the whole year! Heaven grant your followers leave untouched the harvest of new maize! Don Rafael would go out of his senses if it were broached and trampled on by this rabble, — begging your Grace's pardon a thousand times!"

Don Vicente, as the young man was called, laughed as he stamped his feet on the brick pavement until his spurs and the chains and buttons on his riding suit clanked again, — though he looked half sadly, half furtively around.

"Have no fear, Pedro good friend, the men have their orders. The General, José Ramirez, is not to be trifled with;" and he glanced at his companion, a man older than himself, but still in the prime of life, who had also dismounted

and was shaking hands with Don Rafael, with many polite
expressions of pleasure at meeting the courageous and
prudent administrador of Tres Hermanos.

These compliments were returned with rather pallid
lips by Don Rafael, who however upon being recognized
by Don Vicente, who advanced to embrace him with the
cordiality of a friend, though with something of the condescension of a superior, regained his composure with the
rapidity natural to a man who having fancied himself in
some peril finds himself under the protection of a powerful
and generous patron. He hastened in the name of Doña
Isabel to place everything the hacienda contained at the
disposal of the visitors, making a mental reservation of
the new maize and sundry fine horses that happened to be
in the courtyards.

Chinita, who had pushed her way through the crowd of
children and half-grown idlers that had been attracted to
the court, and were gazing in silent and opened-mouthed
wonderment and admiration at the imposing personage
called the General José Ramirez, was so absorbed in the
contemplation of his half-military, half-equestrian bravery
of riding trousers of stamped leather trimmed with silver
buttons, and wide felt hat gorgeous with gold and silver
cords and lace, his epauletted jacket, and scarlet sash
bristling with silver-handled pistols and stilletto, that she
took no heed when a servant came to lead away the
charger upon which the object of her admiration had been
mounted, and so narrowly escaped being knocked down
and trampled upon.

"Have a care thou!" cried Don Vicente, as he sprang
forward and clutched the child by the arm, drawing her out
of danger, while a score of voices — the General's perhaps the most indifferent among them — reiterated epithets
of abuse to the servant and admonition to the child. In
the midst of the commotion, Don Rafael conducted the
two officers to rooms which were hastily assigned them.

As they disappeared, Chinita's eyes followed them. She
was not especially grateful for her escape : it was not the
first time she had been snatched from beneath the feet of
a restive horse ; the incident was natural enough to her,
and perhaps for this reason her rescuer was not specially
interesting to her mind. Somewhat to her disgust, an

hour later, when she had managed to steal unobserved into the supper-room, where she crouched in a corner, she saw Rosario and Chata from their seats at their mother's side regarding the young officer with amiable smiles,— Rosario with infantile coquetry, drooping her long lashes demurely over her soft dreamy black eyes ; and Chata, with her orbs of a nondescript gray, frankly though coyly taking in every detail of his face and dress, while they averted themselves as if startled or repelled from the dark countenance of his companion. It might have been thought that Doña Feliz shared her dread, for more than once she looked at the General with an expression of perplexity and aversion, as he lightly entertained Doña Rita with an account of his family and his own exploits, — topics strangely chosen for a Mexican, but which seemed natural rather than egotistical when lightly and wittily expatiated upon by this gay soldier of fortune.

Meanwhile, Don Vicente Gonzales was talking in a low voice to Doña Feliz. He ate little and drank only some water mixed with red wine, while Don Rafael and the General Ramirez partook freely of more generous stimulants, growing more talkative as the evening advanced; and at last, as the ladies rose from the table, and Doña Rita went with the children to the upper rooms, the two walked away together to inspect the horses and talk of the grand reforms initiated by Comonfort, which in reality had but filled the country with discontent and bloodshed. The poison of personal ambition was working in the new President slowly — as it had done more rapidly in his renowned predecessor Santa Anna — the change from the patriot to the demagogue. He who had talked and worked and fought for the liberties of Mexico, dallied with the chains he should have broken.

XIV.

As Don Rafael in an unwonted state of complacency, which drew the anxious eyes of his mother upon him, disappeared with his jovial guest the General, the younger officer, Don Vicente Gonzales, drew a long breath of relief, and at a sign from Doña Feliz followed her to the window, with the half-sombre, half-expectant air of one who is about to speak of past events with an old and tried friend; and throwing himself into a chair, he turned his face toward her with the air and gesture which says more plainly than words, "What have you to tell, or ask? We are alone; let us exchange confidences."

In truth they were not quite alone. Chinita had half-sulkily, half-defiantly, crept after Doña Feliz, and had sunk down in her usual crouching attitude within the shadow of the wall. She would have preferred to follow Don Rafael and the General in their rounds, but she knew that was impracticable; Pedro would have stopped her at the gate, and sent her to Florencia, or kept her close beside him, — and so even the inferior pleasure of seeing and listening to the less attractive stranger would have been denied her. Chinita was an imaginative child; she used sometimes to stand upon the balcony with Chata, and gaze and gaze far away into the blue which seemed to lie beyond the farthest hills, and wonder vaguely what strange creatures lived there. Sometimes her wild imagination pictured such uncouth monsters, such terrifying shapes, that she herself was seized with nervous tremblings, and Chata and Rosario would clasp each other and cry out in fright; but oftener she peopled that world with cavaliers such as she had occasionally seen, and stately dames such as she imagined Doña Isabel and the *niña* Herlinda must be, — for the accidental mention of those names was as potent as would have been the smoke of opium to fill her brain with dreams. By the sight of

Don José Ramirez in his picturesque apparel, part of these vague dreams seemed realized; and even the quiet figure of Don Vicente and the sound of his stranger voice had the charm of novelty. She placed herself where she could best see his face, with infantile philosophy contenting herself with the next best where the actual pleasure desired was unattainable. She was very quiet, for she had naturally the Indian stealthiness of movement, and she had besides a vague instinct that her presence upon the corridor might be forbidden. Still she did not feel herself in any sense an intruder; she felt as a petted animal may be supposed to do, that she had a perfect right in any spot from which she was not driven.

But as Doña Feliz and the new-comer were long silent, she became impatient, and half-resolved to settle herself to sleep there and then. She had drawn her, feet under her, covering them with the ragged edges of her skirt, and drawing her scarf over her head and shoulders, tightly over the arms which clasped her knee, looked out as from a little tent, and instead of sleeping became gradually absorbed in the contemplation of the face and figure which, when seen beside those of the dashing Ramirez, had appeared gloomy and insignificant. The young man was dressed in black; the close-fitting riding trousers, the short round jacket, the wide hat, which now lay on the ground beside him, being relieved only by a scanty supply of silver buttons, — a contrast to the usual lavishness of a young cavalier; and in its severe outlines and its expression of gloom, his face, as he sat in the moonlight, was in entire harmony with his dress. How rigid looked the clear-cut profile against the dead whiteness of the column against which it rested, his close-cropped head framed in black, his youthful brow corrugated in painful thought. Suddenly he lifted the dark eyes which had rested upon Doña Feliz, and turned them on the fountain which was splashing within the circle of flowering plants and murmured : —

"I feel as though in a dream. Is it possible I am here, and she is gone, gone forever? How often I have seen her by the side of the fountain, raising herself upon the jutting stone-work to pluck the red geraniums and place them in her hair! Even when I was a boy her pretty unstudied ways delighted me, — and Herlinda as naturally as she breathed acted her dainty coquetries. And to fancy now that all that grace and beauty is lost to me, to the world, forever! that she is sacrificed — buried!"

He spoke bitterly and sighed, yet with that tone of renunciation which more completely than to death itself, marks the voices of the children of the Church of Rome as they yield their loved ones to her cloisters. It was in the voice of Doña Feliz, as she presently replied, —

"It seems indeed a strange destiny for so bright a life; but against the call of religion we cannot murmur, Vicente. Many and great have been the sins of the Garcias. May Herlinda's prayers, her vigils, her tears condone them!" She crossed herself and sighed heavily.

"I cannot accept even the inevitable so calmly," cried the young man in sudden passion. "I loved her from a child; I never had a thought but for her! She was promised me when we were boy and girl! She used to tease me, saying she hated me, and then with a soft glance of her dark eyes disarmed my anger. She would thrust me from her with her tiny foot, and then draw me to her with one slender finger hooked in the dangling chain of a jacket button, and laughingly promise to be good, breaking her word the next moment. She would taunt me when I sprang toward her in alarm as she leaped from the fountain parapet, and in turn would cry out in agonies of fright as I hung from the highest boughs of the garden trees, or when I dashed by her on the back of a half-broken horse, stopping him or throwing him perhaps on his haunches, with one turn of the cruel bit. Through all her vagaries I loved her, and perhaps the more because of them; and I fancied she loved me. Even later, when she had grown more formal and I more ardent, I believed that her coy repulses were but maiden arts to win me on."

"I always told Doña Isabel," interrupted Feliz, "that such freedom of intercourse between youth and maiden would but lead to weariness on one side or the other. But she was a hater of old customs. She said there was more danger in two glances exchanged from the pavement and the balcony than in hours of such youthful chat and frolic."

"Yet this freedom was designed to bind our hearts together," said Vicente. "The wish of Doña Isabel's heart for years was to see us one day man and wife. Yet she changed as suddenly — more suddenly and completely than Herlinda did. What is the secret? Is not Tres Hermanos productive enough to provide dowers for two daughters? Is all this to be centred on Carmen? Rich men have immured their daughters in convents to leave their wealth undivided. Can it be that Doña Isabel —"

"Be silent!" interrupted Doña Feliz, as she might have done to a foolish child. "Let us talk no more of Herlinda, Vicente; it makes my heart sore, and can but torture thine."

"No, it relieves me; it soothes me," cried Vicente. "I have longed to come here to talk to you. Doña Isabel is unapproachable. She has relapsed once more into the icy impenetrability that characterized her in that terrible time so many years ago. I can just remember —"

"Let the dead rest," cried Doña Feliz, sharply. "That is a forbidden subject in Doña Isabel's house. You are her guest."

Vicente accepted the reproof with a shrug of his shoulders, and Doña Feliz added, as if at once to turn his thoughts and afford the sympathy he craved, "Talk to me then, if you will, of Herlinda. Do you know where she is now?"

"Yes, in Lagos, in that dreariest of prisons the convent of Our Lady of Tribulation. Think you Maria Santisima can desire such scourgings, such long fastings, such interminable vigils as they say are practised there? God grant the scoffers are right, and that the reputed self-immolations are but imaginings, — tales of the priests to attract richer offerings to the Church shrine. When I saw it, it was groaning beneath vessels of gold and silver and wreaths of jewels. Oh, Feliz! Feliz! higher and heavier than the treasures they pile on their altars are the woes these monks and nuns accumulate upon our devoted country!"

Doña Feliz glanced around warily, but an expression of genuine acquiescence gleamed from her eyes.

"You are where I have always hoped to see you," she said in a low tone; "but beware of a too indiscriminate zeal. They say Comonfort himself has been too hasty, must draw back — retract — ”

“ Retract!” cried Vicente. “ Never! Down, I say, with these tyrants in priestly garments, — these robbers in the guise of saints! The land is overrun with them; their dwellings rise in hundreds in the sunlight of prosperity, and the hovels of the poor are covered in the darkness of their oppressions. The finest lands, the richest mines, the wealth of whole families have passed into their cunning and grasping hands. There is no right, either temporal or spiritual, but is controlled by them. Better let us be lost eternally than be saved by such a clergy. What, saved by bull-baiters, cock-fighters, the deluders of the widow and orphan, the oppressors of the poor!”

“ You are bitter and unjust,” interrupted Doña Feliz; “ remember, too, the base ministers of the Church take nothing from the sanctity of her ordinances.”

“ So be it,” answered Vicente. “ Perhaps,” he added, with a short laugh, “ you think I have lost my senses. No, no; but my personal loss has quickened my sense of public wrongs. In losing Herlinda. I lost all that held me to the past, — old superstitions, old deceptions. The idle boyish life died then, and up sprang the discontented, far-seeing, turbulent new spirit which spurns old dogmas, breaks old chains, and cries for freedom.”

Vicente had risen to his feet; his face lighted with enthusiasm; his pain was for a moment forgotten. The listening child felt a glow at her heart, though his words were as Greek to her. Doña Feliz thrilled with a purer, more reasonable longing for that liberty which as a child she had heard proclaimed, but which had flitted mockingly above her country, refusing to touch its ground. Her enthusiasm kindled at that of the young man, though his sprung from bitterness. How many enthusiasms own the same origin! Sweetness and content produce no frantic dissatisfactions, no daring aims, no conquering endeavors.

“ You belie yourself,” she said, after a pause. “ It is not merely the bitterness of your heart which has made you a patriot. The needs, the wrongs, the aspirations of the time have aroused you. Had Herlinda been yours, you still must have listened to those voices. With such men

as you at his call, Comonfort should not falter. The cause
he espoused must triumph."

"Humph!" muttered Vicente, doubtfully, while Feliz,
with a sudden qualm at her outspoken approbation of
measures subversive of an authority that her training had
made her believe sanctioned by heaven cried : —

"Ave Maria Santisima! what have I said? In blam-
ing, in casting reproach upon the clergy, am I not casting mud upon our Holy Mother the Church?"

"Feliz!" cried Vicente, impatiently, "that question too
asks Comonfort. Such irrational fears as these are the real
foes of progress ; and so deeply are old prejudices and superstitions rooted, that they find a place in every heart ;
no matter how powerful the intellect, how clear the comprehension of the political situation, how scrupulous or
unscrupulous the conscience, the same ghostly fears hang
over all. What spells have those monks with their oppressions and their shameless lives thrown over us that we
have been wax in their hands? Think of your own father,
— a man of parts, generous, lofty-minded, but a fanatic.
He shunned the monté table, the bull-fight, and all such
costly sports as the *hacenderos* love ; he almost lived in
the Church. But that could not keep misfortune from his
door : his cattle died ; his horses were driven away in the
revolution ; his fields were devastated ; and he was forced
to borrow money on his lands. And to whom should he ·
look but the clergy, — who so eager to lend, who so suave
and kind as they? And when he was in the snare, who so
pitiless in winding it around and about him, strangling,
withering his life?"

"But, Vicente," said Feliz, in a hard, embittered voice,
"in our lot there was a show of justice. If you would
have a more unmitigated use of pitiless craft, think of the
fate of your own cousin Inez."

The child within the shadow of the wall was listening
breathlessly. Her innate rebellion against all authority
made her quick to grasp the situation ; a secret detestation of the coarse-handed, loud-voiced village priest who
had succeeded Padre Francisco at Tres Hermanos quickened her apprehension. She looked at Vicente with glistening eyes. "Ah, well I remember poor Inez," he said ;
"forced by her father to become a nun, that at his death

he might win pardon for his soul by satisfying the greed of his councillors, she implored, wept, raved, fell into imbecility, and died ; and her sad story, penetrating even the thickness of convent walls, was blackened by the assertion that she was possessed of devils foul and unclean, — she, the whitest, purest soul that ever stood before the gates of heaven."

His voice choked ; he was silent and sank again into his chair. "And Comonfort," he muttered presently, "strives to conciliate wretches such as these. He is a man, Feliz, who with all his courage believes a poor compromise better than a long fight. Ah, the world believes Mexicans savage, unappeasable, blood-thirsty. How can they be otherwise with these blind leaders who precipitate them into those ditches which they fondly hope will prove roads to liberty and peace ! "

Feliz looked at him with disquietude. "What, Vicente," she said, "are you a man to be blown about by every wind, — a mere ordinary revolutionist seeking a new chief for each fresh battle ? "

Vicente flushed at the insinuation. "One cause and a *thousand* chiefs if need be," he said. "But there is now a man in Mexico, Feliz, who must inevitably become the head of this movement, — who, like the cause, will remain the same through all mischances. To-day he is the friend of Comonfort, but who knows? To-morrow — "

" He may be his enemy," ejaculated Feliz. "I wonder if in all this land there can be found one man who can be faithful ! "

"To-morrow," said Vicente, completing his sentence, " he may be the friend and leader of all the lovers of freedom in Mexico ; and if so, *my* leader. I have talked with that man, and he sees to the farthest ramifications of this great canker that is eating out the very vitals of our land. You will hear of him soon, Feliz, if you have not done so already. His name is Benito Juarez."

Feliz smiled. "What, that Indian?" she said. "It is a new thing for a gentleman of pure Spanish blood to choose such a leader. Ah, Vicente, you disappoint me ! It must be this Ramirez, who has in his every movement the air of a guerilla, a free-fighter, who has infected you."

" No," answered Vicente, sullenly, " Ramirez has no influence over me ; only the fortune of war has thrown us together, — a blustering fellow on the surface, but so deep, so astute, that none can fathom him. He is not the man I could make my friend."

" Where does he come from ? " asked Doña Feliz with interest. " There is something familiar to me in his voice or expression."

" A mere fancy on your part," answered Vicente ; " just such a fancy as makes me glance at him sometimes as he rides silent at my side, and with a sudden start clap my hand upon my sword. I have an instinctive dread of him, — not a fear, but such a dread as I have of a deadly reptile. I wonder," he added gloomily, " if it is to be my fate to take his life."

Feliz shuddered. Chinita's eyes flashed.

" And yet once I saved him, when we were fighting against the guerillas of Ortiz. He was caught in a defile of the mountains ; four assailants dashed upon him at once with exultant cries ; and though he fought gallantly, had I not rushed to the rescue he must have been killed there. Together we beat the villains off, and he fancies he owes me some thanks ; and perhaps too I have some kindness for the man I saved, — and yet there are times when I cannot trust myself to look upon him."

" Strange ! strange indeed ! " said Doña Feliz, musingly. " I have heard his name before. Is he not the man who stopped the train of wagons by which the merchants of Guanapila were despatching funds to make their foreign payments, and who took fifty thousand dollars or more to pay his troops ? "

" The same," answered Vicente ; " and those troops were reinforced by a chain-gang he had released the day before, — vile miscreants every one. We quarrelled over each of these acts ; but he laughed us all — the merchants, the government, myself — into good-humor again. He is one of those anomalies one detests, and admires, — crafty, daring, licentious, superstitious, yielding, cruel, all in turn and when least expected. He will rob a city with one hand, and feed the poor or enrich a church with the other. But here he comes ! "

The man thus spoken of was, indeed, crossing the court

with Don Rafael, who seemed to reel slightly in his walk, and was laughing and talking volubly. "Yes, yes," he was saying, as he came within hearing, "you are right, Señor Don José; the herd of brood mares of Tres Herma-nos is the finest in the country. There are more than a hundred well-broken horses in the pasture, besides scores upon scores that no man has crossed. I sent a hundred and fifty to Don Julian a month ago. Doña Isabel begrudges nothing to the cause of liberty."

"Then I will take the other hundred to-morrow," said Ramirez, lightly. Don Rafael stared at him blankly. There was something in the General's face that almost sobered him. The countenance of Gonzales darkened.

"Believe me, Señor Comonfort shall know of your good-will, and that of the excellent lady Doña Isabel," continued Ramirez, suavely. "She will lose nothing by the complacency of her administrador," and as he spoke, he smiled half indulgently, half contemptuously, upon Don Rafael.

"You promised me that here at least no seizures should be made," exclaimed Don Vicente, in a low indignant voice, hot with the thought that even the men he had him-self mustered and commanded were so utterly under the spell of Ramirez that upon any disagreement they were likely to shift their allegiance, — for those free companies were even less to be depended upon than the easily re-bellious regulars.

"There have been no seizures, nor will there be," answered the General, laughing. "Don Rafael and I have been talking together as friends and brothers; he has told me of his amiable family, and I him of my foot-sore troops."

Vicente, silenced but enraged, glared upon Ramirez as he bade farewell to Doña Feliz. As he took her hand, he bent and lightly kissed it. The action was a common one, — Doña Feliz scarcely noticed it; her eyes rested upon her son, who shifted uneasily from one foot to the other, his garrulity checked, his gaze confused and alarmed.

"We shall be gone at daybreak. You will be glad to be rid of us," the General said laughingly; "yet we are innocent folk, and would do you no harm. Hark! how sweetly our followers are singing," — and, indeed, the plaintive notes of a love ditty faintly floated on the air. "My adieus to the Señora de Sanchez and her lovely children."

While the General spoke thus, with many low bows and formal words of parting, he was quite in the shadow of the wall. Doña Feliz could scarce see his face, but Chinita's eyes never left it. As he turned away, a sob rose in her throat; but for a sudden fear, she would have darted after him. Her blood seemed afire. There was something in the very atmosphere stirred by this man that roused her wild nature, even as the advent of its fellow casts an admonishing scent upon the air breathed by some savage beast.

Don Rafael stole away to bed, but Don Vicente and Doña Feliz continued their interrupted conversation far into the night. Chinita sat in the same place, and slumbered fitfully, and dreamed. All through her dreams sounded the voice of the General Ramirez; all through her dreams Gonzales followed him, with hand upon his sword.

It was near morning, when at last the child awoke, chilled and stiff, and found herself alone in the corridor. The moon had sunk, and only the faint light of the stars shone on the vast and silent building; but she was not afraid. She was used to dropping asleep, as did others of the peasant class, where best it suited her, and at best her softest bed was a sheep-skin. She sleepily crept to the most sheltered part of the corridor and slept again. But the stony pillow invited to no lengthy repose; and when the dawn broke, the sound of movement in the outer court quickly roused her, and she ran out just in time to see the officers hastily swallowing their chocolate, while Don Rafael, Pedro, and a crowd of laborers, shivering in their *jorongos*, were looking on, while the sumpter mules were being laden. At the village, the camp women were already making their shrill adieus, taking their departure upon sorry beasts, laden with screeching chickens, grunting young pigs, and handfuls of rice, coffee, chile, or whatever edibles they had been able to filch or beg, tied in scraps of cloth and hung from their wide panniers, where the children were perched at imminent risk of losing their balance and breaking their brown necks. It was not

7

known, however, that such accidents had ever happened, and the women jogged merrily away, to fall into the rear when outstripped by their better mounted lords.

Don Rafael wore a gloomy face. A squad of soldiers had already been despatched for the horses; his own herders were lassooing them in the pastures, and they were presently driven past the hacienda gates, plunging and snorting. He felt that had he not in Doña Isabel's name yielded them, they would have been forcibly seized; yet his conscience troubled him. The night before he had drunk too much; the wine had strangely affected him, — he had been maudlin and garrulous. These were times when no prudent man should talk unnecessarily, and especially to such a listener as the adventurer General José Ramirez.

The neighing and whinnying of the horses, the hollow ringing of their unshod hoofs upon the road-way, the shouts of the men, the shrill voices of the women, all combined to fill the air with unwonted sounds, and brought the family of the administrador early from their beds. As Vicente Gonzales, after shaking hands coldly with Don Rafael, rode away at the head of his band, he half turned in his saddle to glance at Doña Isabel's balcony. At the rear of the house, a faint glow was beginning to steal up the sky and touch the tops of the trees which rose above the garden wall, and tinge with opal the square towers of the church; he remembered the good Padre Francisco, and piously breathed a prayer for his soul. The drooping rose on the balcony of what he knew to be Doña Isabel's chamber seemed the very emblem of death and desolation. With a sigh he pulled his hat over his eyes and rode on; but the General, José Ramirez, who had been longer in his adieus, caught sight of Doña Rita in the corner balcony, leaning over her two half-dressed children. Their two heads were close together, their laughing faces side by side, their four eyes making points of dancing light behind the black bars of the balcony railing.

Don José Ramirez was in a gentle mood; a sudden impulse seized him to turn his horse and ride close to the building, turning his eyes searchingly upon the children. Both coquettishly turned their faces away. Rosario covered her eyes with her fingers, glancing coyly through them; then kissing the tips of the other hand, opened them lightly above him in an imaginary shower of kisses. No goddess could have sprinkled them more deftly than did this infantine coquette.

Ramirez answered the salute laughingly, then turned away with a frown on his brow. The slight delay had left him behind the troop, amid the dust of the restive horses. Yet he made no haste to escape the inconvenience, but yielding for the moment to some absorbing thought rode slowly. The voice of a child suddenly caused him to arrest his horse with an ungentle hand. He looked around him with a start, — an object indistinctly seen under a mesquite tree caused his heart to bound. The blood left his cheek, he shook in his saddle. His horse, as startled as he, bounded in the air, and trembled in every limb. A moment later and José Ramirez laughed aloud. His name was repeated. "What do you there, child?" he cried; "thou art a witch, and hast frightened my horse. And by my patron saint," he added in a lower tone, "I was startled myself!"

Chinita the foundling came forward calmly, though her skirt was in tatters, and her draggled scarf scarce covered her shoulders; but there was an air about her as if she had been dressed in imperial robes. "Ah!" she said quite calmly, "it is the smell of the blood that has startled your horse; they say no animal passes here without shying and plunging, since the American was killed!"

Ramirez glanced around him with wild eyes. "Oh, you cannot see him now," cried the child; "that happened long ago. No, no, there is nothing here that will hurt you. Why do you look at me like that? It is not I — a poor little girl — who could injure you, but men like those," and she pointed to the columns of soldiers whose bayonets were glistening in the rising sun. Her eye seemed to single out Gonzales, though he was beyond her vision. The thought of Ramirez perchance followed hers, yet he only sat and stared at her, his eyes fixed, his body shrunken and bowed.

"See here," she said slowly, raising herself on tiptoe, and with eager hand drawing something from beneath her clothing, "I have a charm of jet: Pedro put it on my neck when I was a baby. It will ward off the evil eye.

Take it; wear it. An old man gave it to Pedro on his death-bed; he had been a soldier, a highwayman; he had fought many battles, killed many men, yet had never had a wound! Take it!" She took from her neck a tiny bit of jet, hanging from a hempen string, and thrust it into his hand.

Ramirez was astounded. He looked upon her as a vision from another world, — he who was accustomed to outbursts of strange eloquence, even from the lips of un-clothed children amid those untutored peasantry. She seemed to him a thing of witchcraft. His eyes fixed themselves on the child's face as if fascinated; he saw it grimy, vivacious, beautiful but weird, tempting, mysterious. No angel, he felt, had stopped him on his way. He took the charm mechanically, and the child, with a joyous yet mocking laugh, fled away. He roused as from a spell, called after her, tossed the charm into the air, and caught it again, and called once more, but she neither answered nor stopped. He gazed around him once again. A superstitious awe, akin to terror, crept over him; he shuddered, thrust the talisman into his belt, and put spurs to his horse.

That day, for the most part, he rode alone, and when for a time he joined Gonzales, he was silent; silent, too, was his companion, and neither one nor the other divined the thoughts of the man who rode at his side.

XV.

YEARS passed. The nine days' feast of the Blessed Virgin, one of the most charming of all the year, was being celebrated with unusual pomp in the church at Tres Hermanos. Since the death of Padre Francisco, no priest had been regularly stationed there; but at the expense of Doña Isabel, one had been sent there to remain through the nine days sacred to Mary, and the people gave their whole time to devotional exercises, much to the neglect of the usual hacienda work. The crops in the fields were untended, while the men crowded to Mass in the morning, and spent their afternoons at the tavern-shop playing monté and drinking pulque; while the women and children streamed in and out of the church, — the women to witness the offering of flowers upon the altar, the children to lay them there, happy once in the year to be chief in the service of the beautiful Queen of Heaven. For though the image above the altar was blackened by time and defaced by many a scar, the robes were brilliant, and glittered with variously colored jewels of glass; the crown was untarnished, and the little yellow babe in the mother's arms appealed to the strong maternal sentiment which lies deep in the heart of every Mexican woman.

Upon the first day of the feast not one female child of the many who lived within the hacienda limits was absent from the church; and they were so many that the proud mothers, who had spent no little of their time and substance in arraying them, were fain to crowd the aisles and doorways, or stand craning their necks without, hoping to catch a glimpse of the high altar, as the crowd surged to and fro, making way for the tiny representatives of womanhood, who claimed right of entrance from their very powerlessness and innocence. Quaint and ludicrous looked these little creatures, mincing daintily into the church, their wide-spread crinolines expanding skirts stiffly starched, and rustling audibly under brilliant tunics of flowered muslin or purple and green stuffs. These dresses were an exact imitation in material and style of the gala attire of the mothers. The full skirts swept the ground, and over the curiously embroidered linen chemise which formed the bodice was thrown the ever-present reboso, or scarf of shimmering tints. The well-oiled black locks of these miniature *rancheras* were drawn back tightly from the low foreheads, — the long, smooth braids fastened and adorned by knots of bright ribbon, and crowned with flowers of domestic manufacture, their glaring hues and fantastic shapes contrasting strangely with the masses of beauty and fragrance that each child clasped to her bosom. In spite of its incongruities, a fantastic and pleasant sight was offered; and Doña Rita, looking around her with the eye of a devotee, doubted whether any more pleasing could be devised for God or man.

Within the sacred walls of her temple at least, the Church of Rome is consistent in declaring that in her eyes her children are all equal; and upon that spring-time afternoon at Tres Hermanos, among a throng of plebeian children from the village, knelt the daughters of the administrador; and side by side were Doña Rita and a woman from whose contact, as she met her on the court the day before, she had drawn back her skirt, lest it should be polluted by the mere touch of so foul a creature.

Rosario and Chata (as Florentina was so constantly called that her baptismal name was almost unknown) had already laid their wreaths of pink Castillian roses upon the altar, and were demurely telling their beads, when a startling vision passed them.

It was Chinita, literally begarlanded with flowers, — wild-roses, pale and delicate, long tendrils of jessamine, and masses of faint yellow cups of the cactus, and scarlet verbenas, dusty and coarse, yet offering a dazzling contrast of color to the snowy pyramid of lily-shaped blossoms, hacked from the summit of a palm, which she bore proudly upon one shoulder; while from the other hung her blue reboso in the guise of a bag filled with ferns and grasses brought from coverts few others knew of. The flowers made a glorious display as they were laid about the altar, for there was not room for half upon it. The breath of the fields and woodlands rushed over the church, almost overpowering the smell of the incense, and there were smiles on many faces and wide-eyed glances of admiration and surprise as Chinita descended to take her place among the congregation.

Five Mays had come and gone since she had stood under the fateful tree, and given the jet amulet to the cavalier who had so roused and fascinated her imagination; but whatever may have been its effect upon its new possessor, its loss had certainly wrought no ill upon Chinita. Though not yet fourteen years of age, she was fast attaining the development of womanhood, and her mind as well as person showed a rare precocity even in that land where the change from childhood to womanhood seems almost instantaneous. But there was no coyness, as there was no assumption of womanly ways in this tall, straight young creature, whose only toil was to carry the water-jar from the fountain to Florencia's hut, perhaps twice in the day, — and who did it sometimes laughingly, sometimes grudgingly as the humor seized her, but always spilling half the burden with which she left the fountain before she lifted it from her shoulder and set it in the hollow worn in the mud floor of the hut, escaping with a laugh from Florencia's scolding, and hurrying out to her old pursuits, now grown more various, more daring, more perplexing, more vexatious to all with whom she came in contact.

A thousand times had it been upon the lips of Doña Rita to forbid the entrance in her house of the foundling to distract the minds of Rosario and Chata by her wild pranks; but aside from the fact that Doña Rita was of a constitutionally indolent nature, averse even to the use of many words and still more to energetic action, the child was a constant source of interest. She carried into the quiet rooms a sense of freedom and expansion, as though she brought with her the breezes and sunlight in which she delighted to wander. She had too a powerful ally in Doña Feliz, who kept a watchful eye upon her; and though she never, like her daughter-in-law or the children, made a pet and plaything of the waif, yet she was always the first to notice if she looked less well than usual, or to set Pedro on his guard if her wanderings were too far afield, or her absences too long.

Upon this day as Chinita turned from the altar, while others smiled, a frown contracted the brow of Doña Feliz, as for the first time perhaps she realized that this gypsy-like child was in physique a woman. She had chosen to wear a dress of bright green woollen stuff, — far from becoming to the olive tint of her skin, but by some accident cut to fit the lithe figure which already outlined, though imperfectly, the graces of early womanhood. The short armless jacket was fashioned after the child's own fancy, and opened over a chemise which was a mass of drawn work and embroidery; her skirts outspread all others, yet the flowing drapery could not wholly conceal the small brown feet which, as the custom was, were stockingless and cased in heelless slippers of some fine black stuff, —more an ornament than a protection. But Chinita's crowning glory were the rows of many-colored worthless glass beads, mingled with strings of corals and dark and irregular pearls, that hung around her neck and festooned the front of her jacket. This dazzling vision, with the inevitable soiled reboso thrown lightly over one shoulder, came down from the altar and through the aisle of the church, smiling in supreme content, not because of the glorious tribute of flowers she had plucked and offered, nor with pride at her own appearance, gorgeous as she believed it to be, but because of the delightful effect she supposed both would leave on her aristocratic playmates; and much amazed was she as she neared them to see Chata's expressive nose assume an elevation of unapproachable dignity, while Rosario's indignation took the form of an aggressive pinch, so deftly given that Chinita's shrill interjection seemed as unaccountable as the glory of her apparel.

Chinita in some consternation sank on her knees, her green skirt rising in folds around her, reminding Chata irresistibly of a huge butterfly which she had that very morning seen settle upon a verdant pomegranate bush. How she longed to extinguish Chinita's glories as she had done those of the insect, by a cast of her reboso. There was no malice in her thought, though perhaps a trifle of envy, for she too loved brilliant colors. She could not restrain a titter as she thought what Chinita's vexation

would be; and with a face glowing with anger and eyes
filled with reproach, Pedro's foster-child sailed haughtily
past the sisters while the untrained choir were singing
hymns of rejoicing, with that inimitable undertone of pathos
natural in the voices of the Aztecs, and the censers of incense were still swinging, and left the church, — longing to
rush back and to trample under foot the flowers she had so
joyously gathered, longing to tear off the fine clothes and
adornments she had so proudly donned. She pushed angrily past a peasant boy in tattered cotton garments and
coarse sombrero of woven grass, who was the slave of her
caprices, who had toiled in her service all day and upon
whom she had smiled when she entered the church, yet
whom she now thrust aside in rage as she left it, with a
"Out of my way, stupid! What art thou staring at?
Thou art like blind Tomas, with his eyes open all day
long, yet seeing nothing."

"A pretty one thou," cried the boy, angrily. "Dost
suppose I am a rabbit, to care for nothing but green?
Bah! thou art uglier in thy gay skirts than in thy old ones
of red-and-white flannel!"

But the girl had not lingered to listen to his taunts.
She flew rather than ran to her hut, which on account of
the service in the church was deserted. A crowd of ragged urchins who had taken up the cry of her flouted swain,
followed her, jeering and hooting, to the door which she
slammed in their faces. Not that they bore her any ill
will; but the sight of Chinita in her fine clothes, ruffling
and fluttering like an enraged peacock, was irresistibly
exciting to the youths whom her lofty disdain usually
held in the cowed and submissive state of awe-stricken
admiration.

Chinita, scarcely understanding her own miserable disappointment and anger, began to disembarrass herself of
her finery, flinging each article from her with contempt,
until she stood in the coarse red white-spotted skirt, with a
broad band of light green above the hips, — which formed
her ordinary apparel. As she stood panting, two great
tears rolling down her cheeks and two others as large hanging upon her long, black lashes, she saw the door gently
pushed open and before, with an angry exclamation, she
could reach it, a little brown head was thrust in.

"Go away!" cried Chinita, imperatively. "Thou hast
been told not to come here. Thy mother will have thee
whipped, and I shall be glad, and I will laugh! yes, I will
laugh and laugh!" and she proceeded to do so sardonically on the instant, gazing down with a glance of contemptuous fury, which for the moment was tragically
genuine, upon the little brown countenance lifted to her
own somewhat apprehensively, yet with a mischievous
daring in the dark eyes that lighted it.

Chinita, with a child's freedom and in the forgetfulness
of anger, had used the "thou" of equality in addressing
her visitor; yet so natural and irresistible are class distinctions in Mexico, that she held open the door with
some deference for the daughter of the administrador to
enter, and caught up her scarf to throw over her head
and bare shoulders, as was but seemly in the presence of
a superior however young. That done, however, they
were but two children together, two wilful playmates for
the moment at variance.

"Now, then! Be not angry, Chinita!" laughed Chata,
looking around her with great satisfaction. "What good
fortune that thou art here alone! I slipped by the gate
when Pedro was busy talking, and Rosario was making
my mother and *mamagrande* to fear dying of laughter
by mimicking thee, Chinita; and so they never missed me
when I darted away to seek thee, Sanchica."

"And thou hadst better go back," cried Chinita, grimly,
more piqued at being the cause of laughter than pleased
at Chata's penetration; for in choosing her green gown
she had had in her mind the habit of green cloth sent by the
Duchess to Sancho Panza's rustic daughter, and had teased
and wheedled Pedro into buying her holiday dress of
that color, — because when they were reading the story
together Chata had called her Sanchica and herself the
Duchess, and for many a day they had acted together
such a little comedy as even Cervantes never dreamed of,
in which they had seemed to live in quite another world
than that actually around them. The tale of the "Knight
of the Sorrowful Countenance" was a strange text-book for
children; yet in it they had contrived to put together the
letters learned in the breviary, and with their two heads
close bent over the page, these two, as years passed on,

had spelled out first the story, then later an inkling of the wit, the fancy, the philosophy which lay deep between the two leathern covers that inclosed the entire secular literature that the house of Don Rafael afforded.

There were, indeed, shelves of quaint volumes in the darkened rooms into which Chata sometimes peeped when Doña Feliz left a door ajar; but so great was her awe that she would not have disturbed an atom of dust, and scarce dared to breathe lest the deep stillness of those dusky rooms should be broken by ghostly voices. But Chinita, less scrupulous, had more than once, quite unsuspected, passed what were to her delightful though grewsome hours in those echoing shades, and with the bare data of a few names had repeopled them in imagination with those long dead and gone, as well as with the figure of that stately Doña Isabel, who still lived in some far-off city, — mourning rebelliously, it was whispered, over the beautiful daughter shut from her sight by the walls of a convent, yet who with seemingly pitiless indifference had consigned the equally beautiful younger Carmen to a loveless marriage; for the latter had married an elderly widower, and who could believe it might be from choice? Chinita heard perhaps more of these things than any one, for she was free to run in and out of every hut, as well as the house of the administrador; and with her quick intelligence, her lively imagination, and that faculty which with one drop of Indian blood seems to pervade the entire being, — the faculty of astute and silent assimilation of every glance and hint, — she was in her apparent ignorance and childishness storing thoughts and preparing deductions, which lay as deep from any human eye as the volcanic fires that in the depths of some vine-clad mountain may at any moment burst forth, to amaze and terrify and overwhelm.

But Chinita was brooding over no secret thoughts as she began to smile, though unwillingly and half wrathfully, as Chata eagerly declared how well the green dress had transformed her into a veritable Sanchica, and how stupid she herself had been not to guess from the first what her clever playmate had meant; then she laughed again as she thought of the billowy green in which Chinita had knelt, and the half-appeased masquerader was vexed anew, and sat sullenly on the edge of the adobe shelf that served as a bedstead, and tugged viciously at the knots of ribbon in the rebellious hair which she had vainly striven to confine in seemly tresses. She shook back the wild locks, which once free sprang into a thousand rings and tendrils, and looking at Chata irefully from between them, exclaimed, —

"You laugh at me always! You are a baby; you read in the book, and yet you know nothing. If I were rich like you, I would not be silent and puny and weak as you are. I would be strong and beautiful, and a woman as Rosario is; and I would know everything, — yes, as much as the Padre Comacho, and more; and I would be great and proud, as they say the Señora Doña Isabel is!"

"But," cried Chata, flushing with astonishment and some anger, "how can I be beautiful and strong and like a grown woman at will? My grandmother says it is well I am still a child, while Rosario is almost a woman; and I do not mind being little, no, nor even that my nose turns back to run away, as you say, from my mouth every time I open it; but it is growing more courageous, I know," — and she gave the doubtful member an encouraging pull. "I do not mind all this in the least, while my father and my grandmother love me; but my mother and you and every one else look only at Rosario, and talk only of her —" and her lip trembled.

"But do I talk *to* Rosario?" asked Chinita, much mollified. "Do I ever tell her my dreams, and all the fine things I see and hear, when I wander off in the fields and by the river, and up into the dark cañons of the hills? And," she added in an eager whisper, "shall I ever tell her about the American's ghost when I see him?"

"Bah! you will never see him," ejaculated Chata, contemptuously, though she glanced over her shoulder with a sudden start. "There is no such thing. I asked my grandmother about it yesterday, and she says it is all wicked nonsense. There could have been no American to be murdered, for she remembers nothing about it."

"Oh!" ejaculated Chinita, significantly, and she laughed. "Then it is no use for me to tell you where he is buried. If there was no American, he could not have a grave."

"Yet you have found it!" cried Chata, in intense excitement, for the story, more or less veracious, that had often been told her of the murder of the American years before, and the return of his ghost from time to time to haunt the spot accursed by his unavenged blood, had taken a strong hold upon her imagination. "Oh, Chinita! did you go, as you said you would, among the graves on the hillside? Did you go?"

"Why, yes, I did go," answered Chinita, slowly, winding her arms around her knees, as she leaned from her high perch, her brown face almost touching that of the smaller child, who still stood before her. "But I sha'n't tell you anything more, so you may as well go home. Ah, I think I hear them calling you," and she straightened herself up as if to listen.

"No! no! no!" cried Chata in an agony of impatience, "I will not go till you tell me. I *will* know! Oh, Chinita, if I were but like you, and could run about at will, over the fields and up the hills!" The tears rose to her eyes as she spoke, — poor little captive, in her stolen moment of liberty feeling in her soul the iron of bondage to custom or necessity.

"Well, then," said Chinita, deliberately, prolonging the impatience of her supplicant, while the tears in the dark gray eyes lifted to her own moved her, "I went through the cornfield. I drove Pepé back when he wanted to go with me. Oh, how afraid that big boy is of me! Yes, I went through the corn, — oh, it is so high, so high, I thought it was the very wood where Don Quixote and Sancho Panza met the robbers; but I was not afraid. And then I came to the beanfield, and oh, *niña*! I meant to go again this very day, and bring an armful of the sweet blossoms to Our Lady, and I forgot it!" clasping her hands penitently.

"And well for thee that thou didst," exclaimed Chata, "or a pretty rating my father would have given thee! He says it is enough to make the Blessed Virgin vexed for a year to see the good food-blossoms wasted, when there are millions of flowers God only meant for her and the bees. But, Chinita, I would I were a bee, to make thee cry as I wish! Thou art slower than ever to-day. Tell me, tell me, what didst thou next?"

"Well, did I not tell you I came to the beanfield, — what should I do but go through it?" remonstrated Chinita; "and then I walked under the willows. Ah, if you could only once walk under the willows, *niña*! it is like heaven in the green shade by the clear water, and there are great brakes of rushes, with the birds skimming over them. I saw among them a stork standing on one leg, and he had in his mouth a little striped snake, yellow and scarlet and black, which so wriggled and twisted! Ah, and I saw, besides, little fish in the shallow water, and —"

Chata sighed. She had unconsciously sunk upon the mud floor; her eyes opened wide, as if in imagination she saw all those things of which, though she was set in the very heart of Nature, her bodily eyes had caught no glimpse. How in her heart of hearts the sheltered, cloistered daughter of the administrador envied the wild foster-child of the gate-keeper, who was so free, and from whom the woods and fields could keep no secrets! "Go on!" she whispered, and Chinita said, in a sort of recitative, —

"Yes, I went on and on, not very long by the water's edge, though I loved it, but up the little path through the stones and the thorny cacti. Oh, but they were full of yellow blossoms, and they smelled so sweet; but they were full of prickles too, and as I went up the steep hillside they caught my reboso every minute, and when I stood among the graves my hands were tingling and smarting, and I was half blind and stumbling. I was so tired, oh, so tired! and I sat down and rubbed my hands in the sand. It was very still there; it seemed to me that a little wind was always singing, but perhaps it was the dry grass rustling; but as I bent down to listen, I fell asleep, and when I woke up the sun was no higher in the sky than the width of my hand, and I had no time to look for anything."

"Ah, stupid creature!" cried Chata, after a moment's silent disappointment. "Why did you not tell me so before? I must be missed. I shall be scolded," and in a sudden panic she rose to her feet and turned to the door.

"Stay! stay!" cried Chinita, eager to give her news, as she saw Chata about to fly. "Though I did not look, I found something. Oh, yes, in black letters, so big and clear!"

Chata returned precipitately. "Letters — what letters?" she cried.

"Big black letters, J and U and A and N; and the letters for the American name — how do they say it? Ash — Yes, Ashley — it is not hard — and that he was born in the United States, and murdered here in May, — yes, I forget the figures, but I counted up; it was just fourteen years ago, upon the 13th of this very month. It was all written out upon a little wooden cross, which had fallen face down upon the grave I fell asleep upon. I might have looked for it a hundred years and not have found it, but I had scraped away the sand from it to rub my hands. It is thick and heavy; I could scarcely turn it over to read the words, — but they are there. You may tell Doña Feliz there was an American."

"No, I shall say nothing," said Chata, dreamily. "She likes not to hear of murder or of ghosts. Ah, the poor American! why does his spirit stay here? This is not purgatory. Ah, can it be he cannot rest because he died upon the 13th? — the unlucky number, my mother says."

"Let us make it lucky," said Chinita, daringly. "Let us say thirteen Aves and thirteen Pater Nosters for his soul."

But Chata shook her head doubtfully, and started violently as a servant maid, grimy and ragged like all her clan, and panting with haste, thrust open the door, exclaiming, —

"*Niña* of my soul, your lady mother declares you are dead. Doña Feliz has searched all the house, and is wringing her hands with grief. Don Rafael has seized Pedro by the collar, and is mad with rage because he swears you have not passed the gate; and here I find you, with your white frock all stained with dirt, and that beggar brat filling your ears with her mad tales. The Saints defend us! Sometime the witch will fly off — as she came — no one knows where. But you, *niña*, come, come away!" and the excited woman dragged the truant reluctantly away; while Chinita, thrusting her tongue into her cheek, received the epithets of "beggar brat" and "witch" with a contempt which the gesture only, rather than any words, fluent as she was in plebeian repartee, could at that moment adequately express.

XVI

Though Chinita as was usual was made the scapegoat for Chata's fault, — Doña Rita averring that the girl possessed an irresistible power for evil over her own innocent children, — Chata on this occasion felt herself most heavily punished, for Don Rafael strengthened his wife's fiat against the dangerous temptress, the gate-keeper's child, by absolutely prohibiting her entrance to his house. Chata wept for her playmate, and for many days Rosario moped and sulked; while Chinita hung disconsolate — as the Peri at the gate of Paradise — about the entrance to the court, finding small solace in the young fawn Pepé had given her, though she twined her arms around it and held its head against her bosom, that its large pensive eyes might seem to join in the appeal of her own. And perhaps the two aided by time and Chata's grief might have conquered; but there was a sudden interruption of the quiet course of life at Tres Hermanos.

One day Chinita found the whole house open to her; there was no one there either to welcome or repulse her save Doña Feliz. Don Rafael, with his wife and children, had obeyed a sudden call, and had hastened to the dying bed of Doña Rita's mother. For the first time in her life Chata had left the hacienda. Rosario had twice before gone with her mother to visit relatives, but for various reasons Chata had remained at home. Doña Rita seemed half inclined to leave her at this time also; but Don Rafael cut the matter short by ordering her few necessaries to be packed, and in a flutter of excitement, perhaps heightened by the frown upon her mother's face, Chata took her seat in the carriage that was to bear her far beyond the circle of hills which had heretofore bounded her vision.

What a pall seemed to fall upon the place when they were all gone! First, a great stillness pervaded the court and corridors where the children's voices were wont to ring ; and then hollow, ghostly noises woke the echoes. A second court was now opened which long had been closed, though the fountains played there, and the flower-pots were all rich with bloom. The doors of rooms which before at best had been only left ajar were opened wide ; and Doña Feliz, with a few of her most trusty servants, swept out the long accumulated dust, and let the light stream in upon the disused furniture. Chinita had caught glimpses of these things before, indistinct, uncertain, as though they were far memories of a past existence. She and Chata had often talked of them in days when they played at being grand ladies, and in imagination they were rich and beautiful ; but when she actually stood in the broad sunshine, and saw the gilt and varnish, the variegated stuffs and great mirrors, the reality seemed a dream, from which she feared to waken. For all these material things appealed to something in the child's nature which it appeared impossible she should have inherited from a long line of plebeian ancestors, — a something that was not a mere gaping admiration for what was bright and beautiful and dazzling by its very height of separation from the poor possibilities of her life, but which one would say had sprung directly from the influences of lavish splendor. There was an impulse toward appropriation and enjoyment in the actual touch of these attributes of an aristocratic life, an instinctive knowledge of the uses of things she had never before seen or heard of, which seemed to come as naturally into her mind as would the art of swimming to a duckling that had passed its first days in the coop with its foster-mother the hen. Nothing surprised her, and the delight she felt was not merely that of novelty, but that of the satisfaction of a long-felt want. Doña Feliz had not forbidden her entrance when she first saw her at the door of Doña Isabel's apartment, but watched her with grave surprise as she wandered through the long rooms, sometimes picking up a fan, a hand-glass, a cup, and unconsciously assuming the very air and walk of a grand lady, — an air so natural that even in her tattered red skirt it never for a moment made her appear grotesque.

Don Rafael returned home in the midst of the work of renovation. He had left his family with the dying mother, forced to return by the exigencies of business, —

8

but ill pleased to leave them, for the roads were full of
bandits, and the country was infested with wandering
bands, as dangerous in their professed military character
as the openly avowed robbers. They enjoyed immunity in
all their depredations and deeds of violence, because they
were committed under the standard of the Governor of the
State, José Ramirez, — for to his *rôle* of military chieftain
the adventurer had added that of politician. In this *rôle*
he had hastened the tottering fortunes of President Comonfort to their fall, by seizing in his name a large sum of
money belonging to foreign merchants, and with it buying
over the troops under his command, — first to declare him
military governor, and then to join with enthusiasm the
clerical forces, which sprang into being as if by magic,
bringing with them money in plenty, and gay uniforms,
which put to shame the rags which the Liberals wore
and which the resources of the legitimate government
were insufficient to replace with more attractive garb.
For months the name of José Ramirez had rung through
the land in alternate shouts of triumph and joy and howls
of execration. The prison doors had been thrown open,
and hundreds of convicts had joined his ranks, ready to
die for the man who had set them free, — not for gratitude, but in an excess of admiration for a spirit more
lawless, more daring, than their own.

Chinita used to stand half aloof, and listen to these
things, as wild rumors of them reached the hacienda, a
burning pride glowing in her heart as she heard of deeds
that made men tremble and stand aghast ; and in imagination she saw the tall dark man whom she had made her
hero riding through the streets in the full panoply of military splendor, followed by a train of mounted soldiers as
gorgeous as himself, — then the blaring band, the gay foot
soldiers shouting his name, and that terrible battle-cry of
" Religion y Fueros," in which so many infernal deeds
were done ; and last of all a multitude of half-clad men,
women, and boys and girls like herself in ragged garments, not hungry nor wretched, though with all the grime
and squalor of poverty upon them. She loathed them
in her heart, though she did not consciously separate
herself from their kind ; but often ran to the covert of
the tall corn, or the shade of some tree, and sat down

and drew her reboso over her head, laughing softly and breathlessly, for had she not given this man the amulet which gave him a charmed life? Sometimes she heard of attacks made upon him, — how bullets had gone crashing through his carriage windows, how in the very streets of the city, as well as on the battle-field, his horses had been shot under him; but he had never once been hurt. She was a ragged, barefoot girl, but here was something which in her own eyes enwrapped her as with velvet and ermine, — the belief that she had some part in that dazzling career that attracted the gaze, the wonder, the terror of what was to her mind the whole wide world.

Through those hot summer days Pedro saw little of his foster child; and sometimes when he did see her, she would pass by as if he were nothing to her, or would shudder sometimes when he laid his hand with gentle violence upon her arm, and forced her in from the glaring sunshine, in which she often wandered for hours, unconscious of the heat which was burning her skin browner and browner, but painting roses on her cheeks, and filling her eyes with light; and sometimes she would come softly up behind him and throw the brown tangle of her hair over his eyes, almost smothering him in the golden crispness of its ruddy ends, and kiss him wildly between his bushy eyebrows, calling herself his wicked Chinita, his naughty child, until he would draw her on his knee and wipe away her streaming tears with the tenderness but none of the familiarity of a parent, and while he did so, sigh and sigh again, and wonder what these wild moods would lead to.

When Doña Feliz began the renovation of the family apartments Pedro stole in there one day when she chanced to be quite alone, and asked if it was true that Doña Isabel would soon return; it was many years — yes, twelve and more — since she had left them; and the *niña* Carmen, was it true that she was married? And the Señorita Herlinda? " Was it quite certain," and his voice grew low, — " was it quite certain she was in a convent? "

" Did not Don Vicente tell you that? " queried Doña Feliz; " and his sad looks, did they not tell you? Ah, unhappy girl, where should she be but in a convent? Where else in the world should she hide, who was so at feud with life? " She started, remembering herself; but

Pedro was looking at her with impassive stolidity. "Yes, yes," she continued impatiently, "she has chosen her path; she has left the world forever."

"But they say," droned Pedro, monotonously, "that the convents will be opened and all the nuns be made free when the Señor Juarez takes his turn to rule. They say the day he enters the palace the dead men's hands will open, and all their riches escape from their grasp. The silver and gold will be taken from the altars and given to the poor, and the monasteries and nunneries be pulled down, that the people may build their houses with the stones."

Doña Feliz laughed. It was not often any sound of merriment passed her lips, and then not in scorn. "Dreams, dreams, Pedro!" she said. "Are you as foolish as the rest, and think the new law would give all the poor wealth, or even the despoiled their own? Do you think Juarez himself believes it? No, no! he is a sly fox; and while the Church and Comonfort were the lion and bear struggling over the carcass, he strives to glide in and steal the flesh. Do you think he will divide it among you hungry ones? No! these politicians are all alike, and whether with the cry of religion or liberty, fight and plot only for their own aggrandizement, and the poor country is forgotten, as it is drenched by the blood of her sons. There is not one true patriot in all this distracted land."

She spoke rather to herself than Pedro, who shook his head with a sort of grim obstinacy. "I am thinking to go away, Doña Feliz," he said. "You know the Señor Juarez is at liberty, and there will be bloody days soon if Zuloaga does not yield him his rightful place in Mexico. I have a mind to see a few of them. You know I was a good soldier in Santa Anna's time, and as I sit in the gate I hear the sound of the cannon and the rattle of musketry and the voice of my old commander Gonzales, only it comes now from the lips of his son; and I feel I must go."

Doña Feliz looked at him steadily. She knew her countryman well, and though she doubted not that something of the martial spirit of the time was stirring within him, she was equally certain that a second and more potent reason was prompting Pedro to leave Tres Hermanos; but she only said, —

"Then you wish to join Vicente Gonzales? They say he, with all his band, has thrown his fortunes in with those of Juarez. Well, well, perhaps anything was better than that he should be linked with Ramirez. If Vincente is a traitor, it is at least with a noble aim, not for mere plunder. There was something strange, forbidding, terrible, about that man Ramirez. Did you notice his face, Pedro, when he was here?"

Pedro shook his head, returning with pertinacity to his own plans. "You will talk to Don Rafael for me, will you not, Señora?" he said, with a trace of the abject whine in his tone that marked the habit of serfdom, which a few years of nominal freedom had done little to alter, "and with your good leave I will go, and take Chinita with me." He spoke hesitatingly, as though fearful his right would be disputed.

"Take Chinita!" exclaimed Doña Feliz. "What, to a soldiers' camp, to her ruin! You are mad, Pedro. No, she shall remain here with me. I will take her into the house. I will teach her to sew. She shall be my child rather than my servant! .I—" she stopped in extreme agitation, for within the doorway the child stood.

"I will be no one's servant!" she said, proudly drawing herself up; "and as to going to the Indian's camp— ah, I know a better place than that," and she nodded her head significantly. "You shall leave me, Father Pedro, with your Doña Isabel!"

Doña Feliz and Pedro started as if they had been shot.

"I came to tell you she is coming," continued the child. "I was out beyond the granaries, letting my fawn browse on the little hill, and as I was looking toward the gorge I saw a horseman coming, and far behind him was a carriage and many men. Is all ready?" and she glanced around her with the air of a prophetess. "Hark! the courier is in the court now. Doña Isabel will not be long behind him."

Pedro hastened from the room with an exclamation of alarmed amazement. "Go, go!" cried Feliz. "You are too late!" for she knew in her heart that it was in very fear of this visit, and to remove the child from the chance of encountering Doña Isabel, that Pedro had proposed to leave the hacienda; and here was Doña Isabel herself, — for strangely enough, neither of them doubted that what the child had assumed was true. The thoughts of Doña Feliz were inexplicable even to herself. She felt as though she was placed in some vast and gloomy theatre, with the curtain about to rise upon some strange play, which at the will of the actors might become either comedy or tragedy. Though of late she had felt certain that Doña Isabel would return to the hacienda, that very act seemed dramatic, the precursor of inevitable complications.

" Why could she not be content in the new life she had chosen?" muttered Doña Feliz. " What voice has been sounding in her ears, to call her back to resurrect old griefs, to walk among the spectres of long-silent agonies and shame? Foolish, foolish woman! Yet as the magnet attracts iron, so thy hard heart is drawn by these bitter remembrances. Go, go! thou child!" she exclaimed aloud, and almost angrily. " Doña Isabel would be vexed to see thee in her room. Go, and keep thee out of her way!" She gazed after Chinita with a look of perplexity and pain, as with a bound of irresistible excitement the girl sprang out upon the corridor, her laugh rising through the still air as if in notes of defiance. " What said the child?" muttered Doña Feliz. " ' Leave me with your Doña Isabel'?"

XVII.

From the city of Guanapila to the hacienda of Tres Hermanos the road runs almost continually through mountain defiles, where on either hand the great masses of bare rocks rise so precipitously that it seems impossible that man or beast should scale them; and here, where Nature's aspect is most terrible, man is least to be feared. But there are intervals where broad flat ledges hang above the roadway, or where it crosses plateaus shaded by scrub-oak or mesquite and even grassy dells, where after the rains water may be found, offering charming camping-grounds during the noon-tide heat; and precisely at such places the anxious traveller has need to look to his weapons, and picket his horses and mules in such order that no sudden attack may cause a stampede among them, and that they may, if need offer, form a barricade for their defenders. In those lawless times few persons ventured forth without a military escort, and if possible sought additional security by accompanying the baggage trains which by arrangement with the party for the moment in power enjoyed immunity from attack by roving bands of soldiery, and were too formidable to be successfully assailed by the ordinary cliques of highwaymen. Seldom indeed was there found a person so reckless as to venture forth attended only by the escort his own house afforded; and daring indeed was the woman who would undertake a two days' journey in such a manner. The least she might expect would be to find her protectors dispersed, perhaps slain, and herself a captive, — held for an exorbitant ransom, and subjected to the hardships of life in the remote recesses of the mountains, and to indignities the very report of which might daunt the most reckless or the bravest.

Yet in spite of all this, a carriage containing a lady and her maid — for such were their relative positions, though both were alike dressed in plain black gowns and the common blue reboso — entered in the early afternoon of a summer's day the narrow gorge that led by circuitous windings through the rocks to the great gorge that formed the entrance to the wide valley of Tres Hermanos, whose entire extent offered to the eye the wondrous fruitfulness so rich and varied in itself, so startling in contrast to the desolation passed to reach it.

The midday halt had been a short one, for it was the rainy season, and progress was necessarily slow over the swollen watercourses and the obstructions of accumulated sands and pebbles, the masses of cactus and branches of trees and shrubs, which had been brought down by recent storms. At times it seemed impossible that the carriage, although drawn by four stout mules, could proceed, and from time to time the servant looked anxiously through the window. But the mistress was equal to all emergencies, herself giving directions to the perplexed driver and his assistant, and though she had been travelling for more than two days over a road usually easily passed in one, allowing no sign or word of weariness or impatience to escape her.

But this carriage and its occupants would have appeared to a passer-by the least important factor in the caravan of which it formed a part; for it was encircled and almost concealed by a band of mounted men, clad in suits of brownish leather, glimpses of the red waist-band glistening with knives and pistols showing from beneath their striped blankets, long knives and lassos hanging at their saddle-bows, rifles in their sinewy right hands, while from beneath their wide hats their keen eyes investigated sharply every jutting rock and peered into the distance with an air of half-defiant, half-fearful expectancy, — for these were men taken from her own estate, who idle retainers as they had been in her great bare house in the city where Doña Isabel Garcia had lived for years in melancholy state, thrilled with clannish fidelity to their mistress and passionate love for their *tierra* to which they were returning, and with that vague delight in the possibility of a fight which arouses in man both chivalrous and brutish daring, as the smell of blood arouses the love of slaughter in the tamest beast.

In front of these rode the conductor of the party clad in a half-military fashion, as became the character he had earned for eccentric daring, the reputation of which perhaps more than actual bravery made him eminently successful in guiding safely the party wise or rich enough to secure his escort. This man was known as Tio Reyes, though his appearance did not justify the honorary title of Uncle, for he was still in the prime of life; but it was applied to him in tones of jesting yet affectionate respect by his followers who had joined the party with him, and adopted by the others to whom he was a stranger, — for at the last moment he had appeared just as they were leaving Guanapila, and with a brief word to the mistress, to which in much surprise and some annoyance she had agreed, had placed himself at their head.

In the rear of those we have described came four or five mules laden with provisions, necessaries for camping, and some private baggage; these were driven by *arrieros* who ran at their sides, for the travelling pace of horses did not exceed that of those trained runners.

The journey, wearisome as it had proved, had so far been made without alarms, and upon nearing the boundaries of Tres Hermanos much of the anxiety though none of the vigilance of the escort subsided; when suddenly upon the glaring sunshine of the day, all the hotter and clearer from the recent rains, rose in the distance a sort of mist, which filled the narrow road and blurred the outline of the towering rocks. The guide paused for a moment and glanced back at the escort. Each hand grasped tighter the ready rifle; at a word the carriage was stopped, the baggage mules were driven up and enclosed within the square hastily formed by the armed men, — for upon that clear day, after the rains, the tramp of many feet was requisite to raise that cloud of dust, and these precautions were but prudent, whether the advancing troop were friends or foes.

Tio Reyes, after disposing his force to his satisfaction, rode forward with his lieutenant to meet the advancing host, which in those few moments seemed to fill the entire range of vision, though at first with confusing indistinctness, as did the sounds that came echoing from rock to rock. The cries of men rose hoarsely above a deep and rumbling undertone, which resolved itself at last into the lowing of cattle and the bleating of sheep, — harmless and terrified wayfarers, but driven and preceded by a troop of undisciplined soldiery, ripe for deeds more tragic than the plunder of vaqueros and shepherds, who would be more likely wisely to seek shelter in the crevices of the rocks than to defy numbers before whom they were helpless.

"Señora of my soul!" cried the servant, catching a word from one of the men, "we are lost! Virgin of Succors, pray for us! These are some of the men of his Excellency the Governor, and you know they stop at nothing. Ah, what a chance to gain money is this! Once in the mountains what may they not demand for you? *Ave Maria Sanctissima!* Ah, Señora, if you would but have listened to the Señorita! to me!"

"Silence!" said the lady, in a tone as of one unused to hear her actions commented upon. "Silence! thou wilt be safe. If we are captured, thou wilt not be a prize worth retaining; it will be easy to induce them to take thee to Guanapila, and obtain a reward from my cousin, Don Hernando."

"No, no!" cried the woman, brought to her senses by this quiet scorn and the startling proposition of her mistress. "Could I leave your grace? No, no! imprisonment, starvation, even to be made the wife of one of those bandits!" and a faint smile curled the damsel's lip, for she was not ugly, and knew something of the gallantries of Ramirez's followers, — "anything rather than desert my lady! Ay, my life! whom have we here?"

It was Tio Reyes undoubtedly, and with him was a military stranger, a gallant young fellow, and handsome, though his hands and face were covered with dust, and something like a large blood-stain defaced the breast of his blue coat. "Pardon, Señora," he exclaimed, bowing most obsequiously and removing his wide hat, disclosing a young and vivacious countenance, "I am Rodrigo Alva, your servant, who kisses your feet, captain of this troop of horse, of the forces of his Excellency Don José Ramirez, Governor of Guanapila."

"And I am the Señora Doña Isabel Garcia de Garcia," responded the lady, with dignified recognition of the young man's courteous self-introduction; "and as I am unaware of any cause for detention, I beg to be permitted to proceed toward my hacienda, which I desire to reach before night closes in."

"It is not my desire to molest ladies," said the captain, gallantly; "and I have besides received express orders to defend your passage and facilitate it in every way."

"I have no acquaintance with Señor Ramirez," said Doña Isabel in surprise; "yet more than once have I been indebted to his courtesy," and she glanced at Tio Reyes. "He it was who sent me this worthy guide. I know not why the Señor Ramirez takes such interest in my personal safety, especially as we are politically opposed;" and she added with a daring which had somewhat of girlish archness, strange from the lips of Doña Isabel, "he has not the name of a man given to gallantries."

"No, rather to gallant deeds," said the young captain, his voice accentuating the distinction. "But you, Doña Isabel, like us who serve him, must be content not to inquire too closely into his motives."

"Whatever they may be," retorted she, in a voice of displeasure, "they are not such as will spare my flocks and herds;" and she frowned as a stray ox, upon whose flank she recognized the well-known brand of Tres Hermanos, bounded by the carriage, from which the escort had gradually withdrawn, and were now exchanging amicable salutations with the more advanced of the host which they would have been equally pleased to fight.

The young man bowed in some confusion. "The men must be fed," he said. "These come from the ranchito del Refugio, Señora, and I regret to say the huts are burned down and the shepherds and vaqueros scattered; one poor fellow was killed in pure wantonness."

"And you dare tell me this!" cried Doña Isabel, in violent indignation, which for the moment overcame her wonted calmness.

"It was but to explain," interrupted Captain Alva, "that we encountered the famous Calvo there. He has succeeded in raising three hundred men or more to march to the assistance of the double-dyed traitor Juarez. Fortunately, but a portion of his troops were with him; the rest have joined Gonzales, — so our work was easy, though the fellows fought well. Three or four were killed, a few wounded, the rest fled to the mountains, and we succeeded in securing the cattle and sheep; and I hope your grace will be consoled in knowing they are destined to feed good patriots."

Doña Isabel waved her hand impatiently. "What matter a few animals?" she said. "But the poor shepherds, — they must be looked to. And the wounded — what of them?"

"*Canalla!*" laughed the captain, carelessly, "one or two are with us here, tied on their saddles. They will do well enough. Others lay down under bushes to shelter their cracked heads. But one there is, Señora, a foreigner, a mere boy, who was in the party by chance they say, just a boy's freak, — but, my faith! he did a man's portion of fighting, and has a wound to end a man's life. He must die if he rides much farther lashed to his horse;" and the young soldier, half a bandit in lawlessness, and in his perplexed notions of honor, perhaps too, scarce free from blood-guiltiness, sighed as he added, "but this is no subject for a lady's ear. Permit, Señora, that my troops and their belongings pass by, and you may then proceed in all peace and safety."

"Thanks, Señor," said Doña Isabel, adding half hesitatingly: "And the wounded youth, — a foreigner, I think you said?"

"By his looks and tongue, English," answered the officer, with his hand to his hat as a parting salute. But Doña Isabel's look stopped him.

"You pity this poor wounded creature," she said, "and I can do no less. You are compelled to travel in haste, and the city — if that is your destination — is far distant."

Doña Isabel spoke as if under some invisible compulsion and as against her will, and paused as if unable to utter the proposal that trembled on her lips; but the voluble young officer, with the eagerness of desire, divined what she would say, and so lauded the appearance and bearing of the wounded prisoner that to her own amazement Doña Isabel found herself making room for him in her carriage, much to the surprise of her maid Petra, who was mounted upon the led horse, which in thought her mistress had at first destined to the use of her unexpected guest.

However, when under the superintendence of Captain Alva and Tio Reyes the youth was transferred from his horse to the carriage, Doña Isabel saw at once that his strength was so nearly spent that even with most careful handling it was doubtful whether he would reach the hacienda alive. She shrank away as his fair young head was laid back upon the dark cushions, and his long limbs were disposed upon blankets and cushions, as much to avoid contact with that frame so evidently of alien mould as to give all the space possible to the almost unconscious sufferer. She scarce looked at him, as with effusive thanks Alva bade her farewell, but forced her eyes, though with no special interest or regret, upon the portion of her flocks that was driven bleating before her carriage, with mechanical kindness closing the window as the horned cattle, bellowing and pawing the dust, followed, and breathing a sigh of relief as the last of the revolutionary force rode by, and the sound of their noisy march grew fainter, and she realized that her own escort had fallen into their places around her carriage, the slow motion of which indicated that her interrupted journey was resumed.

For some time the thoughts of Doña Isabel were necessarily directed to her wounded guest. The wound in the shoulder had been bandaged with such skill and care as could be offered by the self-trained doctor of the rancho, for the nonce become army surgeon; and it would doubtless have done well but for exposure and fatigue, which had induced fever, in which the patient muttered uneasily and even at times became violently excited, looking at Doña Isabel with eyes of inexpressible brilliancy, catching her cool white hands in his own burning ones and calling her in endearing accents names which, though untranslatable by her, were sweet to her ear. Perhaps, they were those of mother or sister, — she almost longed to know. Later, when under her tendance and that of the grooms, who when she motioned for the carriage to be stopped often came to her assistance, he sank into uneasy slumber, she had opportunity to wonder at the impulse that had induced *her* to receive this stranger of a race, that whether American or English, she had long abjured, and to feel once more as she gazed upon his wan features something of the bitter detestation with which she had looked upon Ashley's dead face.

Doña Isabel started; the thought had entered her mind just as they were emerging from the great chasm of rocks which gave entrance to the plain, and she saw once more the Eden from which she had been driven. The house was so far distant still that she caught, across the fields of tall corn, but a mere suggestion of its flat roofs and the square turrets at the corners of the encircling walls; but though more distant still, the tall chimney of the reduction-works rose clearly defined against the sky, — so clearly that she could see where a few bricks had fallen from the cornice, and how a solitary pigeon was circling it in settling to its nest. What a picture of solitariness! Doña Isabel groaned, and covered her face with her hand. It was as she had known it would be. The first objects to meet her gaze were those that could waken the darkest and bitterest memories. Why had she come? Oh that she could retrace the rough path that she had traversed!

The wounded man groaned; he was fainting. "Hasten, hasten!" she cried, "send Anselmo forward; bid them prepare a bed. The road is not so rough; let them drive faster!"

Thus Doña Isabel's words belied the desire of her heart, for she could not by her own wish have approached her home too slowly. This boy was a stranger, not even brought thither by her will, as the other had been; yet as the other had driven her forth, this one was hastening her back. Was it fancy, or did the boy's lips pronounce a name? No, no! it was but her excited imagination. No wonder! Did not the earth and sky, the wide circle of the hills, all cry out to her, "What hast thou done? Where is Herlinda?"

XVIII.

Although Chinita had divined aright when she declared that the carriage she had seen in the distance could be no other than that of Doña Isabel, and the sounds which penetrated from the court announced the arrival of her outrider, she was wrong in supposing that the lady herself would be speedily at hand. There was a long delay in which Doña Feliz had time to recover outwardly from the agitation into which she was thrown, and accustom herself to this verification of her foresight, when upon hearing of the marriage of Carmen she had felt a conviction that Doña Isabel in her loneliness and the unaccustomed lack of interests around her would be irresistibly attracted to the home she had virtually forsworn.

Don Rafael having listened eagerly to the courier's account of the meeting with Ramirez's band, left him to give fuller details to the anxious villagers who gathered around, — many of whom had sons or husbands at that part of the hacienda lands known as the ranchito del Refugio, — and rushed up to Doña Feliz with the news, then down again to the court to mount a horse which had been instantly saddled, and followed by a clerk and servants galloped away to give meet welcome to the lady who had just entered upon her own domains.

Calling the maids, Doña Feliz caused the long-disused beds to be spread with fresh linen, and completed the preparations for this vaguely yet confidently expected arrival. "She had felt it in the air," she said to herself, for she knew nothing of any theory of second sight, nor had ever reasoned, on the other hand, that even the most trivial circumstances of life must work toward some given result, which they instinctively foreshadow to the observant, as the bodily eye makes out the reflection of a material object in a dimmed and besmirched mirror. She bestirred herself as if in a dream, her mind full of Doña Isabel and the past. Yet like an undercurrent beneath the flood of her thoughts flowed the idea of the new element that Doña Isabel was bringing with her. "A *foreigner!*" she muttered, as if she could scarce believe her words. "Can it be possible that the hand once stung can dally again with the scorpion? Ah, no! necessity wears the guise of heresy, but it is not possible that Doña Isabel can forget."

She glanced around her; Chinita had disappeared. Doña Feliz saw her no more until the long-delayed carriage rolled into the court, when she descended to greet her mistress.

The long summer's day had almost waned, and so dark was the court that torches of pitch-pine had been stuck into rude sconces against the pillars, and the face of Doña Isabel looked wan and ghastly in the lurid and flickering glare. She could not descend from the carriage until the wounded youth had been lifted out. Doña Feliz had never seen but one man so fair. She started as her eyes fell upon the yellow masses of hair that lay disordered upon his brow, but pointed to a chamber which a woman ran to open, and into which the stranger was carried: while Doña Isabel, cramped and stiff, leaned upon the arm of Don Rafael, and stepped to the ground. As she did so she would have fallen but for two strong young hands which caught hers, and as she involuntarily held them and steadied herself she turned her eyes upon the face which was level with her own. Her eyes opened widely, and with an exclamation of actual horror she threw Chinita from her with a sudden and violent struggle, and passed proudly though tremblingly across the court.

Don Rafael and Doña Feliz followed, too astounded to make one movement to assist their lady's ascent of the stairs; but when they reached the corridor and heard the door of the bed-chamber heavily closed, they turned toward each other, their faces pale in the twilight. "Her thoughts are serpents to lash her," murmured Doña Feliz; adding with a sort of national pride, "The Castillian woman may choose to ignore, but she can never forget or forgive."

Don Rafael shrugged his shoulders. How much with some races a shrug may signify! His then was one of dogged resolution. "It is well," it seemed to say; and he muttered, "As the mistress leads, the servant must follow," while his mother, shaking her head doubtfully, pointed to the court below.

Chinita had rushed furiously away from the carriage and the group of men, who after the first silence of surprise had broken into but half-suppressed laughter, which was soon lost in the babel of greetings that the disappearance of Doña Isabel gave an opportunity for exchanging, and scarcely knowing in her blind rage where she went, had thrown herself upon one of the stone seats that bordered the fountain, and with her small clinched fist was beating the rugged stone. Pedro stood near her, his face as indignant as her own, vainly endeavoring with a voice that shook with anger to soothe her wounded pride, while with one hand he strove to lead her away. She spoke not a word. Suddenly, as the young face of the girl was lifted to the light, Feliz clasped her hands together, and leaned eagerly forward. She motioned to Don Rafael, — she would not break the spell by speech; but unheeding her he left the corridor and walked away, and presently Pedro was obliged to hasten to his duties at the doorway, and the girl and the woman were left alone in the enclosure. Doña Feliz leaned motionless over the railing. Chinita, still beating the stone with her fist, sat upon the edge of the fountain. With her native instinct of propriety, to meet Doña Isabel she had put on her second best skirt — not the green one — and all her necklaces circled her throat. Her hair was closely braided, but curled wilfully round her brow and the nape of her neck. She pulled at it abstractedly in a manner she had when excited. Her face was turned aside, but to Doña Feliz there was something strangely familiar in her attitude, — something which suggested other personalities, but of whom; which recalled the past, but how?

While Chinita still sat there, Doña Isabel came out of her chamber and crossed to the side of Feliz. Her face quivered as her eyes fell on the child, and she laid her nervous white hand upon Feliz's arm. The two women looked at each other, but said not a word; the eyes of the one were full of reproach, those of the other of defiant distrust. When they turned them upon the court again, the girl had moved noiselessly away. Her passion of

9

anger was spent, and with the instinct of the Indian strain in her mixed blood, she had gone to hide herself away in some sheltered corner and brood sullenly upon her wrongs.

As she passed through the many courts, reaching at last that upon which the church opened, she was so absorbed that she did not notice she was closely followed by a man who had been very near when Doña Isabel had repulsed her, and who with a few apparently careless questions had possessed himself of all there was to know of Chinita's history.

"Look you!" said one, "did not Pedro say that a man as black as the devil dropped her into his hands? Who knows but she is the fiend's own child? *Vaya*, she struck me over the face with talons like a cat's only last week."

"And well thou deservedst it," cried the boy called Pepé. But he was laughed down by a shrill majority, for Doña Isabel's unaccountable repulse of her had turned the tide of public opinion strongly against the foundling; and the woman toward whom Tio Reyes — for he it was — now turned for additional particulars, rightly judging that in such matters female memories would prove most explicit, crossed herself as she opined "that the fox knows much, but more he who traps him, and that Pedro who had found the girl could best tell whence she came," — a saying which elicited many nods and exclamations of approval, for Pedro had never been believed quite honest in the matter. A wild story that he had received the babe from the hands of a beautiful and pallid spectre which had once been seen to speak with him in the corridor, and that this was the ghost of some lovely woman he had murdered in those early days when he and Don Leon were comrades in many a wild adventure, had passed into a sort of legend, which if not entirely accepted, certainly was not utterly disbelieved by any one.

"Go thy way! She is the devil's own brat," cried the wife of the man Chinita had once attacked.

"Ay, to be sure!" cried another; "was it not to be remembered how she had struggled and screamed when the good Father Francisco baptized her, and had sputtered and spat out the salt which the good priest had put in her mouth like a very cat. And little good had it done her, for she had never been called by a Christian name."

" Tut! tut!" said the new-comer, " what need of a name has such a pretty maid as that, or of a father or mother either? Though ye women have no mercy, she 'll laugh at you all yet. The lads will not be blind, eh Pancho?"

"That they will not!" cried the lad Pepé, throwing a meaning glance at Pancho as if daring him to take up the cudgels in behalf of his old playfellow. "What care I who she is? She 's not the first who came into the world by a crooked road; and must all the women hint that it began at the Devil's door because they can't trace it back? Ay, they know enough ways to the same place."

"Well said, young friend!" cried Tio Reyes with a hearty slap on the boy's shoulder. "But, hist! here comes Pedro — with an ill look too in his eye. Ah! I thought so," as the men suddenly became noisily busy with the unsaddling of their horses, and the women slipped away to their household occupations. "Tio Pedro is not a man to be trifled with. But, ah, there goes the girl!" and in a moment of confusion he adroitly left the court without being seen, and as has been said followed her steps till, as she crouched behind one of the buttresses of the church, he halted behind another and looked at her keenly, impatient with the uncertain light, eager to approach her before it darkened, yet waiting stoically until she was settled in a sullen crouching attitude, probably for that vigil of silence and hunger in which a ranchero's anger usually expends itself, or crystallizes into a revengeful memory.

After some minutes, during which the girl neither sobbed nor moved, he suddenly bent over and touched her on the shoulder. She was accustomed to such intrusions, and shook herself sullenly, not even looking up when an unknown voice accosted her. "Hist, thou! I have something for thee."

" I want nothing, not manna from Heaven even."

" 'T will prove better than that."

"Then keep it thyself. Thou 'rt a stranger. I take neither a blow from a woman nor a gift from a man."

" Ah!" said the man, coming a little nearer and laying

a hand lightly on her shoulder, "if thou wilt have no gift, shall I *tell* thee something?"

The girl shrugged her shoulder uneasily under his hand. "I am not a baby to care for tales," she said contemptuously; yet the man noticed she turned her head slightly toward him.

"Thou art one of a thousand!" he ejaculated admiringly. "Hey now, proud one, suppose I should tell thee who thou art, — what wouldst thou give Tio Reyes for that?"

"Bah!" said the girl, "I have never thought about it." Yet she was conscious that her heart began to beat wildly and her voice sounded faint in her ears. A little picture formed itself before her eyes, of Pepé and Marta and Ranulfo and a score of others, waifs of humanity, and she herself on a height looking down upon them. She had never consciously separated herself from them, — she had never even wished that she, like them, had at least a mother; but presently she was conscious of a new feeling. Yet she laughed as she said, "I was born then like other children, — I had a mother?"

"That had you; but I am not going to sing all that's in the book, *niña.* The wise man talks little and the prudent woman asks few questions, and thus fewer lies are spoken."

"But thou art not my father?" queried Chinita, insolently, yielding to a sudden apprehension that seized her, and turning full upon the stranger.

"God deliver me!" answered he; "badly fared the owl that nourished the young eaglet."

"Tell me who I am!" cried Chinita, in a sudden passion of eagerness clutching the man's arm.

"Tut! tut! tut! that is not my business; and as you will not hear my pretty little tale," — for Chinita thrust him violently aside, — "I will give you but one word of warning and be gone: the old hind pushes at the young fawn, but they both make venison."

Chinita was accustomed to the obscure phraseology and symbolical meanings of the thousand proverbs used by her country people, and she instantly caught the idea the speaker sought to convey; but its very audacity held her silent for some moments. It was only after she had gazed at him long and searchingly that she could stammer, " Doña Isabel — and I — Chinita — the same — of one blood ! "

The man nodded, but put his finger upon his lip. He feared perhaps some wild outburst of surprise or exultation ; but instead she said in an awed whisper, " Is she then my mother? "

Tio Reyes leaned against the church and burst into irrepressible though silent laughter. " What next will the girl dream of? " he ejaculated at length, and laughed again.

" What, am I then such a fool? " asked Chinita, coolly, though with inward rage. " Look you, if you had told me yes, I would not have believed you any more than I believed when Señor Enrique said that she had the young American killed who died so many years ago. Bah ! one thing is as foolish as the other," and she turned away disdainfully.

" What! " exclaimed the man, eagerly, " do they say that? Humph ! Well, things as strange as that have happened in her day."

" But that is a lie," cried Chinita, excitedly ; " it was only because Doña Isabel would not interfere to save his son from being shot as murderer and *ladron* that Enrique said so. He went away himself the day after, and he it was who led Calvo to the rancho del Refugio. But what has that to do with us? " and now first, perhaps because there had been time for the matter to take shape in her mind, she showed an eager and excited curiosity. " Tell me who I am ; you surely have more to tell me than that I was born Garcia ! "

The man stared, then cried, " And is not that enough? Why, for a word thou canst be as good as Doña Isabel's daughter. With that face of thine she dare not refuse thee anything."

Chinita looked at him as if she would have torn his secret from him. Strange to say, not a suspicion that he was jesting with her entered her mind. Even as she stood there almost in rags, she felt instinctively that she was far removed from him. The one thought that she was a Garcia, one of the family whom she looked upon as the incarnation of wealth and power, overpowered every other emotion, even that of curiosity. She was vexed,

baffled that he said no more, yet felt as though she had
known all, and had but for a moment forgotten. She even
turned away from him with a momentary impulse to rush
into the presence of Doña Isabel and assail her with the
cry, "Look at me! Why did you thrust me away? I too
am a Garcia!"

"Stay!" cried Tio Reyes, as she started from his side.
Her wild thoughts had flashed by so rapidly that, quick
though he was to read the countenance, he had caught
scarce an inkling of what had passed through her mind,
and was certain only of the half-dazed dislike with which
she looked at him. It irritated and disappointed him.

"What, girl!" he said, "is not this news worth so
much as a 'thank you'? Is it nothing to you whether
you are the dust of the roadway or a jewel of the mine?
Well, I lied to you. Ah! ah! what know I who you are?
It was my joke! Tio Reyes always likes a jest with a
pretty girl."

"But this is no jest," said Chinita, quick to perceive
that the man was already half repentant of his words;
"you can better put the ocean into a well, than shut up
the truth when it is once out. Ah, I did not need you to
tell me I was no beggar's brat, picked up by chance on the
plain. I have heard them say that Pedro has rich clothes
which I was wrapped in. He has always laughed at me
when I have asked about them, but all the same he shall
show them to you this very night."

"Chut!" interrupted the man, "what should I know of
swaddling clothes? 'T is just a maid's folly to think of
such trifles. They would not prove thee a Garcia, any
more than the lack of them belies it, or my mere word
insures it!"

"That which puzzles me is," said Chinita, gravely,
turning her head on one side and looking at him keenly
by the dim light, "why you have told me this. Have
you been sent with a message from — from those who left
me here?"

"No, by my faith," said the man, laughing; "and
why do I laugh, think you? Why, you are the first one
who ever asked Tio Reyes for a reason. Does anybody
who knows me say, 'Why did you take Don Fulano with
all his dollars safe through the mountains, and then allow

that poor devil De Tal, who had not so much as a four-penny piece, to be shot down like a dog by the wayside?' No, even the village idiot knows Tio Reyes has reasons too great to be tossed from one to another like a ball; and yet you ask me why I have told you the secret I have kept for years, and perhaps expect an answer! No, no! that plum is not ripe enough to fall at the first puff of wind."

" I will tell you one thing, though you tell me nothing," said Chinita, shrewdly, after a pause : " It is not from love to Doña Isabel that you have told me this, nor for love of me either. What good have you done me by telling me I am a Garcia? Why, if I had had the sense of a parrot, I might have known it before." It seemed to her in her excitement as if, indeed, she had always known it.

" A word to the wise is enough," said the man, myste-riously. " Keep your knowledge to yourself, but use it to your advantage. You were sent like a package to Doña Isabel years ago, but stopped by a clumsy mes-senger. She finds you in her path now; let her find something alive under the shabby coverings. God puts many a sweet nut in a rough shell, many a poison in despised weeds ! "

"Oh ! " cried Chinita, with a wicked little laugh, though even at that moment the chords of kinship thrilled, " I am but a weed to Doña Isabel, eh? Shall I go to her and say, ' Here is a Garcia to be trodden down'?"

She said this with so superb an air of derision that the man who unconsciously all his life had been an inimitable actor in his way, muttered a deep *caramba* of enthusiastic admiration.

"I would by all the saints I could stay here to see how you will goad and sting my grand Señora," he said vindictively. " Ay, remember you are a Garcia, with a hundred old scores to pay off. I have put the cards in your hands, — patience, and shuffle them well ! "

"Patience, and shuffle your cards," — those cards simply the knowledge that she was a Garcia, with presumably the wrongs of parents to avenge. The thoughts were not very clear in her mind, but the instincts of resentment of insult and of filial devotion were those which amid so much that is ungenerous, evil, and fierce, ever pervade the breast of the Mexican. She turned again to ask almost imploringly, " My father — my mother — who were they?" when she found she was alone. The stranger had extorted no promise of secrecy, offered no bribe; it was as if he had put a weapon in her hand, knowing that its very preciousness and subtlety would prevent her from revealing whence she had received it, and would indicate the use to which it was to be turned.

Chinita leaned against the buttress and pondered. Strangely enough, she did not for a moment think to seek the man and demand further explanation. As she felt he had divined her character, so she divined his. He had said all he would say. After all, it was enough. At the end of an hour she left that spot, which she never saw after without a thrill of the heart, and walked straight to the doorway where Pedro sat. He was eating his supper mechanically, with a disturbed countenance, which cleared when he saw her.

" They are *tamales de chile*, daughter," he said, pushing toward her the platter, upon which lay some morsels of corn-pastry and pepper-sauce, wrapped in corn-leaves. " Eat, thou must be hungry."

Pedro sighed, for perplexity and vexation had destroyed his own appetite, and thought enviously, as Chinita's white teeth closed on the soft pastry, which was yellow in comparison, " It is a good thing nothing but unrequited love keeps the young from supping, — and that only for a time."

The gate-keeper watched Chinita narrowly as she was eating and drinking atole from the rough earthen jar. There was some change in her he could not understand, quite different from the passion in which he had last seen her, or the languor which would naturally succeed it. She did not talk, and something kept him from referring to the scene in the courtyard; he felt that she would resent it. Two or three times she bent over him and touched his hand caressingly; yet he was not encouraged to smooth her tangled hair, or offer any of those awkward proofs of affection which she was wont to receive and laugh at or return as the humor seized her; neither did he remind her that it was getting late, but at last rose and took from his girdle the key of the postern.

" Put it back, Pedro ! " she said in her softest voice.
" I shall never sleep in the hut with Florencia and the
children again; yet be not afraid, I will not go to the
corridor either. There is room and to spare in yon great
house." She nodded toward the inner court, muttered
a good-night, and before Pedro could recover from his
surprise sufficiently to speak, swiftly crossed the patio
and disappeared.

Pedro looked after her stupefied. He realized that a
great gulf had opened between them; that figuratively
speaking, his foster-child had left him forever. He looked
like one who, holding a pet bird loosely in his hand, had beheld it suddenly escape him, and soar across a wide and
bridgeless chasm. Would it dash itself into atoms against
the opposite cliffs, or perchance reach a safe haven? Such
was the essence of the thoughts for which Pedro framed no
words. " God is great," he muttered at length, " and
knows what He does ; " adding with a sort of heathen and
dogged obstinacy, " but Pedro still is here ; Pedro does
not forget *niña !* " He looked up as if to some invisible
auditor, crossed himself, then wearily threw himself upon
his pallet ; but weary as he was, the strong young subject
of his cares was sunk in deep and dreamless sleep long
before he closed his eyes.

XIX.

ONCE within the court, Chinita paused and looked around her cautiously. The doors of the lower rooms stood open, and she might have entered any one of them unnoticed and found a shelter for the night. But she was in no mood for solitude. Indeed it was hard for her to check a certain wild impulse that seized her, as she saw a faint glimmer of light which streamed through a slight opening of a door on the upper corridor, and that urged her to rush at once into the presence of Doña Isabel and claim recognition. To what relationship, and to what rights, she did not ask herself; a positive though undefined certainty that Doña Isabel herself would know, and would be forced to yield her justice, possessed her.

Chinita was now a child neither in stature nor mind, but though so young in years, had reached the first development of her powers with the mingled precocity of the Indian and Spaniard, fostered by a clime that seems the very elixir of passion. She had been maturing rapidly in the last few months, and as she stood that night in the faint starlight, the last trace of childhood seemed to drop visibly from her. She folded her arms on her breast, and sighed deeply, — not for sorrow, but as if she breathed a life that was new to her, and her lungs were oppressed by the weight of a strange and too heavily perfumed atmosphere.

In her absorption Chinita was unconscious that she was observed, — but it chanced that Don Rafael Sanchez and his mother had just left the Señora Doña Isabel, and were passing through the upper corridor to their own apartments. The gallery was wide and they were in the shadow, but a stray gleam of light touched the upturned face of the girl and exhibited it in strong relief within the framing of her waving hair. As they caught sight of it, they involuntarily paused to look at her.

" I do not wonder," whispered Feliz," that such a face is an accusing conscience to Doña Isabel. There is a strange familiarity in every feature ; and what a spirit, too, she has, — one even to glory in strife ! "

Don Rafael nodded. " There has always seemed to me something in that child to mark her as the offspring of a dominant family," he said ; " it is inevitable that she must break the lines an adverse Fate has cast about her. Others such as she stretch out a hand to Vice ; if something better comes to her, who are we to hinder it? "

The brow of Doña Feliz contracted. " Ay, Rafael," she murmured, " what a change a few miserable years have wrought ! Once I was a sister to Doña Isabel, and now—"

" You are no traitress," interposed Don Rafael, " and it is by circumstance only that the change has come. Console yourself, dear mother, and remember we are pledged. Though we seem false to her mother, only so can we be true to Herlinda."

He breathed the name so low that even Doña Feliz did not hear it ; she listened rather to the beating of the heart that seemed to repeat without cessation the name of one so loved and lost. " How strange it is, Rafael," she said presently, "that I have such persistent, such mocking dreams, which against my reason, against all precedent, create in me the belief that all is not ended for Herlinda Garcia."

Don Rafael looked at her musingly.

" There is a man called Juarez who has dreams such as yours," he said ; " but they are of the freedom of a race, not of one woman alone. But he is hardly able to work miracles. Yet, mother, this truly is the time of prodigies ; what think you this boy, the young American that Doña Isabel brought hither, calls himself ? "

" I have asked him," she said, " but he did not under-- stand me. Oh, Rafael ! my heart stood still when I saw him first ; yet after all he is not so very like —"

" Yet he has the same name, Mother. It may be but chance ; those Americans are half barbarians as we know, — they forget the saints, and seek to glorify their great men by giving their children as Christian names the surnames of those who have distinguished themselves in

battle or statesmanship. Sometimes, too, a mother proud
of the surname of her own family gives it to her son. It
may have been so with this man. When I gave him pen
and paper, and bade him write his name, it was thus:
'Ashley Ward.'"

The name as spoken by Don Rafael was mispronounced,
would have been hardly recognizable in the ears of him
who owned it; yet to Doña Feliz it was like a trumpet
blast. "Strange! strange! strange!" she repeated again
and again. "Can it be mere chance?"

"That we shall soon know," said Don Rafael. "These
Americans blurt out their affairs to the first comer,
expecting help from every quarter. There is no rain that
falls but that they fancy it is to water their own field.
Nay, mother," as Doña Feliz made a movement toward
the stairway, "go not near the man to-night; he has
fever, and is in need of quiet. Old Selsa is with him, and
he can need no better care. He is safe to remain here
many days; let him rest in peace now. And do you,
mother, try to sleep; you are weary and worn."

With the filial solicitude of a true Mexican, the man,
already middle-aged, took his mother's hand fondly and led
her to the door of her own apartment. There she detained
him long in low and earnest conversation, and when on
leaving her he looked down into the court it was entirely
deserted.

In glancing around her, Chinita's eyes had caught no
glimpse of the figures above, perhaps because they had
been diverted by a faint glimmer of light at one angle of
the courtyard; and remembering that this came from
the room to which the wounded man had been carried, she
darted swiftly and noiselessly toward it, and in a moment
had pushed the door sufficiently ajar to admit of her
entrance, and had passed in. She arrested her footsteps
at the foot of the narrow bed, which extended like a bier
from the wall to the centre of the room. There was not
another article of furniture in the apartment, except a
chair upon which the sick man's coat was thrown; but
Chinita's eyes, accustomed to the vault-like and vacant
suites of square cells that made up the greater part of the
vast building, were struck with no sense of desolation. A
slender jar of water, and a number of earthen utensils of

different forms and shapes, containing medicaments and food, were gathered upon the floor near the bed's head; and on a deep window-ledge was placed a sputtering tallow-candle, which had already half filled with grease the clay sconce in which it was sunk.

As Chinita leaned over the foot of the bed and peered through her unkempt locks at its occupant, he looked up with a start, and presently said something in an appealing tone, which certainly touched her more than the words, could she have understood them, would have done. He had in fact exclaimed in English, with an unmistakable American intonation, "Heavens, what a gypsy! and what can she want here in this miserable jail they have left me in?"

She thought he had perhaps asked for water, so she gave him some, which was not unacceptable, — though it irritated him that after giving him the cup, she took up the candle and held it close to his face while he drank. She was in the mood for new impressions however rather than for kindness, and the sight of a strange face pleased her. Burning with fever though he was, and tossing with all the impatience natural to his condition, he could not but notice the totally unaffected ease with which she made her inspection. He might have been a curly-headed infant instead of a man, so utterly unconcernedly did she look into his dark-blue eyes, and note the broad white brow upon which his damp yellow hair clustered, even touching lightly with her finger the firm white throat bared by the opened collar sufficiently to expose the clumsily arranged dressings on the wounded shoulder, Instantly, with a few deft movements, she made them more comfortable, for which the young man thanked her in a few of the very scanty words of Spanish at his command, — at which she laughed, not ironically, but with a sort of nervous irrelevance, thinking to herself the while, " He is beautiful — bless me, yes! as beautiful as they say the murdered American was! Who knows? this one may come from the same district! It must be but a little place, his country, — there cannot be such a very great world outside the mountains yonder; they touch heaven everywhere. Look now, how white his arms are, and his brow, where the sun has not touched it! and how red his cheeks!

But that must be with the fever." And so half audibly
she made her comments upon the wounded stranger, seemingly entirely unconscious or regardless that there was any
mind or soul within this body she so frankly admired, —
lifting his unwounded arm sometimes, or turning his face
into better view, as she might have done parts of a
mechanism that pleased her.

"Evidently she thinks me wooden," he said with a
gleam of humor in his eyes. "As I am dumb to her, she
believes me also senseless and sightless. Thanks, for
taking away that ill-smelling candle," as with the offending taper in her hand she passed to the other side of
the bed. Then she stopped and laughed, and he remembered that he had seen the old woman who had been left
in charge of him arrange her sheepskins there and throw
herself upon them. Until the young girl had come, old
Selsa's snores had vexed him; since that he had forgotten
them, though now they became audible again. As Chinita
laughed, she placed the candle-stick upon the window-ledge
and looked around her, stretching herself and yawning.
The hour was late for her, the diversion caused by sight
of the blond stranger and the little service she had rendered him had relaxed the tension of her mind, and she
felt herself aweary; the shadows fell dark in every corner
of the room, — there was something grewsome in its aspect
even to Chinita's accustomed eyes. It subdued her wild
and reckless mood, and she scanned the place narrowly
for something upon which she might lie. Presently the
young man saw her glide toward the sleeping nurse, and
deftly, with a half mischievous, half triumphant expression
upon her face, draw out one of the sheepskin mats upon
which the old woman was lying, and taking it to the opposite side of the bed arrange it to her liking upon the
brick floor, and sinking upon it softly and daintily as a
cat might have done, compose herself to sleep.

The candle on the window-sill sputtered and flickered;
old Selsa snored in her corner, seemingly undisturbed
by the abstraction of a part of her bed; the shadows in
the apartment grew longer and longer; the eyelids of
the young girl closed, her regular breathing parted her full
lips. The young man had painfully raised himself upon
one arm, and assured himself of this. He himself was

dropping off into snatches of slumber which promised to become profound, when suddenly with a start he found himself wide awake, and staring at a draped figure which had noiselessly glided into his chamber. Save for the candle it bore he would have thought it a visitant from another world; but his first surprise over, he recognized it as that of a woman. He was conscious that his heart beat wildly; his fever had returned. Where had he seen this pale proud face, these classic features, these dark penetrating eyes? For a moment again he felt as if swinging between heaven and earth, between life and death. Ah! yes, he comprehended, — he had been brought thither in some swaying vehicle, and this woman had been beside him; she perhaps had saved his life.

He murmured a word of thanks, but she did not notice it. "Señor," she said in a voice soft in courtesy, "I pray you forgive me that I had for a little time forgotten my guest. I trust you lack for nothing? Ah! what — alone?" and with a frown, she made a motion as if to awaken the servant Selsa. He understood the gesture though not the words, and stopped her by one as expressive.

"No, no!" he exclaimed. "I too shall sleep; and she is old. I would not awaken her. See, if I need anything a touch of my hand will rouse this girl," — and the young man indicated by a turn of his head and arm the recumbent figure which his visitor had not observed.

With some curiosity she moved to the opposite side of the bed, and bending over lightly removed the fringe of the reboso which shaded the face of the sleeper. Doña Isabel started, and a slight exclamation escaped her lips as she turned hurriedly away, — as hurriedly returning, and shading the candle with her hand, that its light might not fall upon the eyes of the sleeper, she gazed upon the young girl long and earnestly. Unmindful of herself, she suffered the full glare of the candle to illuminate her own countenance; and as he looked upon it, the young American thought it might serve as the very model for the mask of tragedy. Nothing more pitiless, more remorseless, more sombre than its expression could be imagined; yet as she gazed, a flush of shame rose from neck to brow. Her eyes clouded, her breath came with a quick gasp. She stood for a moment clasping the rod at the foot of the bed with her white nervous hand; she looked at the American fixedly, yet she seemed to have no consciousness that she herself was seen; and presently, with the slow movement of a somnambulist, so absorbing was her thought, she turned to the door.

Ashley was watching her intently; suddenly her light was extinguished, and she vanished as if dissolved in air. He was calm enough to remember that she had spoken to him, to know that she could be no phantom of his imagination, and to suppose that upon stepping into the corridor she had extinguished her light, and sped noiselessly along the wall to some other apartment; yet for a long time a feeling of mystery oppressed him, and he could not sleep. A vague consciousness of some strange influence near him kept him feverish, with all his senses on the alert; yet he heard no movement of the woman who crouched within the doorway, leaning against the cold wall, and who during the long silent night passed in review the strange events that had brought her — the Señora Isabel Garcia de Garcia — to guard the slumbers of a foundling, the foster-child of a man so low in station as the gate-keeper of her house.

XX.

Doña Isabel Garcia had been born within the walls of Tres Hermanos, her father having been part owner of the estate, and her mother the daughter of an impoverished gentleman of the neighboring city of Guanapila. Doña Clarita had been a most beautiful woman, whose attractions had been utilized to prop the falling fortunes of her house by her marriage with the elderly but kindly proprietor Don Ignacio Garcia.

At the time of her marriage, Clarita Rodriguez was very young, and with the habits of submission universal among her countrywomen would probably have taken kindly to her fate, never doubting its justice, but that from her balcony she had one day seen a young officer of the city troop ride by in all the magnificence of the military uniform of the period. A dazzling vision of gold lace and braid, clanking spurs and sabre, and of eyes and teeth and smile more dazzling still, haunted her for weeks. Yet that might have passed, but that the vision glided from the eye to the heart, when on one luckless night, at the governor's ball, Pancho Vallé was introduced to her, and they twice were partners in that lover's delirium the slow and voluptuous *danza*. As they moved together in the dreamy measure, a few low words were exchanged, — commonplace perhaps but not harmless, and by one at least never to be forgotten. Afterward an occasional missive penned in most regular characters upon daintily tinted paper came to her hands through some complaisant servant. But Don Ranulfo Rodriguez was too jealous a guardian to suffer many such to escape him, and had been far too wise in his generation to place it in his daughter's power to engage in such dangerous pastime as the production of replies to unwelcome suitors. Like most other girls of her age and position, Clarita had been strenuously prevented from learning to write, and it is doubtful if she ever knew the exact import of Vallé's perfumed

10

missives, although her heart doubtless guessed what her eyes could not decipher.

Whether Vallé's impassioned glances meant all they indicated or not, certain it was that he had not ventured to declare himself to the father as a suitor for the fair Clarita's hand, when Don Ignacio Garcia stepped in and literally carried away the prize. The courtship had been short, the position of the groom unassailable. Clarita shed some tears, but the delighted father declared they were for joy at her good fortune; and they were indeed of so mixed a character — baffled love, wounded pride, and an irrepressible sense of triumph at her unexpected promotion — that she herself scarce cared to analyze them. She danced with Vallé once again on the occasion of her marriage; again a few words were spoken, and the passionate heart of Clarita was pierced with a secret dart, which never ceased to rankle.

Don Ignacio Garcia conducted her immediately to the hacienda, where his jealous nature found no cause for suspicion; and there the little Isabel was born; and on beholding the wealth of maternal affection which the young wife lavished upon her child, the husband forgot the indifference that had sometimes chafed him, and for a few brief months imagined himself beloved. This egotistic delusion was never dispelled, for at its height, upon the second anniversary of their wedding day, when taking part in a bull-chase, Don Ignacio's horse swerved as he urged him to the side of the infuriated animal; a moment's hesitancy was fatal; the horse was ripped open by the powerful horn of the bull, and plunging wildly, fell back upon his luckless rider, whose neck was instantly broken. It was an accident which it seemed incredible could have happened to a man so skilled in horsemanship as was Don Ignacio. The spectators were for a moment dumb with horror and surprise, then with groans and shrieks rushed to the rescue, but only to lift a corpse. Doña Clarita with a wild shriek had fainted as the horse plunged back, and upon regaining her senses, threw herself in an agony of not unremorseful grief upon the body of her husband. It was, however, of that violent character which soon expends itself; and before the funeral obsequies were well over, she began to look around the narrow horizon of Tres

Hermanos, and remember, if not rejoice, that she was free
to go beyond it.

Don Gregorio, the cousin of Clarita's husband's, though
a mere boy, had been brought up on the estate, and was
competent to take charge, and the administrador and
clerks were trusty men ; so there was no absolute reason
why the young widow should remain to guard her interests and those of her child, and it seemed but natural
she should return to her father's house, at least during
the first months of her sorrow.   Thither indeed she
went.   She had dwelt there before, a dependent child, to
be disposed of at her father's will ; she returned to it a
rich widow, profuse of her favors but tenacious of her
rights, one of which all too soon proclaimed itself to be
that of choosing for herself a second husband.   A month
or two after her arrival in the city, Don Pancho Vallé returned from some expedition in which patriotism and personal gain were deftly combined, with the halo of success
added to his personal attractions, and was quick to declare
an unswerving devotion to the divinity at whose shrine he
had worshipped but doubtfully while it remained ungilded
by the sun of prosperity.   Whether Clarita had learned to
read or not, certain it is that Don Pancho's impassioned
missives met with a response more satisfactory than pen
and ink alone could give, for immediately after the expiration of the year due to the memory of Don Ignacio, she
became the wife of the gay soldier.

Don Pancho and his wife were both young, both equally
delighted in excitement and luxury ; and within an incredibly short time the ample resources which had seemed
to them boundless were perceptibly narrowed.   To the
taste for extravagant living, for gorgeous apparel, for
numerous and magnificent horses, shared by them in common, were added a passionate love of gambling, and a
scarcely less expensive one for military enterprises of an
independent and half guerilla order, on the part of Don
Pancho ; and thus a few years saw the wife's fortune
reduced to an encumbered interest in the lands of Tres
Hermanos.

Don Pancho in spite of numerous infidelities still retained his influence over the heart and mind of Clarita ;
and one night in play against Don Gregorio Garcia—

who, like other caballeros, occasionally engaged in a game or two for pastime — he staked the last acre of her estate, knowing she would refuse him nothing, and lost. For a moment he looked blank, — a most unwonted manifestation of dismay in so practised a gambler, — then laughed and shook hands with his fortunate opponent. There was a laughing group around him, condoling with him banteringly, for Pancho Vallé had never seemed to make any misfortune a serious matter, when a pistol-shot was heard. For a moment no one realized what had happened ; the young officer stood in his gay uniform, smiling still, his gold-mounted pistol in his hand, then fell heavily forward. The ball had passed through his heart. His widow had the satisfaction of seeing by the smile that remained on his handsome countenance that he had died as joyously as he had lived ; not a trace of care showed that aught deeper than mere pique and caprice had moved him. "Angel of my life !" she cried, when her first burst of grief was over, " thou wert beginning to make my heart ache, for I had nothing more to give thee !"

This was her only word of reproach, if reproach it might be called. For love that woman would have yielded even her life, and never have known the hollowness of her idol. Grief did the work that ingratitude and neglect — nay absolute cruelty — would perhaps never have effected, and in a few short months destroyed her life. As she was dying she called her daughter to her. "Isabel," she said, "thou hast wealth, thy brother has nothing ; swear to me by the Virgin and thy patron saint, that thou wilt be as a mother to him, that thou wilt refuse him nothing that thy hand can give ! Money, money, money, is what makes men happy !" That had been the creed her life's experience had taught her. For money her father had sold her ; for that the husband she adored had given her fair words and caresses. "As thou wouldst have thy mother's blessing, promise me that Leon shall never appeal to thee in vain !"

Isabel Garcia was but a child, and the boy Leon but three years younger ; yet as she looked upon her dying mother she solemnly promised to fill her place, to take upon herself the rôle of sacrifice, which her religion taught her was that of motherhood. Poor Clarita ! little had she understood a mother's highest duties, — to warn, to guide, to plead with God for the beloved. The mere yielding of material things, — to clothe herself in sackcloth, that the child might be robed in purple, to walk barefoot that he might ride in state, to hunger that he might be delicately fed, — she had pictured these things to herself as the purest sacrifices, and surely the only ones to appeal to the hearts of such men as she had known; and the young Isabel entered upon her task with her mother's precepts deeply engraved upon her heart, her mind all uninstructed, awaiting the iron finger of experience to write upon it its lessons.

After their mother's death, the young brother and sister, mere children both, went to live in the house of some elderly relatives, who with generous though not always judicious kindness strove to forget the faults of the father by ignoring them when they became apparent in the boy. The uncle of Isabel, the Friar Francisco, became their tutor, but taught them little beyond the breviary. What could a woman need with more? As for Leon, he took more kindly to the lasso and saddle, to the pistol and sword, than to the book or pen, — and even while still a child in years, more passionately still to the gaming table. Though his elders with a shake of the head remembered his father's fate, and sometimes pushed the boy half laughingly away from the monté table, or of a Sunday afternoon sent him out to the bull-ring for his diversion, where he was a mere spectator, rather than to the cock-pit, where he became a participant, yet the question did not present itself as one at all of questionable morals: every one gambled on a feast day, or at a social game among one's friends. Perhaps of all those by whom he was surrounded, no one felt any serious anxiety for Leon except the young girl who with premature solicitude warned him of the evil, even as she supplied the means to indulge his wayward tastes.

Leon was a brilliant rather than a handsome boy, promising to be well grown; and his lithe, vigorous figure showed to good advantage in his gay riding-suits, whether of sombre black cloth with silver buttons set closely down the outer seam of the pantaloons and adorning the short round jacket, or in loose *chapareras* of buckskin bound by a scarlet sash and bedizened with leather fringes, — a costume that perhaps served to betray the Indian strain in his blood, which ordinarily was detected only by a slight prominence of the cheek bones and a somewhat furtive expression in the soft dark eyes. At unguarded moments, however, perhaps when he fancied himself unobserved and was practising with his pistol or sabre, those eyes could flash with concentrated fire, so that more than once Isabel had been constrained to call out: "Leon, Leon, you frighten me! You look like the great cat when he pounces upon a harmless little bird and crushes it for the very joy of killing!"

Then Leon would laugh, and the soft, dreamy haze would rise again over the eyes as he would turn upon her. "Ha!" he would say, "you will never be a man, Isabel; you will never understand why I love the sights and sounds that throw you poor women into fainting fits and tears. Ha! Isabel, if I were you I'd not stay in this dull house with a couple of old women to guard me, when you might go to the hacienda and be free as air."

"Nonsense," Isabel would retort; "what could I do there other than here? I could not turn herdsman or vaquero, nor even ride out to the fields to see how the crops were flourishing, nor roam like an Indian through the mountains."

"But *I* would!" Leon would cry enthusiastically; and with his longing ardor for the free life of a country gentleman, with its barbaric luxury and wild sports, he thus first put into the young girl's mind the thought of favoring the suit which her cousin, Don Gregorio Garcia, began to urge.

Don Gregorio had married young, soon after the death of Ignacio Garcia whom he succeeded in the management of the estate of which they had been joint owners; but his wife had died leaving him without an heir, and the first grief assuaged, it was but natural after the passage of years that the widower should weary of his loneliness. There were many reasons why his thoughts should turn to his distant cousin Isabel, for though she was many years younger than himself, such disparity of age was not unusual; the marriage would unite still more closely the family fortunes, and effectually prevent the intrusion of any undesirable stranger; and above all, Isabel was gracious and queenly and beautiful enough to charm the heart even of an anchorite, and Don Gregorio was far from being one. Indeed, in his very early years he had given indications of a partiality for a far more adventurous career than he had finally, by force of circumstances, been led to adopt. Thus he sympathized somewhat with Leon's restless activity, and quite honestly secured the boy's alliance, — no slight advantage in his siege of the heart of Isabel.

This, perhaps more than the good-will of the rest of the family, enabled Don Gregorio to approach so nearly to Isabel's inmost nature that he learned far more of the strength of purpose and capability for passionate devotion possessed by the young untrained girl than any other being had done, and for the first time in his life knew a love far deeper and purer than any passion which mere physical charms could awaken. Such a love appealed to Isabel. She was perhaps constitutionally cold to sexual charms, but eminently susceptible to the sympathetic attrition of an appreciative mind, while her heart could translate far more readily the rational outpourings of friendship than the wild rhapsodies of passion. Thus, although Isabel would have shrunk from a man who in his ardor would have demanded of her affection some sacrifice of the unqualified devotion that she had vowed to her brother, she seemed to find in Don Gregorio one who could understand and applaud the exaggerated devotion to the ideal standard of filial and sisterly duty which she had unconsciously erected upon the few utterly irrational words of a weak and dying woman.

The first four years of Isabel's married life passed uneventfully. Leon was constantly near her, and was the life of the great house, which despite the crowd of retainers that frequented it would without him have proved but a dull dwelling for so young a matron, with no illusions in regard to the staid and kindly husband, who was rather a friend to be consulted and revered than a lover to be adored, — for although Don Gregorio worshipped his beautiful young wife, he was at once too mindful of his own dignity, and too wary of startling Isabel's passionless nature, to manifest or exact romantic and exhaustive

proofs of affection.   He used sometimes to mutter to himself: "'The stronger the flame the sooner the wood is
burnt;' better that the substance of love should endure
than be dissipated in smoke!"

Don Gregorio was somewhat of a philosopher; and as
such, as soon as the glamour thrown over him by Leon's
brilliant but inconsequent sallies of wit, and his daring
and dashing manner, was dimmed, and above all as soon
as his unreasoning sympathy with Isabel's predispositions
settled into a calm and sincere desire for her certain happiness and welfare, he began to look with some suspicion
upon traits which had at first attracted him as the natural
outcome of an ardent and generous nature.

Friar Francisco had accompanied the young brother
and sister to the hacienda, partly to minister in the church,
and partly as tutor to Leon; but in the latter capacity he
found little exercise for his talents.   Upon one pretext or
another the boy at first evaded and later absolutely refused study; but he joined so heartily in the labors as
well as pleasures of hacienda life,— he was so ready in resource, so untiring in action, so companionable alike to
all classes, that Nature seemed to have fitted him absolutely for the position that he was apparently destined to
fill in life.   Yet though he was the prince of rancheros, the
life of the city sometimes seemed to possess an irresistible
attraction for him; and after months perhaps spent among
the employees of the hacienda, in riding with the vaqueros
or in penetrating the recesses of the mountain, even sleeping in the huts of charcoal burners, or in caves with rovers
of still more doubtful reputation, he would suddenly weary
of it all, and followed by a servant or two ride gayly
down to the city to see how the world went there.

At first Don Gregorio had no idea how much those
visits cost Isabel; but as time went on, and rumors
reached them of the boy's extravagant mode of life, Isabel became anxious and Don Gregorio indignant.   Some
investigation showed that a troop of young roysterers
who called him captain were maintained in the mountains, and that a thousand wild freaks which had mystified the neighboring villages and haciendas might be
traced to these mad spirits, among whom Don Gregorio shrewdly conjectured might be found many of the

most daring young fellows, both of the higher and
lower orders, who had one by one mysteriously disappeared during the few months preceding Leon's eighteenth
birthday.

Leon only laughed when taxed with his guerilla following, and although as he managed it it was a somewhat
costly amusement, it was not an unusual or an altogether
useless one in those days of anarchy; for no one could
say how soon the fortunes of war might turn an enemy
upon the land and stores of Tres Hermanos, and even
Don Gregorio was not displeased to find the most refractory of his retainers placed in a position to defend rather
than imperil the interests of the estate. As to the escapades of city life he found them less pardonable, for
they consisted chiefly in mad devotion to the gaming-table,
which Leon was never content to leave until his varying
fortunes turned to disaster and his wild excitement was
quelled by the tardy reflection that his sister's generosity
would be taxed in thousands to pay the folly of a night.

Before the age of twenty Leon Vallé had run the gamut
of the vices and extravagances peculiar to Mexican youths,
and large as the resources of Doña Isabel were, he had
begun to encroach seriously upon them; for true to her
mother's request, she had never refused to supply his
demands for money, though of late she had begun to make
remonstrances, which were received half incredulously, half
sullenly, as though he realized neither their justice nor their
necessity. Isabel was now a mother, her daughter Herlinda
having been born a year after her marriage, and their son
Norberto, the pride and hope of Don Gregorio, three years
later; and naturally the young mother longed to consider
the interests of her children, which so far as her own
property was concerned seemed utterly obliterated and
overwhelmed by the mad extravagances of her brother.

Strangely enough, Don Gregorio attempted no interference with his wife's disposal of her income, though it
seemed not improbable that at no distant day even the
lands would be in jeopardy. Perhaps he foresaw that as
her means to gratify his insatiable demands declined, so
gradually Leon's strange fascination over his sister would
cease; for inevitably his restless spirit would draw him
afar to find fresh fields for adventure, since in those days,

when the great struggle between Church and State was beginning and foreign complications were forming, such a leader as he might prove to be would find no lack of occasion for daring deeds and reckless followers, nor scarcity of plunder with which to repay the latter.

Whatever were his thoughts, Don Gregorio guarded them well, saying sometimes either to Leon himself, or to some friend who expressed a half horrified conjecture as to where such absolute madness must end, "See you not, 't is foolish to squeeze the orange until one tastes the bitterness of the rind?" He expected some sudden and violent reaction in Isabel's mind and conduct. But though she began to show she realized and suffered, she bore the strain put upon her with royal fortitude. Youth can hope through such adverse circumstances, and it always seemed to her that one who "meant so well" as Leon, must eventually turn from temptation and begin a new and nobler career.

At last what appeared to Isabel the turning point in her brother's destiny was reached. He became violently enamored of the beautiful daughter of a Spaniard, one Señor Fernandez, who of a family too distinguished to be flattered by an alliance with a mere attaché of a wealthy and powerful house, was so poor as to be willing to con- sider it should a suitable provision be made to insure his daughter's future prosperity. The beautiful Dolores was herself favorably inclined toward the gay cavalier, who most ardently pressed his suit, — the more ardently per- haps that he was piqued and indignant that the wary father utterly refused to consider the matter until Don Gregorio or Doña Isabel herself should formally ask the hand of his daughter, presenting at the same time unmis- takable assurances of Leon's ability to fulfil the promises he recklessly poured forth.

That Leon had turned from his old evil courses seemed as months passed on an absolute certainty. Not even the administrador himself could be more utterly bound to the wheel of routine than he. To see his changed life, his ab- solute repugnance even to the sports suitable to his age, was almost piteous ; his whole heart and mind seemed set upon atonement for the folly of the past, and in preparation for a life of toil and anxiety in the future. For in examining into her affairs, Doña Isabel found that her income was largely overdrawn; Leon's extravagances, together with heavy losses incurred in the working of the reduction-works, had so far crippled her resources that it was only by stringent effort, and an appeal to Don Gregorio for aid, that she was enabled so to rehabilitate the fortunes of Leon that he could hope to win the prize which was to make or mar his future.

Doña Isabel was as happy as the impatient lover himself when she could place in his hands the deeds of a small but productive estate, famous for the growth of the maguey, from which the sale of pulque and mescal promised a never failing revenue. The money had been raised largely through concessions made by Don Gregorio, and was to be repaid from the income of Isabel's encumbered estate, so that for some years at least it would be out of her power to render Leon any further assistance. Don Gregorio shook his head gravely over the whole matter; yet the fact that the young man was virtually thrown upon the resources provided for him, which certainly without the concentration of all his energies and tact would be altogether insufficient for his maintenance, and also that he had great faith in the energy of character which for the first time appeared diverted into a legitimate channel, inclined him to believe that at last, urged by necessity as well as love, Leon would redeem his past and settle down into the reputable citizen and relative who was to justify and repay the sister's tireless and extraordinary devotion. "Or at least," he said to himself, "Isabel will be satisfied that no more can or should be done; and it is worth a fortune to convince her of that."

Strangely enough, though Isabel had addressed herself with a frenzy of determination to the task of securing a competency for Leon that might enable him to marry and enter upon a life which was to relieve her of the constant drain upon her resources, both material and mental, which for years had been sapping her prosperity and peace, yet as she beheld him ride away toward the town in which his inamorata dwelt to make the final arrangements for his marriage, her heart sank within her; and instead of relief and thankfulness, she felt a frightful pang of apprehension, she knew not why, as if a prophetic voice warned her that her own hand had opened the door to a chamber of horrors, through which the smiling youth would pass and drag her as he went.

Isabel threw herself upon her husband's breast in an agony which he could not comprehend, but which he gently soothed, happy to feel that to him she turned in the first moment of her abandonment,—for indeed she felt that she who had given her substance, her sympathy, her faith, all of which a sister's life is capable, was indeed abandoned, and all for a fresh young face, a word, a smile. Leon was a changed man, but all her devotion had not worked the miracle; another whose love could be as yet but a fancy had accomplished what years of sacrifice from her had striven for in vain!

There was something of jealousy, but far more of the pain of baffled aspiration in the thought, and through it all that dreadful doubt, that sickening dread as to whether she had done well thus to strip herself of the power to minister to him. It seemed, even against her reason, impossible that Leon could be beyond the pale of her bounty; she had been so accustomed to plan, to think, to plot for him, that she could not grasp the thought that henceforth he was to live without her, that she was to know him happy, joyous, at ease, and she no longer be the immediate and ministering Providence which made him so.

After the infant Carmen was born, the mother's thoughts turned into other channels. As she looked at this child, the thought for the first time came to her, that some day it might be possible that her children would inherit some material good from her. Their father was a rich man, yet there was a pleasure in the thought that her children, her daughters most especially, would be pleased by a mother's rich gifts, would perhaps from her receive the dower that would make them welcome in the homes of the men they might love. Isabel began to indulge in the maternal hopes and visions of young motherhood, and to feel the security that a still hopeful mind may acquire, after years of secret and harassing cares have passed.

The usual visits of ceremony had passed between the contracting families; the Señor Fernandez had declared himself satisfied with the generous provisions which had been made for the young couple; the house was set in order, and an early day named for the wedding. Some days of purest happiness followed the tearful anxiety with which Dolores had awaited the negotiations that were to shape her destiny. An earnest of the future came to her in the present of jewels, with which Leon presaged the marriage gifts which he went to the city of Mexico to choose,—for whether rich or poor, no Mexican bridegroom would fail of a necklet of pearls, or a brooch and earrings of brilliants for his bride ; and with his luxurious tastes, it was not to be supposed that Leon Vallé could fail to add to these laces and silks and velvets, fit rather for a princess than for the future wife of a country youth whose only capital was in house and land. Isabel had just heard of these things, and had begun to excuse in her heart these extravagances, which seemed so natural to a youth in love, when a remembrance flashed upon her mind which justified the apprehensions she had felt, and which it seemed incredible should have escaped not only her own but also Don Gregorio's vigilance, — Leon had gone to Mexico in the days of the feast of San Augustin.

Isabel was too jealous of her brother's good name, too eager to shield him from a breath of distrust, to mention the fears that assailed her. She called herself irrational, faithless, unjust, yet she could not rid herself of the dread which seemed to brood above her like a cloud. And so passed the month of June, and July brought Leon Vallé back again, and one glance at his haggard face and bloodshot eyes revealed to Isabel that her fears were realized. He told the tale in a few words and with a hollow laugh.

"You will have to go to Garcia for me now, Isabel," he said. "Your last venture has brought me the old luck, cursed bad luck. A plague upon your money ! I thought to double or treble it, and the last cent is gone !"

"And the hacienda of San Lazaro?" queried Isabel, faintly.

"Would you believe it? Gone too ! Aranda has had the devil's own luck. 'T was the last of the feast, Isabel. Thousands were changing hands at every table. It seemed a cowardice not to try a stake for a fortune that might be had for the asking. I was a fool, and hesitated till it was too late. Had I only ventured at once ! What think you happened to Leoncio Alvarez? He played his hacienda against Esparto's, and lost. He had dared me not five minutes before to the venture. The devil, what a chance I missed! His hacienda was three times the size of San Lazaro! He bore its loss like a man. 'What can one do, friend?' he cried to Esparto; 'it has been thy luck to-day, 't will be mine when we next meet.' Just then his brother Antonio came up. 'What luck, Leoncio?' he said. 'Cursed!' he answered. 'I have played my hacienda against Esparto's here, and lost it.' Antonio shrugged his shoulders and turned away. 'Play mine and get it back,' he suggested, and walked off to the next table. The cards were dealt, and in three minutes Leoncio's hacienda was his own again, thrown like a ball from one hand to the other. It was glorious play!'"

"But this has nothing to do with thee," ventured Isabel.

"No," muttered Leon, moodily; "when *I* ventured my hacienda and lost, there was no Antonio to bid me play his and get it back."

He looked at Isabel with an air of reproach. She had neither look nor word of reproach for him, yet she felt that a mortal blow had been dealt her. And Leon? He had laughed, though she knew that the laugh was that of the mocking fiend Despair which possessed him; and he had bade her go on his behalf to Garcia. She left him in desperation. She knew how utterly fruitless such an appeal would be.

It *was* fruitless. Don Gregorio asked with some scorn in his voice whether Leon thought him as weak as she had been, or as much of a madman as himself when he had dared the chances of the tables at San Augustin. For him, Garcia, to furnish money to the oft-tried scapegrace would be a folly that would merit the inevitable loss it would bring. All of which, though true enough, Don Gregorio repeated with unnecessary vehemence to Leon himself, with the tone of irrepressible satisfaction with which he at last saw humiliated the man who had for so long held such a resistless fascination over his wife.

With wonderful self-restraint Leon replied not a word to the cutting irony with which his brother-in-law referred to the mad ambition and folly which had led to his losses,

and with which Gregorio excused himself from further
assisting in the ruin of the Garcia family, — reminding
the gamester that though he had thrown away the key to
fortune which he had taken from his sister's hand, he had
still youth, a sword, and a subtle mind, any one of which
should be able to provide him a living.

"That is true," replied Leon, with a dangerous light in
his half-closed eyes. "Thanks for the reminder, my
brother. What is the old saying? 'A hungry man dis-
covers more than a thousand wise men.'"

They both laughed. It was not likely that Leon's poverty would ever reach the point of actual want. There
at the hacienda was his home when he cared for it; but
as for money, — why as Don Gregorio had said, the key
to fortune was thrown away, and it seemed unlikely the
unfortunate loser would ever recover it.

Almost on the same day on which Leon Vallé had told
his sister of his fatal hardihood at the feast of San
Augustin, there arrived, with assurances of the profound
respect of Señor Fernandez and his daughter, the jewels
and other rich gifts which Dolores had accepted as the
betrothed of Leon. With deep indignation that his
explanations and protestations had been rejected, but
with a pride which prevented the frantic remonstrances
which rushed to his lips from passing beyond them, Leon
received these proofs of his dismissal, which in a few days
was rendered final by the news that the beautiful Dolores
had married a wealthier and perhaps even more ardent
suitor, whom the insolence and mockery of Fate had provided in the person of the lucky winner of San Lazaro.
Even Don Gregorio felt his heart burn with the natural
chagrin of family pride, and Isabel would have turned
with some sympathy toward the brother of whom, unconsciously to herself, she could no longer make a hero.
Strangely enough, his aspect as a suppliant for her husband's bounty had disrobed him of the glamour through
which she had always beheld him. When she herself was
powerless to minister to him, he was no longer a prince
claiming tribute, but the undignified dependent whom she
blushed to see lounging in sullen idleness in her husband's
house. Yet as has been said, when word of the marriage
of Dolores Fernandez reached them, they would have

given him sympathy; but he had received the news first, and collecting a half-dozen followers had mounted and ridden madly away.

The horses they rode were Don Gregorio's yet Leon had gone without a word of excuse or farewell. Isabel had no opportunity to tell him that she had no more money to give him; and in her distress at supposing him penniless it was an immense relief to her to find that he had retained in his possession the jewels that the father of Dolores had returned to him. He would at least not be without resource. But soon a strange tale reached her. The jewels torn from their settings, the stones in fragments, the whole crushed into an utterly worthless mass, so far as human strength and ingenuity could accomplish it, had been found upon the pillow of the bride. The husband was jealously frantic that her sanctuary had been invaded; the bride was hysterically alarmed, yet flattered at this proof of her lover's passion; and the entire community were for days on the *qui vive* for further developments in this drama of love.

But none came, and soon Leon Vallé's name was heard of as one of the guerillas of the Texan war, where he fought for — it was not to be said under — Santa Anna; and ere many months his name rang from one end of the republic to the other, — the synonym of gallant daring, which in a less exciting time might have been called ferocious bloodthirstiness.

Isabel quailed as she heard the wild tales told of him; but Don Gregorio shrugged his shoulders and said, "Thank Heaven he turned soldier rather than brigand!" The chief difference between the two in those days was in name; but that meant much in sentiment.

XXI.

Leon Vallé had not parted from his sister in declared hostility, yet months passed before she heard directly from him. But this was not to be wondered at, as letters were necessarily sent by private carriers, and it was not to be expected that in the adventurous excitement of his life he should pause to send a mere salutation over leagues of desolate country.

Meanwhile the prevailing anarchy of the time crept closer and closer to the hacienda limits. Bandits gathered in the mountains and ravaged the outlying villages, driving off flocks of sheep or herds of cattle, lassoing the finest horses, and mocking the futile efforts of the country people to guard their property. The name of one Juan Planillos became a terror in every household; yet one by one the younger men stole away to strengthen the number of his followers and share the wild excitement of the bandit life, rather than to wait patiently at home to be drafted into the ranks of some political chieftain whose career raised little enthusiasm, and whose political creed was as obscure as his origin. "The memory is confused," says an historian, "by the plans and *pronunciamientos* of that time. Men changed ideas at each step, and defended to-day what they had attacked yesterday. Parties triumphed and fell at every turn." The form of government was as change- able as a kaleidoscope, and only the brigand and guerilla seemed immutable. Whatever the politics of the day, their motto was plunder and rapine; and their deeds, so brilliant, so unforeseeable, offered an irresistible attraction to the restless spirits of that revolutionary epoch.

Though Doña Isabel Garcia, like all others, was imbued with the military ardor of the time, the brilliant reputation that her brother was winning in distant fields, though in harmony with her own political opinions, horrified rather than dazzled her. She shuddered as she heard his name

11

mentioned in the same breath with that of the remorseless
Valdez, or the crafty and bloody Planillos; yet she was
glad to believe his incentive was patriotism rather than
plunder, and when at last a messenger from him reached
her with the same old cry for "Money! money! money!"
she responded with a heaping handful of gold,—all she
had been able to accumulate in the few months of his absence. Don Gregorio however, vexed by recent losses
and harassed by constant raids from the mountain brigands, sent a refusal that was worded almost like a curse;
and ashamed of her brother, annoyed by and yet sympathizing with her husband, Doña Isabel felt her heart sink like
lead in her bosom, and for the first time her superb health
showed signs of yielding to the severe mental strain to
which she had been so long subjected.

June had come again; the rainy season would soon begin, and Don Gregorio, suddenly thinking that the change
would benefit his wife, suggested that they should pass
some months in the city. The roads were threatened by
highwaymen, yet Isabel was glad to go, and even to incur
the novelty of danger. Her travelling carriage was luxurious, and with her little girls immediately under her own
eye, with an occasional glimpse of the four-year-old Norberto riding proudly at his father's side in the midst of the
numerous escort of picked men, she felt an exhilaration both
of body and mind to which she had long been a stranger.

The travelling was necessarily slow, for the roads were
excessively rough, and the party had at sunset of the first
day scarcely left the limits of the hacienda and entered
the defile which led to the deeper cañons of the mountains,
wherein upon the morrow they anticipated the necessity of
exercising a double vigilance. Not a creature had been
seen for hours; the mountains with their straggling clumps
of cacti and blackened, stunted palms seemed absolutely
bereft of animal life, except when occasionally a lizard
glided swiftly over a rock, or a snake rustled through the
dry and crackling herbage. Caution seemed absurd in
such a place where there was scarce a cleft for concealment, yet the party drew nearer together, and the men
looked to their arms as the cliffs became closer on either
side and so precipitous that it seemed as though a goat
could scarcely have scaled them.

They had passed nearly the entire length of this cañon, and the nervous tension that had held the whole party silent and upon the alert was gradually yielding to the glimpse of more open country which lay beyond, and on which they had planned to camp for the night, when suddenly the whole country seemed alive with men. They blocked the way, backward and forward; they hung from the cliffs; they bounded from rock to rock, on foot and on horse, the horses as agile as the men. Amid the tumult one man seemed ubiquitous. All eyes followed him, yet not one caught sight of his face; the striped jorongo thrown over shoulders and face formed an impenetrable disguise, such as the noted guerilla chief of the mountains was wont to wear. Suddenly there was a cry of " Planillos! Planillos! " amid the confusion of angry voices, of curses, and the clanking of sabres and echo of pistol-shots. Don Gregorio found himself driven against the rocks, a sword-point at his throat, a pistol pressed to his temple, his own smoking weapon in his hand.

Immediately the shouts ceased, and before the smoke which had filled the gorge had cleared, the travellers found themselves alone, with two or three dead men obstructing the road. Don Gregorio had barely time to notice them, or the blank faces of his men staring bewildered at one another, when a cry from Doña Isabel recalled him to his senses, and he saw her rushing wildly from group to group. In an instant he was at her side. " Norberto! where is Norberto? " both demanded wildly, and some of the men who had caught the name began to force their horses up the almost inaccessible cliffs, and to gallop up or down the cañon in a confused pursuit of the vanished enemy.

Don Gregorio alone retained his presence of mind; though night was closing in and the horses were wearied by a day's travel, not a moment was lost in dispatching couriers to the city for armed police and to the hacienda for fresh men and horses, and the return to Tres Hermanos was immediately begun. Sometime during the morning hours they were met by a party from the hacienda, and putting himself at the head of his retainers Don Gregorio led them in search of his son, while Doña Isabel in a state bordering upon distraction proceeded to her desolated home.

Her first act was to send a courier to her brother. No one knew the mountains as he did, and in her terrible plight she was certain he would not fail her. But her haste was needless, for information reached him from some other source, and within a few days he was at the head of a party of valiant Garcias, who had hastened from far and near to the rescue of their young kinsman.

In all the country round the abduction of Norberto Garcia was called "the abduction by enchanters," — so sudden had been the attack, so complete the disappearance of the victim. Beyond the immediate scene no trace remained of the act, — it seemed that the very earth must have opened to swallow the perpetrators; and yet day by day proofs of their existence were found in letters left upon the very saddle crossed by the father, or upon the pillow wet with the tears of the mother, demanding ransom which each day became more exorbitant, accompanied by threats more and more ingenious and horrible.

Such seizures, though rare, were by no means unprecedented, and such threats had been proved to be only too likely to be fulfilled. As days went by the agony of the parents became unbearable, and Don Gregorio's early resolution to spend a fortune in the pursuit and punishment of the robbers rather than comply with their demands, and thus lend encouragement to similar outrages, began to yield before the imminent danger to the life of his son; and to Doña Isabel it seemed a cruel mockery that her brother and the young Garcias should urge him to further exertion and postponement of the inevitable moment when he must accede to the imperious demands of the outlaws.

The family were one evening discussing again the momentous and constantly agitated question, when Doña Feliz appeared among them with starting eyes and pallid cheeks, bidding Don Gregorio go to his wife, from whose nerveless hand she had wrested a paper, which Leon seized and opened as the excited woman held it toward him. Don Gregorio turned back at his brother-in-law's exclamation, and beheld upon his outstretched hand a lock of soft brown hair, evidently that of a child. It had been severed from the head by a bloody knife. It was a mute threat, yet they understood it but too well. Every man there sprang to his feet with a groan or an oath. Such a threat they remembered had been sent to the parents the very day before the infant Ranulfo Ortega had been found dead not a hundred yards from his father's door. Did this mean also that the last demand for ransom had been made, and the patience of Norberto's abductors was exhausted?

Don Gregorio clasped his hands over his eyes, and reeled against the wall. Leon sprang to his feet, pale to his lips, his eyes blazing. Julian Garcia picked up the hair which had fallen from Leon's hand; the others stood grouped in horrified expectancy. Doña Feliz stood for a moment looking at them with lofty courage and determination upon her face.

" What," she cried, " is this a time for hesitation? The money must be paid, the child's life saved. Vengeance can wait! " She spoke with a fire that thrilled them, and though they spoke but of the ransom, it was the word " vengeance " that rang in their ears, and steeled Don Gregorio to the terrible task that awaited him.

That night the quaint hiding-places of the vast hacienda were ransacked, and many a hoard of coin was extracted from the deep corners of the walls, and the depths of half-ruinous wells. Doña Isabel saw treasures of whose existence she had never heard before, but had perhaps vaguely suspected; for through the long years of anarchy the Garcias had become expert in secreting such surplus wealth as they desired to keep within reach. Large as was the sum brought to light, it barely sufficed to meet the demands of the robbers; yet it was a question how such a weight of coin was to be conveyed by one person to the spot indicated for the payment of the ransom and delivery of the child, — for it had been urgently insisted upon that but one man should go into the very stronghold of the bandits.

At daybreak, having refused the offer of Leon Vallé to go in his stead, Don Gregorio mounted his horse and set out on his mission. He knew well the place appointed, for he had been in his youth an adventurous mountaineer, and more than once had penetrated the deep gorge into which, late in the afternoon, he descended, bearing with him the gold and silver. As he entered the " Zahuan del Infierno " he shuddered. Not ten days before he had passed

through it, followed by a dozen trusty followers, in search
of his child, and had discovered no trace of him; now
he was alone, weighted with treasure, sufficient sensibly
to retard his movements and render him a rich prize for
the outlaws he had gone to meet.   Once he fancied he
heard a step behind him; doubtless he was shadowed by
those who would take his life without a moment's hesitation.
Yet he pressed on, obliged to leave his horse and proceed
on foot, for at times the cliffs were so close together that
a man could barely force his way between them.

Just as the last rays of daylight pierced the gloomy
abyss, at a sudden turn in the narrowest part of the gorge
Don Gregorio saw standing two armed men, placed in such
a position that the head of one overtopped that of the
other, while the features of both were shadowed though
made the more forbidding by heavy black beards, which it
occurred to him later were probably false and worn for
the purpose of disguise.   At the feet of the foremost was
placed a child; and though he restrained the cry that rose
to his lips, the tortured father recognized in him his
son, — but so emaciated, so deathly pale, with such
wild, startled eyes, gazing like a hunted creature before
him, yet seeing nothing, that he could scarcely credit
it was the same beautiful, sensitive, highly-strung Norberto who had been wrested from him but a short month
before.

At the sight the father felt an almost irresistible impulse
to precipitate himself upon those fiends who thus dared to
mock him; but even had his hands been free to grasp the
pistol in his belt, to have done so would have been to
bring upon himself certain death.   As it was he could but
look with blind rage from the bags of coin he carried to
the brigands who stood like statues, the right hand of the
foremost laid upon the throat of the trembling boy.   Even
in that desperate moment Don Gregorio noticed that the
hand was whiter and more slender than the hands of common men are wont to be; the nails were well formed and
well kept, though there was a bruise or mark on the second
one, as though it had met some recent injury.   He was not
conscious at the time that he noticed this, but it came to
him afterward.   The foremost man did not speak; it was
the other who in a soft voice, as evenly modulated as though

to words of purest courtesy, bade the Señor Garcia welcome, and thanked him for his prompt appearance.

"Let us dispense with compliments," said Don Gregorio, huskily. "Here is the money you have demanded for my child. I know something of the honor of bandits, and as you can gain nothing by falsifying your word, I have chosen to trust in it. Here am I, alone with the gold," and he poured it out on the rock at the child's feet, — "count it if you will;" and he put out his hand and laid it upon the child's shoulder. As he did so his hand touched the brigand's, and both started, glaring like two tigers before they spring; but at that moment Norberto bounded over the scattered heap of coin and into his father's arms.

As he felt that slight form within his grasp the father reeled, and his sight failed him; a voice presently recalled him to his senses, and glancing up he saw the two men still standing motionless, with their pistols levelled upon him and the child.

"The Señor will find it best to withdraw backward," said the bandit; "there is not space here for me to have the honor of passing and leading the way, and it is even too narrow for your grace to turn. You will find your horse at the entrance to the gorge; it has been well cared for. Adios, Señor, and may every felicity attend this fortunate termination of our negotiations."

"I doubt not there will," cried Don Gregorio, though in a voice of perfect politeness, "for I swear to you I will unearth the villains who have tortured and robbed me, and give myself a moment of exquisite joy with every drop of life-blood I slowly wring from them. You have my gold, and I have my child, and now — Vengeance!"

Gregorio Garcia knew so well the peculiar ideas of honor among bandits as well as the spirit of his countrymen that perhaps he was assured that no immediate risk would follow this proclamation. The word "vengeance" rang from cliff to cliff, yet the bandits only smiled mockingly and bowed, waving a hand in token of farewell, as with what haste he might he withdrew. A turn in the gorge soon hid them from his sight, and staggering through the darkness, he hastened on with his precious burden, feeling that Norberto had fainted in his arms.

It was near midnight when Don Gregorio reached the hacienda, and needless is it to attempt to describe the joy of the mother at sight of her child, though Norberto, after one faint cry of recognition, laid his head upon her breast with a long shuddering sigh, which warned her that his strength and courage had been so overtaxed that they were, perhaps, destroyed forever.

As days passed, it seemed evident that the mind of the boy was suffering from the shock. The male relatives who during the absence of Don Gregorio had mostly dispersed to find, manlike, some distraction a-field, returned one by one to embrace him ; but he turned from each with unreasoning fear and aversion, unable to distinguish between them and the strangers in whose hands he had been held a prisoner. At some of them he gazed as if fascinated, especially at his Uncle Leon ; and when by any chance the latter touched him he would burst into agonizing wails, which ceased only when his father held him closely in his arms, whispering words of affection and encouragement.

Before many days it became evident that Norberto was dying. There was a constant, low, shuddering cry upon his lips, "He will kill me ! — he will kill me if I tell !" and the horrified father and mother became convinced that Norberto knew at least one of his captors, and that deadly fear alone prevented him from uttering the name. They entreated him in vain ; and one night the end of the tortured life drew near, and Norberto's wailing cry was still.

The family was alone, except for the presence of Leon Vallé and a young cousin, Doctor Genaro Calderon, one of the numerous family connections ; and those, with the Padre Francisco and Doña Feliz, were gathered around the bed of the dying child. The father in an agony of grief and vengeful despair stood at the head, and Doña Isabel, ghostlike and haggard from her long suspense and watching, was on her knees at the side, her eyes fixed upon the face of the child, when suddenly he opened his eyes in a wild stare upon Leon Vallé, who stood near the foot of the bed, and faintly, slowly articulated the same agonizing cry, "He will kill me if I tell !"

At that moment, as if by an irresistible impulse, Leon stretched out his hand and placed a finger on the lips of the dying boy. The eyes of Don Gregorio followed it; and then like a thunderbolt hurled through space he threw himself upon his brother-in-law, grappling his throat with a deathlike grasp. He had recognized the bruise upon the second finger of the white hand, — he had recognized the very hand. Recalled to life by the excitement of the moment, Norberto started up and exclaimed in a loud shrill voice, "Take him away! He cut my hair with his bloody knife! Oh, Uncle Leon, will you kill me?" and fell back in the death agony, — the agony that only the priest witnessed, for even Isabel turned to the mortal combat waged between her husband and her brother.

Don Gregorio was unarmed, but Leon had managed to draw a knife from his belt. The murderous dagger was poised for a blow, when a woman rushed between the combatants; Don Gregorio was flung bleeding upon the bed, Doña Feliz hurled into a corner of the apartment the dagger which she had grasped with her naked hand, and Leon Vallé rushed like a madman from the room. Before he could escape, however, he was seized, pinioned, and thrust like a wild beast into one of the solid stone rooms of the building. Don Gregorio was held by main force from accomplishing his purpose of taking the life of the unnatural bandit ere the bolts were shot upon him. He however gave immediate orders that messengers be despatched in quest of police; but by some misapprehension or intentional delay on the part of the administrador these messengers were detained till dawn, and just as they were about to set forth, a cry went through the house that the prisoner had escaped.

Gregorio Garcia rushed to the room, glanced in with wild, bloodshot eyes, and then with unrestrainable fury, sought out his wife, and grasping her arm cried in a voice as full of horror as of rage, "Traitress! You have set free the murderer of your child!"

She threw herself on her knees at his feet, — he never knew with what purpose, whether to confess her weakness or declare her innocence, — for Doña Feliz cast herself between them.

"It was I who set him free!" she exclaimed. "I love the Garcias too well to suffer them to be made a mockery of by the false mercy of such laws as ours. Think you the idol of the bandits would be sacrificed for such a trifle as a child's life? And you, Gregorio Garcia, would you, this fury passed, avenge your injuries in the blood of your wife's brother, robber and murderer though he be? Leon has sworn to me to hide himself forever from the family he has disgraced, under another name in another land. He has the brand of Cain upon his brow, — God will surely bring his doom upon him!"

Doña Feliz spoke like a prophetess. The superb assurance upon which she had acted, setting aside all rights of man and relegating vengeance to the Lord, did more to reconcile Don Gregorio to the escape of his enemy than all further reflection, decisive though it was in convincing him that in the disordered and anarchical state of the country, the laws would have shielded rather than punished an offender so popular as was Leon Vallé. There was perhaps, too, a comfort in the hidden hope of personal vengeance with which he waited long months to learn the retreat of the man who had done him such foul wrong.

Meanwhile the exact facts of the case were never known abroad; and when at last it was rumored that Leon Vallé had been shot by a rival guerilla chief and hung to a tree placarded as a traitor and robber, there were few to doubt the story, or to make more than a passing comment on the hard necessities of war. There seemed so much poetic justice in it, that Gregorio Garcia, who was near the end of the disease contracted through exposure and mental agony, did not for a moment doubt it, and died almost content. Indeed, the circumstances were so minutely detailed by a servant who had followed Leon in his adventurous career and who dared to face the family in order to prove the death, that even Doña Isabel herself did not question it until long months afterward, when a petty scandal stole through the land. The lady of San Lazaro had disappeared, — whether of her own free will, whether in madness she had strayed, or whether she had been kidnapped, none could conjecture. No demand for ransom came, no tidings were ever heard of the peerlessly beautiful Dolores.

It was after that time that Doña Isabel began to demand tidings of all who came to her door, and a suspicion en-

tered her mind which became a certainty upon the night
our story opened, but which no subsequent event had
tended to confirm during the years that had passed since
then.

This brief relation may serve to explain the strange
emotions and experiences that made Doña Isabel what
her full womanhood found her, and which with other
events of her later life rendered possible and natural
the bitter suspense and fear that held her the long night
through, a watcher at the door of one who, as others had
done, might find a means to pierce her heart and wound
her pride, if not to awaken her deep and passionate
affections.

XXII.

CHINITA woke with a confused sensation of haste, and in the dim light discovered with a momentary surprise that she was in one of the chambers of the great house. Her first clear remembrance was that there was to be a wedding in the village that day, and that she must hasten to help array the bride, her old playmate Juana, — a girl scarce older than herself, but who as the daughter of the silversmith held some pretentions to superior gentility among the village folk. She wondered that she was not in the hut with Florencia and the children, and raised herself upon one arm to peer through the gloom at the figure upon the bed; then suddenly sprang to her feet with an exclamation. The sight of the wounded man brought to memory the train of events connected with his appearance there. The young man was asleep, but even if he had been awake and in dire need of aid, Chinita would not have paused an instant; for it flashed into her mind that she must see and speak to Tio Reyes before he left. He had told her so little — nothing that she could separate as a tangible fact. She must know more. Surely it was early still, — she never slept after daybreak; he would not yet be gone. Yet in quick apprehension, which burst forth in an irate interjection at her tardy awakening, she ran out into the court.

The morning light was beaming there unmistakably, though no ray of sunlight penetrated it; and not a creature was stirring, and still hopeful the young girl hurried to the outer court. The mingled sounds of the movements of men and horses greeted her ear. Although she was late, Tio Reyes perhaps was still there. Vain hope! One glance around the great court showed her that he whom she sought was gone.

With an angry little cry, which made more than one muleteer turn to look at her with, "What has happened to

thee?" on his lips, Chinita sped across the court, and caught
the arm of Pedro, who was standing dejectedly outside the
great gate. He crossed himself as she appeared, and his
face lighted up, then clouded again as she cried, "Where
are the soldiers? When did they go? Why did no one
awaken me?"

The man pointed with a disdainful gesture across the
plain. Florencia was standing at the door of her hut,
calling in a rage to a neighbor that those worthless vaga-
bonds had robbed her of her last handful of toasted corn;
and Pedro began to explain to Chinita in his slow way that
the good friends of the night before had naturally enough
demanded something from the housewives upon which to
breakfast, and that instead of giving it to them quietly,
and thanking the Virgin that after drinking the soup they
had not taken the pot, the foolish women must needs scold
and bewail, as though soldiers should be saints and live on
air, and as if this was the first raid that ever had been heard
of, instead of a mere frolic, very different from that of the
month before, when the forces of the clergy had carried off
a thousand bushels of maize, without as much as a "God
repay you."

Chinita gazed eagerly toward the east, and presently
burst into passionate tears. The sun, which a moment
before had shown a tiny red disk above the hills, flooded
the plain with light, and dazzled her vision. Through it
she saw some rapidly moving figures. The man she
sought was already miles away. Silently but bitterly she
reproached herself. She had slept like an insensate lump,
and suffered to escape her the man who could have told
her so much, whom she would have *forced* to speak.
She could, as her eyes became accustomed to the light,
distinguish his very figure in the clear atmosphere; and
yet he and all she would have learned were so far away.

"What wouldst thou?" demanded Pedro, gruffly; "the
soldiers have carried off nothing of thine! Heaven fore-
fend! Go to the hut and drink the atolé if there is any left,
and give God the thanks!"

The broad daylight had cleared the mind of Pedro of
all the sentimental fears of the night. The glamour had
passed away; there stood Chinita with the old familiar
ragged clothing upon her, to be talked with, caressed it

might be, certainly scolded with the mock severity of old. Yes, it was the same fiery, uncertain, irascible Chinita, who, clearing her eyes of their unusual tears with a backward sweep of her small brown hand, ran down the hill, — not to the hut where Florencia stood with the water-jar, beckoning her, but in quite another direction, to join the little crowd of sympathizing friends who were gathered at the door of the silversmith.

Pepé was standing there with a gayly caparisoned donkey, destined to bear the *novia* to the village some eight miles distant, where the lazy priest who divided his time between the sinners of that point and Tres Hermanos, had consented to earn a royal fee by uniting two poor peasants in holy matrimony. "It is but for once," Gabriel had hopefully remarked; "and though one runs in debt for the wedding, one can hold one's head above one's neighbors, to say nothing of dying in peace, if a bull's horn finds its way some unlucky day between one's ribs."

Gabriel was a man who honored the proprieties, and Juana was well pleased with the good fortune that had awarded her to him; though he was twice her age, and had a squint which made ludicrous his most amorous glances.

"What has happened?" cried Pepé in a disappointed tone, as Chinita darted past him. "Didst thou not say thou wouldst ride with Juana? She has been waiting for thee this half hour. The *novio* will be on his way before her if we tarry longer, and thou knowest what that portends. The impatient lover becomes the husband never appeased! the wife shall wait many a day for him."

"Bah!" returned Chinita, "if Juana were of my mind the *novio* would wait so long that her turn to play at *paciencia* would never arrive."

"Go to!" cried a woman who stood near, "who would have imagined thou wouldst be so envious, Chinita; and thou but a child yet? But thou art one that hast been brought up between cotton, and expectest the soft places all thy life."

"Pshaw!" answered Chinita. "Speak of what thou knowest, Señora Gomesinda; and thou, Pepé, cease making eyes at me. Thinkest thou I have nothing better to do than to ride after Juana to see her married to yon black giant of a vaquero, who will manage his wife as he does his horses, — with a thong? I tell thee as I tell her, he is not worth the beating she got when he asked for her!"

"Ay, Señora," cried Gomesinda, shrilly, "was ever such talk from the mouth of a modest girl? What could a reasonable father and mother do for a girl when a man asks her in marriage? It is plain she must have played some tricks of our Señora Madre Eva to have beguiled him. Ay, but I remember my mother flailed me black and blue when José asked for me. I warrant you I screamed so hard the whole neighborhood knew she was doing the honorable part by me. Thank Heaven, I knew what was proper as well as another, and if I had given the man a glance from the corner of my eyes, I was willing my shoulders should suffer for it. One may tell of it when one is the mother of ten children."

During this harangue, Chinita had slipped by her, and darted into the hut. She threw her arms around the expectant bride, who dressed in the stiffest of starched skirts, the upper one of which was of flowered pink muslin, stood waiting the finishing touches of her sponsor.

"What, thou art not ready?" cried Juana in a dejected tone, surveying Chinita with disapproving eyes. "Gabriel has twice sent messages that the sun has risen, and that the Señor Priest likes not to be kept long fasting, and thou knowest, as the priest sings the sacristan answers."

"Ay," said Chinita, laughing, "a lesson in patience will be good for both the priest and thy Gabriel; but it will bode thee ill if he learns it at the tavern, as I saw him doing just now. Truly, Juana, thou must go without me. I am in no humor to go so far on thy ambling donkey;" and she drew herself up with an air of hauteur, which did not escape the observant eye of the bride, who said, with a reproachful look, —

"What have I done? Did I ever give thee a sharp word, Chinita?"

For answer, Chinita threw her arms around the girl's neck; for she was really fond of Juana, who had ever been a gentle girl, and had borne her perverse humors with a sort of admiring patience which had flattered and won the heart of the wayward one. Completely mollified, Juana pressed her cheek against Chinita's shoulder, for she had turned her face away, and said, "But thou wilt put on thy finest clothes and sit beside me at the fandango, wilt thou not? And thou wilt help my sponsor to dress me. See! Dost thou think she has done well this time?" and the girl threw her scarf from her head and shoulders, and exhibited her long, well-oiled tresses with an air of conscious vanity.

" Nothing could be better," declared Chinita, heartily, pulling out a loop of the bright red ribbons. " Yes, yes," she added with some effort, " I will stay beside thee all through the feast. Thou hast ever been a good friend of mine, Juana. There, there, they are calling thee ;" and she pushed her toward the door, where by this time a noisy crowd had gathered.

Instead of only one donkey, there were five or six standing there, with' gay bridles and necklaces of horsehair, brightened with cords of red or blue, and with panniers covered with well-trimmed sheepskins. As the Señora Madrina said, " She who should ride upon them would think herself on cushions of down." On the most luxurious of these rural thrones Juana was raised, and upon the others her mother and a number of her female friends, mostly in pairs, were accommodated ; and with many injunctions from the bystanders to hasten, the bridal party were at last dismissed upon their way.

Laughing and chattering, the women dispersed to their huts to grind a fresh stint of maize to replace the tortillas and atolé that had been carried away by the soldiers ; but Chinita sat down at the door of the adobe hut thus temporarily deserted, and with a smile of derision upon her lips watched the group of men congregated around the village shop. The bridegroom, a middle-aged man, with a dark face deeply imbrowned by the sun and seamed with scars (for he had been a soldier before he was a vaquero), stood in the midst of them, dressed in a suit of buff leather, gay with embroidery. The embossed leather sheath of his knife showed in his scarlet waist-scarf, and immense spurs clanked on his heels in response to the buttons and chains on the half-opened sides of his riding trousers of goat-skin. He was a picturesque figure — though Chinita's accustomed eyes failed to recognize that — as he stood with his wide, silver-laced hat pushed back upon the mat of black hair that crowned his swarthy countenance, holding high the small glass of mezcal which he was about to drink in favor of the toast some comrade had proposed. Meanwhile, his companions were noisily hilarious, rallying him with impossible prophecies of good fortune, to which he listened with an air of imperturbability which was part of the etiquette of the occasion, — for in all the world can be found no greater slave to his peculiar code of manners than the Mexican ranchero.

The party on donkey-back had almost disappeared upon the horizon before it seemed to occur to the group at the tavern store that any movement was expected from them. More than once the women had stopped in their household tasks to call out a shrill "Go on! go on! By the saints, man, will you keep the priest waiting?" and still Gabriel affected the indifferent, until as if by accident he strolled toward his horse, which stood champing the bit impatiently. Immediately there was a rush of his best friends, and the triumphant one who caught the stirrup and held it as the bridegroom mounted claimed the luck-gift for the good news of the departure, — which was effected at once after a series of pirouettes and caracolling, by Gabriel's putting spurs to his steed and galloping madly away, followed by his friends as quickly as they could throw themselves into their saddles.

The spell of the day before continued still so to rest upon her that Chinita neither joined in the cheer nor the laughter of the women, but turned slowly toward Pedro's hut. The cravings of a healthy appetite subdued for the moment the pride that scorned the lowly home. It was natural to go there for the corn-cake and the draught of atolé or chocolate with which to break her fast. She found the share left for her; but after a mouthful or two it seemed to grow bitter to her taste. She divided it petulantly among the children who clamored around her, and in response to a call from Florencia went to Selsa's hut where they were making tortillas for the wedding feast, arrogantly refusing to help, yet glad of accustomed companionship. Much as she resented old associations, the wrench was too great for her to separate herself from them at once, especially as she had no conception of what could or should take their place. She was like a child upon the banks of a river that separates it from the farther shore

which it longs to reach, though dreading to push forth
from the land it knows, rough and forlorn though it may
be.   There was with Chinita a strange sense of clinging
to a past which was irrevocably severed from her, of impatience of a problem of the future to be solved, and of lack
of will to set herself to its solution, as she went from hut to
hut.   The fever of her mind expended itself first in seething irony and jests, and later in a wild repentance, which
manifested itself in quick embraces of the half offended
women, and in practical toil, which effectually promoted
the preparations for the feast, and went far to restore her
to the good graces of the harassed workers.   Indeed,
often enough they paused in their labors to listen and
laugh, as she stood at the brasiers fanning the glowing
charcoal, or watching the tortillas taken from the flat
comal and piled in heaps upon the fringed and embroidered napkins used on such occasions of ceremony ; or
went from dish to dish of black beans, or red and fiery
chile rich with pork or fowl ; or gazed with positive admiration upon the kids and lambs, stuffed with almonds
and raisins, forcemeat and olives, and other delicacies,
which drawn smoking from the earthen ovens attested
the generosity of the administrador toward his favorite
vaquero.

Toward noon the bride and her party returned, ambling home upon their donkeys, as humbly as they had
gone.   Juana was conducted to her future home, and her
mother-in-law, welcoming her with distant ceremony, intended to inspire respect, suffered her to touch her cheek
with her lips, then led her to the inner room, where lay
the apparel for her adornment, — a number of toilets being
indispensable upon the occasion, and indicative of the pretensions of the bridegroom who had hired them.

Chinita, in her mingled mood of disdain and levity, had
neglected to keep her promise of putting on holiday attire,
and stood in some awe and much admiration before the
bride as she at last appeared in the little bower or tent
that had been raised for her at one side of the hut, facing
upon the plaza where the feast was to be held.   The little
woman — for she was not fully grown — was resplendent
in a stiff-flowered brocade of many colors, trimmed with
real Spanish lace and bedecked with flowers, and wore a

necklace and bracelets of imitation gems set in filagree, fit, as her sponsor proudly declared, for the Blessed Virgin upon the high altar.

Juana threw a glance of reproach upon Chinita; but her new dignity forbade recrimination. A shout presently announced that the bridegroom was in sight. The bride, well-drilled in her part, kept her glance fixed on the ground; and as he swept by her bower Gabriel deigned not a look, but reined in his horse at his own door with a sudden turn of the hand which almost threw the animal on its haunches, and before his stirrup could be seized had thrown himself from his saddle and was shaking hands with his friends, and immediately the feast began.

There was no table set. The fires burned at the corners of the plaza, and the women stood over them, dispensing the fragrant contents of the jars to all comers. Yet in this apparent informality the strictest decorum was observed, and not a mouthful was swallowed or a drink of *pulque* or milky *chia*, without a friendly interchange of courtesies, which rather increased than grew less as the hours flew by.

The proverb is true that at a wedding the bride eats least; and at that of the Mexican peasant the saying becomes a law. Juana was too well drilled in the proprieties to touch a morsel of the delicacies offered her, but wore constantly the air of timid resignation with which she had met the assumed indifference of her spouse, who resolutely avoided casting even a glance in the direction where she held her court, — the women crowding with ever increasing admiration to view her after each change of toilet, as they might have done to examine a gorgeous picture, commenting loudly upon the taste of the dresser and the liberality of the groom. But nothing could be more satisfactory to her than this feigned indifference of her husband. "Is not Gabriel an angel?" she took occasion to ask Chinita, as for the tenth time she was changing her apparel. "Imagine to yourself twelve changes of clothing, and he acts as if the hiring of them were nothing! What a difference between him and Pancho Orteago, who was married at Easter! Four beggarly suits were all he provided for Anita, and not one silk among them; and he actually was quite close to her again and again, with mouth open, as if he would eat her!

Such an idiot! He would have spoken to her if he had
had the chance. I should think she was half dead with
mortification! Such foolishness in public! Her mother
cried with vexation; and no wonder, with such a slur cast
on the family!"

"Yet it has been like a marriage of turtle-doves!" cried
Chinita. "Let us see, little woman, if thou wilt say that
of thy own six months hence!"

Juana shrugged her shoulders and returned to her seat,
with her eyes more coyly cast down, and a dejected mien,
which might not have been altogether assumed; for, too
earnest in acting her part even to take food in private, she
was not unnaturally almost spent with the long and ceremonious state which for perhaps the only time in her life
she was called upon to maintain.

By this time, torches of fat pine were blazing at every
door-post, and the strumming of harps and guitars and
many primitive instruments became incessant. Groups of
men, drowsy or hilarious, as the mezcal and pulque they
had drunk chanced to affect them, were stretched on the
ground, lazily watching and criticising the slow and untiring movements of the fandango; now and then one would
spring up, to place himself before some dusky partner,
who would raise the song in her shrill monotone, swaying
and bending her body in unison with the gliding steps,
which seemed as untiring as they were fascinating.

Occasionally the shrill song of the women was enlivened
by the snapping of the fingers and thumbs of the men;
and more than once, though it had been forbidden, the
sharp crack of a pistol-shot indicated the irrepressible excitement of some enthusiastic dancer. As the night wore
on, the click of the castanets became more frequent, and
the weird and tender refrain of *La paloma* gave place to
a bacchanalian chorus. Yet this chorus ever bore an
undertone of pathos and sentiment which seemed to
render impossible the absolute frenzy and rudeness of
mirth that would be apt to characterize such scenes in
other lands, — though the element of danger that lurked
within began to show itself in scornful glances, and the
contemptuous turning of shoulder or head.

The night was chilly and dark, for it was the rainy season, and there was no moon; but the light from scores of

torches and from the tripod of burning pitch set in the middle of the plaza illuminated the entire village. The great house was set so high that the lurid glare reached no farther than its gates; yet while its massive façade was in comparative darkness, from its windows the scene of revelry was glowingly distinct, and irresistibly attracted even the indifferent gaze of Doña Isabel.

Late in the evening she stepped into her balcony; Doña Feliz joined her, and they wrapped themselves in their black rebosos, and silently regarded the scene. The dances and sports of the peasantry had been familiar to them from their childhood. A pleasurable excitement thrilled the veins of each as they gazed. This gayety was as far beneath them as the follies of our life may be beneath the pleasures of angels, yet pleased the exalted sense of kindly interest in the affairs of plebeian humanity. They began to murmur to each other something of this feeling, when suddenly both became silent. A single figure had caught the glances of both. It was that of Chinita, who, scornful and cool while the slow *afforados* and *jarabes* were in progress, had yielded to the seductive strains of the waltz, and was drawn from her station at Juana's side by a rual beau from a neighboring village. The two whirled in the mazy dance, presently beginning a series of improvised changes, possible only to the subtle grace of youth under the spell of excitement wrought to its height by music, wine, and amorous flattery. One by one the other couples ceased dancing, the fingers of the musicians flew over their instruments, and the swift feet of Chinita and her partner kept time. Sometimes they swept together around the circle formed by the admiring on-lookers; anon Chinita, lifting her arms to the cadence of the music, waved her swain away, and circled round him like a bird poising for descent, then glided again to his arms; or turning one bare shoulder from which the reboso had fallen, looked back upon him with soft, languorous eyes which challenged pursuit, while she fled with the speed of the wind.

The circle were enraptured, and broke into loud *vivas*, or joined in the words of the air to which the pair were dancing. Pedro stood with the rest, watching with shining eyes; but at his side was a young woman, whose dark brows were drawn together in a spasm of rage. This was Elvira, a young widow, to whom the stranger was plighted, and who in the utter abandonment of her lover to the dance with another younger and fairer than herself, found a fair excuse for the mad jealousy that surged through heart and brain, and convulsed her features. But there was none to notice her; all eyes were bent upon the dancers, when a sudden turn brought them both before the infuriated woman. Seizing a knife from the belt of the unconscious Pedro, she sprang toward Chinita, with intent to wreak the usual vengeance of the jealous country-woman by slashing her across the cheek or mouth, and thus destroying her beauty forever. But quick as a flash Pepé, the derided but faithful, threw himself between them, receiving the blow in his arm; but shouting and gesticulating with pain, he made ridiculous a scene which might have been heroic.

This was no uncommon incident at such gatherings, and roused more laughter than dismay. The dance suddenly ceased. Chinita, panting with exertion, threw herself with a cry for protection upon Pedro, who in rage had involuntarily grasped for the missing knife that had so nearly accomplished so foul a work; and Benito, recalled to his allegiance by this undoubted proof of his Elvira's devotion, turned to her with words of mingled reproach and endearment. Pepé, in spite of his outcry, was quite unnoticed in the general excitement until his sister the bride, forgetting her dignity, forced her way through the crowd and bound her large lace handkerchief over the bleeding wound.

"Thou shalt come home!" said Pedro, resolutely, as Chinita struggled in his grasp, with a half defined intention of assailing the woman who had assaulted her, and who was being led sobbing away by her repentant lover. "What will the Señora think of thee?" he added in a whisper. "She is on her balcony."

Chinita glanced up. She could see nothing against the great blank wall that loomed in the near distance, but a sensation of acute shame overcame her. She suddenly remembered that which in her brief delirium she had forgotten. She turned from the throng as though they had been serpents, and fled up the path to the gate, dashing against it breathless. The postern was open.

She felt for it with her hands and darted through, coming full upon Doña Isabel. Feliz followed her lady, both looking like spectres under the rough stone arch of the vestibule, with its grim garniture of serpents and fierce-eyed wild beasts.

"Wretched girl!" cried Doña Isabel, as Chinita stopped like a deer at bay. "Wretched girl!" grasping her with a grip of steel, yet shaking as with ague. "Hast thou a wound? Is the mark of shame on thy face already? My God! Oh, child! Canst thou not speak?"

"I will kill her!" gasped Chinita, too much excited herself to be surprised by the agitation of Doña Isabel, or to wonder at her presence. "To-morrow I will find her and give her such a blow as she would have given me. What will her Benito care for her then?"

"What is he to thee?" cried Doña Isabel, catching the girl by the wrist, and looking into her eyes, — "he or any such *canalla?* Come thou with me! — with me, I say!" She threw a glance, half inquiring, half defiant, at Feliz, who stood with her eyes cast down, her face strangely white, yet inexpressive. "Come thou with me," she reiterated, scanning the girl from her unkempt shock of tawny curls to her unshod feet. A blush passed over the usually colorless and haughty face of the lady, as she added slowly, "before it is too late."

The girl and the mistress of Tres Hermanos looked at each other searchingly; then Doña Isabel turned and led the way across the court. Chinita followed her with head erect and sparkling eyes. Pedro entered at the instant, but his foster daughter did not hear him; but Feliz, who gave way that the strangely associated lady and girl might pass, looked up, and her eyes met those of the gatekeeper. Pedro approached with his Indian, cat-like silence of movement, and found her standing as if in a dream. The eyes of the man filled with tears. He was too lowly to manifest resentment at the studied reserve he believed Doña Feliz had for years preserved toward him, while still she had made him her tool. He and such as he were made for use. Yet inferior as he was, they had been workers in a common cause, and their common purposes seemed now frustrated at a word.

He bent humbly and touched the fringe of her reboso.

" Have I done well, Doña Feliz? " he queried in a broken voice. " Alas ! I can do no more. You see how blood flows to blood, as the brooks turn to the river. "

Feliz started. " Strange ! strange ! " she muttered. She turned upon Pedro a glance of mingled pity and deprecation. She seemed about to say more, but paused. " Thou art a good man, Pedro," she presently whispered. " Thou hast done a greater work than thou guessest. Be content. Thou knowest the child's nature,— Chinita will not suffer with Doña Isabel; but she who thrust from her bosom the dove will perchance warm the adder into life."

"No, no ! " cried the man, vehemently. " Cruel, bitter woman ! Chinita hath been my child, and though she turn from me I will hear no evil of her. I will live or die for her ! " The unwonted outburst ended in a sob, and before he could speak again, Doña Feliz had passed across the court, but — strange condescension ! — she had seized his hand and pressed it to her lips, in irresistible homage to a devotion as pure and unselfish as that of the loftiest knight who ever drew sword in the cause of helpless innocence.

Pedro turned to his alcove dazed, stunned. To him it was as if a star should leave its place in heaven to touch the vilest clod upon the highway. A very miracle !

XXIII.

ALTHOUGH Doña Rita had left her home upon a sad errand, and her tears flowed fast when on embracing her mother she beheld upon her countenance the shadow of death, that first startling impression vanquished, she allowed herself to be deceived by the fitful brightness that hovers over the consumptive ; and as days passed on she felt a pleased sense of freedom and relaxation, and her return to her early home, which had been undertaken as a pilgrimage, assumed much of the character of an ordinary visit of pleasure.

Doña Rita was a member of a large family, of whom most had married ; so that her parents, relieved from cares that had long pressed upon them, were enabled to live in the little town of El Toro with an ease and comfort from which in their narrow circumstances they had necessarily been debarred while the children were dependent. They were, strictly speaking, people of the class known as *medio pelo*, or " the half-clothed order," as far below the aristocrat as above the plebeian ; and Rita Farias had been thought to have risen greatly in life when she became the wife of Rafael Sanchez, though he was then but a clerk, the son of the administrador of Tres Hermanos, with no prospect of succeeding soon to his honors. But as the pious neighbors said when they heard of the early death of the bridegroom's father, " God blessed her with both hands," of which one held marriage, and the other death ; so Doña Rita was accustomed when she at rare intervals visited her parents to be looked upon with ever increasing respect. Such silken skirts and rebosos as she wore were seldom seen within the quiet precincts of El Toro.

Doña Rita herself was not quite clear upon the point as to whether or not her native place could be considered to rival " the City," as Mexico was called *par excellence*, or even Guadalajara, which she had heard was a labyrinth of palaces ; but Rosario who had seen El Toro declared to

Chata that nothing could be finer, and Chata herself was quite convinced of that when opening her eyes suddenly upon the clear moonlight night on which the diligence stopped before the door of the inn, she first looked out upon the plaza.

The two girls shivered a little in their sudden awakening, as, scarcely knowing how, they were lifted from the diligence and stood upon their feet at the door of the inn, with an injunction to watch the basket, the five parcels tied in paper or towels, the drinking-gourd, the bottle of claret, and the young parrot which their mother had brought with her as a suitable gift to her declining relative. With habitual obedience they did as they were bid, more than once rescuing a parcel from the long, skinny claw of a blear-eyed hag, who crouched in the shadow of the wall whining for alms, while at the same time they cast their admiring glances at the really beautiful church upon which the white rays of the moonlight streamed, converting it for the nonce into a symmetrical pile of virgin snow or spotless alabaster. The priest's house, a long low building with numerous barred windows, stood on one side of it, while an angle of the square was formed by a mass of buildings, the frowning walls of which were apparently unpierced by door or window. This was a convent. Later the children learned to know well the gardens it enclosed, and also the taste of the wonderful confections the sweet-faced sisters made. The other buildings seemed poor and small in comparison to those, with the exception of the inn which rose gloomily behind them, a solitary rush-light burning palely in the yawning vestibule, and the torches flaming in the court-yard, where benighted travellers were loudly bargaining for lodgings, — no hope of supper presenting itself at that late hour.

While Rosario and Chata were noticing these things with wide-open eyes but with ill suppressed yawns, Don Rafael and Doña Rita were returning the salutations of the concourse of friends who had come to meet them; and as soon as the children had been embraced in succession by each affectionate cousin or punctilious friend, they were hurried across the plaza upon the side where the shadows lay black as ink, and with a regretful glance at the seeming palaces of marble that rose on either hand were conducted with much kindly help and cheerfulness over the rough cobble-stones along a narrow street of single-storied houses, above the walls of which, as if piercing the roofs, rose at intervals tall slender trees, indicating the well-planted courts within. Reaching the more scattered portions of the town where the moonlight shone clear over open fields and walled gardens and orchards, with low adobe houses scattered among them, they at last entered, somewhat to the disappointment of Chata, a rather pretentious house which fronted directly upon the street. She was consoled upon the following day to find a garden at the back, where a triangle of pink roses of Castile, larkspur, and red geraniums grew, almost choking with their luxuriance the beds of onions and chiles, and rivalling in glory of color the "manta de la Virgin" or convolvulus, which entirely covered the half-ruinous stone-wall — the gaps filled with tuñas and magueys — which divided the cultivated land from the thickets of mesquite and cactus that lay beyond.

In the garden the children spent many hours while their mother sat chatting at the side of the invalid, who rallied wonderfully as she heard the endless tales of her daughter's prosperity; though like many another *nouveau riche*, Doña Rita had her fancied self-denials to complain of. One of the clerks at the hacienda had a wife whose father had given her a string of pearls as large as cherries upon her wedding day, while she the wife of the administrador was left to blush over the shabby necklace — not a bead of which was bigger than a pea — which Rafael had gone in debt to give her on her wedding day, and which until the advent of the fortunate Doña Gomesinda she had thought most beautiful; and then too her dearest friend had a daughter who would inherit a fine house of three rooms or more in that very town, and money and jewels fit for a *hacendado's* daughter; and it was quite possible that she would marry — who could tell? it might even be an attorney or an official, — while with two to endow (and it was well known that Rafael loved to enjoy as he went), Heaven only knew to what her own flesh and blood were doomed! There was Rosario for example, — and her own grand-mother, who would not be prejudiced, could judge if there was a prettier or more daintily-bred girl in the whole

town, — what chance was there that an officer or an attorney, or indeed any one but a clerk, a ranchero, or a poor
shop-keeper, should pretend to their alliance when they
could give so poor a dower with their daughter? Doña
Rita's eyes filled with tears, and decidedly she was obliged
to compress her lips very tightly to prevent herself from
uttering further complaint; for since Rosario had with
true Mexican precocity burst into the full glory of young
womanhood, this had become a very real grievance to her
mother, but one of which, with the awe of the promoted
as well as trained daughter and wife, she had seldom
ventured to hint of either to Doña Feliz or Don Rafael.

As Rosario had outgrown her sister in physique, so had
she also in womanly dignity and apparent force of intellect.
At least she thought of matters, and even to her admiring
mother and female relatives began to give weighty opinions upon affairs which either wearied Chata or interested
her little. The grandfather, old Don José Maria, used to
sit under a fig-tree watching with disapproving eyes as
Chata darted hither and thither chasing a butterfly or
ruby-throated humming-bird, or with her lap full of flowers
or neglected sewing pored over some entrancing book
lent her by the village priest (he was a man whose ideas,
had he not been the Santo Padre, would have been the
last that should have been tolerated in the bringing up of
sedate and simple maidens) ; and those same eyes lighted
with pride as they fell on Rosario, beating eggs to a froth
to mix with honey and almonds for her grandfather's
delectation, or bending over a brasier of ruddy charcoal
watching anxiously the cooking of the *dulce*, of which
already more successes than failures showed her a born
artist. Then again sometimes, when Don José came in the
cool of the evening from the plaza where he had been to
buy his jar of pulque or his handful of garlic, he could see
his favorite sitting demurely in the upper balcony with
her head bent over her needle, listening it is true to that
maldito libro, " that pernicious book," which Chata was
reading, but as far as he could see doing no other harm,
unless the very fact of a young and pretty girl looking
into the street was a harm in itself, — but *Maria Purissima!* one must not be too rigorous with one's own flesh
and blood: like others before him and more who will

come after, Don José Maria forgot in tenderness to the grandchildren the discipline he had thought absolutely necessary with the preceding generation.

Chata, too, thought it delightful to sit on the balcony and peer through the wooden railing at the long stretch of sand which led far away where the houses dwindled into a few half-ruinous hovels, where children and dogs throve as well as the bristling cacti. On Sunday mornings very early, as the mother and daughters came from Mass along that road, they used to be covered with dust thrown up by the scores of plodding donkeys who wended their way to the plaza laden with charcoal and vegetables, eggs and screaming fowls. Doña Rita and her daughters would cover their faces with their rebosos, and trip daintily by, scarcely appeased by the admiring salutations and apologies of the drivers, who pulling off their rough straw hats apostrophized the dust and the scorching sun and the clumsy donkey, " by your license be the name spoken ! "

Sometimes more distinguished wayfarers passed over the road and turned into the inn, or rode on to the barracks which lay quite at the opposite extremity of the little town ; for it happened that a company of soldiers were quartered there. They were for the most part well clad in a gay uniform of red and blue, and every man had a profusion of stripes on his sleeves or lace on his cap. No one knew and no one asked whether they were Mochos or Puros, Conservatives or Liberals, — for the nonce they were Ramirez's men. This General had been a Liberal the month before, and was suspected of favoring the clergy at this time. Who could tell? Who knew what he might be on the morrow? In the night all cats are gray ; in times of perplexity all soldiers are patriots. The ragged urchins of El Toro threw up their hats for the soldiers of Ramirez, and the discreet householders leaned from their balconies every evening to hear the little band play, and to exult for a brief quarter of an hour in the mild excitement inseparable from a garrison town.

Chata and Chinita had delighted in the distant music, and had caught glimpses of the soldiers, as disenchanting as those of the rude grimy structures they had in the moonlight imagined to be marble palaces ; they had gazed up and down the dusty street and watched the noisy ragged urchins play " Toro " with a big-horned, long-haired, decrepit goat, with crowds of half naked elfin-faced girls as spectators, until they were actually beginning to weary of the attractions of the town and long for home, — when one day the beat of a drum was heard and a squad of soldiers went filing past, with a young officer riding at their head, who threw a glance so killing at the balcony where the young girls stood that, whether intended to reach her or not, it pierced the heart of Rosario on the instant.

Chata had also noticed the young officer (a slender under-sized young fellow, with a swarthy lean face and keen black eyes, shaded by a profusely decorated sombrero), but merely as a part of the mimic pageant, — a prominent part, for the trappings of his horse, as well as his own dress, were covered by that profusion of ornament affected by gallants whose capital was invested in the adornment of the person with which they hoped to conquer fortune; for in those days there were numberless roystering adventurers, who to a modicum of valor united a vanity and assurance which provided many a rich girl with a dashing and fickle hus-band, and his country with a soldier as false to Mexico as to his Doña Fulana.

It was just after this that evening after evening Ro-sario would lean pensively over the balcony rail, resist-ing Chata's entreaties to come to the garden where there was no dust to stifle them, and where the dew would soon begin to fall upon the larkspurs and roses, and already the wide white cups of the *gloria mundo* were beginning to fill with perfume. The dew would chill her, the perfume sicken her, Rosario said. Chata remonstrated; Rosario smirked and smiled. Chata grew vexed; she thought the smile in mockery of her. She need not have lost her sweet temper, — Rosario was thinking of a far different person. The young captain was walking slowly down the opposite side of the street; he had just laid his hand on his heart. It was on him Rosario smiled.

Doña Rita, discreetest of mothers, was not one to leave her daughters to their own devices unwatched. It was she who always accompanied them in their walks or to Mass; yet curiously enough the young captain found means to slip a tiny note into Rosario's ready hand, as she knelt on the grimy stone floor of the church. Obviously, Doña Rita could not be in two places at once, and she usually knelt behind Chata, who needed perhaps some maternal supervision at her devotions; and it came about that the space behind Rosario was occupied by some stranger. It was Don José Maria who first noticed that quite as a matter of course that stranger grew to be the Captain Don Fernando Ruiz; and quite accidentally it happened that thereafter the mother and daughters went to an earlier Mass. Don José Maria was not so early a riser as Don Fernando was; so he was not there, while the young soldier was in his usual place.

Chata was perhaps a stupid little creature, — Rosario it is quite certain would never have done such a silly thing; but one day when Don Fernando had pressed a note into the hand which was nearest to him, and which in the confusion of dispersal happened to be that of the smaller sister, she gave it in some indignation to her mother. It was full of violent protestations of affection, and entreated the life of his life to give her lover hope; it was signed her " agonized yet adoring Fernando."

Doña Rita showed herself capable of great self-control; she said sadly that she would not ask which had been guilty of attracting such impassioned admiration, but she assured the girls she was heart-broken. When she reached the house, after first carefully closing the door that her father might not hear, she rated them both soundly. Chata did not think it strange they should both be thought guilty; she assumed that Rosario was as innocent as herself. Doña Rita, giving Rosario the note to read, that she might learn for herself the daring and presumption of which man is capable, forgot in her indignation to reclaim it. An hour afterward Chata saw Rosario read it over in secret, and was scandalized to see her kiss it; and late that day, as they stood as usual on the balcony (the little mother, as Chata remarked, was so forgiving!), she caught Rosario's hand spasmodically as Fernando passed by, but the girl released it with some impatience and slyly kissed the tips of her fingers, — and Chata, with a pang of awakening, realized that her sister had not been and was not so innocent of coquetry as she had assumed, and thenceforth suffered indescribable tortures between her sense of loyalty to her sister and duty to her mother.

Rosario's ideal of truth was in accordance with that which surrounded her; to be silent when speech was undesirable, to equivocate pleasantly where plain speaking would be harsh, to tell a lie gracefully where truth would offend, — this was her natural creed, which she had never questioned. But Chata, unknown to herself, had never accepted it; her soul was like certain material objects which resist the dyes that other substances at once absorb. It was not enough for her to give the truth when it was asked, — it was a torture, an unnatural crime, to her to withhold it. She would not indeed have done so in this case, had not Rosario in a manner put her upon her honor the very next day.

The washerwoman had been there, and Rosario, who was an embryo housewife, had been deputed to attend her, and Chata, who had gladly escaped the duty, ran to the bedroom when she saw the servant depart to congratulate her sister on the dispatch she had made; when Rosario closing the door mysteriously, cried: "Look! look what he has sent me! Is it not beautiful, charming, divine?" and she held up to the light her hand, on the first finger of which glittered a ring.

Truth to tell, Chata was dazzled; at that moment her own insignificance and the womanliness and beauty of Rosario were more than ever apparent. She gazed at Rosario with greater admiration than on the ring, beautiful though it was. Here was a sister just her own age, yet a woman with an actual lover! Oh!

"What will our mother say?" she began in an awed voice, when Rosario, her womanly dignity gone, began to spring up and down, screaming yet laughing, "*Ay, Dios mio!*" throwing her hand over her shoulder and slipping it into the loose neck of her dress. "Oh, my life! the creature is down my back! it is crawling now on my shoulder! No, no, grandfather," for Don José Maria had entered, "it is Chata who will help me. No, my mother! Ay, it is gone now! I would not have you frightened, it was but one of those bright little beetles that live on the roses;" and she contemptuously tossed something out of the window, and Chata saw with speechless wonder that the ring which had been on her finger was gone. The bauble at least had slipped into a secure hiding-place, and Chata really could not determine whether the beetle had ever existed or no.

An air of delightful mystery began to pervade not only the house but the quiet street all the way from the plaza, which Don Fernando Ruiz crossed at intervals in the long, dull, sultry days. It became quite a diversion to the initiated to watch what clever turns and doublings he would make, and with what assumed indifference he would linger by the fruit-stand at the corner, where old Antonina sold tuñas or a few poor figs and lumps of roasted cassava root. She made quite a fortune from the young captain, who seemed bent on dazzling her bleared eyes; for every day, and sometimes three or four times in a day, he appeared resplendent in uniform of blue and red, or a riding suit of buckskin embroidered in silver, or perhaps, when his mood was sombre, in black hung with silver buttons, and more than once in a suit of velvet and embossed leather, with buttons of gold set with brilliants, and riding a horse with accoutrements so splendid that Doña Rita declared he must be as rich as the Marquis of Carabas himself, and without any apparent consistency embraced Rosario with tears.

Truth to tell, Doña Rita was a match-maker born, and though her talents had lain dormant during the years she had spent at the hacienda, they had not declined; and it was natural that she should find a quiet exultation in exerting them in favor of her daughter, for young though Rosario was, her precocity and the custom of the country and period rendered it perfectly natural that marriage should present itself in her immediate future.

A vision of it rose before the impassioned girl like a star, though there was a period of clouds and mourning when her grandmother died, and Chata, sobbing in the garden or moving sadly about the darkened rooms, wondered that Rosario could smile over those pink notes she was always stealing into corners to pore over. During the nine days that her mother remained within doors receiving visits of condolence, the notes indeed were the aliment upon which Rosario's fancy fed; for Doña Rita, though the little drama of courtship had undoubtedly made less absorbing to her the tragedy of illness and death, was too strict an observer of the proprieties to allow her maternal affection to betray

13

her at such a time into permitting even a shutter to be left ajar, or to suffer her daughter to approach a window to satisfy herself by a momentary peep as to whether the love-lorn captain was on his accustomed beat or no. It was a time however when without offence the veriest stranger might leave a card and word of sympathy, and this he never failed to do from day to day. Doña Rita would glance at the bit of cardboard with an affectation of indifference, but it would always shortly disappear from the table, and with the cruel sarcasm of childish intolerance Chata would suggest to Rosario its suitability for baking the little puffs of sugar and almonds upon, which she was so deft at compounding.

At last the *novena* of grief was ended, and taking her aged father's arm Doña Rita dutifully led him into the street to breathe the air. Rosario knew that at that hour the captain was on duty at the barracks, but nevertheless could not resist the opportunity of stepping into the balcony and gazing upon the scene from which she had been so long debarred. A neighbor across the way greeted her with a significant smile; and somewhat piqued, Rosario drew back, half closed the shutters with a hesitating hand, and then dropping on the floor in the long ray of sunlight that streamed through the aperture, set herself to the ever entrancing task of re-reading her lover's letters.

As she sat there opening them one by one and after perusal leaving them unfolded in her lap, she became so absorbed that she did not notice the passage of time until a footstep sounded behind her, and glancing up she saw with trepidation that her grandfather was ushering in a tall and imposing stranger, whose military garb made her heart beat madly, for a wild thought of Fernando Ruiz flashed through her mind. Her confusion was not lessened by perceiving that the visitor was a man of more advanced age and infinitely greater assumption of rank. The tell-tale letters were in her lap, though involuntarily she had dropped her reboso over them; but she dared not rise lest they should drop in a shower around her, and she equally feared the anger of her grandfather and the condemnatory surprise of the visitor.

"I pray you enter the house, Señor! Pass in, sir, pass in!" she heard her grandfather say in his smoothest tones.

"My daughter will be here almost immediately; but she stopped at the convent for a moment to buy a blessed candle to place before the altar of Our Lady of Succors. She will be honored indeed by this visit. Take care, Señor, the room is somewhat dark, but I will open a shutter. *Valgame Dios*, what have we here?" as he caught sight of the bent figure sitting in the narrow streak of sunshine. "*Caramba, niña*, rise! rise, I say! seest thou not the Señor General?"

"Ay, but I have the cramp in my poor foot, my grandfather," cried Rosario in a voice of lamentation, vainly endeavoring under cover of the reboso to make some disposal of the letters which rustled alarmingly. "*No, Señores*, by Blessed Mary my patroness, let me alone!" she cried, as both her grandfather and the stranger attempted to help her, — the latter with a faint gleam of amusement in his eyes, the former with genuine consternation depicted on his face. "Ay, Chata," for by this time her sister had appeared. "Oh, but my back is broken! it is worse than when you struck me with the stick when you were trying to knock the peaches from the tree. Oh! ah! no, it is impossible for me to rise!"

In dire affright Chata knelt before her. "Oh, what shall I do?" she cried, in remorse at the remembrance of an escapade that had been almost forgotten, and in sudden fear that it might have been the cause of her sister's present distress. "Oh, my life! I thought it was your poor foot!" and she began rubbing one small slippered member, while Rosario eagerly whispered, "Stupid one, hide me these letters!" and the mystified Chata felt her sister's hand with a mass of fluttering papers thrust under her arm, covered with the ever useful reboso.

Involuntarily the hapless confidant pressed them to her side, and at the same moment Rosario limped from the room, inwardly raging at making so poor a figure before the General, while Chata, standing for a moment abashed, was about to follow, when a voice which bewildered her by its strange yet familiar accent said gayly, "And you, my fair Señorita, have you never a twinge of the same disorder that afflicts your sister?" and he glanced meaningly at a pink envelope, which had fallen at her feet, — at the same time covering it with his foot that it might not attract the suspicious eye of the old man, who with profuse apologies for the informality of the reception was assuring the visitor that until that moment never had there been a healthier damsel than his granddaughter Rosario, adding with a sigh, "But the Devil robs with one hand and pinches with the other."

Chata trembled and blushed painfully as she raised her eyes timidly to the General's, while with a sense of the grotesque she was conscious of wondering whether he, like herself, was thinking her grandfather had suggested no complimentary agency in her grandmother's removal to another sphere. But at the instant all present perplexities vanished in the surprise with which she recognized the face which she had seen but for a few brief hours years before, — the face of the man of whom Chinita had never grown weary of talking. "The Señor General Ramirez," she said in a low voice, with some awe. She was more than ever bewildered by the look he had fixed upon her. She shrank back, barely dropping her hand for a moment upon that he extended toward her. She was actually inclined to be frightened, his eyes were so brilliant, his smile so eager. The foolish thought struck her that had not her grandfather been there, this strange imperious man would surely have taken her in his arms, would have kissed her! She hurried from the room to find Rosario waiting for her at the end of the corridor, alternately smothering her laughter in the folds of her dress, and angrily chafing at her sister's delay.

"Your horrid letters!" cried Chata, thrusting them into her hands. "Here, take them, read them, laugh over them or cry, or kiss them if you will! I hope I shall never see a love-letter again in my life. He saw them, — the Señor General. I know he did. Oh, what shame!"

"Pshaw!" interrupted Rosario. "What does it matter? He will think none the worse of me. Without doubt he is come on the part of Fernando to ask for me. How proud and happy my mother will be, and how she will rail at me! It will not be difficult for me to cry as I ought, for I am mad with vexation to have appeared such a fool when I should have been so dignified. Why, the Señor will think me a child still! Does he not look like

some one we know, Chata? And yet we can never have
seen him before."

"Yes," returned Chata, "we have seen him. He is the
General José Ramirez."

"Ah, my heart!" ejaculated Rosario, dramatically.
"What a misfortune! My father hates the General
Ramirez because he once had some horses driven away
from the hacienda; and besides he is a good Christian
and fights for the Church! Ay, unlucky Fernando, to
have chosen such a messenger! But thank Heaven, it
is my mother who will first hear him! Ah, there she
comes!" and in irrepressible excitement Rosario grasped
her sister's hand. "Oh, child!" she added sentimentally,
"you too may be asked in marriage some day!" and she
sighed with an air of vastly superior experience, while
Chata revolved in her mind what her playfellow Chinita
would say when she told her of this unexpected meeting
with the hero whom she fancied she had rendered invincible by the gift of the amulet.

Like most children of her country Chata wore a scapulary.
It had lain upon her breast ever since she could remember.
She drew it out and looked at it. Some day she thought
she would open it; now she only made the sign of the
cross, as she replaced it. Rosario in nervous unrest had
left her. The cool of the evening had come; the perfume
of the flowers stole in at the open window, and the breeze
soothed the unusual agitation of her mind. Glad to be
alone, yet anxious and perplexed, she stepped into the
garden. More than once as she walked down the alley
she stopped, her heart palpitating violently. She fancied
she heard her name called, or that Ramirez would step
from the shadow of a tree to encounter her. It was an
unnatural and unchildlike mood quite new to her. It
seemed to her that her grandfather's unnecessary mention
of the Devil's name might have incited that enemy of
innocence to annoy her, and she whispered an *Ave*.

There was a large cluster of bananas just behind the
house. Chata sat down there to watch the fantastic clouds
which hovered where the sun had set. In her absorption
in the glowing scene she was unconscious that any sound
disturbed the silence around her. It was indeed but a low
indistinct hum, scarcely recognizable as the sound of

human voices. Had she noticed them, she would have remembered that she was within a foot or two of a window which was screened from sight by the foliage, and would have withdrawn from possible discovery; but as it was, she remained there an unconscious trespasser. The first distinct sound that reached her ear at once startled and impressed her, for it was the deep voice of Ramirez uttering her own name.

"Chata, yes it was Chata I said," he affirmed dictatorially. "Why attempt dissimulation with you, Señora? I am in no humor for trifling. Will Doña Isabel provide a dowry for your daughter? It is my fancy that Ruiz should marry the little one, and I can make or mar him. So far the boy has blundered, but if he once turns his eyes on the pretty face of Chata, he will not find the mistake irremediable."

Chata could not credit the evidence of her senses, and remained as if rooted to the spot. She presently heard her mother sobbing: "This is an unheard of thing! A young man pays court to one child, — perhaps she is not insensible to his advances, — and his patron comes to me to bid me give him another, whom he has not perhaps even glanced at. Oh, it is too much! too much!"

"I have already told you," said Ramirez, coldly, "that Ruiz is poor. His father was my father's servant, and is mine; more than once he has saved my life at the risk of his own. Years ago he rendered me a service that I swore to repay in a certain manner. More than once of late I have been reminded of my promise, and the marriage of Fernando with your daughter would render its fulfilment impossible."

"By my patron saint!" cried Doña Rita, "it is strange indeed that a poor little country girl should interfere with the projects of a man as great as yourself. But even if that is possible, why bid me give him Chata?" — adding with asperity, "have I not done enough? No, no! I will not, I cannot make my Rosario a sacrifice!"

"*Caramba!*" cried Ramirez, laughing, "is it so dreadful a thing that she should wait until the next lover comes, — he will be sure to come, Señora, — and that she should have a double dower to make her fairer in his eyes? for I tell you Ruiz will ask no dowry from you with the little one. Come, come, Señora, I am not used to reasoning and pleading, yet I am not cruel. The child has been yours too long for me to tear her from your arms. It was a cunning device of Doña Isabel to hide her from me. Ah, it is not the first trick she has served me, and, like the others, she will find it turn to my advantage!"

"As Heaven is my witness," ejaculated Doña Rita, in a voice of intense impulse and fear, "never have I breathed to mortal the secret which you seem to know! Who are you, sir? What have you to do with the child?" Suddenly, she uttered a horrified shriek. Chata, who had started from her seat with dilated eyes and lips parted, gasping for breath, heard her mother spring to her feet, and rush toward the door; heard also Ramirez follow her and apparently draw her back, remonstrating in low tones. Then she realized no more.. Perhaps she fainted, though to herself there appeared no interruption of consciousness. Though she did not notice the stars come out, she beheld them at last looking down upon her, as if they heard the questions that were repeating themselves again and again in her mind. Whose child was she; who was the man who claimed the right to shape her destiny? That she was not the child of Rafael Sanchez and his wife she felt certain. Doña Rita had not denied the insinuation.

The child — all childish thoughts suddenly crushed by the overwhelming revelation she had surprised — remained in the same spot, unconscious of the passage of time, until she heard her sister — no, Rosario — calling her in anxious yet irritated tones: "Where art thou, Chata? Chata, the supper is ready; the grandfather is angry that thou art so long in the garden! Oh, here thou art!"

The two girls encountered each other in the dusk. Rosario threw her arms around the truant. "How cold thou art!" she said. "Hast thou seen a ghost here alone? Bless me! one would think the General Ramirez had brought the plague with him. My mother has shut herself up, and when I went to her door to beg her to tell me whether she was ill, she answered me, 'The world is all ill. Go dress saints, my child, it is all that is left to thee!' What could she have meant? Can it be after all that the General did not come from Fernando?"

Rosario stopped to wipe a tear from the corners of her eyes. Evidently she was more perplexed than dismayed. She was too young to fear the mischances and mishaps of love. Her words recalled to Chata's mind the fate that was decreed to her, — to which she had given no second thought, in her discovery that she was not the child of those she called father and mother. Friendless, homeless, nameless, — yes, she reflected bitterly, that she had *never* been known by a Christian name, — she felt as though the solid earth had opened beneath her, and she was clinging desperately to some tiny twig or bough to prevent herself from being engulfed forever. She clung hysterically to Rosario, who had begun to laugh nervously. And so old Don José Maria found them, and querulously bade them go into the house; nothing but ill fortune would befall maidens who wandered alone in the dark; did they not know that the Devil stood always at the elbow of a woman after the sun set? With which second-hand and scurrilous wisdom the old philosopher ushered them into the dimly lighted dining-room. Doña Rita was there, and as the girls entered lifted her eyes, which were heavy with weeping, and for the first time in her life Chata saw in them aversion, — yes, actual fear and dislike.

The child sighed deeply, and sat down at a shaded corner. No one noticed that she ate nothing. The old man was sleepy, Doña Rita was occupied with Rosario, who grew more and more depressed. From her mother's very kindness her daughter foreboded little good from the tidings she could give her.

XXIV.

For many succeeding days Chata seemed to herself to be struggling to awaken from a torturing dream. The household was very quiet. Doña Rita and Rosario went gloomily to work to set the house in order and prepare for departure; they talked together in low tones, and sometimes one or the other would sigh in echo to poor old Don José Maria, who was contemplating a lonely widowhood, though a kindly cousin had consented to take charge of his domestic affairs, — a kindness which was taken exceedingly ill by the two elderly servants. It was natural enough that the atmosphere around her should be charged with gloom, and as natural that to Chata it should seem a part of the evil dream from which she longed to emerge. At times she thought desperately that she would rush to Doña Rita and beg her to tell her all; but she shrank from dispelling the illusion of her life, from losing the father and mother whom she had believed her own. Her father! — was it possible he could be other than Don Rafael? No, no, no! she loved him, he loved her; he was her own, her very own, — even Rosario did not love and cling to him as she did. And if by word or deed he was deposed from that relationship who would take his place?

The unhappy girl shuddered from head to foot; her very heart seemed to become ice. Who, if all she had heard was true, could be her father but this man, General José Ramirez, — the bloody guerilla, the unscrupulous robber? He had not, it was true, declared so in as many words; it would kill her to hear them — she would not hear them. And so in a sort of dumb frenzy she resisted the temptation to disclose what she had heard; and with a miserable conviction that she was the object of suspicion and dislike, and feeling herself a hypocrite and impostor, she lived from day to day, nursing in her heart such repressed misery as perhaps only a sensitive and uncomprehended child can feel.

Chata was at the point in life where the intuitions of womanhood begin to encroach upon the credulity and frankness of immaturity. A year earlier it is likely she would have gone to Rosario at once with her surprising discovery; but now she unconsciously felt that she was — however unwillingly — her rival. She needed no instruction by word or experience to tell her that Rosario would feel no sympathy with the stranger who had shared as a sister in the love of father, mother, and friends, and who it was purposed should be given to the man whom she had herself won. Strangely enough the remembrance of this only occurred to Chata at intervals, and simply in connection with Rosario. Her mind was so engrossed by the sense of desolation and the agonizing fear of the General Ramirez, that the thought of Ruiz seldom presented itself to her; and the possibility of his being in any way made to affect her life seemed so absolutely incredible that even the sight of him brought no blush to her cheek nor a thrill of interest, either of dislike or latent kindness, to her bosom.

The bewildered and suffering girl did not realize that there was any change in her manner. Sometimes she wondered that she could sleep all night, that she could laugh, yes even talk, so wildly at times that Don José Maria sniffed impatiently, and muttered that it was hard an old man could not take his sorrow in quiet, — as if it was some sort of soothing potion, which to be healthful must be lingered over. But the truth was that the dull, heavy, unrefreshing sleep which came to the child took the place of food to her, besides following naturally upon the physical exhaustion consequent on incessant thought and movement; her sharp, penetrating laugh and inconsequent babble were the outbursts of mental excitement that otherwise must have found vent in passionate cries and tears.

Chata, it is true, had suddenly become invested with a new interest to Doña Rita, who, while events flowed smoothly on, accepted without question the prevailing opinions and sentiments of those surrounding her. She had honestly thought she loved her foster daughter as her

own, and that her welfare was as dear to her as that of
her own child; but now, without reasoning on the matter,
without a throb of anguish in contemplating the fate which
Ramirez might will for her, she saw in the girl but a
rival who, once knowing them, might well approve and
glory in the designs that threatened the pride and affections of Rosario.

Doña Rita dared not repeat to her daughter the substance of her interview with Ramirez; and even had she
been at liberty to do so, her satisfaction in being the
possessor of an actual secret would have led her to assume, as she did now, mild airs of superior wisdom, —
which were perhaps as effectual as words could have been
in assuring Rosario that the opposition which the General
Ramirez had urged against his subaltern's engagement was
more serious than the ordinary interest of a patron would
have induced him to make; and for a week or more her
affectations of despair, her abundant tears and hopeless
sighs, were sufficient to justify her mother's exaggerated
tenderness, — a tenderness which Chata contrasted bitterly with the indifference that permitted her own suffering to pass unnoticed.

The secret fear of Chata's heart was that she might
meet Ramirez, might even be called upon to speak with him.
The thought of either filled her with a frenzy of dread.
Had it been possible she would have fled from the town.
Oh, if she could but have hoped to find her way to the
hacienda alone, even though she dared not make herself
known to Doña Feliz and the administrador! Oh, was
it possible that they could be cold, suspicious, as Doña
Rita was? The thought was an impiety, yet it returned to
her again and again, and her dread of meeting Don Rafael
became — from vastly differing causes — almost as strong
as that with which she imagined herself enduring the
mocking and triumphant scrutiny of Ramirez. In her
desolation the memory of Chinita rose before her. Oh,
to steal with her into the hut and lean her head upon the
breast of that poor waif, who must in her woman's consciousness be feeling something of the misery that day
by day was becoming more agonizing and unendurable to
Chata! The similarity of lot so unexpectedly revealed
to her seemed to explain the irresistible attraction which

the foundling — who had apparently been so far removed from her by caste and circumstance — had always
possessed for her. At the thought, a tint of crimson
suffused her neck and face. How could she know but
that in the obscurity of Chinita's life as the adopted child
of a poor gate-keeper, even the foundling had perhaps
less to blush for than the supposed daughter of the
administrador?

Doña Rita had talked much during the early part of
her visit of the family affairs of the important personages
whom her husband served. Chata had heard the talk
with more entertainment than interest; but she was of a
reflecting and acute mind, and she began now to weave
theories and form conclusions which sometimes startled,
sometimes horrified her. Had she but caught the name
that had brought the shriek from Doña Rita's lips the evening the General Ramirez had talked with her! But without that clew her speculations were idle, and she tortured
herself in vain, yet with unconscious dissimulation hid her
wild and bitter thoughts beneath an exterior that to the
ordinary observer appeared one of thoughtless rather than
feigned and hysterical levity.

In the fear of meeting the General — though the temptation often came upon her to fly from the house lest he
might enter it — Chata avoided going into the streets, and
but that she feared it might prove a deadly sin she would
even have made an excuse of illness to remain from Mass.
But this might not be, though no temptation of a week-day
feast would draw her forth. And thus it happened that
she and Doña Rita were alone when the General Ramirez
for the second time visited the house.

Rosario by chance had accompanied her grandfather on
a visit. She had gone in the best of spirits; for she had
shown Chata a note from Ruiz, in which he declared that
though forbidden to ask for her until in the course of the
revolution he had acquired a competency, or her father
should lose his unjust prejudices against the Church party,
he should ever remain true to her, and should live only in
the hope of calling her his own. For the first time Chata
had embraced Rosario with a genuine sympathy with this
love which seemed so true and yet so hopeless, and had
watched her turn the corner leading to the plaza, when

she was suddenly aroused from a melancholy — which was actual repose compared to the state of excitement that had long possessed her — by the sound of a quick, imperious knock upon the street door ; and glancing down, she saw the General Ramirez impatiently flicking his boot with the small cane he carried, and glancing up and down the street as if suspicious rather than desirous of observation. He had not seen her she was sure. Quick as thought she ran through the room, and passing through the window pushed open a door which led to the parapeted flat roof of the back building, and crouching behind a low brick wall prayed breathlessly to the Virgin for protection. It was a solitary place, where only a servant came sometimes to place a tub of water to be heated in the noonday sun, or to hang some household article for speedy drying. It was not likely, even were she wanted, they would think to look for her there. She was out of hearing, away from all the ordinary sounds of the house ; no voice could reach her there, — not even that voice whose accents she could never forget, which had made her desolate.

As the time passed on and the stillness grew oppressive, and the sunbeams, which had at first annoyed and distracted her, stole to the wall and at last receded altogether, a sense of bitter forlornness and weariness overcame her ; and ceasing from the vain repetitions of *Aves* and *Pater nosters*, Chata clasped her hands over her face, and resting it upon her knees burst into heart-rending sobs.

Her passion did not continue long ; it was perhaps too severe. It was arrested as by a blow, — by the sudden bang of a heavy door. She lifted her head and listened. Was it fancy, or did she hear the rattle of musketry? It was an unfamiliar sound, and yet she recognized it. What had happened? Was an enemy entering the town? Had the garrison revolted? Accounts of such events were too frequent to make these conjectures other than natural even to Chata's unwarlike mind. She hastily rose, pushed aside the bolt of the heavy door, and stepping into the corridor found herself face to face with Doña Rita.

" Ah, you are here ! " that lady exclaimed in a hurried

and abstracted manner, far different from that which she would usually have worn at the discovery of such a misdemeanor. " I have been seeking you everywhere,— I could not send a servant. And now something has happened in the street, and he has rushed away without seeing you, — the Señor General Ramirez, I mean."

"I know whom you mean!" cried Chata. "Oh, my mother, why should I see him?" Then with wild passion she threw herself at Doña Rita's feet, and buried her face in her skirts and the flowing ends of her reboso. "Oh, tell me that it was not true — what I heard! I was in the garden the other evening as you talked! Oh, my mother, my mother!"

Doña Rita looked down at her in startled surprise, but almost instantly an expression of relief rose to her countenance. "Rise, child, rise!" she said in a low, not ungentle voice; yet there was an inexpressible lack of maternal solicitude in it, which struck to the heart of the suffering child. "Listen; be reasonable; have I not ever been kind to thee? I do not blame thee even now that thou art forced to repay me so ill; it is not thy fault."

"But you shall not be repaid so ill!" exclaimed Chata. "I will be your child forever. Oh, it is not possible that he — this strange man, who frightens me — would dare take me from you?"

"Bless me, niña, you are a strange one! If you but knew it, you have rare good fortune. A handsome lover and a rich dowry are not to be had every day for the asking. But you show a proper spirit, and one I should have expected after the good training you have had. Heaven knows what would have been the result had you been given to Doña Isabel, and allowed to run at large like most of the children of Our Blessed Lady. Yet it was a cruel trick my mother-in-law played me, and Rafael too! Well, well, it shall be brought home to him some day. Listen! was not that the sound of cannon? and my child abroad! Ave Maria Sanctissima!"

"Mother, be not afraid!" said Chata, desperately. "She and my grandfather will not yet have left Doña Francisca's, and that you know is quite away from the plaza or the barracks; they have only to cross the gardens and be home in a 'God speed us!' But as for me,

I am in more fright and misery than if a thousand guns
were levelled upon me. Do you not see, I know only
that I am not your child! Who am I? What is to become of me?"

"The last seems settled already," returned Doña Rita,
with an accent of chagrin which was almost spiteful;
"and the long and short of it is, child, that you were
sent to Doña Isabel, but that my mother-in-law had the
fancy you would be safer with me; and I, like a ten-
der-hearted simpleton, did not object to humoring her
whim, thinking at the same time I was doing a person
whom I loved a service she would know how to appre-
ciate, — and now when the time has come for recompense,
instead of gain, comes loss. There is nothing in this
world but vexation and disappointment."

"I cannot understand anything of this," said Chata,
with a deep sigh. She had risen to her feet, and was
looking pitifully at Doña Rita, who walked up and down
the corridor, listening to the distant and irregular firing, and interrupting her discourse with interjections and
doubts as to the safety of her daughter. "But when I
see my father, Don Rafael, I will ask him, or Doña
Feliz, — yes, Doña Feliz always loved me."

"Ay, but you must ask nothing," almost screamed
Doña Rita, running to Chata and seizing her by the
shoulders. "They will think it was I who betrayed the
secret; they will never forgive me. Oh, I should lead a
dog's life! You are not old enough to know how cruel an
angry husband or a baffled mother-in-law can be. And
poor Rosario —"

"What can it matter to Rosario?" interrupted Chata.
"Were you not lamenting that her dowry would be so
small? Will it not be double now that I shall not inno-
cently rob her?"

"Yes, yes," whispered Doña Rita, eagerly. "The General Ramirez promised me this very day that when you,
Chata, married Ruiz, he would make a gift to Rosario of all
my husband may bestow on you, and that as much more
should be given her on her wedding day, provided that the
secret of your birth be kept. It is useless to ask me his
reasons. He gave me none. I cannot guess them any
more than I can surmise why Doña Isabel would not re-

ceive you, and therefore you were thrust into my arms. Heavens, what a reverberation! the whole house shakes!"

"It is nothing," cried Chata, "but the slamming of a door. I hear the voices of Don José Maria and Rosario. Stay!" she added, grasping Doña Rita as she was about to run down the stairs. "I warn you that I will know all the truth. Your poor reasons shall not keep me from demanding it. Doña Feliz shall not refuse me!"

"Doña Feliz will do as she wills!" retorted Doña Rita. "But this I tell you, child, that the moment Ramirez knows that those who once crossed his plans are warned against him, you will be spirited away. Ramirez has his own purposes, and is not to be thwarted. He is already angry against Rafael and Doña Feliz for their attempted and long successful deception. He is a man of great and mysterious power, and knows not the meaning of the word forgive; and as sure as you stand there, if you disobey his commands sent you through me he will separate you at once from your home and friends, and bring ruin upon those who have cared for you."

Doña Rita spoke with that impressive eloquence and fire which upon occasion seems at the command of every Mexican. She stood with one foot on the corridor floor, the other upon the stair, which she was about to descend, and she had turned half-way round, stretching out her hands, and lifting her dark and anxious eyes to encounter and fix the gaze of Chata. Below, in the stone entrance-way, stood Rosario, volubly describing to a servant the dangers she and her grandfather had encountered. For the moment Doña Rita appeared in Chata's eyes like some timorous yet desperate animal standing between her and her young. "My Rosario, my poor child," said the mother in a low voice, "is her life to be blasted by you? Ramirez is in two minds now. One is to resent the frustration of his will, and be the mortal enemy of those who have sheltered you; the other to applaud and reward them. Upon your discretion all depends."

"But I shall go mad if I have only this to think upon," exclaimed Chata. "Who, who can tell me anything to make this dreadful revelation endurable, if not Don Rafael or Doña Feliz? Ah, yes, there is — there is the General."

"Surely!" replied Doña Rita. "Yes, my life, I am

coming "— to Rosario. " Yes, Chata, could I have found you to-day, you would have known all. Ask him what you like — it will please him. Oh, he is most considerate. Did he not show that by taking me into his confidence? Yes, yes, you are right; insist upon knowing all from him, and you shall tell me: who could understand, or sympathize so well? But as you love me and value the safety of Rafael, not a word to him or Doña Feliz. — Rosario! what an impatient one! What is there to see? If there is commotion in the street, keep back from the windows. Ay, who would have thought the troops would pass this way? God save us, we shall be killed! the whole town will be destroyed! The street is alive with soldiers. Bar the doors! close the shutters! Oh, what horror! Is it Comonfort returned? Is it a *pronunciamiento?* What new alarm is this?" Ejaculating these last sentences Doña Rita hurried downstairs and rushed from room to room, directing the bewildered servants and chiding Rosario, who, attracted by the sound of music and the trampling of men and horses, strove to peep through a crack in the shutters.

Chata, standing where she had been left at the head of the stairs, heard it all as though in a dream. She said over and over to herself, " It is the General I will ask. Yes, yes, I will have the courage! No word of mine shall bring danger on my father. Oh, why do I say 'my father'? Yes, I will say so; he is mine until he turns me away! Oh, what shall I do? Oh, Sanctissima Maria, help thy child! May I not say to Don Rafael, 'Here is thy poor little child; she will be the daughter of no other'? Oh, I know he would cling to me, fight for me; but that Doña Rita says would be ruin! Ah, I know the soldier is cruel and false, even if he is my father; he has been so to me — " She stopped suddenly, as though blasphemy had escaped her. Though she would not believe in her heart the testimony which her reason could not disallow, she was struck dumb by the mere possibility of filial disrespect and with the actual abhorrence which she felt in her bosom toward the man whom she instinctively feared.

As if to flee from her thoughts, she rushed into a room that faced upon the street, and with an impulse such as leads the desperate man to throw himself into a vortex of seething water, or into the thickest of battle, as her ear caught the sounds of commotion, she threw open the shutters and stepped out upon the balcony.

A scene of confusion met her eye, in which men on horseback and on foot seemed mingled indiscriminately, each individual struggling in an attempt to secure a personal advantage. Ranks were broken and scattered. Men and officers alike were for the most part un-uniformed, and to the uninitiated it was impossible to distinguish the adherents of one party from those of another, save by the wild cries of " *Religion y Fueros!* Long live Liberty! Long live Juarez!"

The name of Juarez had begun to be a familiar one in all ears; and even though it possessed not the magic of later years, the voices that uttered it thrilled with an intensity of purpose which seemed to infuse the word with life, — to make it a watchword for great and noble aspirations and deeds, not the mere echo of a name, a party cry to be shouted with frenzy to-day and execrated to-morrow.

It was impossible to tell what chance had forced the combatants upon that straggling highway. The struggle had begun at the barracks, when a party of horse had surprised the garrison, pouncing upon it from the hills like hawks upon their prey, and by the sheer force of surprise, rather than any superiority of numbers or courage, throwing it into a confusion which in spite of the efforts of the young officers speedily resulted in a panic. The soldiers who had been drilling before the town prison, — which had done duty as a fort, — after a feeble and confused attempt to defend its doors, had been driven into the plaza; and when Ramirez reached this, it was to find his own guns turned upon him. His servant had been leading his charger up and down the street, awaiting him; and catching a glimpse of his master as he hurried past an alley in which the groom had taken refuge, he called in mingled devotion and affright, —

"For God's sake, Señor! here is the black. Mount him for your life! another moment and we should have been discovered! Everybody knows Choolooke, and my life would not have been worth a cent had they caught sight of him. My faith, I like not these surprises! This way, Señor! Around by the church there is an alley un-guarded. They are fighting like ten thousand devils in the plaza. It is madness to go there!"

Ramirez sprang into the saddle with a laugh, though his lips were white and his eyes blazing with rage. It was a new experience to him to be thus caught napping, — his scouts must have played him false. His horse snorted and bounded under him. In another moment he was in the midst of the mêlée, and an electric shock seemed to pass through friends and foes alike. There were wild shrieks at sight of him. The exultant invaders echoed with some dismay the name of Ramirez, the battle-cry with which his followers made an attempt to rally, seizing arms from the hands of their opponents, or using the pis-tols which had remained forgotten in their belts.

For a few moments the plaza appeared to be a veritable battle-ground, though there was far more noise and con-fusion than actual fighting done. Ramirez knew with infinite rage and shame that he would probably be forced to yield the town, rather by strategy than superior num-bers. It would have been an actual pleasure to him at the moment to have seen his followers falling in their blood, rather than flying disarmed, — even though they should rally later and take a terrible revenge upon the enemy. For an instant his presence stemmed the current of retreat, but for an instant only. There had been a secret dissatisfaction in his ranks, which the sight of the well-known face of a popular leader, together with panic, rapidly fermented into a *pronunciamiento;* and even as Ramirez, waving his sword above his head, entered the street of the Orchards, he was saluted with the shout, "Down with Ramirez! Down with the Clergy! Long live Juarez! Long live Gonzales!" and through the dust and smoke he caught sight of Vicente Gonzales, almost unrecognizable under the grime of the hurried march and the heat of excitement and success.

The two were so close together they could have touched each other. One of those hand-to-hand encounters which the history of Mexico proves were not infrequent even at that date seemed inevitable, as they turned toward each other with the fury of personal hatred added to partisan animosity.

But at the moment when the two fiery steeds would have clashed together, a woman threw herself before Ramirez and caught his arm, calling aloud his name. With that wonderful power of the bridle-hand possessed by the horsemen of Mexico, Gonzales drew back his charger and gazed full at his opponent, whom force more potent than a blow seemed to arrest. The crowd surged in; Ramirez's horse was forced back. The woman had fallen in the mêlée; and with a curse upon her the guerilla chieftain was swept onward in the current of retreat.

Chata from the balcony had witnessed this incident in the distance. She shrieked as the woman fell. An officer who was speeding past looked up,— it was Fernando Ruiz. "Coward!" she involuntarily cried, "to leave your General!" She realized how impossible, having lost the first moment of vantage, would be an attempt to control the undisciplined and flying rabble when even the officers had succumbed to panic; and for the first time her sympathies woke for Ramirez.

Yielding to the necessity of the moment the General had put spurs to his horse. The bullets flew past him as he sped over the highway; yet he glanced up as he passed the house,— he even drew rein for an instant in alarmed surprise.

"Go in! go in!" he cried. "What! wilt thou be killed in mere wantoness? Go in, I tell thee! Are *both* to be killed before my eyes to-day?" Chata sprang through the open window in affright, obedient rather to his stern yet imploring gesture than to his words. He glanced back, fired a pistol toward a pair of Liberal soldiers who had rapidly gained upon him, and without the change of a muscle upon his set face, as one of them pitched headlong from his plunging steed, continued his flight and disappeared in the low bushes.

With horror Chata watched the death agony of the wounded soldier. His comrade had not thought it worth while to linger; there might be booty or sport elsewhere. All the church bells were being rung for the victory by this time. The half hour's fight was over; the fort had been taken, the garrison routed, a *pronunciamiento* successful; the town had changed its politics. A few dead men were lying in the streets, a few wounded were bathing or plastering their bleeding heads or limbs; the closed houses were opening again; the street merchants were setting forth their wares; and one of the thousand phases of the revolution had passed.

The next day the Liberal soldiers were lounging about the streets; the boys were shouting, " Long live Gonzales ! " as they went by, as they had shouted before, " Long live Ramirez ! " A tranquil gayety pervaded the place. No one would have known its peace had ever been disturbed.

So lovely was the afternoon, and the distant sounds of the band playing in the plaza were so inspiring, that Doña Rita and her two charges sallied forth to visit the convent. They had often been there before. Rosario thought it dull to wait while her mother chatted at the grating with the soft-voiced nuns, but Chata watched them with awe. There was one whose pale face used to peer out wistfully through the semi-darkness; her voice and her large dark eyes, it seemed to Chata, were always softened by tears. She longed to touch the white hand which she sometimes saw raised to the sensitive lips, as if to check some ill-considered word.

Upon this day some rays of light piercing the barred window of the corridor rendered the features of the nun unusually distinct. A sense of bewilderment stole over Chata as she gazed upon them. Where had she seen them before? Who was this Sister Veronica?

The short time allowed for the interview expired; the attendant nun gave her hand to Doña Rita to kiss in token of dismissal, and turned away. As the Sister Veronica extended her hand in turn, Doña Rita caught it eagerly : " Forgive me ! Forgive me ! Oh, I had thought so ill of you," she said earnestly; " yet to think ill of you seemed to make my own life noble. Forgive me, Señorita Herlinda, that I ever thought you anything but a true and spotless saint ! "

The eyes of the nun opened wide. " Forgive, forgive? I have nothing to forgive ; why should not you — ay, all the world — condemn me ? " she whispered hoarsely. " Oh, Rita, that face ! that face ! "

At that instant the slide was drawn and the white face and eager eyes of the nun disappeared.

Chata turned to look behind her where the nun had apparently directed her gaze. A woman was crouching on the door-sill. She was not old, though over her wonderful Spanish beauty some power of devastation seemed to have swept. She was carelessly but richly dressed, the disorder of her person seemingly according with that of her manner, — perhaps of her intellect; for though evidently a lady by birth, she lay in the sun, her head uncovered, her shawl thrown back from her shoulders, her hair, which was of a peculiar reddish brown, half uncoiled, twining like little serpents around her throat.

She glanced carelessly up as Doña Rita and the young girls passed her. Chata saw with surprise that one side of her face was bruised, and there was a deep scratch on her arm. Where had she seen before the glint of that shining hair? It flashed over her in a moment. This was the woman who had thrown herself upon Ramirez!

Chata involuntarily paused, but Doña Rita caught her hand and drew her away. She had motioned Rosario on before. Her very garments had rustled with disdain as she passed the prostrate woman.

"Such as these one can at least be certain of," she said sententiously. It was not a pleasant thing to own one's self mistaken. Chata detected chagrin in the tone of her voice: was she piqued that she had misjudged Sister Veronica? Then she remembered with a start what the new interest of the moment had driven from her mind, — the name by which her mother had addressed the nun: it was of the Señorita Herlinda that her mother had asked pardon!

A feeling of awe crept over her. She had seen Doña Isabel's beautiful and sainted daughter, around whose name hung so much romance and mystery. And oh the sadness of that face! the wistfulness of those eyes! the appealing agony of that voice!

When they reached the house the door was ajar; there was a mild excitement within. A familiar voice saluted their ears. Doña Rita clutched Chata's arm and whispered, "Not a word, I command thee!" and with a glance of mingled entreaty and menace followed Rosario to greet Don Rafael with exclamations of welcome and delight.

Chata took with icy fingers the hand he extended at sight of her and bent over it with tears and kisses. "My father, my own father!" she whispered. Even had she been at liberty to do so, she would not for the world have broken the spell of those words.

"My patron saint!" cried Don Rafael, regarding her with puzzled fondness, "what has come to the child?" He caught her on his arm and held her from him. Her eyelids lowered, her color rose beneath his gaze. Presently he released her and turned away. He had not kissed her. Had he forgotten? Had some new, deep feeling withheld him? Chata felt cold and faint; he too had muttered under his breath, "That face! that face!" and *he* had spoken those words of *her*.

XXV.

For many days following the unexpected event which closed the feast of Juana's marriage, an old proverb went the rounds of the gossips of Tres Hermanos: "She who would handle the wild-cat should wear steel gloves." Doña Isabel had heard it perhaps, though it was not likely to reach her ears then: and assuredly she had reason to remember it.

Perhaps when Chinita crossed the court and followed Doña Isabel upstairs to her own room, dazzling visions flitted before her of being clasped in the embrace of her patroness, and being called by the name which to her was sovereign. But nothing of the sort occurred. Doña Isabel threw herself into a chair as if exhausted, and bent her face upon her hands, leaving the child standing so long regarding her in silence that at length her impatient spirit rose in rebellion, and she said, "The Señora surely brought me here for something more than to stand like a drowsy hen waiting for morning."

Doña Isabel raised her head at these words, which though impatient did not strike her as impertinent, — she was too well acquainted with the characteristic speech of her inferiors, rich in quaint phrases and figures drawn from familiar objects, — and regarding the girl with that curious mixture of admiration and repulsion which never entirely disappeared, she replied, —

"Thou art a proud child. Humility would better become thee. Hast thou no other name than Chinita, which I hear all call thee?"

"I was baptized like any other Christian," cried Chinita, indignantly. "And as for surname," she added recklessly, "if I am not Garcia, you Señora, will tell me!"

Doña Isabel's lips compressed; no effort of her will could prevent the falling of her eyelids, — an actual fear of the girl seized her; yet she was fascinated. She said

not a word, and presently Chinita began to laugh in a
low, triumphant tone, which was to Doña Isabel like the
mocking of a thousand devils.

"Hush, hush!" she said violently at length. "You
distract, you madden me!"

She caught up a candle, took the girl's hand and drew
her impetuously into the corridor. She tried several doors,
and opened the first that yielded. It was not until they
stood within the room that Doña Isabel knew it was
that (long deserted, half unconsciously avoided) of Herlinda. She started, and clasped her hand over her heart.
Then as if scorning her weakness, pointed to the bed, and
without a word turned from the room.

With a sense of wild exultation Chinita saw she was
to sleep in a bed, like a woman of quality; in the very
bed of the daughter, whose name, like that of a saint,
was spoken with bated breath by the vulgar, and was
perhaps too sacred for utterance by those who had
loved her.

The little structure of brass, with its mattresses and
pillows, its linen and lace, was unpretentious enough, but
Chinita walked around it and eyed it almost in awe, as if
it had been the throne of a princess. The candle was beginning to flicker in its socket when she at last lay down,
adjusting her head to the unaccustomed pressure of the
pillows with some difficulty, saying to herself with an
impatient smile, "What a poor creature I am! Even
the things I have longed for hurt more than please me to
learn to use. But there must be still greater things to
conform to, and I shall do it. Oh, yes, Sanchita thought
she could ride in a coach, and be taken for a lady as well as
another; and I who was born a lady must forget I have
been ever a Sanchita. It should not be hard!"

Chinita had slept far better upon the preceding night
upon a sheepskin. Her excitement and the unusual comfort
of the bed kept her wakeful; and at early dawn she was
up, peeping into the wardrobe, where long-disused dresses
and other garments were hanging. She took down one of
bright silk and put it on, and thought how exactly it fitted
her. She could scarcely see herself in the dim mirror, and
she went to the door to open it for the admission of more
light, and with a momentary fright found herself a prisoner.

She decided in a moment that Doña Isabel had no intention of detaining her beyond the sleeping hours, yet a feverish impulse seized her to escape at once. That any one should hold her at a moment's disadvantage was intolerable to her. Without thinking of the dress she had on, she glanced around her eagerly for means of egress. The window was barred, but there was a door that opened into an adjoining chamber, into which she passed hastily, finding the door that opened on the corridor actually ajar. As her way was open, she was in no hurry to depart, but stood balancing herself on one foot, holding by one hand to the door-post, and with the other pushing back her hair that she might see clearly into the court.

Not a creature was astir; the very bird that was in a cage hanging near her stood silently on his perch, with his head on one side, gazing through the bars as if in pensive wonderment at the silence.

Chinita had a feeling that the world had been transformed with her; she was half terrified, yet amused, and longed for some one to speak to. Could she speak the old words, the accustomed sounds? Was she indeed Chinita and not another? Had Rosario or Chata been under the same roof, she would have been tempted to run to them at once with the query; but there was no one who would know what she meant if she put such a question to them. They would only laugh and stare and pass on. Ah, there was one who could not pass on! At a bound she was on the stairs, and in a minute stood at the door of the stranger's room. It was open; he liked the air. Early as it was, Selsa had left him; so without let or hindrance Chinita seated herself at the foot of the bed, and with expressive pantomime began to inquire into the state of the wounded shoulder.

The young man looked at her in amaze. This was the strangest of the strange visitors he had had. At first he did not recognize her in the incongruous dress; but a glance at the elfin face and the mop of curls recalled to his mind the name Chinita, and he held out his hand with a gesture of welcome and surprise, and even found words in his meagre stock of Spanish to ask her where she had been.

"I have been in my home," she answered with a great show of dignity. "Do you not see, I am a lady, a grand lady?"

She had risen and spread out the silken dress with her hands. The young man caught one of the locks of her hair, and pulled it teasingly, "*No comprendo*, I don't understand. Tell me where is your mother? Where is your *padre?*"

Such a mixture of languages should have been unintelligible, but Chinita understood very well, and with a sudden prompting of the spirit of mischief which was never far from her, replied, "*Padre mio muerto! Americano guero, como Ud.! Oh, si Americano!*"

"What!" cried the young man in English, "Your father dead! An American? Fair like me?" He had clutched the lock of hair so tightly, as he rose in his bed in his excitement, that her head was quite near him. "Are you quite sure? Can it be possible?" adding, with sudden remembrance that intelligent though she was it was impossible she should understand his foreign tongue, and angry as he saw her at his vehemence, it was unlikely she should care to divine his meaning, "*Niña bonita*, pretty child, pardon me! Your father an *Americano?* Well, that is wonderful! I *Americano*, — I, Ashley Ward. *Pardona mi!*"

Chinita was not to be at once appeased; but she saw with inward delight that he was much impressed by her claim jestingly set forth to American parentage, and there was something in the sound of his name that recalled to her mind the man who had been murdered so many years ago. She began with a thousand gestures, which made somewhat intelligible her voluble Spanish, to give an account of him. The young man listened with intense excitement, anathematizing his ignorance of the language in which she spoke, yet convinced that chance had led him to the very spot which he had had it in his mind to seek. In the interest of her narration, Chinita forgot the assertion she had made; but her listener more than once supposed that she alluded to it, and looked intently upon her face to catch a glimpse of some expression that should remind him even of the race to which the man of whom she spoke had belonged. But there was nothing. The features, expression, color, were those of a Mexican of mixed Spanish and Indian types, with nothing individual other than a weird beauty and vivacity, and the peculiar hair which had suggested the name that even Doña Isabel did not seek to disassociate from her. For at the moment when the interest of her narrative was at its height, and Ashley Ward had risen on his pillows and was following her every gesture with mute and rapt attention, the lady of the mansion entered, calling breathlessly, "Chinita! Chinita!" suddenly arresting her steps, as she caught the concluding words: "And so he was killed! And they say it was not a man, but the Devil who did it. But for my part I don't believe it, for the ghost of the American can be seen under the tree or at the old reduction-works any night; and it's not likely Señor Satan would give so much liberty to a soul he seemed so anxious to get."

Chinita had finished her sentence with a certain defiance, for she felt guilty before Doña Isabel, — not so much for being found in the room of the wounded guest, as because of her borrowed attire. But Doña Isabel did not seem to notice that. "Thou art wrong to come here," she said; "thou art wrong to talk like a scullery-maid of things thou dost not understand. What did I hear thee say of an American as I came in?"

"Did I say American?" retorted Chinita with a laugh at the thought of the jest she had made, for the idea of falsehood did not occur to her. "Ah, yes! I told him the American was my father! He would have believed me even had I said Señor San Gabriel. Oh, it is a grand diversion to see his eyes open with wonder! Selsa says he is dumb and deaf and understands nothing, but there is not a word I say that he does not understand quickly enough; and he knows—" But she ceased suddenly, for Doña Isabel was deadly white. She had turned to the American almost fiercely, and demanded hoarsely, "What has this child told you? What tale has she poured into your ears, wild, improbable, — the dreams of a child, filled with the superstitious tales of the common people? What have you heard? What have you believed?"

Ashley Ward looked at her in some surprise at her

vehemence. Her gestures did not translate to him the
purport of words which had not even a familiar sound.
After a moment he shook his head, and said slowly : " *No
comprendo !* I do not understand Spanish."

Doña Isabel breathed freely ; her rigid face relaxed ;
she almost smiled. " Foolish child," she said to Chinita ;
" he does not understand our language. Come, thou
shalt have chocolate with me. I am not angry, though
thou art a runaway."

Chinita seldom afterward found Doña Isabel so gracious when she had committed a fault ; but she discovered
at night, when she was left in her room alone, that that
particular escapade was not to be repeated. The door
which led to the adjoining room was locked, as well as that
which opened upon the corridor. She shook the bars of
the window in impotent rage. She opened her mouth to
scream, to wake the echoes with the name of Pedro, but
at a second thought refrained, and went and lay quietly
down like a baffled animal reserving its strength for the
time when its prey should be near. She did not sleep.
She had done nothing to tire her, and also she had
dropped into slumber more than once during the day in
the silence of Doña Isabel's room, where she had sat
watching her, as she opened drawers and boxes, and as if
by stealth moved various articles to a large trunk, turning
from it with affected carelessness when Doña Feliz or any
servant entered.

Chinita was living over again in her mind the long monotonous day, feeling as if a thunder-clap or some con-
vulsion of Nature must break upon the feverish stillness,
when she heard a tap at her window. The sash was
already raised, but she sprang noiselessly from the bed
and across the floor, and thrust her hand through the bars,
for she divined that Pedro had called her.

" It is but for a moment, *niña*," he whispered, almost
humbly, as he kissed her hand. " But tell me, art thou
happy ; art thou content ? "

" Why should I not be happy ? " she asked. " I have
worn a silk gown all day long, and have eaten and drunk
things so dainty a humming-bird might sip them ; and
Doña Isabel has dared not say no to me, — though she
does not love me, Pedro, and I love not her."

"Then thou wilt come again to poor Pedro, who does love thee?" queried the gatekeeper in a tremulous and doubting voice.

She withdrew her hand, tossing her head scornfully. "No," she said. "You know how the black cat strayed once into the hut, and though Florencia drove him away, and would strike and frighten him if he stole as much as a morsel of dried beef, he would come back and curl himself under the bench, and lie there upon the cold floor, though he might have gone to the granaries and had his fill of fat mice, and plenty of straw to lie on. Well, Pedro, I am the black cat, and I will stay in Doña Isabel's house because it is my humor, and I cannot tell why, and there is an end of it."

Pedro sighed; but presently he said in his slow way, "Well, well! God is God, — may he care for thee! Pedro can be of no more use to thee; the guitar that does n't accord with the voice is best hung upon the wall. Farewell, Chinita; God grant thee so much good that thou needst not remember thy old friends."

Chinita laughed. "Thou art vexed, Pedro; but I love thee, and I would love thee more if thou wouldst tell me the name of my father or my mother." Pedro shook his head. "Oh, I am sure thou dost not know; thou couldst not have kept a secret all these years!" She looked at him sharply, but he was not the man to begin unwary defences, which might to a keen eye expose the weakest spots in his armor. He stood for some moments quite silent. Chinita saw by the moonlight that his face had lines upon it she had never seen before. Her conscience smote her, yet she could not say she was sorry for the fate which had parted them, — for it did not occur to her any more than to him that he might question the act of Doña Isabel, and refuse to yield the child he had sheltered from its birth.

"What secret should the tool have?" he asked at length bitterly. "It is taken up and laid by as the master wills. Years ago I used to think I was a man, but since then I have been but a dog to watch and to guard; but the watch is over, and the dog may be a man again. That would please you, would it not? There is better work than to sit at a gate and see the soldiers come and go, and never hear so much as the echo of a shot; or as much as know why there is a smell of blood always in the air, and men are dragged away to death. Gonzales told me the struggle is for liberty; I can do no more for you, and I will go and see. Who knows what I may find beyond there? Who knows what news I may bring to you?"

The face usually so stoical in its expression was lighted as if by an inward fire. For the first time Chinita knew that this man too had his ambitions, the stronger that they had been repressed for years. Would he join the next band of soldiers or bandits that came that way? The thought struck her comically, like a touch of the mock heroic; yet it thrilled her. She would have liked to be a soldier herself. She would have chosen to be a boy to go with him; and yet she was glad they were to part, if that indeed was his meaning, — that her foster father would no longer sit at the gate.

He had touched her hand and bent to kiss it humbly, as he might have saluted Doña Isabel herself. Then he thrust a long narrow package through the bars, muttered softly, "*Adios*," and stole noiselessly away.

Though Chinita saw him at his old place on the morrow, she understood that an eternal farewell had been made to their old relations and their old life. All that remained of them was contained in the package of trinkets he had brought her, — the coral beads, the few irregular pearls. the many-hued reboso, and the ribbons she had prized and which in his simplicity he had thought she would regret. Indeed, she had recognized them with a thrill of delight; nothing half so bright or costly had been offered her in the new life she had imagined would be so rich and brilliant. Yet she clung to it as hers of right, the more firmly after turning over and over, again and again, the dainty swaddling clothes, which she had never seen before, but which she knew Pedro had yielded to her as the sole possessions with which she had come to him, — possessions useless in themselves, but invaluable to her as proofs that she came from no plebeian stock. She wondered if her mother had arrayed her in them to cast her out, — and though she was of no gentle mould, her mind revolted from the thought. Then, had her father disowned her; or had an enemy filched her from her cradle, and unwilling to be guilty of her blood, left her in the first hands he had encountered? She ran over in her mind all the tales she had heard of mysterious disappearances, — and they were not a few, — but none would fit the case; and surely a hue-and-cry would have been made at the abduction of a rich man's infant.

Chinita wrapped up the clothes and hid them away in impatient despair. Once she thought of taking them to Doña Isabel; but what would be gained by that? That her protectress knew the secret of her birth she was convinced, not by any course of reasoning, but by the simple fact that she had assumed the charge of her as her right. The girl did not know how baseless are apt to be the caprices of a great lady.

The days passed wearily to the eager child. They would have been intolerable — for she was always alone or with Doña Isabel, who gave her no certain status as equal or inferior, and with whom she was feverishly defiant, or seized with sudden tremors of awe or actual fear — but that she knew Don Rafael had gone to bring his family home. She longed to pour her secret thoughts into the ears of Chata, to show the infant clothes and hear her comments and suggestions. It appeared to her that Chata would certainly penetrate the gloom, and in her sweet simplicity throw some light upon the mystery which enveloped her. Besides, the wilful girl exulted in the anticipation of dazzling the eyes of Rosario and Doña Rita by her connection with Doña Isabel. She was shrewd enough to see it had greatly increased her importance in the estimation of the servants and employees. Even Don Rafael, before he went away, had seized an opportunity to ask her whether she was content, and afterward had never failed to bow to her with grave politeness when they met.

Once a strange thought had been set in the child's mind: it returned and vexed her again and again. Doña Feliz had come into the room when in an unusual mood of devotion Chinita had knelt to pray before the image of the Virgin, before which, though she did not know it, had been poured forth so many bitter cries. Feliz started as she saw her, and Chinita rose to her feet.

"Do not rise," said Doña Feliz; "learn, child, to pray.

Many amens must perforce reach Heaven; it is well to begin thy task young."

"What task?" Chinita queried. "I shall have something more to do than to pray all my life. That is for saints and nuns; and even Pedro would not take me for a saint."

"But thou couldst still be a nun," said Doña Feliz, with a peculiar smile; "and why shouldst thou not be?"

"Why not?" ejaculated Chinita. "Because I will not!" Then seized with a sudden terror, she cried, "Is that why Doña Isabel has taken me from Pedro? Is it to shut me up to pray for her and the wicked brother she loved so much? Selsa told me she had set her own daughter to free his soul from purgatory, and is not that enough? I'll not do it. My knees ache when I kneel; I yawn, I fall asleep. I cannot bear to be forever in one place. It is to go away, to see strange sights, to wear silk and lace every day, as the *niña* Herlinda must have done, — see, here are some of her dresses still, — it is for this, and because I was born for such things, that I stay with Doña Isabel; it is not to pray. I care not to pray, nor sing hymns, nor dress saints. I will go to her and tell her so!"

Doña Feliz caught the arm of the excited child. "I am your friend," she said. "Speak not a word of what I have said. Perhaps it was a foolish thought; but many more beautiful than you have entered convents, and perhaps have been happy."

"Is the Señorita Herlinda happy?" asked Chinita, her excitement calmed by the thought of another. "Selsa told me once, — it was the night Antonita saw the ghost of the American, when she came back from the mountain, — Selsa told me a witch had laid a spell upon her the day he was murdered, — a witch who loved the foreigner; and that the *niña* Herlinda drooped and withered and would have died, but that a fever carried away the evil woman before she could read her into her grave."

"The witch!" ejaculated Doña Feliz, mystified. This was a superstition of which she had heard nothing. "Who was the witch?"

"How can I tell?" answered Chinita. "Chata knows more of her than I. It is to her old Selsa told her tales; she is never cross to Chata. But after the American was killed I know the witch used to read and read and read

15

strange words to the poor *niña*, and she grew paler and paler, and more and more sad."

"And the witch died?" queried Feliz, thinking of Mademoiselle La Croix.

"Yes, in a good hour," answered Chinita, energetically. "But I forgot; you must know it all, Doña Feliz. Tell me," — with her old gossiping habit, — "tell me, did the Señorita love the American? Was it for him she pined away; or because she was bewitched; or was it because the Señora would not let her marry the Señor Gonzales, but would send her to the convent to pray for the wicked Don Leon?"

"*Quien sabe?* Who knows?" answered Doña Feliz, in the non-committal phrase a Mexican finds so convenient. "It is not for us to chatter of the Señorita Herlinda. Peace be with her! and have a care how you mention her name to Doña Isabel." Her brow contracted as she thought how many conjectures, how much gossip of which she had known nothing, had been busy with events she had believed quite passed from remembrance.

XXVI.

ASHLEY WARD had been, an involuntary though perhaps not entirely an unwilling guest, at Tres Hermanos a month or more before it dawned upon him that he was not a perfectly welcome one. Throughout his illness, which had been prolonged by the peculiar nursing and diet to which he had been for the first time in his life subjected, he had, though left almost entirely to the care of Selsa, been provided with luxuries and delicacies that even his imperfect knowledge of the country and situation enabled him to know were rare and costly, and most difficult to obtain. Doña Isabel Garcia was like a princess in her quiet dignity and in her gifts; and like a princess too, he grew to think, in the punctiliousness with which, every day, she sent to inquire after his health, and the infrequency with which she entered to express a hope that he lacked nothing. She never touched his hand, seldom indeed turned her eyes upon him when she spoke, and never smiled; and when she left him he inwardly raged, and vowed he would leave the hacienda on the morrow, even though he should die from the exertion. But his wound was slow in healing; the fever had sapped his strength; he was alone, and no opportunity of securing escort presented itself. He was virtually a prisoner. And besides, after these periods of vexation he would fall into a fit of musing, which would end in the resolve never to leave Tres Hermanos until certain doubts were set at rest, which from day to day grew more and more perplexing.

The nurse, Selsa, was more communicative than the Indian peasant woman is apt to be. She had been employed constantly in and about the great house in positions of some trust, and had lost that awe of superiors, which held the mere common people dumb. In a sense, indeed, she felt herself one of the family, privileged to use gentle insistence with the sick, even against their aristocratic wills, and to be present, though eyes and ears were to be as blind

and deaf as the walls around her, while matters of family
polity were at least hinted at, if not openly discussed. She
had in fact been to the house of Garcia "the confidential
servant," without which no Mexican household is complete, — one of those peculiar beings who however false,
cruel, deceitful, and thievish with the world in general is
silent as the grave, devoted even unto death, true as the
lode-star, to the person or family which she serves.

There was something in the personality of this wrinkled
crone, growing out of these relations, which early impressed
the young American; and gradually he grew to feel that
he was face to face with an oracle, had he but the magic
to unseal her lips, as the witch-like Chinita had had to
change her air of vexed though friendly equality into unobtrusive yet unmistakable deference. Other servants who
came and went spoke with some envy and spite of the sudden elevation of the gatekeeper's foster-child. But Selsa,
sitting in the doorway of the sick man's room, combing
out her long black locks, — for that, though she never succeeded in smoothing them, was her favorite occupation, —
would glance askance at Ward and say, —

"Be silent! the Señora knows what she does. Go
now ! she has a heart like any other Christian. What was
to become of the girl, now that Pedro will be leaving for
the wars? Would you have Don 'Guardo think we are
barbarians here, who would leave the innocents to be devoured like lambs by the coyotes?"

Don 'Guardo was the name Selsa had evolved from
Ward, which she had perhaps believed to be the foreign
contraction of Eduardo; and as Ashley, with boyish enthusiasm easily acquiring the limited vocabulary of those
around him, began to relieve the monotony of his convalescence by listening to their conversations, and asking some
idle questions, he found himself answering to the convenient appellation and alluding to himself by it, until it became as familiar to his ears as his own baptismal name,
and certainly conveyed far more friendliness to him than
the formal Señor Ward, which Don Rafael and his mother
rendered with infinite stumbling over the unattainable W.

There was a subdued excitement throughout the hacienda
upon the day that Don 'Guardo first appeared at the great
gateway. Pedro was sitting there in the dull, dejected

manner suggestive of loss, or waiting, or both ; and it was only when Florencia, with an exclamation, twitched his sleeve that he looked up.

"*Maria Sanctissima!*" he stammered, staggering to his feet. Ashley stood in the dim light in the rear of the deep vestibule, with his hand on Pepé's shoulder, — for the boy had been called to attend him, — but with a sudden faintness he had paused to rest against the stone wall hung with serpents. Ashley was a handsome youth, but in Pedro's eyes a thousand times more startling than the most hideous snake or savage beast. So had he seen John Ashley stand a hundred times or more, not pale and trembling, but full of life and joy. Was this his sad ghost, come with reproachful eyes to haunt him?

"It is the Señor American," said Florencia. "My life ! how pale he looks ! Go, go, Pepito ! bring him hither before the carriage of my Señora drives in ; here it is at the very gate."

Pedro instantly recovered his usual stoicism. "Wait, Señor !" he said, "you are well placed where you are. The carriage can pass and not throw an atom of dust on you." And at that moment the feet of the horses and the rattle of wheels were heard on the stone paving, and the hacienda carriage was driven rapidly into the courtyard. As it passed, Ashley caught a glimpse of Doña Isabel — how pale and statuesque ! — and beside her a creature radiant in triumph, who nodded to Pedro as she passed ; her smile seeming to say, " Behold me ! " Hers was not an ignoble pride, but the wild exultation of an eaglet that had been chained to earth, and for the first time had tried its wings in the empyrean. That morning Doña Isabel had said, "Chinita, thou shalt go with me ;" and though the lady's brows had risen a little when with unconscious audacity the girl had taken the seat beside her, and not that opposite, where Doña Feliz was wont to sit, she said nothing. "The child is pale," she thought, "and needs the air ; there is no one to heed that she sits beside me."

It would be hard to tell what were the thoughts of Chinita ; they were a sudden delirium after the intense quiet of the semi-imprisonment, which she had borne with stoical fortitude for the sake of a dimly seen future of power. In this enforced quiet, day by day, her ambitions were shaping themselves; the dominant passion of her being was seeking a point from which she might have advantage over all the narrow field within the range of her mental vision. As yet her aspirations knew no name; they were mere vague, impatient longings, or rather impatient spurning of the old ignoble conditions of life. To ride in a carriage was an intoxication to her, because the low-born peasant went afoot. She chafed in a very thraldom of inaction because the high-born toiled not. She loved the rustle of a gaudy silk, while her hand shrank from the contact of the stiff and rustling fabric, because such attire was only for the rich and great. As undefined as had been the joy with which she had heard she was a Garcia, was still the delight of each fresh conquest that she made. No eager *virtuoso* groping in the dark among undescribed treasures could be more ignorant yet more wildly anticipative of the glories the daylight should discover than she of what the future should reveal.

From where Don 'Guardo and his attendant stood, they could see Doña Isabel and Chinita as they descended from the carriage. Doña Isabel, without glancing around, ascended the stairs to her own apartment. Chinita followed a step or two behind, then turned and paused. Her quick eye scanned the little group that had gathered in the court. Ashley Ward himself was startled by the change that had passed over her since he had seen her last. What had been elfish in her wild abandonment of bearing had become a subtle grace of manner, which gave piquancy to a hauteur that counterfeited the dignity of inherent nobleness. "The gypsy has borrowed the air of a queen!" was the thought of the American. He felt Pepé quiver beneath his hand, and looking at him saw a sullen fire in his dark, slumberous eyes, though his lips were white and his dusky face ashen as if a chill had seized him. The girl had overlooked him and all the plebeian crowd, and her eyes rested in a triumphant challenge on Ashley. She smiled, and a ray of sunlight darted down and reddened the crisp and straggling tendrils of her hair. The smile or the sunlight dazzled him; he leaned heavier on Pepé's shoulder. She reminded him of a Medusa idealized, of incarnate passion surrounded by the halo of radiant youth.

Ashley was roused by a sudden movement of Pepé, who had for the moment forgotten his station, and impetuously thrown himself upon a bench in an attitude of impotent grief and rage; then he sprang to his feet, and again placed his shoulder under Ashley's hand. Once more he was the mere stock and stick; but Ashley had discovered in him the soul and heart of a man.

"Poor fool!" he thought, with a sort of anger mingled with his pity; "here is a touch of the tragic in this little comedy, which the wily little peasant is inspired to play so daintily. She appears to have bewitched me with the rest; I can't keep the thought of her, or rather of her words, out of my head, — and yet I have only a word to build a whole fabric of theory upon."

These thoughts had passed through his mind in an instant, — the instant in which Chinita had lightly run up the stone steps after Doña Isabel, and in which Ashley and Pepé had reached the broad gateway of the hacienda. Ashley sank upon the stone bench where Pedro was wont to sit, and Pepé leaned sullenly against the rough wall. Both looked in silence over the village, across the fields, the narrow line of cottonwood trees and yellow mud which marked the bed of a torrent in the rainy season and a waste of desolation in the long drought, and onward still to the gray and barren mountains whose distant peaks of purple pierced the deep blue of the cloudless sky. The scene to Pepé was as old as his years, too familiar to distract for a moment his tortured mind; but Ashley beheld it in a sort of rapture. Perhaps any glimpse of the outer world would have charmed him after his unwonted imprisonment; but the fertility of the valley, this gem set in the broad expanse of bare and sterile Mexico, was a revelation to him of that wonderful productiveness and beauty which in his journeyings he had often heard of but had never encountered, until at last he had believed that the horrors of war, in its years of duration, had swept over the land and blasted it. But here was one spot at least that had escaped, — such a spot as he had pictured for months, and sought in vain.

For a time he gazed upon it in simple admiration, then at first almost unconsciously began to look about him for certain landmarks. Yes, here at his back was the great

pile of buildings; here on the sandy slope in front, the
village of adobe thatched with knife-grass; there along
the line of the watercourse, the few straggling huts of the
miners and laborers; there away to the right, the low walls
of the reduction-works with its tall brick chimney, and in
its rear the gaping cleft of the mountain which marked the
entrance to the mine. All now was silent and deserted;
yet for a moment he seemed to look upon it with other
eyes, and to see the trains of laden mules filing in and out
of the wide gateways, and to trace the black smoke rising
in a column to the cloudless sky. "This must be the
place!" he inwardly exclaimed; and drawing from his
breast-pocket a flat case of papers, he selected from them
a torn and yellow letter, and read it slowly over, ever and
anon raising his eyes to identify some point in the description, which a hand as young, more firm, more resolute than his own, had in an hour of leisure so accurately
written years before. The date of the missive was gone,
and with it the name of this new place in which the writer
seemed to have found an earthly paradise, — "not wanting," as he said at the close of the letter, "an Eve to be at
once the gem of this perfect setting, and the inaccessible
star to which poor mortals may raise longing eyes, but
may never hope to win."

Ashley smiled as he read the words. Who could this
divinity have been? But for other letters that had been
put into his hands he would have thought the paragraph
mere bathos, boyish gush, and sentiment; but it was a
prelude to what might prove a strange and fateful series
of events. Somewhere here his cousin had years ago lived
and loved and been done to death; and his mission was
to trace the sequence of these events, and to learn
whether or no with John Ashley had passed away all
possible influence upon the fortunes of his own life.

Until within a few months such questions had never
occurred to him. The John Ashley whom he had dimly
remembered had been murdered years before; and so had
ended an adventurous career, which had been his own
choice, or perhaps his evil destiny. To Ward, as to others,
that had been the sum and substance of the tragedy
which had thrown a gloom for a time over all the family,
and had stricken a proud mother to the heart. She had

suffered years in silence, the name of her wayward son
never passing her lips ; her young daughter had grown up
with no knowledge of her brother but his name. It was
she who after the mother's death had found these letters,
and entreated her cousin to seek the fatal spot of John
Ashley's death, — surely there must be somewhere records
that would give the exact location, — and to make inquiries
for the wife, and for the possible child, of whom he wrote in
his last short letter, full of passionate appeal to his mother
in behalf of the young creature who for him had forfeited
the confidence, perhaps the love, of her own. "Herlinda!
Herlinda! Herlinda!" was the burden of the letter. "The
name rings in my ears," Mary Ashley had said. "How
could my mother have been deaf to it? She thought
of those people as barbarous, false, cruel, treacherous.
But what matters that to me, if there is among them one
who has my brother's blood, or one who loved him?"

"The marriage laws of those countries are strange,"
Ward had ventured to say. "Perhaps your mother
feared complications which could but bring disgrace and
misery."

"I do not fear them," said Mary Ashley, proudly. "It
is a wild country for a woman to go to, but if you will not
investigate this matter, I will brave any inconvenience,
any danger, to do so. I cannot live with this tantalizing
fear in my heart."

The idea that tormented Mary seemed at best that of a
mere possibility to Ashley, — the possibility of an event
which, as the mother had seen, might if proved bring far
more pain than joy, especially at this late date ; yet it
worked upon his mind gradually, as it had upon Mary's
suddenly, — perhaps the more surely because he personally
profited by the supposition that his cousin had died unwed.
By his aunt's will he had been left the share in her property that John would have inherited, on condition that
neither he nor any legitimate heir should appear to claim it.

People shrugged their shoulders and smiled pityingly.
"Poor soul, had she then doubted her son's death?"

The news had reached Mrs. Ashley in an irregular way ;
the war had supervened, and particulars had been few and
far from exact. But later, through some business house,
inquiries had been made and some few books and almost

worthless articles of clothing had been obtained from an alcalde, who swore they had been the dead man's sole effects. Certainly the proofs had been irregular but sufficient. What could one expect from such a lawless set of uncivilized renegades, who knew nothing of civil or international law, and were bent on the sole task of exterminating one another? They smiled at the condition in the will, and pitied the poor woman who could thus hope against hope. Ashley Ward himself, the orphan nephew whom his aunt had loved with a jealous devotion, which at times wearied him by its suspicions and exactions, at first smiled also. But when Mary brought to him the fragments of three old letters to read, just as his mind was filled with plans for a career which the possession of ample wealth and leisure seemed to justify, and which in poverty he could never have dared aspire to, he grew thoughtful, moody at times, — then suddenly his own impetuous, generous self again.

"I will go to Mexico, Mary," he said, "and bring you word of your brother's life there. No doubts shall shake their spectre fingers at me in my prosperity, nor torment your loving and anxious soul."

"Good, true cousin!" was all she answered. She perhaps did not realize what effect upon the prospects of Ashley the results of this journey might possibly have; they dawned upon her little by little as the days went by and no news came of him.

The daring traveller had been obliged to enter Mexico at some obscure point. The Liberal government under Juarez was installed at Vera Cruz; the Conservatives held the City of Mexico; and the length and breadth of the country was in a state of riot and ferment, torn and devastated by roving bands who changed their politics as readily as their encampments. Ashley's journey through the Republic was like a passage over smouldering coals between two fires, and constant address and fearlessness were required to avoid collision with either faction, — his ignorance of the language and causes of contention perhaps serving him a good turn in making natural the indifference and absolute impartiality which he could never so successfully have assumed had his sympathies been ever so slightly biassed.

In the distracted state of the country it was almost a hopeless task to endeavor to trace the movements of an alien who had lived in it but a short time, and that years before. If any record had been made of the exact place and mode of John Ashley's death, it certainly had been unofficial, and retained no place in the archives of either the Mexican or American government.

Ashley Ward was at first appalled by the unexpected difficulties that he encountered. Inquiries brought to his knowledge the existence of several haciendas bearing the name of Los Tres Hermanos ; and these he successively visited, reserving to the last that which lay in the most isolated and mountain-begirt district, — a point which it seemed impossible could, amid wild and sterile surroundings, offer the panorama of beauty and fertility which the pen of his cousin had described. He would perhaps have abandoned his search, at least for that unpropitious time, but for a re-perusal of the first letter which contained neither news nor descriptions of importance, but in which was mentioned the fact that the writer had been offered employment by the family of Garcia. The owners of the distant hacienda of Tres Hermanos, Ashley Ward discovered, were called Garcia, — a name too common, however, to be any proof of identity, yet which seemed to make it worth his while to spend another month or more of precious time in the search, which in another country, with records of average exactness, would perhaps have been performed in one or two days.

The trip had been made as quickly as the excessively bad state of the roads at the rainy season would allow, and with but few divergences and delays ; and the boundaries of the estate had been already passed when the young American and his servant were, in a merry rather than a savage humor, detained or rather actually captured by the redoubtable Calvo, who to amuse the leisure that hung rather heavily upon his hands invited the young American to ride in his company. In his broken but expressive English, the freebooter uttered such courteous phrases that the young man was quite unconscious that he was in fact a prisoner, and passed a not uninteresting day in exchanging political opinions, local and international, with the dashing chieftain, — who, while apparently absorbed

in the novelty and pleasure of listening to the conversation of his involuntary guest, was mentally preparing the
speech in which he should convey to him on the morrow
the terms of ransom for himself and servant, — a likely
fellow whom Calvo had more than half a mind to add to
the number of his followers.

But the servant himself had no illusions as to the glory
of fighting or the chances of booty, and sometime during
the night in which they were encamped at the *ranchito* of
El Refugio managed to elude the lax watchfulness of
the troop, who had made a merry meal on freshly killed
lambs and such other modest viands as Doña Isabel Garcia's trembling shepherds could furnish, and without so
much as a word of warning to the American had escaped,
— bearing with him the small bag of necessaries of which
he had charge, a pair of silver-mounted pistols, and a sum
of money which Ward had been assured would in case of
attack and capture be more secure in the possession of
this " loyal and honest man " than in his own.

Ashley had barely had time to realize the defection
of his servant, to suspect his actual position as a prisoner in the hands of the courteous but mercenary and
implacable Calvo, and wrathfully to regret the ignorant
trustfulness with which he had divided with the much
lauded servant the risk of transporting his funds, retaining
in his own hands perhaps not enough to meet the rapacious demands of his captors, when suddenly his meditations were interrupted by cries of confusion, shouts, the
crack of rifles, the whizzing of balls, challenges and defiant
yells, the shrieks of women, and the groans and appeals of
the helpless shepherds, — followed by the sight of huts
ablaze, of frightened flocks wildly bleating and rushing
blindly under the very feet of the horses, which trampled
them down, while their keepers, as bewildered as they, fell
victims to the mad zeal and excitement of the opposing
troops who had so unexpectedly met on that isolated
spot.

It was conjectured that the missing servant had in his
flight to the mountains accidentally come upon the soldiers
of the Clergy, and to turn attention from himself had betrayed the proximity of the Liberals. A hurried march in
the early morning hours had proved the truth of the ser-

vant's information; and the surprise and some advantage
in numbers—for the Captain Alva had spoken with a trace
of the usual exaggeration of the speech of his countrymen,
in describing the enemy as numbering three hundred—
turned the chances in favor of the attacking party; although Calvo at first seemed inclined to contest the matter
obstinately, and Ward, with an involuntary feeling of
fealty to his host (though he had already some inkling of
his intentions in regard to himself) had ranged himself
upon his side. He soon saw with indignation, however,
that the defence of the poor villagers held no part in
Calvo's thoughts. To frustrate some movement of the
enemy, he actually ordered the firing of a hut in which
women and children had taken refuge; and it was while
defending the humble spot from Puro and Mocho alike,
that Ward received the wound which disabled him,—
that covered with blows from muskets and swords he
fell, and trampled beneath the feet of the now flying and
pursuing soldiers, for a few horrible moments believed
himself doomed to die in a senseless mêlée, in which his
only interest had been to protect the weak, but in which
he recognized no inherent principle of right. Later he
saw in those apparently senseless broils the throes and
struggles of an undisciplined and purblind nation toward
the attainment of a dimly seen ideal of justice and freedom, and learned the truth that these people, who seemed
so lightly swayed by the mere love of adventure, held
within their breasts the divine spark that distinguishes
man from the brute,—the deathless fire of patriotism.
They too could suffer, bear imprisonment, famine, even
death, for freedom.

But these were none of Ashley Ward's reflections as he
found himself laid apart from three or four dead men, who
had been hurriedly thrown together for burial, and after
being subjected to a hasty examination—which resulted
in the abstraction of his remaining funds, his watch and
other valuables, and the binding up of his wound—lifted
to the back of a raw-boned troop-horse, and forced to join
the march of the triumphant guerillas. He would have
preferred to be left to the care of the houseless and destitute shepherds; but Captain Alva, whether with the hope
of some ultimate benefit from the capture of the foreigner

or not it is impossible to tell, professed himself horrified at
the barbarity of deserting him, — and, as we have seen
later, in apprehension of his death from exposure to the
sun, and the fever that seized him, availed himself of
the opportunity of evading the responsibility of the death
of an American upon his hands, by delivering him to the
care of Doña Isabel Garcia.

And so, still weak, and destitute of money until he
could arrange for a supply from the City of Mexico, but
full of hope, confident that he had reached his goal, and
that a few discreet inquiries would give him the information he sought, and perhaps allay forever the doubts that
tormented his sensitive conscience, Ashley Ward drew a
deep breath of satisfaction as he sat at the hacienda gate;
and in an animated mood, which supplemented his insufficient Spanish, addressed himself to the reticent and
gloomy Pedro, startling him from his usual stoicism by
the exclamation, "And you, my man, can you tell me of
the American your foster-child spoke of? There is not so
much happens here that you can have forgotten."

Had Ashley known anything of the instincts and customs of the genuine ranchero, he would have begun his
investigations in a far more guarded manner. That a certain Don Juan had met a bloody death there years before,
he already knew; that this had been his cousin, he surmised; that the gatekeeper should know more of the domestic life of an employee of the hacienda than the owner
herself, or even the administrador, was a natural conclusion. But had Ashley Ward wished to seal the lips of the
suspicious and astute gatekeeper, he could not have chosen a more effective manner of accomplishing it. As well
touch the horns of a snail and expect that it would not
withdraw into its shell, as to question this man directly
and hope to learn aught of value.

Pedro looked at the inquirer from under the shadow of
his bushy eyebrows and wide hat; and though his heart
bounded, his face became a very mask of rustic stupidity as he answered, "Your grace has had much fever with
your wound. Heaven and all the saints be thanked that
you are young and healthy, and will soon be as strong as
ever."

"Um!" ejaculated Ward, for the moment disconcerted.

"Yes, I have had fever, but that has nothing to do with the American. He was a living man fourteen or fifteen years ago, if there be any truth in what your — young mistress told me." He hesitated how to designate the girl, whose status and relations seemed so strangely undefined.

Pedro's eyes for a moment lightened. Pepé laughed ironically, yet he would have turned like a wild beast on another who had done so.

"Who speaks much, speaks to his undoing," quoth Pedro, gruffly, and turned away; yet he eyed the young American furtively, with an inborn hostility to his race, an unreasoning belief that in the guise of such fair tempters lurked the demon who would destroy unwary damsels body and soul, yet with an almost irresistible desire to unburden his soul of the weight that had so long oppressed it, to cry aloud, "I can tell you all you would know, — how the American lived, how he died, how the child he never saw lives after him. Is it her you seek? And why?"

Pedro clenched his hands with a gasp. He remembered that the natural instincts of kindred had changed to bitterness against Herlinda's child. She had been cast out, disowned, deserted. Who was this stranger, this foreigner, that he should be more just, more generous, toward the doubtful offspring of one who had died years before? How should he even guess such a child to be in existence? No, he could not guess it. What a mad thought had darted through his own brain! Pedro actually laughed at his own perplexed imaginings. What! the secret of Herlinda, which had been kept so inscrutably, in danger from this idle news-seeker? Preposterous! yet an odd conceit entered the gatekeeper's mind: "The blind man dreamed that he saw, and dreamed what he desired." This groping youth had come far to inquire into the fate of a man long dead, — it must be because it would bring him profit, for it did not for a moment occur to Pedro that the questions asked were from mere idle curiosity, — and would it be possible anything should escape him? "Well, what God wills, the saints themselves cannot hinder."

Pedro sat down upon the stone bench opposite, in an

affectation of sullen obstinacy. Ashley was weary and chagrined, and in silence looked over the landscape with an increasing sense of recognition. Pepé stood in the same lounging attitude, patiently waiting. One might have thought him carved of wood against the stone wall, yet of the three men he it was whose passions were fiercest, whose thoughts like unbridled coursers followed one another in mad confusion. His mind was full of Chinita! Chinita! Chinita! her beauty, her insolent grace, — the memory of her pretty, haughty ways when she had been but a barefoot, ragged peasant like himself, and the contemplation of the hopeless height to which she had risen. Never before had he been conscious that he had aspired. Now, bruised, torn, wounded as if by a fall into hopeless depths, he saw her image swimming before his disordered vision; he thought of her as a princess, a goddess, yet he laughed when he heard her named as mistress.

Such was the mood in which Pepé presently listened to the disconnected dialogue between Pedro and the guest, who was hampered by a language strange to him, and by suspicious caution on the part of the gatekeeper. For the first time in his life, Pepé was struck by a peculiarity in Pedro with which he had always been acquainted; namely, his unwillingness to speak of the tragedy, which to other minds had seemed no more horrible than scores of others that had occurred in the neighborhood and were common subjects of conversation. As he listened, Pepé became conscious that Pedro was detracting from the interest of the tale rather than adding to it; and when the young American at last said inquiringly, "And the cause of this murder was never known? There was no woman — " he was startled that Pedro answered not with the old jest, "Was there ever an evil but that a woman was at the root of it?" but rose and strode rapidly away.

"There *was* a woman," muttered Ward, looking after him, "and the gatekeeper knew her. I have found the man who can tell me of Herlinda."

He spoke in English, but Pepé the eager listener caught the name "Herlinda." Five minutes later, when Ward turned to speak to the youth, he found him with his hands clasped, stretched out before him, his eyes staring into vacancy.

"Idiot!" was the half contemptuous, half pitying comment of the American. Little guessed he that the conversation that had seemed to result in so little to him had offered both a suggestion and an inspiration to the peasant, — the very key to the problem which he had himself come so far and dared so much to solve.

16

XXVII

UPON the following day, Ashley Ward went again to the gateway, — not merely to breathe the fresh air and enjoy the view, but irresistibly attracted by the remembrance of the taciturn warder. The more he reflected upon the emotion the man had shown when his eyes first rested upon him, a stranger, as he had entered the vestibule ; the more he thought upon the guarded replies to the questions he had asked concerning the young American who had been there years before, — the more convinced he became that there had been a mystery which had led to his kinsman's death, and that Pedro, if he would, could divulge it.

Was it possible the man himself was the assassin? The perplexed youth began to sound Pepé cautiously as to the reputation Pedro had borne. But the young fellow was absorbed in other matters, of which Ashley rightly conjectured Chinita was the vital point, and was wandering and curt in his answers. Yet he seemed to feel that Ashley divined, if he did not comprehend, his pain, and so attached himself to him and followed him about, much as might a wounded dog some stranger who had spoken to him with an accent of pity in his voice.

So when Ashley went to the gateway, it was Pepé's arm that aided him, though with the impatience of a young man he protested against this need of a crutch, and had actually walked steadily enough across the court, under the gaze of Doña Feliz and Chinita, who happened to be in the window ; but he had been glad to clutch at Pepé as they entered the vestibule. The lad was not trembling then, but erect and flushed : Chinita had smiled upon him as he passed.

Pedro was standing in the gateway, shading his eyes with his hand, and gazing toward the cañon which opened behind the reduction-works. He did not notice Ashley and Pepé, but presently began to mutter: "Yes, it is they. Don Rafael has had a lucky journey. Go thou, Chinita, and tell Doña Feliz the master and her daughter-in-law and children will be here for the noon dinner."

Pepé laughed derisively. "You forget, Pedro," he said; "it is the *niña* Chinita, and the Señorita Chinita now; even if she heard, she is scarce likely to run at your bidding. But are you sure the Señor Administrador comes there? If so, I will myself go and tell them."

"Go then, go!" cried Pedro, impatiently. "I am not blind, though old usage sometimes misleads me, and I talk like a dotard. Yes, yes. There comes the carriage down the cañon, and Don Rafael himself on his gray, and Gabriel and Panchito; I can almost distinguish their very faces."

So could Ashley, for the air was brilliantly clear, and the travellers had yielded to the inspiring influences natural at the sight of home, and allowed their horses to break into a mad pace, far different from the methodic gait of ordinary travel.

Pepé, in spite of repressed excitement, had gone at his usual lounging and listless pace to inform Doña Feliz of the approach of her son, and a little group of villagers had assembled around Pedro, when a lithe, active young figure brushed by them and leaped upon the stone bench at Ashley's side. He glanced up, and to his surprise saw Chinita, her hair flying, her eyes bright with anticipation. Putting her finger upon her lip as he was about to speak, as if to enjoin silence, she pressed herself close to the wall. There was a long narrow niche where she stood, and it received almost her entire figure. No one but Ashley and Pepé, who came with haste behind her, had noticed her.

"Hush! hush!" she whispered. "Chata will look for me here, — here where I used to stand. Ay, Pepé, you were a good lad to warn me in time, so I could slip away. Doña Isabel will never miss me, — she is at her prayers; and Doña Feliz is wild with joy that her son comes home again."

The excited girl had spoken in the softest of voices, yet Pedro heard her. But the rest of the gathering crowd were craning their necks and straining their eyes in the direction in which the approaching travellers were to be seen.

Pepé looked up at the ardent and gypsy-like young creature, as though she were a saint, and Ashley with a glance of genuine admiration and sympathy. He knew not whom she was thus eager to welcome, but it thrilled and surprised him that she should manifest such lively affection. Both the young men instinctively drew near as if to shield her, and stood one on either side, almost hiding her.

"That is right; but you will stand away and let her see me when the carriage drives by," she whispered, placing a hand on Pepé's shoulder. "*Dios mio*, how my heart beats! She will cry with joy when she sees me, with silk skirts and all so fine. And Doña Rita and the *niña* Rosario, — how they will open wide their eyes!" And she broke into a low laugh, which to Ashley's ears was too full of a sort of malicious triumph to be merry.

The time of waiting seemed long; it was indeed far longer than Chinita had counted upon. "They will miss me from the house; they will look for me here!" she whispered again and again in an agony of impatience.

Strangely enough, the adults of the gaping throng, who were intent on watching the approach of the travellers, had not noticed her; but three or four children arrayed themselves in a wondering row, pointing their fingers at her with ejaculations of "Look! look!" but were checked from uttering more by Pepé's warning frowns and Chinita's own imploring gestures.

Ashley was beginning to realize that there must be much that was absurd in the scene. Surely, never was so strange a background made for a group of gossiping peasants as this of the eager-eyed and beautiful girl, leaning from her niche in the massive stone-wall between the two young men — the one the type of aristocratic refinement and delicacy; the other of swarthy, ignorant, half-tamed savagery — who served as caryatids, upon whom she leaned alternately in her excitement, seeming herself to partake of the nature of each.

The carriage with its group of outriders now rapidly approached. "Ah! ah!" exclaimed Chinita, "the horses are plunging at the tree where the American was murdered. They say the creatures can always see him there, Señor.

Ah, now they have passed; they come gayly, they come straight. It is not only the Señor Administrador and the servants, there are strangers too. I am glad! I am happy! I love to see new faces!"

"Be silent!" whispered Pepé, hurriedly; "all the world will hear if you sing so loud. *Carrhi!* the soldier sees you!"

It was true; though the villagers had been too intent upon welcoming the new-comers to heed Chinita, and the carriage flashed by so rapidly the inmates could have caught but a glimpse of color against the cold gray wall, a stranger in a travel-stained uniform started as his eyes fell upon her, and checked his horse so suddenly that it reared.

"The Virgin of our native land!" he muttered in a sort of patriotic and admiring wonder. "Ah, what a beautiful creature!" he added, as the girl he had for a moment classed as a saint sprang from her niche to the bench and thence to the ground, and darted through the crowd to the inner court, — where by this time the carriage had stopped and its inmates were descending.

Ashley sank upon the bench with a sudden access of weariness. Pedro, oblivious of his vicinity, crouched rather than sat beside him. The gatekeeper's nerves doubtless were weak. The carriage that had driven into the court was the same in which Herlinda Garcia had departed years before; as it dashed by him he could have sworn he saw her face framed in the window. He had seen, as had Chinita, the sad and gentle countenance of Chata. Grief reveals strange likenesses.

When Chinita reached the carriage door, she found it blocked by the descending travellers and those who welcomed them. Doña Rita was so slow in carefully placing her feet from step to step, and paused so often to answer salutations, that there was ample time for the young officer to reach the spot and extend a hand to Rosario who followed her. Her blushes and coy smiles; the air with which she drew back and with which, with a little shriek, she pulled her dress over her tiny foot lest it might be seen; the soft glances which she threw from beneath her long lashes, — formed a pretty piece of by-play, quite intelligible to all beholders, but for that time certainly quite thrown away upon the stranger.

Ten minutes before, to have held for a few brief minutes the tips of Rosario's fingers would have been to him ecstasy. Now he was scarcely conscious that they were within his own, and his eyes were fixed upon Chinita as she stood breathlessly waiting for Chata. Never in his life, he thought, had he seen such a face. The changeable yet ever radiant expression was like the dazzle of warm sunshine through scented leaves; the shimmer of rebellious hair was a divine halo, though the sparkle of the dusky eyes declared a daring soul more fit for earthly adventure than ethereal joys.

Rosario's eyes followed his gaze. She had heard the strange tale of Doña Isabel's intervention in the fate of the waif. She had wondered whether the high-born lady could have seen anything in the girl's face that attracted her; and that moment more decidedly than ever she answered "No," yet realized that here was a face to bewitch men. She tossed her head and passed on. Doña Feliz stopped her to embrace her, and meanwhile the two early playmates met.

"Life of my soul!" cried Chinita. "How I have longed for you! Did you not see me perched in the niche of the wall? Ay, how Doña Isabel would frown if she knew!"

"I saw only the tall, fair man," answered Chata in a low voice. She was pale and trembled: "I thought first it was the ghost of the American. Oh God, what a shock!"

Chinita laughed merrily. "What! a coward still, and with the old stories we used to tell still first in your mind? Ah, I have tales to tell now will be worth your hearing." She bent low and added in a whisper, "Have they not told you? I have the place of the Señorita Herlinda now! I have her room. I think sometimes she must be dead, and I have risen in her stead. Do I look like a ghost, Chata?"

"Hush, hush!" entreated Chata. "Oh Chinita, I wish I never had gone away. Oh, how shall I live now? How can I bear it?"

At that moment Doña Feliz approached, and evading her proffered embrace the young girl bent her head on the arm of the woman and burst into tears. Chinita stood confounded; the light and joyousness died out of her face; a certain half-savage look of inquiry came over it. She turned abruptly to the young officer, —

"What have they done to her?" she demanded.

"Chinita," said a cold, impassive voice, "this gentleman is a stranger to you. It is not seemly that you stand here questioning him;" and with an imperious wave of her hand, Doña Isabel seemed actually to force the two apart.

Almost unconsciously the young man drew back, bowing low, and Chinita turned to the staircase; yet as she obeyed the movement of Doña Isabel's hand a furious rage possessed her. As she stepped upon the first stair, some demon prompted her to wind her arm around Chata's neck and raise her tear-stained face.

"I am going to the Señorita Herlinda's room," she said. "I am there in her place; and — " here she stopped, laughed, and threw a glance over her shoulder — " there is the American!"

Her last words had been prompted by a glimpse of Ashley Ward as he crossed the court. He caught the appellation, and bowed and smiled. Chinita ran up the stairs, and Doña Isabel stood rigid with a face like death. Her eyes were resting however on Chata's countenance.

The young girl had shrunk within Doña Feliz's protecting arm. Had Doña Isabel turned her eyes upon the woman's defiant yet apprehensive face, it might have been a revelation to her; but she looked at Don Rafael.

"Your daughter has a strange face and strange ways for a ranchero's daughter," she said, with an attempt at irony; but it failed. Her face worked painfully as she added, "She reminds me of those I would forget. We have strange fancies as we grow old."

A laugh sounded from the window above. She started and looked up, then dropped her head again and turned slowly away.

Chata gazed after her awestruck, though she knew not why. Her manner was so different from that of the proud and haughty dame she had pictured. Don Rafael looked from Doña Isabel to his mother. Both these women, it seemed to him, had grown wonderfully aged since they had met, but a month or so before. There was a subtile

antagonism between them — these two who loved each
other, as only such deep intense natures can — which
tore and harried them far more than actual hate could
have done.

"What hast thou, my life?" Doña Feliz whispered to
Chata. "Art thou not happy? Have strange tales been
told thee?" and she looked keenly at her daughter-in-law,
who had smiled and courtesied in vain as Doña Isabel
went by.

"My mother," said Doña Rita in her softest voice,
"the child is weary; she must rest. Heed not this silly
child, Don Fernando. Thank Heaven, Rosario is not so
fanciful!"

But Don Fernando was not thinking of Rosario, or
of Chata either for that matter, but of how he had slunk
away from his chief to prosecute a love-affair that he had
believed no power could make less than a matter of life or
death to him; and how in a moment it had become lighter
than air. The boyish perversity with which he had determined, even at the risk of offending his patron, to continue
his courtship of Rosario Sanchez, trusting to fate or her
father's generosity to make marriage with her possible,
faded from his mind like a dream, and with it her image;
and in its place rose the arch mocking face of the "little
saint of the Wall." Proved she angel or demon, he felt
that she was henceforth the genius of his destiny. He
was a vain and profligate adventurer; but all the same
the arrow had found his heart, not as a thousand times
before to inflict a passing scratch, but to bury itself in
its inmost core.

All had taken place in a few short moments. While the
horses were being unharnessed and led away; while the
villagers were still crowding around the carriage, and Doña
Rita's baskets and packages were being lifted out; while
a few words of greeting were exchanged, — emotions and
passions had sprung into being that were to make the
seemingly prosaic household a very vortex of conflicting
elements.

The young American, who thought himself but a looker-
on, was also not unmoved. Like Doña Isabel, he said
within himself, "That young girl has a strange face and
strange ways for the daughter of a Mexican. And yet

what know I of Mexicans or their ways? This is a strange atmosphere, and fills my brain with strange fancies. Perhaps out of them all I shall evolve some reality. May the Fates grant me again such a chance as I had to-day of speaking to the wild gypsy Chinita! Nothing has happened here, I can well believe, that she cannot tell me of. But after the escapade of to-day, she will hardly escape the vigilance of her duenna again. Ah, here comes the young soldier — too travel-stained to be as dashing as is his custom, no doubt. He looks a gay bird with sadly bedraggled feathers."

Pepé apparently approved of him as little, as he passed by to the room assigned him. The peasant did not cease from lounging against the wall or bare his head as an inferior should.

"Insolent barbarian!" muttered Don Fernando, in a revival of his usual contempt for the peasantry, as the swarthy young fellow scowled at him, he neither guessed nor cared why. What could such a vagabond have to do with the Señora Garcia's *protégée?* He would serve when the time came, to make one, in the independent troop he, Fernando, would raise: such worms as he were only fit to serve men. There were wild rumors afloat of the wonderful fortune of that phœnix Benito Juarez. What if he, Ruiz, should join his standard? There was a strange fire and exultation in the young man's veins. He had been tied to a resistless fate long enough, — he would break his trammels, and by one daring act free himself forever from control, from tutelage, from Ramirez.

"Señor Don Rafael!" cried a hoarse voice at break of day. "Rise, your grace! for strange things have happened while we have slept! Ay, Señor, if the demon himself has not carried away Pedro the gatekeeper, who can tell us how he has gone?"

"Gone!" echoed the voice of Don Rafael from within.

"Gone, Señor, and left not even so much as his shadow; yet the doors are locked, and not even in the postern is there so much as a crack, nor the key in the lock. The muleteers, who were to be upon the road at cock-crow, have waited until both they and their beasts are cramped with standing, and all to no purpose."

"Is this true?" exclaimed Don Rafael, presently appearing with a *serape* thrown over his shoulders, and shivering in the morning air. "Ay, man, thou hast a tongue like a woman's. And Pedro, thou sayest, is gone?"

The man drew one hand sharply across the other, as who should say, "vanished!" though his lips ejaculated, "Gone, Señor; and who is to open the door now that it is shut? And who could shut the door upon Pedro but Satan himself?"

"Who, indeed?" said Don Rafael, gravely. "Think you so bulky a fellow could creep through the keyhole of the postern and take the key with him? By good fortune, he brought me the key of the great door as usual, and here it is. If the Devil hath carried away one gatekeeper on his shoulders, it is but fair he should send me another; and thou, Felipe, shalt be the man."

Felipe stared a moment; then with a transient change of expression which might be of intelligence, or simply a vague smile at his own good fortune, extended his hand for the keys; and suddenly mute with the weight of his

unexpected promotion trudged down the stone stairs,
across the silent inner court and the outer one, where
by this time the household servants were exchanging exclamations of wonder and alarm with the impatient muleteers. Felipe unlocked the wide doors, threw them open
with a clang, sank into Pedro's place upon the stone bench,
and thereafter reigned in his stead.

The wonder of Pedro's disappearance grew greater and
ever greater, until the boy Pepé said sulkily he had been
played a shabby trick. Had not he said to Pedro the night
before, when the Señor Don Rafael had told them that
the General Vicente Gonzales was in El Toro, that for a
word he himself would go to him there; and doubtless
Pedro had stolen away alone, like the surly fox that he
was. But the saints be praised, the road was open to
one man as well as another.

"Hush!" said one in a warning tone; "though Pedro
may have a fancy for a cleft head or broken bones, must
we all cry for the same? Go to thou Pepé! thou art scarce
old enough to leave the shade of thy mother's reboso.
Did I not see thee sucking thy thumb but last Saint
John's day?"

There was a roar of laughter, and though Pepé raged,
no one heeded his wrath; the talk was all of Pedro. That
he had gone to be a soldier was universally believed; that
Don Rafael, and not the Devil, had aided his going was
not for a moment thought of. The women crossed themselves, and the men spat on the floor emphatically, — yet
there had been more mysteries than that in the life of
Pedro.

Florencia, who was distraught at her uncle's disappearance, and tore her hair and bewailed herself as a bereaved
niece should, found her way to Chinita to pour out her
griefs and fears; although since the change in the young
girl's position they had by common consent ignored their
former relations, — Florencia, because of the wide social
gulf fixed between the great house and the hovels around
it; Chinita, from pure indifference. She was too full of
her new life to think of the old, or of the persons connected
with it.

It was so early that she was still not fully dressed, and
the chocolate wherewith to break her fast stood untouched

upon the table, when the sound of some one sobbing at the door brought a tone of sorrow into thoughts which had simply been vexed before.

Chinita had risen in an ill humor. Doña Rita and Rosario, and even Chata herself, had failed to show any surprise at her position. True, Don Rafael had warned them of it ; but at least something more than a kindly indifference might have greeted her, — if only a glance of envy from Rosario. What wonderful things had they all seen, that they had no thoughts to spare for her? Bah! Rosario had neither eyes nor thoughts for any one but the young officer with the red neck-tie. Well, they should see! But what of Doña Rita, — and Chata too? Why, Chinita hardly knew her. Was she also thinking but of herself, like the others? That was a change in Chata, and one that ill-suited her.

Chinita had slept badly for thinking of these things ; and truth to tell, when her mind was ill at ease the softness of the bed troubled her. She had dreamed of snakes, of three snakes who had lifted their heads out of water to hiss at her. Here was the first one. Certainly she had not dreamed of snakes for nothing. Well, to be sure, here was Florencia, whom she had almost forgotten, come with some trouble! She felt a little flutter of gratification, and unconsciously assumed the air of a *patrona,* as she said, —

"Ah, is it then Florencia? And what ails thee ; and how can I help thee? What, has Tomasito broken the newest water-jar, or by better fortune his neck? Or has Terecita choked herself with a dry bean?"

"God has not desired to do me such favors," returned Florencia, piously and with a flood of tears. "No, rather than my children should become little angels, he prefers that they shall be friendless upon the earth. *Ay de mi!* what is a father, what is a husband (and you know the very driveller of a man I have), what is any one to an uncle who was a gatekeeper of Tres Hermanos?— a veritable treasure of silver, a spring of refreshing! Was there ever a time Florencia asked a shilling of Pedro in vain?"

At another time Chinita would have laughed at this pious exaggeration ; now it filled her with inexpressible alarm.

"What! is my god-father dead?" she cried, wringing her hands and for the moment relapsing into the demonstrative gestures and cries of her plebeian training. "*Ay Dios*, Florencia, it cannot be! Answer me, stupid one! Is thy mouth as full as thy eyes that thou canst not answer?"

"Is chocolate served to the poor at day-break?" cried Florencia in an injured tone, and with a glance at the dainty breakfast; and then at an impatient word from Chinita she explained how Pedro had departed in the night, though the hacienda doors were locked upon the inside, and conjectured that if he had not been spirited away by the Devil, he had gone to join the Liberal General Gonzales, — there could be no other alternative. She had heard Señor Don Rafael talking to him till late in the night of how Gonzales had beaten the General Ramirez at El Toro, and was still there trying to strengthen his forces, while those of the Clergy had disappeared, no one knew where, but surely to gather men and means to recover the lost position.

Chinita's eyes flashed. She knew nothing of politics, but she thrilled at the name of Ramirez. She laughed scornfully that Pedro should throw his puny strength into the force against him. Still she said, "God keep him;" and jested away Florencia's fears.

"Bah! What should happen to my god-father?" she said. "And thou knowest thou wilt want for nothing. Hark thou! there is nothing to cry for that thy uncle is gone. Has he not often told us of the dollars he made in the wars?"

"I fear me he is likely rather to receive hard blows than hard dollars now," answered Florencia, disconsolately, — an expression of expectancy, however, relieving her doleful countenance, as she added, "Ah, Chinita of my soul, thou wert ever the kerchief to wipe away my tears."

Chinita laughed. "Thou used to say I was a prickly pear to draw tears, rather than a kerchief to dry them," she presently said, pushing her chocolate toward Florencia, and thrusting into her hand the little twists of bread.

"There, take them; I would a thousand times rather

have a thick cake and a drink of white gruel. One is not
always in the humor for sweets;" and she tugged viciously
at the hair she tried vainly to smooth, — she was always
at feud with it because it was not longer. But at last she
confined it in two short tresses, tying each with a red
ribbon; and then suddenly dropping on her knees before
Florencia, placed her hands palm downward upon the
floor, and looking up in the woman's face with a laugh
exclaimed, as a tinge of red deepened the olive of her
complexion, "And what of the American, Florencia? Is
he like him thou sayest the Señorita Herlinda loved?"

"Ave Maria Purissima!" cried the startled woman.
"The saints forbid that I should say such a thing of a
Garcia, and she dedicated to the Madonna!" But recovering herself, "Certainly this American is like the other.
Is not one cactus like another that grows on the same
mountain? Should a white-blooded American be like a
cavalier of blue-blood, or like an Indian of the villages?
Yet both, one and the other, are we not Mexicans?" and
she uttered the words as one might say, "Are we not
gods?"

"That is very true," commented Chinita, gravely; "and
yet they are not frights, these Americans. Why should
not the Señorita Herlinda have loved one if it pleased
her? Listen, Florencia; I will tell thee a dream I had
one night. When one's bed is too soft, one dreams
dreams."

Florencia looked at the girl with an admiring glance.
How amiable she could be, this Chinita, when she
chose. "Little puss! little puss!" she murmured,
giving her the pet name Pedro had used, when in her
kittenish moods one had never known whether she would
scratch or fondle one with soft purrings, begun and ended
in a moment. "Little puss! thou wert ever good to thy
Florencia."

"Thou art a flatterer!" ejaculated Chinita, half-inclined
to withhold her confidence, yet longing for a listener. "Ay,
Florencia, thou knowest not what it is to sit for hours in
the gloom within four walls. Ah, what thoughts come
into one's head! When I ran about the village, the wind
blew the thoughts about as it did my hair; but now my
brains are like cobwebs, and when a thought touches them

it clings like dust, and so they grow thicker and heavier until my very skull aches;" and she pressed her head with her hands, and heaved a deep sigh.

"But to think is not to dream," said Florencia, in some disappointment, for she had a child's love for the marvellous, and did not understand Chinita's abstractions, — unstudied and simple though they were.

"But dreams come from thoughts," answered Chinita; "and what should I think of here but of mysteries, — such as why the Señora should keep me with her, though she loves me not; why she walks the floor and counts her beads, and when she forgets I am in the room murmurs over and over the name of Herlinda; why she looks before her sometimes, as you used to tell me the woman looked who saw the ghost of the American, — and that is always when she chances to meet this Don 'Guardo whom she will not speak of, or suffer Doña Feliz to invite to our table, though he stays here so long. And after I have asked so many things, I set myself to the answer. Oh, you would wonder at what I say to myself of all these things, — and then sometimes come dreams to tell me I am right."

Florencia looked at the door vaguely, — she was thinking perhaps she had better go.

"Yes, yes," continued Chinita, as if to herself, "I am growing perhaps like the owl, — I, who in the broad sunlight saw nothing, have discovered many things here in the dark. Well, well, Florencia, one thought came to me on a vexed night when I could not sleep. I had been talking to Doña Feliz that day. I know not why, but I am with Doña Feliz like the young fox my god-father tamed, — when I touched him with my hand he was pleased, yet he bristled and longed to bite. Good! we had talked that day. Yes, — it was of the nuns, and she said the Señora might desire I should be one; and I was angry, and said I would not be shut up to pray as the Señorita Herlinda had been; and then Doña Feliz bade me be silent and ponder what she had said. And after she went away it was not of myself I thought, but of the Señorita Herlinda; and in the midst of my thoughts I saw the American pass the court, and Doña Isabel, who was near, turned herself away, as if an adder had darted upon her."

Florencia looked up with a mute inquiry or fascination in

her gaze. Chinita, in a sort of monotone, followed the thread of her thoughts.

"When I went to sleep at last, I dreamed that I, though still Chinita, was Herlinda, and that the American who was lying wounded in the room below came up the stairs, and tapped lightly at my window. I stepped softly and looked out at him through the grating. Ah, it was this Don 'Guardo, yet so different, as a man is different from his reflection in a glass; and I did not wonder to see him there. I put my hand out and touched him, and was happy. And as I stood at the bars, — I myself, and yet the *niña* Herlinda, — the man of my dream said, as a husband says to his wife, 'Open, my life;' and when I opened the door he led in by the hand a little child, — I knew it to be his child, though it had not blue eyes nor the yellow hair. Well, I stood there, and stood there, and strove to speak and could not; and the vision of the man and of the child faded, and the thought that I was still Herlinda faded too, and the dream was ended."

She ceased speaking, and looked at Florencia with a vague yet searching gaze.

"By my faith, a strange dream!" murmured Florencia, disquieted. "You should have lighted a blessed candle when you woke, and passed it before you three times, saying an *Ave* each time. Santa Inez! I would rather see the ghost of the American than dream such a dream!"

"Coward! it frightened me not," continued the girl. "And I did not seem to wake, though I knew that I, Chinita, lay in the bed, and that my head sank deep in the soft pillow, and that I could not or would not raise it; and the meaning of the dream crept into my mind, as the light creeps into a dark room. Yes, I felt as I used to when I saw the little green blades shoot up in the spring, and I could think how the corn would grow, and the leaves would wave, and the maize would lie in the silk and the yellow sheath; and so I had thought of what I had heard, — of the love of Herlinda for the American, and what might have come of it."

"Hush!" interrupted Florencia with a scared look. "You said you dreamed of a child. Did you see its face?"

"No," answered Chinita, slowly. "But what need that I should see it?"

The two had risen as if by one impulse, and looked into each other's eyes. The woman was awed as much by the penetration and daring of the young girl's mind as by the thought that for the first time arose within her.

She cast her thoughts back. She had been young when the American was murdered, when the Señorita Herlinda had left the hacienda never to return, when the child had been found at the gate; yet she wondered that she had been so blind to what now appeared so plain, and that all alike — the wise and simple, the old and young — had been so utterly dazzled by the glamor that surrounded the family of Garcia that no suspicion of dishonor might attach to its women, or of cowardice to its men. Surely none other than Herlinda Garcia would have escaped the lynx-eyed Selsa, or a score of other scandal-loving women! Curiously enough, while a feeling of detraction for the nun, whom she had long been used to canonize in her thoughts, stole into her mind, a sensation of traditional reverence for the Garcia arose for the young girl before her. Florencia's ideas of morality were perhaps vague on all points; they certainly did not reach that of aspersion of the innocent fruit of another's fault.

" Ay, *niña,*" the woman said at last with a gasp, " it is not every one who drinks red wine that is happy. Thanks to God, the peasant woman who carries a burden in her arms too soon needs only to suckle it under her scarf, like any mother, and needs not to close upon herself the doors of a convent. Santa Maria! who would have thought such things of the *niña* Herlinda?"

" Be silent!" cried Chinita, with a tardy repentance of her confidence. " How do I know that I am not the worst of evil thinkers, and a fool, a very fool? Look thou, Florencia, it is thou who shall discover the truth for me. Pedro is gone; perhaps he never knew it. The Tio Reyes must know; but where is he? Yet I *must* know. Oh, I could bear the truth from Feliz, from Doña Isabel; but they are as silent and as sorrowful as the image of the Madre Dolores. It is thou, Florencia, who must help me. Oh, it will be but a diversion for thee. Thou shalt talk of thy Tio Pedro, and of the day I was dropped in his hand, and of the days that went before. Thou canst talk now of the murder of the American, and of the Señorita Her-

linda too, and there will be no Pedro to chide thee.   And
see, — " as the woman began some faint objection, — " I
have all the pretty things Pedro gave me, and money
too ; yes, more than thou wouldst think.   And thou shalt
never miss thy uncle ; thou shalt have them all, if thou
wilt but talk to the old women of things that happened
here before the time of the great sickness.   But, Florencia,
thou must tell them nothing.   Oh, if I could only run
again in and out of the village huts as I used to do ! "

Florencia looked at the excited girl with a nod of intelligence.   " Have no fear," she said ; " it is not possible
that Florencia knows not how to manage her own tongue,
though no one knows better than thyself it was ever a
quiet one.   But it shall wag now, and not like the dog's
tail, in mere idleness."

Chinita laughed, then glancing around her warily, drew
from her bosom a small gold coin.   She had evidently
prepared herself for a chance meeting with Florencia.

" Take it," she said, " and go.   Thou hast been here too
long already ; and," she added with the flush of red again
tingeing her face, " talk and gossip when the American is
near.   He must be sad, — it will cheer him to hear the
voices, even if he understands but little ; and if by
chance he speaks to thee, why ! thou shalt tell me
what he says."

Florencia had experienced one great surprise that
morning, and here was another ; the first had awed,
the second delighted her.   Like all her race she had the
instincts of secrecy and intrigue, and suddenly the opportunity to practise both were offered her.   She looked
at Chinita with a glance of infinite cunning in her soft
dark eyes ; but the young girl would not meet her gaze.
" Go, go ! " she said impatiently ; " you have been
here too long.   The Señora is coming — or is it Doña
Feliz ?   Go ! go, I say ! "

It was neither Doña Isabel nor Feliz, but only Chata,
who entered with a preoccupied air, scarcely noticing the
woman who passed her on the threshold.   She did not
speak, however, until Florencia had reluctantly passed
out of hearing ; and then she cried eagerly, " Chinita !
Chinita ! who is the stranger who stood with thee at the
doorway ?   God bless us !   I thought I saw the ghost of

the American we used to talk of; and but now I met
him below in the court. Who is he? What is he here
for?"

"That remains to be seen," answered Chinita, with an
uneasy laugh. Her hasty confidence in Florencia troubled
her, and closed her lips toward the friend for whom she
had hitherto longed. "At least the stranger is no ghost;
yet how can we know that the man who was murdered
here so many years before was anything to him?"

"But I do know," insisted Chata. "I had gone to
the arbor, thinking thou mightest be there, to break my
fast. I was standing in the centre, with my eyes turned
toward this room, thinking I should see thee leave it, and
thinking too of the *niña* Herlinda,— O Chinita! she is still
so beautiful,— when I heard a step behind me. It was a
strange step, and I turned quickly and saw the American
looking at me as if he too believed he saw a ghost. Was
it not strange, Chinita? We looked at each other quite
steadily for many moments, then he said, —

"'Pardon me, you are then the daughter of the administrador? You came here yesterday?'

"I could scarcely make out his words, yet I understood
what he said, and I seemed to know that he had taken me
for another,— perhaps for thee, Chinita; and then again
he said, 'Pardon me! Pardon me!' and we still continued to look at each other; and I did not think how
bold I must appear until the other stranger, the young
officer who loves Rosario, stepped out of the room they
have given him. I heard his spurs clank on the pavement,
and then I fled away to thee. But for the fright, I should
not have dared to come hither, Chinita. All yesterday
my grandmother kept me from thee. She said now thou
art the child of Doña Isabel, and that without leave I
must not go to thee."

"Chata, thou hast a poor spirit!" exclaimed Chinita,
with some severity, — though she remembered with impatient anger that Doña Isabel had kept her in the garden at her side, on pretence of showing her the strings
of irregular pearls, which she should some day arrange
in even strands. Doña Isabel had made no promise,
but Chinita could almost see them in the future bedecking her own neck and arms. She had been beguiled,

even as Chata had been commanded, to keep apart from her old playmate.

"There is a mystery in it all!" she exclaimed. "Though I am here with Doña Isabel, I know not who I am. It is intolerable! Sometimes I fear I am but her plaything, with no more right to her notice than had the fawn I found on the river bank and petted, till it died from very heartbreak because it longed so for the mountains and its kind. And so I long, Chata. Ah, thou knowest not what it is to be a nameless wretch, to be tossed from hand to hand, and have no share in the game but the dizzy whirling through the air. Pshaw! I would rather be dashed to pieces against the first wall than go through life with nothing but favor to rely on. I want a name, a place, a right. I will have them: even you, who are the daughter of the administrador, have those; and I— Well, I will not be simply *Chinita*, whom Doña Isabel makes a lady to-day, who was a child of the Madonna yesterday, and may be a beggar to-morrow."

Chata had been leaning on the arm and pressing her head against the shoulder of Chinita. She raised it now with a sharp low cry, and turned away. Little guessed the impetuous, ambitious foundling how her words tortured and taunted the other, who longed to cry out, "I too am no one! I too am a stray, a waif, and if I know my father, know him only as a terror, — a horror." Her promise to Doña Rita silenced her. She felt there was but one person in the world to whom she would break her promise, — the pale, sweet-faced nun of the convent of El Toro. In her passionate, bitter mood Chinita chilled and silenced her, She did not even tell her that as she hastened from the arbor the American had caught the end of her flying reboso, as if by an irresistible impulse, and cried: "I am Ashley Ward! Ashley! Ashley! remember the name!"

Remember it! it seemed to Chata as if she had always known the man as well as the name, which had ever before been to her the symbol of the dead rather than of the living. That she should have seen the Señorita Herlinda, whom she had always known to be alive, seemed more wonderful, more incredible to her mind, than that the young man should have risen before her to claim the name of the murdered foreigner. Now that he had come, she seemed all her life to have been expecting him. She did not see him again for days, but all that time the expression of his eyes haunted her. She could not fathom it. She did not guess it had been but a reflection of the surprise, yet conviction, in her own.

Chata did not again transgress the commands of Doña Feliz; nor did she remain long enough with Chinita in her first visit to be tempted into further confidence. Indeed, they parted with something like a quarrel, as they had been used to do in their childhood's days. Rosario's name had been mentioned, and Chinita had with some scorn commented both on her sentimental air and the indifference of her lover.

"Did he love her at El Toro?" she asked with the laugh that was so mocking. "He stood for an hour, you say, at the corner of the street waiting for a glance from her; he wrote verses by day and sang them by night beneath her window? Well, he stood from noon till night yesterday with his eyes turned upward, — one would have thought he had never gazed at anything lower than the sky; yet it was only for a glimpse of *my* face, and a single glance from my eyes dazzled and blinded him. Thank Heaven, he dare not tune a guitar beneath my windows for fear of Doña Isabel, or I should be tormented with all the old rhymes changed from Rosario to Chinita. Ah, there are likings and likings, and this pretty soldier is one who would try them all!"

"Chinita," cried Chata in indignation, "you are false, you are cruel! Rosario has done nothing to you that you should torment her. I understand nothing of such things as Rosario does; though I am her age, she seems to be a woman while I am still a child. But she says she loves Fernando, and for love a woman's heart may break."

Chata was thinking of the pale, sad nun; but Chinita threw herself into a chair and broke into a peal of laughter. It rang through the silent house, and startled Doña Isabel in the further chamber. She started nervously and clasped her hands over her ears.

"What a strange child it is." she murmured, "Ah, I should have loved her if—" She glanced at a note she had just written. It was addressed to Vicente Gonzales, and promised him a thousand mounted soldiers.

Doña Isabel made no idle promises, and she had counted well the cost when she had thus irrevocably committed herself to the cause of the Liberals. She had watched for years the course of events, and none saw more clearly than she that the time for passiveness had gone. On every hand there must necessarily be sacrifice. " That which goes not in sighs, must in tears," she said sententiously. "I like not the Indian Juarez, yet his policy promises deliverance from the vampire that for generations has grown strong and ever stronger, as it has drained the very life of the nation."

The knowledge that Gonzales was in El Toro enjoying the prestige of an accidental victory, but with a force entirely insufficient to meet that which Ramirez might at any day bring against him, had been the immediate cause of her action. To reward Pedro with a service which should at once remove him from her sight and fill his mind with new and absorbing interests, were the reasons why he had been chosen to ride from rancho to rancho secretly inciting the men to join the standard, which was to be raised upon the morrow.

" Ah, this Ruiz is a poor tool!" muttered Doña Isabel, " yet for that reason may be the more readily bought. He loves the daughter of my administrador, and will do much to gain my good word. Rafael says he is a brave soldier, if a false one ; and there will be those with him who will guard against treachery. He shall fulfil his empty offer to lead a thousand men to Gonzales, and claim of Rafael the reward he sighs for. Ah, there is the child's laugh again, — I could almost fancy it in mockery of me! Ah, this of patriot is a new *rôle* for me, and tries my nerves. Well, Chinita shall laugh while she can : if it is for long, it will prove her none of the blood of Garcia. Was there ever a happy woman among them ? "

While Doña Isabel pondered thus, Chata in deep indignation had turned from her whilom friend. She had been brought up among a people who in matters of love held man excused and woman guilty in all cases of inconstancy. " Farewell!" she exclaimed, "I will come no more to you who are so cruel. Doña Isabel was right to part us; she has changed your heart as she has your fortune. Ah!" she added bitterly, "all the world is changed to me, and why not you?"

The grieved and imbittered girl went out so quickly that Chinita's answer did not reach her. As she passed through the corridor Chata glanced down. The young officer stood there, as Chinita had described. He would catch the first glimpse of her as she left her room. Chata flushed in anger, yet tears of pity rose to her eyes. She was still a child, yet her heart foretold what might be the agony of woman's slighted love.

Even so soon Chinita was laughing no longer; she had crouched forward and sat with her face bent almost to her knees. "What have I done?" she asked herself. "It is early morning still, and I have told a secret to a fool, and offended her I should have trusted!"

She had eaten nothing; the excitement under which she had acted suddenly expired, and she burst into sobs and tears. Doña Feliz coming in a few minutes later, found her on her knees before the little image of her patron saint, passionately vowing the gift of a silver *Christo* in return for the boon she craved.

"Go to the corridor, my child," said Feliz pityingly. The girl was a problem to her, which every day seemed more difficult of solution. "You look weary and ill; but console yourself, — Pedro is safe. You will see the good foster-father again, be assured."

Chinita looked at her in astonishment. She had for the time forgotten Pedro's very existence. Doña Feliz discerned at once that she had credited the girl with a sensibility to which she was a stranger. Five minutes later she was quite certain of it, as Chinita sat on the corridor, apparently equally unconscious of the impassioned glances of Ruiz, or those of the invisible but infuriate Rosario, drawing the threads of some dainty linen and singing, —

Sale la Linda,
Sale la fea,
Sale el enano,
Con su galea.

" The beauty comes out,
　　The ugly one too;
　Then comes the dwarf,
　　With a gay halloo."

As unstudied and inconsequent as the meaningless words of the song seemed the actions of the singer, but Feliz shook her head, and met Doña Isabel with a face that was even more serious than its wont. The problem became to her mind each day more complicated. Would the result be bitterness, and that grief most dreaded by the proud heart of Doña Isabel Garcia, — the grief and bitterness of shame?

XXIX.

FLORENCIA fulfilled her mission well, — recalling skilfully to the minds of the elder gossips the events and doubts of years agone, and those suspicions, light as air, which had once before menaced the fair name and fame of her who later had been revered as a saint under the name of Sister Veronica.

It was natural after the excitement of Pedro's disappearance had subsided that reminiscences of events in which he had figured should, in default of some new interest, rise to the stagnant surface of hacienda life, and be re-colored and adorned with suggestions probable or improbable, and that the favorite topic should be torn to shreds in its dissection, while the motive power of its appearance should in the excitement of discussion be utterly lost sight of. Florencia herself, in the interest of tracing the sequence of events, and in hearing attributed to the characters that had figured in her girlhood traits and deeds of which she had heard little or nothing at that bygone time, almost forgot that she was talking with a purpose, and therefore perhaps had a truly unprejudiced account to give to Chinita, — when she could again see her, for Doña Isabel had become a wary duenna, and the girl had had no opportunity of learning anything that might have thrown light upon the theory she had formed of her birth and parentage.

In his insufficient knowledge of the language, Ashley Ward let much of the gossip of the women who chatted about him as they performed their daily tasks pass entirely unheeded, while he pondered upon the very subjects which with more or less directness were discussed. But one morning he caught the name of Herlinda, and thenceforth all his senses were alert. Great was his surprise when he discovered this to be the name of a daughter of Doña Isabel who had been a beautiful girl when the

American was killed, and thenceforward his mind became preternaturally keen; so that he divined the meanings of words he had never heard before, — gestures, glances, the very inflection of a tone, became revelations to him.

Hitherto, without cogitating upon the matter, Ward had naturally assumed from hearing no reference to another that the newly married Carmen was the only child of Doña Isabel. Now he learned the tragical fate of Norberto and the existence of the elder and more beautiful daughter Herlinda, the cloistered nun; and she was for the time the theme of endless reminiscences and conjectures. Her winsome childhood; her early gayety and incomparable beauty; the open love of Gonzales; the suspected mutual attachment of the young American and the daring child, who with her mother's pride had failed to inherit her mother's strength of will; the murder of John Ashley; the time of the great sickness; the death of Mademoiselle La Croix; the effect of the shock and horror upon the mind and appearance of Herlinda; the scarcely whispered, faint, yet not wholly disproved suspicions which had floated over the name and fame of the daughter of a house too absolute in its ascendency and power to be lightly attacked; her removal from the hacienda; her strange rejection of the suit of one who had always been dear to her, and to whom her mother, in accordance with good and seemly usage, had pledged her; her renunciation of the world she had loved, and entrance to a convent, which she had held in horror, — all these circumstances were discussed from a dozen points of view.

And all he heard confirmed in Ashley's mind the belief that the woman whom his cousin had loved was traced; that whether she had been actually a wife or no, she, Herlinda Garcia, the daughter of a woman whom it would be a mortal offence to approach upon such a subject, was the possible mother of a child which he could scarcely refuse to believe existed, — though here a new perplexity confronted him as (like the young officer, whom he regarded with a half-contemptuous amusement that should have prevented him from following any example set by so love-lorn a cavalier) he began to seek occasion for observing Chinita with an intensity that made her doubly the object of the jealous and ireful dislike of Rosario and her mother. To his alert and dispassionate mind circumstances pointed to this girl as the possible link between the families of Ashley and Garcia, though the most minute and patient observation only seemed to make absurd the supposition that American blood mingled in the fiery tide which filled her veins, colored her rich beauty, and vivified the scornful and stoical yet ambitious spirit, which as by a spell at the same moment repelled yet charmed both himself and the haughty Doña Isabel. What was the secret of the foundling's influence? He cared not to analyze either his own mind or the irresistible fascination of Chinita; but that the girl, though not positively beautiful, and unmistakably repellent in her caustic yet stoical discontent and ambitious unrest, possessed a bewitching and bewildering grace far different from any he had ever beheld in woman, of whatever race or kindred, impressed him daily more and more deeply, while — But stubborn facts made speculation and efforts at inquiry alike futile.

As days passed on, a certain friendship sprang up between Ward and Don Rafael. They talked for hours over the political situation, — Ashley straining ear and mind to comprehend the administrador's smooth and impressive utterances, and Don Rafael with grave politeness listening without a smile or gesture of amusement to the hesitating and often utterly incomprehensible attempts of the young American to deliver his opinions, or to make minute inquiry into reasons and events which often horrified as well as puzzled him. Don Rafael had the air of simplicity and candor which is so infinitely attractive to the stranger, and which presented so great a contrast to the lofty coldness of Doña Isabel and the grave and melancholy reticence of Feliz. Their demeanor left the baffling and depressing conviction that there was an infinity that they might reveal were but the right chord touched; while that of Don Rafael was satisfying in its cordiality, even while no response fulfilled the expectation that his fluent and kindly frankness appeared to encourage.

As soon as the state of his wound permitted, Ashley joined the administrador in his early morning rides to the fields and pastures, and learned much of the workings of a great hacienda. These rides were confined to the im-

mediate neighborhood of the great house, and four or six
armed men were invariably in attendance, — for, as Don
Rafael explained with a smile, the administrador of the
rich hacienda of Tres Hermanos was invested with the dignity of its possessors, his personal insignificance being
absorbed in the state of those he represented; so that his
person bore a fictitious value, and if seized by an enemy,
either personal or political, would doubtless be held at a
prince's ransom, which the honor as well as the interest of
his employers would force them to pay.

In the course of these rides they not infrequently approached the deserted reduction-works, and it was upon
the first occasion that this happened that Don Rafael
questioned the young American as to his relationship to
the last director; and upon learning it, rehearsed with
deep feeling the story of his murder, pointing out the very
tree under which the bloody tragedy was enacted.

Ashley watched his countenance narrowly as he talked.
His words, whose meaning might have been obscure to
the foreigner, were rendered dramatic by the deep pathos
of his tone and the expressive force of his gestures; even
the men who rode behind drew near as his voice rose on
the stillness of the air in a tale so foreign to the peace and
beauty of the scene. As they skirted the low adobe wall
and looked over upon the stagnant masses of mineral clay,
the piles of broken ores, the adobe sheds and stables
crumbling under rain and sun, Ashley was ready to credit
the whispered words with which Don Rafael ended his
narration; "Señor, it is said in the silent night, when
the moon is at its full, phantoms of its old life revivify
this deserted spot, and that its massive gates open at
the call of a ghostly rider, who wears the form of that
poor youth who after his last midnight ride came back
feet foremost, recumbent, silent, from the tryst he had
sallied forth to keep."

"And did you know the woman?" gasped rather than
demanded Ashley Ward.

"Did *I* know the woman?" answered Don Rafael. "*I*
know the woman? I was a stranger, and, truth to tell, no
friend of Americans; a faithful husband withal, and was
it likely, though he had them, this stranger would have
shared secrets of a doubtful nature with me? When

I said a 'tryst' I used it for want of a better word. What attraction should a man so refined, so engrossed in his affairs as this busy foreigner, find in the humble and rustic beauties of the village? For my part, I find it impossible to imagine such coarseness in a man so little likely to be governed by a base passion as Ashley appeared. You know your own people better than I can; what say you?"

"I say the same!" answered Ward, eagerly, with a keen glance at the sensitive dark face of the administrador. "Yet I know that my cousin loved; that he claimed to be married; that the lady—"

He paused,—some of the men were within hearing, listening like Don Rafael himself with rapt faces. That of Don Rafael lighted for a moment with an incredulous smile. "Ah, then there *was* a woman?" he said. "That might be; but a marriage? Ah, Señor, if there had been that, all the world would have known it. You know but little of our laws if you suppose such a contract could be here secretly and legally made. If he claimed such to be the case, he was vilely deceived, or himself was—"

He stopped at the word, as if fearing to offend.

To urge the matter further seemed to Ashley worse than useless. He had learned enough of marriage laws in Mexico to feel that to mention the name of Herlinda Garcia in connection with that of Ashley was to cast upon it a slur such as could but bring upon him the resentment, and perhaps the revenge, of the family to which he was probably indebted for his very life, and certainly for a hospitality that merited respect for its liberality if not gratitude for its warmth.

"I shall never learn the truth," he thought; "and why indeed should I seek it? My aunt was wise in her generation. Though ignorant of the possibilities or impossibilities of Mexican society and character, she wisely refrained from problems which its keenness and honor ignored or left unsolved. I will go back again in content to my houses and lands, to my silver and gold. I am despoiling no legitimate heir; and to imagine the existence of any other is an offence either to my cousin's intelligence or honor, as well as to the chastity of a woman whom even in thought I must be a villain to asperse. Let but a momentary quiet come that I may be able to obtain the requisite funds, and I will abandon this sense-less quest, and leave my murdered cousin to rest in peace in his forgotten grave, in this land of violence and mysteries."

This was the resolve of one hour, — to be broken in the next, as the sight of a girl's face or the sound of her voice, like a disturbing conscience, assured him that in absence the doubt, or rather the tantalizing certainty, would each day torment him more and more, and so make enjoyment of his wealth even more impossible than it had been when Mary's sensitive imaginings had urged him upon his Quixotic errand.

Trivial and even ridiculous things often divert minds most harassed and burdened, and exert an influence when great and weighty matters would benumb or torture. It would have been impossible for Ashley Ward, in the em-barrassment of his situation (for his funds in the City of Mexico were entirely cut off by its investment by the Lib-erals) and in the perplexity of his thoughts, to have entered with enjoyment upon any festivity or pleasure requiring exertion either of body or mind; but he was, quite unconsciously to himself, in the mood idly to view the little comedy which was enacted more and more freely before his eyes, — just as in seasons of deepest grief and anxiety one may seek mechanical employment for the eye and relief for the brain in the perusal of a tale so light that neither the strain of a nerve or a thought, nor the excitement of pleasure or pain, shall awaken emotion or burden memory.

Fernando Ruiz was too wily a youth, too courteous, too kind, to throw off at once the semblance of devotion to a goddess who had lured him to a shrine that held a divinity whose charms, in his inconstant sight, so far surpassed her own that he could not choose but transfer his worship, even were it but to be disdained and rejected. In the decorous visits he made to Doña Rita and when they met at table, he would still sigh and cast despairing glances at the bridling Rosario, who but that she intercepted others more fervent still, directed toward the upper end of the board where Doña Isabel and Chinita sat in lonely state, would have believed quite true the tale with which her mother strove to console her, — using such feeble prevari-

cation as is usual in Mexican families when ill news is to
be ultimately communicated, in the fond hope of softening
a blow which doubt and procrastination can but cause to
be the more nervously dreaded. But well was Rosario
convinced that though Ruiz held daily conferences with
her father, and even once or more was honored by a few
moments' speech with Doña Isabel, it was not of her or of
love that they spoke ; and with a philosophic determination to replace with a more faithful lover the fickle admirer
whom she could cease to love but would never forgive,
the piqued, but lightly wounded damsel began to turn a
shoulder upon the recreant soldier and her smiles upon
the stranger.

Ward was perhaps singularly free from vanity, or too
much absorbed to notice the honor paid him ; but with a
sense of angry surprise he became aware that Chinita no
longer ignored the existence of the persistent languisher,
who at early morning paced the court in trim riding-suit
of leather, a gay serape thrown negligently over his left
shoulder, his wide-brimmed hat poised at the angle whence
he could see the door of her room open, and Chinita rival
the sun in dazzling his enchanted eyes. At noon he stood
in the self-same spot in gay uniform, from which by some
miraculous process all stain and grime had disappeared ;
and not infrequently at evening he reappeared in the
holiday dress of some clerk, who for the time had lent
his jacket of black velvet trimmed with silver buttons, or
his riding-suit of stamped leather and waist-scarf of scarlet silk, well pleased to fancy he was represented by the
lithe young officer, who filled them with a grace that made
them thenceforth of treble value in the owner's eyes.

This masquerade might have continued indefinitely, —
for Ruiz wearied no sooner of changing fine clothes than
of descanting to Ashley of his sudden but undying passion
for the young Chinita, whose fortunes he conceived, as the
favored of Doña Isabel Garcia, would be as brilliant as
her charms, — but that first, one by one, then in twos and
threes, in tens and dozens, men flocked into the adjacent
villages ; and though reluctant to be torn from gentler
pursuits, yet proud to form and command a regiment, the
young adventurer was set the task of bringing order
out of the wild and discordant elements, — a task for

which the training of his life, and his peculiar knowledge of the material with which he had to work, more fitted him than any especial talent, however brilliant, in the conduct of ordinary military affairs would have done.

The young officer's vanity was flattered, for in some occult way the responsibility of the spontaneous rally was thrown upon his shoulders, and he became the central figure in a movement which within a few days assumed a picturesque and imposing character. He himself assumed that the magic of his name had called from their rocky lairs these mountain banditti, these sturdy vaqueros, these apathetic but resolute rancheros who trooped in, bringing with them rusty carbines and shotguns, and sometimes polished Henry and Sharp's rifles, which the enterprise of speculative Americans had introduced into the country. There was no choice of weapons, but every one brought something, — a silver-mounted pistol, worthless as pretentious, or a strong and formidable short-sword, or glittering curved sabre, forged in some mountain or village smithy.

It seemed too that by mere force of will money came into the captain's hands, and that clothing, horses, and provisions were thus brought forth from the stores and fields of Tres Hermanos; that plans were laid, and adverse possibilities provided against, a way marked out and guides provided; and that he suddenly found himself at the head of a force more fully equipped than any he had before beheld, — men eager for adventure and battle, and clamorous to be led to join the forces of Gonzales, who while the cause with which he sympathized was meeting bloody reverses around the City of Mexico in which the Clerical forces were concentrated, was daily attracting in the interior formidable additions to the numbers of the Liberals. The tales of Conservative despotism and barbarity, which later investigations proved to have been well founded, aided much in influencing the masses to seek a change of evils, even where hopeless of any lasting benefit from the new condition of affairs which it was proposed to inaugurate.

A people who had for generations found in changes of government simply fresh despotisms and encroachments were not likely to be as enthusiastic in discussion as mad for action, — for crushing and destroying the old, and seizing upon all available booty, not as necessary to the success of their cause, but as a despoilment of the enemy. And upon this principle it within a few days happened that Tres Hermanos presented more the appearance of a forced than a voluntary contributor to the military necessities of the time. Not only the common soldiers but those who were to lead them, — most of them men as skilled in ordering the sacking of a hacienda as in defending a mountain pass or assaulting some unwary town, — had poured in and filled every vacant nook in the village huts, and occupied the long-deserted reduction-works and the ruinous huts along the watercourse, and overran the courts and yards of the great house itself.

The great conical storehouses of small grains and corn were opened and the mill invaded by the soldiers, who under the half-reluctant directions of the skilled workmen kept the somewhat primitive machinery in constant motion, — varying their employment by breaking the half-wild horses brought in from the wide pastures and talking love to the village girls, who in all their lives had never before beheld a holiday-making half so delightful.

The long-closed church too was thrown open, and a priest from the next village was busied all day long shriving the sins of those whom he shrewdly suspected were ready to raise the standard of revolt against the temporal rule of the Church, whose ghostly powers had overshadowed earth with the terrors of its supernatural dominion.

Ruiz had gained a certain fame, more as a reflection from that of the man with whom he had been associated than from any daring episodes in his own career; and he actually possessed a military training that ordinarily well filled the place of innate genius, and at other times counterfeited it. He had impressed Don Rafael as a man well suited, if hedged with precautions, to lead the forces that his representations induced Doña Isabel to send to the relief of her favorite Gonzales. A leader of more positive aspirations and declared opinions than Ruiz manifested, would not so happily have welded and moulded men of such diverse and conflicting elements, — men who, accustomed to the freedom of guerilla warfare, were more

18

ready to be led by the glitter than the substance of authority. A man of straw, who though answering a purpose for the time could create no diversion of devotion to his own person in detriment to the supremacy of Gonzales, was sought and found in Ruiz. He was indeed the simple tool of Doña Isabel Garcia, manipulated by her administrador, yet so skilfully that he came to think himself the moving power which from an isolated farmhouse had within a few days changed Los Tres Hermanos into a military camp.

In proportion with the importance of the position into which Ruiz was forced his love and daring grew, and he remembered that many men of family as obscure, and certainly of less tact and talent than he, had crowned their fortunes by marriage with beautiful daughters of rich houses ; and he even began to reflect with some dissatisfaction upon Chinita's doubtful status, although a few days before he had despaired of rising to a height where he might dare so much as touch the hand of Doña Isabel's favored *protégée.*

These changes of feeling were watched from day to day with amusement by Ashley Ward, and with rage by Pepé, as with despair he saw himself fading completely from the horizon of Chinita's life, and a new and dazzling star rising upon her view. More than once Ashley Ward saw him nervously fingering the knife in his belt, as the unconscious Ruiz stood by the fountain in the moonlight and strummed the strings of a bandoline, and in the shrill tenor which seems the natural vehicle of such weird strains sang the *paloma,* " the Dove," or *Te amo,* " I love thee," — sounds pleasing in any female ear, though doubtless, thought Doña Isabel, intended to reach the heart of one particular fair one ; at which she smiled as she imagined this to be the pretty brown Rosario, while the tender notes in reality appealed not quite in vain to the girl who with a remarkable semblance of patience shared the seclusion of her own life.

Once only had Chinita rebelled, and that was when, instead of her usual ramble in the garden with Feliz or Doña Isabel herself, she had asked to be driven through the village, past the reduction-works, that she might see the preparations of which the distant sounds reached her.

She would not be appeased at Doña Isabel's refusal, even by the suggestion that she should stand upon the balcony of the central window, whence she could overlook the scene for miles; and so contrary was her humor that Doña Isabel was glad to agree to her sudden fancy that her old playfellow Pepé should be allowed to describe to her what he had seen. "Men see more than women," the wilful girl exclaimed; "he will tell me something more than of the chickens that are stolen, and the number of tortillas that are eaten. Ay, Dios! I would I were a man myself, to be a soldier!"

So toward evening a message brought by Doña Feliz herself startled the sullen Pepé. Ashley Ward watched the youth with some curiosity as he sauntered across the court and ascended the stone stairs. Pepé's dress that day was in a Saturday's state of grime, and at best consisted of a shabby suit of yellow buckskin, from which the metal buttons had mostly dropped, and which gaped at the armholes as widely as at the waistband; and his leathern sandals and sombrero of woven grass showed signs of age, corresponding to that of the ragged blanket he wore with such an air that he might have been taken for the very king of idle loungers.

Doña Isabel glanced up at him as he muttered the customary salutation, uncovering his shock of black hair and inclining his head to her, while his black eyes furtively sought Chinita. There was nothing in his appearance for the most careful duenna to fear, and although Doña Isabel remembered that a few weeks ago those two had been equals, they now seemed as widely sundered as the poles; and knowing the prolixity with which the ordinary ranchero usually approached and gave his views upon any subject, she withdrew to the lower end of the gallery, where she might count her beads or con her thoughts undisturbed. The murmur of voices reached her with sufficient distinctness for her to know that the usual process of minute questioning and tantalizing indefiniteness of answer was in progress; and at length, soothed by the warm still air, the low song of a bird in the orange-tree which exhaled a sweet and heavy odor, and the habitual absorption of her own reflections, she failed to notice that the murmur of the voices grew less and less distinct, and indeed blended faintly with the low medley of sounds peculiar to the coming eveningtide.

"Pepé," Chinita was saying then, in a tone a little above a whisper, "tell me, is it true that this Don Fernando Ruiz, who for love of Rosario, and to please Don Rafael and Doña Isabel, is to lead these recruits to join Don Gonzales, — tell me, is it true that he was the associate of that Ramirez who was here so many years ago?"

"It is likely," answered Pepé, sullenly. "I have heard that he is Ramirez's godson; and what more likely," he added in an undertone, "than that the Devil should stand sponsor for an imp of his own blackness?"

"In that case," said Chinita, sharply, "it is impossible Ruiz has pronounced against him. Who ever heard of a godchild drawing sword against his sponsor? It should be against his father 'or brother rather. Go to, Pepé, you and I know nothing of Puro or Mocho. Bah! they know not the difference one from the other themselves; but we do know Ramirez and Gonzales, and it is the first that I love. What are you frowning at, Pepé? Oh! oh! oh! you are jealous, as you used to be of Pancho and Juan and Gabriel! What an idea! Ha! ha! ha!"

"Why do you laugh so loudly?" asked Doña Isabel across the corridor, not displeased to see her merry.

"Because he was telling me how the Tia Gomesinda broke the jar over the shoulders of the brave recruit who drained it of her last boiling of corn gruel," answered Chinita, readily. "But excuse me, Señora, I will not disturb you again;" and she turned with a conciliatory smile toward Pepé, who was regarding her with an expression of malignant idolatry, — if such an extravagant phrase may be coined, to indicate a love which was capable of destroying, but never of renouncing, its object.

"Thou art more unmannerly and more easily vexed than when thou usedst to follow me through the corn and bean fields, bending under the loads of wild fruit and flowers I piled upon thee, and then throwing them down some stony ravine because of one sharp word I would give thee. How canst thou expect ever to be aught but a poor ranchero, with a temper so unreasonable?"

"And what if I were as patient as Saint Stephen himself, what would it matter? Thou wouldst not love me,"

answered the young man. " And what care I whether I
am poor or rich, ranchero or soldier? It is all one now
that thou art with Doña Isabel. Why, if thou wert her
child she could not be more choice of thee. Those who
ate from the same plate and drank from the same bowl
with thee are less than the dogs who followed thee ; " and
he would have kicked, had it been near enough, the cur
which had been Pedro's, and which like many others had
the undisputed right to the corridor, and with patient
obstinacy chose to lie at Chinita's door.

The young girl looked up with a tantalizing smile. She
had been used to these speeches of covert jealousy, which
she feigned to take as the envy of an ill-mannered ranchero.
" Pshaw ! " she said gazing at him through her half-closed
lids, and yet from beneath the long lashes that veiled them
casting a languorous though wholly unstudied glance,
which dazzled and thrilled him, " ' friends, bacon, and
wine should be old ! ' What friend like an old friend?
He is better than a new-found relation. It is he who
will do a bidding and ask no reason for it ; it is he — "

" What can I do for thee ? " whispered Pepé, hoarsely.
" Tell me, and thou shalt see whether I am a friend or no ;
and then Chinita thou wilt — "

" Sh-h ! " interrupted Chinita, her finger again on her
lip. " What does it matter to me who wins or loses in
these senseless battles? Yet I wonder thou art not with
Pedro ; I would not have him sick or wounded, and alone,"
and her eyes filled with tears. Pepé moved from foot to
foot, and rubbed his shoulder against the wall uneasily.
There was a covert reproach in her tone which he resented, and yet it pleased him too that she should be
troubled : if Pedro were remembered, he could not himself
be wholly forgotten.

" It is not my fault," he muttered : " he stole away in
the night. Some say after all he has not gone to Gonzales,
and that the men who are gathered here may find themselves led to Ramirez. At any rate this Ruiz — who you
say loves Rosario, but who sighs like a furnace when his
eye lights on you, and who has worn away the post of his
door writing verses to your praise with the point of his
rapier — should be but little to be trusted."

" Ah ! " ejaculated Chinita, " I do not think thou lovest

him, Pepito. Thou wouldst not that he should do me a favor instead of thyself?"

"I would see him choked first with the wine in which he drinks a toast to thine eyes," answered Pepé, hotly. "Señor Don 'Guardo and I are in the same mind about that; but it is not that he thinks thee a beauty," he added hastily.

Chinita flushed and tossed her head proudly. "What matters it what Don 'Guardo thinks?" she said. "There could be nothing but ill luck in the favor of a man like that. Hast thou shown him the grave of the other American? Ah, thou must know where to find it. Didst thou think I did not see thee following me behind the tuñas and bushes the day I found it after I had bidden thee go back? Thou wert like Negrito there. Come here, Negrito; thou art lean and black, but I love thee;" and she stooped to pat the slinking cur. "Ah, ah! Pepito, it would be a good jest if thou wouldst show Don 'Guardo the American's grave, and tell him Chinita bids him beware of the same fortune."

"He would think thee a gypsy more than ever, and a saucy one," answered Pepé. "But I know this is not the favor thou wouldst ask of me. Thou art thinking ever of Ramirez, who bewitched thee. Ask it of the Captain Ruiz rather than me. I would die for thee, but I see not how I can serve thee by turning traitor."

Chinita started up angrily. "Am I a false-hearted wretch to ask it of thee?" she cried furiously, though in a low voice. "Ramirez fights for the side of right. Is it his fault if the Clergy are right to-day and the Liberals to-morrow? Were not he and Gonzales upon the same side when they were here years ago? Were not his men crying 'Dios y Libertad!' when they passed here six months ago? And suppose the cry is changed. Bah! with Doña Isabel's men he would be of Doña Isabel's opinion! What does it matter to him? He is a man to fight, not to sit down like Don Rafael and the major-domo, old Don Tomas, and talk, talk, talk!"

"That is very well," said Pepé, staidly; "but why do you not tell this all to Doña Isabel? Or listen, now: to please thee I will seek Pedro,—I warrant me he is not so far away,—and I will tell him how thou wouldst have

Ramirez rather than Gonzales to lead th troops; if it matters not to him, *cierto* it will not to me! But I tell thee frankly I would be of those who would pull down rather than build up churches. I see no gain to be had in fighting for the Señores the bishops, who have so much already that the poor man can have nothing but leave to fast while the priests revel in plenty. Go to, Chinita! thou hast heard Pedro talk of freedom as much as I have. If Don Benito Juarez and Don Vicente and the rest of them gain the day, I — why I might be an alcalde myself, or a general; and then — well, anything thou wilt!"

Chinita laughed and nodded at him. "It is the Señor Ramirez who could bring about all that," she said with conviction; "and, Pepé, though thou dost not love the Captain Ruiz, thou shalt take him that message from Chinita. Yes, yes! go thy way quietly to Pedro, and if there is treason, Ruiz shall work it. So the General Ramirez shall be brought over to our side, and Ruiz shall be the only man who will be blamed, if Doña Isabel is vexed."

Pepé shook his head doubtfully. His views were no clearer than Chinita's, but they were not additionally obscured by an unreasoning enthusiasm for a self-created hero. Doña Isabel was rising from her chair; the rattle of the wood upon the bricks startled the two speakers.

"How goes it with thy sister Juana?" asked Chinita, lightly. "She told me once she loved Gabriel because, though he was old and ugly, he would do more to please her than all the young and handsome lovers. Are they happy, do you think, or has he beaten her already, as I said he would?"

Pepé looked at her keenly and with an expression of wild hope from behind the wide hat he was holding in both hands before his face, in awkward preparation for departure. Would Chinita too marry the man who would please her? And after all it was but a little thing, — just a hint to the man whose admiration she jeered at.

"Thou canst go now, Pepé," said Doña Isabel, approaching. "I am sure the Señorita has heard enough of the wild doings of these mad soldiers. Thank Heaven, they leave us soon! Ah, now that I think of it, thou mayst say to the Señor Americano that Captain Ruiz told me to-day he would gladly give him safe escort as far upon their way as their roads may lie together ; and — but I forgot, such messages are not for thee. I will send them by the Señor Administrador."

Pepé muttered his adieus and bowed himself away in some confusion. Chinita looked after him meaningly ; he caught her glance and then the motion of her lips. His heart beat wildly ; they formed the refrain of a popular song,—

" Adios, my dearest love ! "

Pepé reached the court quite dizzy. Ashley Ward and Captain Ruiz were both waiting for him. His excitement had reached a crisis. He seized Ruiz by the arm. " If you would please her," he hissed in his ear, " find Ramirez, and let him, and not Gonzales, lead the troops."

" You are drunk ! " answered Ruiz ; yet he clutched the youth by the arm, and led him into his room.

Pepé came to his senses with the shock as he sank upon a stone bench against the cold, hard wall. Presently he gave a brief account of Chinita's desires and reasons. Ruiz listened without a smile. Childish and unprincipled as they were, they were not more so than scores he had heard discussed in the course of the years of anarchy in which he had entered upon manhood. Find Ramirez, pledge him to the Liberal cause, leave it to him to gain such an ascendency over the troops that they would themselves proclaim him their leader ! It was an easy task. It set him thinking, and Pepé slunk away to hope, to doubt, to despair, to hope again.

" Adios, my dearest love ! " —

just the refrain of a song, yet it pursued and bewildered him. For less, stronger men than Pepé the ranchero have committed unimaginable crimes.

The next morning when they met in the court, Captain Ruiz stopped Pepé. " Tell her her wishes are law to me !" he said. " If she but love me, I — "

" *Caramba !* " cried Pepé, savagely. " Am I an old woman or a priest that I should carry your messages ? She love you ! she would needs have been born to lead apes, to love you." And Pepé flung himself off in a rage, while the astounded Ruiz gazed after him in open-mouthed amazement.

" By my life, he loves her himself!'" he muttered vacantly. "Señor Don 'Guardo, heard you ever such presumption? The bare-skin beggar loves the favorite — what shall we say? — niece of Doña Isabel!'"

"Let us say you are both fools!" said Don 'Guardo in good round English and with a sudden rage, the motive of which was to himself inexplicable; and the discomfited captain bowed, not doubting that his own expression of disgust had been echoed.

"*Caramba!* a woman so beautiful gazed at by every beggar, like an image of the Virgin of Remedios carried in procession! I swear I will not forget thee, Pepito, and will keep a close eye on thee, now I know thou hast been tampered with!" continued Ruiz, hotly. "A word to the General Gonzales will be enough if he is of my mind!"

That day, in spite of Doña Isabel's diligence, a pink note found its way to Chinita. "Good!" she said after reading it, "My General Ramirez will have the men; the Señor Gonzales will be helped, and Doña Isabel will do a double good. This is not so bad a subject, — this Ruiz; and his eyes are as black and large as those of Ramirez himself. All is well. All things will come right at last. Ah, if only what Don Rafael told Feliz one night should come true, and the convents are opened, then — "

She paused. It seemed too utterly impossible even to dream of. She looked again at her first love-letter; a twinge of remorse seized her as she thought of Rosario. She laughed, but she tore the paper into infinitesimal shreds.

What was the writer thinking? "Onward! I have gone too far to turn back even at the word of Chinita. A promise will gain her love, but the essential thing is the good-will of Doña Isabel. ' A pearl is all the better for a golden setting!' No treaties then with Ramirez. Though he is my godfather, I need not his patronage. Doña Isabel, a straight path, and Juarez! Forward! Ruiz, fortune favors you!"

XXX.

A FEW days later the troops had left Tres Hermanos, and Ashley Ward stood in the silent graveyard on the mountain side, pushing back with his foot the loose sand his tread had disturbed, as it threatened again and again to cover the rude wooden cross upon which his eyes were fixed. It bore the name of his murdered cousin, faint yet distinct, preserved by the sand, for the wind had soon prostrated it after Chinita's shallow replanting. The words seemed to Ashley to call to him aloud from the dust of his kinsman; in the hot sunshine their spell was as potent as though a ghostly voice had spoken at midnight. For the first time, something more intense than the desire to satisfy conscience by proving that he wronged no rightful heir in entering upon property which would have been John Ashley's had he lived, arose in his mind. The absolute reality of his cousin's death for the first time seemed to become an overwhelming conviction; and with it came memories of the young and daring man whom he had in childhood held in wondering admiration. And as he stood within sight of the spot where the brilliant young life had ended in a bloody tragedy, a deep wave of sorrow surged over his soul, and from its depths, as from the loose sands of the wind-levelled grave, appeared to rise a cry for vengeance.

Though not till now had Chinita's charge that he be taken to the American's grave been carried out, the message from Doña Isabel, which Pepé had not failed to deliver, had reached him some days before, and had been supplemented by a visit from Don Rafael. Although a certain fascination had inclined Ashley to linger still at Tres Hermanos, he had so little hope of adding to the information he had already gained of his cousin's life, — there seemed so little possibility that the marriage which John Ashley had intimated had taken place, could ever

have been more than a mere sentimental dedication of the
lovers one to the other, in which they deemed themselves
man and wife in the sight of God, but which in the sight
of man was a mere illicit connection, to be condemned
or ignored, — that he had not dared to present himself
before the haughty mother of the one Herlinda whom he
suspected to have been the object of his cousin's passion,
and to insult her with questions or insinuations that would
cast a doubt upon her daughter's purity and a stain upon
the fame of the house of Garcia, which even the blood of
John Ashley and his own added thereto would be insufficient to wash away.

The young man had decided then to accept the order of
dismissal, so delicately conveyed in the intimation that
by accepting the escort of the troops as far as they might
proceed toward Guanapila, he would not only reach a point
whence in all probability he might in safety proceed to
that city, but that he would thus render a favor to Doña
Isabel, who was minded by the same opportunity to withdraw from the hacienda, — her presence there being liable
to act as a lure to either party, who might after seizing
her person levy a ransom upon the family which even their
large resources would be severely strained to meet.

Although the fiction was maintained that her assistance
of the Liberal cause was involuntary, it was readily surmised that Doña Isabel Garcia was in reality seeking to
avoid the vengeance of the Conservatives, while their
forces were so demoralized and scattered that she might
hope to reach Guanapila, which was then occupied by a
patriot guard, before the tide of the war should turn and
bring the army of the Church again to the fore *en masse*,
— collected by the clarion cry of fanaticism, and lavishly
rewarded from the hoards of silver and gold drawn from
the vaults into which for generations had been drained the
prosperity and the very life-blood of the peasantry.

Ashley Ward had been struck with admiration of the
woman who thus dared the dangers of the road, — to
which she had been no stranger. He had felt something of
the chivalrous enthusiasm of a knight of old, as he joined
the irregular band which by daylight had gathered upon
the sandy plain before the straggling village. The soldiers
had fallen into march with something like order, with Ruiz

at their head, — for once with an anxious face, for he felt that the die was cast, and that he had raised up for himself an enemy whom it would be mad temerity to face, and hopeless to attempt to conciliate. The baggage-mules were driven by the leathern-clad muleteers, who even thus early had begun their profane adjurations to the nimble-footed beasts, that listened with quivering ears thrown back in obstinate surprise at every unwonted silence. The women who had come from other villages had laughed and chided their unruly infants, as they arranged and re-arranged their baskets of maize and vegetables upon the panniers of their donkeys, if they were fortunate enough to possess any, or upon their own shoulders if they were to walk; and those who were for the first time leaving their birthplace to follow the fortunes of husband or sweetheart, had burst into loud lamentations. Ashley had been glad to find these changed to laughter, however, before they were well past the broken wall of the reduction-works; which they skirted, entering upon the bridle-path which led across the hill, where the rough heaps of sand showed through the scattered cacti, and where, by the rude wooden crosses, he now for the first time learned lay the village graveyard.

Pepé had ridden sullenly by his side. He had been sent back with a sharp reprimand from the station he had taken among the mounted servants who surrounded the carriage of Doña Isabel, Ruiz in petty tyranny refusing him so honorable a place. A glance from Chinita had been the deepest reproof of all; and as he pondered upon it, certain words which she had uttered, and which he had hitherto forgotten, had come into his mind. As they neared the graveyard his eye caught Ward's, and suddenly laying his hand upon the bridle of the American's horse, he had muttered, —

" Señor, she thinks I have forgotten all her wishes; but there is not even one so foolish that I scorn it. Turn aside but for a moment, Señor, — here where the adobe has fallen, your horse can scramble through the wall. Follow me, they will not miss us before we can reach our places again. *Caramba!* Don Fernando watches me as a cat watches a mouse. Here, Señor, — never mind the women. Stupids! how they herd their donkeys together, when they might have the whole hillside to pick their own paths on! Patience! Let us wait a little, Señor! Ah," he reflected, as they remained silent and motionless, "there is the spot. I have never forgotten it since I followed her through the rushes down there by the stream, and scratched my face in the tuñas, darting behind them that she should not see me. I was not half so tired as Chinita was though, when she sat down to rub sand upon her smarting hands, and fell asleep with the sun beating upon her head. I wonder if she ever thought it was I who covered her face with her ragged reboso, — she wears one of silk now, as clean and soft as a dove's breast, — or that I lay behind the big pipes of the flowering organ-plant as she turned over the fallen cross which her hand struck against, and read the name and age of the American who had been murdered years before? Who ever would have thought — for I hated her then if I did follow her, as she maddens me now with her soft eyes and her mocking smile — that I should be bringing here the man who perhaps is just the handsome, woman-maddening demon they say that other was, and at her will too? *Ave Maria Purissima!* what God wills the very saints themselves may not say No to, — much less a poor peasant like Pepé Ortiz."

These thoughts, perhaps scarcely in the order in which they are set down, passed through the mind of Pepé, as lingering until the straggling procession had passed, he emerged from the shade of such an organ-plant as had once sheltered him years ago, and taking his bearings with unerring eyes, beckoned to Ashley, — who had waited within touch of his hand, and whose heart had begun to beat suffocatingly, though he knew that it was utterly improbable that anything more important than the mound that covered the body of his cousin would meet his eye, — and led the way to the most wind-swept and desolate portion of that paupers' acre, and presently stooping where the ground was sunken rather than heaped, turned with some effort the half-buried cross, and exposed to Ashley's view the name from which his own had been derived.

The young man gazed at it in a sort of fascination, actually spelling the letters over and over. He felt as if a part of himself must be buried there. His eyes burned; the glaring sunshine leaped and quivered above the ill-carved letters, distorting and confounding them. His heart beat violently; every sense but that of hearing seemed to fail him, and every sound upon the air became a weird, mysterious voice, — blood crying unto its kindred blood.

This deep emotion fixed the indifferent and wandering eye of Pepé, who, holding the bridles of the horses, stood near, impatient to be gone, yet intending to watch out of sight the last stragglers; for it was with a double purpose he had turned aside to point out the grave of the American, — first, perhaps, to gratify the seemingly jesting wish of Chinita; and then to seize the opportunity to turn his fleet steed into the narrow bridle-path which led to mountain villages, where he shrewdly suspected Pedro might be found, or at least be heard of. He had promised to carry the message of Chinita to Pedro, and would have set forth upon the very night she had charged him with it, but until mounted by Ruiz's command had found it impossible to provide himself with a horse, without which it was hopeless for him to attempt his quest. To escape the discipline of the ranks, he had induced Ashley to retain him as his servant, feeling no scruple at his intended abandonment. As his eye rested upon the pale and excited countenance of Ashley, Chinita's words, with which she had bade him taunt him, flashed into his mind; yet he forbore to utter them, saying presently in a tone of concern, —

"Let us go now, Señor, it is growing hot. It is almost noon, and you are faint. Let us ride on, and I will point out the way that you must take when we have crossed the face of the hill. Then comes a slight descent, Señor, and upon the little plain that lies between that and the cañon of the Water-pots will the troop stop for the nooning. This has been a rapid march. Doña Isabel will feel all the safer when she is once on the highway. But as for us, Señor, we must part company. You will find a better servant; I should but ill serve your grace. You know yourself I am but a stupid fellow, and it is only the patience of your grace that has been equal to my ignorance."

Ashley heard neither the excuses of Pepé nor his own

praises, but with a gesture at once commanding and entreating the servant to leave him, said: "Pepé, I had forgotten. There is something which will keep me still at Tres Hermanos. The Señora Doña Isabel must pardon me. Go! go to your duty, as I must to mine. God! how could I have forgotten it? Oh John, John! does time and distance make men so unnatural? Is it possible I could leave the place where you were so foully murdered, without knowing why or by whom? Who killed him, and why was the deadly and secret blow struck? Ah, that involves the question of the very mystery I came here to fathom, and which I was turning my back upon; for I am convinced that it is here, and not by following Doña Isabel Garcia, that it may be solved. She is too resolute, too astute; nothing is to be forced or beguiled from her lips! But now that the spell of her presence is removed, I may learn everything from these people, who with all their cunning and clannish devotion can surely be influenced by reasons such as I can give."

"Who would have guessed the sight of a grave would so stir the blood?" soliloquized Pepé. "Can it be that Chinita — But no, she was more in jest than earnest; she always laughed at the *niña* Chata for her sorrow for the foreigner. — Well, all must die!" he said aloud. "Believe me, Señor, after all these years a knife-thrust is a little matter to inquire into. *Caramba!* Chinita herself would tell you that to turn back on a journey because of the dead is an omen of evil; 't was not for that she would have me show you the grave of your countryman, — God rest him!"

Ashley looked at him keenly. "Ah," he said, "it is then no accident that you have brought me here? God! what a mystery! Pepé, tell Chinita I know her thoughts, and that I never will rest till I prove them right or wrong. She is a strange creature, and likely to prove an enigma to more men than myself. Poor lad, she is not for you to dream of."

"I will not see her again till I can tell her that which shall please her," said Pepé. "Look you, Señor, she is one who will have the world turn to suit her."

"A wilful girl," thought Ashley, with judicial disapproval. "She has all the craftiness and deceit of the Indian and the pride and passion of a Spaniard; yet what if I should follow her? No, no! mere circumstance and conjecture shall not turn me!—*Adios*, Pepé," he said aloud, "and beware! It is Doña Isabel you serve, and not the young girl who has bewitched you."

Pepé smiled vaguely; his glance roved over the landscape. "Her heart is virgin honey in a cup of alabaster!" he murmured. Ashley was becoming accustomed to the poetic expressions of these unlettered rancheros, and with some impatience took in his own hand the bridle-rein of his horse, and reminding Pepé that it was nearly noon, and that he would be missed should he longer delay, bade him mount and hasten with messages of excuse to Doña Isabel for his own sudden return to Tres Hermanos.

With the customary apparent submission of a peasant, Pepé prepared to obey. He was in fact anxious to set forth as soon as he could be certain that no straggler was near to mark his movements. The troops and their followers had disappeared. "The Señor Don 'Guardo should leave this solitary spot on the instant," he said with genuine concern; "in these days of revolution, one can never say what dangerous people may be wandering abroad."

"I have nothing to fear from them," answered Ashley, "unless it should be that they might attempt to rob me of the horse Doña Isabel has lent me. Well, for its sake, I will be prudent; though in truth the sight of a ghost in this desolate spot of sunken graves would seem more probable than that any living being should pass here. Now, then, good-by, Pepé."

"Until our next meeting, Señor!" replied Pepé, gravely lifting his hat. He had attached himself to Ashley, and it seemed to him an evil omen that they should part at a grave. and he thus attempted to console himself by the pretence that it was but for a little while. "For a short time Señor, and God keep you!"

Ashley shook his hand warmly. The ranchero drew his hat over his eyes, adjusted his scrape so that his face was almost hidden, and dropping into that utterly ungraceful posture into which the skilled horseman of Mexico relapses when he suffers his steed to take his own way and pace across a wearisome stretch of country, he turned his horse's head toward the bridle-path they had left, and slowly re-

ceded from Ashley's gaze. Once however beyond the crest
of the hill, the rider's eye brightened, his figure straightened ; a distant sound of voices reached his keen ear, —
it was so remote that but for the rarity of the atmosphere
it would have failed to reach him. Bending his head, he
listened intently for a moment ; then raising it he gazed
searchingly on every hand, rode for a short distance to the
right, guided his nimble-footed beast down the cleft sides
of a deep ravine and along the dry bottom of a rock-
strewn path, which rapid floods had in some past time cut
in their fierce descent from the steep sides of the frowning
mountains, and so gradually gained the dark and solitary
defiles that led directly to those eyries of bandit mountaineers, who under the guise of shepherds, charcoal-burners, and goat-herds had been, as Pepé well knew, the
chosen comrades of Pedro Gomez and his mates in the
boyhood days of that Don Leon whose wild deeds were
still the theme of many a tale, and like the story of his
death became more mythical with every repetition.

Pepé rode steadily on for hours, picturing to himself his
meeting with Pedro should he find him, or the quiet exultation of Chinita when she should hear that he had deserted
the troops, or of the return of Don 'Guardo to the hacienda. In his heart he was not displeased that the American should be separated from Chinita, though it left her
the more completely to the gallant care of Ruiz. He had
comprehended instantly the emotion which had seized
upon Ashley at his kinsman's grave, — the instinct for
revenge. He said to himself that those Americans, after
all, were people of sensibility, and he felt a certain satisfaction that he had been the instrument of calling into
action a sentiment that did the foreigner so much
credit.

Meanwhile the heat of noon passed, and Ashley's horse
stood with patient dejection in the shadow of the huge
cactus to which he had been tethered, not even taking
advantage of the freedom allowed by the length of the
rope, so little temptation to browse was offered by the
sparse and coarse tufts of herbage which struggled into
existence here and there. The time wore on, and an occasional stamp attested his disapprobation of a master
who lay prone upon the ground under a mesquite tree

19

when the sun shone hottest, and who when the cool breeze of afternoon swept over the silent spot, stood long and still beside the grave he had not sought, and yet felt infinite reluctance to leave.

It was a foolish thought, but as he gazed across the broad valley to the great square of buildings set among the fields, the youth imagined how indeed the dead man might at times steal forth to visit again those fertile scenes where he had lived and loved. As he stood there, Ashley could see the people like pigmies passing in and out the great gateway, or going from hut to hut in the village. There was one figure — it seemed that of a woman — which his eye sought from time to time, as it appeared and disappeared in the corn and bean fields, and at last came out on the open road that lay between them and the reduction-works. He was becoming quite fascinated by its hesitating yet persistent progress, when he was startled by a sound; and glancing up, he saw a man leaning upon the crumbling wall and regarding him with a gaze so bewildered, so fixed, that involuntarily he moved a step toward him.

The stranger started, as if some frightful spell had been broken. Ashley saw that he crossed himself, and muttered some invocation; yet that he had not the look of a nervous man or a coward, but rather of a somnambulist pacing the earth under the impulse of some horrible dream. The man was not ill-looking, — no, decidedly not; and though his skin was deeply browned as if from much exposure, and his cheek bones were prominent, giving his face a certain cast below the eyes that was plebeian or Indian in character, the eyes themselves were dilated and brilliant, and the straight nose and pointed beard gave him the air of a Spanish cavalier, though he wore the broad sombrero and scrape of a common soldier of the rural order. Perhaps on ordinary occasions even a more practised eye than that of Ashley Ward would have accepted the stranger for what he purported to be; but the American with an extraordinary feeling of repulsion little accounted for by the mere sense of intrusion caused by the man's unexpected appearance, at once leaped to the conclusion that his dress — though he had no appearance of strangeness in it — was virtually a disguise, and that instead of a soldier of the ranks, the man before him was of no ordinary position or character.

The new-comer seemed to have risen out of the ground, so stealthily had he approached. It would have been quite possible for him, tall as he was, to have skirted the wall without observation from any one within the enclosure. But undoubtedly he had taken no precaution in that solitary place, which except at funeral times was shunned as the haunt of ghosts and ill-omened birds and reptiles, and thus had come unexpectedly upon the motionless figure of the tall young man clothed in a plain riding-suit of black, with bright conspicuous locks at the moment uncovered, and fair-skinned face of a characteristic American type, — all unremarkable in themselves but associated in the mind of the observer with one whom he had seen but twice or thrice, and this on the mad night when the moon had shone down upon a victim quivering in the death-agony above which he had exulted.

The two men held each the other's gaze in silence for a full minute, both unmindful of the common courtesy usual in such chance encounters in solitary places. Then recovering from the superstitious awe which had overpowered him, the Mexican stepped over the broken wall. Ashley noticed as he did so that heavy silver spurs were on his heels, and that the fringed sides of his leathern trousers were stained as though with hard riding, and that, as if from habit, rather than any purpose of menace, his nervous hand closed upon the pistol in his scarlet band, as with a few long strides he reached the spot on which Ashley stood with that air of defiance which a sudden intrusion upon a solitude however secure naturally arouses in a man who is neither a coward nor an adept in the self-command that is perhaps the most perfect substitute for invincible courage.

" Señor," said the Mexican, " your pistols are on your saddle. You are right; this is an evil habit to wear them so readily at one's side. Pardon me if in my surprise I assumed an attitude of menace; but these are troublous times. One scarcely expects to find a cavalier alone in such a place." He looked around him with a smile, which did not hinder a quiver of the lip expressing an excitement which his commonplace words denied.

Ashley regarded the speaker with ever-increasing repugnance. It was true his pistols hung from the saddle, but there was a small knife in his belt, and his hand wandered to it stealthily as he answered: " Señor, I make no inquiry why you are here, and on foot, — which you must acknowledge might well cause some curiosity in this place ; but in all courtesy I trust your errand is a happier one than mine. Whatever it is, I will not intrude upon it longer than will suffice to plant this cross." And with an air of perfect security, yet with his knife in hand, he bent to the work, which the other regarded with an almost incredulous gaze, — the preservation of a grave or its tokens being a sort of sentimentality to which by tradition and training he was a stranger ; and to see it exhibited for the first time in this God's acre of laborers, almost sufficed to dissipate the impression the unexpected encounter had made upon him. As Ashley quietly pursued his work, the new-comer had an opportunity to look at him narrowly. After all, this one was like many another American! Yet there was something in the young man's appearance that brought the sweat to the brow of the soldier ; he pushed back his hat, and breathed hard. As he did so, Ashley braced the cross against his knee. The action brought the letters into clear and direct view. The eyes of the Mexican rested upon them. He fell back a step or two in superstitious awe, involuntarily exclaiming :

"*Cristo!* was *he* buried here? And who are you?"

Ashley glanced up. There was a revelation to him in the questioner's disordered and ashy countenance. He dropped the cross, sprang over the grave, and seized the stranger by the right arm. " Who are you who ask? " he cried. " What do you know of the man who is buried there? "

" My faith! you are a brave man to put such questions! " retorted the new-comer, wrenching himself free. Ashley had spoken in English, but the violence of his act had interpreted his words. " Take your pistols and defend yourself, if you are here for vengeance. Kill him? Yes ; I killed him as I would a dog. Faith, I thought it was his accursed ghost that had risen to challenge me! "

" I am his cousin! Assassin, give me reasons for your deed! " cried Ashley, furiously, yet with a remembrance that to every criminal should be allowed some chance of justification.

But the Mexican seemed little inclined to profit by it.

"Reasons!" cried he. "Yes, such reasons as I gave him when I thrust the knife into his heart." He raised his pistol and fired. The shot passed so close to Ashley's temple that he heard it whiz through the air. In the same instant the two men clinched. The horse, which during the controversy had plunged and reared madly, broke away, and careering over the graves galloped wildly down the hillside. A fresh horse with its rider at the same instant dashed into the enclosure, and a voice cried, "For God's sake my General! what adventure is this? Mount! mount! there is no time to be lost!"

The combatants at the sound of a third voice had involuntarily paused. Had the knife in the hand of the American been in that of the Mexican it would have sheathed itself in his opponent's heart; but Ashley, less ready in its use, arrested his hand midway. His passion half spent, the scarcely healed wound throbbing in his shoulder, his strength exhausted, he had much ado to keep himself from staggering.

"A touch of my sabre would finish him," said the newcomer coolly, as he reined in his restive horse, and put his hand on the long weapon swinging from his saddle. But the soldier stopped him.

"No killing in cold blood," he exclaimed. "'T is a madman, but his fury is over. What brings you here, Reyes? Were you not to wait at the rendezvous?"

"Wait!" he retorted, "this is no time to wait! We are already a day too late. A thousand men are on the road before us, my General! We let them pass us this morning as we lingered on the opposite side of the mountain in the Devil's gate!"

"And the troops are there still?" cried the other furiously. "Where is Choolooke? Did you not think to bring me a horse? Back to the Zahuan, man! We must begin the march this very night. I know Ruiz; he will yield in a moment at sight of me!"

"Not he!" answered Reyes. "He has a new patroness; Doña Isabel herself is with him."

"Isabel!" cried the officer with an oath. "Ah, then,

Tres Hermanos is partisan at last! *Carrhi!* my lady Isabel shall find what she has begun shall be soon ended!" He put a small silver whistle to his lips and blew a shrill blast, which was answered by a neigh. A black horse lifted its head and looked over the wall with a gaze of almost human intelligence.

"He followed me at a word," exclaimed Reyes, "and stood by the wall like a statue when I bade him. Never was there such another horse as your black Choolooke, my General. Even the stampede of that unbroken brute that was tethered here could not startle him."

"Ay, I discipline horses better than I do men, — eh, Choolooke?" The horse with its jingling accoutrements had cantered into the enclosure, and with one bound his owner was in the saddle.

All had passed in the few minutes in which Ashley was recovering breath, and in utter bewilderment endeavoring to gain some insight into the meaning of this rapid transformation scene, of which he himself had formed a part. As his late opponent sprang into the saddle, he could have fancied he heard the sound of the bugle, so alert were the man's movements, so soldierly his bearing. But in the midst of his involuntary admiration he did not forget the extraordinary relations in which they stood to each other. He threw himself before the horse at the imminent risk of being trampled down. "Your name!" he cried. "By your own admission you are my cousin's murderer. We must meet again! I am Ashley Ward; and you?"

"Out of the way!" cried the rider, checking his horse by a dexterous turn of his hand. "My name? Ah, yes! Tell them there," and he nodded in the direction of the hacienda, "they will soon have reason never to forget it!" He hesitated; plunged the spurs into his already impatient steed, and dashed furiously away, followed by Reyes; then rose in his stirrups to shout back in defiance the name — "Ramirez!"

XXXI.

Ramirez! Ashley's heart bounded, his brain throbbed dizzily yet acutely. Here was no obscure assassin, who once escaping him would perhaps be lost forever.

The name was on every lip with those of Juarez, Ortega, Degollado, Miramon, and a score of other popular chieftains who of one party or another, or of independent factions, attracted to themselves a host of followers, more by their own personal magnetism than for the sake of any principles they represented. In that time of anarchy any head that rose above the common herd led enthusiastic multitudes, who followed a nod and applauded to the echo even one deed of daring. But Ramirez held his prestige by no such recent and uncertain tenure; throughout the long years of revolution he had been a central figure in the bloody drama. Even his recent defeat at El Toro and his subsequent disappearance had added but a fresh glamor of mystery to his adventurous career, without detracting from the almost superstitious awe with which he was regarded. It was believed that he would reappear when and where least expected. Ashley Ward had smiled covertly at the strange and daring escapades attributed to this man. He had become in his mind a figure of romance; and here in the broad day he had risen before him, the self-denounced murderer of John Ashley, — and as suddenly as he had come, so had he escaped him.

Thinking no more of the cross, which had fallen upon the ground, hiding beneath it the name that had been so long preserved for so strange a purpose, Ashley Ward turned from the sunken graves and striding across the mounds, scarred and broken by the sacrilegious tread of the horses' feet, stood for a moment upon the broken wall, scanning the country in his excitement for some sign of the desperate men who but a few moments before had urged their restive steeds up the steep path and disap-

peared over the crest of the hill. He saw his own reo-
reant steed galloping toward the hacienda walls, keeping
the high-road, on past the reduction-works and the long
stretch of open country beyond, and plunging and rearing
at the fatal mesquite-tree. The superstitious vaqueros
had instinctively imbued their animals with the same irrational terrors in which they had themselves been trained.
Yet no sight of ghost or smell of blood lingered there to
rouse memory or vengeance. Their waiting-place had been
that long-forgotten grave upon the desolate hillside.

Ashley leaped from the wall and rapidly began the
descent to the valley. The sun was still high in the
heavens, for the scene we have recorded had passed in
less than a brief quarter of an hour. As he walked on,
gradually falling into a more natural pace, the whole
matter took definite form and coherence in his mind.
That which had been so unexpected, so unnatural, seemed
to be the event to which his whole journey to Mexico,
all his wanderings, his strange and wearisome experiences,
had inevitably and naturally tended. And then arose
a point beyond. His work at Tres Hermanos seemed
ended; the primal cause of his being there was forgotten.
The definite thought now in his mind was to reach the
hacienda, provide himself anew with horse, guide, and
arms, and follow on the path which Ramirez had chosen,
and upon which he would sooner or later re-appear, decoyed by the rich booty that Doña Isabel had intrusted
to the weak and presumably faithless Ruiz. Could he
reach and warn her in time?

Ashley's scarce-healed wound was throbbing painfully,
the way was long, the heat intense; yet he pressed
on resolutely, though at last he staggered as he went.
He sat down to rest awhile among the dry rushes of the
spent watercourse, under a straggling cottonwood-tree,
the few poor leaves of which scarcely sufficed to shade
him from the fierce rays of the sun. A fever heat was in
his veins; wild theories and speculations passed through
his brain, — some of them, perhaps, not far from being
keys to the mystery of that tragedy which that day for
the first time had become to his mind other than a vague
and gloomy fantasy. Now, like the murderer himself, it
was real, absorbing, appalling.

The young man rose and again pressed on. After the descent to the long rude wall of the reduction-works, he skirted it slowly, thinking as he went how changed the aspect of the place must be since his cousin had ridden forth to his death. How proudly John had written, and almost vauntingly, of the prosperity his management had inaugurated, of the crowds of laden animals that passed in and out of the wide gates, of the men who led their slow, laborious lives among those primitive mills and wide floors of trodden ores.

Ashley glanced at the great square mass of walls and towers of Tres Hermanos, glistening in the distance. To his weary eye it looked far away; yet doubtless he thought it had been but the ride of a few eager minutes to the lover, as he went at midnight to cast a glance at the walls that circled his mistress, or to rein his horse beneath her window that he might win a word or glance from her who whispered from above. These, Ashley had heard, were lovers' ways in Mexico; he did not know that no maiden of Tres Hermanos ever occupied one of the few apartments whose windows opened toward the outer air. Yet as he debated the matter with himself, it became more and more probable to him that John Ashley had upon the fatal night been actually within the walls of the hacienda, and been stealthily followed thence by his treacherous rival, — for what, he thought, even to a Spaniard, could justify so foul a murder but the falseness of his mistress, the triumph of a hated rival? Pedro's taciturnity and gloom Ashley construed as proofs of his complicity in the crime. Even then Ramirez had been a chieftain of renown, and Pedro in his youth had been a soldier, a free rider, of whom strange tales were told. Was it not probable that he had opened the gate at a comrade's bidding, — or, more likely still, had bidden him wait beneath the tree where the favored lover was wont to mount his horse, and so take him unawares? Ashley remembered that such, it had been said, had been the manner of his cousin's taking off. He had been slain with the swiftness and sureness of a secret and unhesitating avenger.

The ardent youth railed at the mocking chances that had combined to suffer Ramirez to escape him in the unpremeditated struggle in which they had clinched with a deadly enmity. In such a struggle he could have found himself the victor without remorse, or could have died without regret; but it was not in his nature to follow a man for blood. Yet neither could he shut his ears to that cry for vengeance, for justice, which seemed ringing through the sultry stillness, — the more importunate as the possibilities of their attainment shaped themselves in his mind.

That this must be a personal matter between himself and Ramirez was clear. At any time it would probably have been useless for an alien to have denounced so popular and influential a man as the proud and daring *revolucionario*. To attempt his arrest for a murder committed years before and probably in rivalry for a lady's favor, would be but to throw a new mystery about him, and add a fresh legend of romance to those which already made him rather a character of ideal chivalry than of mere vulgar, every-day lawlessness and semi-barbarity. Though the brilliant adventurer was now under a temporary cloud, one threat of attack from law would make him again a popular idol; indeed it was likely that a *pronunciamiento* in his favor would be the immediate result, and that in falling into his hands the American would lose, if not his life, at least all opportunity either of obtaining the satisfaction of the law for his cousin's death, or of investigating further those doubts and probabilities which he had forgotten, but which now came upon him with redoubled force.

The excited Ashley planned in his mind to refresh himself upon reaching the hacienda, and demanding horse and guide to set forth upon that very night, hoping to rejoin the force at daybreak. It was useless, he reflected, to waste further time in idle questionings. It was to Doña Isabel herself he would appeal, and warning her of the danger that threatened her from the bandit chieftain, induce her to make common cause with him against one who for years must have been their common enemy. Impossible was it for him to solve the mystery of the relations in which the several actors in this strange drama in which he was so unexpectedly taking part, stood either to one another, or to himself. There was but one fact certain; by that alone he could connect himself with beings who seemed almost of another world,

— the one undoubted fact of the discovery of John Ashley's murderer.

Ashley's ready apprehension of the public mind had been helped by what he knew to be the actual state of affairs in the ranks to which Doña Isabel had intrusted the safety of her person, trusting to the resources which were at her command, and to the present ascendency of Gonzales, to bind those soldiers of fortune to the cause she had espoused. Perhaps none knew better than she the elements that an alluring chance of gain or a transient enthusiasm had drawn together; but she could not know how near the fire lay to the straw, and how at her very side were those who in the name of patriotism — or, like Chinita, for a personal sentiment as unexplainable as it was imaginative and ardent — would sacrifice her dearest plans, and think it a grand and noble deed to raise the ubiquitous and dashing Ramirez upon the fall of the slow and cautious Gonzales. Ashley had imperfectly comprehended the scheme or its bearings; he had little understood, and felt but little interest in, those strange complexities and personalities of Mexican politics; but now a sudden party zeal and horror of treason seized him. Where was Pedro Gomez, who, having played traitor once, might do so a hundred times more? Where was Pepé? Had he rejoined the troops, or had the detour to the graveyard been but a clever plan for eluding them? Were these, and perhaps Ruiz too, the tools of Ramirez? Yet the latter had appeared to have ridden far; the news of the gathering and departure of the troops had appeared to have astounded as much as it had enraged him. Who had carried the news to Reyes?

The way was long and the youth's excitement waning; his recent illness and still aching wound began to declare their effects. In his full vigor Ashley Ward would have found the walk under the glaring sunshine — which, though no longer vertical, was fierce and blinding as it neared the western hilltops — more than he would have chosen for an afternoon's stroll. Weak as he was, and becoming painfully conscious that he had fasted since morning, he was glad to lean sometimes against the high adobe wall and measure with his eye the slowly decreasing distance. It was a landmark on his way when he caught sight of the heavy gate set in the wall of the reduction-works; he knew then just how much farther he must go. He had no thought of actually approaching it, but he noticed with surprise that one heavy valve was slightly ajar; and with that sudden collapse which is apt to assail the overtasked frame at the unexpected sight of an open door, however meagre the entertainment it may suggest, he dragged himself onward with the natural belief that he should find within some servant or attaché of the great house. But when he reached the gate and looked through the narrow aperture, a perfect stillness reigned within. No horse stamped in the courtyard; no spurred heel rang on the pavement. Great cacti were pushing their gaunt and prickly branches into the narrow space, as if stretching longing arms out into the wide world from which they had been so long shut in.

With some effort Ashley thrust back the strong and aggressive barrier, and forced his way in. Rank grass, which was at that season yellow and matted, had grown up between the cobble-stones, and raised them in little heaps, over which the lizards ran. One -- fiery red -- stopped as Ashley's boot-heel woke the echoes, and turned a wondering ear, then glided swiftly on.

Between the main building and the offices there was a small arched lobby, through which one entered the great court, upon which piles of broken ores and the long dried masses were spread. In this lobby in the olden time the workmen had been stopped by the watchman or gate-keeper and searched, — a proceeding to which they daily submitted with indifference, holding their arms on high while the practised searcher ran his hands over their thin and scanty garments, shook out the coarse scrape and tattered sombrero, peered among the rows of glistening teeth and under the tongue, for those fragments of rich ore or amalgam which in spite of all precautions, or by the connivance of the searcher, reached the outer world, netting in the aggregate a considerable surplus to the income of the laborers, which found its way to the gambling tables, or was spent in the adornment of their wives, — as was proved by the great decline in the village of the manufacture of filagree ornaments of quaint and delicate designs upon the closing of the Garcia mining-works.

Ashley, with a feeling of curiosity or a sense of impending action, which renewed his strength as a tonic might have done, noticed that the door upon the side of the lobby that opened into the main building or living rooms was also ajar. He glanced in, but except where the long ray of light stole in through the aperture, which his person partially obscured, all was so dim that he saw only imperfectly a few scattered articles of furniture, — and they appeared to be so old and battered that they were scarce worth the protection which the great padlock and rusty key, hanging from a staple in the door, indicated had been afforded them.

With a feeling of awe, Ashley remembered that his cousin must have lived, and perhaps had lain dead, in that room. With nervous energy he thrust open the door, and the light streamed in. He started as his eyes fell upon the floor. It was of large square bricks, thickly spread with the dust of many years, but impressed with footprints so blurred that, dazzled as his eyes were, he could not tell whether they were those of man, woman, or child. They seemed mysterious, ghostly. There was no sound of human presence. His heart beat as it had not done in all the excitement of that day.

"I am here! I have been waiting as you bade me," said a low, frightened voice. The words came so unexpectedly that Ashley scarce understood them. He stepped forward and glanced around searchingly. In the further corner of the room a female figure was in the act of rising from a low seat on which it had crouched. The face was half-averted, the dark reboso was drawn over it with the left hand, the right was outstretched as if in supplicating, almost compulsory, welcome.

"Good God!" — "*Dios mio!*" The ejaculations were simultaneous; the girl sank to the floor, the young man involuntarily drew back.

"Señorita!" he exclaimed in a voice of incredulity, "Señorita, you here and alone?"

"*Maria Sanctissima!* not the General Ramirez!" he heard her moan; yet in the fright and confusion there seemed an accent of relief. "Don 'Guardo! Oh, what has brought you here? Oh, Señor, believe me — "

"Do not distress yourself to explain, Señorita," interrupted Ashley, coldly. "Rise, I beg, and I will go at once; but that you may not waste more time in waiting, I will tell you that the man you speak of will not be here to-day. And," he added, with an intensity that startled even himself, "if there is justice in heaven or upon earth, never again shall he fulfil a lover's tryst upon a spot that by any other than a demon would be shunned as a scene of gentle dalliance, if not abhorred as the theatre of a crime that should have blasted his whole life!"

The girl threw back her head-covering and looked up in uncomprehending amaze. As her gaze caught Ashley's both colored, both averted their eyes in confusion. Ashley recoiled before hers, so childlike, so honest.

"Chata!" he murmured; "Chata!" involuntarily extending toward her his hand in deprecation, in entreaty, in protection. She clasped it as a frightened child might, and clinging to it rose to her feet, swaying a little and bending low, not with weakness, but with shame.

"I dared not disobey him," she murmured at last. "I dared not disobey."

Ashley dropped her hand, — almost flung it from him.

The girl's face crimsoned; she opened her lips, hesitated, then clasping her hands together, cried, "It is not as you think. Oh, rather than the truth, would to God it were! I am not the child of Don Rafael and Doña Rita! José Ramirez is my father!"

XXXII.

"José Ramirez is my father!"

Had her words been a thunderbolt hurled at Ashley's feet, they could not have astounded him more. The daughter of Ramirez!

"I do not believe it! I cannot believe it!" he exclaimed, with no thought for courteous words. "Oh, that is a tale for a jealous lover! but I am not one. Anything, anything rather than that, Señorita, would serve to explain the reason of your presence here!"

"Why have I spoken?" cried the young girl with tears. "Why have I broken my promise, and only to be disbelieved and scorned? O, Señor, I know not what it was in you that wrung the words from me! Did he not command me to be silent till he gave me leave to speak? He is my father, yet I have disobeyed his first command. In the letter the woman brought me, two days after he left El Toro, and in which he commanded me to meet him here upon this day, he enjoined secrecy again and again; and yet I forgot. Miserable girl that I am!"

Ashley had lived among Mexicans long enough to learn something of their ideas of filial duty. No matter how vile, how cruel, how debased the parent may be, the duty of the child is perfect obedience and respect; the petted infant in its most wilful moments ceases its passionate cries to kiss the father's hand; the young man deprives himself, his wife and children, to minister to his aged parents; he who cannot or will not work, esteems it a pious act to become a bandit upon the highway rather than that his father or mother shall look to him for food or even for luxuries in vain, — and thus he comprehended the remorse of this conscience-stricken child, as the conviction rushed over him that her belief might indeed be true. There was that in the contour of her face which resembled that of Ramirez more markedly than the mere

general type that in her babyhood had given her that resemblance to Rosario, which daily grew less, and indeed
had never been apparent to Ashley; though in her face he
had traced resemblances which had puzzled and bewildered
him, and which as he gazed upon her now became still
more confusing.

As they had been conversing, Ashley and Chata had
gradually drawn near to the door, where the light fell full
upon the agitated girl. Yes, in the square brows, the
heavily fringed lids resting upon the olive cheeks, —
too broad beneath the eyes for beauty, but singularly
delicate about the mouth and chin, — so far she resembled
Ramirez; or was it but a common Aztec type? The
mouth itself, sensitive, refined, — which should have parted
but for laughter, — quivered with emotion, and the large
gray eyes she lifted to Ashley's were singularly grave
and earnest. Where had he seen such a mouth, such eyes?
The contrasts and combinations in the face confused him.
Never had he seen its counterpart, yet fancy might under
other circumstances have led him upon wild theories.
That face familiar, yet strange, had haunted him since
he had first seen it. Vainly he had sought in his memory for some picture, some dream, with which to connect
it. Now, though he had seen Ramirez, though Chata
declared herself his child, the same feeling of uncertainty,
of tantalizing familiarity yet strangeness, remained; the
association of one with the other did not even momen-
tarily satisfy him. He was not conscious that the face
appealed to his imagination rather than to his memory,
or that it had always awakened an interest different from
that with which he had looked upon others. Certainly
its beauty had not delighted him; even as he looked at
her now, the witching, glowing, ever-changing countenance
of Chinita rose before him. "Strange! strange!" he
murmured. "What can be the mystery that from the
first has seemed to hover around you, to separate you
from the rest?"

"Ah, yes!" she said humbly. "I have realized that
myself. Oh, for a long, long time I have felt as a stranger
among them all, — they so good, so true; and I — O
God, who am I? Ah, I used to pity Chinita, but they
have given her her proper place. It must have been a

worthy one, or Doña Isabel would not have made her her child. But when they separate me from Don Rafael what shall I be?"

"Do not think of it. He — this Ramirez — is gone, perhaps never to return," said Ashley, soothingly. "And if not, why should you go with him? Appeal to Don Rafael, to Doña Feliz."

"Doña Rita has told me already that would be worse than useless," replied Chata. "Don Rafael and Doña Feliz have already interfered in his plans for me; to thwart him further would be to make him their deadly enemy. Oh, you know not, Señor, what men like Don José Ramirez will do; and yet he is my father!"

Her voice failed in an agony of terror and shame. Ashley's words died on his lips. Here was a grief he could hardly understand, against which he could offer no advice to one whose education and mind were so different from his own. What could he say to her to lessen the burden of her grief? Surely not, as he would have done to Chinita, that she should strive to content herself in a destiny which would raise her from an obscure station to wealth, — for the revolutionary chieftain, he supposed, had never-failing resources, — and to a certain dignity, as the daughter of a popular hero. He could have imagined Chinita as glorying in such a position, and Rosario as reigning with a thousand airs and graces in the miniature court around her; but here was a child, a very child, shrinking from the possible contact with cruel and conscience-hardened adventurers, and stricken to the heart by the thought of losing the heritage of an honest name.

Presently Chata spoke again, as though to speak to this stranger in whom she had involuntarily confided was, in spite of her self-reproach, to lay her long repression, her doubts and fears, before a shrine. Almost incoherently, in the rapid utterance of overwhelming excitement, she poured forth the story of the interview of Ramirez and Doña Rita which she had overheard in the garden at El Toro. In her earnestness she did not even omit the project which had been discussed for uniting her future with that of Ruiz. Ashley's teeth became set and his lips pressed each other as he listened. Here indeed was confirmation of the villain's claim; and yet — and yet —

"It cannot be!" he interrupted. "I cannot believe it. You say yourself, your very being recoils from him — ah, it must be for some deep cause you hate him so! And I too — I hate him. Did I not tell you I have a long arrear of wrong to settle, and — "

"You!" she ejaculated wonderingly. "What wrong can he have done to you? Was it he who robbed and wounded you?"

"No, no!" he answered. "Those were but the chances of travel. There is something far greater than that; but while you believe him to be your father, I will not talk to you of avenging myself. I should be a brute indeed to add a feather's weight to your trouble. Do not think of that again; but believe me, there is some mystery neither of us understands. The truth may be far from what you think it. I will demand it of Don Rafael, of Doña Feliz — they must know."

She was looking at him wonderingly, almost in awe, with those large, clear, gray eyes, which seemed to have in them the reflection of a purer, calmer sky than the intense and fiery one beneath which she was born. As he looked at her, her very dress seemed a disguise, so entirely did she seem disassociated from the scenes in which he found her.

"Ah," she said hopelessly, clasping her hands, "you do not know my people as I do. I have not asked Don Rafael or Doña Feliz to tell me the secret of my birth. They have concealed it for some weighty reason, and until the time comes when they judge it right for me to know, I might plead with them in vain. By going to them I should but lose their love, and become the object of their suspicion and doubt. Oh, I could not endure that, I would not endure it! Doña Rita is changed, is cold, distrustful; and why should I by useless haste bring their anger upon her? No, no, Señor, I beg, I entreat you, say nothing to Don Rafael. Let me be in peace as long as I may. My father has not come to-day; perhaps he has forgotten me!"

"You reason wildly," said Ashley. "I cannot understand these strange duplicities; yet I know it is quite true I should gain nothing by direct questioning. What have I ever gained? No, it is to Doña Isabel I will go, and to Ramirez himself. But promise me, Chata," he added earnestly, "promise me, by all you hold most sacred, never to leave the hacienda to meet him or any messenger of his. Promise for your own sake, and I swear I will leave no measure untried to free you from this strange bondage."

He had expressed himself with difficulty throughout, but she caught his meaning eagerly. "Oh, if I dared to promise!" she murmured. "But it is the duty of the child to obey. Besides, he would tell me the truth; even this very day I thought I should have known the wretched story, — oh, I am sure it is a wretched one! Well, I have a respite, — a little respite. Go, Señor; you have been kind, — be kind still by being silent. I must go; the sun will soon set. Ah, unfortunate that I am, the men will be coming in from the fields, the women will be at their doors, — how shall I ever return without being seen?"

Here was indeed a difficulty. The strictly nurtured girl had never in her life been outside the precincts of the village alone; that she then should be, and with a young man, would occasion endless gossip. The two involuntary culprits looked at each other with blank faces, — Ashley in absolute dismay, for he had heard of the strict requirements of Mexican customs and etiquette, and knew to what cruel innuendo this young girl had exposed herself. He realized then for the first time how great her courage had been in venturing forth in obedience to the command of Ramirez.

"Chata, Chata! for God's sake," he cried, "go at once! I will remain. Your mad freak will be pardoned this time, when they see you are alone."

"Alone!" she echoed, a crimson flush suffusing her face as she fully realized the significance of his words, and saw that with a sudden faintness he leaned against the wall, spent with excitement and fatigue.

"Yes, yes," he said wearily, "none will know I am here. The night will soon pass; in the morning I will wander in to one of the huts. They will fancy I was lost on the mountain. None will think — you will be safe."

"I *am* safe," said the girl with sudden resolution. "Would a woman of your own country leave you to hunger and shiver through all the night in a desolate place

like this? Ah," she added with a long-drawn breath and
a tremor, " even ghosts are here."

Ashley smiled. " I do not fear them," he said. " I
fear but for you. Go! go at once! And yet before you
go, promise ! — promise me never to run these risks again ;
never in any place to meet Ramirez ! "

In his earnestness he clasped her hand and gazed
eagerly into her limpid eyes. " I promise, yes, I promise," she said hurriedly. " But I will not leave you, —
weak, fasting, fainting ! "

She looked up at him with the angelic pity in her face
that innocent children feel before they have learned distrust. Ashley read the perfect trust, the perfect guileless-
ness, of her tender nature. Rather, he thought, would he
die than cast a cloud upon her name ; and what, after all,
would matter the privations of a few hours? That he must
not be seen in the neighborhood for some time after her
unusual wanderings was a foregone conclusion. How
should he combat her resolution? Truly, this gentle girl
had deep springs of action within her. For duty and
right she could be a very heroine.

As these thoughts passed through his mind, a sudden
breeze stole through the open gate and reached the lobby ;
there was a faint smell of cactus flowers, and a rustle of
the dry grass. The effect was weird and ghostly. A
shadow fell between them. Had the sun plunged down
beneath the western hills? They glanced up and started
apart, — Doña Feliz was before them.

The ordinarily grave and self-possessed woman was for
a moment the most agitated of the three. She gasped for
breath. She had been walking fast, but it was not that
alone which caused the earth apparently to reel beneath
her. She had found Chata, whose disappearance from the
hacienda she had discovered at the moment when a cry
had run through the house that the horse of the young
American had returned riderless ; that the youth had
doubtless met an evil fate. She had found them both, —
and together !

She pressed her hands over her eyes as though to shut
out some horrid vision ; a moan broke from her lips, —
then she caught Chata in her arms and glared at Ashley
with concentrated anguish and fury. Had one guilty

thought possessed him, or had he meditated a doubtful act, her glance would have covered him with confusion. As it was, he read in her expressive face and gesture a volume of deep and terrible significance, far different from that which an anxious duenna ordinarily casts upon the imagined trifler with the affections of her charge. Nothing of that assumption of virtuous indignation, yet of flattered satisfaction, which in the midst of remonstrance gives indication of a certain sympathy and inclination to condone the offence in consideration of its cause, was apparent. Doña Feliz evidently had in her mind no lover's venial follies. This meeting was to her a tragedy, — the very culmination of woes.

Ashley read something of this in her expression and gesture, and hastened to reassure her, by giving a partial account of the reasons of his return. The anxious guardian of innocence would perhaps have thought his turning aside at the instance of Pepé to view his cousin's grave, his lingering there, the departure of the servant, the flight of his horse, all a fabrication, but for the meeting with his cousin's murderer, which the young man recounted with startling brevity and force, unconsciously regaining in the recital much of the excitement and deep indignation which had thrilled him at the time of the encounter, and which had gradually subsided amid the new complications that Chata's words had opened before him.

Involuntarily Ashley refrained from any allusion to the fact that the young girl had ventured forth to meet this man Ramirez; and acute though she was, it did not suggest itself to Doña Feliz, who seemed lost in wonder at the almost miraculous chance which after so many years had brought into contact the secret murderer and him whose mission it seemed to avenge the innocent blood. In his recital, Ashley had not mentioned the name of the self-confessed assassin. Doña Feliz did not ask it, — perhaps she inferred that it remained unknown to him, — yet Ashley was certain his identity was no problem to her. Had she guessed the secret all these years? Had she screened the guilty and fostered the innocent, at the same time?

Deep as was her interest in his tale, full as was her acceptance of the fact that the meeting of Ashley Ward and Chata was purely accidental, Doña Feliz did not exhibit a tithe of that horror and dismay which was depicted upon the countenance of Chata, who listened breathlessly, — her lips apart, her hair pushed back, her startled eyes opened wide. Ashley would gladly have recalled his words as he looked at her. Every particle of color had faded from her face.

In her absorption in Ashley's words, Doña Feliz had ceased to regard or even remember the young girl, who suddenly recalled herself to that lady's mind.

" Doña Feliz," she murmured in an agonized and pleading voice, " when my mother forsook me, why did you not suffer me to die? Oh why, why did I live to hear such horrors, to know such wretchedness as this ? "

As if in a frenzy, before either thought to stop her, or found words with which to answer or recall her, she ran out from the lobby, — her small figure passing unimpeded through the cactus-guarded gateway, — and fled across the plain toward the hacienda. She was young and strong, — excitement lent wings to her feet. Doña Feliz and Ashley standing together in the gateway looked at each other in amazement. The girl continued her flight until she reached the outskirts of the village. There a horseman stopped her. Even at that distance they recognized Don Rafael, and saw that Chata clung to him passionately when he dismounted.

" She is safe !" murmured Doña Feliz. " Rafael will know how to account for her presence with him."

" Yes," thought Ashley ; " these Mexicans fortunately know how to coin a plausible tale as well for a good cause as for a bad one."

They saw that Don Rafael, placing Chata on his horse before him, had turned in the direction of the hacienda, and was signalling to the vaqueros lingering in uncertainty at the gate.

" They will be here in a few moments, Señor," said Doña Feliz, calmly. " We must lock the gates and conceal the keys. You must be found outside of, not within, these walls."

Ashley assented, and within a few moments, and in silence, their necessary task was accomplished. Doña Feliz then led the way toward the village, walking rapidly

as though impelled by the agitation of her thoughts or a
desire to escape question. Ashley kept pace with her
with some effort, though the chill which had come with
the grayness of evening over the landscape revived and
strengthened him. The breeze was whistling in the tall
corn in the fields as they passed them; the cattle were
lowing in the yards; the distant sound of horses' feet was
beginning to be heard; the riders like gray columns were
seen approaching. Ashley laid his hand upon the arm of
Doña Feliz. She turned and looked at him. His face
was to her a volume of reproach and question. Her voice
broke forth in a great sob.

"Ashley! Ashley!" she exclaimed, "do you not comprehend that a vow stronger than death controls me?
Ask me nothing, but follow the indications which the good
God — Fate — Providence — has given you. The time
may come — for strange things are happening in our land
— when I may be free once more. Now I may only watch
and wait and pray. Ah! what hard tasks for a woman
such as I am! But I have vowed; I cannot retract!"

"You are wrong!" cried Ashley. "How strange that
a woman of so much intelligence, of a conscience so pure,
can suffer herself to be led by the spurious customs and
traditions that pride and priestcraft together have fastened
upon her people! But your very reticence, Doña Feliz,
confirms my beliefs. I will go as you recommend, as my
own judgment urged me, to follow the clew I have so unexpectedly obtained. Do not think that a vulgar and
wolfish desire for vengeance alone actuates me; but justice must be done. Even for Chata's sake, this man must
not be suffered to continue his course unchecked." He
would have added more, but Gabriel and Pancho, the
vaqueros, came galloping up with *vivas* and cries of
welcome.

"Praised be our Holy Mother, and all the saints!"
exclaimed one. "Don Rafael told us you were safe.
Who would have thought the Señora and the *niña* Chatita
would have found you no farther away than deaf and blind
Refugio's? Ay, Doña Feliz, without seeking, finds more
than will a dozen unlucky ones, though they have specta-
cles and lanterns to aid them. In the name of reason,
Don 'Guardo, how happened your nag to throw you and

gallop back thus? He is manageable enough with any of us —" and there was a suspicion of irony in the solicitude, of the horseman, which did not escape Ashley as he answered, —

"To-morrow you shall have the whole tale. These roads of yours are no place for a man to linger on alone. But for the present, remember I have a wound not too well healed, and am more anxious for supper than for recounting adventures."

"Ah! ah! he was stopped on the road by banditti, — and has escaped." The vaqueros regarded Ashley with vastly increased respect. Their numbers were augmented as they neared the hacienda; and when the party reached the gates, wild rumors of Ashley's prowess were already flying from mouth to mouth.

Ashley did not present an imposing figure as he passed in between the crowds of admiring women; but he served to turn their thoughts from the unprecedented appearance of Chata, which was but unsatisfactorily explained by Don Rafael's ready fiction that she and Doña Feliz had been piously visiting at the hut of old Refugio, and that upon the arrival of Ashley there, the young girl had hastened to meet her father, and give him news of the American's safety.

"Doña Feliz is even too careful of her grandchildren," said some of the more liberal. "What harm would have come to the maiden from a walk of a few minutes, or a few words spoken, with an honorable young man such as he seems to be? Now, if it were Don Alonzo, or that gay young Captain Ruiz, for example!"

Rosario, who had been leaning over the balcony as Ashley arrived, heard something of what was said, and smiled. She was not at all ready to believe that Chata's walk had extended only as far as the hut of blind Refugio; and that it had not been made in company with Doña Feliz she was quite certain. But she had no time just then to interest herself in Chata's affairs, — her own were far too engrossing; for the new clerk whom Carmen, at Doña Isabel's request, had sent from Guanapila, evidently was much more intent upon studying the charms of Rosario than his new duties, and in seeking favor in her eyes than in those of the administrador himself. The new clerk was Don

Alonzo, and Don Alonzo was a handsome fellow, with the face of an angel, Doña Rita said, — a contrast indeed to that little brown monkey Captain Ruiz; and Rosario smiled coyly, and did not gainsay her.

The next morning at an unusually early hour this same Don Alonzo tapped on Ashley's door. " Pardon, Señor," he said, " but the horses and servants are ready, and I have orders myself to accompany you beyond the boundaries of Tres Hermanos."

The announcement was not a surprise. Ashley had arranged his departure with Don Rafael upon the preceding evening. He dressed hastily, and while partaking of his cup of chocolate, glanced often around him, in expectation of the appearance of Don Rafael or his mother; but in vain. The American could no longer hope to learn at a parting moment what each had chosen to withhold. Irrationally, and against all likelihood, he ventured to hope that Chata might steal forth for a farewell word. He laughed at himself afterward for the thought, saying that the air of intrigue had begun to affect his own brain.

Sooner than was usual, even in that land of early movement, Don Alonzo warned him it was growing late. It was not too late or early for Rosario to wave her little brown hand from her mother's window in token of adieu. Ashley did not see it, but he for whom it was intended did. So with more foreboding and reluctance than he could have imagined possible but a few hours before, Ashley once more rode forth from Tres Hermanos, — this time with a definite object, from which he felt there could be no turning back, no possible end but his own death or the downfall of a man to whom but yesterday he had been utterly indifferent, but who to-day was inseparable from all his thoughts, his passions, his purposes, — Ramirez the *revolucionario,* the declared murderer of John Ashley, the declared father of the young girl who seemed the very incarnation of honor and sensibility, of tenderness and purity.

THE departure of Ashley Ward from Tres Hermanos was not so entirely disregarded as he had supposed. It was not Rosario only, who left her chamber at daybreak. Scarcely had she disappeared in the gloom of Doña Isabel's apartments on her way to the favorite balcony, when her father stepped out upon the corridor, starting as his eyes fell upon Doña Feliz, who, seemingly with the spirit of unrest that pervaded the household, at the same moment emerged from her room. With a muttered salutation each abandoned the original intention of exchanging a farewell word with the departing guest; and arresting their steps at the balustrade, they leaned over and listened intently to the sounds of the early exit. The light was still so uncertain that though Don Rafael noticed, he did not wonder at, the gray tinge upon his mother's face; it seemed only in harmony with the prevailing darkness.

The rains of the past season had been insufficient, and a murky though almost inpalpable mist, felt rather than seen, brooded over the silent landscape. It was scarcely oppressive enough to affect the young men who rode forth stirring the sluggish air, nor the eager horses lifting their heads to fill their lungs with the breath of morning, and expelling it again with a force that agitated the stillness with a sound like a blow upon water; yet it weighed inexpressibly both upon the body and mind of Don Rafael. As he had come to the corridor with a certainty in his mind that he should meet his mother, he had purposed to question her as to the actual occurrences of the day before, for the connection of Chata with the return of Ashley Ward remained entirely unexplained. That his mother was satisfied that it was not a mere vulgar *rendezvous* into which she had been tempted, he was assured by her manner toward both the young man and the recreant girl; indeed, it appeared that she had scarcely noticed an incident which in that place, and at the age of Chata, was sufficient to array against a young girl the suspicions of the most trusting and generous of matrons. Yet Don Rafael could imagine no possible inducement but the voice of a lover that could have called her forth alone from the great house, — for that Chata had gone alone, he knew as well as did his keen-eyed daughter Rosario.

The last gray figure had long since disappeared from the outer court, into which they looked as into a distant and narrow vista; the clank of the horses' hoofs upon the paving had changed to the thud upon the roadway, then ceased altogether to be heard; and Don Rafael turning his eyes upon his mother's face, had opened his lips to question her, — when with a thrill of surprise, which became terror even before the momentary utterance was repeated, he heard her laugh that strange, unmirthful, hollow laugh that indicates a mind diseased, while she said whisperingly, —

"He is gone. Yes! yes! I unbarred the door, and Pedro picked the lock so cleverly and noiselessly that the very watchman asleep across the threshold did not hear him. Ah, I knew Gregorio would be quiet enough by daylight; but Leon was awake, wide awake. For all your tears, Isabel, he would not have gone but for me; he swore he would kill Don Gregorio for the blow he gave him. Why did you say you loved at last as a woman should the husband who was your brother's foe to death, and that you sent him freedom that he might seek a death more worthy of his villany than by the sword of an outraged father, or the executioner's bullet? They were bitter words, and you knew they were false, — for even with your child lying dead through his persecution, you loved him still. And when he would not stir because of your taunts, but swore he would meet his fate and shame the callous heart whose love had been as weak as her sacrifice was forced and incomplete, what was there for you to do but to throw yourself on your knees before him, and entreat him for his mother's sake to be gone? Even then he would have stayed but for me. 'What!' I cried, 'to shame your sister, you will give another victory to the husband of Dolores?'

"Ah, it is not tears that conquer such a man as Leon!

In a moment he had sprung to his feet; he had thrust Isabel aside, and me too, — yes, that was nothing. Pedro held his horse, but Leon glared at him as he sprang into the saddle. ' But for you, I should have given the last blow at midnight,' he cried. ' It shall be thine some day, when thy master's account has been closed ! ' and with that he was gone. Yes, he is gone. Not a sound of the horse as he gallops ! Gone, and none too soon ! the morning is come," — and she uttered again that sound called a laugh.

" Mother, what hast thou ? " cried Don Rafael, clasping her arm, and noticing for the first time the deep hollows beneath her brilliant eyes, and the wide circles that made more appalling their unnatural glare. " Mother, thou art dreaming ! thy hand burns, and thy temples. Maria Sanctissima ! dost thou not know me ? "

" Know thee ? — yes. Why, thou art Rafael," she answered, letting her eyes drop for a moment on his scared and anxious face. " Why should I not know thee ? Had ever woman a better son ? Yes, yes, he is safe ; let Don Gregorio wake when he will, Leon is away. Ah, at the last he was not so cruel, — eh, Isabel ? Why should you moan and wring your hands because he vowed never again but by his death should his name shame you ? Ah ! Ah ! Ah ! well, they say he died, shot and hanged to a tree as a miscreant should be. Do you believe it, Isabel ? Yet why not ? God of my soul ! is it only the son of Pancho Valle that can be pitiless ? Only — " so she muttered on, in a low monotonous voice, pacing the corridor with an uncertain step, varying from the halting motion of one about to fall, to the impetuous haste with which she fancied herself urging again the unwilling flight of the sullen and revengeful youth, whom she too, with the perversity of woman's heart, had loved as sincerely as she had condemned.

Don Rafael followed her in a perturbation of surprise and terror, which drove from his mind all other thoughts save those that his remembrance of former plague-stricken seasons forced upon his mind. Fever was in the air, and his mother was the first victim ! The rainy season, which in most years cleared the black watercourses and the village itself of the accumulations of nine dry and almost torrid mouths, had failed to do its accustomed work. No rush-

ing torrents had cleared the watercourses ; but instead of
proving the friend of humanity water had become its
enemy, by mingling scantily with the foul elements that
had gathered during the long period of drouth, and which
exhaled the subtle miasma which even the pure air of
that elevated region was powerless to render innoxious.
Don Rafael absolutely wrung his hands before the evil
he foresaw, and which neither experience nor intelligence
had led him to combat with any sanitary precautions.
That the fever should from time to time decimate the
hacienda appeared to his mind one of the inevitable
calamities of life, no more to be avoided than the spring
floods or the blasting lightning or the outburst of volcanic fires. But had all these forces combined assailed
him at once, his consternation could not have been
greater than to witness in his mother the delirium which
testified to the dreaded typhoid. As has been intimated,
his love for his mother was of no common order ; without being weak in judgment or irresolute in character,
he had been accustomed to share with her his every
thought, and their sentiments and aims were ever in
such perfect accord that a dissentient word had never
arisen between them.

As Don Rafael followed his mother in her erratic and
excited movements, scarcely conscious of what he did, or
of anything except that with each moment her talk grew
more distracted, while her thoughts were persistently
fixed upon the events and woes and passions of by-gone
years, a door at the end of the corridor was timidly
pushed open, and Chata's face peeped anxiously out.
Had Don Rafael's thoughts been free, he would have
wondered that the girl was fully dressed at such an
early hour ; but he did not even heed the explanation
she hurriedly gave as she advanced to meet him.

"I would not have left my grandmother alone, but she
forbade me to come," she said. "Oh, I could not sleep.
I thought the morning would never dawn. I went to her
with the first light, but she would not listen to me. She
bade me leave her ; and I thought it was because she
was angry, but it was this! Oh, Father, is it a sickness?
See, she does not know me? *Mama grande*, it is I ; it is
your Chata."

"Be silent!" exclaimed Don Rafael, the more sharply because of his extreme alarm. "Fly, Chata! fly to thy mother, thy sister! Call old Selsa, any one who has sense and knows what remedies to bring. Why do you stare? Do you think my mother is mad? It is the fever. It is not for nothing that the rains have been delayed so long. Pitying Saints, as I rode by the ditches last week they were black as pitch and foul as a vulture's quarry. Run! I will lead her to her room. Ay, ay, Mother, thou art strong, and not so old yet," — and with the tenderness of a child and the devotion of a lover the son guided the steps of the delirious yet gentle woman, who, half-conscious of her state, half-resentful of care, suffered herself to be led into the chamber she had quitted in apparent health but a brief quarter of an hour before.

Apparent health only, for she had passed an utterly sleepless night, strangely excited by the events of the day, yet unable to fix her mind upon them. Chata, upon her return to the hacienda, had sought her own chamber; and in the press of other thoughts Doña Feliz had failed to follow and to question her upon the strange escapade, which the whole character and bearing of the young girl combined to render utterly inexplicable, — for she had no data by which to connect it with the appearance of Ramirez at the cemetery, and she absolved Ashley Ward from any pre-arrangement with the young girl as completely as though they had been found a thousand miles asunder. As was natural, suspicions of some precocious love, of which some one of the many volatile and dashing youth that had lately gathered at the hacienda was the object, haunted the mind of Doña Feliz; but she rejected them with disdain, promising herself upon the early morning to demand the truth, not doubting she should learn it. Even while awake to the importance of the incident, and inwardly debating it, she was conscious that the remembrance of it, as well as of Ashley and his strange participation in the life-drama in which she had enacted so forced and painful a part, constantly strove to elude her, and was recalled with an effort that with every hour grew greater and less effective; while all the events and actors of long ago passed in endless review before her, — Doña Isabel in her matronly girlhood, soothing and bribing with tender words and lavish gifts her wilful half-brother; Don Gregorio; the dying Norberto; the scowling and furious abductor; then Herlinda and John Ashley. The pale procession, spectral yet real, voiceless yet each repeating with irresistible eloquence the tale of his love, his guilt or anguish, passed before her, thrusting aside, as often as they re-appeared, the forms of those who at this new and critical point had appeared upon the scene.

As the night passed, she was perfectly aware of this tantalizing inability to command her thoughts; and as again and again she set herself to follow the probable course and effect of Ashley Ward's intervention in the fate of the man who to her seemed gifted with demoniacal powers for evil, and an absolute invulnerability to human vengeance, or as she began in mind to question Chata, the persons both of the young man and the girl seemed to fade from before her, and the voices that should have replied, were those which had been familiar years before, — oftenest that of Herlinda in wild repetition of her unhappy love, and agonized entreaties for the babe she was but to embrace and forever relinquish. Through it all Doña Feliz had retained the thought of Ashley's departure; and with some vague thought that the sight of him would calm her fevered brain, she instinctively strove to accomplish the resolve with which she had begun the night. And thus her last conscious act before the positive delirium of the fever seized her, had been to look, with the half-fearful gaze of one who invokes· yet dreads the vengeance of heaven, upon him who seemed to her morbid and superstitious mind fraught with a mission to avenge and right the innocent, — both the living and the dead.

Don Rafael, in consternation, had recognized at once the serious character of his mother's illness. As he called aloud for help, and Chata with white and affrighted face hastened to obey his command, Rosario, followed by her mother in some confusion, appeared from the farther corridor. Too much bewildered and alarmed to wonder at seeing his daughter also dressed and abroad at such an hour, her father exclaimed in impatience at the voluble reproaches of Doña Rita, who, pushing Rosario from the side of Doña Feliz, bade her cease from such tempting of Providence, affirming that for her own sins she (Doña

Rita) must have been burdened with the plague of so reckless a child, and praying her in the name of the Holy Babe to fly from infection lest she should break her mother's heart by her premature decease. To all of which Rosario submitted with a sobbing declaration that she was already faint and ill, whereupon Doña Rita hastily retreated to her own room, dragging Rosario with her; and in spite of his hurriedly formed resolution to the contrary, Don Rafael was forced to confide his mother to the care of Chata and of the servants, who, subservient to the slightest wish even of this inexperienced girl, were however absolutely useless without the guiding presence of a superior.

XXXIV.

The hilltops were flooded with sunshine when the party from Tres Hermanos reached them; the atmosphere was so clear, that looking back over the broad valley, spread with fields of maize and beans, and the half-tropical luxuriance of fruit and flower, Ashley could distinguish every break and fret on the massive front of the great house, and recognized with a feeling almost of awe the tall, slender figure standing upon the centre balcony. She waved her hand in token of God-speed. Strange, inscrutable woman! She had bidden him go forth as the minister of fate, she had furnished him with servants, horses, money, arms, — yet had spoken no word. Ashley felt as though he were an enchanted knight in an enchanted land!

The traveller bade adieu to Don Alonzo in sight of his cousin's grave; then, followed by his two servants, rode rapidly onward in the direction taken the day before by the troops and Doña Isabel, by Ramirez and Reyes, — indifferent which he first should encounter, confident that sooner or later the full significance of the impulse that had led him upon his Quixotic journey to Mexico would be revealed. The little cloud no bigger than a man's hand had grown so great as to overshadow his earth and heavens. He rode on as in a dream. The day passed, the night came, and the party was still alone. The guide had mistaken the way. That night they encamped but a league from the village of Las Passas. Ashley slept neither better nor worse for that; there was no voice to tell him it could be more to him or his than a score of other villages which lay in the recesses of these wild mountains. The next day he left it to the right, and set his face toward El Toro.

Meanwhile the march of the troops had been as rapid as the nature of the country, broken by deep ravines and at first offering a tortuous ascent to the table-lands, would allow. To Chinita, though the slow movement of the car-

21

riage was irksome and irritating, and the clouds of dust
that rose from beneath the tread of the horses obscured
the sights which in their novelty delighted and filled her
with exultation of a new and expanding life, the hours
passed as though winged by enchantment. In the joyous clamor of the camp followers and the scarcely less
restrained hilarity of the troops, in the tramp of the
horses, the clanking of arms, there was a subtile music
that aroused all the energies of her adventurous spirit,
and imbued her with an animation which like a flame
within a crystal vase seemed visibly to fill and surround
her whole being with strength and beauty.

Had the country passed over been as dull and uninteresting as it was in fact wild and picturesque, the effect of
movement and change would have been still the same to
her; for hers was a mind to be affected by the various
phases of humanity rather than of inanimate nature.
The landscape in truth offered to her view little of novelty, for in her childhood she had wandered where she listed, and her lithe young limbs had been as untiring as her
curiosity. The succeeding cañons and hills, the slopes
and cactus-planted valleys, were but counterparts of those
which she had explored on every side of the plain on which
Tres Hermanos stood. With ready tact she avoided recalling her unwatched, untended childhood to the mind of
Doña Isabel, who received with a distaste which seemed of
the nature of regretful shame any allusion to the life from
which the girl who now called her *Tia* (aunt) had been
rescued.

The use of this appellation had been brought about by
Ruiz, in his evident uncertainty as to how the apparent
relationship between his patroness and her *protégée* should
be defined. He had tentatively alluded to Doña Isabel as
the godmother of Chinita, a designation which some conscientious scruple led her to reject. The word *Tia* is used
by Mexicans as a term of respect toward an elder as often
as in actual acknowledgment of relationship; and when
with some daring Chinita one day applied it to Doña Isabel,
in answering some remark of the young captain, the lady
allowed it to pass unchallenged; and gradually *"mi Tia
Isabel"* took the place of the formal *"Señora,"* which
hitherto had helped to keep their intercourse as reserved

and cold as when Chinita still stood at the gate at Pedro's side, and Doña Isabel had furtively glanced at her glowing beauty, and felt the hand of remorse pressing upon her heart.

The haughty lady felt it still; and that it was which made her lenient to a score of faults in this young girl that in her own children would have been deemed almost unpardonable. She did not admit that she loved her, — it is doubtful if she really did, — yet she strove by all the arts of which the long repression of her nature made her capable to win the heart of the girl, who she saw with suspicious intuition beheld in her one who had wronged her, and was even now withholding her birthright. Doña Isabel bestowed rich presents, but never a caress; perhaps Chinita would have spurned the last as lightly as she received the first. Ruiz, admitted to a certain intimacy by the necessities of the time, was impressed by the entire absence of any sense of obligation with which the young girl took her place with Doña Isabel, as if she had never known one more humble, while there was something in the cold and stately manner of Doña Isabel which seemed to shrink before the imperious force of character of her young companion.

It was at their first halt that Doña Isabel had, with unexpected hospitality, sent to invite Ruiz to share their midday meal; and, evidently with some effort, at the same time she bade the servant extend the invitation to the young American. Ruiz presented himself with due acknowledgments, but Ashley was nowhere to be found: he and his servant Pepé had disappeared from the ranks. No one remembered having seen them since they ascended the face of the hill of the graveyard; doubtless, it was surmised, the young man had grown weary, and had unceremoniously returned to Tres Hermanos.

Doña Isabel's face clouded. Upon the next day she had hoped to part company with her unwelcome guest forever; and now, — part of her purpose in leaving the hacienda was already frustrated. Ruiz was scarcely less disquieted; a glance at Chinita's triumphant countenance confirmed his apprehensions. Pepé, at least, had not returned to the hacienda, he was assured. The officer had had it in his mind to have the servant strictly watched; but it had not occurred to him that upon the first day he would attempt to evade him and fulfil Chinita's wild project of summoning Ramirez. He inwardly cursed his own folly and the duplicity of Ashley, whom he hitherto had not for a moment supposed in sympathy with the plot. He and the young American had even laughed at it together as, the foolish dream of an imaginative girl. Now to the suspicious officer's apprehensions was added a burning jealousy. For Chinita's sake the American had doubtless made her cause his own; and with such an ally, Ruiz reflected, it was not impossible that he might see himself confronted by the man who he knew well never forgave a slight, never left unrevenged an injury.

The manner of Ruiz was so grave and abstracted that day, that Doña Isabel was inclined to credit him with far more depth and earnestness than as the reputed suitor of Rosario, or the airy and flippant recreant follower of the notorious Ramirez, she had attributed to him. Ruiz had the art of involuntarily suiting his demeanor and conversation to those in whose company he was thrown. There was no conscious hypocrisy in this, for the desire to please was natural to him, and often served him in good stead in the absence of genuine feeling, and even under the sting of wounded self-love held him silent, and masked his resentment. Many a time in his life-long intercourse with Ramirez had he chafed under the General's haughty patronage and made no sign; and it was only when he found himself thwarted in what was for the moment his strongest passion, that he began to question the designs of the chieftain to whom he owed all the fortune which birth or talents combine to make possible to other men.

Ruiz was the son of Tio Reyes, a life-long follower of Ramirez, for whom the chieftain had been sponsor, and toward whom he had with minute conscientiousness directed every worldly advantage which his means and position rendered possible. To Ramirez, Ruiz — who was known by the name of his mother (a not uncommon custom where her family renders the cognomen more honorable than that of the father)—owed the chance which had made him a soldier of fortune instead of a laborer in the village where his brothers and sisters plodded and toiled, in absolute ignorance of the father who had forsaken them.

Ruiz's knowledge of this strengthened his resolution to

ignore the past, and suffer no ill-timed revelations to interfere with his determination to win at one step love and
fortune by gaining the hand of the *protégée* of Doña Isabel,
— a purpose he was certain Ramirez would oppose, for in
a moment of confidence the General had intimated that
it was to a daughter of his own, in accordance with a
promise made long years before to Reyes, that the
young man was to be united ; it was for this destiny his
future had been shaped, his fortunes moulded.

At any previous time the ambition of Ruiz would have
been fully satisfied ; his whole desire would have been to
meet this promised bride, and by his marriage strengthen
the interest which the caprice or affection of Ramirez alone
caused to be centred upon him, and which, though often
burdensome and tyrannous, was apparently the young
man's sole passport to success. Even when in pique and
half-timorous defiance he took advantage of his separation
from Ramirez to follow Rosario to Tres Hermanos, it was
with no fixed resolution to tempt fortune alone. His short-
lived passion and his independence and anger would have
died together, had not his love for Chinita and the unexpected opportunities thrust upon him opened before him a
prospect of advancement and triumph far above his wildest
dreams, and completed his treason to his early patron,
without teaching him the lesson of truth either to the new
cause or to the mistress to which he was sworn.

In the eyes of Doña Isabel Ruiz was but the hireling
whose faith was purchased for Gonzales ; in those of Chinita, the devoted follower of Ramirez ; in his own — well,
time and circumstance would decide.

Like thousands of others who took part in the strife that
rent and decimated Mexico, Ruiz had but little conception
of the points at issue. He had simply followed the lead
of the popular chieftain to whom circumstances had attached him. He had learned by observation that wealth
flowed from the coffers of the clergy into the hands of
Ramirez, who scattered it lavishly to all about him, —
dissipating the greater part in luxurious living in cities,
and the maintenance of hordes of followers in towns and
cañons of the mountains, and with ready superstition returning much to the source whence it came, for never a
follower of his kept child unchristened or burial Mass

unsaid for want of means to purchase the services of a priest.

Ramirez had appeared to the young imagination of Ruiz absolute and ubiquitous. There were few daring deeds done that he had not shared in; scarce a town been seized and its merchants arrested until the forced loans demanded from them were paid, scarce a train of wagons laden with silver stopped, scarce a *pronunciamiento* with its excitement and rapid exchange of power and property effected, that he had taken no part in. He had been found wherever fighting or plunder were. He had taken a bloody part in the repulse of the Liberals at the City of Mexico, where the names of Zuloaga the President and of Miramon alike were made infamous. He had shared in the futile attacks upon Vera Cruz, where Juarez at the head of the Provisional Government maintained with stubborn tenacity, with a handful of followers, the most important stronghold upon the seaboard, promulgating those unprecedented resolutions and decrees which revealed to the minds of the people that of which they had never hitherto dreamed, — namely, the separation of Church and State; the suppression of the monasteries, which like vampires had for generations drained the resources and absorbed the intellect of the people; and the secularization of those immense treasures which, donated by the faithful to feed the hungry and the sick, train the orphans, maintain the glory and worship of God, had become the means of oppression and bloodshed, and were the thews and sinews of the civil war, in which the clergy strove to maintain the abuses of the past and forge fresh chains for the future.

In a country where the dogmas of Catholicism were as the oracles of God, where every heart was bound either by the truths or the superstitions of Rome, or in most cases by both inseparably, the magnitude of the task assumed by the astute and resolute Juarez was almost beyond the comprehension of those bred in the lands which have never groaned beneath the yoke of ecclesiastical tyranny. Any premature act, any unguarded word, might become the cause of offence; and yet it was no time for hesitation or timorous questioning.

Juarez knew the time and the temper of his countrymen; and environed though he was, virtually imprisoned in one small town upon the seashore, his influence reached to the most remote districts of the interior. And although the armies of the clergy swept the country from sea to sea, in obscure fastnesses rose daring bands in tens and twenties and hundreds, who promulgating the new promises of liberty sent forth by Juarez, maintained them with a tenacity of purpose that made defeat impossible. Worsted in one quarter, they arose in another, employing with unscrupulous daring every means that cunning or audacity could bring within their power,— claiming the excuse of necessity for those acts of rapine and cruelty in the satisfaction of personal enmities, the warfare upon the women and children, and the thousand barbarous deeds which make the history of that time a continual record of horrors. Had example been necessary, they would have found it in the career of the opposing forces; but in truth it was a time when the attributes of patriot and plunderer, soldier and bandit, became inextricably confused; so that, perhaps as completely to himself as to others, the average actor in that bloody drama became a baffling and unsatisfying enigma.

Such was the mental condition of Ruiz, though it did not occur to him to define it. Attached to the clerical party by long association, and by the uninterrupted prosperity which he had shared with Ramirez, — who since separating himself from Gonzales had followed an independent career, in which he had found the highest bidders for his services among the crafty leaders of the old régime (who to their rich gifts added the indulgences of the Church, to which no soul however blood-stained and conscienceless could remain indifferent),— when Ruiz declared himself to Don Rafael a convert to the Liberal cause, it was but as a precautionary measure recommended by Doña Rita; and it was only when he saw in Doña Isabel a patroness more powerful than the one he had abandoned, added to his resolution to make himself independent of the man who had hitherto controlled as well as defended him, that he in reality inclined to the faction which day by day seemed gathering strength, and likely to become the dominant power.

But though his political views thus shaped themselves to meet Doña Isabel's, Ruiz was no more faithful to her purposes than to those of Chinita. To abandon Gonzales to his fate at El Toro, — for he did not doubt that Ramirez would return with overwhelming numbers to the destruction of its insufficient garrison, — and at the same time to win the confidence of Doña Isabel and that of the troops under his command, thereafter seizing the first opportunity of having himself proclaimed their permanent leader and marching to join Juarez, whose cause was becoming strengthened day by day by fresh accessions from the interior, became his dream. Thus he hoped to blind Chinita by an apparent inability rather than disinclination to further her designs, mislead Doña Isabel, and secure for himself a position which should render it not absurd or incredible that he should aspire to the hand of a *protégée* of the Garcias, and to the dower which he shrewdly suspected he might of right demand.

All these plans were not perfected in a day, and the defection of Ashley Ward and his servant seriously interfered in the ambitious captain's calculations; but he allowed no trace of uneasiness to appear in those rare intervals when he found an opportunity to exchange a few words with the impatient Chinita.

Unconsciously also, Doña Isabel herself aided to establish a bond of confidence between them. When the long irregular column, with banners flying, driving before it the lowing cattle, whose numbers grew less after each night's slaughter, and followed by the motley line of women and children with the rude equipage of the camp, would be fairly in motion after the confusion of the early start, Ruiz would rein his prancing steed at the side of the carriage and deferentially place himself at the orders of the ladies. On these occasions his manner was one of perfect respect to both, of entire concurrence in the dictates and desires of Doña Isabel, and of half-indifferent, half-amused rejection of the immature and inconsequent conjectures and opinions of the girl, for whose beauty he exhibited a timid but irresistible recognition, which flattered while it disarmed the suspicious mind of Doña Isabel. She believed him still the ardent admirer of Rosario, — a thing which, she reflected, was under the circumstances most fortunate.

In the freshness and animation of those morning hours conversation became natural and easy, and the events and names which were upon every tongue furnished food for abundant reminiscence and comment. Doña Isabel was eloquent in praise of Gonzales, who to his success at El Toro had added others in the neighborhood, which together with the occupation of Guanapila had made the entire district the undisputed territory of Liberalism. Ruiz assented to her enthusiasm with an ardor which seemed but natural in a youth who having separated himself from one powerful patron, should desire to place himself beneath the protection of another; and a comparison of the two, which should explain his defection from the first, followed in natural course; and with carefully chosen words, whose meaning held a subtile relation to the thoughts and predilections of his two auditors, he spoke of the intrepid and unscrupulous Ramirez.

More than once Doña Isabel, in the midst of his talk, sank back in the carriage lost in deep and painful thought, as the wild and terrible deeds in which that lawless man had figured recalled to her mind the horrors of her youth. Deeds such as these might have been planned and executed by the boy who had once been the pride, as he was afterward the bane, of her life, had he lived; but he was dead. Yes, thank God! though her heart had bled inwardly for long years; he had made no sign since the tale of his end came — he was dead!

While she was thus lost in thought, Chinita listened with glowing cheek and eyes. Ruiz knew of the meeting with Ramirez to which she looked back with such peculiar and unwearying fascination; and discerning in her admiration of his former leader an unfailing means of rousing in her a personal attraction which in her passionate nature might become an absorbing love, he carefully refrained from giving her any hint of his real sentiments toward her hero, and spared no covert word, no mute eloquence of his dark and expressive eyes, to increase an enthusiasm which had already led her into such strange defiance of the plans of Doña Isabel. To reinstate her hero in the power from which he had fallen became Chinita's dream, the aspiration of her soul.

On the fifth night of their journey it chanced that they entered a village, where Doña Isabel and her servants were enabled to find a shelter, which after the restricted and insufficient accommodation of tents seemed absolutely luxurious, primitive and rude though it was. Doña Isabel wearied with travel, and depressed with anxiety at the unaccountable delay of Gonzales, who she had supposed would have hastened to take command of the troops that her energy and bounty had provided, had early retired to the room assigned her. Chinita had reluctantly accompanied her, for a fandango was in progress in the great kitchen, the charcoal brasiers flaming red against the dark walls of yellow-washed adobe, and shining upon the bronzed faces of a group of swarthy men, who strummed upon stringed instruments of various shapes and sizes; while another group of mingled men and women went through the rhythmic motions of the dance, with which the young girl, gazing from her cell-like retreat across the court, had long been so familiar.

Chinita had never danced since the night that she had fled from the wedding *fiesta* into the waiting arms of Doña Isabel. She had thought of the scene and its pleasures only with anger and disgust; and yet as she looked into the red glare and watched the swaying figures, she longed to rush in and throw herself among them. To her, as to Doña Isabel, the time of suspense was growing unbearably long; she was mad for action. Unreasonably, she felt that there among their caste she might find Pedro, Pepé, — some one who would do her bidding, who would not dare put her off as Ruiz was doing with tantalizing promises.

Chinita knew that instead of following the most direct paths as Doña Isabel had commanded, the route on various pretexts had been changed, — she supposed to make communication with Ramirez possible. She had no reason to doubt the good faith of Ruiz, yet she was impatient and miserable. A straggler upon the road had given them the news that Ramirez had been seen upon the hills with a forlorn and ill-armed troop, which bore evidence of the ill fortune which the defeat at El Toro had inaugurated. She had conceived a violent and unreasonable antagonism to Gonzales, who from his whilom associate had become the successful opponent and rival of the man whom by the childish gift of an amulet she had fancied herself endowing with invincible good fortune. Even as she grew older, her faith in the magic powers of a charm which had been the creation of a wizard, and had been blessed by Holy Church, scarcely grew less; and the remembrance of it undoubtedly strengthened the fealty so strangely sworn. Besides, a purpose had arisen in her mind of appealing to Ramirez to establish her position in the house of Garcia, by wresting from Doña Isabel an acknowledgment which would give her rights and a certain status (though clouded it might be) where now she was but the recipient of favors, — the peasant born raised to a dignity which was a mere scoff and jest to the ready wit of the sarcastic and epigrammatic rancheros. Chinita knew them well. Were not their gifts and prejudices her own?

Musing thus, the girl glanced from the barred window where she stood back through the gloom of the apartment to the bed where Doña Isabel was lying, — already asleep. The yellow light of a candle just touched the lady's pale face; it was contracted with that habitual expression of pain which the darkness of night permitted to the proud and suffering woman, but which in the day, or under the eye of even the most unobservant, she banished resolutely, though its shadow rested ever uncomprehended, unpitied.

There was something in the lassitude of Doña Isabel's figure, the hopeless grief upon the countenance, which for the first time suggested to Chinita the possibility that emotions deeper than that pride of birth which was as great in degree in herself, though neither as pure in principle nor bounded by the conventionalities of caste, had actuated the deeds and embittered the life of her who to the eye had been so absolute, so unassailable. With a feeling of awe Chinita took a step toward the sleeper, when a sound drew her glance to the court. Into the motley throng of lounging soldiers and *arrieros*, with their mules feeding and stamping around them, two belated travellers forced their way. It was the voice of one of them that had startled the watcher, and claimed instantly all her thoughts, setting her heart beating stiflingly as she sprang to the lattice and pressed her face eagerly against the iron bars.

The red light from the kitchen was augmented by the flame of a smoking torch, as a servant came forward to take the horse of the foremost rider. When he leaped lightly from his saddle, pushing back his broad hat, Chinita recognized the American, while a woman ran across the court and clasped the arm of the other as he alighted: it was Juana, the wife of Gabriel.

"Hist! hist!" said the man in a low voice, "no crying nor screaming. The Señor and I are here on business that would please your captain but little. By good fortune he is camped to-night at the outskirts of the village, and dare not leave his post. Tell me, Juana, — and not a word to Gabriel when thou seest him, — where is Chinita?"

Before Juana could gather her wits to reply, a hand was thrust through the bars almost at the speaker's shoulder; but it was Ashley who first saw it. He took it for an instant in his own, and bent over it. "I must speak with you, Chinita," he said; "join me in the corridor as soon as the house is quiet. I have much to say."

It was not the voice of a lover that spoke, but it thrilled her as that of a prophet. "Speak low," she answered, breathlessly, "Doña Isabel sleeps close by; but I will escape, — yes, I will come to you. Is not Juana with you? She must take my place here. The door is locked; the key is in the hand of Doña Isabel. But I will have it, trust me; the Señora sleeps heavily."

The girl's face glowed with excitement; she was ready for any adventure, the more daring the more welcome. Ashley Ward looked at her with a strange pride and admiration: this was a nature that no shame could crush, no outward fate dismay!

Chinita, standing at the grating, feeling an almost unrestrainable desire to burst into wild laughter and tears, was for some time utterly silent, waiting the hour when, the revelry over, sleep would fall upon the house. Ashley drew into the shade of the corridor. The inn was but a caravansary; there was none to notice who came or went. In the laughing, chattering crowd he was virtually alone. The thoughts that came to him as the fires faded, as the noisy revellers strolled one by one to their sleeping-places, and the pale light of the stars shining down upon that strange scene showed Pepé wrapped in his blanket, standing sentinel at his side, were indescribable. A phantasmagoria seemed to glide before him, in which Mary, his cousin,

the ordinary places, scenes, and associates of his youth,
Ramirez, Chata, all the strange actors in this drama, in
new and ill-comprehended scenes, passed by ; and in the
midst the door of a chamber cautiously opened, and the
girl of the siren face, which the very voice of fate had
seemed to bid him seek in this far land, stepped eagerly
and lightly forth to meet him.

In an angle of the corridor, where from sunrise to sunset a woman usually sat, selling cigarettes and small glasses of *chia* to the passers-by, stood a low *banquito*, which was in fact only a superfluous adobe jutting out from the massive wall. Ashley withdrew his foot from this rude stool and greeted Chinita ceremoniously, and yet with an air of protecting authority, inviting her by a gesture to be seated, saying, " So you will be less likely to be seen by any chance comer. But from necessity, I would not have asked you to speak to me here."

The girl looked at him with a little quiver of laughter rippling her mouth, though her eyes were anxious. Evidently she was troubled with no sense of impropriety, and the thought of having eluded Doña Isabel diverted her. Instead of obeying Ashley's invitation, she darted to Pepé's side, caught a fold of his blanket in her hand, and drew it from his half-covered face.

"Ah, Pepito, and is it thou?" she cried breathlessly. "What news dost thou bring me? Hast thou then seen my godfather, and what does he say of the Señor General? Does he not think the plan a good one?"

Pepé shuffled uneasily to regain possession of the blanket, answering pettishly and in a stifled voice, "Is the servant to talk when the master stands by with the words ready? Go now, Chinita, you knew better than that when Florencia used to pull your ears for a saucy one!"

The girl pouted, turning to Ashley with a lowering face. She felt instinctively that what had been to her a matter of simple expediency, a means of securing the fortunes of a man who was in her imagination all that was noble and great, might have a meaner aspect to this stranger, who would perhaps think she had meant harm to Doña Isabel. Why had Pepé dragged this American into the matter at all? Idiot! Ruiz had said nothing but evil would come of it; and here was the stranger standing so straight and silent to be questioned, — and looking at her, too, with a sort of pity in the curious gaze he turned upon her. She felt half inclined to turn back to the room whence she had come; yet she said somewhat mockingly,

"It is you, Señor, who must speak, though it was the servant I sent on my errand; but perhaps you have seen Pedro and asked him my questions?"

"You had better sit down, Chinita," answered Ashley, severely. "I should not be here to-night if it were not to tell you things hard for you to listen to, and only to learn of matters of life or death should you have consented to come. Heavens! what a strange perversity of fate that you of all others should be anxious for the welfare, infatuated with the character, of — Ramirez!"

He spoke the name as though it were a curse, and the ready flame leaped into Chinita's eyes and cheek.

"Ah, then," she said, in a low but intense and penetrating tone, "you have come to tell me, like the others, that he is a brigand and a wretch! It is false! He is too brave, too daring, too noble for such cowardly spirits as yours to understand! Pepé, thou wert a craven. Stupid, it was Pedro I bade thee go to, not to this pale American, who has lost all his blood through a single wound!"

Ashley smiled faintly, vexed to find himself stung by a girl's unreasoning passion, but interposed quietly, "We lose time, Señorita, which is prudent neither for you nor for me. I beg you will listen to what I have to say. You will agree with me then that this is no hour to talk of my courage or the lack of it."

He had stepped between her and Pepé, to whom with a strange perversity she turned as if to show her disdain for the foreigner, whose every word had a tone of reproach. A mere suggestion that the proprieties which Doña Feliz and Doña Isabel had attempted to graft upon the rude stalk of her untrained, unguarded childhood had some other meaning than an elder's caprices, touched Chinita's mind: a young man could know nothing of woman's freaks and prejudices; she felt the hot blood rising to her cheek as she encountered his quiet gaze. All at once the court and corridor seemed to become wonderfully dark and still. A slight shudder ran through her frame; she drew back from the American and sat down where he had directed her, 'drawing her reboso close around her.

"Señor," she said, quite humbly, "I am listening."

Ashley did not speak at once, though Pepé seemed to urge him to do so by a motion of the head, which betokened readiness to confirm his speech; and when he began, it was at a point entirely unexpected by either listener.

"Señorita," he said, "is it not true that when you think of an American, you have in your mind a pale-faced, mysterious, unresisting youth, gliding spectre-like about the hacienda walls, tempting by a love-song the bloody steel of some dark and daring desperado? In a word, is it not the vision — distorted, insufficient, faint — of my murdered cousin, John Ashley, that comes before you?"

The young girl started. "Yes! yes!" she said hurriedly, not knowing what she said. "At least, once I thought like that. I had not seen an American then; I did not know —"

"And the first American you have known has had the benefit of the preconception," interrupted Ashley, grimly. "Well, it is something to know the secret of a contemptuous indifference which has always been so frankly expressed." This comment was in English, and though Chinita watched the motion of his lips, their silence could not have given her better opportunity to recover her confused and startled thoughts.

"Then it is true," she said. "You are of the family of the poor American, who was killed like a rabbit by a hawk. Why, they say that he could not have even clapped his hand on his belt, though a *man* from very instinct would draw a knife on his enemy, even in his last gasp. Is it not so, Pepito? I used to tell Chata that, when she would shed her soft tears of pity for him. Well, I could not cry, but I have watched at the mesquite-tree for the coming of his ghost a thousand times; yet I never saw it, — and it was I who found his grave."

"And it was you who bade Pepé show it me," interrupted Ashley; "and perhaps not as a mere jest as he thought." She nodded, looking up at him vaguely and keenly. "You thought perhaps I had come these many miles from my own country to find it?" he added. "Well, that was scarcely so; it had not presented itself to me as possible that the obscure grave of a murdered foreigner should be remembered still, and that his name should be found above it. No, I came for proofs of John Ashley's life, not of his death. It was not even to trace his murderer or to avenge him that I came."

She looked incredulous. "Why then should you come?" she asked. "Had you a vow? If I had known and loved the dead man, it would have been to kill the man who struck him in secret that I would have come. But it is as Captain Ruiz says, — the blood of an American runs so slowly it cools his heart, while ours is a burning torrent that causes the soul to leap and the hand to smite at a word."

Ashley realized that impatient contempt of him was struggling with a feeling to which, with sudden apprehension of its importance, she dared not give utterance; or perhaps the idea that had long been shaping itself was for the moment obscured, but yet in the darkness and confusion was growing to an overwhelming certainty in her mind. Chinita had risen to her feet, but suddenly she sat down, covering her face with a hand which Ashley saw in the dim light shook with suppressed excitement. Her attitude was that of a listener; and in a low voice he told her of his boyhood, of the days when he had come in from school and stood at the shoulder of his grown cousin, — the young man with the silky shadow just darkening his upper lip, and with the clear frank eyes of a boy, who looked so eagerly forward into the active life of manhood, restive under the restraints and cautions that hampered him, until at last he broke away, and was no more seen, nor scarcely heard of, until the news of his early and violent death came to cast an unending gloom over the household, which before had been captious, foreboding, but ever loving, ever secretly proud of the bold, irrepressible spirit it could not chain to its standard of decorum, or tame to walk in the narrow path of uneventful and passionless existence. The years of his own youth he passed lightly by; there was nothing in them for comment until he came to the time of his aunt's death, his inheritance of the fortune that should have been John Ashley's, the reading of those few letters which had given

22

to Mary Ashley such strange dreams, and which in the
re-reading had filled his mind with thoughts of the same
possibilities that racked her own. He spoke of them
briefly in a single sentence: "We found by his letters
that he believed himself married; it was to find the
woman he had loved, or any trace of her, that I came."

Chinita sat so still one might have doubted if she
heard; but that very stillness convinced Ashley that she
listened with an absorbing interest, too great for questioning. She could but wait breathlessly for what was
to come.

"After long and vexatious wanderings I was taken
wounded to Tres Hermanos," continued the young man.
"There, when my hope was almost exhausted, I heard
the name that had been in my mind so long, — heard it
only to make inquiries which ended in confusion, and
threatened to involve me in endless complications; so
at last I was glad to suffer myself to be convinced that
my conjectures were the mere vagaries of an overburdened fancy, a too scrupulous conscience, and to turn my
face homeward, determined that thereafter I would live
my life, and take in peace the goods fortune sent me.
In such a mind I rode with the troop across the plain
and up the desolate hillside, along which the scattered
graves of the poor lay, the mounds scarce noticeable
among the rocks and cacti. Pepé remembered your jesting command; it would give him an opportunity to withdraw from the troops unheeded. He invited me to go
with him to see something that would interest me. When
I saw the grave, my heart began to beat; when I read
the name upon the fallen cross, the blood rushed into my
eyes and suffocated me; every drop in my heart accused
me! There lay my cousin murdered, and in looking for
a possible claimant to his name, I had forgotten him!
I had forgotten that his death was still unatoned for,
the murderer undiscovered, unsought, unpunished."

Chinita dropped her hand from her face and looked up,
her eyes glowing, her lips apart, her bosom rising and
falling with the quick breath that came and went. Here
were words she could understand; here was a spirit that
touched her own.

"And then, then, then?" she muttered; and Pepé

leaned out from the wall, like a gaunt shadow, to hear the narration, as if every word was too significant to allow a single one to escape him. "Then?"

"Then," resumed Ashley, "I seemed chained to the spot. I could not tear myself away, though reason told me that to stay there was useless; to hasten forward and demand the truth from those I had hitherto shrunk from offending, the only course open to me. Reason as I would, I could not force myself to leave the spot. After a time, yielding to necessity and to my command, Pepé left me. I was alone for hours with the dead. My mind was full of him; I heard his voice; I looked into the eyes which death had closed for so many unregarded years. I saw before me that face which I had so long forgotten; but my fancy pictured him never as in life, gay, happy, resolute, but pale, bloody, corpse-like, stretching out dead hands to me and speaking with the soundless voice of those we dream of. Who remembers the tone of a voice, silent forever? Yet it echoes in our heart; it awakens our joys, our griefs, our fears; it is more powerful, more terrible, than any living voice. And so upon that day was the voice of the dead John Ashley to me. As I listened to it, I swore never to leave Mexico until the mystery of his death, as well as that of his life, was open to me; until I had called to account the villain who had cut him off so secretly, so vilely.

"While I was full of the thought, and the whole world around me seemed to stretch on every side silent, void, waiting for me to choose whither I would go, in what direction I would set out to seek the nameless object of the new absorbing passion, which seemed more vital, more essential to my being than the air I breathed, I felt a presence near me. I looked up, — a man was leaning over the wall. I instantly conjectured he was not the mere peasant his dress indicated. A sense of mysterious connection between his life and mine seized upon me; it strengthened as he crossed the wall and strode toward me over the sunken graves. He came as though under a spell; I looked upon him as if under the fascination of a serpent-like gaze. I recoiled, yet for worlds I would not have turned from him. His eyes fell upon the cross; the expression of his face, the words that sprang from his lips, —

vague though they were, — sped to my brain with an electric thrill. I knew the man before me was John Ashley's murderer."

Chinita had risen. She stretched out her hand and touched the hilt of the knife in Ashley's belt. It was the action of a moment, yet it was a question that the quick beating of her heart and the panting breath made at the instant impossible from her lips. Ashley answered it by a brief account of the combat and its interruption.

As he ended, she drew a deep breath of relief. It did not occur to him that it could be for any other than himself. It flattered and pleased him, for an instant he realized how deeply, as having in it something of the tender unreasoning fears of gentle womanhood. Yet the readiness with which she had comprehended his passion for revenge, while it justified him, had set her in a harsh and cruel aspect, which made her lithe, dark beauty forbidding, unrelenting, tiger-like. Yet this strange young creature, he thought, at once so foreign to him, and still so near, concealed after all, under the surface of incomprehensible moods and half barbaric customs, those attributes of gentleness, those instincts of justness, which amidst the perplexing differences of national manners and standards of good and evil may be distinguished and understood by every mind. At that moment Ashley felt her to be less an alien than he had ever been able before to consider her. She was not only beautiful, bewitching, but in part, at least, comprehensible.

Chinita stood silent for many moments; she had not even started when he spoke the name Ramirez. The personality of the man of whom he had spoken had been a foregone conclusion in her mind.

"It was the amulet I gave him that saved him," she said simply; and Ashley stared at her blankly, not comprehending the meaning of her words, but only that the relief she had experienced had been rather for the aggressor than for him. Had he then been mistaken? Was she an entire stranger to the thought which so permeated his own mind that he had imagined it must be present in hers?

"Yes, the amulet that I gave him must have all the virtues Pedro told me of," she said musingly. "So it was the General Ramirez who killed the American? *Dios mio!* he must have had good cause; yet it angers me. Ah! it is well I have time to think what cause he must have had!"

" Cause !" ejaculated Ashley, " cause ! "

The girl nodded her head in an argumentative way. In the dim light Ashley could read the struggle in her mind, — indignation at the deed, dismay at its consequences, battling with attempted justification of the perpetrator. " By my patron saint !" she exclaimed at length, " it was the woman who was to blame. Why did she torture him? He must have loved her; and what was there in the American to make her false to Ramirez? Strange she should have preferred another to him ! "

" For God's sake say no more !" cried Ashley, with actual horror in his voice. " I forgot that this tale has no deeper significance to you than any other; that the American is to you simply an American, and Ramirez the hero of your own countrymen, by whose desperate deeds your imagination is dazzled, and for whom, even in the midst of horror, you find excuse, admiration, justification. To you he seems but a jealous lover, taking just revenge upon a successful rival."

Chinita spoke not a word, but bent her head as though his words were an accusation. Her face, in the dim light, was so impassive it was impossible for Ashley to conjecture what was passing in her mind. Did she remember that he had said he had come to seek a child, and was it possible that the mystery of her own birth had not suggested to her that she might have an interest in the ghastly deed of Ramirez far deeper than would make natural or possible to her the excuse of jealousy in the perpetrator? He had learned something of the reticence and self-restraint of these people since he had come among them ; yet was it possible this young girl could suspend judgment in such a cause until her own relation to it was fully ascertained? Were prejudice, education, sentiment, so much stronger than the voice of Nature? Did no instinct cry in her heart, denouncing this man, of whom she had made a hero, — no womanly pity hover over his victim? What a ready apprehension she had shown of Ashley's own desire for vengeance ! Was that simply because it was the passion strongest in her own soul, and so gave to her ready excuse even for murder?

Under the moonlight it seemed to him that the young girl's face grew hard as marble. No, she was not one to yield her faith lightly. This deed, which had filled the mind of Chata with dismay, and intensified a thousand-fold the horror in which she held the character of the man whom she believed it sin not to reverence and love, would in no wise shake the faith and admiration of this stronger soul, who could condone it with the thought that a woman had played the murderer false.

"Yet with all this, Señor," she said at length, looking up, "if you have no more to tell me, I see not why this should turn me against the Señor General. For you it is different — oh, quite different; but for me, —" She paused suddenly, and Ashley saw that the hand which hung at her side was clenched till the nails marked her flesh.

Yes, the deed itself was nothing, — a trifle, at most, — but in its relation to her, how great, how terrible, it might become!

Ashley was not deceived. He felt that by a word he might fan into a resistless flame the fire that lay smouldering in that resolute heart, — a word which would be no surprise to her, which would but confirm the conviction against which, in loyalty to Ramirez, she struggled with even a certain anger against the persistent suspicion that made the legendary and unheroic figure of the American a mute denouncer, more powerful, more persuasive, than the living man who had revealed the author of the tragedy which through all her life had been so dark a mystery. It seemed to Ashley that she held her breath to listen to his next words; but he could be as hard as she was herself to this girl, whose heart seemed incapable of feeling aught but a personal injury, or any passion but revenge.

"Señorita," he said, "I went back to the hacienda. My horse had fled; there was nothing else for me to do, if I would find means to follow this man who had suddenly become my debtor in all the dues of outraged kinship. My object was to obtain money, a horse and guide, and to regain the troop as quickly as should be possible; to denounce this murderer to Doña Isabel, and reveal the plot against her interests which had appeared to me so weak, so absolutely absurd, but which now assumed an importance commensurate with my detestation of him whom it was designed to serve. But with further thought my resolution changed. If all her agents were false, — Pedro, Ruiz, as well as you, whom I know to be" (Chinita winced), — " and Pepé should be successful in inducing Pedro to play into the hands of Ramirez, what power could Doña Isabel employ to prevent that change of leadership which it was more than probable the troops — indifferent to the cause, eager only for action and booty — would accept with acclamations? Clearly, my only course was to proceed to El Toro and arouse the too confident Gonzales, who in incomprehensible inactivity was awaiting the promised succor, — incomprehensible if the emissaries of Doña Isabel had reached him; for, as I knew, not one word in reply had been returned.

"I had much to ask of Doña Isabel Garcia, — questions which had burned upon my lips before; but reflection told me I was no more ready to ask them now than I had been; that her pride might be still as obdurate. No, there were months before me in which by gradual assault I might acquire all the knowledge I would in vain endeavor to gain by sudden force. I was confident that if by no stratagem or treason Ramirez ultimately could place himself at the head of these troops, he would be found in the field against them. I learned that he hated Gonzales as a personal, no less than a political, foe. Gonzales then was the man for me to follow. In serving Doña Isabel against the machinations of those she had so blindly trusted, I should serve myself; keep in view the mocking fiend whose downfall I had sworn, and perchance satisfy myself in regard to the still importunate doubts which had led to my presence amid these strange scenes.

" I had intended to leave the hacienda upon the very night of my return, but on my way — Well, that is nothing to the purpose; I reached it exhausted. But the early morning found me in the saddle. My strength revived with every step toward El Toro. Once we caught sight of the long line of the hacienda troop crossing the open plain. We had passed through cañons and byways, and were far in advance of them. More than once in the mountains we heard the name of Ramirez, and made wide detours of hamlets where men were gathering in twos and threes and sixes, — ragged, unkempt, unarmed for the most part, but full of enthusiasm in their leader, and confident of booty and glory. Without doubt, the reverse of Ramirez at El Toro would not remain unavenged. I realized the spell of that potent name, the very echo of which seemed to be as eloquent as the living voice of most men, chieftains and leaders though they might be."

Chinita's eyes glistened; she raised herself with a proud gesture, as if the involuntary tribute to the genius of the adventurer was a personal commendation.

"Though we avoided the villages," continued Ashley, "I did not hesitate to question the few passengers we met upon the roads. These were chiefly wandering traders, stooping under their burdens of clay-ware or charcoal, adherents of no particular party, and reticent or the opposite, as their natural impulses or the supposed necessities of the time prompted. These I plied in vain for news of Pedro, of Pepé, or even of the noted Ramirez himself. Each and every one seemed to have passed, and left not even a memory behind; though from these very ranchos and hamlets I knew Doña Isabel's troops had been drawn, and that the followers of Ramirez were daily drawing more, — forcing those they could not persuade, laughing at the protestations of the women, and feeding the adventurous ardor of the men with tales of daring exploits and promises of plunder. All this we heard, and knew the whole country was in a ferment, yet passed through it undetected, on our own part unable to catch a glimpse or hear a word of the covert from which Ramirez directed and inspired the movement. Travelling rapidly, we entered upon the third day a deep gorge, which cut the foothills of the very mountain that overshadowed the towers of the convent town toward which I was journeying. Still a painful stretch of twelve hours, of an almost pathless labyrinth of rock and sand, I was told, lay before us; and early in the evening I ordered a halt, intending to set forth before the day broke. One of my servants spoke of a spring which he knew of; and though the season was so dry that we had little hope of discovering it, we decided to push on, although at every step the horses seemed to protest against the effort, — for they had been ridden mercilessly, without change and almost without food or rest. As we neared the spot where we hoped to find water, the aspect of the country seemed to grow even more forbidding.

" ' The dry season has swallowed it,' said the servant dejectedly, after a careful survey of the locality. 'There is nothing here but sand, — a dry welcome for our thirsty beasts ;' and at a signal from me he threw himself from the saddle, and tethering his panting horse, clambered up the gorge to gather a handful of dry grease-wood with which to light a fire. Meanwhile, his fellow busied himself in unpacking the few articles we had brought, and I threw myself on the ground against a rock, feeling myself more secure in that wild and secluded pass than I had done since I left the hacienda.

" The place was very still. Although it was yet daylight in the world without, the whole gorge was in shadow. The crackling of the herbage under the horses' feet, or a low word occasionally spoken by the men, was all that broke the stillness. I suppose from thought I was gradually falling into slumber, when the sound of horses galloping, of men laughing and shouting, broke upon the air. I started to my feet and seized my arms, calling for the men ; but they had disappeared ; the three horses were rearing and plunging. I caught and succeeded in mounting my own ; but as the cavalcade drew near, I realized that its members were so numerous and in such mad humor that it would be worse than folly for me to approach them. One of my men had recovered from his panic, and stole up to me with blanched face and wide-staring eyes. I pointed to the horses, and with wonderful dexterity he bounded into the saddle of one, and caught the bridle of the other. In as little time as it takes me to tell it, we gained the shelter of the rock. Calmed by a few low words, the horses stood motionless, and from our covert we saw the company of lawless soldiery go by.

" Ramirez was at their head ; and by a cord at his bridle-rein was tied a man, who vainly strove to keep pace with the gallop of his horse. At almost every step he fell, and was struck by the hoofs of the foremost horses, whose riders leaning down brought him again to his feet with blows from the flat sides of their swords. There were perhaps thirty ruffians engaged in this brutal sport ; and after them ran a man at such a pace as only an Indian could maintain, even for moments, wringing his hands and praying and crying, — alternately a prayer and a curse. And in him, more by his voice, gasping and hoarse though it was, than by sight, I recognized Pepé Ortiz."

Chinita would have screamed, but the ready hand of the peasant closed over her mouth. "The man! the man tied to the horse's rein!" she gasped, when he released her.

"I could not see his face, and he had no breath to cry out," said Ashley. "They passed so closely, I could have shot Ramirez like a dog. But I seemed paralyzed by horror. It did for me what perhaps a moment's reflection would have done had I been capable of it, — it saved me from suicide. To have moved then would have been certain death. I could not comprehend the mad jests of those around the victim; but a moment after they passed I heard a sound which to all ears conveys the same meaning, — a pistol shot, — and the voice of Ramirez crying, —

"'*Caramba!* the next fall would have killed him, and the dog should die only by my hand. There! I have paid the debt I owed thee, — thou knowest for what. It should have been paid thee like the other villain's years ago. Would that I had dragged him at my horse's rein as I have thee!'

"The man fell; a soldier, with a laugh, cut the rope; all swept on with shouts and laughter, — Ramirez the quietest among them. In a few minutes they were far up the gorge. One glance had satisfied Ramirez that his shot had reached its aim.

"None seemed to remember the panting wretch behind. I had reached the prostrate body as soon as he, and together we raised it up. Under the mask of bruises and blood and the dust of the roadway, I recognized the man I had been seeking, — Pedro Gomez."

Pepé caught Chinita on his outstretched arm, — she had staggered as though struck by a heavy blow. Ashley sprang to her side in remorse, — he had spared her nothing in the recital; but she had not fainted. She raised herself slowly, and lifting her arms above her head, wrung her hands in speechless agony.

The man who had been murdered years before had been a shadow, a myth, in her mind. He became at that supreme moment a living presence, joining with, blent with, the martyred Pedro in denunciation of the man whom she had raised in her admiration to a pinnacle of glory. The idol of years crashed to the earth, in semblance of a demon, — and with it fell the stoicism and pride that had encased as in bands of steel the softer emotions of her nature.

"Murdered! murdered both!" she moaned at length. "Was it not enough he should bereave me even before I came into the world, but that he should so vilely slay the only creature who has loved me? Oh, my God!" she added, shuddering, "why have I been so cursed as to have given one thought to such a wretch? Oh! forgive, forgive, forgive!"

XXXVI.

To whom was that vain cry addressed? Ashley questioned not, but clasping in his the icy hands which strove to smite and beat each other, spoke such words of soothing as came readiest in the stranger tongue he found so inadequate. He realized that it was not to him Chinita directed that wail of self-abasement and remorse; and he also apprehended somewhat of the wild joy that would have been his, had she involuntarily turned to him in the anguish of her desolation. But she was scarcely conscious of his presence, and in her frenzy — terrible to witness, though it was not loud — even Pepé's rough accents were unheeded.

"*Niña* of my soul!" he said earnestly, "Pedro is not dead. No, it is not a lie I tell thee! Who would lie to thee in such an hour as this? I have come to tell thee that he lives; 't was he himself who sent me."

"He himself!", she echoed at last, turning her wild, tearless eyes upon Pepé's face. "Ah, it is because thou art here that I know he is dead, else thou wouldst not dare to leave him!"

"And by my faith, it is not of my own will I am here!" answered Pepé, bluntly. "Señor Don 'Guardo, you can tell her that."

"I can in truth," replied Ashley, who seeing that the peasant's words were received by her but as mere attempts to defer the evil moment when the inevitable assurance of the death of her foster-father must be given her, — so well did she know the customs and manners of her country people, ever prone to useless prevarication, even in their deepest sorrow, — hastened to describe to her the few scant means they had found in his extremity to recall the exhausted Pedro to the life that had apparently been thrust and beaten and driven from him forever.

The ball of the pistol had but grazed the cheek of the tortured man; the blood and dust had deceived the ac-

customed eyes of Ramirez, as it had deceived their own.
The greater danger arose from the frightful condition of
laceration and fatigue to which the mad race through the
stony cañon had reduced him. ,

In a few words Pepé told the tale. He and Pedro had
met but the day before, and it was while hastening to El
Toro to apprize Gonzales of the plot that Pepé, in the
petition of Chinita, had revealed to the indignant Pedro,
that they had encountered face to face the irate chieftain
and his followers. Pepé understood little of the cause
that led to their being seized, dragged from their horses,
and threatened with instant death. Both alike protested
innocence of any scheme to baffle or injure the mountain
chieftain ; but he understood too well the ease with which
a foe too weak to fight could assume the aspect of a friend.
At the worst, however, Pepé imagined they might be
forced to turn back on their way to spend a few unwilling
hours among the bandit followers, until chance should
give them opportunity to escape. But Ramirez's memory
was keen as it was vengeful. Suddenly he bent and gazed
searchingly into the face of the elder prisoner.

" Ah ! " he exclaimed, with an oath, " I know thee !
Thou art Pedro Gomez."

Pedro, who till this moment had bent his head to avoid
the gaze of his captors, raised it swiftly with an ejaculation of amazement. A red handkerchief bound the brows
of Ramirez ; his face was swarthy and grimed with hard
riding.

" Ah, and thou knowest me, too ! " Ramirez cried.
" Thou hast called me a devil more than once in thy lifetime ; and now I will prove thy word true. Hereafter
thou wilt have no further chance for that, or for opening the gate to the man who would make my — " He
gnashed his teeth in speechless rage, and with his sword
struck the keeper across the face.

The action spoke louder than words. Some one, in
ready comprehension of the leader's mood, threw a lasso,
and catching the prisoner across the breast began to
mimic the wild shouts of a bull-fighter. But Ramirez was
in no humor for pastime.

" On ! on ! " he cried. " 'T is nearly sunset. Let us
see how far on our way this fellow can accompany us

till then; and then by a vow I made to my patron San
Leonidas, more than a score of years ago, he shall die.
Caramba! did ever man play Ramirez false, and he forget
to pay him his dues?"

Pepé, amid the shouts and laughter of the band, heard
these words with a wild sense of terror; but it was only
when he beheld Pedro struggling at the side of the plunging horse, that he realized that the gate-keeper was to be
dragged to his death. He had heard of Ramirez's wild
jests, and imagined that this might be one, until he beheld the cortège speeding forward, urging the unhappy
Pedro before them with blows and jeers, or exhibiting
their wonderful horsemanship in evading his prostrate
body, — which, however, more than once, as he fell,
sounded under the thud of the horses' feet.

Pepé could have escaped at any moment, for in the concentration of attention upon Pedro his companion had
been utterly forgotten; but he followed madly, expostulating, entreating, cursing, while his breath allowed; and
then was swept onward in the whirl, seemingly almost
unconscious, till he heard the shot that ended the mad
scene, and found himself staggering over the body of the
bleeding Pedro.

The sight of Ashley, as unexpected as it was reassuring,
as though an angel had arisen, saved the wretched youth
from utter collapse of mind and body. But for the new
excitement he would have fallen prone, and had he ever
regained consciousness it would have been to find his comrade dead. But under the impulse of Ashley's energetic
action and sustaining words, he even helped to raise the
victim, in whom, lacerated though he was, Ashley soon
discovered a feeble flutter of the heart.

"We took him to the shelter of the rock," said Ashley,
who had by signs hastened Pepé's conclusion of the account,
which, related in his own profuse manner, was far more
agonizing than the brief outline here given, "and found
that his extraordinary powers of endurance, though strained
to the uttermost, had stood him in wonderful stead. An
arm was broken, and every muscle so wrenched and
strained that when he regained his consciousness the
resolute will, which during the progress of the torture had
withheld him from uttering protest or groan, utterly gave

way, and he screamed in agony. Happily his persecutors
were too far distant to be recalled by those unrestrainable
cries of returning consciousness. Even while we poured
brandy down his throat, and rubbed and stretched his
limbs, it seemed as though it would have been a thousand
times more charitable to suffer him to die than to recall
him to such agony. When he regained full consciousness, however, the cries ceased, — not because the pain
was less, but that the will regained its mastery. "As
his eyes fell upon me, he gazed at me a moment as upon
an apparition. So wild was his look, I thought he was
going mad.

"'Don Juan! here! here!' he muttered hoarsely.
'Are we in hell together? But, no!' he sprang up, then
fell back with a groan. 'I shall live to warn her yet.
Oh God, that the child should entreat me to turn traitor
for him! But she shall not fall into his accursed hands.
Never! never! Ah, Pepé, thou art here; hasten, hasten!
tell her she is the child of John Ashley, the man Ramirez
murdered. What though I die? She will be saved! Go!
go! I pray you!'

Chinita started. Ward anticipated some outburst of
emotion, but the glance she flashed back at him indicated
simply keen intelligence; the springs of feeling remained
untouched. With an effort Ward continued : —

"My recreant servant had returned. It was Stefano,
whom you know well. He is a coward, but ready in
resource, and with a kindly heart. He knew the country
well, and told us of a cave he once had slept in, and led
us to it unerringly. To our surprise we found there a
scanty supply of toasted corn, left by some wandering
tenant, and a quantity of water, still fresh enough to show
that the cave had not long been empty. There was a remnant of a woman's dress in one corner, — heaven knows
how brought there, — and this we used to bind the pistol
wound; while Stefano used the best means available in
setting the broken arm. These rancheros are possessed
of strange accomplishments, — I don't believe a surgeon
could have done it with more skill.

"During the course of our passage through the dusk,
bearing as best we could our groaning burden, Pedro's hallucination that I was John Ashley merged into recogni-

tion. It was but little I could do for him, but it filled him with gratitude. 'You are a good Christian,' he ejaculated again and again; and once in the night, when the others slept, he muttered '*Niña, niña* Herlinda, forgive me! I am dying. You bade me protect the child! Ah, even in life it has not been possible! Is she not in the hands you bade me defend her from?'

"These sentences, murmured at intervals, kept me waking while all others slept, hanging over him with entreaties to disburden his mind of the secret which weighed so heavily upon him that it seemed under it he could neither live nor die.

"'Tell me at least,' I said, 'who is this man called Ramirez, whom I saw this evening wreak upon you so terrible a revenge? How comes it that you are so hated by the man for whom your foster-daughter is plotting? Have you not been his follower in by-gone days? Surely it is not Chinita who has set such enmity between you!'

"'No, no! it began before she was born,' answered Pedro shudderingly, his pale countenance becoming more ghastly still. 'Oh, Lady of Sorrows!' he continued, as if forgetful of my presence, 'was it not enough that the child should fall again into the power of Doña Isabel, — she who tore it from its mother's breast to cast it among the beggars who feed with the dogs at her gates, — but that her father's murderer, her mother's destroyer, should wield this devil's witchcraft over her? My God, who will defend her? Who will rescue her?'"

Chinita raised her head, her nostrils quivering, the veins upon her neck and temples swollen and palpitating.

"'Tell her the truth,' I said! 'Then she will be her own defender; and I — you know me; for what other purpose am I here but to shield her? Yes, Pedro, the secret you have kept so long is mine as well as yours. John Ashley, my cousin, died because he dared love a woman named Herlinda; and that Herlinda was the daughter of Doña Isabel Garcia.'" A look of indescribable hauteur and triumph passed over Chinita's rigid face, while Ashley continued,—

"Pedro stared at me in wild dismay, '*Niña, niña!*' he muttered, piteously, 'I have not betrayed thee; and Doña Isabel, though you have taken the child from me which you thrust upon me in such mockery, have I not borne the torture meekly?   No, even to this man, so like the other that he needed not to tell his name and kin, I have told nothing to shame you!'

"His words sprang from his lips in spite of the will that would have kept them back; for a time he was like a man under the influence of a maddening draught.   Striving to calm him by the assurance that I would never use the knowledge he might give me to dishonor the family to which his whole life had been devoted, I drew from him little by little his strange tale.   It concerns neither you nor me, Chinita, until in recompense for secret service done her in the cause of her wretched brother Leon, Doña Isabel Garcia made Pedro gate-keeper at Tres Hermanos. There my unfortunate cousin gained his good offices in his secret meetings with the young Herlinda.   The man seems in truth to have been conscious of no serious offence against Doña Isabel in lending his aid to the tender intercourse of the young lovers, although he was cognizant of her plans regarding the marriage of Herlinda and Gonzales.   My cousin claimed the right to visit his wife; and Pedro took his gold and was silent, if not convinced.

"'Ah, how joyously Ashley left his wife — for the last time,' Pedro exclaimed at length, ceasing to expect my questions and taking the tone of narrative.   'Yes, Don Juan called Herlinda always his wife: what was the keeper of the gate to demand, — the word of a priest forsooth, rather than that of the man whom his mistress loved? Ah! Doña Isabel I knew would ask all, or the young Gonzales.   One cannot do worse than put his hand in a boiling pot, and wherefore do that when it hangs over his neighbor's fire?   Yes, never had Ashley seemed more confident, more gay.   "I shall not again need to waken thee at midnight to let me pass like a thief who leaves a bribe," he said; "to-morrow I shall be free to come and go as I will."

"'Alas!' the remorseful Pedro continued, 'as my eyes followed the young American, I thought any woman might be pardoned for loving him : had he not beguiled my own heart? for I swear I loved him.   Yet I wondered at the courage of the *Niña* Herlinda, — she who had seemed so timid, so yielding to her mother's every wish.   *Caramba!*

23

it is true, — "There is nothing too strong for love or death." I laughed as Ashley stepped forth, to think how youth in its folly can baffle caution, when a voice behind me echoed the sound. The blood froze in my veins, so overpowering was the very presence near me even before it touched me. Almighty powers! when I looked up, the man in the peasant's dress, whom only a few hours before I had admitted as a stranger within the walls, hurled himself upon me; but the blaze in his eyes could burn only from the fierce and terrible rage of the evil spirit of that house. It was Leon Vallé who dashed me down and rushed out into the night.'"

Chinita uttered an exclamation; then repeating the name, "Leon! Leon Vallé," listened with bated breath, while Ashley continued in the words of Pedro: —

"'I knew at the moment that Ashley was lost. Not a thousand prayers, nor the swiftest aid my cries could have gained him, would have saved him. I waited, scarce daring to breathe; with strained ears I listened. Would the murderer, his first work accomplished, return? I knew then he held my life forfeit; yet had he returned, I should have opened the gate to him. Ah, you know not the power of that man! As it was in Leon Vallé then, so it is now in Ramirez. God, what power in those terrible eyes! I felt it then, I felt it to-day. What resistance was possible? The morning came. I was still alive, but the people came to me crying of the dead. What need had I to ask the name? In the midst of the tumult a terrible shriek rang on my ears. I thought my brain was turning. There was but one thought that steadied it, — confession, confession to Doña Isabel.

"'As soon as it was possible I sought her presence. I cannot tell you what passed; I only know the words I would have spoken died on my lips. Whether Doña Isabel had known of it or not, I could not determine; but that the love of Herlinda Garcia and the young American was to die with him, and that the terrible vengeance which had been worked for her was not to be in vain, seared itself upon my mind. The preservation of that secret was to atone for my sins, and not confession. Never to mortal was my knowledge to be breathed. This was the penitence laid upon me. And so, despairing, I left her. What was the immortal soul of a poor peasant in comparison to the honor of the family of Garcia?

" ' It was well! Why should a servant gainsay his mistress? So months went on, Señor. Within and around the hacienda people were dying. They told me the *niña* Herlinda herself was pining, — some whispered for the American; but a terror seized even on the boldest, and the American's name ceased to be heard, and that of the young Gonzales took its place. The gossips were content to blame any name unchid for her wan cheeks and sunken eyes. But I knew that no man had scorned her love, and that no living man had aught to answer for had she loved too well. I had not seen her for weeks and weeks; but one night a creature so pale and wan I thought it her ghost, accosted me. Strange, strange the mission that brought her. It was to entreat my protection —that of the worthless Pedro — for the child which in secret and in banishment she was about to bring into the world.

" ' Well! well! I promised all she asked. I should have done so even had I thought it possible the dire need she pleaded would be hers. Oh! I had heard strange and fearful tales of deeds that have been wrought within the walls of these great and solitary haciendas; but that Doña Isabel would stoop to crime, and that I should find it in my power to save a child which she would strive to sacrifice, I could not believe. Trouble, I thought, had made Herlinda mad. But she was mad only with the frenzy of a prophetess.

" ' With terrible forebodings I saw her taken from her home. Day and night I thought of her, and my heart was like ice; but one day, when worn out with watching and expectancy I sat at the gate, I fell into a doze, and in my dream heard the voice of Herlinda calling me. It changed to that of a man. I woke with a start, and a child was dropped into my hands. Strange and wonderful must have been the means by which the hunted and distracted Herlinda had evaded the mother she feared! Who had been her friends, Señor? The wonder is with me still. I saw the face of her messenger but for a moment, yet it has haunted me. Yes, more than once, when I have thought of new faces that have passed before

me, I have said, "Such an one was like the man; why
was I blind to it when he stood before me?"' Pedro
started up, and clasped my arm so powerfully that I
shrank. 'Señor!' he cried, 'As God lives, I saw such
a face to-day! It was that of the man who rode behind,
him they call Ramirez.'

"'Reyes!' I ejaculated. 'Reyes!' What strange
sport made the messenger of Herlinda the follower of
Ramirez? I—"

Ashley paused, for Chinita echoed the name with an
intense surprise far greater than his own. She clasped
her hands to her temples, as though fearing the mad bewilderment of her thoughts was crazing her. "Tell me
no more," she said faintly. "Do I not know the unnatural wretch that I have been? But what of Pedro? Why
did you leave him? How dared you leave him? You!"
She turned upon Pepé, accusingly. "He lives, you say,
and yet you are here!"

"No less would content him," interposed Ashley, while
Pepé muttered an inarticulate remonstrance. "It was
Pepé you had sent upon your errand; it was Pepé whom
Pedro would dispatch with his answer."

"Ay!" said Pepé, grumblingly, "and with you I must
remain. I am sworn to that, whether you like it or
loathe it."

"I," said Ashley, "have ridden thus far out of the
direct path I would have taken to El Toro, to warn you
of the character of the man you have made your hero;
to tell you I believe you to be the daughter of my cousin,
to offer you the home and the fortune that would have
been his."

He spoke unhesitatingly, yet a strange sense of bewilderment swept over him. He was conscious that it
was no fear of material loss that troubled him, though not
for an instant did he dream of using the advantage of the
law against this defenceless girl; but that this strange impulsive creature should be of the same blood as he, as the
calm and gentle Mary; that she should come into their life
with her wayward passions, her erratic genius, her weird
beauty, — was a thing incomprehensible, almost terrible.
Yet the blood leaped stronger in the young man's veins
as he beheld her; and his heart bounded as he said,

" Yes, I must go; for I have certain news that the enemy
is massing his forces for attack. I go to warn Gonzales;
but I shall return to claim you as my cousin's child.
Meanwhile, be silent — patient. Pedro prays you keep
the secret of your birth. He believes as firmly as ever
that only thus can you be safe. And for that mother's
sake I pray you be silent. Right may be won for you,
and her good name be still left untainted. There may be
a mystery still to be unravelled."

" I will be silent; I will wait," Chinita said in a cold,
hollow voice.

Ashley noticed that she had no word of sympathy for
him, no recognition of the endeavors that had led to her
discovery. Apparently the thought that he was aught to
her was as far from her mind as any grief had ever been
for that other American, — as far indeed as such was at that
moment. For, strangely, Ashley seemed to penetrate the
inmost shrine of her thought; and still the figures around
which centred her love, her hopes, her passions were
only those of Pedro, of Ramirez, of Doña Isabel.

" I will be silent," she repeated. " Ah, it will be easier
now ! Yes, hasten to El Toro, bring Gonzales; he will
be a surer, safer leader than Ruiz — though I will turn him
again to my will. Yes, yes, more than once I have thought
Ruiz wavering, uncertain ! Now at a word I will make
him what before he has only affected to others to be, —
the undying enemy of Ramirez ! "

Ashley was silent. He would have had this girl passive,
supine, womanly; yet from the very necessity of warning
her, he had been forced to arouse in her this vindictive
wrath against the man who had done her unwittingly such
foul wrong.

" Listen ! " he said hurriedly, after a pause. " It is
Pedro who implores, who commands, that until he gives
you leave, nothing of what I have told you shall pass your
lips. I might have had your promise before I would speak.
See, the stars are shining that must see me on my way.
Give me two promises before we part, — one that you will
be silent; the other that Pepé shall be continually within
your sight or call. For this he was sent from the side of
the suffering, perhaps dying, Pedro. He would have you
safe, — safe from Ramirez."

"And I will kill you before you shall fall into his hands," interposed Pepé, grimly.

Chinita smiled with cynical bitterness, and said indifferently, "I promise. Yes, I promise. Ah, yes, Señor, you will see I have been silent when you come again. And now I will go back. What if the Señora Doña Isabel should wake and find me missing? — the child she loves so well!"

She waved her hand, and stepped backward through the darkness. At the door of the chamber where Doña Isabel lay, she seemed to vanish into air, so swift, so silent, was her going.

Ashley gazed after her long in silence, — so long that another spectral figure stole through the doorway, and with noiseless steps reached Pepé's side. "The Señora slept like the dead," Juana whispered; "but not for a thousand hard dollars would I lie in Chinita's place again, while she forgets time in lover's chat. I wonder at thee, Pepé! thou hast not a man's heart in thee. I thought thou lovedst her thyself!"

"Fool!" said Pepé, sulkily, and turned away; while Juana, ill paid for her devotion, sought a corner of the corridor in which to sink to sleep.

"Strange, incomprehensible creature!" muttered Ashley at length. "What emotions, what thoughts are hers? At least it is certain that the fascination of Ramirez is dissolved, — horror, hatred perhaps, has taken its place. She is safe. And now Pepé, my horse; I must take the road. And if it be true that Juarez is at hand, even Ramirez himself may tremble; the combined forces of Gonzales and Ruiz will hold him at bay, and keep an open road for the intrepid Liberal to the capital."

It was scarcely two hours past midnight, though his interview with Chinita had lasted long, when Ashley cautiously emerged from the inn, and took his way toward the open country. The troops lay at the east end of the town; but giving the watchword to the few sentinels who challenged him, he avoided them, and soon found himself in the vast solitude of the night. He had taken the precaution to procure a fresh horse, and for some leagues the way lay across a level country, so he made such speed as brought him by dawn within sight of the mountain upon which Pedro lay, — but on a side many miles nearer El Toro, his destination, where Gonzales, with his insufficient garrison, was anxiously awaiting the reinforcements without which he could neither dare to advance, nor hope to maintain his position in case of attack.

As Ashley glanced toward the ragged and solitary cliffs where like a hunted animal the man was lying, he remembered that after the first horror was passed, Chinita had spoken no more of her foster-father, had asked no question as to what hands were set to tend him, nor in what direction lay the cave in which he was sheltered. Such queries would have been useless, — she could do nothing; yet it would have been but natural that she should have made them. Even if the gate-keeper's care of her neglected infancy was forgotten, or accepted as a matter of course, and though her mind was absorbed by thoughts of her own history and her wrongs, yet his very connection with them should have made him an object of interest if not of tenderness.

"Heavens!" murmured Ashley, "can it be that this strange creature, as different in her instincts as in her appearance and education, is of the same blood as Mary? A bewildering charge shall I take to her, if Doña Isabel still, to save the reputation of her daughter, lays no claim to this beautiful girl, and denies her such scanty justice as she can give! For a daughter of an Ashley must not be left to the sport of chance, — neither to be sold to the first who bargains for her beauty; nor, worse still, to be consigned to a convent, as the unhappy Herlinda was." He reasoned calmly, yet his heart and temples beat hotly. "Let me think. If this Gonzales but proves a man of honor, I may gain some aid from him; he, at least, may know in which convent this woman — whom he also loved — is immured. By the way, he is a fanatic upon this new scheme of Juarez, of secularizing the property of the clergy. Ah, in event of the success of the Liberal arms, that might work countless and unimagined changes!"

The thought was full of suggestion. Ashley gave rein to his horse, and dashed forward with fresh vigor. Afterward he scarce remembered how the day passed; but its close found him, spent and weary, alighting at the door of the inn of El Toro.

Almost at the same moment, far on the other side of the mountain, two travellers, so wrapped in long striped blankets and covered by wide sombreros as to be almost indistinguishable, the man from the woman, drew rein before a mass of cactus and gray rock; and while the one gazed furtively around, vainly seeking a sign of human contiguity, the other dismounted, and bending to a mere crevice in the rock gave a long, low whistle, then turned to help his companion, saying, "That will bring Stefano. Chinita, thou wilt see that, though a coward, he is no fool, and has cared well for thy foster-father. Said I not so? Ah, here he comes."

Chinita was cramped by long riding, and was fain to cling to her guide. She looked around her with a shudder. The wild solitude of the place was terrible. She feared to move, lest she should find herself face to face with death. Her head swam, the world turned black before her eyes; and in the midst a strange hand touched her own. A low laugh sounded on her ear, — it was that of a woman.

"Santa Maria!" she heard Pepé exclaim. "It is the Virgin of Guadalupe herself. It is then that we are too late to serve the poor *padron!*"

The low laugh sounded again, — there was in it more of madness than sanctity. Chinita, with superstitious fear and desperation, sought to wrench her hand from the hot clasp in which it was held. The close air of the entrance of the cave closed round her, as with persistent force she was drawn within; and with a scream of terror she fell fainting, overcome by the excitement and exertion of many hours, and by the unexpected apparition which had greeted her.

THE illness which attacked Doña Feliz upon the morning that Ashley Ward set forth from Tres Hermanos, was the first indication of an epidemic similar in character and force to that which had devastated the hacienda fifteen years before. Reminiscences of the time of the great sickness became the absorbing topic of conversation, until the care of the dying and the burial of the dead silenced all voices, and turned all thoughts to the overwhelming cares of the present.

At first with unspeakable remorse Chata attributed the illness of Doña Feliz to her unwonted exertion in walking to the reduction-works through the fierce sunshine, and to her grief and shame in discovering her, whom she believed to be her granddaughter, there in conversation with a stranger, — from whom a modest maiden would have shrunk in decent coyness, if not in fear. Chata's heart burned with grief and remorse. She longed to throw herself upon her knees, and pour out her soul before the woman she held in such love and reverence that the thought of her distrust and displeasure was like a mortal wound in her heart. Yet she was forced to be silent, before the unconsciousness and delirium which for days and weeks overpowered the body and mind of the strong, though no longer youthful, woman.

It was some consolation to the distressed maiden that she was called upon, almost alone, to bear the labor and responsibility of the care of Doña Feliz. Don Rafael was almost helpless before his mother's peril; the servants were terrified and incompetent. Soon Chata, in the incessant toil, almost ceased to think of the trials and perplexities of her own life, save to cry bitterly to herself that had she never known before that Doña Rita was not her own mother, the difference in her bearing at that crisis toward Rosario and herself would have betrayed the truth.

"Even Don Rafael," she thought, "though he loves me, is content that I, rather than his own child, should risk the danger of the infected atmosphere."

But in truth the alarmed and harassed man was capable of but little reflection or discrimination as to the actions of those about him. He gave no heed to the selfishness of his wife or Rosario, while he found Chata ever at Doña Feliz's side, tireless, calm, unmurmuring, ministering with a rare ability, which even natural tact and long experience seldom combine to produce in such perfection, to the needs and comfort of the ever delirious patient. He grew speedily to have a perfect trust and faith in this ministering child; and though once, when for a little while his mother was silent, and the servants had fallen asleep, he opened his lips to question her, there was something in the imploring yet innocent gaze of those clear gray eyes before which he shrank, as Ashley Ward had done, powerless to utter a word that should indicate distrust.

"Perhaps my mother knows, — yes, doubtless she knew," he said to himself, with a faint attempt to justify his silence. "*Caramba!* a man must have a black heart himself who could doubt the whiteness of so pure a soul!"

Almost hourly his perturbation of mind was increased by the report of some fresh name upon the list of the sick. With a faith as profound as their own in the decoctions of herbs and roots used by the village quacks, and a superstitious respect for the alleged virtues of blessed relics and candles, and even for amulets of less sacred renown, he went from hut to hut, endeavoring to propitiate the favor of Heaven by charitable deeds, — thus perhaps gaining for himself a more personal affection than the mere clannish regard which he in a measure shared with the actual proprietors of the vast estate, but which was not strong enough to insure him against the wit or malice of the dependent yet utterly indifferent and irresponsible host he attempted to govern. A doctor had been sent for, and also a priest; but neither appeared, — the priest perhaps because the last one, who had but lately left there, had given accounts of Doña Isabel's proceedings little likely to be acceptable to the Church. This added to the perplexities of Don Rafael.

In the midst of them he was one day accosted by

Tomas, the husband of Florencia, who in tones of genuine distress, which for the time gave pathos to his usual
drunken whine, bewailed the sickness of his wife, and related how, spurning his care, she called vainly upon her
Uncle Pedro (not a day's luck had befallen them since he
had left them), and upon the Señorita Chinita (praying his
grace's pardon for mentioning one whom the Señora Doña
Isabel herself had chosen to be a lady), to come and give
her a cup of cold water, — as if he, Tomas, himself had
not spilled over her a jar of honeyed *pulque* in the vain
effort to pour a draught down her parched throat. It was
plain to see that the woman was doomed, and that it was
for her the corpse-candles had been lighted.

"The corpse-candles!" echoed Don Rafael, — for he
well knew the popular superstition at Tres Hermanos, that
when the burial lights were to burn in the great house, their
spectral counterfeits were first seen in the ancient dwelling where the spirits of the early possessors of the hacienda still guarded treasures, which awaited some daring
and fortunate claimant in a descendant who should combine their faith with a tenacity of purpose and an untiring
energy worthy the riches that had eluded their own weak
and inconstant efforts. Had indeed the conclave of shades
gathered to welcome another unsuccessful toiler among
them? Don Rafael shuddered and crossed himself, and
wondered that there was no news of Doña Isabel. He
gave Tomas a silver piece, and told him that it was not for
Florencia, or even for his own mother, that the corpse-
lights of the Garcias would burn blue, and sent him away
comforted.

An hour later, through the medium of the fiery liquors
distilled from the agave, Tomas had so far strengthened his courage that he forgot the corpse-lights altogether, until he saw them again at midnight glimmering
in the distance, not only behind the hacienda walls, but
fitfully in the darkness of the middle distance. He crossed
himself, as he fancied he caught at intervals glimpses of
spectral bearers. His comrade on the watch jested at the
fears that he opined transformed the soft brilliancy of the
large and brilliant firefly into the light of ghostly candles;
and Tomas was content to yield to the soporific charm of
the mescal, rather than contest the matter with his drowsy

comrade, — who, with a regularity which custom made invariable, at certain intervals awoke and emitted the shrill whistle that proclaimed that the sleepers of Tres Hermanos were safe beneath his vigilant care.

Just at dawn the man straightened himself suddenly before the rampart against which he had been leaning, gazed over the landscape with keen apprehension, and uttered a faint cry of consternation. The sandy line between the hacienda gates and the village had become a living one. Whence had the figures stolen? There they stood motionless, horse and man. The watchman stooped and shook his unconscious comrade. "Mother of Jesus!" he cried; "your corpse-lights were in the hands of living men. They are here! they are here! Ah, they are knocking upon the doors! That fool Felipe is turning the key in the lock! Up! Up!" At the same moment his whistle sounded shrilly, and the crack of his rifle upon the air woke the slumbering tenants of the assaulted house.

Too late! the unwary gatekeeper was surprised; the heavy doors were forced open, the courts in an instant were full of armed men, and Don Rafael, half dressed, staggering from his scarce tried slumbers, was seized by a half-dozen soldiers, while a voice he well knew, though it came as if from the dead, and knew to be that of a man who was as inflexible in act as unscrupulous in purpose, exclaimed, —

"How now, Don Rafael? Doña Isabel Garcia has at last showed her true colors. It is for Gonzales and the Liberals the men and treasure of Tres Hermanos have been accumulating! What, nothing for her Mother the Church? Ah, it is the old story, — nothing for those of her own household!"

The unwelcome intruder glanced around him with the air of one familiar with, yet inimical to, his surroundings; he laughed as he dropped the point of his sword upon the brick pave, and his spurred heel rang upon the stone step. Yet a close observer might have noticed a false note in the light and scornful tone, as though some poignant memory troubled his present purpose; and it was with a half evasive though still a threatening glance, that he lifted his eyes to encounter those of the administrador, who stood a disordered and helpless but resolute prisoner upon the steps above him.

At the sound of voices and the tramp of men, Chata had run hastily out from the room of Doña Feliz, whose illness had approached a crisis. The press of men prevented her from reaching Don Rafael, who imperatively signed to her to retreat. Still she would have dared much to reach him; but catching a glimpse of the triumphant countenance of the man at the foot of the stairs, she drew back, covered her face with her hands and fled precipitately, — in fear for herself perhaps, but more with an instinctive feeling that her presence endangered rather than helped her foster-father. That the General José Ramirez had entered Tres Hermanos in a mood to seize any pretext to assume toward it and its people the *rôle* of an injured and desperate man, was to be seen at a glance. The very soldiers had already divined as much, and were leading their horses and mules to drink at the fountain, and invading the arbor and lower rooms; the sound of their jests and laughter was mingling with the crash of the great flower-pots, carelessly pushed from their stands, and the sharp crack of jars of the quaint black and gilded ware of Guadalajara, which ornamented the corridors.

Chata re-entered the room of the sick woman, with pallid face and lips, and eyes expanding with a terror such as the mere sight of the imminent destruction of material things alone could not have occasioned. Terrible had been the tales she had heard of houses laid waste and property destroyed; yet even when the horrors seemed about to be repeated around her, she felt that she could have endured them bravely as among the chances of war had not this invasion brought to her an intensely dreaded and peculiar danger. She passed the group of alarmed and excited women who gathered at the bedside, uttering exclamations of terror, and kneeling at the head of the couch she clasped in her own the hand of the unconscious Doña Feliz.

"Grandmother, my dearest!" she murmered in a low voice, yet full of agony; "surely he will not tear me from thee! Oh, rather may I die with thee!"

"Oh, by the saints," cried the voice of Doña Rita in her ear, "for my child's sake, Chata, rise and fly to him!

It is thou only who canst save us. What did I tell thee in
El Toro? Doña Isabel has ruined us! but for her fool-
hardiness in sending aid to Gonzales all might have been
well; but that has brought the wrath of Ramirez upon
Rafael!" She turned toward her prostrate mother-in-law,
with something very like fury, clenching her hand and
crying, " Ah! ah! your clever deception will not seem so
happy a one when you wake to find it has killed your son!
That is what you deserve! You deceived even me. Do
you think had I known, I would for all the favor promised
me have played mother to the brat of Leon Vallé?"

The women ceased their cries to listen to this frantic
outburst, which though but Greek to them, had a sound
of mystery, which for the moment deadened their ears to
the increasing tumult without. " Leon Vallé!" said one
in an awe-struck voice, — " that was the Señora's wicked
brother."

" Leon Vallé!" echoed Chata, a new light dawning
upon her. " Maria Sanctissima, can it be?"

" What more natural?" cried Doña Rita, testily. " Was
he ever weary of extorting some proof of Doña Isabel's
devotion? But *Dios mio*, there was to be an end of her
infatuation! Had he not killed her child? What better
chance for vengeance was she to find than to conceal,
destroy, every trace of his, when with devilish mockery
he thrust it upon her? But then he might have known
it was like thrusting the lamb into the jaws of the wolf.
On my faith, girl, it maddens me to see you standing
there motionless, when it is as if the legions of Satanas
himself were loose. Go! go! I say, to soothe him. Entreat him to restrain his troops. The house will be sacked.
Who knows what horrors may follow!"

" I will not go to him," said Chata, slowly, a red spot
burning upon either cheek, her eyes dark with horror.
" If he is indeed the man you say, will he not defend the
home of his sister? If I am his child, will he not claim
me? If he does, I must submit; but go to him — No!
To save the hacienda — what has Doña Isabel done for
me? To save my life — no!"

XXXVIII.

In the few moments during which this scene had passed, the administrador at a sign from the General had been half forced — though he made no attempt at resistance — to the lower corridor. Thence he followed his captor to a dining-room, where a servant with terrified alacrity was already bringing in cups of chocolate for the breakfast, while a woman with a tray of small loaves of sweet-bread in her hands dropped it incontinently at sight of the dreaded Ramirez. He laughed, throwing himself into a chair, and looking around him with the furtive glance with which men involuntarily regard places or persons connected with memories distasteful or horrifying. There was an image of the Virgin of Guadalupe at one end of the apartment, with a small lamp burning before it. He crossed himself, and muttered an *Ave* as he looked at it; then pointed to a second chair and the cups of chocolate.

"It is early, Don Rafael," he said lightly, "but I have a soldier's appetite, which the fresh air has sharpened, — and you know the saying, that a stomach at rest makes an active brain; so accompany me, I entreat, in breaking the morning fast, and then let us to business." And with a show of indifference, which imposed far better upon his followers, who made an interested throng around the door, than upon Don Rafael, he tasted the chocolate he had drawn to his side.

The administrador remained standing, though the two soldiers, who had each held an arm, released their grasp and stepped back. Disconcerted by the thought that in his dishabille he could scarcely present a dignified figure, Don Rafael still maintained his composure sufficiently to refuse the proffered refreshment with the air of a man who questions the right of another to play the part of host, — assuming, in fact, toward the intruder rather the attitude of personal than of political hostility.

Ramirez divined this, and his face darkened. "You know me, Don Rafael," he said in a low tone, "and that I am a man to take no denials."

"Yes," answered the administrador, shortly, "I know you. The saints must have blinded me that I was so easily deceived upon your last visit; but you had always the power to mask your face at will."

"Bah! every man has a dozen countenances at his command, if he but know how to summon them," replied Ramirez, carelessly, "and a touch of art to fix their coloring, and twist the eyebrows or moustache. Why, even your mother was deceived! Where is she now? Ah! that woman was like Isabel herself; I swear she would have killed me, even when she seemed to love me most. It is the way of women, like serpents, to twine and sting at the same moment."

"My mother is dying," said Don Rafael, lifting his eyes for a moment upon the face of the image of Mary. "Yet living or dying, it is not for a man to hear another speak lightly of his mother. But this is nothing to the purpose."

"Nothing," replied the other, accepting the rebuke; "and I have no time to lose." He seemed to forget the chocolate, pushing the cup from him, and turning as if to rise from the chair. "Look you, Rafael, what money did Isabel leave with you? Not half her resources went in that mad freak of raising a troop for Gonzales."

Perhaps Don Rafael had expected the question, for his countenance remained imperturbable. "There are horses and cattle and corn and men, still," he answered. "The administrador of Tres Hermanos can do nothing to defend them; but the money, — by Heaven and the Holy Virgin, its hiding-place is known only to him, and he will die before you shall have another dollar to add to those which have cost so much blood and so many tears!"

Ramirez's eyes flashed; yet the look of astonishment which he threw upon the small, half-clothed man was as full of admiration as though he had been a king clad in royal robes. But even a king would not have thwarted Ramirez with impunity.

"You know me," he reiterated in the same intonation with which he had before spoken the words, allowing a

long, dark, intimidating gaze to rest upon the face of Don
Rafael.

" Yes, I know you," was the answer as before. " Yes,
I know you; and it is for that reason I have said that
never a dollar belonging to the woman you have so foully
wronged shall pass into your hands. Thank Heaven that
she is not here to be tempted! Thank God that while the
identity of Ramirez with the bane and curse of the house
of Garcia has been shaping itself in my mind, no hint of
the truth has been in hers! "

" I do not believe it! " cried Ramirez, violently. " She
hates me! for the sake of that puling boy and her dotard
husband she hates me still! ' The bane of the house of
Garcia,' said you. Why, what man among them has a
name beyond his own door-stone but me? And the
women! Ah, ah! What saint would have saved the
fame of the women of the house of Garcia had it not
been for me?"

Don Rafael glanced around him warningly, — the room
was full of strange faces, beginning to light with wondering curiosity at this strange conversation, so different in
substance from that usual between the guerilla and his
victims. This was no place in which to talk of women;
yet Don Rafael himself desired to avoid a private interview with this man, while Ramirez on his part assumed an
ostentatious air of having nothing to conceal, — nothing
that he might be ashamed his followers should learn. He
knew, in fact, that at that crisis, surrounded as he was by
the most unscrupulous and desperate characters, the prestige of his mad career might be advantageously heightened
rather than diminished, if he would keep his ascendency.
Don Rafael read his thought, and lest in very hardihood
his opponent should be led to accusations or revelations it
would be impossible for him to leave unanswered, he began
one of those long and desultory conversations that, while
apparently frank and unstudied, are triumphs in the art of
avoiding or concealing the real subject at issue.

Ramirez, well as he knew the tricks of the genuine
ranchero, whether of the higher or lower grade, was himself for a time deceived, — for, with far less than his
usual astuteness, he allowed himself to lapse into occasional denunciations, and to make demands of the admin-

24

istrador that increased the curiosity and interest of his listeners. These did not in any degree shake the constancy of Don Rafael, who, with the thought that the crisis of his life was approaching, crossed his arms upon his breast and fortified his courage with the remembrance of the vows by which he had pledged himself, and the less heroic satisfaction that he promised himself then in thwarting the plans of a man whose will had been as triumphant as it was insatiable.

Meanwhile, the tumult in the house increased. A wild rumor had spread that the General José Ramirez was by right the master of the place and all it contained. Some said he was the lover, others the brother, of Doña Isabel. At last, even the name by which he had been known there began to be shouted, though the sound of it was less popular than that by which he had won his way later to fame. Still, it gave a certain authority for license where there had been before a show of restraint; and a speedy assault was made upon the store-rooms and granaries, and even upon the inner chambers and courts, which contained nothing but furniture and ornaments, — useless to soldiers on the march, or even as booty for their wives and followers.

Ramirez listened to the tumult without attempting to interfere. Evidently his object was to break the resolution of Sanchez by an exhibition of the destructive and unscrupulous character of his followers. But Don Rafael never winced except once, when the cry of a woman pierced the apartment.

Ramirez heard it also. "Ah! it came from the kitchens, from some scullery-maid," he commented after a moment. "Now, Don Rafael, you see and hear for yourself what a crew of devils I have with me, — just the riff-raff of the mountains, whom that cursed Pedro failed to wile away from me. *Caramba!* never was a surprise greater. It would not have happened but that like a fool I lingered near El Toro waiting for a chance to pounce upon Gonzales. Never let a private vengeance sway the judgment," he added sententiously. "A thousand devils! It seems as if the hacienda were tumbling about our ears! - Yet at a word I can stop it. Where is the money?"

"If the din never ceases till I reveal that," answered

Don Rafael, doggedly, " you will never have your revenge on Gonzales; for what I have sworn I have sworn. The flocks and herds I can't defend; and what are a few hundred beeves or horses? But the money; no, by God! if Doña Isabel herself should command it, I would not suffer that another coin should touch your bloody hand!"

Ramirez started up with an oath. Involuntarily he glanced at his hand. It would not have surprised him to have seen it literally red, — and, strangely enough, the blood gushing from the fatal wound he had dealt the American, just from the arms of Herlinda, rather than that of his nephew or Don Gregorio, was that which presented itself to his mind. He walked the room in a new and undefinable excitement. The sight of Don Rafael, to whom the destruction of the property that was precious as his life seemed as nothing to the pleasure of baffling the man he abhorred of the money he believed absolutely necessary to his success in leading troops to encounter the well-reinforced and well-equipped Gonzales, revealed to him the hatred and horror in which he was held. Doubtless that of the servant was but a mere reflection of that of Doña Isabel.

Well, let them hate him with reason; let the wild mountaineers take their own sport unchecked. He heard one of the clerks, flying rather than running through the corridor, exclaim that Don Rafael must come, or there would be a famine in the place before the next harvest; that the great storehouses of maize had been forced open, and the contents scattered throughout the village for horses and men to tread under their feet; and that the very oxen and sheep were revelling in the abundance, liable to destroy themselves by very excess, even if the soldiers should fail to drive them before them.

Ramirez and the administrador glanced at each other. They had not spoken for many minutes, each feeling the other implacable, yet each perhaps believing that the wanton destruction would appeal to the other's weaker or better nature. Ramirez grew crimson, almost black, with inward rage, — rage as great with those who were wreaking destruction on his sister's house, as with this insignificant yet determined man who withstood it. Don Rafael was white as death, his lips blue, his eyes strained; again the cry of a woman sounded on the air! It came from above.

He started toward the door. A dozen hands seized him. Ramirez turned upon him with his drawn sword.

"Where is my daughter?" he demanded in a voice of fury. "I will find a way to force the gold from you, but first my daughter, — where is she?"

"Your daughter?" echoed Don Rafael in a tone of such absolute amazement that even Ramirez was for a second distracted from his rage.

"Yes, my daughter! She whom you have aided Isabel to hide from me all these years. Faith, it was a pretty trick, — an eye for an eye, with a vengeance. But after all it was a petty plot, and soon fathomed. You were less jealous of flesh and blood than of this cursed gold, and gave me the first inkling of her whereabouts yourself."

"I?" exclaimed the administrador; "I? What know I of a child of yours?"

"Ah, that is what you must satisfy me of. Where is she, — the Chata, whom you nodded and hinted about so mysteriously in your cups so many years ago?"

Don Rafael — if it were possible — turned a shade whiter than before; his form seemed to shrink, his heart sank with guilty shame and absolute terror. How well he remembered those few words, which, though so indirect and apparently unimportant, he had thought of with remorse a thousand times. And to what a terrible, though utterly unforeseen, conclusion they had led this man! He lifted his hands above his head.

"By the Blessed Mother, I swear," he said, "that I know not what you mean! I know nothing of a child of yours!"

Ramirez looked at him contemptuously. "You will tell me next that the child your wife denies is yours," he said.

In effect it had been upon the lips of Don Rafael to claim Chata as his daughter, as he had done a thousand times before. Was she not his before all the world? Had she not been from the very moment the eyes of his wife had rested upon her? But she had betrayed the confidence to which she had been but partially admitted, — Rita! He hesitated, and Ramirez seized the advantage.

"You dare not!" he exclaimed. "Your wife has confessed all: it will never do to trust a woman with a secret

in company of a man who cares to learn it, though very
perversity might keep her silent with a world of women."
The sight of the discomfiture of Don Rafael had restored
to Ramirez some portion of good nature. " The screeching has ceased," he added. " Yet I am a fond father. I
would assure myself of my child's safety. Where is the
girl? I must and will see her, if but to tell her why I
played her false last week. Where is my daughter?"

Don Rafael's face, which throughout this interview had
retained its pallor, crimsoned with excess of agitation.
The mystery of Chata's visit to the hacienda was revealed.
Had she met this man? Did she know — did she believe?
He remembered her changed aspect, her silence, her tears.
Ramirez stood watching him with impatience, yet triumph.
The crimson flush convicted the administrador. Don
Rafael strove in vain to steady the glance of his suffused
and burning eyes, to still the throbbing of his temples,
while he sought to command the most impressive and
convincing words in which to answer and forever silence
this mad assumption. But none presented themselves.
The group around listened breathlessly, more excited
than Ramirez himself. They looked silently from face
to face of the two men who were engaged in this singular
dispute. Inside the room one might have heard a feather
float through the air, so deep was the silence ; and at last,
in despair of finding imposing words, the administrador
uttered the simple denial, " Chata is not your child."

Most of the men drew back for the moment convinced.
Not so Ramirez. " It is false ! " he cried. " I have your
own maudlin hint, and your wife's positive confession, that
the girl is neither hers nor yours."

Don Rafael grew pale again. There was that in his
face which would have augured ill to Doña Rita had she
seen it ; but he said with an effort, " I will not give my
wife the lie. The child is neither mine nor hers ! "

" Then whose — whose but mine ? " demanded Ramirez
fiercely.

Don Rafael paused a moment as before. In an instant
he had recalled the circumstances that had attended the
adoption of the child. Rita had been young, placable,
easily pleased with a gift : the fewer confidants the better ; it was ever the duty of a Mexican wife to obey un-

questioningly, — she had been obedient then; it had not been necessary that she should know more than it had been wise to tell. Don Rafael drew a deep breath of relief. Ramirez and the group around him watched him narrowly.

" Declare then!" queried Ramirez at last, " whose daughter is she if not mine?"

" I will not say," answered Don Rafael; " but I do swear she is not yours. Stay," he added, struck with an idea. " What reason have you for thinking she is yours?"

" Reason!" echoed Ramirez scornfully; " because fifteen years ago, more or less, — perhaps you have reason here to remember well that year, — I sent my child here, to Doña Isabel: it was a whim of mine that she should have tender nurture and decent training. I was a fool to trust a woman's love. Of course Isabel remembered her own bantling, though I had even some foolish thought that the little one I sent might console her, — most women have hearts for baby wants and fancies that sicken men. Of course for her it was a chance for revenge too good to be lost. I have been in two minds ever since I knew how she scorned my trust whether to be angry or pleased with you for aiding her purpose. But let it pass; yield the child and the money quietly and " — he looked over his shoulder with an impatient frown — "that infernal tumult and destruction shall cease. If not — "

" I will yield neither the girl nor the money;" replied Don Rafael. " They are neither of them mine nor yours; but I have possession of both, and will keep them. — Surely Rita has both girls in the secret recess, as we have always planned in such a case as this," he thought, with a qualm at the remembrance of his wife's treason, as revealed by Ramirez. " Surely at such a time she will protect a young damsel, even though she be not her own child."

Ramirez looked at him with a lowering brow, repeating again, " If not mine, whose child is she? By Heaven, I know she is mine! There could not be on all the earth a creature in whom Doña Isabel or Feliz or yourself could have so deep an interest as to trouble yourself for life with his child. It is incredible, impossible. Unless she is — " He paused on the name, looked round him, clinched his hands, advanced to Don Rafael, and gazed searchingly into his face.

Don Rafael did not flinch. Ramirez burst into a laugh. "I would have killed you had you dared even to have looked askance," he said. "*Caramba!* the women of the Garcias may be fools or devils,— they have shown the spirit of both; but if a man should ever kill another because of one of them, it would be for his daring, not in revenge of his triumph."

Did these words indicate a tardy repentance, a conviction that Herlinda had been indiscreet but innocent? Don Rafael had no time to discuss the question with himself; but he had such new insight into the mind of Ramirez that he was warned from giving any fresh cause of offence. Had he had no previous reasons, it would have been a sufficient one for him to keep inviolate the secret which he had sworn to preserve to his life's end. In his present humor, the man with whom he had to deal would in his baffled and vengeful rage have spared neither the name nor fame of even his own mother, had occasion offered to tempt him to blacken it. Don Rafael believed the women of his household as well as the money safe in the hiding places he had constructed for them, — the first known to Doña Feliz and Doña Rita, the second to himself alone. To any fate that might befall himself he looked with stoical courage if not indifference. Leaning against the wall, he crossed his arms defiantly and awaited events.

XXXIX.

At high noon a terrible and heartrending wail of anguish sounded through the house, penetrating with dismal insistence through the clamor of the soldiery and the thousand indescribable noises of the animals, which had been hastily collected, and which added the element of mere brute bewilderment to the scarcely more reasonably restrained terror of the people.

Ramirez had recognized the obstinate defiance of the administrador. More than once before he had dealt with others as tenacious of the interests of those they served. He had no time to lose in vain persuasions, and had himself conducted the search throughout the vast building, of which he believed he knew every nook and corner. But he had to his amazement and chagrin found neither treasure nor any member of the family of the administrador save the apparently dying Doña Feliz. After a fruitless endeavor to recall her to consciousness, he left her with a curse, and returning to her son, assaulted him with menaces, alternated with fair promises, — the one as little regarded as the other.

Upon one subject only would Don Rafael permit himself to speak; and to that Ramirez, in his rage, refused to listen. The suggestion that his daughter, if indeed he had a reason to seek one there, might prove to be Chinita, the foster-daughter of Pedro Gomez, he received with utter contempt. He remembered her well, he said; an imp as black as Pedro himself, — black as he must be now, scorching in Hades. That little demon was none of his, while Chata had the very face of his mother, — the face of an angel. Ah! ah! that was indeed a daring jest, that Isabel should strive to palm off upon him the brat of her doorkeeper! Once long before, like the witch she was, the girl had stopped him and thrust into his hand an amulet, — he drew it from his pocket, and cast it from him. By

the way, now Pedro was dead, if Rafael still believed her
worth a thought, he had better see in such a day as this
that she had some other protector. She must be nearly
a woman now!

Ramirez fell into greater rage when he learned that Doña
Isabel had taken charge of this despised waif. He swore
that it was in mockery of himself; and Don Rafael soon
perceiving that every word he uttered was construed as an
attempt to deceive, and fearing that at some time it might
bring evil upon the girl to whom, whether she were the
daughter of Ramirez or no, he certainly desired no harm,
the administrador became utterly silent, in his heart commending the prudence of Rita in following this time with
exactness his instructions, and condoning the treason of
which by the assurances of Ramirez he had been forced
to believe her guilty.

In truth, although at first the alarmed and not too scrupulous woman had urged Chata to secure the safety of herself and her child by claiming the protection of Ramirez, as
time passed and he made no movement toward such recognition she began to distrust the effect it might produce upon
the renowned guerilla. He and his soldiers were there for
plunder and rapine, not paternal sentiment. As the cries
of the women-servants and villagers reached her, the resolution to seek safety in concealment seized her. Though
still far from wishing to conceal Chata from Ramirez, to
whom the accidental sight of her might recall some sense
of mercy or tenderness, she feared both him and her husband too greatly to dare leave her to the chance of insult
from the licentious soldiery. But Chata absolutely refused
to leave Doña Feliz, from whose side even the servants
had fled; and it was her scream that had penetrated to
the rooms below, when, by the friendly force of Don
Alonzo, she was immured with Doña Rita and Rosario
in the secret recess, which Don Rafael had constructed
with a vague apprehension of such an emergency.

It chanced that this recess, which was in the immensely
thick outer wall of the great house, was dimly lighted and
ventilated by a loop-hole so small as to be barely visible
from without, but which opened funnel-like toward the inside of the apartment. Through this loop-hole these three
women, whose voices were quite inaudible to those either

within or without the building, heard confusedly the village cries, and caught uncertain glimpses of the space outside the hacienda gates. After what seemed hours of incarceration, during which Rosario had fretted and slept, and Doña Rita had alternately chided and lamented, while Chata entreated to be released that she might return to the side of Doña Feliz, they saw with anxious surprise a crowd gathering upon the sandy slope; not of the soldiery alone, but the people of the hacienda, — clerks, workmen, women who were wringing their hands and uttering sharp cries of terror and entreaty, which ended in that deep wail, which seemed to signify some agonizing catastrophe.

Doña Rita was the first to divine what was happening. "Maria Purissima!" she cried. "Is it possible Rafael is as mad as the administrador of Los Chalcos, — that he has refused some demand? Does he not remember how Ramirez caused that poor foolish one to be hanged without mercy! O my husband, my husband! Oh! has he no thought for me, for his child, that he will sacrifice his life for Doña Isabel? How will she thank him? Whoever thinks twice of the foolhardy obstinacy of an administrador?"

Chata sprang to her feet. "Give me the key!" she cried. "Let me go! Now if Ramirez is my father, he shall prove it! Would he deny his daughter the life of her foster-father? Give me the key!"

"No, no!" screamed Doña Rita, "the place is full of ruffians. Ramirez himself is a tiger! I—" but Chata had wrenched the key from her numbed and shaking hands, and thrusting it in the lock had turned the grating wards.

When she rushed into the corridors they were empty, — there was a sight to behold elsewhere. On she flew, not noticing that Doña Rita and Rosario followed, and that their shrieks rose with hers, as in a minute or less they reached the outer court, and strove to penetrate the throng that filled it and extended to the village beyond.

Within the high arch of the doorway, clear against the deep blue of the mid-day sky, swayed the figure of a man, — of Rafael Sanchez. Below, sword in hand, stood Ramirez and two panting laborers who that instant had

accomplished his decree. Around them were gathered
scores of armed men, evil-eyed, with the ferocity of
brutes in their faces; and Ramirez stood pre-eminent,
a very demon.

The crowd parted like water before the shrieks of the
three women. In a moment Chata reached the side of
Ramirez, and grasped his sword. "Spare him! spare
him!" she demanded rather than entreated. "If I am
your daughter, cut the rope! Spare him, and do as you
like with me; else I swear I will die with him rather
than be known as your child!"

The women were on their knees, — not Doña Rita and
Rosario alone, but all those of the village. Sobs and entreaties filled the air. Ramirez threw a glance of triumphant admiration upon Chata, and put one arm around
her, while he raised the other, pointing with a nod to
the swaying figure.

A man sprang to cut the rope, and the administrador fell
into the dozen arms stretched out to receive him. Chata
saw with infinite joy that he was not dead. He threw up
his arms, gasped, opened wide-staring eyes. A moment
later, she was hurried away. Half-fainting though she
was, she was glad to escape that embrace from which
she dared not shrink.

"Ah, Rafael, you are conquered, — I have the girl!
And now where is the gold?" she heard Ramirez exclaim, and saw the gesture of defiance with which the
scarce conscious victim answered this demand.

An hour later Chata was riding by the side of the baffled Ramirez. She knew not whether her foster-father was
living or dead, and dared not ask; but stifling her sobs,
looked back through a mist of tears upon the desolated
hacienda. It was incredible even to her horrified and
longing gaze, the terrible devastation that had been
worked in a few short hours. Seemingly to complete
its ruin, a thunder-cloud, which had been lurking over
the valley, discharged its contents over the devoted
house. Upon the hills the sun shone; Chata was safe
from the fury of the storm. And yet she felt as though
the very wrath of heaven had burst over her.

"*Caramba*, Chatita! thou wilt make a soldier's daughter
yet!" Ramirez was exclaiming. "By my faith, I am proud

of thee!" In spite of the unattained gold, he pressed on
in rare good humor. His fury, like the storm, was quickly
expended. "And by our Lady of Glory I am glad that
you came in time to save that obstinate fool, Rafael.
He has, after all is said, served me a good turn in aiding
Isabel to put what she meant for a shabby trick upon me.
Caramba! It was clever of her. I should never have discovered it but for a slip of the tongue on Rafael's part
which no one else would have noticed, and but for thy
wonderful likeness to my mother, — the angels give her
good rest!"

Chata could not be grateful for this favor of nature; it
seemed to her indeed the bitterest spite that could have
been wreaked upon her. She turned her eyes upon the
face of Ramirez with a questioning glance, which startled
him: those gray eyes, limpid and clear as they were, were
far different from the large, languorous, black ones of his
mother, — yet not unfamiliar. Where had he seen such
before? The inquiry was not worth a special effort of
memory. Enough that the eyes were beautiful. The very
softness and appeal in their expression held a peculiar
charm for this fierce, hard spirit. He had begun a denunciation of the revenge practised against him by his sister,
but he abruptly paused. What if this young creature
knew nothing of those wild deeds of bygone years? Why
shock her tender and immature mind by the recital of such
episodes as she would view but at their darkest? For the
first time in his life he felt the impossibility of impressing
his hearer with the daring rather than the villany of his
deeds, and rode beside her in silence, furtively watching
her face, which with wonderful control, indicating a latent
strength of character, she suffered to reveal none of the
horror or fear with which he inspired her, but only the
natural grief with which she had been separated from the
home of her childhood.

Indeed, the thought of Doña Feliz was the dominant one
in Chata's mind, and prevented any serious grief or alarm
as to her own situation. The question of her own safety or
future position troubled her little. It was the fact of her
separation from the beloved and stricken friend, who was
so dependent upon her care, and her absolute horror of
the murderer of the American, — for as such Ramirez

ever figured in her thoughts, — which rendered it so difficult a task for her to retain her self-possession and answer
with calmness the few questions or remarks that were from
time to time addressed to her.

Chata soon perceived that as the day wore on, and she
began to exhibit signs of fatigue from the hurried march
and the heat, her presence caused far more anxiety than
triumph to her captor. "The old folly!" he muttered
from time to time, — "to act without counting the cost.
I doubt whether there is a decent woman among this
drove of camp-followers. If I had but thought to bring
one from the hacienda! In fact, it was a fool's act to bring
the child at all, with such work before me as I have!"

Chata caught these broken sentences with a wild hope
that he might decree her return to Tres Hermanos. Willingly would she have risked going alone on foot if necessary. But the sun set, the shades of evening closed in,
and the hurried march was still pursued, until, when she
was ready to faint with fatigue, the General ordered a
halt, and lifting her from the saddle, placed her upon a
pile of blankets; while a half-dozen men set to work
with practised hands to build a little hut or tent of mesquite and manzanita boughs to shelter her from the
night air.

As the weary girl sat near the tent fire, endeavoring to
eat the food of which she stood in much need, but for which
she could not force an appetite, she found herself the centre
of a wild horde of perhaps nearly five hundred persons, of
whom a fifth were women and children, who were busy at
the fires preparing the evening meal while the men were
staking horses, or patrolling the circle of the camp, keeping within bounds the hard-driven and panting cattle and
sheep, whose distressing lowing and bleating at intervals
filled the air. Apparently there was an entire lack of discipline, the unreasoning enthusiasm of the moment and the
personal magnetism of the renowned leader serving to
hold the unruly elements subservient to the necessities
of the occasion, and obedient to his slightest mandate.
The majority of the troops were of the most wild and
even savage appearance; for, as their leader had said, they
were the riff-raff, the scourings of the mountain villages and remote farms. Chata was not unaccustomed to

the sight of such individuals, but in mass the impression they made upon her was of concentrated evil. The trace of gentler feeling that each face or person might have revealed on scrutiny was lost in the prevailing ferocity of expression and accoutrement. The clash of arms, the jingle of spurs, the hoarse voices made her shudder no less than the sullen faces, the gleaming eyes, and the sinewy and powerful frames.

Strangely enough, as her eyes followed Ramirez, a sense of his complete harmony with his surroundings seemed in the girl's mind to condone the wild deeds of which he had figured as the hero. She realized for the first time the fascination that unlimited power over such elements must exercise over a mind given to daring, and uncontrolled by any moral principle. She thought of Chinita, and how her adventurous spirit would have exulted in such an adventure as this. As she gazed into the fire the very face of that fearless, enigmatic young nature seemed to rise before her, beautiful, passionate, yet with that capacity of endurance, which in a man might become cruelty, that capricious changeableness, which one moment dissolved in tears, and the next shone in a smile. So real was the vision that Chata started, and found herself gazing affrightedly into the face of Ramirez, who was regarding her with the expression of mingled affection, triumph, and vexation which had not left his countenance since he had set her upon Doña Rita's favorite horse at the door of the hacienda.

"I have a notable project in my mind for you," he said abruptly. "You know that I am the Governor of Guanapila."

"Yes," she said timidly; "but I thought—" she hesitated, fearing to offend.

"Ah, you thought I was beaten and barred out. They will find I am neither one nor the other. The gate is shut but not bolted, and it will be hard if I find not a way to creep in. It is impossible for me to keep you with me on the march. You must be with some woman."

"Oh, I would rather be with you. Indeed I will give no trouble! I will be brave!" she exclaimed, instinctively shrinking from the thought of contact with such women as she saw around her.

He smiled with gratification, his egotistic nature flattered by the thought that he was gaining her confidence; but his face darkened as she added with hesitation, " I had hoped — I thought perhaps you were taking me to my mother."

" It is not of your mother I was thinking," he said ambiguously, "when I spoke of Guanapila, but of my niece Carmen de Velasquez. She knows that the General Ramirez once sent an escort with her mother to Tres Hermanos, and levied upon her husband for a loan of ten thousand dollars when he might have had five times as much, — for the old fellow she has married is rich, and does honor to the financial acumen of the fair Carmen, and we will see whether she has a just appreciation of the favors I am supposed to have rendered her. There, go to your tent and sleep in peace; in three days you shall be safe within the house of Velasquez in Guanapila."

It cannot be said that Chata slept in peace; yet the prospect was reassuring, and enabled her to bear with resignation the fatigues and excitements of the following days, and the loneliness and terrors of the nights. The General slept before the opening of her tent. Upon the fourth night he awoke her, and handed her a torn and shabby reboso and a skirt of coarse red cloth, with instructions to put them on. She did so with some repugnance, though the clothing she left was not better; and at a call stepped out into the starlight. The young Captain Alva preceded her in silence outside the limits of the camp, where two horses were in waiting, held by a man whom at the first startled glance she failed to recognize. It would have horrified her beyond control had she known that in his size and air and dress he was the image of the ranchero who had entered Tres Hermanos on the night of the murder, years before. She uttered a cry of relief as Ramirez greeted her.

" Ah, is it not a perfect disguise?" he said. " Why, I might go into El Toro itself with impunity ! Mount, child, and keep close at my side ! "

In a minute or less, with the assistance of Alva, Chata was ready for the start, — her courage rising with the sense of mystery and daring under which Ramirez seemed to glow and expand. He paused to give his last commands to Alva, of which she heard only the concluding words: "Reyes should be here by daylight. Keep him at all hazards, for he must sound Ruiz before another day passes. *Caramba!* I cannot believe that fellow has failed me; but whether or no, the end will be the same, —except that I swear if Ruiz prove false, were he twice my godson he shall not escape my vengeance."

The General pulled his hat over his eyes, waved his hand, struck the spurs into his horse, and led the way at a swift canter. Chata until within the last few days had never ridden on horseback; but she was singularly free from fear or awkwardness, and with ease, though in silence, kept at his side.

"Chata," Ramirez once said abruptly, turning his dark and piercing eyes upon her, "I am risking much for your sake. Remember that you are my daughter. Be faithful to me, obey my bidding, and I will cherish you as the apple of my eye. It may depend upon you whether the troops of Doña Isabel follow my lead or that of Gonzales. You will know my meaning later; but I swear to you, as I have done by Ruiz, my vengeance shall rest upon whomsoever balks me, —yes, if it is even you, the new-found daughter whom I love."

Chata trembled. Though his words were an enigma, they indicated that her *rôle* was not to be an utterly passive one. Her companion awaited no answer, and Chata did not attempt to make one. They rode on at ever increasing speed as the night advanced. Just at daybreak they reached a hut, which was placed at the mouth of a cañon. There they left their horses, and an old woman appeared with a crate of turkeys in each hand, one of which she gave to the disguised chieftain, the other to the wondering Chata.

An hour later they were in the streets of Guanapila, and before they had broken their fast Chata sat overcome with fatigue and dismay upon the stone stairs that led to the corridor of a palatial residence. The ranchero, as the servants supposed him, had gone to speak with the lady of the mansion. It was a long time before he re-appeared; and when he did, a beautiful woman preceded him. She was very pale, and there was in her eyes an incredulous and startled expression, which changed to pity as her gaze fell upon Chata, — who, looking up, thought of the pale and lovely face she had seen but once, and knew she must be in the presence of Carmen, the sister of the nun of El Toro.

Ramirez whispered a word in the ear of the bewildered girl, it might be of warning or of farewell; but her senses failed her, — she neither saw nor heard more.

"Go, go!" cried the mistress of the house. "For God's sake go, before there is any one to wonder. Whether your tale be true or false, she has the face of a Garcia, and a loveliness and sweetness of her own. I will guard her as though she were my child. Go, go! and the saints grant you a safe passage. I will not betray your confidence. Ah, she has fainted! I will manage that; it shall be my pretext for charity."

Ramirez kissed the hand of the unconscious Chata, and turned away. For once he had executed an act of extreme self-denial, yet amid it all his crafty mind foresaw how he might use it to his advantage.

The exit from the city was readily effected, but Ramirez did not proceed many miles unrecognized after mounting his horse at the hut where he had left it. The man who spoke his name unhesitatingly, though in a cautious voice, was Reyes. He gave the General unwelcome tidings. Gonzales had joined forces with those of Tres Hermanos. He had risked the attack and occupation of El Toro, and it was conjectured would attempt the march to the Capital itself, round which the audacious Juarez was from his stronghold in Vera Cruz directing the concentration of the Liberal forces.

Ramirez ground his teeth in rage. "I have been delayed and hampered by that girl," he cried. "Could I but have gone straight to Ruiz, he would not have dared defy me. As it is — "

"As it is," interrupted Reyes, "all is not yet lost. I have still to see Ruiz, — he is not my son if it is impossible to convince him upon which hot plate the cake is best toasted."

The conference of the two men lasted but a few moments. They had been so accustomed in their long intercourse to treat of subjects of which one was as well informed as the other, and upon the course to be taken

25

at the present time they were so well agreed, that they parted with no attempt at explanation, but simply after a few words of instruction had been given by Ramirez to the other.

"Tell him," the chief said finally, "I am ready to fulfil my word; and if Ruiz be anxious to see her, let him risk as much for love as I have done. She is at the house of Doña Carmen Velasquez in Guanapila; and tell him as surely as he is my godson and your son he shall be shot as a traitor if he fails me in this affair. Good-by for a time; good news or bad news, my blood is up for a desperate venture now. It cannot be that after all these years luck is turning against me at last."

"It did that years ago when you stabbed the American," thought Reyes as they parted; "it was that that weighted the scale. That accursed foreigner who is here to avenge him has upset all our plans for misleading Gonzales. With both together Ramirez has fearful odds against him, which even with the help of Ruiz and his men he may find it hard to combat. But how in heaven's name has the General his daughter with him? *Caramba!* I have often wondered how he would relish that drunken freak of mine! Faith, I did not care to try his temper to-night by many questions. Well, who would have thought he would have kept in the same mind for so many years! To think of his striving to give her the family training at this late date! Ah, ah, ah! it is more likely to mar than to make her. If Fernando is of my mind he will wait in such a matter for no pruning and training, but pluck the flower while it is within his reach, thorns and all."

With which poetic simile, Tio Reyes rode on well pleased on his errand to the young Ruiz, while Ramirez, proceeding rapidly in the opposite direction, regained within the hour his enthusiastic but disorderly horde.

Vain would be the attempt to describe the consternation of Doña Isabel when she awoke at early dawn, and felt about her that peculiar stillness — a stillness that seems absolutely tangible — which indicates the abstraction of the element of humanity from the associations about us, and is especially impressive when that loss is utterly unexpected.

It was not yet daylight, and it was by this peculiar stillness, and not by sight, that Doña Isabel learned with a deadly feeling of dismay at her heart, that she was alone. For a moment she lay silent, then raising herself on her elbow sought to peer through the gloom, while with faltering voice she uttered the name " Chinita."

There was no answer. She would have been inexpressibly surprised had there been ; and yet refusing to be convinced, she arose from her bed and made her way to that of Chinita. Had the girl been there, in the infinite relief and excitement of the moment the lady must have clasped her in her arms with kisses and tears ; as it was, after passing her hands wildly over the empty couch, she sank upon it with a deep and bitter moan, feeling anew, and with the intensified agony of remembrance, the shock with which she had heard the cry of Herlinda, — " My husband ! My husband ! " What but a like betrayal could in that place and time have drawn a young girl from her chamber? Alas ! alas !

The thoughts of Doña Isabel flew to Ruiz ; a thousand trifles, unheeded before, crowded her remembrance as confirmation of some secret understanding between him and Chinita. If she had noticed them at all it was to think with a smile that they had reference to Rosario. How had she been so blind ! She sprang to her feet and hastily dressed herself with some undefined intention of seeking him in his quarters, and demanding an explanation of him if he were to be found, or of confirming her worst fears if he had fled. All her old distrust of him, which he had so skilfully lulled, returned with overwhelming force, and in her unfounded suspicion she included the more just one of treason to her purposes to the cause of liberty and to Gonzales, and with irresistible certainty became convinced that the delays and detours which Ruiz had made had been expedients of traitorous policy. In the few moments needed for the completion of her toilet, a terrible fear took possession of her. For the first time that night she had been separated from the main body of the troops, — what if she were abandoned! Nothing seemed more likely. Only the great self-possession that she habitually practised prevented her from rushing out — yes, even into the streets of the village — to satisfy herself that the rude encampment remained unbroken.

Yet with all this raging excitement of grief and doubt within her, she presently stepped out upon the corridor with that stately calmness which she ever wore before the world, were it represented by but the meanest peasant. Day had scarcely broken, yet there was a sound of movement unusual in so small a place. To the excited mind of Doña Isabel it appeared that like herself the people all must be searching wildly for the girl who had so strangely escaped her. She went to the inn door and looked out. The camp-women were wandering through the streets already, chaffering and bargaining with the vendors of milk and bread and vegetables. In the distance she saw the soldiers preparing for the march. Three or four officers were lounging down the narrow street. To her infinite surprise and relief she saw among them Ruiz. He hastened his steps and joined her with an air of consternation, which even in her excitement she noticed had in it a subdued suggestion of apprehension as of one detected in some doubtful act.

In a few words Doña Isabel apprised him of the disappearance of Chinita. It was impossible that it could be concealed; it was absolutely necessary that search should be made. Ruiz listened with an emotion greater even than hers. "Good heavens. Señora!" he cried, "we are undone. Ramirez must be at hand. In some way she has learned his whereabouts; she has fled to him!"

Doña Isabel thought Ruiz had suddenly gone mad. "Fled to Ramirez!" she cried. "Impossible! What can she know of the man? What object can she have in seeking him?"

Instinctively the lady had led the way back to the room she had left. Ruiz followed her, in the utter demoralization of his mind at the unexpected tidings, pouring out incoherent explanations of the designs that Chinita had cherished, and unconsciously revealing much of the duplicity of the part he had himself acted. With an acuteness of mind perhaps intensified by the keen emotion with which she listened to the unexpected accusations against the young girl, Doña Isabel conjectured at once that the speaker had played a double part; and it was a not improbable solution of the mystery of Chinita's disappearance, that in discovering this the young girl had resolved to precipitate a crisis in the fate of the man who exercised so unaccountable a fascination over her.

Yet with whom had she fled? Had Ramirez himself stolen into the inn and borne her away? The face of Ruiz blanched at this suggestion. Had the girl learned what was indeed a fact, that upon that very day the troops of Doña Isabel Garcia were by their officers to protest against a further attempt to reach Gonzales, and declaring Ruiz their chosen and permanent leader were at once to take up the march to join the forces of General Ortega, a newly arisen and popular Liberal chieftain who was a personal and implacable enemy of Ramirez, — thus leaving El Toro to its fate? Had Chinita indeed gone with such news to Ramirez? Ruiz felt that his doom was sealed, for he rightly conjectured that the excitement of Chinita's disappearance had already dampened the ardor in his behalf which he had found it a slow and almost impossible task to awaken among the troops. Indeed, that it had been roused at all was owing to the discontent which had arisen through the cleverly concealed tactics he had used in contriving so long and monotonous a march to the aid of a man but little known or admired, and from the general belief in the love of the beautiful *protégée* of Doña Isabel for the young aspirant for fame. In her hand the favor of Doña Isabel was supposed to lie. Eager for action, eager for booty, brought to a point where they were almost within sound of the bugles of General Ortega, who was making his hurried and triumphant march to the capital, it had been decided that upon that very morning a *pronunciamento* should be made, which, while involving no change of politics, should compel the consent of Doña Isabel to the apparently spontaneous outburst of patriotism upon the part of her troops, and confirm Ruiz in the command that she had temporarily confided to him.

Ruiz had so cunningly planned every detail that he doubted not that not only Doña Isabel, but Chinita as well, would be convinced of his entire ignorance of the *coup*, and that the girl's ambition, and perhaps a somewhat malicious satisfaction in the reversal of the plans of Doña Isabel, would lead her to an acceptance of the apparently unavoidable forfeiture of her own desires.

To this end the ambitious young officer had been patiently working since the day he had found himself at the head of the troops of Tres Hermanos. He had been amazed at his own success. Everything had seemed to contribute to it.' Not even the triumph of seeing himself actually attracting the good-will, if not the love, of Chinita had been denied him; and now at the moment least expected, at the most critical juncture, she had failed him. It was impossible for him to assume his usual self-sufficient air as he re-issued from the apartment of Doña Isabel, — an air that imposed on the majority of observers as that of a man conscious of power, rather than as a disguise of incompetency. His crest-fallen bearing as he gave the necessary orders for scouts to be sent out in search of those who in the night must have left the ill-guarded town was evident to the most careless eye, and did much to increase the feeling of distrust and coldness that was already beginning to supplant the ill-considered ardor of a few hours before.

The scouts had been despatched; and the main body of the troops waited for marching orders, which were long delayed. Ruiz, closeted with the men who had been most amenable to his reasoning, urged openly the arguments that he had but covertly suggested before. That exhausted apathy which following an exploded project is far more hopeless than that which, merely unignited,

precedes its agitation, resisted all his efforts at revival.
The officers, like the soldiers, listlessly waited to hear
what would happen next, absolutely indifferent to Ruiz,
and concerned for the moment in a mere matter of gossip,
— the escapade of a young girl.

Toward noon some of the messengers returned. Most
of them had nothing to report, but the vaquero Gabriel,
the husband of Juana, as soon as he could escape the
questioning of Ruiz, disappeared. An hour later he
entered the apartment of Doña Isabel.

"What news, Gabriel, what news?" the lady cried
excitedly. "Did you come upon any trace of — of the
child; of those who have stolen her away?"

The vaquero shook his head, and Doña Isabel groaned.
Those few hours had wrought a terrible change in her
appearance. She was not young and able to meet shocks
of disaster as she had been when they had shaken her
in by-gone years.

"I found no trace of them, my Señora," said the man,
slowly. "Perhaps my eyes are not as keen as they were,
and they say when one thinks much one sees little. Since
I am married I find one must think. A woman gives one
abundance for thought. She grinds care for a man more
surely than corn for his bread."

Doña Isabel looked up at him quickly. She knew that
this oracular sentence had some bearing on the subject
that absorbed her thoughts. "Speak," she said. "What
has your wife to do with this?"

"She was the playmate of the young Señorita," he
suggested.

"True, but what of that?"

"She would be likely to be in her confidence, — at least
where there was no other to trust."

Doña Isabel started, looking at him with fixed attention.

"The thought came to me as I rode out of the town,
— it came back to me again and again. After hours of
vain search I suffered myself to be convinced. I came
back and taxed Juana with knowing with whom, and when
and where, her friend had gone."

"Well?" ejaculated Doña Isabel, in extreme agitation.

"She denied it. By all the saints she denied it; but I

had a saint she had forgotten to commend herself to." He smiled significantly.

Doña Isabel understood the arguments used by rancheros to refractory wives too well to doubt what his grim jest meant. At another time she would have indignantly dismissed from her presence the man who admitted laying a hand in castigation upon his wife ; now she merely by an imperative gesture urged him to finish what he had to communicate.

"It was as I thought," he said coolly. "Two men talked with her last night. The one was Juana's brother, Pepé ; the other was the Señor Americano your grace knows of."

Doña Isabel sank back in her chair as if struck by a sharp weapon. "The American! the American!" she repeated again and again. She felt as though a hand had been thrust from the grave to torture her. The superstitious dread which had been planted in her breast by the first glimpse of the face of Ashley Ward, and which had perhaps led her irresistibly to a course that the resolution of years would under ordinary circumstances have rendered impossible to a nature as tenacious as was her own, became a horrible certainty. Evil fate in the guise of the American appeared to pursue her. Whatever the purpose with which he had lured Chinita from her side, it could but be productive of woe for her. Would the tale of her daughter's shame and her own apparent heartlessness be told throughout the land? Had this pale and seemingly spiritless young man resolved on such a vengeance of his cousin's fancied wrongs? Or — worse still — was this but a repetition of the old, old tale of passion and folly? Doña Isabel covered her face with her hand and groaned again.

Gabriel had called his wife to the room, and she came with eyes red with weeping, and told the tale that seemed to her best. Fearful of bringing the vengeance of the Señora upon Pepé, should she avow that he had left the inn alone with Chinita, she declared he had but accompanied the American, · whom she boldly affirmed had set out for the coast, with the young girl, intending to set sail for the wild country whence he had come.

Doña Isabel and Gabriel both knew too well the inventive genius of their countrywomen literally to believe all she said; yet as hour after hour passed by and no news of the fugitives was heard, and no trace of them in spite of the most untiring search was found, they were at length led to conclude — the one with despair — that Juana's words were true, and that the brief connection of the beautiful foster-child of Pedro Gomez with the lady of Tres Hermanos was ended forever.

XLI.

NEVER perhaps did so marked a change occur in the discipline and carriage of any body of troops, from a cause apparently so slight, as that which followed the flight of Chinita. Of the visit of the American nothing was publicly known, but the wildest rumors of her probable action ran like wildfire through the ranks, the name of Ramirez coupled with her own being on every tongue. So potent was the fame of the guerilla chieftain and the fascination of Chinita, that a word from her at that excited moment would have acted like fire on straw, and set a blaze to the smouldering insubordination and disappointed energies of the baffled and impatient recruits, who had entered upon the service from love of adventure and booty rather than with any fixed convictions or an intelligent conception of the interests at stake.

Doña Isabel wore before the world the same impassive face as ever, but at night the demon powers of remorse and intolerable anxiety wrought cruel havoc with its beauty. It was impossible too for her to conceal utterly the suspicion and distrust with which Ruiz inspired her; and the influence which through Chinita mainly he had for a brief period acquired, both over Doña Isabel and the troops, and which at best had been looked upon as a privilege he should yield later with his authority to Gonzales, began to wane rapidly. Dissatisfaction and mutinous threatenings were manifested on every hand, and the position of Ruiz but for the presence of Doña Isabel would have been absolutely untenable; and a crisis was evidently imminent, when the long desired leader suddenly appeared to relieve the tension of the situation, and to awaken a frenzy of enthusiasm for the cause, which had been at the point of abandonment.

It was with intense relief that Ruiz himself greeted the appearance of Gonzales, unexpected though it was, and incomprehensible the means by which he had obtained information that had led him so completely to alter his plans. That the American was concerned in the matter Ruiz did not doubt, though he could imagine no clew to his motives, the conviction being still in the mind of the baffled officer of Chinita's indifference to Ashley, and of her flight to Ramirez.

It was with amazement and alarm that Gonzales witnessed the ravages of time and care upon the once beautiful and stately Doña Isabel. The very excess of joy with which she welcomed him seemed weak and pitiful. He had been detained long upon the way from El Toro by a series of petty annoyances, such as the bad state of the roads and a succession of trifling skirmishes with the enemy, resulting in burdening the march with the care of the wounded; and thus the loss of Chinita had become to Doña Isabel by the time of his arrival an assured fact. With tears of anguish she told him of the ingratitude of the child she loved, though she carefully concealed the fact that she supposed her to be other than one of the class of people from whom she had taken her; and with this explanation only Gonzales could not enter fully into her grief, or accept the fact that the loss of her *protégée* was indeed the entire cause of her anguish. Had she not mourned for years as he had the living entombment of her daughter Herlinda? Had not the sight of him revived in her mind the keenness of her woe?

Doña Isabel was ill both in body and in mind; worn out with anxiety and the fatigues of travel, the reaction occasioned by the appearance of Gonzales was doubtless too great for her enfeebled powers. To his extreme embarrassment and anxiety he found himself charged with the unexpected responsibility of the care of a lady of much social consequence, and one personally extremely dear to him, who was stricken with an illness that demanded the most efficient attendance and complete isolation from disturbing influences. Added to the present necessity of gaining the confidence of the disorganized troops, and of continuing the march with the most unrelaxing vigilance, the situation thus became most onerous to the young commander, — not the less so because of the presence of a man he had thwarted and displaced, and whom it was necessary to keep in view and perhaps conciliate.

Upon the next night after the arrival of Gonzales, when Ruiz with seeming cordiality though with relief and rage contending in his mind had yielded his command, he strode to the outskirts of the camp, and smoking or rather forgetting to smoke a cigarette, mentally reviewed with bitter disappointment the perplexing and conflicting events that had led to so utter an overthrowal of his carefully concocted schemes. With the rapidity and excitement of his thoughts, his pace increased as though he was striving to tread down his mortification while he was preparing therefor a speedy and certain revenge.

The thought of this was chiefly directed toward Chinita. But for her flight Ruiz doubted not his position would have been so firmly assured that he would have been enabled to carry out his schemes. Thus he had hoped to find himself at the head of a force which in the event of final victory would have recommended him to the highest honors in the gift of Juarez, or at any rate assured him against the vengeance of Ramirez. To treachery time had added actual hatred of the man who had befriended him, and whose evil deeds, while he professed to abhor them, he would have rejoiced to have courage and address to imitate, and of whom he still held a superstitious dread, which had once been absolute awe.

It maddened the recreant follower of Ramirez to think of Chinita in the power of such a man. That day the last wild escapade of the lawless adventurer, the torture of Pedro, had in some way reached the ears of Ruiz and destroyed a lingering hope he had cherished that the girl, proud and hard though he believed her, had in some impulse of affection gone to her foster-father, — a thought that he had not even hinted to Doña Isabel, for with petty spite he refrained from uttering that which he imagined might give relief to her long agony. He imagined how Chinita, who doubtless had seen through his double dealing, would make it contemptible by her scorn, and ridiculous with her irony; and how Ramirez would, after listening to her account of him rise his sworn enemy: Ruiz had witnessed such scenes. No; return to Ramirez was impossible. Besides, that chieftain's ultimate defeat was certain: the Liberal cause was strengthening every hour. Ramirez must have lost his former keenness to

follow thus a losing venture. Ruiz began to console himself by thoughts of how, though only in a subordinate part,
he should assist in the discomfiture of the proud general
and that of the girl who loved him, — for the ignoble youth
was incapable of believing hers to be the love of a mere
unreasoning child, though to a purer heart her words would
have a thousand times declared her enthusiasm to be but
a fanatical admiration, untouched by a tinge of passion.
The maddening jealousy that had raged in the heart of
Ruiz since he had learned of the flight of Chinita, and had
rendered him incapable of a sustained effort to renew the
ambitious projects so fatally shaken, now flamed up with
cruel intensity; and yet he loved her. At that moment
he would have liked to throttle her, yet would have recalled her to life with words of passionate love and burning kisses.

As he pondered, he struck his breast with his clinched
hand. "*Caramba!*" he muttered, "is all lost? Is there
no way to overset this miserable favorite of the Señora?
Maria Sanctissima! who is that?" His hand like a flash
passed to his pistol.

"Hist!" said a voice. "It is I, Fernando. I have not
a moment to spare. I have tried to gain a way to thee for
an hour or more. I know all that has passed. Fool!
thou shouldst have raised the battle-cry for Ramirez before this Gonzales reached thee; there were men with
thee who would have sustained thee well!"

"Bah! a man has opinions," answered Ruiz, coolly,
recognizing the voice; "and if Ramirez still chooses to
fight for the priests, that is no argument for my being as
mad. I tell you plainly, Father, I am tired of playing a
boy's part; you will hear of me yet as something more
than the lieutenant of Gonzales."

"Big words, big words," laughed Tio Reyes. "Now
listen to that which I have to say to you;" and leaning
from his saddle in a few concise words he delivered the
message of Ramirez, adding a few paternal injunctions
as to the conduct Ruiz should in future observe.

"Up to this time nothing is lost," he continued; "in
truth had you acted in good faith, no course could have
been better save this last step, — but that may easily be recalled. Ramirez will soon be prepared to attack Gonzales

in force ; his mind was set on regaining El Toro, but that can be deferred. 'When the loaf is cut the crumbs may be soon eaten!' Be you prepared to pass over to your rightful commander at the last moment with all your men. The rest of the troop will follow like sheep. Bah! what is the name of Gonzales to that of Ramirez! With the forces we could then combine, what might we not attempt! I promise you in the name of Ramirez, on his honor as a soldier and his faith as your godfather, a free pardon for all that has passed. *Caramba*, man! I can't imagine how you could have been so mad. I have seen the girl who has bewitched you, and by my faith I thought her nothing more than any other brown chit, save that her eyes were darker and bigger than most, and her tongue sharper than a man cares to find between his wife's lips! What, you hesitate? You believe Ramirez at the bottom of a pit, and the pit dry? Fool! He has treasure you know nothing of; and as for men, did the mountain villages ever fail him? — and you know how many may be counted on here. *Caramba*, try them! Tell them he has sacked Tres Hermanos."

"I know it," said Ruiz, thoughtfully, "and doubtless the booty was great!"

Reyes shrugged his shoulders but did not contradict him, reiterating again and again the assurances of the favor of Ramirez in the event of Ruiz's acceptance of his proposals, and on the contrary the chief's determination to wreak an awful vengeance upon his god-child should he prove obdurate and attempt to carry to injurious lengths the treacherous intrigues which he had designed against his benefactor.

Ruiz vehemently denied his guilt, yet hesitated to make promises which, whether kept or broken, might make still more dubious his future position. Reyes read his mind, and at length said coolly, —

"The fact is, you have been bred a servant of Ramirez. When I swore the service of my life to him, yours went with it. You are the one creature in the world he has never met with a frown or given a harsh word to; but do you think he will spare you for that? No; if you should fall into his hands as a traitor, which sooner or later you would be sure to do, you would be shot! Yes, like a dog, —" and the speaker spat on the ground to emphasize his contempt. " But if you are reasonable he will forget all that has passed, — more than I would do in his place I can tell you ; ay, he will even give you his daughter."

" His daughter ! " echoed Ruiz with a sneer.

" On my soul, you must be hard to please," cried his father. "For the girl's sake I was sorry enough he killed the fool of a gatekeeper five days ago. For all her proud ways, she loved him like a child, — more than she will love Ramirez though he is her father, when she hears of this mad deed."

Ruiz sprang to his side. "What do you mean?" he cried, seizing his arm. " Is Chinita the daughter of Ramirez? Is she with him? Is she indeed the girl who has been promised to me for these years and years? *Por Dios*, what would I not do for her? What would I not dare? But I do not believe it. Ramirez knows I love her ; this is but a deception. Ah, I know him too well ! "

Reyes laughed. " He told me if you were not satisfied you might go and see for yourself. Faith, he had no thought you loved her already. I met him on the road as he came back from leaving her. Does that surprise you? He is a careful father ; she is in the house of the Señora's daughter, Doña Carmen."

Ruiz seemed stunned. Reyes saw that his point was gained, and uttered but a few words more, which elicited only the response, — " Ramirez's daughter? Wonderful, wonderful ! And after all, she will be mine. Heavens ! how can I live a day longer without seeing her? Commend me to the Señor General. You know, my father, my heart is good, though my brain may have erred ! Tell me, has she said but one good word for me? She — "

" Enough ! " cried Reyes, laughing the more. " I have not seen her, I tell thee ; and if thou wouldst know what she thinks, find a pretext and see her at Doña Carmen's house. It was a strange freak of the General's to take her there, but a happy one. Thou shalt not be molested on the way, I promise thee. But I have no further time for talking. Adios ! thou art the only man I have ever seen whom love has brought to his right senses. It will be well if thou art as sane a year after the wedding ! "

The two men embraced, in the fashion of the country,

and with an ardor on the part of Ruiz that he seldom affected.

" *Caramba!* the father is a man of a thousand," he muttered to himself as he watched him disappear, guiding his horse so deftly that not a sound broke the silence of the night. " Virgin of consolation ! " he continued, as he walked slowly back to his quarters. " This is like a dream. Plague upon it ! That is the fault of my father ; he is always in haste. I would have asked him a thousand questions, had he given me but a quarter of an hour. But it is of Chinita herself I will ask them. Surely she must have shown some favor toward me, or my godfather would not recommend me to her with such confidence. *Santo Niño,* show me some way to make it possible to steal into Guanapila and exchange a word with her ! "

The curiosity of the young man as much as his love prompted the latter aspiration. His suspicion of the identity of Ramirez with the brother of Doña Isabel, the Leon Vallé so long supposed dead, returned to him with force ; but he longed to know whether the secret of her birth had been conveyed to Chinita, and how her flight had been contrived. He pictured her then like a bird in a cage beating herself against the iron bars of Doña Carmen's windows. That was not what she had hoped for when she had talked to him of Ramirez. If she had tolerated him before, would he not now be doubly dear, as one who should liberate her from the natural restraints of a maiden's life ?

Ruiz forgot his fancied wrongs in an intoxication of delight. Constant pondering upon the question how he should manage to evade the vigilance and suspicions of Gonzales and effect a visit to Guanapila kept him preoccupied, yet feverishly alert, until the increased indisposition of Doña Isabel brought about what appeared to him a special interposition in his behalf, and in pleading for the aid of " Our Lady of the Impossible " he promised her in pious gratitude a candle of enormous proportions.

To reach a point where he might leave his generous but failing friend had become the most earnest desire of Gonzales. But its fulfilment had seemed an impossibility, for from the time he assumed command of the troops almost hourly news had been brought to him of gatherings of bands of Conservatives, which promised to offer formidable resistance to any movement he might make; and until Doña Isabel was safely disposed of, he desired at almost any risk to avoid an open collision.

The march had slowly proceeded, and so constantly had Gonzales been occupied, and so serious became the condition of Doña Isabel, that there was but little conversation between them, and somewhat to his impatience that on her part had been limited to a few brief sentences of warning against Ruiz and constant inquiries for Chinita, and entreaties that search should be made for her in every direction.

Gonzales, as far as was possible, had obeyed these inopportune requests; but the anxiety and grief that prompted them seemed to him strained and unnatural, though he could not doubt after due inquiry made that the lost girl was of remarkable beauty and of an original and fascinating character. Still, his knowledge of the class whence he supposed her sprung had made quite credible to him the generally accepted theory of her flight. Yet he started when Doña Isabel had mentioned the American as her probable companion or instigator, adding in a low voice, " Twice an American has robbed him." What did she mean? His cheek flushed as he remembered that it had been said that for love of the murdered Ashley, Herlinda had taken the veil. And had Doña Isabel dreamed that he would find consolation after so many years in this beautiful peasant girl whom she had raised from the dust? Gonzales silently resented the insinuation. Yet none the less the suggestion of the complicity of the American in her disappearance haunted and vexed him. He did not tell Doña Isabel that to Ward he owed the definite news of the approach of reinforcements, and that he had virtually left him in charge of El Toro, and that the commission from Juarez for which the foreigner had applied had already doubtless reached him. Had he betrayed this young girl, — the *protégée* of Doña Isabel, — in spite of his zeal in his service the American should have much to answer for to him. A few weeks would decide all. He preferred to wait patiently the development of affairs, and refrained from perplexing further the mind of Doña Isabel.

Meanwhile the condition of the lady had become rapidly worse. Perhaps she had brought from Tres Hermanos the germs of the disease that during these very days was working such terrible havoc there; perhaps the long days and nights of exertion, anxiety, and grief had produced it, — but certain it is that as the position of Gonzales became more critical, so the imminent danger of Doña Isabel increased. A desperate evil commands a desperate remedy. So it was at length decided that an effort should be made to convey the lady to the city of Guanapila, to the house of her daughter Doña Carmen; and Ruiz, in the utter impossibility that Gonzales found of personally conducting the party, was permitted to execute the delicate and important trust.

With an apparent readiness of resource and disregard of danger, which commended him greatly to the perplexed General, Ruiz himself had proposed the measure.

Taking the precaution to send with him men from Tres Hermanos only, and such as he knew to be warmly devoted to their mistress, Gonzales acceded to the plans of the wily young officer, and despatched him upon the important and seemingly dangerous mission.

After the separation of the detailed party from the main body, skirmishing parties began upon the latter frequent and harassing attacks, and the suspicions of Gonzales were again aroused by the impunity which Ruiz enjoyed, yet alternated with fears for his ultimate safety. He could scarcely believe that knowing it to be in their power to secure so rich a prize as Doña Isabel, the hungry forces of the clergy would suffer her to escape, unless indeed Ruiz was himself as false as he had once suspected. Again and again he reproached himself for yielding to the apparent frankness and loyalty of the man he had at first distrusted, and with an anxiety which grew into actual torture he awaited the outcome of the action which circumstances against his will and judgment had forced upon him.

Ruiz, unmolested, made his way as rapidly as the condition of his charge permitted toward Guanapila. He comprehended well the circumstances which were distracting the mind of Gonzales. These constant though petty attacks he knew from information sent by Reyes were

destined to weaken the prestige of Gonzales by a series
of petty misadventures, after which his destruction by
the desertion of Ruiz, followed by the mass of the disaffected, might, it was conjectured, be readily accomplished. It seemed the simplest matter in the world to
effect, and had been instantly agreed to by Ruiz in the
hasty conference with his father. Yet further reflection
gave him an unaccountable antipathy to the course he was
to pursue. It cannot be said that a lingering trace of
honor influenced him, or any genuine disapproval of the
character or convictions of Ramirez, for Ruiz was in the
widest sense a man to be bought and sold, a creature influenced by every turn of advantage ; but in spite of all that
had passed between him and Reyes, he doubted the good
faith of Ramirez. The good fortune that was to give
him Chinita at so slight a cost seemed to him incredible.
Did the girl love him, and had she owned as much? Or
was she to be fooled into acquiescence in the plans of
Ramirez by the chimera of his parental power? No ; he
knew Chinita too well to believe she would marry against
her own desire, even to gratify a parent who exerted over
her the extraordinary ascendency that she had instinctively
acknowledged in Ramirez. Ruiz was, moreover, impressed
with a belief in the ultimate disaster of the Conservative
cause. For Chinita's sake he would risk involvement in
the ruin he foresaw, hoping that by some spar he himself
might float ; but unless assured of her good-will, — the
thoughts of the young conspirator carried him no further,
unless vaguely to conjecture the extent of power which he
might thereafter exert over the fortunes of Doña Isabel,
through his connection with her mysterious *protégée*.

With ill-concealed impatience, and hopes and emotions
which every hour grew more dazzling and overpowering,
Ruiz at length found himself in the house of Doña Carmen,
and in her presence and that of her young companion.
With inexpressible amazement, instead of her he sought
he found himself face to face with Chata, the supposed
daughter of Don Rafael.

The confusion and excitement of the arrival gave almost instantly an opportunity for him to pour into the
ear of the young girl the burning questions which rushed
to his lips. In the necessity in which she found herself

to attend instantly the wants of her mother, Doña Carmen left the young soldier and her charge alone together. Breathlessly demanding of Chata news of Chinita, Ruiz revealed to the astounded girl the separation of her playmate from Doña Isabel, the mystery of her flight, and the extraordinary purposes which the young girl had cherished in relation to Ramirez. In every word too he betrayed his own love for her he denounced, and the raging jealousy which possessed him.

Chata in her extreme agitation, forgetting the promises she had made, revealed her own connection with Ramirez, in describing in a few brief sentences the scenes which had taken place at Tres Hermanos, and especially the means by which she had saved Don Rafael. She could not comprehend the rage and disgust with which Ruiz flung himself from her when she announced herself to be the daughter of Ramirez, but a moment later it flashed upon her that she had heard herself named as the destined bride of this man who so openly despised her. Had he too known of the destiny awarded him? She turned from him with a burning blush, and without a word they parted. She remembered afterward that she might perhaps have sent news to the hacienda, — to her foster-father Don Rafael, to Doña Feliz did she still live; but her one chance had gone, and her semi-imprisonment began anew. Doña Carmen was not again betrayed into a momentary forgetfulness of her charge.

Ruiz turned from the house with a thousand conflicting emotions. The encounter with Chata had produced in his mind an absolute fury of resentment, as he reflected that this was the girl whom Ramirez had promised him as his wife, — in his boyhood jestingly; in his manhood as a reward, an incentive. Heavens! what was this puny creature in comparison with Chinita? And Chinita was perhaps at that very moment with Ramirez, — perhaps even laughing with him over the weakness and discomfiture of the youth they had combined to deceive! With blind and insensate rage, Ruiz believed himself the victim of a conspiracy between Ramirez and his own father to substitute this girl for the peerless creature that he loved, and who doubtless was at that moment in the camp of her triumphant lover. They had thought to entrap him into furthering their designs, deeming it impossible that he should enter Guanapila and discover the trick that was to be played upon him.

Ruiz did not for a moment conceive it possible that Ramirez had known nothing of his love for Chinita, or that his father had himself been ignorant of the identity of the girl whom Ramirez had claimed as his daughter, or that Reyes had drawn a false conclusion from his own hasty questions.

In this mood Ruiz was presently met by old acquaintances, before whom he was forced to mask his excitement; and moreover they were in festive humor, which prevented them from being observant or critical. The town, but imperfectly garrisoned, had for some time held an anxious and harassed populace, prognosticating nothing but invasion and the levy of forced loans; but it chanced that on that day a guest had arrived, who by the mere magic of his presence, unattractive and unimpressive as was his bearing, inspired confidence and hope. Benito Juarez himself had made one of those secret incursions for which he was famed, and had reached Guanapila with the purpose of conferring with such officers of his party as had ventured to meet him. There were but few, and Ruiz was honored by an invitation to represent Gonzales. The deference paid him as a delegate from so important a leader, in command of so considerable a force, raised to its highest pitch the absolute fury of resentment that convulsed the desperate lover; and at the banquet that followed the conference, the wine and flattering notice of the Liberal President completed the overthrow of the little caution that he had hitherto maintained in his speech and demeanor.

The toasts drunk were loud and frequent, and the name of Ramirez was the most deeply execrated. Many of the young men indulged in extravagant boasts and declarations as to the deeds they would accomplish in the near future, scorning the prowess of the man at whose very name they were accustomed to tremble. Some one spoke with a laugh of a beautiful girl who had been seen in his company but a few days before. It was not until afterward that Ruiz reflected that the spy had probably caught a glimpse of Chata on her way from Tres Hermanos. At the moment his mind was full of Chinita, and rising impetuously, in a torrent of fiery words he broke into denunciation and invective, telling the tale of Pedro's martyrdom as he had heard it, and vowing that as Ramirez had slain the poor peasant, so he himself would accomplish the defeat and death of the "mountain wolf." "I promise you, Señores," he concluded, "that when you next hear of Fernando Ruiz you shall have cause to remember the vow I have here made. Ramirez is doomed!"

The stoical man at the head of the table smiled faintly at the storm of applause that followed this speech, and as Ruiz a few minutes later took his departure Juarez muttered to his neighbor, "That young fellow will bear watching. He has either a tremendous personal wrong to avenge, or he is striving to mislead us. I know him to be the godson of this very Ramirez, whom he thunders against. A Mexican may turn against, may even murder, his own father; but his godfather, — he must be a renegade indeed to attempt his destruction!" His neighbor assented.

When the words of Ruiz were reported to Ramirez, — as reported they were a few days later, — he smiled as grimly as Benito Juarez himself had done. "The cockerel crows loud," he said. "He was always a blusterer. Well, we shall see; a week at latest will decide all that. Bah! if the fellow but had in him the blood of his father! — but with the name of his mother he must have taken a braggart's tongue. It will be well for him if he does not weary my patience in the end. But for my promise to Reyes —"

He frowned darkly. Had Ruiz seen the face of his godfather then he might have repented his boast. As it was, his own mad words served as a spur urging him to the inevitable future. He returned to the camp of Gonzales unmolested, and was received with intense relief, with thanks and praises, yet wore thereafter a dark and vengeful face.

THE arrival of Doña Isabel at the house of her daughter brought a change into the life of Chata that might have been considered even more dreary and oppressive than the semi-imprisonment to which she had thus far been subjected, though she was spoken of as an honored guest. In fact this change was most welcome to the young girl; for while it afforded her even less freedom of movement, it gave a sufficient reason for her seclusion, as also occupation both to body and mind.

What had been the nature of the communication that Ramirez had made to Doña Carmen, Chata knew not, but it had evidently impressed that lady with a deep sense of responsibility. In those days there were even in the quietest times no regular mails into the country districts, and this gave a ready pretext to Doña Carmen for resisting all attempts to communicate with the household at Tres Hermanos. The highways, infested as they were by roving bands of soldiers and banditti, were indeed scarcely safe for the transmission of even peaceful intelligence; and thus none reached Guanapila from the hacienda, and Chata, and in a lesser degree Doña Carmen herself, endured a painful uncertainty as to the condition of Don Rafael and of Doña Feliz and others whom Chata had left stricken with the dreaded fever. Day by day she had awaited news; day by day she had hoped for the appearance of Doña Isabel and Chinita, — while Doña Carmen, after listening with astonishment and some manifestations of displeasure to the account Chata gave of the departure of her mother from Tres Hermanos under the escort of troops destined to the relief of Gonzales, gave the opinion that the destination she would seek would be El Toro rather than Guanapila.

"My sister the religious is at present there," she said; and Chata with glowing face. and lips that trembled at the memory, told her of the chance glimpse she had once caught of the beautiful and saintly nun.

Doña Carmen's eyes filled with tears, and she silently embraced the girl; the little incident drew Chata nearer to her heart. "Ah, child," she would say, "I never have known, I never could conjecture, why our beautiful Herlinda chose so sad a life, — it must be sad to be shut away from this fair world, from sweet companionship, from love. Yes, Herlinda might have chosen from among a score of the handsomest and noblest of cavaliers. And then our mother, — how she loved her! one might see it through all her sternness. I never knew the truth, yet I am sure a great and terrible sorrow caused Herlinda to enter a convent. She had no inherent fitness, no liking natural or acquired, for such a life."

Doña Carmen was not accustomed to speak thus freely of family affairs. She had much of the characteristic reticence of the Garcias. Chata met many of the younger members from time to time. They were too well bred to show any curiosity concerning her; but among the servants of the household and of others, there was much gossip as to how and why she had come, and what relationship she bore to the husband of Doña Carmen, who, kind and amiable man that he was, seemed to take peculiar pleasure in her companionship. But the arrival of Doña Isabel in an apparently dying condition turned all thoughts into a new channel.

From the first, Chata had entreated to be allowed to take her part in nursing the stricken lady, but had been gently refused. Thereafter, the husband of Doña Carmen used often to see their young guest gliding restlessly about the house vainly seeking some distraction for her anxious thoughts. He did not know the secret pain that tormented her. He would gladly have facilitated her return if he could to that Don Rafael from whom in a mad freak the mountain chieftain had stolen her; yet there were circumstances, — there were reasons for not offending one so powerful. Who knew? Guanapila was of course under Liberal rule to-day, but what would it be to-morrow? The cautious man shrugged his shoulders and said something of this to Chata, who smiled and thought him good to care, yet wondered with all his goodness and his years,

— the years that had not brought in their train any additional attractiveness to his person, — that Doña Carmen loved him. Was it as she had heard, that his riches had beguiled one already passing rich?

Since she had left El Toro, Chata had become a woman. Change of scene had given impetus to the somewhat retarded development of her physique, and mental anxiety had stimulated her mind and given to it an intuitive appreciation of causes and events that is generally gained by innocent and unsuspicious natures, such as hers, only after long experience.

Thus she comprehended fully, as she would not have done a few months before, the gravity of the step Chinita had taken in separating herself from Doña Isabel. Ruiz had not spared the woman he loved in the few brief sentences he had passionately uttered : love was with him but a devouring flame, ready to destroy its object either in the struggle of attainment or in the fury of baffled desire. Chata blushed even in secret when she remembered the aspersions he had cast upon the friend of her childhood. She knew the innate purity of the girl's mind, though it had been developed amid surroundings which might well have tainted it. She knew her pride : even when she was but the barefoot foster-child of Pedro the gatekeeper, Chinita had held Pepé and his mates as far apart from her as the dogs that followed them or the mules they tended. Dogs and mules she liked well and made serve her needs, as also she did the lads. Chata did not doubt that Pepé now as ever had proved himself the slave of Chinita's will. Perhaps it was to Tres Hermanos she had gone. Although knowing as she did the fascination that Ramirez had always exerted over the girl's mind, she could not but fear that led not by reckless passion but by a spirit of devotion at which Ruiz had sneered, yet in which Chata herself recognized the peculiar strength and determination of Chinita's character, the impulsive creature might actually have sought an entrance to the camp to urge the plan that she conceived was to further the glory of the Church and the interest of him whom she had made the hero of her imagination. That Ashley Ward was in any way concerned in the disappearance of Chinita, either as a principal or an accessory, Chata indignantly refused to be-

lieve. Her heart beat suffocatingly as she thought of him.
No, no! he was not a man to entice a girl to her ruin.

And as days went by news reached Chata that strengthened this conviction. The American was engaged in
deeds of a far different character. In his way he was
beginning to fill the minds and occupy the conversation
of people as much as Ramirez had ever done. They gave
him a new name, as those at the hacienda had done; but
Conservatives and Liberals alike wondered at and exaggerated his exploits, until Ashley had won a reputation for
reckless bravado quite foreign to his true character, —
which was exhibiting itself in the most careful and nice
calculations of chances, the whole tending toward the
fulfilment of the task to which he had dedicated himself;
namely, the downfall of the unpunished and unrepentant
murderer of John Ashley.

Chata recognized this, and was filled with emotions perhaps more conflicting, more strange, than had ever before met in the breast of so young a girl. They held her
thoughts by day and night. Oh that she had never left
Ramirez! Oh that she could speak but for a few moments
with Ashley! But she was powerless; and meanwhile
what was the fate of Chinita? What that impending over
the man she was in duty bound to warn, — to love if it
were possible?

But before these reflections had reached this point, an
employment that prevented them from becoming utterly
overwhelming was afforded her. Chata no longer wandered
aimlessly about the house, but kept the strict seclusion of
Doña Isabel's apartment, to which she had been hastily
summoned one night by Doña Carmen herself.

" My mother talks so strangely," she had said in a low
voice, pressing her hands to her white and frightened face.
" No, I cannot comprehend what she says; but I cannot
have the servants about her. They might imagine un-
speakable things. Oh, what tales and rumors they might
set afloat! No, no! I will not have them here, with their
suspicions and evil thoughts. But you, — you are innocent and frank; you will not torture into strange meanings
the mutterings of a diseased imagination."

" No, no! " answered Chata, reassuringly. " It was the
same with Doña Feliz. Sometimes she talked so strangely.

so sadly, one was forced to weep, and then again to laugh; yes, in all my trouble I laughed. But I will not now, Doña Carmen; only let me be useful. Doña Isabel did not seem to like me when she was at the hacienda, so I kept as much as possible out of her sight. She said my face was not such as Don Rafael's daughter should have; and after all," she added sadly, "she was right."

What passed in that sick chamber through those long days and nights Doña Carmen and Chata never repeated, even to each other. Perhaps they could not, all was so disconnected, so improbable, and through all her delirium the patient held so great a restraint over her utterances. Sometimes one escaped her that startled and commanded attention; but the next invariably contradicted it, and it was impossible to form a connected theory even had Chata tried. But that great sorrows, events to cause constant and secret care and remorse, had taken place in the life of Doña Isabel, and that they concerned Chinita closely, was abundantly clear. What pathetic appeals, what wild ravings, in which the names of those who had lived in the past, — of her husband, her mother, her brother, and of Herlinda, — were constantly mingled with those of the American and Chinita. And friends or servants followed each other in endless yet confusing succession; yet of them all the name of Chinita was the most frequent. The present grief combined all others; in Chinita seemed centred the agonies and loves of her lifetime.

Chata listened with a sort of envy. Ah, if it had been given to her to raise such a passion of feeling! She found herself from day to day leaning with infinite tenderness over this woman, who had seemed so cold, but whose heart was now revealed as a very volcano of repressed and seething emotions. She was grateful and deeply touched that Doña Isabel in her delirium clung to her fondly, calling her " Mother," or " Quina," which Doña Carmen told her was the name of a cousin she had dearly loved. Even after she had recognized her when the delirium was past as the daughter of Don Rafael, she seemed pleased to have her there; though she said querulously, " It is strange you are only a little country girl. But Feliz has good blood in her; it has been transmitted to you, — there is nothing of Rita, nothing of Rafael himself."

After that she made no further comment; but her eyes often followed the movements of Chata with a puzzled expression painful to see. One day after she had become convalescent, Doña Carmen spoke of this. "Whom does she remind you of?" she asked lightly.

"I cannot tell; I do not know," Doña Isabel answered wearily. "Perhaps it is of Chinita. Oh! I can think of nothing but Chinita. Are they still looking for her, as I have prayed, — as I have commanded?"

"Mother," said Doña Carmen, solemnly, "who is Chinita? Why should you care so much?"

The face of Doña Isabel grew rigid. "Shall I tell you what you have uttered in your delirium?" continued Doña Carmen, looking fixedly into her mother's eyes. "Shall I ask you if you spoke the truth, or if what I have gathered — here a word, there a word — is but a dreadful fancy? Mother, Mother! if it is the truth, no wonder that the fate of this girl is on your soul! No wonder Herlinda —"

She paused affrighted. In her excitement she had said far more than she had intended. What if her mother in her delicate condition should sink beneath this cruel attack, — should faint, should die? Carmen threw herself down beside the couch with a prayer for forgiveness.

Doña Isabel in the first surprise had clasped her hands over her heart. Slowly the pale hue of life returned to her face. "Carmen," she whispered faintly, "speak! speak! After all these years, accusation — even from my own child — is more bearable than silence. O my God, I meant well! — it was for Herlinda's sake. Yet what remorse, what agony I have suffered!"

The two women sank into each other's arms. There had ever been a barrier of reserve between them, — in a moment it was swept away. Doña Isabel poured out her heart. It was Carmen who withheld what might have been revealed; a conviction seized her that there was much in this strange family mystery yet undeclared, and of which Doña Isabel knew nothing; and that her mother's mind was in no condition to be perplexed by further doubts and complications. She left the room and went to her husband.

"Chulita my beautiful one," he said anxiously, as she was about to leave him an hour later, "thou wilt do nothing rash? Yet I will not forbid thee. In truth, but that robberies and abductions are so common upon the roads, I would go with thee myself."

" Not for the world!" exclaimed Doña Carmen in genuine consternation. " They would seize thee and carry thee into the mountains. But as for me, — I promise thee no robber shall think me worth a second thought. But hold thee ready, — the desire may come to her at a moment's thought, and I would not leave thee without warning; I would not have thee unprepared."

XLIII.

WITH the same unreasoning fury with which he had denounced Ramirez at the banquet, Ruiz had returned to the camp of Gonzales; and through a cleverly managed correspondence with Ramirez — in which however he dared not mention the name of Chinita, lest he should awaken in the astute mind of the General a suspicion that his godson conjectured the deception which was to be played upon him — Ruiz gradually drew from the chief data through which to propose such movements to Gonzales as procured for him as a strategist the respect and admiration of that commander, which well might have satisfied a laudable ambition.

Meanwhile Ramirez himself, though surrounded by no despicable force, which was daily augmented by accessions from the mountains or from the ranks of less popular leaders of either party, was for the first time in his life oppressed by a vague melancholy, — which, with some impatience, he ascribed to the forced separation from the child whose purity and innocence had so irresistibly attracted him. There were times when he thought with what horror such a record as his would be viewed by that gentle and upright nature; and a positive dread came upon him of her ever knowing the one incident that had been so vividly recalled to him by the appearance of the avenger upon the grave of the man he had murdered years before, — one crime among many he had almost forgotten. He said to himself that an evil spell had been upon him ever since the day when he had foolishly thrown away the charm the elf-like child had given him. His emissaries had brought him word time and again of the miscarriage of his best-laid plans. Who had betrayed them?

Ramirez knew too well who had frustrated them. - The American who had escaped his knife at the cemetery seemed ubiquitous since obtaining the commission which authorized him to wage war against his cousin's murderer.

Not content with defending El Toro with unexampled bravery, he appeared at every point where an advantage was to be gained. "*Carrhi!*" Ramirez said to himself, "I shall be forced to give that fellow a thrust of my dagger in secret, since he appears to be impervious to ball and proof against the chances of open warfare. He or I must fall. There's not room in all Mexico for him and me."

Whether there was room or not, it seemed destined that they should remain in it together, though not without constant collision. Gonzales became to the mind of Ramirez far less formidable than this yellow-haired foreigner, who with a mere handful of followers so constantly harassed and baffled him. Like most men of his class, the mountain chieftain was intensely superstitious, and one night in the moonlight he saw, or fancied he saw, a female form glide before him into the chapparal. He caught but a glimpse of the face, but it had reminded him of Herlinda, for whom he had done the deed that, so late, seemed to have brought upon him a threatened retribution. As he searched the bushes for the woman, whom he could not discover, he shuddered as he remembered the expression of her eyes, — as of a wronged creature who had loved and now hated. He had seen such an expression in a woman's eyes before. More than ever after this strange occurrence the thought of Ashley Ward tormented him; the young man's face haunted him; and curiously enough other faces also began to peer upon him, — faces of women he had wronged, of men who with good cause bore him deadly hatred, or of others whom, like the American, or the gatekeeper, he had murdered.

Ramirez grew strangely taciturn and nervous. Not even the letters of Ruiz aroused him. In his heart he distrusted his godson, as he did all men but Reyes, all women but Chata. Had she been near, he thought, he would have talked to her and cast off his fancies; but in her absence they grew upon him. One day he could have sworn he saw clearly not only the face but the figure of Pedro Gomez; and upon another, that of the woman he had loved long years before. Bah! they were fantasies. He wondered whether he too would be seized with the fever, which was still raging at Tres Hermanos, and of which they said its lady was dying at her daughter's house in Guanapila. Was this weakness of nerve the presage of what was to come?

At last battle was joined with Gonzales as had been planned. The day turned in favor of Ramirez; even the gallant assistance of Ward availed little against the desperate courage of the mountain troops. The genius and valor of their leader were manifested with a vigor that declared they had been but shaken, not broken. Until the arrival of Ward it had even appeared that the forces actually under the command of Ramirez would have been sufficient to effect a victory; but Ward's appearance speedily turned the tide in favor of Gonzales, and with some impatience Ramirez gave the signal that was to hasten the promised action of Ruiz.

But at the critical moment the expected ally failed him. With a vindictive fury which was demoniacal in its exhibition, Ruiz threw himself against his old commander. The carnage was terrible in that part of the field; and when the fray was ended, the demoralization of Ramirez's troops was complete, — yet he himself had escaped.

That such should be the case seemed to Ashley Ward incredible, as later he walked over the field seeking among the slain the man against whom he had begun a private warfare, which to his own surprise had, with further investigation of the principles involved, rapidly attained in his mind the dignity of a struggle for liberty that even dwarfed the incentive of personal revenge, although it was impossible that this should be wholly forgotten or ignored.

Gonzales marched into El Toro amid the clanging of bells and shouts of rejoicing; for though that was a convent town, the people of the lower class were mad *Juaristas*, who did good service under Ward when troops were scarce. The triumph had however not been gained without much loss upon the Liberal side; and among the missing was the young officer who in the eyes of Gonzales — and to the astonishment of Ward — had so ably vindicated his character as a stanch adherent in the day of battle. Pepé too, the right-hand man of Ward, was gone.

In very truth, at the last moment the most important and useful calculation of Ruiz had failed. He saw Ramirez, by his orders, surrounded by desperate men; it seemed inevitable that he must be stricken down, — when a party led by Reyes broke through to his assistance, and in the fury of the onslaught Ruiz himself was swept from his horse and hurried away, and to his consternation found himself a prisoner dragged onward in the irresistible impetus of flight.

They were miles distant from the scene of battle when the fugitives at last paused; and here for the first time Ramirez knew of the special prisoner that had been made. When his eyes fell upon the youth, a frown which darkened as with a palpable cloud his already rigid and pitiless face, overspread the countenance of Ramirez and made it absolutely terrible. Even to fallen angels the crime of ingratitude may seem the one damnable offence. In Ruiz, remembering the love and favor he had shown him, Ramirez held it so to be. This insignificant boy had compassed his ruin; his life seemed too poor a forfeit to condone the offence. The baffled, desperate, outraged chieftain cursed the fate which had cast the treacherous favorite into his power. But the terrible blackness of his face still deepened, as he gazed.

A lasso had been drawn tightly around the waist of Ruiz. His face was cut and bleeding; the gold lace and epaulettes had been torn from his coat; his uncovered hair was filled with dust, and his face reeking with sweat. He raised his bloodshot eyes appealingly. He knew the man before him, — the man, worthless and unscrupulous though he was, who had been kind to him, whom he had betrayed, and whose death he had attempted to compass. Ruiz did not attempt to speak, but fell on his knees and raised his bound hands. Ramirez gazed at him a moment in silence, then without the quiver of a muscle in his impassive face uttered the sentence, " Let him be shot at once!"

Shot at *once*, — from that terrible mandate there was no appeal. There was not one there to utter a word in the traitor's behalf, but only a moan from the dust to which he had sunk. Reyes was not there; probably the result would have been the same had he been. The soldiers raised the young officer and stood him against a tree.

At the last moment that strange indifference to death,

27

which among his countrymen so often counterfeits courage, caused Ruiz to straighten his figure and raise his head ; and in the insolence of despair he said to Ramirez, with a glance of malignant contempt, "Had you fallen into my hands I would have shot you with my own pistol an hour ago."

Perhaps the still proud youth hoped by this speech to escape the ignominy of execution by a file of common soldiers. If so he was mistaken. Ramirez gave the signal ; the balls whizzed through the air and found their way to their destined aim. Ruiz fell without a groan. Ramirez himself, though still with an impassive face, to the astonishment of all stooped and stretched the limbs and crossed the hands of the young man upon his breast. There was a spot of blood upon the face, and the chief wiped it away as tenderly as a mother might lave the face of her dead infant ; and yet but a few moments before he had commanded this youth to a violent death, and according to the creed he held, his soul to purgatory without benefit of clergy.

Forgetting to give the expected order for the execution of the other prisoners, Ramirez turned away. In another moment he had placed himself at the head of the party and continued the retreat. "At the next halt it can be done as well," remarked the lieutenant, philosophically. "There are plenty of horses ; bind the prisoners well and bring them along."

And thus for that day at least Pepé Ortiz among others knew he had escaped a fate of which the very idea — with the remembrance of Ruiz to intensify its horror — made his tongue cleave to the roof of his mouth and his knees quiver with terror. Yet the day came when he, like the traitor whose end he had witnessed, straightened himself against a tree, and with apparent coolness awaited the mandate of Ramirez that was to consign him to eternity ; naught but a miracle it seemed could save him. He only begged a cigarette of a soldier, remarking that they might be scarce where he was going, — secretly hoping thus to hide the quiver of the lips which belied the bravado of his words.

Shortly after this time, Chata to her surprise received by the hand of an Indian fruitseller a brief note from

Ramirez. At the first reading its contents seemed hard and indifferent. He spoke with an almost savage irony of those who were driving him back like a wolf to his mountain lairs. "I know of fastnesses, if I care to seek them, where no foot but mine has ever trod, and where this accursed American who is hunting me down like fate could never hope to follow me," he wrote. "But it shall never be said that Ramirez fled from man or spirit, were it Satan himself. After all, a man may not escape from him who is destined to bring death to him. Ruiz was marked to die by me. I loved him, yet his fate is accomplished."

Chata shuddered. It seemed incredible that save by accident such a thing could happen, so sacred is esteemed by Mexicans the tie between sponsor and godchild; and the tone of the letter impressed her as that of a desperate man who was ready for unheard-of deeds. Had Ramirez in truth deliberately destroyed the man whom for years he had associated in his every hope and plan, to whom he had promised the hand of his child? Deep indeed must have been the villany that had merited such an end. The sigh of relief which Chata involuntarily breathed, that she was free from the possible accomplishment of the destiny that had been marked out for her, was perhaps as sympathetic as any caused by the death of Fernando Ruiz.

A reperusal of the letter gave to Chata's mind an impression of the longing, the stinging regret, the remorse which the words had been designed to conceal rather than display. The pride, the fierceness, the unconquerable will of the writer pervaded them; yet the wail of a lost spirit crying for the one good that it had known, and now believed forfeited forever, seemed to echo through her soul. "He loves me," she thought remorsefully. "He believes himself doomed to die, and that he will see me no more. Oh! if it were possible I would go to him. Oh, if I dared tell Doña Isabel! — but no, she would keep me from him; she would mock my pain with the cry that this was but the just recompense of the evil he had brought upon her long ago. She believes her brother dead; why torture her by telling her my miserable history?"

Chata showed the letter to Doña Carmen, and she it was who called the girl's attention to some chance mention of the name of the place where Ramirez said he might be able to remain some days, even if closely pressed, for the people there were secretly sworn to his support. Day after day wild rumors flew through the city of the pursuit of Ramirez, his capture, his death, only to be contradicted upon the next. They did not seriously agitate Chata, for not once was the name of the place he called his stronghold mentioned.

One night the anxious girl had a vivid dream. She dreamed she saw the chieftain and Chinita lying dead, — the one on one side of a village street, the other on the opposite. The people were rushing wildly about screaming and gesticulating madly, while Doña Isabel, followed by women clothed in black like herself, was in frenzy passing from one to the other, uttering that low wail that seems the very key-note of woe.

Chata woke with a stifled scream. The wind was blowing shrilly through the trees and seemed to bring to her a voice, which said, "Wake! oh wake, Chata! I have dreamed of her." The voice sounded close to her ear. It came from Doña Isabel, who leaning over the dreamer's bed was repeating again and again the words, "I shall find her. I have dreamed of her."

Chata raised herself upon the pillows and caught the lady's wasted hand. "Yes, yes," continued Doña Isabel, "I have dreamed of Chinita and of another, — one I loved long years ago. I saw them together in Las Parras. It is a revelation! Why have I not thought of it before? No other place would be so fitting. I shall find her. I am going now, now! My carriage, my horses, my men must be here; I will call them. Tell my daughter when she wakes; she will understand."

Doña Isabel turned to leave the room, her excitement supplementing her returning strength; but Chata detained her. "I too will go," she cried. "Nothing shall prevent me. Doña Carmen will not stop us, — she knows; she dare not forbid me. I will tell her now. She will know what is best for us. The carriage is still here, but — "

Chata hastened from the room and wakened Doña Carmen. "Ah," said the daughter to herself, "the thought is come, and the hour." She hastily wrote a line to her husband, who was absent at a hacienda he owned near the city; provided herself with some rolls of gold, and presently entered her mother's room dressed in a somewhat soiled cotton gown, and with her reboso over her arm. Doña Isabel, who in the excitement of her thoughts was walking hither and thither, taking up and putting down articles of apparel, looked at her daughter blankly. Why, she thought, had a servant come at that hour?

"See, I am ready," cried Carmen, cheerfully. "The diligence is to leave the city for the first time to-day. We shall pass through the country quite safely. Who would stop such poor creatures as we appear to be?"

Doña Isabel looked at her daughter gratefully,— her mind had been running helplessly upon carriages and mounted escorts and all the paraphernalia of travel, which require so much time and thought to prepare. "True, true!" she said, "that will be best, oh much the best!" In feverish haste she prepared herself for the journey as Carmen had done, arraying herself in a plain dark dress and reboso. But her daughter noticed that she did not think of the expenses of the journey, and herself silently assumed the direction of the little party.

Doña Carmen led the way from her own house so quietly that only the doorkeeper to whom she gave a few directions, which he doubtless in his amazement straightway forgot, was awakened. The three ladies were so humbly dressed that they attracted but little notice at the diligence house, and being hastily motioned to the poorest seats in the coach were soon on their way. Covering their faces with their rebosos, they did not so much as speak to one another.

Some ten leagues from the city the diligence was stopped by a half-dozen armed men. The male passengers were ordered to lie down upon their faces, and were despoiled of all their money and valuables. Chata to her extreme disgust — which fortunately was disguised by her alarm — received an amicable expression of approval from one of the bandits, which was abruptly checked by the remark of the captain that this was no time for fooling, as there was a rival band but a half-mile farther on. The elder women escaped remark. Happily, the other band did not present itself, and the three ladies told their beads in devout thankfulness.

That night the travellers remained at a miserable hut, which served as an inn, feeling a certain protection in the presence of an aged priest, who chanced to be awaiting there an opportunity to proceed upon a long-interrupted journey; and upon the following morning he formed one of the travelling party. Beyond bestowing upon them his blessing, he said nothing to them, — although somewhat to her discomfort Doña Carmen noticed that he often turned an inquiring gaze upon them. Early in the afternoon the diligence stopped at a miserable village, the nearest point at which, in the interrupted arrangements of travel, it approached Las Parras; and having deposited Doña Isabel's party and the priest, diverged toward the north.

Doña Isabel looked around her helplessly, saying, "It is nearly eight leagues to Las Parras. I have often been here, — I know the road well. We shall never reach there!"

"You will see, Mother, you will see," answered Doña Carmen, cheerfully; and greatly to the astonishment of the priest and the women who stood near, she drew forth a half-dozen ounces of gold, and held them up. "See," she said in her clear patrician voice, "you are good people here; we are not afraid to trust you," — her quick eye had shown her there was not an able-bodied man in the almost ruinous place. "We are not so poor as we look, and I will give you all this for three, four—" she glanced at the priest — "horses, donkeys, or mules, be they ever so poor, upon which we can go our way."

The women laughed stupidly, and looked at one another and then at the gold. Evidently if there was a beast of burden in the village it was securely hidden, and though the money tempted them they were afraid.

"No, no," said one at length. "Three weeks ago the Señores Liberales drove off our last cow, and the week after the Señores Conservadores slaughtered the turkeys, and —"

"But we want neither cows nor turkeys," interrupted Carmen, impatiently.

"Quite true; but the Señorita would have horses," answered the matron imperturbably; "and yesterday the General Ramirez was here —"

She paused as though it were unnecessary to say more

of the fate of their horses; and Doña Isabel, starting up
impetuously, hurriedly questioned the assembled gossips.
Upon the subject of the visit of Ramirez the villagers were
eloquent. He and his followers had reached there spent
with fatigue and long fasting. In a few moments the place
had been sacked of all its poor provision; there had not
been enough to give one poor ration to the half-dozen
prisoners who were with them. They would have been
shot—yes, upon the very spot upon which their graces were
standing—but for the prayers of a young girl, who seemed
to be the lieutenant's wife; at least she was in his care,—
and Ramirez had admitted it could be done as well at the
next halt. She herself gave a drink of water to the poor
lads for the love of God, and also a tortilla to one among
them that she knew,—poor Pepé Ortiz; but he was too
weak to swallow it, and had given it to another less
wretched than he.

Chata began to cry softly, while Doña Isabel demanded
a description of the young girl who had been of the party.
This was vague enough; but insufficient as it was it made
the thought of further delay impossible,—and the eloquence and gold of Doña Carmen, to which was added
the authority of the priest, presently induced the villagers
to produce four sorry beasts, upon which with some difficulty the party were secured, for no saddles or panniers
were to be had. It was almost sunset when, following
the old stage-road, the already wearied travellers set out
upon their long and possibly perilous ride.

The women of the village stood for a long time with
arms akimbo, looking after the departing travellers. They
had divided the money among themselves,—they felt rich
and could afford to be pitiful. "The poor Señora has
perhaps lost a daughter," said one—"doubtless the fair
girl who rode with the lieutenant. The Holy Mother
protect her, for the man was in two minds about taking
her farther; but the Señor General swore he would run
his sabre through him if he cast her off to starve in such
a hole. To starve, eh! One who has never lived in my
birthplace cannot know how well the pigs fatten here
when the tunas are ripe."

"Pshaw! girls are fools, and not worth breaking one's
head for," said a second, whose only son kept her rich,

when well-laden travellers were plenty. "Where go they now? They are turning toward Las Parras. They will miss the soldiers, or I am no prophet."

"As a prophet one may give thee a thousand lashes, for thou art ever at fault," laughed a third. "But what matters it to us where they go? The road is open to them as to another. They should not go far wrong with a holy little priest to guide them."

XLIV.

Upon the very morning that Doña Isabel and her companion left Guanapila, news which might perhaps have changed their movements had they heard of it flew like wildfire over the city. The convents throughout Mexico had been simultaneously opened under a decree of the Liberal government, and thousands of women dedicated to a cloistered life were thus set free to choose anew their destiny.

Women who for half a century, perhaps, had lived apart from life and love were returned to die amid the turmoils of a home where love for them had ceased, or to pass over seas to seclusion in strange lands. Others, in whom voices as of demons were but just then ceasing to tempt the memory with whispers of the world and its alluring joys, saw those joys actually within their reach, and with dismay sought to turn their eyes away, and prayed for strength to brave the perils of the deep, and bear the homesickness that in a strange country would torment the soul of the cloistered nun as surely as if she had been free to gaze upon the valleys and mountains of the native land she was about to leave forever. Younger women, those to whom the early years of seclusion had brought but disenchantment, were cruelly roused from the stupor of habit which was succeeding pain and presaging content, and with secret regret now clung to the vows they fain would have cast aside forever, or in a few — a very few — cases became that shunned and despised creature, a recreant nun. That night was the signal for horror and tears throughout the land. A wail arose from thousands of families, about to catch a glimpse of their consecrated dear ones, and then to know them banished forever. Such uprooting of ties, such griefs, such domestic woes, are inevitable in all great national or social revolutions.

A certain secrecy had been observed in the preparations for and execution of this stroke of policy, which had indeed been threatened and openly urged as a political necessity, but which in spite of the exile of the archbishops and the suppression of monasteries had been thought — even by those who acknowledged its probable benefits to the nation — too daring a measure ever to be carried into effect. It had been thought a dream of the arch-iconoclast Juarez. But he was a man whose dreams were apt to come true ; and so it happened upon this summer night, striking admiration and consternation to the hearts of Liberals and Conservatives alike, for there was scarce a family of either party throughout Mexico that was not represented in the vast religious houses which abounded in every town. Into these, overcoming their superstitious scruples, the populace for the first time now penetrated, and learned something of the surroundings and consequent life of those whom for centuries they had supported as saints, dedicated to prayer and fasting for the sins of the people. To their disenchantment and surprise, the people found many of these gloomy piles filled with wide and beautiful chambers, where flowers and musical instruments stood side by side with the altar and *prie Dieu*, and parlors and refectories which opened upon gardens planted with the choicest and most luxuriant shrubs and flowers. There were kitchens too where the choice conserves were made which sometimes found a way to the outer world, and where doubtless other savory dishes were prepared for the saintly sisterhoods. In many of these retreats each nun had her servant, who came and went at her command, and life — if one may judge from the inanimate things and the low whispers that sometimes reached the outer air — was made a soft and sensuous prelude to the celestial harmony of eternity.

But there were others — and they were many — where the utmost austerity pictured by the devout secular mind was practised ; where entered the poor daughter, or she whom the priests perceived had a true vocation, or a deep and agonizing grief, which would keep her faithful to the vows of poverty, of devotion, and obedience. There were none of those amiable daughters of rich families too bountifully supplied with girls, and for whom a dowry to the

Church provided a safe and pleasant home, whence they might easily glide through this life into another, — where female angels would never be esteemed too plentiful, — but where were only the poor, the sorrowful, the despairing; and the well-filled vaults beneath the gloomy chapels attested how rich a harvest death had gleaned in those dreary abodes of penance.

For many days the officers in command at various points had been in possession of orders, — which it is to be conjectured were in many cases transmitted to the abbesses of the principal nunneries, that they might take advantage of this notice by quietly disbanding their sisterhoods and sending each member to her own family, or in communities to the United States or some transatlantic land. But the opportunity for moral martyrdom was not to be destroyed by a mere concession to convenience, and not in a single case was the knowledge acted upon, — except perhaps that in a few convents upon the designated night the nuns refrained from repairing to their dormitories, but prepared for exit, awaited the mandate praying in the lighted chapels; and where this occurred, the mothers superior afterward acquired reputations of special sancity for the supposed spirit of prophecy which had moved them. But in the majority of these establishments, so absolute was the belief that the threatened invasion would never be attempted, or if attempted would bring upon the intruders the instant vengeance of the Almighty, that no change was made in usual habits, and an outward composure was maintained, which we may believe among the initiated at least disguised many a beating heart filled with genuine horror, or with a wild guilty anticipation from which it shrank in remorse. The world! the world! With a turn of the lock, with scarce more than a step, they would be in it; and then — then!

Guanapila was not, strictly speaking, a convent city. The few small retreats within it were vacated with so little commotion that, except in the houses to which the sisters were removed, nothing was known of the measure until the following morning. But in the much smaller town of El Toro there were whole streets lined on either side with high, massive, and windowless walls which were the façades of vast cloisters. It was with feelings of intense though repressed excitement that Vicente Gonzales placed himself at the head of a small force which was to demand entrance to those formidable but peaceful structures, while the mass of the troops remained at the citadel, ready upon a signal to enforce his authority, whether questioned by Church or people. It was true the populace had declared itself Liberal in sentiment ever since the defeat of Ramirez had left them under the guns of the *Juaristus;* but bred as they had been under the very shadow of these colossal monuments of the Church it was not unlikely that when their sanctity was threatened, the momentary conversion of the citizens to patriotism might yield to zeal in the defence of institutions that had appeared to them as unassailable as the very heavens.

Vicente Gonzales might readily have sent another to fulfil the dubious task before him, — in fact in most cases men of dignity unconnected with the army were chosen as peaceful ambassadors of the power that held the sword; but the hour had arrived for which this man had prayed and fought, — for which he would have prayed and fought had no individual suffering added sharpness to the sting of the thorn that for so long had tormented his nation. He himself, he resolved, would execute the decree that should sweep this great incubus from the land. Perchance among the released he might find one whom he had never consciously for one moment forgotten; he might see her, if but for a moment, as she passed in the throng. He had never ceased to see the yearning, despairing, yet resolute expression upon the young face of Herlinda Garcia, as amid clouds of incense it faded from his sight behind the iron bars that separated her and her sister nuns from the body of the church whence he had witnessed her living entombment. That was in a city far away; most likely she was there now. Yet there was a chance, — a mere chance!

Strangely enough, Ashley Ward had never spoken the name of Herlinda to Gonzales; nor had either mentioned that of Chinita — an inexplicable yet differing motive holding both silent. The rapid events of the war, which had given full occupation to body and mind, had prevented discussion of domestic matters, and there was something in the reticence of Gonzales that forbade aught but deeply serious investigation; and for the present Ward was unprepared to attempt this. They were friends; but there were deeps in the nature of each that the other made no attempt to fathom. Upon this night Ward knew the mind of Gonzales perhaps better than did the man himself; and throughout the unwonted scenes of which he was a mere passive spectator, to him the most engrossing were the emotions that betrayed themselves upon the countenance of the commanding officer.

As Ashley and Gonzales left their quarters together, behind them followed closely a man in a sergeant's uniform, who halted painfully, and across whose face was a livid scar. To those who had heard nothing of the torture he had undergone, Pedro Gomez would have been scarcely recognizable, — for besides the disfiguring scar, there was an expression of vengeful and ferocious daring where before had been but dogged obstinacy and a certain rough kindliness; and to those who had believed him dead, his appearance would have brought a superstitious horror as that of one escaped from the torments of the damned.

Besides these three, several officers and other gentlemen, with a small guard of soldiers, passed out of the citadel afoot, and at a short interval were followed by all the available carriages of the town. What occurred thereafter may perhaps be best described by a translation of the chronicles of the time : —

" One night — one terrible night — a long and unusual sound, a prolonged rumble, was heard in the streets. It seemed shortly as if all the carriages in the city had become mad, now rushing hither, now thither, waking from sleep the peaceful neighborhood; so that each person demanded of the other, ' What is this?' ' What has happened?' and no one could answer with certainty the other.

" While the people wondered, the carriages stopped at the doors of the nunneries, and the gentlemen charged with the commission demanded entrance, and intimated to the nuns the order to leave their cells and refrain from reuniting in cloister.

" ' But, gentlemen, for God's love!'

" ' How can this be?'

" ' His will be done ! '

" ' But where can we go? Oh, what iniquity ! '

" Such were the phrases that broke the startled stillness of the cloisters. But the commissioners were deaf to all appeals, merely rubbing their hands and saying, —

" ' Let us go. Let us go on, Señoritas ! We have no time to lose ! '

" Truly the time was limited, — that night only, for perchance by day the gentlemen commissioners would have had a distaste to penetrate the convents ; or perhaps only by night can certain mischievous deeds be carried to the desired exit.

" It is said that some naughty novices upon hearing themselves called señoritas forgot for an instant their grief, and smiled. There did not lack also of those who had entered the category of grave mothers who did the same ! And after all, was not this a venial and excusable fault? Should not a girl, beautiful and fragrant as a jasmine, become tired of hearing herself addressed every hour and every day in the year as ' Little Mother,' ' My Reverend Mother,' ' How is your Reverence?' . . .

" This was an event which each one was obliged to accept as she would, but none the less surely. ' Came it from God? Came it from Satan?' By either it may have come ; but is it not true that Satan is — ourselves?"

The party headed by Gonzales asked themselves no such questions as these, but cautiously, swiftly, and effectively did the work, which history might criticise. No time was allowed the nuns for preparation. Even from the richest convents few articles were carried away as the nuns dispersed. Perhaps more previous preparation than was suspected or afterward acknowledged had been made ; certain it is that the most magnificent and valuable jewels had disappeared from the vestments of the virgins and saints upon the altars. But as quickly as might be the weeping and lamenting sisters were placed in carriages and conveyed to houses ready to receive them ; though many in the confusion wandered out into the darkness and rain afoot, and gave a pathetic chapter to the tale of bloodless martyrdom. As one by one the convents were vacated, the party passed on ; until the smallest and dreariest of those retreats, that which nestled beneath the shadow of the parish church, was reached.

Throughout the work Gonzales had spoken only to give the necessary orders. The measure that in itself had been so dear to his soul was now in its actual execution repugnant to him, — the tears, the sighs, the long processions of black-robed and wailing women distressed his heart, and filled him with shame and anger. As all this continued, his face darkened and a profound melancholy oppressed him. It was raining dismally. In other towns doubtless the same scenes were being enacted. He turned faint, his eyes filled as with blood. Even Ashley Ward, amid the intense interests of the scenes around him, — the views of those grand interiors lighted by the candles borne by the retiring nuns, and the red glare of the soldier's torches, — felt the influence of the deep sadness of this solemn exodus. The clouds of incense sickened him, and through them the glorified Madonnas, the bleeding Christs upon the altars, the troops of black-robed nuns themselves, seemed alike beings of another world, into which he had stepped unbidden. The light shone upon rows and rows of white faces, which looked forth from their wrappings like faces of dead saints. He seemed to see each individual one. He was excited to the utmost; the blood pulsed hotly through every vein, yet a sense of keen disappointment chilled his heart, and unconsciously to himself something of what he read upon the faces of Gonzales and Pedro was reflected upon his own. A profound quiet and solemnity fell upon the party, as they passed the vestibule and penetrated the dim recesses of the Convent of the Martyrs.

There the nuns were all gathered in the chapel, praying and waiting, and the wail of the Miserere stole from the great organ through the dim arches and bare cells. In that place there was nothing of beauty, of grace, of sensuous luxury. The stern austerities of an asceticism scarce surpassed in mediæval days was found behind those massive and windowless walls, which shut out the light, material and moral, of the nineteenth century.

As the men entered the chapel, the nuns fell upon their knees and covered their faces, — all except the abbess, who remained standing to hear the mandate of expulsion.

" Blessed be God ! " responded her deep, pathetic voice, " Blessed be God in all his works ! Sisters, let us go hence ; " and taking up the woful strains when the organ ceased, with each nun adding to them the weird beauty of her voice, the abbess led the way to the portal, and the sisterhood passed into the bleak darkness of the unfamiliar street.

By this time the wind was blowing, — a summer's wind, yet it pierced the bodies upon which for years no air of heaven had blown, — and it was raining heavily. Fortunately many vehicles had gathered at the curb, and ere long the banished nuns were under shelter ; and the work of the night was accomplished.

Ashley Ward, with other officers and gentlemen, had busied himself in bestowing the poor ladies as rapidly and commodiously as possible in the carriages, and as the last one turned the corner of the great building, the soldiers fell into line at the word of command ; and in a few moments he found himself alone. He discovered this when he turned to speak to Gonzales. He was nowhere to be seen, and Ashley remembered that when he had last seen him it was at the chapel door, watching with pale and anxious countenance the exit of the nuns.

Gonzales had been suffering from a recent wound. Had the fatigue and exposure, and that deadly sickness of crushed and dying hope overcome him? Ashley caught up a torch, which was sputtering and about to expire on the dripping pave, fanned for a moment its flame, and then made his way back into the forsaken building.

He found Gonzales standing on the spot where he had parted from him, and before him stood a man with a flickering torch. Both were in an attitude of extreme dejection ; both started as Ashley's footsteps broke the stillness. Pedro — for the second man was he — led the way into the outer darkness, and Gonzales, having in his hand the heavy key which had been delivered by the abbess, turned to lock the abandoned house. He paused and looked to the right and left. The street was utterly forsaken ; the rain came in gusts, and it was with much ado that Pedro, turning hither and thither, kept alive the flame of the torch.

Once as he turned, the light fell full upon the face and

figure of Ward; and at the instant an exclamation of
incredulous joy, followed by a groan, fell upon their ears.
Gonzales dropped the key, and it rang sharply upon the
stones at his feet.

"There is a woman here!" he ejaculated breathlessly.
Something in the tones had drawn the blood from his
heart. "Here! here! a light, Pedro, in God's name!"

The senses of Pedro were even more acute than those of
Gonzales and Ward. Not only had he heard the voice,
but he knew whose it was, and whence it had come. His
torch flashed upon an alcove of the deep wall; and there
ensconced they saw the sombre and meanly clad figure
of a nun. She had covered her face; her form shook
violently.

"Señorita," said Gonzales, recovering himself and respectfully approaching the woman, "forgive us that you
are left behind. We thought all had been provided for
— all."

"It is I who would have it so, — I who promised myself
I would escape," answered the nun, brokenly, yet with an
almost fierce intensity. "Have I not prayed and wept for
this hour? Could I let it pass? No, no! I lingered — I
fled — I could not, would not, go with them. They would
have dragged me with them across the seas — away —
away from her, — my child! my child!"

She uttered the last words almost in a scream, yet her
gaze followed Ward. "Who is he? who is he?" she
asked in a feverish whisper. "It is not my murdered
angel, — my love, my husband, — it is not he; and yet so
like! Oh my God, is it because thou hast forgiven me that
thou bringest this vision before me?"

Gonzales started back; gazed eagerly, rapturously at
the nun; then rushed to clasp the coarse folds of her
drapery. Pedro dropped at her feet. Ward alone uttered
her name, — "Herlinda!"

Gonzales bent over her hand, uttering inarticulate words
of greeting. She scarcely seemed to hear them. "Vicente,
is it thou?" she said faintly. "But he, who is he? — the
man of the yellow hair, with the face that at prayer and at
penance, asleep and awake, has ever haunted me?"

Herlinda stepped nearer to Ward. Her lips were parted,
her eyes aflame; never in all his life before and never

again saw he a woman so beautiful as this one in the unsightly garb, so coarse it grazed the skin where it touched it. "No wonder," he thought, "my cousin loved her; he could have done no other, even had he known he was doomed to die for her!"

Ah! the unhappy daughter of the haughty Garcias was far more beautiful that night than ever John Ashley had beheld her. Suffering first had refined, and now the divine inspiration of hope illumined those perfect features. Ashley Ward comprehended this; but Gonzales with horror recalled her words, and thought her mad. "*Maria Sanctissima!*" she cried as the light flashed full on the American, "I am forgiven, that I behold the living likeness of his face."

Ward bent before her, inexpressibly touched. He would have spoken, but at this instant her eyes fell upon the kneeling man at her feet. "It is Pedro, — yes, it is Pedro," Herlinda said in a low voice. "Perhaps he knows of her, — yet, my God, he dares not look at me!"

"Niña, Niña!"

"Speak, Pedro, speak! thou must know of her. Tell me, was Feliz faithful? Is my child well, happy?"

"Merciful God, she is indeed mad!" interjected Gonzales. "O Herlinda, know you not you never were married, never had a child?"

Herlinda turned on him a glance of mingled entreaty and impatience, then raised her eyes piteously toward heaven. "They said I was not married," she moaned brokenly; "but oh, I had a child, — and they took her from me. Oh, if I could have died!"

Gonzales turned from her with a groan. How bitter was the revelation! Married! It could not have been! And a child? Ah! he knew then why a convent had been her doom.

In a broken voice Pedro began to speak. Ashley, with the red glare of the torch he held falling full upon him, seemed to Gonzales a mocking witness of the shame and woe which from Herlinda were reflected upon him, the man who loved her, had ever loved her; yet he felt instinctively that the American had a right to hear, to judge, as well as he. Ah, it was an American who — "An American!" he gasped, and his hand touched the hilt of his sword.

"Niña, Niña!" Pedro was saying. "They brought the child to me. Oh, the sweet child, with its soft, dark eyes, — oh, the child with its ruddy curls! and I remembered all that you had said, my Señorita. I watched over it, I cherished it, it was my own!"

"Thine! thine!" cried the nun clasping her hands, and in her excitement even thrusting him from her. "It could not be! Oh Feliz, Feliz! thou couldst not be so false!"

The tone of incredulity, of horror, in which she spoke pierced Pedro to the quick; yet he answered humbly, "I thought to please you, Niña, to keep her from those you distrusted; and she was happy, oh quite happy, all through her little childhood. You know one can be quite happy playing in the free air."

The released nun burst into sudden tears. "Happy in the free air! Oh yes, yes!" she cried. "Oh, if all these years I could have begged even from door to door with my child, even with the brand of shame upon me! Oh the suffering, the suffering of these long, long desolate years!"

Gonzales stepped to her side, and placed her arm within his own. "Thou shalt be desolate no more, Herlinda," he said, "thou betrayed angel of purity!"

"Betrayed, no!" cried Ashley Ward, looking up. "Deceived perhaps they both were, but the man who was slain as her betrayer believed himself her husband, as she believed herself his wife, — as I believe now she most truly was. Thank God I am here to champion their cause and that of their child!"

Gonzales left Herlinda a moment to embrace Ward in his southern fashion; then supporting her again listened to what Pedro had to say.

The mother's face grew whiter and whiter as the tale proceeded. "That, *that* my child!" she murmured at intervals, and her head sank lower and lower upon her breast. Even Gonzales and Ward heard with amazement the story of Chinita's appearance at the cave where Pedro had lain wounded. "What!" one cried, "has she not been all this time in the house of Doña Carmen? Did you not tell us that in a strange freak of impatience she had hastened there?"

"It was you, Señores, who affirmed it must be she,

when you heard of the young girl who had been taken
there, from the Indian whom you captured as a spy of
Ramirez," answered Pedro, with the humble cunning of the
true ranchero ; "and why should your servant contradict
you, when Chinita herself had commanded otherwise — "

"And where in God's name is she now?" demanded
Ward. "You know who I am. You know all this time I
could not have rested tranquil had I thought — "

"Have no anxiety, Señor," answered the man with his
old sullenness. "And I swear to you, Niña, she is safe,
quite safe. She is with a woman who can guard her well.
She is gone to seek the man who murdered her father. Ah,
Niña, your daughter has the blood of the Garcia ; she will
avenge you !"

Herlinda sank with a moan. Ashley would have raised
her, but Gonzales motioned him back. There was a house
at a little distance where a widow and her daughters dwelt,
and thither he bore her.

It was then at the middle hour between midnight and
dawn ; and long before light, after a hurried consultation,
the three men met again before the widow's door. All arrangements had been made for the brief transfer of the
command of the troops. Gonzales, Ashley, and Pedro
acted as outriders for a strong military coach drawn by
four fleet mules. Into this stepped Herlinda and the
widow, both dressed as respectable gentlewomen ; and before the people of El Toro wakened from their deep sleep
that followed the excitement of the early night, the travellers were far upon the road, and though the way was long
and rough were gaining fast upon the diligence which
bore Doña Isabel, her daughter, and Chata.

XLV.

On the evening when Doña Isabel and her companions set forth from the village upon their toilsome pilgrimage to Las Parras, two women leaned against the gate-posts at the entrance to the garden where the mistress of Tres Hermanos and the mother of the administrador had parted so many years before, and looked wearily along the silent road. One would not have been surprised to hear that during all these years no other mortal had approached the place, for the air of neglect it had worn then had deepened into that of utter abandonment. It looked not merely disused, but actually shunned. The gate had fallen from its hinges and lay broken upon the rank coarse grass and weeds, which thrusting themselves between the bars filled the paths. Thick clumps of cacti and stunted uncultivated fruit and flowers, with manzanita and other common shrubs of the country, had outgrown and outrooted the feebler growths, and almost hid the low front of the solid but dismantled building, upon which the iron-ribbed shutters hung forlornly like broken armor on a battered image.

The sun and wind and rains had done their work unchecked in all these years, aided by the revolution, which had torn and scathed whatever had attracted its greedy hand and then passed on, leaving desolation to continue or repair the work of destruction. The vines, which had at first served as a graceful drapery, hung so heavily on every porch and wooden projection of the house that they had broken down the frail supports, and added to the general appearance of riot and disorder; while their matted masses offered a defiant obstruction to any adventurous comer. Yet these women had forced a way into the dark and mouldy rooms, and found a certain pleasure and security in their seemingly impenetrable and forbidding aspect.

"We have been here three days," said the younger, who even in the declining light one might see was a mere

girl, while her companion, though small, was old in face
and figure, — not with the dignity of actual age, but with
a sort of lithe grace and abandon, which comes from years
of free and careless action. "We have been three days
waiting, yet he has not come! You may be mistaken.
How can you reckon upon what a man like Ramirez will
do? He is not like a blind man, always led by his dog
upon the same round."

"Necessity and habit are the dogs that lead him," said
the woman with a slight laugh. "Fortune is against him;
he has been beaten from every stronghold. I know this
is the hole he will creep into at last."

"And the people here, they would save him?" said
Chinita, musingly. "He has ever spared them, ever protected them, that he might have a safe refuge in time of
need. Here, here, but for us he would be safe? — but for
us, Dolores?"

"Ah, he is not the first who does not find even nests
where he hoped to find birds," answered the woman called
Dolores. "To-day he is laughing at the little troop of
Liberals patrolling these hills; he will make a way between them. Yes, you will see; here, here, upon this
very road, we shall see him flash by like a meteor, and
then be lost. But my eyes can trace him; my hand will
be able to point the way he has gone."

The woman had unwittingly conjured up a vision that
thrilled the imagination of the listener. "Oh!" she cried
with a sudden gesture of repulsion and weariness, "I am
sick of this mean and miserable life. Would to God I
had gone to him as I vowed to do. Do not tell me he
would have laughed at my rage! No, no! a man could
not laugh at the girl who accused him of the murder of
her father; who stood before him to remind him of all
his secret and unnatural crimes! Ah, I cannot endure
this silent, creeping enmity. Three times already by
our means he has been tracked and driven from his
stronghold; once but for Pepé he would have been
killed, — Ruiz himself would have killed him!"

"Fox against tiger!" cried Dolores, contemptuously.
"Bah! the idiot might have known that with the smell
of blood in the air, not even the shadow of the cross
would save him if he fell into the hands of Ramirez;

yet he rushed on his fate. And for Ramirez there waits for him a doom more just than death on the battlefield, — though you, who warned Pepé to save him, are but a faint-hearted weakling."

"Would you have him die without knowing the revenge that followed him?" cried Chinita. "What would death alone be to such a man as he? It was you, yourself, who first urged Pepé to leave us, — not that he might kill, but if need were save, Ramirez."

"It is true," answered Dolores, mollified; yet she fixed upon Chinita a long and penetrating gaze, which seemed to read her very soul. "But you are a strange, strange creature, — a peasant for all your pride. He is still more a grand gentleman to stare at with fear than a murderer and robber to you."

Chinita's face turned white. The reproach of the woman stung her, yet she felt it was just. "Oh, if I were a man!" she presently muttered; "oh, if I were a man!"

"Yes, the way would have been short then," said Dolores. "Just a knife-thrust, and the debt would have been paid. But the revenge of women can be a thousand times more deep, more sweet, if one has the patience to wait."

"Patience!" exclaimed Chinita in that shrill, metallic voice that indicates a mental tension so violent and long continued that every chord of the nervous system vibrates painfully at a word. "Have I not had patience? Have I not waited at your bidding until I seem to live in a frenzy of fear lest he should escape, and never hear, never see me, never know who I am? And what have I gained? Ruiz is dead; Pepé perhaps is dead. Ah, if I had spoken! Had Ramirez known that I live, it might have saved them both!"

The woman's answering laugh had more of scorn than mirth in it. "Be quiet, child!" she said. "You are young. You think Ramirez has a conscience, and that you would have roused it to torment him. Pshaw! I will arm you with a better weapon; a little patience — perhaps to-morrow — and you will see!"

"Mysteries! always mysteries!" exclaimed Chinita, with increased impatience. "Santa Maria! why do you not push back that black kerchief from your brows?

Have you the mark of a jealous woman's knife across your forehead? Is your hair white, or — or — " She paused, with a horrid suspicion flashing through her mind. Was this woman, with whom she had daily and nightly associated for weeks, a victim of that species of leprosy known as the "painted"? Was some dread trace of it to be seen upon that constantly covered head? Dolores with careless grace had raised and clasped her hands above the unsightly kerchief. The bared arms were clear and fair; only the deep-lined face they encircled looked old, but care, not disease, had marked it. She looked at Chinita through the growing dusk with an inscrutable expression in her almond-shaped and beautiful eyes. They were eyes that still might fascinate at will. Chinita drew a little nearer to her, and sighed deeply. There was a sense of guilt upon the girl's mind since she had heard of the death of Ruiz; a sickening apprehension, too, for the fate of Pepé Ortiz.

Dolores read her thoughts. She dropped one hand from her head upon the young girl's shoulder. There seemed something magnetic in the touch. Chinita, though she would rather have resisted, yielded to it, — like a nettle grasped in a strong hand. "Silly one," said the woman soothingly, "fret not yourself for Ruiz. Ramirez knew him better than did you. He had had long years to con the lesson in. It is well for the weak defenceless creatures of the earth that these wild beasts attack and destroy one another!"

Chinita looked unconvinced. In spite of doubts, she had had a certain pride and solace in the belief that Ruiz would prove true to Ramirez, — true through his love for her. She had purposely left him ignorant of the change in her own views and feelings in regard to Ramirez that he might be free to act upon his own impulses and convictions. She knew not what she would have had him do, yet all the same he had disappointed her. She had no clews to the motives of Ruiz, other than those Dolores suggested to her, and there was an uncertainty and vagueness overhanging him which made him in her eyes a victim to his love for her, and a fresh cause for accusation of the man who seemed destined utterly to bereave and despoil her. Strangely enough, in her wildest excitement Chinita had never formulated for herself any definite mode of action when she should see Ramirez, — as see him, accuse, defy him she would ! There had been a conviction in her mind that in her the ghosts of the innocent he had slain, the shame, — which with strange perversity he had shrunk from when it menaced his family pride in the person of Herlinda Garcia, — the contempt and hatred of his wronged sister, would all rise to confront and overwhelm him. That which should follow, time, circumstance would determine ; but that the wild fever of her passion would be satisfied she would not doubt. She had longed with an ever increasing excitement to find herself before Ramirez, and to pour forth her wrongs in burning words. Yet this woman Dolores, with a fascination even greater than the unconscious one that Ramirez himself had exerted over her, had withheld her from her purpose, had even led her to gain the secrets of the chieftain's plans from his most trusted confidants, — the young girl reddened with shame and anger, yet with flattered vanity, when she remembered that the sight of her beauty had been more potent than the gold of Dolores. Chinita had not guessed that she had been purposely employed to act the part of a spy, and had resented deeply the fact that her discoveries had more than once been transmitted to Gonzales, and that her revenge was supposed to be gratified by the consequent defeat which had overcome Ramirez. Her longing was for a more dramatic, more direct revenge. Pedro and Dolores could plot and scheme for the silent overthrow of him who had wronged them ; they gloried in their astuteness that made him an unsuspicious victim, while Chinita writhed under it, and only the promise that in Las Parras she should accuse Ramirez face to face had made endurable to her the life of secret intrigue and absolute disguise and constant change that she had led for weeks. The element of peril, it is true, had stimulated her adventurous spirit ; but she would fain have been in the midst, not hovering a ready fugitive upon the edge of the fray.

When weeks before Chinita had, after her faintness, opened her eyes in the low, rocky cave in which Pedro lay, it had been to find him an almost unrecognizable mass of wounds and bruises, lying on a sheepskin pallet, gazing at her with wide-distended eyes, and ejaculating

in tones of dismay, mingled with incredulous delight,
"What have I done? Oh God! is it possible that she
has come to me,—the miserable, dying Pedro?"

"Yes, yes, Pedro, I am here!" she cried staggering
to her feet. "Ah, the American thought I had forgotten
thee; but thou wert in my heart all the time that he
talked. Ah, though I am of other blood, it is thou that
hast saved me! They would have thrust me out to die.
I will cling to thee while thou livest; I will avenge thee
when thou diest!"

"Hush!" muttered Pedro faintly, as she stooped and
kissed his hand, bedewing it with her tears. "Ah, I
shall not die, now you have come. Did I not tell you,"
he asked, turning to a figure beside Chinita, "that I
should live if I could know she loved me?"

"And this is the girl you have nurtured?" asked the
stifled voice of a woman. She was not as tall as Chinita,
and she held a candle up close to the face of the girl to
look at her. Chinita was spent with fatigue; moreover
there were tears on her face, and she resented the inspection, pushing away the woman's hand rudely. Yet
it was not that of a servant, nor of a woman of the lower
class. Even in the excitement of the moment Chinita
was conscious of wondering who and what this person
was. How came she there in the cave among these
fugitives?

"But for her I should have been dead already," Pedro
was saying. "She has wondrous skill and knowledge of
surgery and herbs. But," he added, in a low, apologetic
voice, "she knows all. I have talked in my delirium. I
could not help it. You will pardon me,—if I die you will
pardon me?"

"I have nothing to pardon!" cried Chinita. "What!
you think because my mother lives I would hide her name?
No, no! I have endured enough for her cowardice and the
shame of Doña Isabel. No, no! let me but see Ramirez,
—this Leon Vallé,—and though it be before all the world,
I will declare who I am. The American, Ashley Ward,
says he will claim me as his cousin. Pepé must ride and
tell him I am here, and we will have vengeance together
for the cruel deeds of Ramirez. You shall be avenged,
Pedro, you shall be avenged!"

The sick man's eyes glistened. As she spoke, Chinita's face had glowed with an unrelenting and cruel intensity of purpose. The woman at her side had never once removed her eyes from her. No one was noticing her; had they done so, they would have beheld an extraordinary series of changes pass over her dark but mobile face, — suspicion, delight, doubt, alarm, conviction. · Suddenly she seized Chinita's hand, and pressed it to her heart; it was beating so tumultuously that the young girl drew back startled. The woman thrust her hands under the loose folds of the black kerchief that draped her head with a sombre yet Oriental grace, then withdrawing them caught a stray lock of Chinita's hair, and burst into a long, low, triumphant laugh.

Chinita drew herself away, alarmed and offended. Pepé had come in; and looking at her anxiously he said, "Nina, do not mind her. Esteban tells me she is a mad woman; yet she does no harm. She does not know what she talks of, and one moment denies what she has said at another. It would not be strange if she should tell you some dreadful tale, and afterward laugh, and say grief had made her mad!"

"And so it has," cried the woman. "Ah yes, I have been mad; but that is past. Yes, yes. Life of my soul," turning to Chinita, "how beautiful thou art! And the hair, it is a miracle! In all the world there should be no other with such hair. Thou hast had good fortune, Pedro, to bring up such a child. She is an angel. Ah, it is as if I had seen her all my life! And thou hast a spirit to match thy face," she added turning again to Chinita. "Thou canst not brook a wrong. Well, well! we will make common cause; and some day—soon, soon we will stand together before Leon Vallé with such a tale, such a revenge, that even he will sink before it. To think that after all these years, I shall turn against him the dagger with which he has pierced me!"

"Who are you? What do you know of me?" cried Chinita, shuddering, though she understood that the weapon of which the stranger spoke was no material tool. "Why should you join with me, or I with you? No, no; when Pedro is able, we will go away, you your way, and I mine!"

"Our ways lie together!" cried the woman, excitedly. "The one without the other would fail. Oh! you think me mad, but I am not. I could tell you things, — but no, I will wait; perhaps thou hast not even heard of me. Ah! how many years is it since I disappeared from the world, that I have been forgotten?"

Pedro raised himself upon his elbow painfully, and gazed at her with a long and eager scrutiny. "I know you now," he said, "though I never saw you but once, and then you were beautiful as the Holy Madonna on the high altar at Pueblo."

"Yes," she interrupted; "I am Dolores, whom Vallé loved. Ah, you think that strange, because my beauty is gone, and I am old, and like a witch, living in this murky cave! Where else should I go — I, whom he stole away and betrayed, and despoiled and forsook?"

"But you are rich," said Pepé in wonder, and in a tone that seemed to condone the rest.

"Rich!" she said scornfully. "Rich! yes, for such needs as mine. Rich! he used to give me jewels a queen might have been proud of. He thought I wasted, lost, destroyed them, as he would have done, but I kept them, — kept them for my child. Ah, I knew she would be beautiful, would be worthy of the rarest and costliest I could give her. Ah, I would give her jewels! such jewels as would buy her love, were she as capricious, as hard, as Ramirez himself."

Chinita drew back from her, with a certain hauteur, a certain loathing upon her face. "I have heard of you," she said coldly. "You chose your lot. If you have wrongs, they can be nothing to mine. See"— and she pointed to Pedro — "what Ramirez has done but now; while but for his murderous knife my father would have lived, and my mother would not have been obliged to hide her disgraced head in a convent, and I should not have been left a pauper at the gate of my mother's house."

"There can be no wrongs greater than these?" said the woman half interrogatively, half affirmatively. "Yet listen! He stole me away from my husband; I swear I did not go willingly, though I loved him, — oh my God, how I loved him! For him I died to the world. I forsook the father who was dear to me as life. I lived a life of infamy, hiding in obscure villages, in mountain huts, in caves when need were. I bore him children; but they died, — all died as though there was a curse upon them. That angered him; then he grew cold, then false and cruel. One day a captive was brought into the camp for ransom, — a captive he himself had made. He sent to me to look at the man and to set a price upon his head. I went, as he told me, in gay attire, with jewels blazing on my arms and neck, a diadem upon my head. When the prisoner looked up and saw me, with the price of my shame as he thought upon me, he staggered, gasped, and fell down dead. He was my father. My senses fled, yet when another child was born they returned to me. She was strong and beautiful. I clasped my treasure; but my heart burned against her father. I swore I would leave him, that I would hide the child where he never should discover her. Fool! fool! that I was! When I woke next day, for in my weakness I slept, the babe was gone, — dead they told me; gone too the pretty clothing I had made, the little trinkets I had placed about her neck. But the blessed prayers I had bought from the holy nuns of La Piedad were not in vain! No, no! wretch, demon, that he was!"

Chinita's heart beat suffocatingly. "What! you think the child was still living?" she said.

"I know it! I know it!" cried Dolores. "I feel it here, — here in my heart, which beats for her. And some-time, when I find that child, if I do find her, think you she will love me? Think you she will hate her father as I do? Think you she will avenge my wrongs and hers?"

"But if he loved her," said Chinita; "if he meant to separate her from — from such a woman as you had been! Oh, I know you have suffered, that you have reason for vengeance; but —" she cried hysterically, striking her hands together, terribly moved, she knew not why. The strange woman broke into sobs, piteous to hear. Chinita clasped her hands. "But you would not have her — your child — his child — hate the man you loved?"

"Hate him!" echoed Dolores. "I would have her hate him with such hate as she would bear toward the fiends of hell. I would have her know him as you know him, — the insatiable monster who wrecked the happiness of a sister too fond, even when most foully wronged, to seize the vengeance that was within her grasp. Ah, Doña Isabel it was who set him free to murder, to betray, to wrench the child from its maddened mother, and cast it out by the first rude and careless hand that would do his will! My God! were you his child could you have pity? Would you not feel your wrongs, — the wrongs of the mother who bore you?"

Dolores spoke with the wild excitement of one who for years had brooded on this theme. Chinita herself seemed to be struggling with some fantasy of a disordered brain. The woman actually glared upon her, as if on her reply hung her destiny. Overcome by the unexpected demand upon her sympathy, — a demand that the peculiar circumstances of her life made irresistibly impressive, — Chinita shrank with horror at the tumult of emotion which revealed to her mind the possibilities of her own passionate nature.

"Tell me no more! Ask me no more!" she cried. "Ah, if I were his daughter! But no, I am the daughter of Herlinda Garcia, and of the man he murdered in secret. Yes, I will seek Ramirez out. I — I — O God! I know not what I will do, but I will have justice! revenge! revenge!"

The girl ended with a scream, and fell down, burying her head on Pedro's shoulder. The wounded man, his ghastly face pressed close against her twining hair, looked appealingly to the excited woman who stood over them. There was scorn, rage, intense offence upon her face; but slowly they died out, and she turned away with the weary air of one in whom some periodic excess of passion or madness had wrought its work and brought its consequent exhaustion. A half hour later she brought the girl some food, wonderfully dainty for the place and its resources, and gently fed and soothed her. Pepé and Pedro looked on wonderingly. All that had been said had passed so quickly that they had not realized that aught of consequence had happened; but in the quiescent attitude of Chinita, and the strange calm that had fallen upon the excited and erratic woman, they instinctively felt that a new phase of life had begun for them. A new spirit was in future to lead and rule them; and it dwelt in the frame of this half-crazed woman, who had declared herself mistress of the cave. The men thenceforth seemed led by a spell; and to the same spell Chinita gradually succumbed.

This had been the first meeting of Chinita with the woman who stood talking with her nearly two months later at the garden gate of Las Parras. They had left the cave weeks before, — Pepé and Pedro, the latter still bruised and maimed, to join the troops of Gonzales; and Chinita, unable to resist the influence of Dolores, followed rebelliously with swift and unerring movement the fortunes of Ramirez. By what arguments Pedro had been won to consent to separate from his foster-child, and to maintain silence concerning her to Ashley, can be but guessed; though certain it is that Chinita on her part reminded him of the promise he had made Herlinda to protect her child from Doña Isabel, to whose care she justly suspected Ashley Ward would strive to return her. Meanwhile Dolores adroitly fostered in the girl's mind that hope of a peculiar and swift revenge, which was to satisfy at once the many wrongs that in those diverse lives were clamorous for justice; while an intense anticipation urged the gatekeeper to hasten without delay to join the Liberal army, — the anticipation of that event which presented to his mind such wondrous possibilities. The convents once opened, would Herlinda claim her child? Would she by some strange miracle confront Leon Vallé and her proud mother with the proof of that which Ashley Ward had in spite of adverse law and custom declared still possible, — the proof of her marriage with the American who had been slain without accusation, without the possibility of defence?

Pedro could not reason; he could but doggedly wait, and guard with silent fidelity and ferocity the charge that had been given him. That a superior intelligence, an undeclared authority potent as an armed power, had for a time wrested Chinita from him, made him only the more tenacious when once again he held her in his grasp. His foster-child while in the mountains with the woman whose life was bound in the same interests, the same mysteries, as her own, was safe from the possibilities of removal from his cognizance.

Pedro was asked no questions which he cared not to

answer, when he presented himself among the Liberal forces. Ashley, tranquil in the belief that Chinita was with Doña Carmen in Guanapila, avoided more than casual mention of her name ; and Pedro jealously guarded his secret, and patiently waited the moment he superstitiously believed would come, — the moment which, when it did come, gave him the sharpest sting he had ever known in his stoical existence ; when Herlinda Garcia cried in uncontrollable horror and dismay, " What ! you, — *you* have brought up my child? She was given to *you!* "

On the journey from El Toro there was but one thought in the mind of him who had served with such blind faithfulness. For the first time a doubt tormented him. " Would the beautiful, uncontrollable idol of his heart satisfy the longing — the years of longing — of the woman who freed from her bonds was hastening to claim her daughter and acknowledge her before the world? " As the hours passed, Pedro shunned the eyes of Herlinda, though they looked upon him with a grateful affection that should have been at once an invitation to confidence and a recompense of his long fidelity. Yet with the remembrance of Chinita ever before him, the glance of Herlinda seemed that of accusation and reproof. Her words rang like a knell in his heart. He, who knew the vices and virtues of the two castes which he and the still beautiful woman represented, knew that like oil and water they were irreconcilable, and understood the full significance of that involuntary cry, " What! *you*, — *you* have brought up *my* child? "

XLVI.

A LEAGUE or less from the village of Las Parras there stood — and perhaps still stands — a small chapel, built, no one knows in fulfilment of what pious vow, at the entrance to a mountain pass of the roughest and most dangerous sort alike from the forces of Nature and of humanity. Likely enough some rich hidalgo, escaping from brigands, raised here the humble pile, and vowed that the lamp should ever burn before the Virgin and her blessed Child. But through the long years of war, as a pious ranchera had said in holy horror, the blessed Babe had remained in darkness. But some time after midnight, one rainy night, a sudden flash of flame lighted up not only the dingy altar but the whole of the small mouldy interior of the chapel, and a scene was revealed which a passing monk might have viewed with reverence, so nearly must it have copied one that may have been common enough when Joseph and Mary journeyed to Jerusalem, eighteen hundred years and more ago.

This thought indeed entered the mind of a man who riding through the drizzling rain caught a glimpse of the unusual light through the unguarded doorway, and reining his horse gazed curiously in. At first the place seemed to him full of women and jaded beasts; then he saw there were but four of each, and that one of the human creatures was a man, — a priest. The women, — good heavens! they were the Señora Doña Isabel Garcia, and the girl whom he had once seen under circumstances almost as extraordinary, — she whom he knew as the daughter of Ramirez and the foster-child of Don Rafael. Of the other woman he scarcely thought, yet he instinctively guessed she was Doña Carmen. Ashley Ward looked round in bewilderment. Only that day some definite account of what had occurred at Tres Hermanos had reached him, told by a man who had been with the administrador and his mother

29

in their vain endeavors to trace the girl who had been so boldly spirited away. The search had been long delayed because of the illness of Doña Feliz; but once begun, it had been prosecuted with untiring zeal. Not a village, scarce a hut throughout that region had been unvisited, yet all in vain.

Ashley had heard the tale with deepest sympathy. Oh inconceivable obtuseness! that it had not once occurred to him or to Gonzales that the girl of whom they had heard as sojourning with Doña Carmen, and whom he had believed to be Chinita, might prove to be her vanished play-mate, — simply because the remembrance of the house of Doña Carmen had slipped from their minds when their supposed knowledge of the movements of Chinita made Doña Carmen's young guest no longer an object of interest to them, simply because the means adopted by Ramirez for the security of Chata would never have suggested themselves to minds less daring, less original than his own. Ashley Ward turned from the doorway dazed. The presence of these personages in such a place, at such a time, seemed unreal, bewildering, ominous.

Upon the heavy sand the horse that Ashley rode had made so little noise that it had not roused the miserable travellers as they cowered wet and shivering around the sputtering fire, upon which the priest with unhesitating hands threw some dry portion of a wooden railing and the broad cover of a sacred book of music. Vain sacrifice! for being of parchment it but curled and blackened, yet would not burn any more than would the bare stone floor upon which the welcome embers lay.

Turning back a few paces Ward encountered the carriage he had accompanied thither. With bowed heads, endeavoring thus to shelter their faces from the mist, General Gonzales and the servant Pedro rode, one on either side of the heavy travelling carriage. Just as Ward appeared they caught sight of the light. The coachman and his helper, half dead as they were from want of sleep, saw it too, and all the mules were stopped as though transfixed. The men began to mumble prayers, crossing themselves with unction. Gonzales, following his habit of caution as well as the motion of Ward, rode softly forward to reconnoitre.

Before the occupants of the carriage had time to question the meaning of the stoppage, Gonzales had returned. His face was white with excitement as he dismounted and opened the door of the vehicle.

"Señorita," he said in a voice that shook from suppressed emotion, " a wonderful thing has happened!"

Herlinda leaned eagerly forward. She caught the gleam of the light and the grim outline of the chapel against the leaden sky. " Is my child — Leon, my uncle — here?" she gasped.

" No, no! that would not be so strange; we may perhaps at any moment encounter them. But your mother, your sister, — they are in yonder church, drenched, wretched; travellers seemingly more anxious, more eager than ourselves. From a word I heard, they too seek — your child."

Gonzales spoke the last two words with evident difficulty and repugnance. Herlinda did not notice that. She scarce had heard more than the words, " Your mother, your sister." In trembling haste she descended from the carriage. Instinctively she clasped the arm of Ashley Ward to support her through the inequalities of the roadway; and followed by Gonzales and Pedro, who had dismounted, she sped with surprising fleetness to the open door of the chapel.

At the sound of approaching footsteps, those within sprang to their feet in terror. Even the brutes hurtled together within the very rail of the altar, leaving free the space between the fire and the low arch beneath which the intruders stood. The women stood panting, their hands clasped upon their hearts, their lips parted, their eyes staring wildly. Doña Isabel was foremost. She first saw as in a vision her daughter, whom she believed still within convent walls, supported by the arm of the American. She sank upon her knees; her tongue clave to the roof of her mouth.

" Mother," said Herlinda in a voice which gave conviction of the reality of her presence, " I am no ghost. The convents have been opened, — I am free. Where is my daughter? You took her from me, — give her back to me. My child! my child!"

She advanced into the chapel with a gesture so earnest,

so impassioned, that it seemed that of concentrated power and anguish combined.

Doña Isabel bowed her head on her hand. Under the red light of the fire her form seemed to shrink and wither. "Have mercy! oh, Herlinda, have mercy!" she moaned. "Your child is not here. I am seeking her, oh with what grief, what anguish! Ah, my God, it is true, — all, all that you can say to me!" She raised her eyes and they fell upon Gonzales. "I thought to save your honor and mine. That there still might be love and joy for you, I gave the child to Feliz to do with as she would. I did not think, I could not think —"

"Cruel, cruel mother!" cried Herlinda, "and false Feliz! Oh, what reproaches will be bitter enough, sharp enough, to heap upon her! She promised me she would love my child, care for it, protect it, — yes, even from you, unnatural mother that you were! Yet together you have degraded, perhaps brought about the ruin of, my child! I have been shut in from all the world, — and yet I am not the weak girl I was. No, the heart and brain of a woman grow even in utter darkness. You had no right to thrust my child away. No, she was mine, — come disgrace, come scorn, what would, she was mine. You tore her from me, — give her back to me!"

While this extraordinary scene took place, Chata with indescribable emotion recognized the pale impulsive face of the nun of El Toro, — so pale still, so worn, yet so strangely young, and lighted by the intense and resolute spirit of a wronged and noble woman.

"Yes, give me back my child!" reiterated Herlinda. "Ah, Mother, I read your heart; I know now better than I did then your motives for utterly ignoring, utterly denying my connection with the American. Your brother killed him: it was to shelter him, Leon Vallé, as much as to hide what you believed my shame, that you tore my baby from me. You resolved that there should be neither wonder nor question that could incriminate your idol. Oh, a sister's love, a sister's sacrifice is beautiful; but where in all the world before has it been stronger, more prescient than that of the mother for her child?"

Doña Isabel raised her hands above her head as though to ward off some crushing blow. Carmen rushed forward and caught her sister's hand. "Herlinda," she cried, "say no more. I am your sister — I am Carmen! Oh, I have always known there was a mystery; yet I have loved you, believed you true, believed you pure. You were almost a child, — you knew not the evil!"

"I was not a child!" returned Herlinda, proudly, yet clasping her sister with a grateful joy. "For all my trusting love I would not have stooped to sin. I was married. Yes," she added defiantly, "though all the world deny it, I was married. God grant that I may one day stand before my husband's murderer, — oh, with that word I will overwhelm him. What! he, the ravisher, the assassin, think to avenge *my* honor!"

The form of the excited woman dilated as she spoke. Through the dim chapel her voice pealed with a ring of purity and truth, more clear than the tone of silver bells. There was a clamor of answering voices. Even the priest started forward, but Chata caught his flowing gown and whispered him in broken accents, —

"Oh, for the pity of God hide me. Let her not see me! Oh, this is too terrible, too terrible!" She shook with dread. "Madre Sanctissima, it will kill me if her eyes fall upon me! I am the daughter of the man she seeks. O Virgin of Succors, pity me!"

The burly person of the priest supported and sheltered the stricken and trembling girl. "Courage, courage!" he whispered. "Thou shalt plead for him. For thy sake she will forego the claims of justice, — she will forgive!" He naturally attributed her emotion to apprehensions for her father's fate. "Yes, even I will plead with her."

But in the brief space of this interference there had been a movement at the door, and a strange voice was heard. Gonzales — who throughout had stood just back of Herlinda, chafing that he was not at her side, for he would have championed her before the world — disappeared for a moment; then returning, strode forward to the fire and raised Doña Isabel with a not unkindly though imperious hand.

"Señora," he said, "I have this moment heard news of Ramirez, brought by an escaped prisoner, one of your own men, Pepé Ortiz by name. As we suspected, the defeated and desperate chief is on his way to, perhaps has entered, Las Parras. There is no time to be lost. With him — accusing him, for such was her mad purpose — we may find your daughter's child. Oh, would to God," he added with fervor, " I had known this horrible blight upon Herlinda's young life! I would have sheltered, I would have sustained her. I would have appealed to Rome."

Doña Isabel looked at Gonzales in a dazed way, slightly swaying as she stood. " Thou wert ever noble, ever true," she said dreamily. "Thou lovedst her. But Leon? She spoke of Leon. Then it is true! He did indeed murder the American. But he is dead; he is dead."

The mind of the poor lady seemed wandering. She stood looking about her with an awful smile. Gonzales saw that she did not connect the name of Ramirez with her brother. Illness, exertion, and the intense emotions of that hour had made it impossible for her to receive any fresh impressions, or even to recall those that perhaps had once faintly suggested themselves and had faded. She was conscious of but one thought, one hope. " Herlinda's child, Herlinda's child!" she repeated again and again. " O God, to find, to give back the child!"

The agonized woman would have clasped the hand of Gonzales appealingly, but he had turned and led Herlinda from the place. Chata, gliding toward Doña Isabel, drew the arm of the suffering lady around her neck, and murmuring fond words, thus stood supporting her. And thus some moments later Ashley Ward found them. The young girl seemed in his eyes the very embodiment of Tenderness supporting Despair.

Ashley took her hand. " Oh, Chata!" he said, " what a fearful error this has been! And Chinita, where shall we find her? Poor girl, poor girl! God grant she has not found that man; the horrible fascination he held over her might prove more fatal than her newly-sworn hatred. Come, come, let us hasten. It is at least certain that Ramirez is at this moment in Las Parras."

" Chinita!" cried Chata, her heart sickening. " What, is Chinita the child of Doña Herlinda? I love her, but oh she — the Señorita Herlinda! No, no, it cannot be!"

Ashley smiled drearily. " The eagle is sometimes found in a dove's nest," he said. " Ah, with such a mother what a glorious woman that strange defiant creature might

have become! But what powers for good have been debased in those low associations among which she was
thrown!"

The young man stopped, remembering Doña Isabel;
but she had moved away. She was already at the door.
Gonzales, who was returning for her, led her silently to
the carriage. The widow who had been with Herlinda
had dismounted and joined Chata and the priest, as they
issued from the gloomy chapel. The poor woman looked
confused and wretched; it was a comfort to her to hear
the muttered benediction of the friar.

Chata mounted the sorry beast on which she had come,
despite the remonstrance of Ashley. "No, no, I cannot
bear the accusing gaze of the Señorita Herlinda," she
protested. "You, Don 'Guardo, know who I am. My
place is at Leon Vallé's side, not here. O God, would
that it were not so!"

The rain had ceased. There was a streak of dawn in
the sky. The road lay like a pale yellow serpent, which
grew brighter as they followed its sinuous twinings among
the hills. There was a slight accident, which detained the
carriage; but Chata, accompanied by Pepé, — who had recognized her with amazement, and who gave her a brief
account of all that had happened in the life of Chinita
since they had parted, — hastened on as speedily as was
possible to her jaded beast. Just at the dawn she found
herself entering the straggling town; and suddenly the
mass of verdure beyond a broken wall which they were
skirting, and over which she was gazing with eyes as
heavy as the dripping herbage, sparkled as with a thousand diamonds. The sun had risen; and facing it — his
eyes so dazzled that the figures upon the roadway were to
him like the scattered trees, mere black, shapeless masses
— was the object of her dread, yet also at that moment
of her fondest anguish bloody and travel-stained with the
marks of battle and flight upon him, the wreck of what
she had last seen him.

Filial duty and womanly pity supplied the place of that
love which she could not conjure even then, and with a
cry she drew rein at the prostrate gate; and to the amazement of Pepé, who knew nothing of the relations between
the young girl and the defeated chieftain, she sprang to

the ground and rushed to the embrace of the hunted man.
Looking back she saw the others approaching, and sought
to repel them by an entreating gesture. Her voice was
heard in warning; but Ramirez heeded it no more than
he did the sound of wheels and the tread of horses on
the roadway. He had known of late such strange vicissitudes and such unaccountable experiences, which had
been so unforeseen, often so disastrous yet fleeting, that
they seemed the phantasmagoria of a frightful dream.
These noises, these figures, were but the same to his
stunned senses. But this girl in his arms, who called him
father, — she was real flesh and blood, and thrilling with
life. He clung to her with rapture; and as he would
have done in a dream, he saw her there without surprise,
— only with a vague bewilderment, a fear that she too
would fade away. No! She clung to him with tears,
as though seeking to protect him from some menaced
danger.

Ah, he understood: this man who had reached them
was the American who had accused him at the grave of
him whom he had murdered. Great God! Had beings
of this world and the other combined against him? There
was Pedro, or his ghost; there too was Herlinda! Yes,
though it was years since he had seen her, and then only
for a moment in her lover's arms, he knew her instantly.

Ramirez recoiled before her glance. His arms fell
from Chata. The released nun, who had not known
that the young girl had been of their company, thrust
her aside, then caught her hand and looked searchingly
into her face. Her own face quivered as she looked. It
grew whiter and whiter still, as Chata raised her eyes and
returned the gaze.

"I saw you from the convent grate — at El Toro," said
Herlinda, breathlessly.

Carmen's face brightened like that of one who solves a
joyful mystery. Chata sighed deeply.

"Chata," cried Ashley, who divined what must be in
the mind of Herlinda, "speak! Tell the Señorita that
you are not her daughter. Her suspense is terrible!"

But Chata could not utter a word. Ramirez broke into
a laugh. He himself heard that betrayal of his overstrained nerves with a shudder. He would not have

laughed had his will served. Why should he laugh?
Then the shame, he thought, of this poor Herlinda had
been complete. She had a child; she had come to the
avenger of her shame hoping to find the lost proof of her
frailty. Even his sister Doña Isabel was crying wofully,
" Oh Leon, Leon, is it thou? Art thou the Ramirez my
poor Chinita loved? Oh, in pity give her back to me! I
will forgive all — yes, even Norberto's death — if thou
wilt give Herlinda her child."

" You are all mad! " cried Ramirez, recalled to himself.
" What know I of Herlinda's child, or even that she ex-
ists? I only know that this is mine," he laid his hand
upon Chata, — " she of whom you thought to cheat me.
Ah, had I known there was another infant to claim your
secret love," he added mockingly, " I could have better
disposed of my own! "

While the unrepentant brother of Doña Isabel was saying this, Pedro in gruff and surly accents was reminding
him of the girl who had stopped him upon the road years
before, and had given him an amulet. Yes, the impatient listener remembered her; he had heard her name, —
Chinita; that was the girl of whom Rafael had spoken,
she who had been the foundling of the gatekeeper. A
vision of the unkempt, witch-like creature who had startled
his horse, as she stood under that accursed mesquite-tree,
rose before him. Was that Herlinda's child? She stood
still with her hand upon Chata, gazing upon her incredulously. Ramirez threw it off in sudden passion.

" Uncle Leon," said Herlinda humbly, hopelessly, " you
killed my husband. Oh, I would forgive you that, could
you give me my child! Oh, when I saw this girl here — "
she dropped her face into her hands and wept.

" Shame on you! " cried Ramirez. The sight of
woman's tears irritated him, and Herlinda's assertion of
her marriage made blacker still a deed whose silent,
stealthy consummation had ever been to him a secret
cause of shame. " What though I killed your lover, was
it not to avenge the honor of the Garcias? "

" The honor of those you had disgraced! " cried the
outraged woman scornfully, — " of her whose life you had
crushed! No, your hand was ready for murder, your
heart delighted in blood, — and so you killed my love,

without a word of warning; and because in your vile, cruel heart you could believe no woman pure, no man just, you thus brought in an instant desolation and ruin upon me!" Ramirez shrank before the indignant pathos of her voice. "Ah," she added, "all, all this I would forgive — O God, have I not prayed to thee and thy saints for grace to forgive? — if I could but behold my child. They tell me she has followed you, — one says because of the strange infatuation your mad career presents to her; another, that she may avenge her wrongs, her father's murder. I warn you! beware! such a girl is not to be scorned."

"I know nothing of her," cried Ramirez, vehemently. "Here is your mother — Pedro; they have known the girl, they should render you an account of her. As for me, there is a man here who upon the grave of him I killed declared himself his avenger: it is to him I will answer for that deed."

Ashley Ward involuntarily drew his sword, eager for the offered combat; but Pedro and Gonzales threw themselves between the two men. "This is neither the time nor the place," exclaimed Gonzales; while Herlinda cried, "Do not touch my uncle for your life! My mother, my mother!"

Doña Isabel had indeed thrown herself upon her knees before the priest, and frantically implored his interposition. As he raised her he was seen to speak; but no one heard his words, for shrill female voices in altercation added to the confusion of the moment, and every eye was turned in the direction whence they came.

"Let me go! let me go! I will hear no more! I will wait no longer! He will escape. Oh, it is not with such weak words I will speak!"

Two female figures issued panting from the covert, — it seemed that the elder woman had striven to hold the other back, but the younger had triumphed. Doña Isabel uttered a cry of infinite gratitude and joy. Chata caught and held the girl as she came. "Chinita! thank God," she cried, "you are here!"

Pedro in an ecstasy seized the robe of Herlinda. "There, there," he cried, "is your child! your beautiful child!"

" Yes ! " cried Chinita in mad excitement which only burning words could relieve. Not then could she pause for fond greetings or reverent tears ; the sight of Ramirez seemed at once to fire yet absorb her wildest passions. She sprang toward him, as one may suppose the lion's whelp faces a tiger that in some fierce struggle has filled the air with the scent of blood. The very aroma arouses and maddens its kindred nature. With an outburst of eloquence which like arrows tipped with venom seemed to sting and paralyze the object upon which they were directed, she assailed Ramirez with the story of his crimes ; and separated from the picturesque and daring events that had accompanied and disguised them, and told with dramatic eloquence and vivid anger, they thrilled every listener with shuddering abhorrence and dismay. Blackest of all, she pictured the murder of John Ashley. Ramirez himself seemed visibly to shrink and wither before her scathing words, while Herlinda pressed her hands over her ears, entreating her to cease. The agonized woman could not endure the vivid rendition, for the girl unconsciously acted out, as she conceived, the scene of midnight murder.

From the moment of Chinita's appearance, Ramirez had seemed overwhelmed as by the sight of some unearthly being ; and while she spoke his eyes riveted themselves upon her, his jaw fell, his countenance took the hue of death. Suddenly the girl burst into wild sobs and tears. Her rage was spent. " Go, go ! " she said, — " you who have cursed my life, you who killed my father, you who condemned my mother to a convent and me to a beggar's life ; for was it strange they cast me out, hoping I should die? And so I should have done but for Pedro — Fiend, to pursue him with devilish tortures after so many years ! Oh ! that it was which brought my hate upon you. Ah, I had loved you from a child, — not with a woman's fancy, but as though the thought of you were the very soul that was born with me. Of you I thought, for you I prayed — was it not so, Chata? It was I who gave you the amulet they said would insure life and fortune. I planned and schemed to give you wealth and power. Ah, even when I knew the cursed wrong you had done me, I could not believe, I could not realize ; that murdered man had been dead so long he seemed of another world, another time, — he seemed nothing to me. But the torture of Pedro, — ah, that was real, that was of my life; it maddened me. Ah! ah! ah! it brought your downfall. You have wondered how your skill, your well-laid plans, your valor, all have failed you. It was because of me! because of us!"

Chinita turned and indicated her companion with a gesture of her hand. She saw then what had riveted the gaze of Ramirez, and rather than her words had held each witness dumb. Dolores—her face kindled into fictitious youth, her beautiful eyes gleaming with a flame that seemed to scathe — had drawn from her brows the kerchief she had worn. The act had revealed a wondrous mass of brown hair, with the russet tinge of the chestnut, gleaming in the sunlight with threads and spirals of gold. The two heads, that of Chinita and of the woman, seemed to have been modelled the one from the other, so exact was their form, and so similar the texture and color and peculiar growth of the marvellous wealth of curls that crowned them both.

Chinita drew back with dilated eyes, speechless with the overwhelming horror of conviction. Chata would have clasped her in her arms, but she drew herself away. In the woman whose wild laugh rang upon the air Chata recognized the one who had thrown herself before the horse of Ramirez, and who had lain a bruised and shameful figure upon the convent steps at El Toro.

There was a moment of profound silence. Even the sultry air seemed waiting, as though for the thunderclap that follows the lightning flash.

"Ah, Leon Vallé! you know now who accuses you," cried the woman. "Oh, is not this a sweet revenge, to curse you by the lips of your own child, — the child you robbed me of? What! you thought *that* your child!" she pointed with ineffable contempt to Chata, who in the overwhelming excitement of the moment clung to the pallid and trembling Herlinda. "Bah! what is she to the beautiful being I bore you,— into whose soul was infused the idolatrous love that had been wrested from my heart, the love that had been my ruin? Ah, such love dies hard! It lived again in her, — it lived in her heart for *you*. Because of it I dared not claim her, though I knew her the moment my eyes fell upon her, — yes, as you know her now. In whom but in our child could be reproduced this wonderful wealth of hair you used to call the siren's dower? In whom but in our child could reappear your own face, glorified, masked, by woman's softness? Ah, Doña Isabel and this Pedro were deceived; they thought it was the beauty of Herlinda that they saw. But I knew it to be yours. Ah, in all these weeks I have taught your child how to hate you; I have plucked out that root of love; I have made more real the fancied wrongs of which she has accused you. Trifles! trifles! trifles all! — the murder of a supposed father, the torture of an old man, the death of a base lover, — yes, that Ruiz to whom from her birth you destined her. But I, — I cry to you give back my innocence! give back my ruined life! give back my father, who by your act was killed as surely as though your hand had struck the blow! give me the young years of my daughter's life, those she squandered a beggar at your sister's gate! Ah, you cannot, you cannot! But I, — I can avenge my wrongs and hers."

Quick as a flash the infuriate woman levelled a pistol. Quick as an answering flash Chinita threw herself before her and sprang to her father's breast. A second shot following so quickly on the first that they seemed as one, a cry of agony, a scream of madness, the cries of women, the hoarse voices of men, made the garden a pandemonium of hideous sounds. The desperate woman, whose bullet had touched its mark harmlessly to Ramirez through the slender form of Chinita, fled madly. Ramirez, scarce conscious whether the blood which streamed over him was that of his daughter or his own, bore the wounded girl through the throng that pressed him, wildly calling upon his child, — alas, alas! his but for the brief span during which her warm young blood should leap from the deadly puncture in her breast!

Herlinda, the first to regain self-control even amid the intense revulsion of feeling through which she had almost instantaneously passed, tore into shreds some portion of her garments and strove to stanch the wound; but in vain. Chinita, with a smile which succeeded her first wild cry and stare of horror, motioned her away. She pressed her own fingers on the wound, raising her head from the arm of Ramirez to say, "I saved you, I saved you! just as I used to think I would do. Ah, I could not hate you, — no, no! though I tried. And she could not root out my love, — it lives here still." She pressed her hand still tighter on the wound. "My father! my father!"

The face of the hardened man contracted in agony. He turned toward Doña Isabel and Herlinda with a heart-rending cry. "You are avenged, — both, both, avenged! O my God! You never can have known such agony as this. Oh wretched man that I am, to see the sum of all my crimes cancelled by this terrible reprisal!"

The hand of the dying girl fell from its place. Chata knelt and placed her own with desperate energy against the fatal wound. Chinita smiled and faintly kissed her. "My dream has come true," she said. "Ah, when they pity me you will say, 'She always longed to die for him.' Tell them it was best that I should die, I loved him so. Death wipes out every wrong. He is my father!"

Ramirez groaned. Great drops of sweat stood on his brow. He strove still to support her; but Gonzales on the one side and Ashley on the other bore her weight.

By this time the garden was full of people. A man forced his way through the throng.

"Reyes! Reyes!" cried Ramirez, "Villain, did you not as I commanded give my child to Isabel, my sister; or was yours the accursed hand that brought her to this pass?"

Reyes gazed at the dying girl in horror. A suspicion of the misapprehension under which Ramirez had acted, and which had confirmed Ruiz in his treachery, had haunted him for days, since in a remote village he had met the administrador of Tres Hermanos and heard from him the tale of the carrying away of Chata. He had hastened toward Las Parras with Don Rafael and his mother, bent on warning Ramirez and confessing the wild carelessness with which he had disposed of the child who had been confided to him, and who he had supposed until his meeting with Chinita had indirectly reached the person to whom she was destined. It had not been possible for him — a man in whom the paternal instinct had never dwelt — to imagine it the one virtue in the callous, fierce, and unscrupulous Ramirez. But with this bleeding, dying figure in his arms Ramirez seemed transformed. Reyes fell on his knees.

"Ah, had you but told me the whole truth!" sighed the dying girl. "A Garcia you said! Ah, I should have been prouder to be *his* daughter than a thousand times Garcia!"

She turned her head, and her eyes fell on Ashley's face and rested there. A soft, strange illumination animated her own, as though from some inward light just kindled. "Adios! Adios!" she murmured. "Ah, you were noble, generous! yet you thought I did not feel, that I did not understand. Ah, could I live, you should see! But this is best; you will never need trouble now for Chinita. No, no, no! do not grieve — Ah, that might make me weak! I would not — find it — hard — to die."

She looked at him long and fixedly, — perhaps to her as to Ashley a secret as sacred as it was precious, was then revealed. A blueness crept around her mouth, a glaze over her beautiful eyes. "No wonder that she loved the American!" she whispered at length, — dreamily, as though her mind wandered to the past. The words sank like lead in Ashley's heart, to be forgotten never, never!

After a moment the lips of the dying girl moved in prayer. The priest, who had from time to time endeavored to control an emotion which seemed a personal rather than a merely sympathetic grief, bent over her, and all present fell on their knees. Chinita whispered in his ear a few words, and received absolution with a smile of perfect peace. Then began the solemn litany for the departing soul; Chinita was evidently sinking rapidly.

Pedro had fallen on his knees before her, in grief too deep for words. Pepé from behind him gazed into her glazing eyes with stoical despair. Suddenly she smiled, and laying her arm over Pedro's shoulder, extended her blood-stained hand, looking at Pepé with the pretty, winning, disdainful smile of old, and said faintly, though proudly, "I am the daughter of the Señor General. Lead me, Pepé, — lead me. I am tired!"

And thus with her arm around him who had been so blindly faithful, and with her hand in that of the peasant youth who through life had been her adoring slave, with one long sigh, which left her lips smiling as it passed, Chinita fell asleep, — resting forever from the passion and turmoil of life.

"Peace, peace, peace!" reiterated the solemn voice of the priest, in assurance, in warning, in invocation. It penetrated hearts to which the very word had seemed a mockery. The hardest, the most reprobate, the haughtiest, the most sorrowful, repeated it with a sob. Ramirez on his knees, crushed to the earth, heard it as the cry of a despairing angel. Where for him could peace be found?

XLVII.

WHEN Pedro Gomez rose from his knees he held in his hand a little square reliquary of faded blue. The string from which it had hung had been pierced by the fatal bullet, and it had dropped unheeded from Chinita's neck.

Reverent hands bore the corpse into the desolate house; while Ramirez, or Leon Vallé, — for by his true name he was ever after called, — rising at the entreaty of his sister, stood like one bereft of sense or movement. Suddenly he laid his hand upon the gatekeeper's arm and muttered hoarsely, "Kill me Pedro! See, I have no sword. If thou wilt not for vengeance, do it for love. You loved her, — for her sake end my misery!"

Pedro laid the reliquary in his hand. "If it should not be true?" he said doggedly of the faded silk. "Oh, was it for this I bore so many years the mocking silence of Doña Feliz and my mistress? No, no! it cannot be. Open this. 'T was on her bosom when she came into my hands. The niña Herlinda promised me a token. It will be found there, — there in the blessed reliquary. Fool that I was to think it had nothing to declare to me. Ah, how your hands shake! Well, 't is but a moment's work."

The gatekeeper ripped the sewed edges with his dagger's point quickly, desperately, as though he were profaning a sacred thing, — then blankly looked at the worthless trifles on his palm. Just a tiny curl of brown and gold, and the eye-tooth of some animal, a fancied charm against infantile diseases, both wrapped in a paper scrawled with a faintly-written prayer.

Pedro was convinced. Till then he had clung to the belief that had given to his clownish life the elements of heroism, of love and sacrifice. Chinita the beautiful, the beloved, was dead — dead; but to his soul there came a bereavement far more terrible than that of death. He raised his glazing eyes appealingly, hopelessly. Ah, there was Doña Feliz, — she whom all these years he had accused as the hard, unpitying witness of the degradation of Herlinda's child! and of her Doña Isabel with sobs was entreating brokenly in God's name some news of the charge she had received years before. Pedro listened with a jealous eagerness, which the involuntary cry of Chata, interrupting for a moment the answering voice of Doña Feliz, made intolerable. "Mother of God!" he cried at length, "it was Doña Feliz then who guarded Herlinda's child!"

"O false, cruel Feliz! why did you deceive me?" cried Doña Isabel. "Why did you suffer me to believe the gatekeeper's foundling was of my own flesh and blood? Ah, God, so she was! It was the beauty of my mother that deceived me; it was repeated in the offspring of Leon, as it could never be in that of the American. Ah, it was for that I loved Chinita with such passionate tenderness and remorse! Oh, why did you suffer it? Why give me no warning? And now Chinita is dead, and my daughter cries to me for her child, and I cannot answer her."

"Did I not warn you at this gate?" responded Doña Feliz, "that the day would come when you would bitterly repent the words you uttered; when you bade me take and hide the babe even from your knowledge, — never to mention her whether living or dead, that to you it might be as though she had never existed? Have I not obeyed your mandate? Ay, even when my heart bled because I saw the agony, the delusion under which you labored, I have suffered with you, but I have been faithful."

Doña Isabel bent her head in speechless woe. For her there might not be even the poor consolation of reproach. Yet she murmured, "In pity, where is Herlinda's child?"

"She is here. Thank God she is here!" replied Doña Feliz, — this girl whom you have believed to be the daughter of my son. "Weeks ago your brother, Leon Vallé, reft her from us, believing her his own. Only by revealing the secret we had sworn to keep could Rafael have saved her. Ah, God knows! Perhaps at the last moment, when hastening from the strong room she threw herself into the power of the ravisher that she might save her foster-father from death, then perhaps his will might have failed; but he was speechless. I have been ill; yes, near to death," — her haggard face, her sunken eyes, her wasted figure attested that, — " yet we sought her far and near. Until last night we had no tidings. A rough soldier listened in the inn to the tale we everywhere proclaimed. He came to me secretly; ' Señora,' he said, ' the girl you seek is perhaps in the house of Doña Carmen. Ramirez himself is deceived.' This was the first stage of our route to Guanapila. We need go no farther; for standing there, Herlinda, with Carmen, is your child."

Doña Feliz broke into sobs, sinking weak as a child into the arms of Don Rafael. " The struggle is over," she said to him; " our task is accomplished, the long dissimulation is ended ! "

Herlinda and Chata had not needed the conclusion of the brief words of Doña Feliz; they had clasped each other in a rapturous embrace. But the sobs of the distressed lady recalled them from their joy, and hastening to her side they poured out in fervent gratitude such words as seemed to repay to her sensitive heart its long years of devotion as truly as though each word had been a priceless jewel.

" Ah ! " said Doña Feliz, " all, all is nothing to merit the happiness of this hour. It is the poor Pedro, he whose matchless devotion mocked my poor work, who is worthy of such words as these. Ah, my heart bled for him, but I could not, dared not speak."

" Oh foolish unreasoning girl that I was so to bind you ! " cried Herlinda. She turned to speak to Pedro, but he was nowhere to be seen. There was a movement among the villagers, who, repulsed from the windows of the house by the soldiers, began to disperse, when the voice of the priest stopped them.

" Listen, friends," he said. " This has been a dread and fearful hour, an hour to try the souls of men. I am old, yet never have I known such anguish as this day has brought to me. Some sixteen years ago, a stranger in this land, ignorant of its language and customs, I came to this village with a young American whom I met. He was a handsome youth and won my heart, — a warm, Irish heart that often led me contrary to my judgment. The American told me that here his love was staying. I laughed at him for fixing his heart upon some brown-skinned, dark-eyed peasant girl. He did not contradict me, but bade me be ready in the early morning to wed him to the lovely object of his youthful passion. I remonstrated, yet was glad to serve him. Though no priest lived here, the little church was open; the people were glad of the opportunity to hear Mass. Just before it began, John Ashley and Herlinda Garcia were married. As she for a moment loosened the reboso she wore to make the necessary responses, I caught a glimpse of a face that led me to suspect it was no simple peasant who stood before me. Yet it was only in after years, when the requirements of the law and the customs unalterable as law among the different castes existing in your land became known to me, that I remembered with disquiet the marriage I had celebrated here. I was a missionary among the tribes of Northern Indians, doing good work. I strove to assure myself that, irregular as I knew the marriage to be, — contracted in secret, unknown to and probably against the consent of the young girl's parents, in a language unintelligible to the few witnesses, — the parties were probably living in amity, satisfied, as surely God and man might be, with a marriage which only the quibbles of the law made disputable. Yet I could not be at ease; a voice seemed calling me hither. Alas, alas! I came but to witness the consummation of the tragedy begun years, years ago, — a tragedy, the direct outcome of my fatal error. But I will atone. I will go — would to God in penance it might be upon my knees — to the Holy Father in Rome, and pray him to ratify the marriage. Doña Herlinda Garcia, pure in name as in deed, shall give a spotless name to the child of her virtuous love!"

The old monk ceased; tremblingly he wiped away his tears. "Pardon, pardon!" he murmured to Herlinda. "Oh my daughter, how you have suffered! But daughter, the certificate I gave, — had you not the paper? That, however subject to cavil, would have declared your purity."

"Ah, a paper!" cried Herlinda. "I have thought of it a thousand times. It was in English. I thought it was a blessed prayer, though John told me to treasure it as my life ; that was why I sewed it in the reliquary I placed about my baby's neck."

With a cry Chata drew forth the tiny bag, almost the counterpart of that poor Chinita had worn, and the sight of which had confirmed the mistake of Pedro, — on such slight things hangs fate ! She thought of how often she and Chinita had compared them when children, laughingly proposing to exchange or open them, yet ever shrinking from tampering with them in superstitious awe. Pedro, who had returned, snatched it from her hand, — the act irresistible. As he opened it with his dagger's point, a filigree earring fell into his palm. He groaned and turned away.

Herlinda caught from his hand a tattered paper. "Read, read !" she cried to Ashley. "See that he was noble, true as you have said ! He was my husband !"

The proof attested by the signature of the long dead Mademoiselle La Croix, and that of the living priest, was of the simplest, the most efficient, and all these years had been preserved by the piety or superstition of the child to whom it had been confided, and who, had she but known it, had so vital an interest in its discovery. Chata gazed at the paper in blank amaze. Around her were men and women giving thanks to God and his saints. At the knees of Herlinda was her uncle Leon Vallé and Doña Isabel her mother.

Ashley Ward was the first to break the spell. He took Herlinda's hand. "Remember, here is a man who never doubted you," he said.

"And here one who would have died for you !" said Gonzales.

In a single phrase each had expressed the loyalty of the nation he represented, — Ashley, that of faith in man's honor and woman's chastity ; Gonzales, the tenacious love that distrust might change to jealous madness, but which it could never destroy.

Within a few hours a sad and solemn funeral cortége set forth from Las Parras, bearing all that was mortal of the beautiful Chinita. Not far from the limits of the town Ashley and Gonzales came upon a startling and awful sight, — a woman lay dead upon the road, her garments sodden, her beautiful hair defiled by the mud of the highway. She had fallen face downward. As though some evil omen warned him, Leon Vallé hastening from the rear anticipated them in raising the corpse.

It was that of the maddened Dolores. It had needed no weapon to reach her heart; despair and agony had summoned to her destruction the swift and fatal malady that had killed her father. Those who saw her, he who pressed her wildly to his breast and bade her live, accusing himself not her, called it a broken heart. As her child had said, "Death wipes out every wrong." Only remorse, pity, love survive.

They buried them both — the two of that sad name Dolores — in the hacienda church. But one lies in a nameless grave, and the other is marked by one that recalls a vision of a beautiful girl, to whom a happier destiny should have brought the joys of life, and whose proud spirit should have conquered its cares; yet its perplexities, its conflicting passions, had made the pilgrimage so hard, so set with thorns, that she had been content — yes, thankful — to end it there: "CHINITA."

In so short a life the unfortunate girl could not have wandered far from heaven; yet for years there was one on earth who spent upon each day long hours of prayer and fasting at the tomb of her brother's child, — to the memory and the name of Chinita uniting that of Leon, and embracing both in the undying love which looked beyond the grave for its perfection and its reward. At evening would come one older, but more peaceful than the mourner, to lead her home; and hand in hand, the two would pass out into the soft and tranquil air. Thus Doña Isabel and Feliz renewed with tears the friendship of their youth; and thus — ended the ambitions, the passions, the impetuous pride, sources of such strange and grievous perplexities — they await together in peaceful gloom the light of a perfect day.

XLVIII

It was thus that Ashley Ward and his bride beheld them in after years, — years during which he had returned to the United States to take part in that great conflict which had been raging there while he had been gaining experience in the irregular and inglorious strife in which his zeal for liberty had been stimulated by private aims. The purity of his patriotism was unstained, however, by any less glorious motive ; and during the last two years of the Civil War for the Union there was none who fought more valiantly than he, nor one who laid down his sword with a more just renown, to dedicate himself to the profession which in the lack of fortune was both his choice and a positive need.

That Ward should renounce the fortune of John Ashley was an actual grief to Herlinda and to Chata herself, but he would have it so ; and even Mary Ashley was pleased it should be, although, as she said, her niece was already most absurdly wealthy in right of the Garcias for a girl of such retired and humble tastes, — one whose only extravagance was in her charities. Mary Ashley found in the love of Chata — she soon abandoned the attempt to call her by the stately name of Florentina — a recompense for the scrupulous conscientiousness which had led her to seek the supposed wife and possible child of her brother.

It was not until after the Pope had ratified her marriage that Herlinda Ashley visited the home of her husband's family. After that she returned at intervals while Chata was being educated as her aunt desired. During that time Gonzales, from whose hand Herlinda had received the Papal edict, was fighting anew the battles of freedom on his native soil ; and by his side, doing gallant deeds unstained by crime, was Leon Vallé. But when the short-

lived empire of Maximilian was overthrown, when Herlinda crowned the long fidelity of Gonzales by following
the rare example given by a few released nuns and became
the wife of the Liberal soldier, the silent yet resolute man
who had been his constant companion in arms disappeared,
and with him Pedro Gomez.

No one but Rosario, who as the wife of Don Alonzo
took the lead among the young and idle wives of the hacienda employés, asked any questions concerning the disappearance of Leon Vallé. Doña Rita looked wise, and
Don Rafael smiled at her, for she knew nothing, and could
conjecture nothing that might bring evil. Rafael was the
same indulgent, easy husband he had ever been. It did
not occur to either that a more perfect confidence might
have been observed between them, — they had followed
custom; what more could be needful?

Chata and her mother sometimes talked of Vallé with
wondering pity; but they saw that Doña Isabel was content, — his fate was not a mystery to her. Perhaps he
was wandering in foreign countries. At least, after he
had gained the new, fresh fame which honored the name of
Leon Vallé, he was no more seen in Mexico. There was
but one thought that troubled the heart of Chata. She
could not, even for Chinita's sake, forgive the murderer of
her father.

It was when Ashley Ward had gained a certain assurance of success and ultimate wealth, that he wooed and
won the object of his early, generous search, his early protecting interest, his later love. In the heart of Chata no
rival flame had ever glowed; Ashley had been her first,
her only love. And he perhaps was scarcely conscious
that the pang which ever came at the sound of one almost
sacred name, was the throb of a scar where love had set
its deathless root. Chata never suspected that an uncommon grief had made possible the tranquil happiness which
she shared with her husband; while he never questioned
even in his own soul whether his happiness would have
been greater, or perhaps have been changed to torture and
torment, had the beautiful, erratic daughter of Leon Vallé
been spared to earth. Whatever wild emotion had thrilled
him, Chata, — the good, the sweet, the gentle Chata, with
the intelligent and reflective mind, which curbed and per-

fected the enduring emotions of her heart, — was the only woman he had ever thought of as his wife. They rejoiced in perfect trust and sympathy, — she never imagining, he never regretting, the more impetuous passion that might have been.

It was while on their wedding journey, attended by an escort of soldiers, which the insecurity of the roads in the years immediately following the overthrow of the empire made necessary, that they went into a remote district among the mountains, some twenty leagues from Vera Cruz, from which port they were to sail for their Northern home. The captain of the escort was a silent, swarthy young man, who born a peasant, had by his valor and development of extraordinary qualities as a strategist acquired during the contest with the French a reputation that would, had the incentive of personal ambition urged, have made it possible for him to reach the highest grade of military rank. But he fought for principle, not for glory; to forget despair, not to challenge fame. The man was Pepé Ortiz. Upon such men, the world when joy and love fail, sometimes thrusts greatness. This was predicted of the silent captain.

One night the young officer came to the inn and invited the bride and groom to walk with him in the moonlight. They passed through the streets of the town, where the massive adobe houses, white as marble in the deceptive light, threw shadows black as ink, and presently emerged upon a paved road, which led to a garden set thick with trees. The air was heavy with perfume; hundreds of fireflies, where the thicket was so dense no ray from the sky might penetrate, seemed to fill the place with ghostly fires. It was enchanting, weird, — ay, awe-inspiring. Chata clung to her husband's arm in mute expectancy.

Soon in the near distance they heard a sound as of measured strokes, and a low continuous moan. The strokes quickened to the whizz of heavy flails, the moan to the dirge of the *Miserere*. Then they understood with a shock of horror that they were about to witness one of the processions of penitents, which, though forbidden by the civil law, still were conducted secretly in remote and fanatical districts. Chata would have fled, but the pity at her heart seemed to paralyze her limbs. Ashley, with a feeling strangely differing from mere curious expectancy, put his arm around her and awaited the advent of the dolorous company.

Presently the penitents came from amid the shelter of the trees, like mournful ghosts upon the moonlit road. They were all men, — men to whom the memory of their sins was intolerable, — and as they walked they wielded the cruel scourges on their bared shoulders, and ceaselessly intoned the dirge. It was past midnight, and for hours they had continued the dreadful flagellation and the unceasing march. Blood streamed from many a gaping wound; they staggered as they walked; more than once a fainting sufferer fell, and was lifted to his feet by the man who walked beside him. All this dismal company were masked; each wore a friar's gown and a rough shirt of hair, which hung pendant from the girdle at the waist, above which was seen the cut and bleeding skin.

Sick with horror, when the last of the miserable wretches had gone by, Chata leaned sobbing on her husband's breast. But he gently set her upon the grassy bank of the roadside, and followed by Pepé hastened to the help of a poor wretch, above whose prostrate form his faithful attendant bent with despairing gestures. They raised the apparently dying man, and turned aside the mask. The moonlight fell upon the face of Leon Vallé, worn with the passions of other years and with the griefs of the present, yet nobler than they had ever beheld it. At that moment the likeness between this man and Chata became in Ashley's eyes peculiarly intensified.

The trembling and sensitive young wife had approached, with an absolute certainty that something was transpiring which was to touch her own being. Scarcely surprised, though with a shock, she recognized Leon Vallé. Presently she bent and kissed him with tears. From that moment Chata had no secret rancor to regret, — the penitent was forgiven.

"Señores, Señores, I pray you leave us; he revives, he will in a moment recover consciousness," cried the rough voice of Pedro Gomez. With that complete self-abnegation which, when the claims and interests of his seignorial chieftain are involved, is perhaps presented in its highest development by the Mexican peasant, he had ignored the revengeful abhorrence with which the memory of Leon Vallé had for years inspired him, and for the sake of her whom he had loved and served as the scion of a noble race, had dedicated his life to the father for whom she had gladly died.

As Doña Feliz had once done years before, Chata kissed with reverence the hand of this embodiment of fidelity, and with a throbbing heart turned from the last scene in the drama of which her life had formed a part. Thenceforth a new act was entered upon, in which deep and tender memories and present peace and trust are working out the trite but blissful tale of wedded love.

University Press: John Wilson & Son, Cambridge.